THE SUNDERING

ALSO BY JACQUELINE CAREY

Kushiel's Dart
Kushiel's Chosen
Kushiel's Avatar

THE SUNDERING

BANEWREAKER

GODSLAYER

Jacqueline Carey

FANTASY

BANEWREAKER Copyright © 2004 by Jacqueline Carey
   Publication History: Tor hardcover, November 2004
                              Tor Paperback, August 2005
GODSLAYER Copyright © 2005 by Jacqueline Carey
   Publication History: Tor hardcover, August 2005

First SFBC Fantasy Printing: August 2005

Published by arrangement with:
Tom Doherty Associates, Inc.
175 Fifth Avenue
New York, NY 10010

Visit The SFBC online at http://www.sfbc.com

ISBN # 0-7394-5690-3

Printed in the United States of America.

CONTENTS

BANEWREAKER   1

GODSLAYER   413

DRAMATIS PERSONAE

❖

SEVEN SHAPERS
Haomane, Lord-of-Thought
Arahila the Fair
Satoris the Sower
Neheris-of-the-Leaping-Waters
Meronin the Deep
Yrinna-of-the-Fruits
Oronin the Glad Hunter

DARKHAVEN'S FORCES
Tanaros Blacksword—General, one of the Three
Ushahin—Dreamspinner, one of the Three
Vorax—Glutton, one of the Three
Hyrgolf—Fjel field marshal
Carfax—Staccian captain
Skragdal—Fjel squadron commander
Speros—Midlander, recent arrival
Meara—madling, attendant to Cerelinde

HAOMANE'S ALLIES
Malthus the Counselor—Haomane's emissary
Ingolin the Wise—Lord of the Rivenlost
Cerelinde—Lady of the Ellylon
Aracus Altorus—heir to Kingdom of the West
Blaise Caveros—Aracus' second-in-command, member of
Malthus' Company
Fianna—the Archer of Arduan, member of Malthus' Company
Peldras—Ellyl, member of Malthus' Company
Lorenlasse of Valmaré—Leader of the Host of the Rivenlost
Dani—Yarru, the Bearer
Thulu—Yarru, Dani's uncle and guide

OTHERS
Lilias—Sorceress of the East
Calandor—dragon, one of the Eldest
Calanthrag—dragon, the Eldest
Grey Dam—ruler of the Were

BANEWREAKER

PROLOGUE

THE PLACE WAS CALLED GORGANTUM.

Wounded once more, he fled there; and having fled, seethed. It was not a defeat, not wholly. No one could say such a thing while he yet lived and held Godslayer in his possession. He was Satoris Third-Born, and from this place, this vale, to the Sundering Sea, the west was his. Two of his Elder Brother's three Counselors were slain, their weapons lost or scattered. The high Lord of the Riven-lost was slain and his son with him, and many others, too. The number of Ellylon who remained would fill no more than a city. There were Men, of course, in ever-increasing numbers, but such discord had been sown on the battlefield as would make for bitter blood between the two races.

It would be long ages before another attempt was made.

But it would happen.

He knew his Elder Brother.

There had not always been enmity between them. Once, the Seven Shapers had dwelled in accord, in the beginning, when Uru-Alat, whom Men called the World God, died to give birth to the world, bringing them forth from the deepest places and giving power unto them.

First-Born among them was Haomane, Lord-of-Thought, for he was brought forth at the place of the Souma, the bright gem, the Eye in the Brow of Uru-Alat.

Second came Arahila the Fair, Born-of-the-Heart, and there was grace in all her ways, and compassion in her fingertips that Shaped the emerging world.

Satoris, once called the Sower, was Third-Born at the juncture of the loins, and in the quickening of the flesh lay his Gift.

Fourth came Neheris, from the northern forelimb, Neheris-of-the-Leaping-Waters, and the high, cold mountains with their sparkling rivers would be her demesne.

From the deep seas came Meronin, where the southern forelimb made harbor, and the Fifth-Born was deep and kept his counsel.

Sixth came Yrinna-of-the-Fruits, Lady of the southern aftlimb, and abundance was in her touch.

Last-Born and seventh was Oronin, the Glad Hunter of the northern aftlimb, and not least, for death rode in his train.

And also, there were dragons.

In those days, the Seven turned their thoughts to the emerging world. Oronin the Youngest gave Shape to wild forests as Yrinna, his sister, brought forth orchards and fields, and Meronin gave form to gentle harbors and deep seas even as Neheris made to rise mountains and rivers. In the Souma dwelled their power, and each drew upon it according to his strength or hers. Haomane First-Born took the brilliance of the Souma itself, the Eye of Uru-Alat, and gave Shape unto light. And the sun shone with bright radiance as it passed; but the night was black, and Arahila took pity upon it, and did Shape a second light called the moon, pale and beautiful, and thousands upon thousands of stars.

This world they called Urulat, after the World God whose death had given birth to it.

And still life emerged from the death of Uru-Alat, those races known as the Lesser Shapers, and each of the Seven did claim a race and Shape their Children according to their strengths and desires.

All save Satoris, who spent his time walking to and fro in the earth, and conversing with dragons; for they came forth from the very bones of Uru-Alat and there was wisdom in them, and cunning, too. Alone among the Seven, Satoris hungered for their knowledge. But his Gift lay in the quickening of the flesh, and he gave it gladly for the asking. Neheris did ask, and Meronin and Yrinna and Oronin, and thus were the children of their Shaping quickened, and the lesser races did increase; Fjeltroll and fish, Were and stag, Dwarf and rabbit alike. Where death entered the world with Oronin's presence, it was countered with Satoris' Gift, and the races did continue.

For the Ellylon, Haomane sought it not, for he had completed their Shaping before the final throes of Uru-Alat's death and time touched them not. He was First-Born, and he drew upon the fullest power of the Souma and wrought his Children of pure thought. Only Arahila's touch did Haomane suffer upon their Shaping, Second-Born and nearest to him of all his brethren. No lesser touch would he abide. Thus did Arahila Shape love into the being of the Ellylon.

In turn, Haomane Lord-of-Thought did place his Shaping on her Children, and those were Men, second among the Lesser Shapers. And they were mightier than all save the Ellylon for they turned the emergent world to their own ends; but they were not outside time and death's touch. Thus did Arahila the Fair seek Satoris' Gift for her children, and Satoris granted it, for he loved her well.

And Haomane was displeased.

For Men were not content, but made war upon the Ellylon, in ever-increasing numbers. And it came to pass in the Fourth Age of Urulat that Haomane First-Born asked Satoris to withdraw his Gift from the race of Men.

Three times, he asked.

Three times, Satoris refused. Out of love for Arahila, he refused; and out of knowledge, the deep and dire knowledge gained from congress with dragons. And, in the discord of his refusal, the Souma, the Eye in the Brow of Uru-Alat, was shattered. In that shattering, a single shard cracked loose from the whole, a shard shaped like a dagger.

Godslayer.

It was Oronin Last-Born who seized the shard and planted it in Satoris' thigh, wounding him so the ichor flowed like blood. Not until then did Satoris call upon the dragons, summoning them to his aid.

So began the Shapers' War.

Though many dragons died and Satoris was held at bay, he might have prevailed in the end, had it not been for Haomane First-Born. The Lord-of-Thought struck the earth a mighty blow, severing the head from the body of Urulat. And, in accordance with the will of Meronin the Deep, the Sundering Sea rushed in to fill the divide.

The Six Shapers were islanded, on that island later called Torath, and the power of the Souma was broken; but Satoris was cast out on the far side of the Sundering Sea, bereft and wounded. The dragons abandoned him, having paid too high a toll for his friendship. This Haomane saw, and the Lord-of-Thought drew upon the might of the shattered Souma. Though he could not

Shape the land, he caused the sun above to blaze like a terrible Eye, and Satoris was scorched by the heat of it, and his skin darkened and parched, and the earth did also, until Arahila begged Haomane to relent for mercy's sake.

Northward, Satoris fled, where the mountains cast shadows over the land, and he sought shelter from Haomane's wrath in the deep caverns of the Fjeltroll, Neheris' Children, brutish and strong as mountains, and as solid, too. There he spoke gentle words to them and the Fjeltroll gave an oath to aid him, for they knew naught of the Shapers' War, only that he repaid them in kindness; a kindness Haomane in his pride had never shown them. He sought to heal himself, but ever after his skin bore the mark of Haomane's anger, and the wound dealt by Oronin was unhealed, but ever wept tears of ichor.

And Satoris' Gift was no more.

Still, Haomane would not leave him in peace, but lurked on the isle Torath, and breathed distant rumor into the ears of all on Urulat who would hear. Ellyl and Man were reunited in hatred of Satoris and gave new names to him: Banewreaker, Sunderer and Prince of Lies. And it came to them through Haomane's whispers that if Satoris were defeated, Urulat could be remade, and all would bask in the light of the Souma.

They made war upon him, and when the loyal Fjeltroll honored their pledge and defended him, they made war upon the Fjeltroll.

They made war until Satoris grew weary and bitter and angry, and raised an army of his own; of Fjeltroll, with their brute strength, and the grey Were, Oronin's hunters. All those who felt abandoned by the Six Shapers heeded his words, and he Shaped their will to his and marched against his enemies. What Haomane had named him, he became. Banewreaker, Bringer-of-Doom.

For a time, they laid waste to Urulat, pressing toward the west.

But his Elder Brother was cunning.

Haomane First-Born took three ruby-red chips of the Souma, smoothing them into gems of power: the Soumanië. Three Counselors he Shaped to bear them: Ardrath, Dergail and Malthus. Three weapons he gave them to wield: the Helm of Shadows, the Spear of Light and the Arrow of Fire. And he sent them across the Sundering Sea to raise an army of Ellylon and Men loyal to the Six Shapers to do battle with Satoris.

It had been a near thing.

Not a defeat, no. Not a victory, either.

He was alive and Godslayer was his. Still, he had been

wounded anew, twice over, and forced to flee the field. But his enemies, Haomane's Allies, had taken grievous blows. Two Counselors slain, the Arrow of Fire lost, and the Helm of Shadows in
Satoris' possession. The war had not ended, but there would be a
reprieve, while ages passed and Haomane conceived his next
move.

All Satoris could do was make ready for it.

First, he healed the mortal wound. The Ellyl blade that struck
him from behind had cut deep, severing the tendons behind his
knee. It had surprised him, that; so much so that he had dropped
the dagger. And without Godslayer, he was—what? A Shaper, but
powerless.

Sundered.

There had been his Gift, once. He smiled with bitter irony as he
healed himself, drawing on the power of Godslayer to splice his
sinews and knit his flesh. Even if it had not been stripped from
him, his Gift would have availed him nothing in this struggle. That
time had come and gone in ages past, vanished in an eyeblink.

He had offered his Gift to Haomane's Children.

Haomane had refused it.

The second wound was more difficult, for it had been dealt by
a weapon Shaped by his brother. If the first had been a surprise,
the second had been a shock. He could see it, still; the Spear of
Light, its shaft gleaming under the sullen skies. It extended in a
straight line from the place where agony flared, where the shining,
leaf-pointed blade was buried in his side. And at the other end,
both hands locked fast on the haft, was the last Counselor; Malthus,
his brother's final emissary.

It had hurt, a hurt second only to one, as he tore himself loose,
a gaffed fish fighting the hook. Such indignity! It was almost worth
it to see the Counselor's dumbstruck face. There was only one
weapon capable of killing Satoris.

Godslayer.

They had both reached for it at once. The dagger, the shard of
the shattered Souma. He grimaced in remembrance, pressing its
blade to the ragged lips of the wound in his side. It pulsed there,
and light kindled in its rubescent depths. So it had pulsed between
their joined hands. Closing his eyes, he called upon its power.
Somewhere, beyond the Sundering Sea, the light of the Souma
flickered in distant sympathy. His kindred would wonder what he
did with it.

Let them wonder, and fear. He drew upon its power for this

second healing, so much more difficult than the first. Inch by slow
inch, he sealed the wound. It left a scar that shone with a pale light,
another memento of his brother's wrath.

When it was done, he was weary.

Not all wounds could be healed.

Always, there was the third wound, the immortal one; there, in
the hollow of his thigh, where Oronin had struck him with Godslayer itself. It festered with deep poison and wept unceasing tears
of ichor, and where they fell, the land itself was blighted and
changed.

So be it, he thought. I have fled my brother's wrath, and he has
found me. I have challenged his might, and he has thwarted me.
My siblings have forsaken me; even Arahila, though her memory
makes me weep. Yet I do not regret my choice. If Haomane asked
a fourth time, I would refuse him anew. In his pride, the Lord-of-
Thought does not see the Shape of what-would-be if my Gift were
forever uncoupled from his. I see; all too clearly, I see. Thus in my
pride, I name myself my brother's enemy, and not his victim. I did
not seek this role, though it has been thrust upon me. Loathe it
though I may, it is my lot. I am what I am. I cling to such honor as
is left to me. Here I will abide, and make of this place a sanctuary;
a stronghold. And when I am done, I will place Godslayer at the
heart of it, where no other hand may touch it.

Being whole, or as whole as he might be, he summoned the
Fjeltroll.

There, in the vale of Gorgantum, he flung up jagged peaks to
surround his place of hiding. He brought forth great slabs of marble
from the earth and Shaped them, black and gleaming. And he
showed them his plan, the vast citadel with its high towers, its encircling wall, and the secret heart of it like a twin-chambered nautilus. There the Fjel labored, honoring their ancient oath. Strong and
high they built its walls—and deep, deep below it they delved, in
Gorgantum, the hollow, where the earth's strong bones conjoined.

When they reached the Source, he sighed to see the marrow-fire.

Godslayer would be safe.

It was a lingering essence of the blazing godhead of Uru-Alat; a
blue-white fire that ran through the bones of the earth, the spark of
which fueled the dragons' fiery bellies at their emergence. Here, at
the Source, it gathered. Nothing mortal could withstand its touch.
He had enough of a Shaper's power yet to Shape the marrow-fire.
It took delicacy, tapping just enough to lace the veined marble of
his citadel, to light the unfaltering torches. For the first time, he un-

derstood the joy his siblings had taken in Shaping the emerging world, and wondered what it would have been like to do so in the fullness of power before the Souma was shattered.

No matter. This would have to be enough.

Of its smoke, he wrought a pall of darkness, and this he flung like a cloak over the vale of Gorgantum, until the very skies were shrouded. And at this, too, he smiled, for it veiled his Elder Brother's prying eyes and sheltered him from the sun's wrath that had scorched his form to blackness.

The Source itself, he dared not alter, but from it he drew a steady flow, a Font in which the marrow-fire danced in an endless coruscation of blue-white flame. In the Font, where no mortal hands would dare reach, he placed the dagger, Godslayer. And there it burned, throbbing like an angry heart; burned, yet was not consumed.

His citadel was complete, and he was pleased.

And he was alone, and lonely.

There were the Fjeltroll, always, faithful to their oath. He had never lied to them. It was true, he treasured them for their very simplicity. But oh, how quickly their lives flickered past, measured against his own! Generations passed in the building of his sanctuary. And in the brute simplicity of their very fidelity, they served as a stark reminder of his complicated, solitary existence. To whom could he turn, when first he heard the whispers of his brother's new Prophecy? It was a cunning plan.

No one.

He turned instead to the prize the Fjeltroll had seized from the battlefield and brought him like a trophy at his summons. The Helm of Shadows, Men had named it.

It hurt to look upon it, even for him. His Elder Brother, who had Shaped the sun of the Souma's light, had Shaped this thing of its absence, from the lightless cracks of its shattering. On the battlefield, Men had averted their eyes, and even the Ellylon had wept to behold it. It held the darkness of all things lost and broken beyond repair—of the Souma, of the concord of the Shapers, of the Sundered World itself.

I am one of those things, he thought, turning the Helm in his hands. Broken beyond repair. Abandoned and bereft, cast out by those who once loved me.

And so thinking, he set about tuning its darkness to his own despair.

In it he placed his abiding frustration at his Elder Brother's

stubborn pride, and his own hatred of the role he had been condemned to play. He placed into it his anguish at his siblings' betrayal, shaded with profound sorrow and honed keen with
rage—for they had all betrayed him, all of them. He gave Shape to
his own self-loathing, to the memory of futile defiance, to that moment, that terrible moment, when the world was Sundered and the
seas rushed into the chasm, and he knew himself defeated and
alone.

Of helpless torment he Shaped it, of the memory of crawling
upon the heaving earth, clutching at it in his pain while the long
arm of his brother's wrath pursued, shifting the very sun until his
skin blackened and cracked, and he was forced, bellowing, to flee
once more. Of countless days and nights of bitter convalescence he
Shaped it, of the awareness of his lost Gift and the dire knowledge
that he was maimed beyond repair, that his name had become a
curse on the lips of his brother's Children. He Shaped it of sheer
loathing at the cowardice of his Elder Brother, who dared not cross
the Sundering Sea, but worked ever at a distance.

Of the grief at all fair things lost, he Shaped it, and the bittersweet pleasures he found to fill their place—of vengeance and ran-
corous triumph, of the dawning knowledge that he was well and
truly abandoned, a rebel Shaper casting a threatening shadow over
his siblings' dearest labors. Of a faint, desperate thread of hope, he
Shaped it; and the sure knowledge that hope was doomed.

Of searing pain he Shaped it, of impotent fury, of the remorseless agony of his wounded flesh, of the slow drip of ichor that bled
from his wound, of the slow drip of malice that poisoned his heart,
fed by generation upon generation of hatred endured.

Of unflinching truth, he Shaped it.

When it was done, he donned the Helm of Shadows and gazed
through the eye-slits of his own dark vision, gazing across the land
and hoarding his dwindling energies to peer into the hearts and
minds of all living beings blessed with his Elder Brother's Gift of
thought; for yes, oh yes, that had been his brother's Gift, in all the
mingled curse and blessing it entailed.

Somewhere, in the far reaches of the Sundered World, there
must be others who shared the pain of betrayal, who understood
what it was to rage against an unfair destiny. Mortals, it was true,
with brief, flickering lives—but with Godslayer to hand, it need not
be so.

Three emissaries his Elder Brother had sent to destroy him. He would summon three of his own; comrades, commanders, keepers of his citadel.

He would find them.

He would make them his.

He would make them immortal.

ONE

Tanaros walked down the hallway, black marble echoing under his bootheels.

It was like an unlit mirror, that floor, polished to a high gleam. The archways were vast, not built to a human scale. All along the walls the marrow-fire burned, delicate veins of blue-white against all that shining blackness. In both, his reflection was blurred and distorted. There was Tanaros; there, and there and there.

A pale brow, furrowed. A lock of dark hair falling, so.

Capable hands.

And a stern mouth, its soft words of love long since betrayed.

It had been a long time, a very long time, since Tanaros had thought of such matters, of the sum total the pieced-together fragments of his being made; nor did he think of them now, for his Lord's summons burned like a beacon in his mind. And beneath his attire, beneath the enameled armor that sheltered him, his branding burned like marrow-fire on his flesh, white-hot and cold as ice, throbbing as his heart beat, and piercing.

So it was, for the Three.

"Guardsman," he said in greeting.

"General Tanaros, sir." The Havenguard Fjeltroll on duty grinned, showing his eyetusks. His weapons hung about him like boulders on the verge of avalanche; he hoisted one, a sharp-pointed mace, in salute as he stood aside. Beyond him, the entrance to the tower stair yawned like an open mouth. "His Lordship awaits you in the observatory."

"Krognar," Tanaros said, remembering his name. "Thank you."

"My pleasure, Lord General." The Fjeltroll saluted again.

It was a long way to the observatory, to the very top of the ut-most tower of Darkhaven. Tanaros climbed it step by step, feeling his heartbeat increasing as he labored. A mortal heart, circum-scribed by the silvered scar of his branding. When all was said and done, he was a Man, nothing more. It was his Lordship who had made him one of the Three, and deathless. He heard his breath la-bor, in and out. Mortal lungs, circulating blood. How long had they been at that task? It had been a thousand years and more since Tanaros had answered his Lord's first summons, his hands red with the lifeblood of one he had once loved, his heart filled with rage and anguish.

It felt longer.

He wondered, briefly, how Vorax made the long climb.

Darkness spiraling on darkness. Broad steps, wrought by Fjel-troll, made to endure their broad, horny feet. Tanaros reached out, touching the spiraling wall of the tower, fingers trailing. It should have burned, the marrow-fire; it did burn, but faintly. Here the veins branched and branched again, growing ever thinner and fainter as the tower thrust upward into the darkness.

It was always dark here.

Tanaros paused in the entrance to the observatory, letting his eyes adjust. Dark. It was always dark. Even the windows opened onto darkness, and the night sky. There, the stars, that never shone in cloud-blotted daylight.

"My Lord." He bowed, crisp and correct, as he had bowed for centuries on end.

"Tanaros." The voice rumbled, deep as mountains; it soothed, easing his joints, loosening the stiffness of centuries, of honor be-trayed and never forgotten. It always had. In the darkness, the Shaper was silhouetted in the windows of night, vast shoulders oc-cluding the stars. A pair of eyes glinted like crimson embers. "You have come."

Tanaros took a breath, feeling his lungs loosen. "Always, my Lord Satoris."

"It is well."

In a carven chair in the corner sat Vorax, his thick legs akimbo, fanning himself and breathing hard. Long ago he had been a lord of the race of Men, dwelling in the cool clime of Staccia, far to the north. Gluttony, greed and a ruthless pragmatism had moved him to answer the Shaper's summons, becoming one of the immortal Three. He grinned at Tanaros from where he sprawled, his beard fanning over his massive chest. "Grave doings, cousin! Is it not so?"

"If you say so, cousin." Tanaros did not sit in his Lord's presence. Long ago, he had stood vigilant in the presence of his King as he stood now, in the presence of one far greater. Loyalties changed; protocol did not. He inclined his head in deference. "We await the Dreamspinner, my Lord?"

"Yes." His Lord turned to the westernmost window, gazing out at the night. "Tell me, Tanaros. What do you see, thence?"

He made his way to his Lord's side. It was like standing beside a stoked forge, the might of the Shaper beating against his skin in waves. In the air a scent, coppery and sweet, like fresh-spilled blood, only *stronger*. "Where, my Lord?"

"There." Satoris pointed to the west, the line of his arm unerring.

It could not be otherwise, of course, for westward lay Torath and the Souma, the Eye in the Brow of Uru-Alat—and Lord Satoris was a Shaper. Though his brethren had cast him out, though their allies reviled him and called him Sunderer, Banewreaker and Prince of Lies, he was a Shaper. Day or night, above the earth or below it, he knew where the Souma lay.

Beyond the Sundering Sea.

Tanaros gripped the edge of the casement and looked west into the night. The low mountains surrounding Darkhaven rose in ridges, silvered by a waning moon. Far, far beyond, he could see the faintest shimmer of surging darkness on the distant horizon where the sea began. Below, it was quiet, only an occasional clatter to be heard in the barracks of the Fjeltroll, a voice raised to break the silence.

Above there was the night sky, thin clouds scudding, scattered with pinpricks of stars and the waning moon. As it was since time had begun, since Arahila the Fair had Shaped them into being that the children of Men might not fear the darkness.

No.

There . . . *there*. Low on the horizon, a star.

A red star.

It was faint, but it was there. Its light throbbed, faint and fickle, red.

Leather and steel creaked as Vorax levered his bulk to his feet, his breathing audible in the tower chamber; louder, as he saw the star and sucked his breath between his teeth with a hiss. "Red star," he said. "That wasn't there before."

Tanaros, who had not known fear for many years, knew it now. He let go the edge of the casement and flexed his hands, tasting fear and wishing for his black sword. "What is it, my Lord?"

The Shaper watched the red star flicker low in the distance. "A warning."

"Of what, my Lord?" The taste of fear in his mouth. "From whom?"

"My elder sister." The voice was as soft as a Shaper's could be, touched with ages of sorrow. "Oh, Arahila!"

Tanaros closed his eyes. "How can that be, my Lord? With the Souma shattered and Urulat sundered . . . how can it be that Arahila would Shape such a thing?"

"Dergail," said Vorax. "Dergail's Soumanië."

A chip of the Souma, long since shattered; a chip, Shaped by Haomane First-Born, Chief of Shapers, into a gem, one of three. It had been lost even before Tanaros was born, when Haomane sent his three Wise Counselors to make war upon his Lordship. The Counselor Dergail, who had borne the Arrow of Fire, had known defeat and flung himself into the sea rather than allow the gem or the weapon to fall into enemy hands. For over a thousand years, both had been lost.

"Yes," said Satoris, watching. "Dergail's Soumanië."

Tanaros' mouth had gone dry. "What does it mean, my Lord?"

Satoris Third-Born watched the red star, and the faint light of the waning moon silvered his dark visage. Calm, so calm! Unmoving, he stood and watched, while ichor seeped like blood from the unhealing wound he bore, laying a glistening trail down the inside of his thigh, never ceasing.

"War," he said. "It means war."

Footsteps sounded on the tower stair, quick and light, announcing Ushahin's arrival. The half-breed entered the chamber, bowing. "My Lord Satoris."

"Dreamspinner," the Shaper acknowledged him. "You have news?"

In the dim light, there was beauty in the ruined face, the mismatched features. The half-breed's smile was like the edge of a knife, deadly and bitter. "I have passed across the plains of Curonan like the wind, my Lord, and walked in the dreams of Men while they slept. I have news. Cerelinde of the Ellylon, granddaughter of Elterrion, has agreed to wed Aracus Altorus of the children of Men."

When a daughter of Elterrion weds a son of Altorus . . .

It was one of the conditions of Haomane's Prophecy, those deeds by which the Lord-of-Thought vowed Satoris would be overthrown and defeated, and Urulat reclaimed by the Six Shapers who remained.

Vorax cursed with a Staccian's fluency.

Tanaros was silent, remembering.

Aracus Altorus.

There had been another of that House, once; there had been many others, and Altorus Farseer first among them, in the First Age of the Sundered World. For Tanaros, born in the years of dwindling glory, there was only one: Roscus Altorus, whom he had called "King," and "my lord." Roscus, dearer to him than any brother. Red-gold hair, a ready smile, a strong hand extended to clasp in friendship.

Or in love, as his hand had clasped that of Tanaros' wife. Claiming her, possessing her. Leading her to his bed, where he got her with child.

Tanaros trembled with hatred.

"Steady, cousin." Vorax's hand was heavy on his shoulder, and there was sympathy in the Staccian's voice. They knew each other well, the Three, after so long. "This concerns us all."

Ushahin Dreamspinner said nothing, but his eyes gleamed in the dark chamber. Near black, the one, its pupil fixed wide; the other waxed and waned like the moon, set in a pale, crazed iris. So it had been, since the day he was beaten and left for dead, and Men said it was madness to meet his eyes. What the Ellylon thought, no one knew.

"My Lord Satoris." Tanaros found his voice. "What would you have of us?"

"Readiness." Calm, still calm, though it seemed the ichor bled faster from his wound, the broad trail glistening wider. "Tanaros, command of the armies is yours. Those who are on leave must be recalled, and each squadron rendered a full complement. There must be new recruits. Vorax, see to our lines of supply, and those allies who might be bribed or bought. Ushahin . . . " The Shaper smiled. "Do as you do."

They bowed, each of the Three, pressing clenched fists to their hearts.

"We will not fail you, my Lord," Tanaros said for them all.

"My brave lieutenants." Satoris' words hung in the air, gentle. "My brother Haomane seeks my life, to end the long quarrel between us. This you know. But all the weapons and all the prophecies in the Sundered World avail him not, so long as the dagger Godslayer remains safe in our charge, and where it lies, no hands but mine may touch it. This I promise you: for so long as the marrow-fire burns, I shall reign in Darkhaven, and you Three with me. It is the pact of your branding, and I shall not fail it. Now go, and see that we are in readiness."

They went.

On the horizon, the red star of war flickered.

"So it's war, then."

For all his mass, the Fjeltroll's hands were quick and deft, working independent of their owner's thoughts.

"So it seems." Tanaros watched Hyrgolf's vast hands shape the *rhios,* using talons and brute force to carve the lump of granite. It was in its final stages, needing only the smoothing of the rounded surfaces and the delineation of the expressive face. "You'll order the recall? And a thousand new recruits drafted?"

"Aye, General." His field marshal blew on the stone, clearing granite dust from the miniature crevices. He held the *rhios* in the palm of his horny hand and regarded it at eye level. A river sprite, rounded like an egg, an incongruous delicacy against the yellowed, leathery palm. "What think you?"

"It is lovely."

Hyrgolf squinted. His eyes were like a boar's, small and fierce, and he was of the Tungskulder Fjel, broad and strong and steady. "There's some will be glad of the news."

"There always are," Tanaros said. "Those are the ones bear watching."

The Fjeltroll nodded, making minute adjustments to the figurine's delicate features, shearing away infinitesimal flakes of granite. "They always are."

Brutes, Men called them; delvers, sheep-slaughterers, little better than animals. Tanaros had believed it himself, once. Once, when the sons of Altorus ruled a powerful kingdom in the southwest, and he had been Commander of the Guard, and held the borders of Altoria against the forces of Satoris; the deadly Were, the horrid Fjeltroll. Once, when he had been a married man deep in love, a husband and faithful servant, who had called a bold, laughing man with red-gold hair his lord and king.

Roscus. Roscus Altorus.

Aracus Altorus.

Oh, love, *love!* Tanaros remembered, wondering. How could you do that to us?

Somewhere, an infant drew breath into its lungs and bawled.

So much time elapsed, and the wound still unhealed. His heart ached with it still, beat and ached beneath the silvery scar that seared it, that made the pain bearable. It had cracked at her betrayal; cracked, like the Souma itself. And in that darkness, Satoris had called to him, and he had answered, for it was the only voice to pierce his void.

Now . . . now.

Now it was different, and he was one of the Three. Tanaros, General Tanaros, Tanaros Blacksword, and this *creature,* Hyrgolf of the Fjeltroll, was his second-in-command, and a trusted companion. For all that he massed more than any two Men combined, for all that his eyetusks showed when he smiled, he was loyal, and true.

"You think of *her,*" Hyrgolf said.

"Is it so obvious, my friend?"

"No." Hyrgolf blew dust from the *rhios* and studied it again, turning it this way and that. "But I know you, General. And I know the stories. It is best not to think of it. The dead are the dead, and gone."

Her neck beneath his hands, white and slender; her eyes, bulging, believing at the last. A crushing force. And somewhere, an infant crying, wisps of red-gold hair plastered on its soft skull. An infant he had allowed to live.

Tanaros remembered and flexed his hands, his capable hands, hunching his shoulders under the weight of memory. "I have lived too long to forget, my friend."

"Here." Broad hands covered his, pressing something into them. Dirt-blackened talons brushed his wrists. An object, egg-sized and warm. Tanaros cradled the *rhios* in his palms. A sprite, a river sprite. Her delicate face laughed at him from between his thumbs. A rounded shape, comforting, bearing streaks of salmon-pink. It made him think of backwater currents, gentle eddies, of spawning-pools rife with eggs.

"Hyrgolf . . . "

"Keep it, General." The Fjeltroll gave him a gentle smile, a hideous sight. "We carry them to remember, we who were once Neheris' Children. One day, if the Sundered World is made whole, perhaps we will be again."

Neheris Fourth-Born, Neheris-of-the-Leaping-Waters, who had Shaped the high mountains of the north and the bright waters that tumbled down them, and Shaped the Fjeltroll also. Tanaros rubbed the *rhios,* the curving stone polished smooth as satin and warm from Hyrgolf's touch. It felt good in his hand.

"That's it." His field marshal nodded. "Keep it in your pocket, General, and it will always be with you."

He stowed the figurine. "Thank you, Hyrgolf."

"Welcome you are, General." Picking up a battle-axe, the Fjel rummaged for a whetstone and began honing the edge of his weapon with the same attentive patience. The whetstone made a rhythmic rasping sound in the snug cavern, familiar and soothing. "Regular weapons inspections from here out, you reckon?"

"Yes." Tanaros rubbed his temples. "We'll double up on drills as soon as the recalled units arrive. And I want scouting patrols in the tunnels, reporting daily. Establish a post at every egress between here and the Unknown, with runners between them. I want daily reports."

"Aye, sir." Hyrgolf tested the edge of the blade with a thick-calloused thumb and resumed his efforts. "Pity for the lads due leave."

"I know." Restless, Tanaros stood to stretch his legs, pacing around the confines of the field marshal's chamber. Like all the barracks, this one was built into a stony ridge. The Fjeltroll had constructed Darkhaven to their own scale, but Lord Satoris was its genius and its architect, and the convoluted magnificence of it echoed its creator. For themselves, the Fjeltroll had eschewed walls and towers, delving into the bones of the earth and carving out the simple caverns they preferred, laid out to flank and protect the mighty edifice. Most dwelled in common chambers; Hyrgolf, due to his rank, had his own. It held a sleeping pallet covered in sheepskin, his weapons and gear, a few simple things from home. Tanaros stopped before a niche hollowed into the wall, containing the stump of a tallow candle and a crudely carved *rhios.*

"My boy's first effort," Hyrgolf said behind him. There was pride in his voice. "Not bad for a mere pup, eh General?"

Tanaros touched the cavern wall, bowing his head. "You were due leave."

"In two months' time." The sound of the whetstone never slowed. "That's the luck, isn't it? We always knew this day might come."

"Yes." He looked back at the Fjeltroll. "How do your people tell it?"

"The Prophecy?" Hyrgolf shook his massive head. "We don't, General."

No, of course not. In the First Age of the Sundered World, when Satoris was sore wounded and at his weakest, when Haomane First-Born, the Lord-of-Thought, had called upon the Souma and brought the sun so near to earth it scorched the land and brought into being the Unknown Desert, the Fjeltroll had sheltered Satoris and pledged their loyalty to him. After his Counselors had been defeated, Haomane First-Born uttered his Prophecy into the ears of his allies. The Prophecy was not shared with the Fjel.

Instead, it doomed them.

"And yet you still honor Neheris," Tanaros said, fingering the *rhios* in his pocket. "Who sided with Haomane, with the Six, against his Lordship. Why, Hyrgolf?"

"It's Shapers' business," Hyrgolf said simply, setting down his axe. "I don't pretend to understand it. We made a pact with his Lordship and he has honored it, generation after generation. He never asked us to stop loving Neheris who Shaped us."

"No," Tanaros said, remembering his Lord's cry. *Oh, Arahila!* "He wouldn't."

And he fingered the *rhios* in his pocket again, and longed for the simplicity of a Fjeltroll's faith. It was not granted to Men, who had been given too many gifts to bear with ease. Oh, Arahila! Second-Born among Shapers, Arahila the Fair, Born-of-the-Heart. Would that you had made us less.

"How do your people tell it?" Hyrgolf asked. "The Prophecy, that is."

Tanaros relinquished the *rhios,* his hands fisted in his pockets as he turned to face his field marshal. "In Altoria," he said, and his voice was harsh, "when I was a boy, it was told thus. 'When the un-known is made known, when the lost weapon is found, when the marrow-fire is quenched and Godslayer is freed, when a daughter of Elterrion weds a son of Altorus, when the Spear of Light is brought forth and the Helm of Shadows is broken, the Fjeltroll shall fall, the Were shall be defeated ere they rise, and the Sunderer shall be no more, the Souma shall be restored and the Sundered World made whole and Haomane's Children shall endure.'"

It grieved him to say it, as if the Fjeltroll might hold him in some way responsible. After all, if he had killed the babe . . . *if he had killed the babe.* The House of Altorus would have ended, then, and there would have been no Prophecy.

Blue eyes, milky and wondering. Red-gold hair plastered to a damp skull.

He hadn't been able to do it. The babe, the child of his cuckolded marriage bed, had succeeded Roscus in the House of Altorus.

"Aye," Hyrgolf said, nodding. "That's as I heard it. The Sundered World made whole, but the cost of it our lives. Well, then, that's only a piece of it, this wedding. There's a good deal more needs happen before the Prophecy is fulfilled, and who knows what the half of it means?"

"His Lordship knows," Tanaros said. "And Malthus."

Their eyes met, then; Man and Fjel, hearing a common enemy named.

"Malthus," Hyrgolf rumbled, deep in his chest. The Wise Counselor, Wielder of the Soumanië, last of three, last and greatest of Haomane's Shapings. "Well, there is Malthus, General, I don't deny you that. But he is only one, now, and we have among us the Three."

Tanaros, Vorax, Ushahin.

"Pray that we are enough," Tanaros said.

"That I do, General," said the Fjeltroll. "That I do."

Tanaros Blacksword, Commander General of the Army of Darkhaven, walked alone to his quarters, a stone the size of an egg in his pocket.

From time to time, he touched it for reassurance.

ELSEWHERE IN THE LAND OF Urulat, flames burnt low and dwindled in their lamps in the archives of Meronil, housed in the Hall of Ingolin, where an elderly figure in scholar's robes bent over a hide-bound tome, muttering. The lamplight caught in his grey, tangled beard, cast shadows in the deep lines of his face, marking them in contrast to the splendid treasures that gleamed about him, housed in the archives for safekeeping.

Footsteps, slow and measured, quiet on the elegant carpets.

"Old friend," said Ingolin, the last Lord of the Ellylon. "You should rest."

The head lifted, sharp nose pointing, eyes fierce under heavy brows. "You know why I do not."

"It is a day for rejoicing, old friend," the Ellyl reminded him.

Malthus the Counselor laughed without mirth. "Can you tell me how to quench the marrow-fire, Ingolin the Wise? Can you render the unknown known?"

"You know I cannot." There was calm acceptance in the Ellyl's reply. In the manner of his people he had lived a long time, and knew the limits of his own knowledge. "Still, Cerelinde has unbent at long last, and Aracus Altorus has bowed his House's ancient pride. Love, it seems, has found them. A piece of the Prophecy shall be fulfilled, and the Rivenlost endure. May we not rejoice in it?"

"It is not enough."

"No." Ingolin glanced unthinking to the west, where Dergail's Soumanië had arisen. "Old friend," he asked, and his voice trembled for the first time in centuries. "Do you hold the answers to these questions you ask?"

"I might," Malthus the Counselor said slowly, and pinched the bridge of his nose, fixing the Lord of the Ellylon with a hawk's stare. "I might. But the way will be long and difficult, and there are many things of which I am unsure."

Ingolin spread his hands. "The aid of the Rivenlost is yours, Malthus. Only tell us how we might serve."

"You can't, old friend," said Malthus the Counselor. "That's the problem."

IN ANOTHER WING OF THE Hall of Ingolin, a fire burned low in the great hearth. Cerelinde, the granddaughter of Elterrion, gazed at it with unseeing eyes and thought about the deed to which she had committed herself this day.

She was the Lady of the Ellylon, the last scion of the House of Elterrion. By the reckoning of her people, she was young, born after the Sundering of the world, after the grieving Ellylon had taken the name Rivenlost unto themselves. Her mother had been Erilonde, daughter of Elterrion the Bold, Lord of the Ellylon, and she had died in childbirth. Her father had been Celendril of the House of Numireth the Fleet, and he had fallen in battle against Satoris Banewreaker in the Fourth Age of the Sundered World.

If the courage of Men had not faltered that day, her father might have lived. Haomane's Allies might have triumphed that day, and the world been made whole.

She had never known the glory of the Souma and Haomane's presence, only the deep, enduring ache of their absence.

That bitter knowledge had dwelled in her while generations were born and died, for, by the reckoning of Men, she was time-

less. She had watched, century upon century, the proud Kings of
Altoria, Altorus' sons, as they grew to manhood and took their
thrones, made love and war and boasts, withered and died. She
had watched as they disdained their ancient friendship with the Ellylon, watched as Satoris Banewreaker calculated his vengeance
and shattered their kingdom. She had stopped watching, then, as
the remnants of a once-mighty dynasty dwindled into the Borderguard of Curonan.

Then Aracus had come; Aracus Altorus, who had been tutored
by Malthus the Counselor since he was a lad. Like her, he was the
last of his line.

And he was different from those who had come before him.

She had known it the moment she laid eyes upon him. Unlike
the others, the Kings of Altoria in all their glory, Aracus was aware
of the brevity of his allotted time; had measured it against the
scope of the Sunderer's plan and determined to spend it to the
greatest effect. She had seen it in his face, in the wide-set, demanding gaze.

He understood the price both of them would have to pay.

And something in her had . . . quickened.

In the hall outside the hearth chamber she heard the sound of
his bootheels striking the white marble floors, echoing louder than
any Ellyl's tread. She heard the quiet murmur of words exchanged
with Lord Ingolin's guards. And then he was there, standing before
the hearth, the scent of horses and leather and night air clinging to
his dun-grey cloak. He had ridden hard to return to her side. His
voice, when he spoke, was hoarse with weariness.

"Cerelinde."

"Aracus."

She stood to greet him. He was tall for a Man and their eyes
were on a level. She searched his face. In the dim firelight, it was
strange to see the glint of red-gold stubble on his chin. He was
Arahila's Child, and not of her kind.

"Is it done?" she asked.

"Aye," he said. "The Borderguard carry word of our betrothal."

Cerelinde looked away. "How long before it reaches the Sunderer's ears?"

"It has done so." He took her hand. "Cerelinde," he said. "The
Sunderer flaunts his defiance. The red star of war has risen. I saw it
as I rode."

Her fingers trembled in his grasp. "So quickly!"

His voice grew softer. "You know what is said, my lady. One of the Three stalks the dreams of mortal Men."

"The Misbegotten." Cerelinde shuddered.

Aracus nodded. "Aye."

Cerelinde gazed at their joined hands. His fingers were warm and calloused, rough against her soft skin. It seemed she could feel his lifeblood pulse through them, urgent and mortal, calling to her. She tried not to think of Ushahin the Misbegotten, and failed.

"Our children . . . " she murmured.

"No!" Aracus breathed the word, quick and fierce. His grip tightened, almost painful. Lifting her head, she met his eyes. "They will not be like that one," he said. "Wrenched forth from violence and hatred, cast out and warped. We honor the Prophecy. Our children will be conceived in love, in accordance with Haomane's will, and Arahila's."

She laid her free hand upon his chest. "Love."

"Aye, lady." He covered her hand with his own, gazing at her. "Never less. I swear it to you. Though my heart beats to a swift and mortal tune, it beats true. And until I die, it lies in your keeping."

"Ah, Aracus!" His name caught in her throat. "We have so little time!"

"I know," he murmured. "All too well, I know."

ELSEWHERE ON URULAT, NIGHT CREPT westward.

Slowly, it progressed, a gilt edge fading to the blue of twilight, drawing a cloak of darkness behind it. Where it passed—over the fields and orchards of Vedasia, over the dank marshes of the Delta, over Harrington Inlet, across the Unknown Desert and Staccia and Seahold and Curonan—the stars emerged in its wake.

It came to the high mountains of Pelmar, where a woman stood on the steep edge of a cavern, and a gem bound in a circlet at her brow shone like the red star that flickered low, low on the far western horizon.

Her name was Lilias, though Men and Ellylon called her the Sorceress of the East. She had been a mortal woman, once; the daughter of a wealthy Pelmaran earl. The east was the land of Oronin Last-Born, in whose train death rode, and his lingering touch lay on those Men, Arahila's Children, who settled in Pelmar as their ever-increasing numbers covered the earth. It was said those of noble birth could hear Oronin's Horn summon them to their deaths.

Lilias feared death. She had seen it, once, in the eyes of a young man to whom her father would have betrothed her. He was a duke's son, well made and gently spoken, but she had seen in his eyes the inevitability of her fate, old age and generations of children yet unborn, and she had heard the echo of Oronin's Horn. Such was the lot of Arahila's Children, and the mighty Chain of Being held her fast in its inescapable grip.

And so she had fled into the mountains. Up, she went, higher than any of her brothers had ever dared climb, scaling the height of Beshtanag Mountain and hiding herself in its caverns. It was there that she had encountered the dragon.

His name was Calandor, and he was immortal after his kind. If he had hungered, he might have swallowed her whole, but since he did not, he asked her instead why she wept.

Weeping, she told him.

Twin jets of smoke had risen from his nostrils, for such was the laughter of dragons. And it was there that he gave a great treasure into her keeping: One of the lost Soumanië, Ardrath's gem that had been missing for many centuries. It had been plucked from the battlefield by a simple soldier who thought it a mere ruby. From thence its trail was lost until it ended in the hoard of a dragon, who made it a gift to a mortal woman who did not wish to die.

Such was the caprice of dragons, whose knowledge was vast and unfathomable. Calandor taught her many things, the first of which was how to use the Soumanië to stretch the Chain of Being, keeping mortality at bay.

She was no longer afraid.

It had been a long time ago. Lilias' family was long dead, her lineage forgotten. She was the Sorceress of the East and possessed great power, which she used with neither great wisdom nor folly. She allowed Oronin's Children, the Were, to hunt freely in the forests of Beshtanag, though elsewhere they were reviled for aiding Satoris the Sunderer in the last great war. The regents of Pelmar feared her and left her in peace, which was her sole desire.

And, until now, the Six Shapers had done the same.

Lilias regarded the red star on the horizon and felt uneasiness stir in her soul for the first time in many centuries. Dergail's Soumanië had risen, and change was afoot. Behind her in the mammoth darkness a vast shadow loomed.

"What does it mean, Calandor?" she asked in a low voice.

"Trouble." The word emerged in a sulfurous breath, half lost in the heights of the vaulted cavern. Unafraid, she laid one hand on the taloned foot nearest her. The rough scales were warm to the touch; massive claws gleaming like hematite, gouging the stone floor. On either side, forelegs as vast and sturdy as columns. Somewhere above and behind her head, she could hear the dragon's heart beating, slow and steady like the pulse of the earth.

"For whom?"

"Usssss." High above, Calandor bent his sinuous neck to answer, the heat of his exhalation brushing her check. "Uss, Liliasss." And there was sorrow, and regret, in the dragon's voice.

I will not be afraid, Lilias told herself. I will not be afraid!

She touched the Soumanië, the red gem bound at her brow, and gazed westward, where its twin flickered on the horizon. "What shall we do, Calandor?"

"Wait," the dragon said, laying his thoughts open to her. "We wait, Liliasss."

And in that moment, she *knew,* knowledge a daughter of Men was never meant to bear. The sorceress Lilias shook with knowledge. "Oh, Calandor!" she cried, turning and hiding her face against the plate-armor of the dragon's breast, warm as burnished bronze. "Calandor!"

"All things must be as they are, little sister," said the dragon. "All thingsss."

And the red star flickered in the west.

TWO

TENS OF THOUSANDS OF FJELTROLL awaited his command.

It was the first full assembly since the troops had been recalled, and there were seasoned veterans and raw recruits alike in
their ranks. All of them had labored hard through the winter at the
drills he had ordered, day in and day out, put to the test this spring
afternoon.

Whatever reservations he had, Tanaros' heart swelled to behold
them. So many! How long had it been since so many had assembled under his Lord's command? Since the fall of Altoria, centuries
ago, when he had led a vast army across the plains of Curonan,
breaking the rule of the House of Altorus forevermore in the southwest of Urulat, establishing the plains as no-man's-land. If they
could not hold it, neither would they cede it to the Enemy.

Who threatened them once again.

"Hear me!" he shouted, letting his voice echo from the hillsides.
"A red star has risen in the west! Our Enemy threatens war! Shall
they find us ready, my brothers?"

A roar answered, and his mount danced sideways beneath him;
black as pitch, a prince among stallions, frothing at the bit. The
strong neck arched, hide sleek with sweat. At his side, Vorax
chuckled deep in his chest, sitting comfortably in his deep-cantled
saddle. Unlike Tanaros in his unadorned field armor, the Staccian
wore full dress regalia, his gilded armor resplendent as a lesser sun
beneath the heavy clouds.

"Steady," Tanaros murmured to his mount, shortening the reins.
"Steady." A breed apart, the horses of Darkhaven. The stallion
calmed, and he raised his voice again. "Let us do, then, what we

do, my brothers! Marshal Hyrgolf, on my orders!" And so saying, he gave the commands in common parlance. "Center, hold! Defensive formation! Left flank, advance and sweep! Right flank, wheel! Attack the rear!"

Under a sullen sky, his orders were enacted. In the center, bannermen waved frantically, conveying his commands to the outer battalions, even as Hyrgolf roared orders, repeating them in common and in the rough tongue of the Fjeltroll, taken up and echoed by his lieutenants. The chain of command, clear-cut and effective.

The central mass of the army swung into a defensive formation, a mighty square bristling with pikes and cudgels. The left flank strung itself out in a line, spears raised. There, to the right, the third unit swung away, retreating and regrouping, forming a wedge that drove into the rear of the central square, shouting Staccians at the fore. In his own tongue, Vorax exhorted his kinsmen with good-natured cries.

Mock battle raged, with wooden swords and cork-tipped spears, and the hills resounded with the clash of armor and grunting effort, and the terrifying roars of the Fjel. Tanaros rode the length of the battle-lines, back and forth, approving of what he saw.

There, he thought, the cavalry would go when they had them, augmenting the left flank; two units of Rukhari, the swift nomads who dwelt on the eastern outskirts of the desert. Long ago, when Men had begun to disperse across the face of Urulat, the Rukhari conceived a love of wandering and disdained the notion of settling in one place. As a result, other Men viewed them with distrust.

The Rukhari were fierce and unpredictable and owed allegiance to no nation, but their culture was based on trade, and they could be persuaded to battle for a price. Vorax had promised them, and Vorax always delivered. As to what was to be done with them—that was Tanaros' concern.

That was his genius. He had done it here.

In their native terrain, the Fjelltroll were strong, cunning adversaries, relying on individual strength and their ability to navigate the steep mountainsides, luring their opponents into traps and snares, fighting in small bands knit with fierce, tribal loyalties. It had worked, once—in the Battle of Neherinach, in the First Age of the Sundered World, when Lord Satoris had fled to the isolated north and gone to earth to heal.

There Elderran had fallen, and Elduril too, sons of Elterrion the Bold.

And the dagger Godslayer, a shard of the Souma itself, had returned to Satoris.

It was the only weapon that could kill him.

And in the Fourth Age of the Sundered World, it had nearly been lost again, after Satoris had retaken the west and made his stronghold at Curonan, the Place-of-the-Heart, when Haomane First-Born sent his Wise Counselors across the sea, and Men and El-lylon alike had raised an army, a mighty army the likes of which had never been seen before or since. On the plains of Curonan, they had overrun the Fjeltroll—outfought them, *outstrategized* them.

Well, there were other forces at play, then; Tanaros knew it, though it was long before he had lived. There was Ardrath the Counselor, mightiest of them all, and the Helm of Shadows had been his, then, until his Lordship slew him. And there was Malthus, who bore the Spear of Light, who stepped into the gap when Ardrath fell, and so very nearly prevailed. Well and so; what of it? If the Fjeltroll had held, Tanaros thought grimly, his Lordship would never had to take the field, never lost Curonan, never been forced to retreat here, to Darkhaven.

And so he had trained the Fjel, whose numbers ever increased; trained them, dividing them into battalions, units and squadrons, each according to its own strength. He taught them to fight as Men, capable of holding their own on level ground, of working in consort with one another, of shifting and *adapting* at their commander's order. Together, they had brought down Altoria and held their own on the plains of Curonan.

That was what he could do.

That was why Lord Satoris had summoned him.

It had been his idea to outfit the Fjeltroll who held the center with round bucklers, little though they had liked it. The Fjel went into battle laden like carters' horses, leather harnesses over their vast shoulders, hung about with every manner of weapon: two battle-axes crossed at the back, cudgel and mace at the waist, a spear in either hand. All of these they were quick to discard, fighting at the end with tusk and talon. Shields had gone against their nature—yet they endured longer with them, holding formations that would have broken down into milling chaos.

Now, they took pride in their discipline.

Other innovations were his, too, some of them newer than others. The Gulnagel squadron of the left flank, Fjel from the lowlands of Neherinach; they were his. Smaller and more agile than their highland brethren, adept at leaping from crag to crag, they could keep pace with a running horse on level ground. Tanaros had found a way to make use of their speed. In a real battle, they would sow chaos in an unready cavalry.

Wood rang on steel, promising bruises and broken bones to the careless. Tanaros winced to hear the latter. When a Fjeltroll went down, howling in agony, one knew the damage was serious. Still, he kept them at it.

Better sick-leave in Darkhaven than dying at the point of an El-lyl sword.

The mock battle raged on, turning grim as the Fjeltroll in the center dug in and held their positions. Inside the square, Hyrgolf stomped, waving his arms and shouting orders, strengthening his troops. Tanaros allowed himself a brief smile. It was well that the center had held. When all was said and done, the strength of Satoris' army was in its infantry.

"Enough, cousin." Vorax came alongside him, laid a heavy hand upon his forearm. Emeralds and other gems winked on the cuffs of his gilded gauntlets. In the shrouded daylight, his features were blunt-carved and unsubtle, only the shrewd eyes hinting at a mind that thought. "Reward them, and keep their loyalty."

Tanaros nodded. "Well done!" he called to them, to the tens of thousands assembled in the valley of Darkhaven, as they laid up their weapons and listened, gasping, to his approbation. "Oh, bravely done, my brothers! Your night's rest is well earned."

"And a measure of *svartblod* to anyone on his feet to claim it!" Vorax bellowed.

They gave a ragged cheer, then.

They knew, the Fjeltroll did, that it was Lord Vorax who filled their trenchers and tankards, who gave them to eat and to drink, understanding the simple hungers that drove their kind. And yet they knew, too, what General Tanaros brought to the battlefield, and what he had made of them. Neheris had Shaped them, and Ne-heris had given them such Gifts as were in her keeping—a love of mountains and high places, and the hidden places within them, knowledge of stone and how it was formed, how it might be shaped, how a swift river might cut through solid rock.

Tanaros made them a disciplined fighting force.

"A fine skirmish!" Vorax clapped a powerful hand on his back. Tanaros coughed at the force of it, his highstrung mount tossing its head. The Staccian only grinned, revealing strong, white teeth. Some said there was Fjeltroll blood in the oldest Staccian lines; Vorax had never denied it. "I'm off to the cellars to count kegs against unkept promises. You'll keep them hard at it in days to come, cousin?"

General Tanaros, half-breathless, fought not to wheeze. "I will," he said as the Staccian saluted him, wheeling his deep-barreled charger toward the cellars of Darkhaven. What they contained, only Vorax knew; as with the larders, as with the treasury. *More,* was the Staccian's motto; *more and more and more,* a hunger as vast as all Urulat. And only his Lord Satoris had granted him indulgence for it.

As he had given Tanaros an army to command.

Thus the desires of two of the Three.

He stayed on the field, watching and waiting as the troops filed past him and saluted, here and there greeting a Fjel by name, commending his performance. Vorax's Staccian unit passed, too, laughing and saluting with fists on hearts, eager for their reward; *svartblod* and gold, Vorax would have promised. He knew them, too. It mattered. He was their general, their commander. He had commanded soldiers before, and he knew their hearts.

And they had hearts; oh, yes. Arahila Second-Born, Arahila the Fair, had given them that Gift. She had given her Gift to all the Shapers' Children, and she had not stinted in the giving.

Thus do we love, Tanaros thought, watching the Fjeltroll parade past him, bantering and jesting in their own guttural tongue, canny veterans dressing down the embarrassed recruits, mocking their bruises and pointing out their journeyman errors. And thus do we hate, for one begets the other.

Once, he had loved his wife and his liege-lord, and despised the Fjeltroll with all the rancor in his passionate heart. And yet it was the betrayal of that very love that had led him to this place, and made the Fjel his boon companions.

A pair of veterans passed, Nåltannen Fjel of the Needle Teeth tribe, bearing along an injured youngster, his meaty arms slung over their shoulders as he hobbled between them. They were laughing, showing their pointed teeth, the lad between them wincing every time his left foot made contact with the ground. "What think you, General?" one called in the common tongue, saluting. "Can we make a soldier of this one?"

"Mangren," Tanaros said, putting a name to the young Fjel's battered face, remembering where he had stood in the battle-lines. This one had worked hard in the drills. Dark bristles covered his hide and rose like hackles along the ridge of his spine; one of the

Mørkhar Fjel, injured and glowering and proud. "You held your ground when the Gulnagel overran your position. Yes, lads, I think he'll do. Get a measure of Lord Vorax's *svartblod* in him, and you'll see."

The veterans laughed, hurrying toward their reward.

Between them, the lad's face relaxed into a grin, still-white tusks showing against his leathery lips as he hobbled toward the barracks, aided by his comrades. He had done well, then; his general was pleased.

And on it went, and on and on, until it was done.

"They did well, eh, General?" Hyrgolf rumbled, planting himself before him.

The Fjeltroll was dusty with battle, dirt engrained in the creases of his thick hide. Scratches and dents marred the dull surfaces of his practice-weapons, the blunt iron. Tanaros shifted in his saddle, his mount sidling beneath him.

"They did well," he agreed.

Once upon a time, he had been the Commander of the Guard in Altoria. Once upon a time, he had taught Men to master their instinctive fear at the sight of the hideous, bestial visages of the Fjeltroll, taught them to strike at their unprotected places. Now, he taught the Fjeltroll to carry shields, and those hideous visages were the faces of his friends and brethren.

Hyrgolf's small eyes were shrewd beneath the thick shelf of his brow-bone. "Shall I report to debrief, General?"

"No." Tanaros shook his head. "The lads fought boldly, Hyrgolf. I saw it myself. Go, then, and claim Lord Vorax's reward. We'll return to regular drills on the morrow, and work on such weaknesses as I perceived."

"Aye, General!" Hyrgolf saluted smartly and set off for the barracks.

Tanaros sat his horse and watched him go. A rolling gait, better suited for the steep crags of the highlands than the floor of this stony hollow. The Fjeltroll's broad shoulders rocked from side to side as he marched, bearing lightly the burden of his battle-harness, the badges of his rank. Such loyalty, such courage!

It shamed him, sometimes.

Above his heart, the mark of his branding burned.

Bloody rays from the setting sun sank low under the overhanging clouds, striking a ruddy wash of light across the Vale of Gorgantum. Following in the wake of his troops, Tanaros shuddered out of habit. Haomane's Fingers, they called it here, probing for

Lord Satoris' pulse. Somewhere, in the depths of the mighty edifice
of Darkhaven, Satoris cowered, fearing his Elder Brother's wrath
that had once made a desert of his refuge.

It angered Tanaros. Flinging back his helmeted head, he
watched the dim orb of the setting sun in the west; watched it, issuing his own private challenge. He was a Man, and should not
fear the sun. Come, then, Haomane First-Born! Send your troops,
your Children, your Ellylon with their bright eyes and sharp blades,
your allies among Men! We are not afraid! We are ready for you!

The sun sank behind the low mountains, the challenge unanswered.

A red star flickered faint warning on the western horizon.

Tanaros sighed, and turned his horse toward home.

LINDANEN DALE HELD THEM LIKE a cupped hand, green and inviting.
It was ringed with stalwart oaks that stood like sentries, their leaves
not yet fully fledged. In the distance, Cerelinde could hear the
Aven River, a sound evocative of Meronil and home. Overhead, the
sky was clear and blue, Haomane's sun shining upon them like a
blessing.

"What think you, my lady?" Aracus smiled at her. He sat at ease
on his mount, one of the Borderguard, his second-in-command, a
half pace behind him. Sunlight made his hair blaze, copper
threaded with gold. "Your kinsmen and mine once met to take
counsel in this place, when Altoria ruled the west."

"Then it is fitting." Cerelinde smiled back at him. "I would fain
wed in a place of such beauty."

"Duke Bornin of Seahold has pledged a company," he said.
"It will be witnessed by Men and Ellylon, that all may know what
we do."

A shadow passed over the greensward. Aracus shaded his eyes
with one hand, gazing at the sky. It was limpid and blue, empty.
Amid the oaks, a raven's hoarse call sounded once, then was silent.

"This is not without risk," Cerelinde said quietly.

"No." He glanced at her. "But it must be witnessed, Cerelinde.
It must be done openly. Haomane's Prophecy will never be fulfilled unless we fire the hearts and minds of Men. Is Lord Ingolin
willing to admit hundreds upon hundreds of us to Meronil?"

She shook her head. "You know he is not. Our magic has
grown weak in this Sundered World. The wards would not hold.
We must be able to defend our last stronghold."

"Here, then." His smile returned. "We will put our faith in mortal steel."

Cerelinde inclined her head, turning in the saddle to address Aracus' companion. "I do not doubt my lord Blaise is capable," she said.

The two Men exchanged an uneasy glance.

Cerelinde raised her brows. "Will you not be in attendance?"

Blaise Caveros bowed briefly in the saddle. "Lady, forgive me, but I will not."

She studied his face. He returned her regard steadily, his dark gaze haunted by the shadow of his lineage. Once upon a time, his distant kinsman Tanaros Caveros had served as second-in-command to a scion of the House of Altorus; served and betrayed, becoming one of the Three. The enormity of his betrayal had tainted the name of all who bore it, and all their descendants thereafter. Aracus had been the first in a thousand years to set aside the ancient mistrust the Caveros name engendered, and Blaise was willing to spend his lifetime in atonement for his ancestor's sin. His loyalty was fierce, defiant and beyond question, and Aracus would never spare him unless grave doings were afoot.

"What," she asked, "is Malthus plotting?"

"Cerelinde." Aracus leaned over to touch her arm. "Nothing is certain and much is yet unknown. I pray you, ask me no questions I cannot answer. Malthus has bidden me keep his counsel, at least until we are wed."

"Even from me?" Anger stirred in her. "Am I not the Lady of the Ellylon? Does the Wise Counselor find even me unworthy of his trust?"

"No." It was Blaise who answered, shaking his head. "Lady, I know not where I am bound, nor does Aracus. It is Malthus who asks that we trust him."

"Malthus." Cerelinde sighed. "Haomane's Weapon keeps his counsel close; too close, perhaps. Haomane's Children do not like being kept in ignorance."

"It is for a short time only, my lady. Malthus knows what he is about." Aracus gazed at her. His eyes were a stormy blue, open and earnest, filled with all the passion of his belief. "Will you not abide?"

Cerelinde thought about all they risked, and the pain both of them would suffer. Time would claim him, leaving her untouched. There would be pain enough to spare, and no need to inflict more upon them, here and now, at the beginning. For the sake of what brief happiness was theirs to claim, she was willing to set aside her pride.

"So be it," she said. "I will abide."

THE EDIFICE OF DARKHAVEN EMBRACED the whole of the Vale of Gorgantum.

The fortress itself loomed at the center, black and gleaming, veined throughout with the marrow-fire. Its steep walls and immaculate lines had a stark beauty, tempered here and there with an unexpected turret, a hidden garden, an elaborate gable. To the west rose the Tower of the Observatory, where Satoris had met with the Three. In the east, there arose the Tower of Ravens, seldom used, though to good effect.

Between and below lay the Chamber of the Font, and Godslayer, where Lord Satoris dwelt.

Deeper still lay the Source.

Of *that,* one did not speak.

Tanaros had been there, in the Chamber of the Font. He had beheld Godslayer, pulsing like a heart in the blue-white flames. And he had knelt, gasping his allegiance, while the Lord Satoris had reached into the marrow-fire and taken Godslayer for his own, reversing the dagger, the Shard of the Souma, and planting its hilt above Tanaros' heart, searing his mortal flesh.

What lay beneath the Font?

The Source.

One did not speak of that which might be extinguished.

And from the Source at its center, Darkhaven spiraled outward to encompass the Vale entire, a double spiral with the two Towers as opposite poles. At its outermost perimeter, black walls coiled up the mountainsides, here and there punctuated by sentry posts, lit with watch-fires emerging visible in the dusk. There, to the east, a gap where the watchtowers flanked the Defile, their signal fires burning low and steady. Tanaros noted them as he rode, numbering them like a merchant counting coin. All was as it should be in the realm of Lord Satoris.

Inside the inner walls of the sanctuary, Tanaros made his way to the stables, dismounting with a groan. He had grown stiff in the saddle, stiff in the service of his Lord. A young stablehand came for the stallion, shadowy and deft, eyes gleaming behind the thatch of his forelock. One of Ushahin's madlings. The lad bobbed a crooked bow, then crooned to the stallion. It arched its neck, flaring its nostrils and huffing in gentle response.

"You needn't walk him long," Tanaros said in the common tongue, laying a hand on the stallion's glossy hide and finding it cool. "He's had his ease since the skirmish."

The madling sketched him a second bow, eyes bright with knowing.

What did he hear, Tanaros wondered; what did he understand? One never knew, with the Dreamspinner's foundlings. This one understood the common tongue, of that he was sure. Most of them did. A few did not. The madling led his mount away, still crooning; the stallion bent his head as if to listen, sleek black hide rippling under the light of the emerging stars. This one, Tanaros thought, loved horses. So much he knew, and no more. Only Ushahin, who walked in their dreams, knew them all.

With stiff fingers, Tanaros unbuckled his helm and approached the postern gate.

"General Tanaros!" The pair of Fjeltroll on duty saluted smartly, slapping the butts of their spears on the marble stair. "We heard the exercise went well," one added cunningly. "Too bad the Havenguard weren't there, eh?"

Pulling off his helm and tucking it under his arm, Tanaros smiled at the ploy. "I'll match Lord Vorax's offer, lads. A measure of *svartblod* to all who stood duty, and see it sent round to the lads on the wall, a full skin to each sentry-post. Send word to the quartermaster that it's on my orders."

They cheered at that, standing aside to let him pass. In some ways, the Fjel were like children, simple and easy to please. Loyalty was given, and loyalty was rewarded. No more could be asked, no more could answer.

Indeed, Tanaros thought as he entered Darkhaven proper, what more is there? He ran his hand through his dark hair, damp with sweat from confinement in his padded helm. Once, he had given his loyalty for the asking. Given it to Roscus Altorus, blood-sworn comrade and liege-lord, he of the red-gold hair and ready grin, the extended hand.

Given it to Calista, his wife, whose throat was white like the swan's, whose doe-eyes had bulged at the end, beseeching him; *oh love, forgive me, forgive me!*

Wary madlings skittered along the hallways, scattering at his passage, reforming behind to trail in his wake. Tanaros, lost in his memories, swung his helm from its leather strap and ignored them. There was food cooking in the great kitchens of Darkhaven, its savory odor teasing the hallways. He ignored that, too. They would serve the barracks, bringing platter upon platter heaped high with mutton, steaming in grey slabs. What Lord Vorax demanded in his quarters was anyone's guess. Tanaros did not care.

Fjeltroll mate for life, Hyrgolf had told him. Always.

He thought about that, sometimes.

"Lord General, Lord General!"

A lone madling, more daring than the rest, accosted him at the doors to his quarters. Tangled hair falling over her face, peering where her work-reddened hands pushed it away to reveal a darting eye.

"Yes, Meara?" Tanaros knew her, made his voice gentle.

She cringed nonetheless, then flexed, arching the lines of her body. "Lord General," she asked with satisfaction, "will you dine this evening? There is mutton and tubers, and Lord Vorax ordered wine from Pelmar."

The madlings behind her sighed, envying her boldness.

"That would be pleasant," he said, inclining his head. "Thank you."

"Tubers!" cried one of the madlings, a hulking figure with a guileless boy's eyes in a man's homely face, hopping up and down. "Tubers!"

Meara simpered, tossing her tangled hair. "I will bring a tray, Lord General."

"Thank you, Meara," he said gravely.

In a rush they left him, following now in Meara's wake, their voices whispering from the walls. Left in peace, Tanaros entered his own quarters.

It was quiet here, in the vast rooms he inhabited. A few lamps burned low, flickering on the gleaming black walls and picking out veins of marrow-fire. Tanaros turned up the wicks until the warm illumination offset the blue-white glimmer of the marrow-fire, lending a human touch to his quarters. Thick Rukhari carpets muffled his footsteps, their intricately woven patterns muted by lamplight. One of his few concessions to luxury. He undid the buckles on his corselet, removed his armor piece by piece, awkward without assistance, hanging it upon its stand. Sitting on a low stool, Tanaros sighed, tugging off his boots, the point of his scabbard catching on the carpet as he bent, the sword's hilt digging into his side.

War. It means war.

Standing and straightening, Tanaros unbuckled his swordbelt. He held it in his hands, bowing his head. Even sheathed, he felt the blade's power, the scar over his heart aching at it. Black it was, that blade, tempered in the marrow-fire and quenched in the ichor of Satoris himself. It was the gift he had received at the pact of his branding, and it had no equal.

Tanaros Blacksword, he thought, and placed the weapon in its stand.

Without it, he felt naked.

There was a scratching at the door. Padding in stocking feet across the carpets, Tanaros opened it. The madling Meara cringed, then proffered a silver tray, other madlings peeping from behind her. Fragrant aromas seeped from beneath the covered dishes.

"Thank you, Meara," he said to her. "Put it on the table, please."

Hunched over her burden, she slunk into the room, setting the gleaming tray on the ebony dining-table with a clatter. Triumphant, she straightened, beckoning to the others. Whispering to one another, they crept into his quarters like shadows, taking with reverent hands his dusty, sweated armor, his dirty boots. In the morning these would be returned, polished and gleaming, the buckles cleaned of grime, straps fresh-oiled, boots buffed to a high gloss.

Tanaros, who had beheld this drama many, many times over, watched with pity. "No," he said gently when one, scarce more than a lad, reached for the black sword. "That I tend myself."

"I touch?" The boy threw him a hopeful glance.

"You may touch it in its scabbard, see?" The Commander General of the Army of Darkhaven went to one knee beside the madling lad, guiding his trembling hand. "There."

The boy's fingers touched the scabbard and he groaned deep in his throat, his mouth soft with ecstasy. "My Lord! My Lord's blood!"

"Yes," Tanaros said softly, as he had done many times before, with this lad and others. "It was tempered in the marrow-fire, and cooled in his blood."

The madling cradled the hand that had touched it. "His blood!" he crowed.

"His blood," Tanaros agreed, rising to his feet, knee-joints popping at the effort. Always, it was so; the young men, the youths, drawn to the blade.

"Enough!" Emboldened by the success of her mission, Meara put her hands upon her hips, surveying Tanaros' quarters, finding nothing amiss. "Will you want a bath, Lord General?"

"Later," Tanaros said. The odor of mutton roast teased the air and his stomach rumbled at it. "Later will suffice."

She gave a firm nod. "Ludo will bring it."

"Thank you, Meara." Tanaros made her a courtly half-bow. She shuddered, a rictus contorting her face, then whirled, summoning the others.

"Come! You and you, and you. Algar, pick up the Lord General's greaves. Come, quickly, and let the Lord General eat!"

Tanaros watched them go, hurrying under Meara's command, laden with their burdens. Where did Ushahin find them? The unwanted, the misbegotten, the castoffs of Urulat. Damaged at birth, many of them—slow, simple, ill-formed. Others, the world had damaged; the world, and the cruelty of Men and the Lesser Shapers. Beaten by jealous lovers, shaken by angry parents, ravaged by conquest, they were victims of life, of circumstance or simple accident, fallen and half-drowned, until wits were addled or sanity snapped like a fine thread and darkness clouded their thoughts.

No wonder Ushahin Dreamspinner loved them.

And in their dreams, he summoned them, calling them to sanctuary in Darkhaven. All through the ages, they had come; singly, in pairs, in groups. In this place, they were sacrosanct. Lord Satoris had decreed it so, long, long ago, upon the day Ushahin had sworn the allegiance of his branding. No one was to harm them, upon pain of death.

Vorax had his indulgences.

Tanaros had his army.

Ushahin had his madlings.

Mutton roast steamed as Tanaros removed the covering domes and sat to his dinner. He carved a slab of meat with his sharp knife, juices pooling on the plate. The tubers were flaky, and there were spring peas, pale green and sweet. Sane or no, the madlings of Darkhaven could cook. Tanaros chewed slowly and swallowed, feeling the day's long efforts—the long efforts of a too-long life—settle wearily into his bones.

A warm bath would be good.

"WELL DONE, COUSIN."

A voice, light and mocking. Tanaros opened his eyes to see Ushahin in his drawing-room. The wicks had burned low, but even so the lamplight was less kind to the half-breed, showing up his mismatched features. One cheekbone, broken, sank too low; the other rode high, knotted with old pain.

"Do you jest, cousin?" Tanaros yawned, pushing himself upright in the chair. "How came you here?"

"By the door." The Dreamspinner indicated it with a nod of his sharp chin. "I jest not at all. Readiness, our Lord asked of us; readiness, you have given, Tanaros Blacksword. A pity you do not ward your own quarters so well."

"Should I not trust to the security of Darkhaven, that I myself have wrought? You make mock of me, cousin." Tanaros stifled a second yawn, blinking to clear his wits. A bath had made him drowsy, and he had dozed in his chair. "What do you seek, Dreamspinner?"

The half-breed folded his knees, dropping to sit cross-legged on Tanaros' carpet. His mismatched gaze was disconcertingly level. "Malthus is plotting something."

"Aye," Tanaros said. "A wedding."

"No." Ushahin shook his head, lank silver-gilt hair stirring. "Something *more*."

Tanaros was awake, now. "You've heard it in the dreams of Men?"

"Would that I had." The Dreamspinner propped his chin on folded hands, frowning. "A little, yes. Only a little. Malthus the Counselor keeps his counsel well. I know only that he is assembling a Company, and it has naught to do with the wedding."

"A Company?" Tanaros sat a little straighter.

"Blaise of the Borderguard is to be in it," Ushahin said softly, watching him. "Altorus' second-in-command. He has dreamed of it. He's your kinsman, is he not?"

"Aye." Tanaros' jaw clenched and he reached, unthinking, for the *rhios* in the pocket of his dressing-robe. The smooth surfaces of it calmed his mind. "Descended on my father's side. They are mounting an attack on Darkhaven? Even now?"

"No." Ushahin noted his gesture, but did not speak of it. "That's the odd thing, cousin. It's naught to do with us, or so it would seem."

"The Sorceress?" Tanaros asked.

Ushahin shrugged unevenly. "She holds one of the Soumanië, which Malthus the Counselor would like to reclaim. Beyond that, I cannot say. Those who have been chosen do not know themselves. I know only that a call has gone out to Arduan, to ask the mightiest of their archers to join the Company."

"Arduan," Tanaros said slowly. Relinquishing the *rhios,* he ran a hand through his hair, still damp from his bath. The Archers of Arduan, which lay along the northern fringes of the Delta, were renowned for their skill with the bow. "Does his Lordship know?"

"Yes." Ushahin's eyes glittered in the lamplight. "He knows."

The taste of fear was back in Tanaros' mouth, the triumph of the day's exercise forgotten. "Does he think it has to do with—"

"The lost weapon of the Prophecy?" the half-breed asked bluntly. "How not?"

Both were silent, at that.

Dergail's Soumanië had risen in the west.

Dergail the Counselor had been one of three, once; three that Haomane First-Born had sent against Satoris in the Fourth Age of the Sundered World. And he had been armed, as they all had. Armed with the Soumanië, polished chips of the Souma with the force to Shape the world itself—and armed also with weapons of Haomane's devising. One, they knew well; the Helm of Shadows, that Ardrath the Counselor had borne, which had fallen into Lord Satoris' grasp, and been *changed.* One other, they knew and feared; the Spear of Light, that Malthus had hidden.

But the last was the Arrow of Fire, that had vanished when Dergail was defeated and flung himself into the sea, and no one knew where it was.

"Ravens bore it away," Tanaros said at length. "Do they know?"

Ushahin shook his head again. "They are as they are, cousin," he said; gently, for him. "Brief lives, measured against ours; a dark flash of feathers in the sun. They do not know. Nor do the Were, who remember. Ravens bore it east, but it did not reach the fastholds of Pelmar."

When it came to the Were, Ushahin alone among Men—or Ellylon—would know. Oronin's Children had raised him, when no one else would. Tanaros considered. "Then Malthus knows," he said.

"Malthus *suspects,*" Ushahin corrected him. "And plots accordingly."

Tanaros spread his hands. "As it may be. I command troops, cousin. What would you have me do?"

"Do?" The half-breed grinned, his mood as mercurial as one of his madlings. "Why, cousin, do as you do! I have come to tell you what I know, and that I have done. You spoke, also, of ravens."

"Ravens." Tanaros smiled. "Is it time?"

"Time, and more." Ushahin uncoiled from the carpet, straightening as he rose. "There is a wedding afoot, after all, and the ravens have come home to roost, with their eyes filled with visions. Your friend is among them. Will you come with me to the rookery on the morrow, ere his Lordship summons them?"

"I will," Tanaros said, "gladly."

THREE

❖

A LIGHT MIST WREATHED THE beech wood, and their steps were sound-less on the mast of fallen leaves, soft and damp after winter. New growth was greening on the trees, forming a canopy overhead.

It was a deeper green than the beeches Tanaros had known as a boy, the leaves broader, fanning to capture and hold the cloud-filtered sunlight. The trunks of the trees were gnarled in a way they weren't elsewhere, twisted around ragged boles as they grew, like spear-gutted warriors straining to stand upright.

They were old and strong, though, and their roots were deep.

Blight, the Ellylon said; Satoris the Sunderer blighted the land, the ichor of his unhealing wound seeping like poison into the earth, tainting it so no wholesome thing could grow.

Tanaros had believed it, once. No longer. Wounded, yes. The Vale of Gorgantum had endured the blow of the Shaper's wound, as Lord Satoris himself endured it. Deprived of sunlight, it suffered, as Lord Satoris suffered, driven to earth by Haomane's wrath. Yet, like the Shaper, it survived; adapted, and survived.

And who was to say there was no beauty in it?

Ahead, a rustling filled the wood. There was no path, but Ushahin Dreamspinner led the way, at home in the woods. From behind, he looked hale, his spine straight and upright, his step sure. His gilt-pale hair shone under the canopy. One might take him, Tanaros thought, for a young Ellyl poet, wandering the wood.

Not from the front, though. No one ever made that mistake.

There, the first nest, a ragged construction wedged in the branches high overhead. Others, there and there, everywhere around them as they entered the rookery proper, and the air came alive with the sound of ravens. Ushahin stopped and gazed around him, a smile on his ruined face.

Ravens hopped and sidled along the branches, preening glossy black feathers. Ravens defended their nests, quarreled over bits of twig. Ravens flew from tree to tree, on wings like airborne shadows.

"*Kaugh!*"

The sound was so close behind him that Tanaros startled. "Fetch!"

There, on a low branch, a raven; *his* raven. The wounded fledgling he had found half-frozen in his Lord's garden six years gone by, grown large as a hawk, with the same disheveled tuft of feathers poking from his head. The raven cocked its head to regard him with one round shiny eye, then the other. Satisfied, it wiped its sharp, sturdy beak on the branch.

Tanaros laughed. "Will he come to me, do you think?"

Ushahin gave his uneven shrug. "Try it and see."

The ravens were the Dreamspinner's charges, a gift not of Lord Satoris, but of the Were who had reared him. Elsewhere, they were territorial. It was only here, in Darkhaven, that they gathered in a flock—and only when summoned, for Ushahin Dreamspinner had made them the eyes and ears of Lord Satoris, and sent them throughout the land.

This one, though, Tanaros had tended.

"Fetch," he said, holding out his forearm. "Come."

The raven muttered in its throat and eyed him, shifting from foot to foot. Tanaros waited. When he was on the verge of conceding, the raven launched himself smoothly into the air, broad wings outspread as he glided to land on Tanaros' padded arm, an unexpectedly heavy weight. Bobbing up and down, he made a deep, chuckling sound.

"Oh, Fetch." At close range, the bird's feathers shone a rich blue-black, miniscule barbs interlocking, layered in a ruff at his neck. Tanaros smoothed them with the tip of one finger, absurdly glad to see him. "How are you, old friend?"

Fetch made his chucking sound, wiped his beak on Tanaros' arm, then uttered a single low "*Kaugh!*" and bobbed expectantly. Tanaros reached into a pouch at his belt and drew forth a gobbet of meat, fed it to the raven, followed by others. In the trees, the others watched and muttered, one raising its voice in a raucous scolding.

"He's very fond of you." Ushahin sounded amused.

Tanaros smiled, remembering the winter he'd kept the fledgling in his quarters. A foul mess he'd made, too, and he was still finding things the raven had stolen and hidden. "Do you disapprove?"

The half-breed shrugged. "The Were hunt with ravens, and ravens hunt with the Were. It is the way of Men, to make tame what is wild. If you had sought to cage him, I would have disapproved."

"I wouldn't." Finding no more meat forthcoming, the raven took his leave, strong talons pricking through the padded leather as he launched himself from Tanaros' arm, landing on a nearby branch and preening under the envious eyes of his fellows, the tuft of feathers atop his head bobbing in a taunt. Tanaros watched his mischief with fond pleasure. "Fetch is his own creature."

"It's well that you understand it. The Were sent them, but the ravens serve Lord Satoris of their own choosing." Ushahin rubbed his thin arms against the morning's chill. "You've a need in you to love, cousin. A pity it's confined to birds and Fjel."

"Love." Anger stirred in Tanaros' heart. "What would you know of love, Dreamspinner?"

"Peace, cousin." Ushahin raised his twisted, broken hands. "I do not say it in despite. The forge of war is upon us, and all our mettle will be tested. Once upon a time, you loved a son of Altorus. And," he added, "once upon a time, you loved a woman."

Tanaros laughed, a sound as harsh as a raven's call. "Altoria lies in ruin because of that love, *cousin,* and the sons of Altorus are reduced to the Borderguard of Curonan. Do you forget?"

"No," Ushahin said simply. "I remember. But it was many years ago, and hatred burned in you like the marrow-fire, then. Now, there is yearning."

The calm, mismatched regard was too much to bear, undermining his anger. What was his suffering, measured against the half-breed's? Ushahin Dreamspinner had been unwanted even before his birth. It was an ill-gotten notion that had sent an embassy of the Ellylon of the Rivenlost to Pelmar in the Sixth Age of the Sundered World; an ill-gotten impulse that had moved a young Pelmaran lordling to lust.

A son of Men had assaulted a daughter of the Ellylon.

And Ushahin was the fruit of that bitter union, which had dealt the Prophecy a dire blow. Ushahin the Unwanted, whose birth ruined his mother—though he'd had no name, then, and hers was hidden from history. In their grief, the Ellylon laid a charge upon the family of the nameless babe's father, bidding them raise him as their own.

Instead, they despised him, for his existence was their shame.

Even in the Dreamspinner's story, Tanaros thought, he could not escape the sons of Altorus, for one had been present. Prince Faranol, Faranol Altorus, who had accompanied the Ellylon embassy on behalf of Altoria. A mighty hunter, that one, bold in the chase. He'd ridden out in a Pelmaran hunting-party, hunting the Were who savaged the northernmost holdings of Men. Oronin's Children were deadly predators, a race unto themselves, as much akin to wolves as Men. And if they hadn't found the Grey Dam herself, they'd found her den—her den, her cubs and her mate.

Prince Faranol had slain the Grey Dam's mate himself, holding him on the end of a spear as he raged forward, dying, the froth on his muzzle flecked with blood. They still told the story in Altoria, when Tanaros was a boy.

A mighty battle, they said.

Was it a mighty battle, he wondered, when Faranol slew the cubs? In Pelmar they had lauded him for it, even as they had turned their backs upon the family of Ushahin's father. Still, the damage was done, and no treaty reached; the Ellylon departed in sorrow and anger, Faranol Altorus' deeds went unrewarded, and in the farthest reaches of Pelmar, the Sorceress of the East remained unchallenged.

Such was the outcome of that embassy.

And seven years later, when a nameless half-breed boy, the shame of his family, starveling and ragged, was set upon and beaten in the marketplace of the capital city, who remarked it? When he staggered into the woods to die, the bones of his face shattered, his limbs crooked, his fingers broken and crippled, who remarked it?

Only the Grey Dam of the Were, still grieving for her slain mate, for her lost cubs, who claimed the misbegotten one for her own and named him in her tongue: Ushahin. And she reared him, and taught him the way of the Were, until Lord Satoris summoned him, and made of his skills a deadly weapon.

Tanaros watched the ravens, *his* raven. "Do you never yearn, cousin?"

"I yearn." The half-breed's voice was dry, colorless. "I yearn for peace, and a cessation to striving. For a world where the Were are free to hunt, as Oronin Last-Born made them, free of the encroachments of Men, cousin. I yearn for a world where ones such as I are left to endure as best we might, where no one will strike out against us in fear. Do you blame me for it?"

"No." Tanaros shook his head. "I do not."

For a moment, Ushahin's face was vulnerable, raw with ancient pain. "Only Satoris has ever offered that hope. He has made it precious to me, cousin; this place, this sanctuary. Do you understand why I fear?"

"I understand," Tanaros said, frowning. "Do you think I will fail his trust?"

"I do not say that," the half-breed replied, hesitating.

Tanaros watched the raven Fetch, sidling cunningly along the low branch, bobbing his head at a likely female, keeping one eye cocked lest he, Tanaros, produce further gobbets of meat from his pouch. "Ravens mate for life, do they not, cousin?"

"Yes." Ushahin's eyes were wary.

"Like the Fjel." Tanaros turned to face the Dreamspinner, squaring his shoulders. "You need not doubt me, cousin. I have given my loyalty to his Lordship; like the Fjeltroll, like the ravens, like the Were." Beneath the scar of his branding, his heart expanded, the sturdy beating that had carried him through centuries continuing, onward and onward. "It is the only love that has never faltered."

Love, yes.

He dared to use that word.

"You understand that what you see this night may pain you?" Ushahin asked gently. "It involves your kindred, and the sons of Altorus."

"I understand." Tanaros inclined his head. "And you, cousin? You understand that we are speaking of a union between Men and Ellylon?"

Ushahin grimaced, baring his even teeth. "I understand, cousin. All too well."

"Then we are in accord," Tanaros said.

The raven Fetch chuckled deep in his throat, shifting from foot to foot.

THREE WERE EMERGED FROM THE dense forest at the base of Beshtanag Mountain, drifting out of the foliage like smoke. They rose from four legs to stand upon two, lean and rangy. Oronin's Children, Shaped by the Glad Hunter himself. They were vaguely Man-shaped, with keen muzzles and amber eyes, their bodies covered in thick pelts of fur.

One among them stood a pace ahead of the others. He addressed Lilias in the Pelmaran tongue, a thick inflection shading his words. "Sorceress, I am the ambassador Kurush. On behalf of the Grey Dam Sorash, we answer your summons."

"My thanks, Kurush." Lilias inclined her head, aware of the weight of the Soumanië on her brow. Her Ward Commander, Gergon, and his men flanked her uneasily, hands upon weapons, watching the Were. In the unseen distance, somewhere atop the mountain, Calandor coiled in his cavern and watched, amusement in his green-slitted eyes. Lilias did not fear the Were. "I seek to affirm our pact."

Kurush's jaws parted in a lupine grin, revealing his sharp white teeth. "You have seen the red star."

"I have," she said.

"It is Haomane's doing," he said, and his Brethren growled low in their throats.

"Perhaps," she said carefully. "It betokens trouble for those who do not abide by the Lord-of-Thought's will."

Kurush nodded toward the mountain with his muzzle. "Is that the wisdom of dragons?"

"It is," Lilias said.

Turning to his Brethren, Kurush spoke in his own tongue, the harsh sounds falling strange on human ears. Lilias waited patiently. She did not take the alliance of the Were for granted. Once, the east had been theirs; until Men had come, claiming land, driving them from their hunting grounds. In the Fourth Age of the Sundered World, the Were had given their allegiance to Satoris Banewreaker, who held the whole of the west. Haomane's Counselors had arrived from over the sea, bearing the three Soumanië and the weapons of Torath, the dwelling-place of the Six Shapers: the Helm of Shadows, the Spear of Light, the Arrow of Fire.

There had been war, then, war as never before. Among the races of Lesser Shapers, only the Dwarfs, Yrinna's Children, had taken no part in it, taking instead a vow of peace.

While Men, Ellylon and Fjel fought on the plains of Curonan, the Were had lain in wait, on the westernmost shore of Urulat—the last place they would be expected. When the ships of Dergail the Counselor and Cerion the Navigator made landfall, thinking to assail Satoris from the rear, the full force of the Were met them and prevailed. Dergail flung himself into the sea, and his Soumanië and the Arrow of Fire were lost. Cerion the Navigator turned his ships and fled, vanishing into the mists of Ellylon legend.

And yet it was no victory.

If the Were had remained in the west, perhaps. Though Satoris had been wounded and forced to take refuge in the Vale of Gorgantum, there he was unassailable. But no, Oronin's Children returned east to the forests of their homeland, flowing like a grey tide, and the wrath of Men was against them, for Haomane's Counselors and the army of Men and Ellylon they led had failed, too. And Men, always, increased in number, growing cunning as they learned to hunt the hunters, waiting until spring to stalk Were-cubs in their dens, while their dams and sires foraged.

Not in Beshtanag. Many centuries ago, Lilias had made a pact with the Grey Dam, the ruler of the Were. Oronin's Children hunted freely in the forests of Beshtanag. In return, they held its outer borders secure.

Concluding his discussion with his Brethren, the ambassador Kurush dropped into a crouch. Gergon ordered his wardsmen a protective step closer to Lilias, and the two Brethren surged forward a pace.

"Hold, Gergon." Lilias raised her hand, amused. It had been more than a mortal lifetime since she had cause to summon the Were. Betimes, she forgot how short-lived her Ward Commanders were. "The ambassador Kurush does but speak to the Grey Dam."

With a dubious glance, Gergon shrugged. "As my lady orders."

Kurush crouched, lowering his head. His taloned hands dug into the forest loam, the lean blades of his shoulders protruding like grey-furred wings. His eyes rolled back into his head, showing only the whites, as he communed with the Grey Dam.

Oronin's Children possessed strange magics.

A gratifyingly short time passed before Kurush relaxed and stood. With another sharp grin he extended his hand. "Yea," he said. "The Grey Dam Sorash accedes."

Lilias clasped his hairy hand. His pads were rough against her palm and his claws scratched lightly against the back of her hand. She recited the ritual words of their alliance. "Thy enemies shall be mine, and my enemies shall be thine."

"My enemies shall be thine, and thy enemies shall be mine," Kurush echoed.

Dipping his muzzle to her, the Were ambassador turned, his Brethren following. In the space of a few heartbeats, they had melted back into the forest from which they had come. The pact had been affirmed. Beshtanag's defenses were secure.

From his distant eyrie, Calandor's thoughts brushed hers, tinged with warm approval.

Well done, Lilias.

IT WAS THE DARK OF the moon, and dark in the Tower of Ravens.

There was no view, here, though the windows stood open onto the night. The rooftops of Darkhaven fell away beneath them, illuminated faintly by starlight.

All of them were there, all of the Three.

And in the center of them stood the Shaper.

"They are ready, Dreamspinner?" he asked.

Ushahin bowed low and sincere, starlight glimmering on his moon-pale hair. "They are, my Lord."

"Come," Lord Satoris whispered, his voice carrying on the night breeze "Come!" And other words he added, uttered in the tongue of the Shapers, tolling and resonant, measured syllables that Shaped possibilities yet unformed.

Beating wings filled the air.

Through every window they came, filling the tower chamber; ravens, the ravens of Darkhaven, come all at once. They came, and they flew, round and around. Silent and unnatural, swirling in a glossy-black current around the tower walls—so close, wings overlapping like layered feathers, jet-bright eyes gleaming round and beady. Around and around they went, raising a wind that tugged at Vorax's ruddy beard, making the Staccian shudder involuntarily.

Still, they held their positions, each of the Three.

Where are you, Tanaros wondered, *which* are you? To no avail he sought to pick a raven, his raven, from the dark, swirling tide that enveloped the tower walls, looking to find a mischievous eye, an errant tuft of pin-feathers, from among them. Darkness upon darkness; as well pick out a droplet of water in a rushing torrent.

"The Ravensmirror is made," Ushahin announced in a flat tone.

In the churning air, a scent like blood, sweet and fecund.

Satoris the Shaper spread his hands, drawing on ancient magic—the veins of the marrow-fire, running deep within the earth; the throbbing heart of Godslayer, that Shard of the Souma that burned and was not consumed.

"*Show!*"

The command hung in the air with its own shimmering darkness. Slowly, slowly, images coalesced, moving. Sight made visible. Only fragments, at first—the tilting sky, a swatch of earth, an upturned face, a scrabbling movement in the leaf-mold. A mouse's beady eye, twitching whiskers. A drawn bow, arrow-shot and an explosion of feathers, a chiding squawk.

Such were the concerns of ravens.

Then; a face, upturned in a glade. A thread for Lord Satoris to tease, drawing it out. What glade, where? Ravens knew, ravens kept their distance from the greensward. One flew high overhead, circling; their perspective diminished with lurching swiftness to an aerial view. There. Where? A greensward, ringed about with oak, a river forking to the north. And in it was a company of Ellylon.

There was no mistaking them for aught else, Haomane's Children. Tall and fair, cloaked in grace. It was in their Shaping, wrought into their bones, in their clear brows where Haomane's blessing shone like a kiss. It was in the shining fall of their hair, in the touch of their feet upon the earth. If their speech had been audible, it would have been in the tenor of their voices.

"What is this place?" Ushahin's words were strained, a taut expression on his ravaged face. Always it was so. More than the children of Men who had shunned him, he despised the Ellylon who had abandoned him.

"It is called Lindanen Dale," said the Shaper, who had walked the earth before it was Sundered. "Southward, it lies."

"I know it, my Lord," Tanaros said. "It lies below the fork of the Aven River. Betimes the Rivenlost of Meronil would meet with the sons of Altorus, when they ruled in the west. Or so my father claimed."

"But what are they *doing?*" Vorax mused.

In the shifting visions, Ellyl craftsmen walked the greensward, measuring, gauging the coming spring. Banners were planted, marking the four corners of the Dale; pennants of white silk, lifted on the breeze, showing the device of Elterrion the Bold, a gold crown above the ruby gem of the Souma, as it had been when it was whole. The Ravensmirror churned and circled, showing what had transpired.

A Man came riding.

The weak sunlight of early spring glinted on his hair, red-gold. His eyes were wide-set and demanding, his hands steady on the reins as he guided his solid dun mount. Tanaros felt weak, beholding him.

Aracus Altorus.

It was him, of course. There was no denying it, no denying the kingship passed down generation upon generation, though the kingdom itself was lost. It did not matter that he wore no crown, that his cloak was dun-grey, designed to blend with the plains of Curonan. What he was, he was. He looked like Roscus. And he looked like Calista, too—Tanaros' wife, so long ago. The set of the eyes, last seen believing. How not? He was of their blood.

And at his side, another, dark-haired and quiet, with scarred knuckles. Unlike his lord, he was watchful as he rode, stern gaze surveying the wood as they emerged into the glade. Ravens took wing, the perspective shifting and blurring as they withdrew, re-solving at a greater distance.

Once, Tanaros had ridden just so, at the right hand of his lord.

Strange, that his memory of Roscus' face as he died was so vague. Surprised, he thought. Yes, that was it. Roscus Altorus had looked surprised, as he raised his hand to the sword-hilt protruding from his belly. There had been no time for aught else.

In the churning Ravensmirror, in Lindanen Dale, Aracus Altorus halted, his second-in-command beside him. Behind them, a small company of Borderguard sat their mounts, silent and waiting in their dun-grey cloaks.

The Ellyl lord in command met him, bowing low, a gesture of grace and courtesy. Aracus nodded his head, accepting it as his due. Who is to say what the Ellyl thought? There was old sorrow in his eyes, and grave acceptance. He spoke to the Altorian king-in-exile, his mouth moving soundlessly in the Ravensmirror, one arm making a sweeping gesture, taking in the glade. There and there, he was saying, and pointed to the river.

Such a contrast between them! Tanaros marveled at it. Next to the ageless courtesy of the Ellyl lord, Aracus Altorus appeared coarse and abrupt, rough-hewn, driven by the brevity of his life-span. Small wonder Cerelinde Elterrion's granddaughter had refused this union generation after generation. And yet . . . and yet. In that very roughness lay vitality, the leaping of red blood in the vein, the leaping of desire in the loins, the quickening of the flesh.

Satoris' Gift, when he had one.

It was the one Gift the Ellylon were denied, for Haomane First-Born had refused it on his Children's behalf, who were Shaped be-fore time came into being and were free of its chains. Only the Lord-of-Thought knew the mind of Uru-Alat. The slippery prompt-ings of desire, the turgid need to seize, to spend, to take and be taken, to generate life in the throes of an ecstasy like unto dying—

this was not for the Ellylon, who endured untouched by time, age-less and changeless as the Lord-of-Thought himself.

But it was for Men.

And because of it, Men had inherited the Sundered World, while the Ellylon dwindled. Unprompted by the goads of desire and death, the cycle of their fertility was as slow and vast as the ages. Men, thinking Men, outpaced them, living and dying, genera-tion upon generation, spreading their seed across the face of Uru-lat, fulfilling Haomane's fears.

"A wedding!" Vorax exclaimed, pointing at the Ravensmirror. "See, my Lord. The Ellyl speaks of tents, here and here. Fresh wa-ter from thence, and supplies ferried upriver, a landing established *there*. From the west, the Rivenlost will come, and Cerelinde among them. They plan to plight their troth here in Lindanen Dale."

Lord Satoris smiled.

Above, the stars shuddered.

"I think," he said, "that this will not come to pass."

And other things were shown in the Ravensmirror.

The ravens of Darkhaven had flown the length and breadth of Urulat, save only the vast inner depths of the Unknown, where there was no water to sustain life. But to the south they had flown, and to the east and north. And every place they had seen, it was the same.

Armies were gathering.

In the south, the Duke of Seahold increased his troops, fortify-ing his borders. Along the curve of Harrington Inlet, where gulls cried above the sea, the Free Fishers laid aside their nets and sharpened their long knives. The knights of Vedasia rode in stately parties along the orchard roads and, here and there, Dwarfs ap-peared along the roadside, giving silent greeting as they passed. In Arduan, men and women gathered in knots to speak in the mar-ketplace, full quivers slung over their shoulders. The streets of Pel-mar City were filled with soldiers, and long trains of them wound through the woods. Along the eastern verge of the desert, the Rukhari whetted their curving swords. To the north, the stone fortresses of Staccia were shut and warded.

"What do they dream, Dreamspinner?"

"War, my Lord," Ushahin said briefly. "They dream of war. They dream of a red star arisen in the west, and the rumor of a wedding-to-come. They dream, in fear, of the rumor of Fjeltroll moving in the mountains, in such numbers as none have seen in living memory."

"Do they dream of the Arrow of Fire?"

Ushahin paused, then shook his head. "In Arduan, they do. All Arduans dream of Oronin's Bow and the Arrow of Fire. But they do not know where it is."

Satoris Third-Born, whom the Ellylon named Banewreaker and Men called Sunderer, watched the swirling images, motionless as a mountain. "Haomane," he murmured, then again, "Haomane!" He sighed, gathering himself. "They will not strike, not yet. Not unless this wedding occurs, and fills them with the courage of my Elder Brother's Prophecy, such as they understand it." A glare lit his eyes. "Then they will bring war to my doorstep."

"Not Staccia, my Lord," Vorax promised. "They guard their own, but they have pledged their loyalty on gold, and sent a company in earnest token. As long as we may ward the tunnels, our lines of supply shall remain open. And the desert Rukhari may be bought for swift horses, for they love fine steeds above all else, and despise the Pelmarans."

"Loyal Vorax," the Shaper said gently. "Your heart is as vast as your appetite. What you have done, I know well, and I am grateful for it. It the unknown that I fear."

When the unknown is made known . . .

Tanaros shivered, brushed by the feather-touch of the Prophecy.

"My Lord." Ushahin pointed at the Ravensmirror. "There is more."

Around and around, the dark maelstrom whirled, fleeting visions forming against the black gloss of feathers, the gleam of round eyes pricking like stars. Around and around, inevitable as time, link upon link in the Chain of Being, circling like the ages.

When the companies parted in Lindanen Dale, Blaise Caveros of the Borderguard—Aracus' second-in-command—went with the Ellylon. He spoke at length with a lieutenant in his company, a young man who saluted him firmly, his jaw set. Aracus Altorus gripped his wrists, gazing into his eyes. And they parted. Blaise rode with the Rivenlost to Meronil, and did not look back, bound to a greater mission.

Tanaros watched him hungrily.

What need could be so great that it would part the second-in-command from his sworn lord? None, in his lifetime, in his mortal lifetime. And yet it was so. Blaise Caveros, who was his own kinsman many times removed, left his lord without glancing back, his grey-cloaked back upright.

"What are you up to, Malthus?" Lord Satoris whispered.

To that, there was no answer. The Ravensmirror swirled onward, giving only taunting glimpses. A contest, and bow-strings
thrumming. Fletched arrows, a silent thud. Feathers, scattering. A
lone Arduan, setting forth on a journey, coiled braids hidden beneath a leather cap.

On the verges of his journey—hers, as it transpired—there was
the Unknown Desert, glimpses assayed by fearful ravens, wary of
the lack of water.

Malthus the Counselor keeps his counsel well . . .

"Enough!" The Shaper's fists clenched, and the Ravensmirror
dispersed, trembling, breaking into a thousand bits of darkness.
Roosts were found, bescaled and taloned bird-feet scrambling for
perches, bright eyes winking as the Shaper paced, the Tower trembling beneath his footfalls. A single raven, with a tuft of feathers
atop his head, croaked a tremulous query. In the air hung the
copper-sweet smell of blood.

"It shall not be," Lord Satoris said. "Though I have left my Elder
Brother in peace, still he pursues me, age upon age. I grow weary
of his enmity. If it is war Haomane wishes, my Three, I shall oblige
him. And I shall not wait for him to bring it to my doorstep." He
turned to Tanaros. His gaze burned, ruddy coals in the night. A line
of seeping ichor glistened on his inner thigh, reeking of blood,
only stronger. "My General, my rouser of Men. Are you fit to travel
the Marasoumië?"

Tanaros bowed.

Tanaros could not do aught else.

"I am yours to command, my Lord," he said, even as a single
raven dispatched itself from the horde, settling on his shoulder. He
stroked its ruffled feathers with a fingertip. "Only tell me what you
wish."

Satoris did.

FOUR

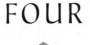

LILIAS KNEW.

It came as a stirring, a tensing of her brow, as if the circlet she ever wore had grown too tight. Awareness tickled the base of her skull, and the Soumanië on her brow warmed against her skin, rendering her feverish.

She paced the halls of her fasthold of Beshtanag, restless and uneasy, curt with her body-servants, her pretty ones, when they sought to soothe her. Calandor had shown her long ago how to Shape the hearts and minds of those who served her, and they were her one indulgence. Some of them sulked, but not all. She had always tried to choose them wisely. Little Sarika wept, curling into a ball, damp hair clinging to her tear-stained cheeks. Pietre dogged her steps, squaring his shoulders in a manful fashion until she snapped at him, too. It wasn't their fault, and she felt guilty at it.

"Calandor," she whispered, *reaching*. "Oh, Calandor!"

I am here.

At the touch of the dragon's thoughts, the Sorceress of the East relaxed, obliquely reassured. "One is coming, traveling the Marasoumië."

Yes, little sister. One of the Branded.

Lilias grasped the railing of the balustrade and stared down the mountainside.

It was secure, of course. The grey crags, the pine mantle spread like a dark green apron below. Gergon and his wardsmen held it for her and the Were defended its borders, but the mountain was hers, hers and Calandor's. With the power of the Soumanië, they had made it so. No creature moved upon it, not squirrel nor bat, wolf nor Were, and least of all Man, but that Calandor knew it. And what the dragon knew, the sorceress knew.

So it had been, for a long, long time.

"I shall have to meet him, won't I?" she asked aloud. "Which one is it?"

The Soldier.

Lilias grimaced. It would have been easier, in a way, had it been one of the others—the Dreamer, or the Glutton.

The Dreamer, she understood. When all was said and done, they were both Pelmaran. The Were had raised him, and although their ways were strange, she understood them better than anyone else of mortal descent.

And as for the Glutton, his wants were simple. Gold, mayhap; a portion of the fabled dragon's hoard. Or flesh, carnal desire. Lilias touched the curves of her body, the ample, swelling flesh at her bodice. That too, she understood.

What the Soldier asked would be harder.

The summons at the base of her skull shrilled louder, insistent. Lilias hurried, taking a seldom-used key from the ring at her waist and unlocking the door that led to the caverns and the tunnels below. The ancient steps were rough-hewn, carved into the living rock. She held her skirts, descending swiftly. If not for Calandor's wisdom, she would never have known such things existed.

Now, little sister. He comes now.

Down, and down and down! All beneath the surface of Urulat, the tunnels interlaced, carved out in ages past, before the world was Sundered. Calandor knew them, for it was his brethren who had carved them, long ago, when there were dragons in the earth. And along those passages lay the Ways of the Marasoumië, the passages of the Souma, along which thought traveled, quick as a pulse. Though they were Sundered from Torath and the Souma itself, still they endured; dangerous, yet passable to those who remembered them and dared.

Dragons remembered, as did the Shaper. No others would dare the Ways, save perhaps Malthus the Counselor, who wielded a Soumanië of his own.

Lilias reached the bottom, hurried along the passageway.

Ahead lay the node-point, and blood-red light beat like a heart, bathing the rocky walls. A vaulted chamber, and a tunnel stretching away westward into darkness. Lines of light, the forgotten Ways, pulsed along it, bundled fibers laid in an intricate network, all linked back to the severed bond of the Souma.

The Marasoumië of Uru-Alat, whom Men had once called the World God. Though Uru-Alat had died to give birth to the world, remnants of his power yet existed. The Marasoumië was one.

A figure was coming, dark and blurred, moving at a walking pace with inhuman speed, each motion fanning in her vision, broken into a thousand component parts. Lilias pressed her back to the stony walls of the cavern, reaching desperately for Calandor.

All is well.

The node-light flared, red and momentarily blinding. Lilias cried out as a figure stumbled into the chamber, his body stunned by the transition to a mortal pace.

A Man, only a Man.

Lilias the Sorceress pulled herself away from the cavern wall and stood upright to acknowledge him, summoning her dignity and the might of the Soumanië she wore. "Greetings, Kingslayer."

He flinched at the title, straightening as though his back pained him, pushing dark hair back from his brow. "Greetings, Sorceress."

A quiet voice, low and husky with exhaustion. He spoke Pelmaran well, with only a trace of a southerner's accent. It was not what Lilias had expected; and yet it was. Calandor had known as much. He was tall, but not nearly as tall as the stories made him, when he had ridden to battle on the plains of Curonan, wearing the Helm of Shadows. A Man, nothing more, nothing less.

"Your Lord has sent you."

"Yes." The Soldier bowed, carefully. "He would beg a favor, my lady. You know that Dergail's Soumanië has risen in the west?"

"I know it." A mad laugh rose in Lilias' throat; she stifled it. It tasted of despair. "I have known it these many weeks, Tanaros Blacksword."

His eyes were weary. "Shall we speak, then?"

Lilias inclined her head. "Follow me."

She was aware of him on the stair behind her, his steps echoing hers, following at a respectful distance. The skin of her back crawled and her throat itched, when she remembered how his wife had died.

He offered no threat.

Even so.

"My lady!" Her Ward Commander, Gergon, was waiting at the top of the stair. He took a step forward, frowning. "You should have sent for—" Her stalwart, grizzled commander forgot what he was saying, staring in hushed awe. "General Tanaros!"

"Commander." The Soldier bowed courteously.

Gergon's gaze slid to the hilt of the black sword, hanging inconspicuously at Tanaros' side. He blinked, his mouth working, no words emerging. Behind him, a pair of junior warders clad in the colors of Beshtanag, forest-green and bronze, jostled one another and craned to see over their commander's shoulder.

Always the blades, with Men.

The dragon's voice sounded amused, by which token Lilias knew there to be no danger. She sighed inwardly, and exerted the power of the Soumanië. "Commander Gergon, I thank you for your concern. I will summon you if there is need."

Gergon stood aside, then, having no choice; his junior warders scrambled to fall in beside him. Lilias swept past them, leading Tanaros Blacksword to her private chambers. He followed her without comment, more patient than she would have guessed. His hands hung loose at his sides, and she tried not to think what they had done.

I have killed, little sister. I have eaten Men whole.

"None that you loved," Lilias said aloud.

Tanaros looked quizzically at her. "Sorceress?"

The dragon chuckled. *What is love?*

Lilias shook her head. "It is nothing," she said to Tanaros.

Calandor's question was too vast to answer, so she ignored it, escorting Tanaros to her drawing-room. A woman's room; she had chosen it deliberately. A warm fire burned in the grate, chasing away the spring chill. Soft rose-colored cushions adorned the low couches, and tapestries hung on the walls, illustrating scenes from Pelmar's past. There was a rack of scrolls along one wall, and shelves with curiosities from Calandor's hoard. In one corner stood a spinning-wheel, dusty for lack of use. The lamps were hooded with amber silk, casting a warm glow. Lilias sank into the cushions, watching Tanaros, lamplight glancing off the lacquered black of his armor.

He was uneasy in the room.

"Sit," she said, indicating a chair. "You must be in need of refreshment, after your journey."

He sat, clearing his throat. "The Ways of the Marasoumië are not easy."

Lilias pulled a bellcord of bronze cabled silk, soft to the touch. Pietre was there almost before she released it, half-belligerent in his eagerness to serve.

"My lady?" He bowed low.

"Pietre." She touched his luxuriant brown hair, caught in a band at the nape of his neck. The silver collar about his neck gleamed. He shivered with pleasure at her touch, and she repressed a smile. "Bring us wine and water, a terrine with bread and cheese, and some of the Vedasian olives."

"My lady." He shivered again before departing.

Tanaros Blacksword watched, expressionless.

"You do not approve?" Lilias raised an eyebrow.

He released his breath in a humorless laugh, pushing at his dark hair. "Approve? I neither approve nor disapprove. It is the way of Men, and the daughters of Men, to make tame what is wild."

Lilias shrugged. "I Shape only those whose natures it is to serve, as mine was not. Some are more willing than others. I try to choose wisely. Pietre has pride in his labors."

"And your army?" He leaned forward, hands on his knees, greaves creaking.

"You have seen my Ward Commander, Kingslayer." Lilias eyed him. "Gergon learned his task at his father's knee, as did his father before him. Though Dergail's Soumanië has risen in the west, Beshtanag is secure. You have done as much for Darkhaven, since before his grandfather drew breath. Do you doubt his pride in it?"

"No." He exhaled, met her gaze. "How long has it been, lady?"

Such a question! She knew what he meant, and tears, unbidden, stung her eyes. "Over a thousand years. How long for you?"

"Twelve hundred." He bowed his head, touching some unknown talisman in his pocket. His dark hair fell to curtain his features. It was ill-cropped, and there was not a trace of grey in it. "Over twelve hundred."

Neither of them spoke.

The door opened for Pietre's return, with Sarika at his heels, a pitcher of water in one hand and wine in the other. They served the refreshments with exquisite, sullen grace. Sarika knelt at her feet, grey-blue eyes pleading mutely for reassurance. Lilias caressed her cheek, finding her voice.

"Thank you, child."

Sarika was pleased; Pietre shot a triumphant glance at the Soldier, who nodded courteously at him, studiously ignoring his bared chest, and how it gleamed by lamplight, oiled and taut below his servant's collar. Lilias poured the wine herself, and waited until Tanaros had filled his mouth with bread and cheese.

"So," she asked him then, "what does your Lord Satoris wish of me?"

Swallowing crumbs, he told her.

❖

I WILL NOT BE AFRAID.

I will not be afraid.

Calandor!

And he was there, with her, as he had been for a thousand years and more, a reassuring presence coiled around the center of her being. Lilias touched the Soumanië at her brow and breathed easier, turning to face the Soldier. When had she risen to pace the room, when had her hands become fists? She did not remember.

"You will bring war to Beshtanag."

"Aye, lady." There was regret in his voice. "A war to prevent a war."

Bring him to me, Lilias. I would hear his Master's words.

"You understand," Lilias said to him, "the decision is not mine alone to make."

"The dragon." There was fear in his eyes, and exultation, too.

"Yes." Lilias nodded. "We are as one in Beshtanag."

Tanaros rose, bowing. "It will be my honor. I bear him greetings from my Lord Satoris."

"Come," Lilias said.

Outside, the air was thin, gold-washed in the afternoon sun. Once again, she led him herself, through the rear entrance her wardmen guarded, out of the castle and upward, up the lonely, winding path where her own people feared to tread. The mountain of Beshtanag ran both deep and high. His breath labored in the thin air. Holding her skirts, the Sorceress cast glances behind her as she climbed.

His face was rapt, and he paused at every chance to gaze at the sun as it gilded the peaks of the trees below. Seeing her notice, he smiled with unexpected sweetness. "Forgive me, my lady. We do not see the unveiled sun in Darkhaven, save as an enemy."

Of course.

Haomane First-Born had Shaped the sun, wrought it of the light of the Souma before the world was Sundered. Lilias knew it, as every schoolchild did. And after the world was Sundered, when Satoris fled into the depths of Urulat, Haomane sought to destroy him with it, withdrawing only when the sun scorched the earth, threatening to destroy all life upon it.

And Satoris had escaped; and in his wake, the Unknown Desert.

Still, it had marked the Sunderer, cracking and blackening his flesh, weakening him so that he could not bear the touch of the sun. A whole Age he had hidden himself in the cold, cavernous fastnesses of Neherinach, among the Fjel, seething and healing, until he was fit to emerge and forge his way west, wreaking vengeance upon the world.

Of course the sun did not shine full upon Darkhaven.

"Your pardon, General," Lilias said. "I did not think upon it."

"No mind." Tanaros smiled again, drawing a deep breath of mountain air. "I have missed it."

Lilias paused, tucking a wind-tugged strand of hair behind her ear. The height was dizzying and the crags fell away beneath their feet, but she was at home, here. "Then why do you serve him?" she asked curiously.

"You know what I did?" His gaze flicked toward her.

She nodded.

She knew; the world knew. Twelve hundred years gone by, Tanaros Caveros had been the Commander of the King's Guard in Altoria, sworn to serve Roscus Altorus, his kinsman. His wife had betrayed him, and lain with the King, giving birth to a babe of Altorus' get. For that betrayal, Tanaros had throttled his beloved wife, had run his sworn King through on the point of a sword and fled, bloody-handed. And that was all Urulat had known of him until he returned, four hundred years later, at the head of the army of Darkhaven and destroyed the kingdom of Altoria.

"Well." Tanaros stared into the distant gorge at the base of the mountain. "Then you know. My Lord Satoris . . ." He paused, fingering the unseen talisman. "He needed me, my lady. He was the only one who did, the only one who gave me a reason to live. A cause to fight, an army to lead. He is the only one who allowed me the dignity of my hatred."

Small wonder, that.

Lilias knew something of the Sunderer's pain, of the betrayal that had Shaped him; but that was between her and the dragon. She wondered how much Tanaros knew. It was difficult to imagine him committing the deeds that had driven him to the Shaper's side, and yet he had not denied it. She wondered if he regretted them, and thought that he must. Even in the bright sunlight, there was a shadow that never left his eyes. "Come," she said. "Calandor is waiting."

And she led him, then, to the mouth of the cavern, scrabbling up the lip of the plateau, all dignity forgotten. It didn't matter, here. The opening yawned like a mouth, and something *moved* within it, high above them. Stalagmites rose from the cavern floor, towering in the air in fantastic, tapering columns. Beyond, distant heaps of treasure glinted, gold and trinkets and sorcerers' gewgaws, books and chalices and gems, all bearing the impress of their once-owners' touch.

A smell of sulfur hung in the air, and Lilias laughed for pure joy. "Calandor!"

"Liliasssss."

One of the stalagmites moved, then another, equidistant. Something scraped along the cavern floor. Vast claws gouged stone, and a bronze-scaled breast hove into view like the keel of a mighty ship. High above, a snort of flame lit the vaulted roof sulfur-yellow. Tanaros took a step backward, reaching unthinking for the hilt of his sword, then held his ground as the dragon bent his sinuous neck downward, scales glinting in the slanting light from the opening.

"Tanaross Caverosss."

The mighty jaws parted as the dragon spoke, lined with rows of pointed teeth, each one as large as a man's hand. Forge-breath ruffled the Soldier's hair, but he stood unflinching though the dragon's head hovered above his own, incomprehensibly vast. Thin trickles of smoke issued from the dragon's nostrils and its eyes were green, green and cat-slitted, lit with an inner luminescence.

"Calandor." Tanaros bowed, unable to conceal the awe in his face. "Eldest, I bear you greetings from my Lord Satoris, whom you once called friend."

A nictitating membrane covered the dragon's eyes in a brief blink; a smile, though Tanaros could not have known it. "I am not *the* Eldessst, Blackssword. Your Masster knows as much. What does he want, the Sssower?"

"He wants our aid, Calandor," Lilias said aloud what the dragon already knew. "He wants to lay a false trail to our doorstep for the Ellylon to follow."

Calandor ignored her, dragging himself past them step by slow step to the verge of the cavern, positioning his immense claws with care. His plated underbelly rasped on the stone. The crest of spines along his neck became visible, the massive shoulders. His wings, folded at his sides, the vaned pinions glittering like burnished gold. Outspread in the sky, they would shadow the mountainside. Lilias heard Tanaros stifle a gasp.

The dragon scented the air through nostrils the size of dinner-plates. "Sheep," he said, sounding satisfied. "In the northeast meadow. Three have lambed this day. I am hungry, Liliasss."

"Then you shall feed, Calandor."

"At nightfall," the dragon said. "I will take wing. Two ewes, and one lamb."

"It shall be so, Calandor." Lilias had conferred with her head herdsman, as she did each spring. They knew, to a lamb, what losses the flock could sustain. The dragon knew it, too. She wondered at what game he played.

Calandor's head swung around, swiveling on that sinuous neck, green eyes fixing on the Soldier. "You were to have been my rightful prey, Man! You whose numbers have overrun the earth."

Tanaros shuddered and held fast. "I represent my Lord, not my race, Calandor."

Twin jets of smoke emerged in a laugh. "The Shaper."

"Yes," Tanaros said. "The Shaper."

The dragon lifted his massive head and stared westward, eyes slitting in the sun. "We aided Sssatoriss when the Sssouma was shattered, because he was a friend. Many of usss died for it, and Haomane became our Enemy. No more, we sssaid. But it was too late, and we too few, and I, I am one of the lasst. Do you asssk me now to die, Ssoldier?"

"No," Tanaros said. "No! Eldest Brother, we will lay a trail to the doorstep of Beshtanag, yes. And when the Ellylon follow it, and the sons of Altorus and whatever allies they might gather, we will fall upon them from behind, the army of Darkhaven in all its strength, and it shall be ended. This I swear to you. Do you doubt it?"

Why, Lilias wondered, did she want to weep?

Calandor blinked, slowly. "I am not the Eldessst, Kingsslayer."

"Nonetheless." Tanaros' voice hardened. "My lord Calandor, Dergail's Soumanië has risen, and the signs of the Prophecy have begun. In a week's time, Cerelinde of the Ellylon will plight her troth with Aracus Altorus, and across the land, Urulat prepares for war. Haomane himself only knows what mission Malthus the Counselor has undertaken. Where will you be, if Darkhaven falls? If Godslayer falls into the Counselor's hands, if Urulat is made whole on Haomane's terms? Do you think one mortal sorceress with a chip of the Souma can resist the Six Shapers? Where will you be then, Elder Brother?"

"Enough!" Lilias clapped her hands over her ears.

But the dragon only sighed.

"Then let them come, Kingsssslayer," he said. "You sspeak the truth. If I will not ssserve your cause, neither will I oppose it. Lay your falssse trail. Let them come, and make of uss the anvil on which your hammer may ssstrike. Does this please you?"

"My lord Calandor," Tanaros said. "I am grateful. My Lord is grateful."

"Yesss," the dragon said. "Now go."

FIVE

THE OLD MAN SQUATTED ON his haunches, gazing at the stars.

Even in the small hours of night, the rock held enough sun-captured heat to warm his buttocks, though the naked soles of his feet were calloused and immune to warmth or cold. He watched the stars wheel slowly through their nocturnal circuit, counting through the long telling of his ancestors. There was a smell of water in his nostrils, iron-rich and heavy. Something scrabbled in the spiny thorn-brush. It might have been a hopping-mouse or a hunting lizard, though it was not. He was an Elder of the Yarru-yami, and he knew every sound in the Unknown Desert.

"Can you not leave me in peace, old woman?" the old man grumbled.

"Peace!" She emerged from the night to place herself before his rock, folding arms over withered dugs, her long, grey-white hair illuminated by starlight. "You would squat on this rock all night, old man, chewing *gamal* and watching the stars. You call that peace?"

After all these years, she was as spirited as the day he had met her. He smiled into his beard. "I do, old woman. If you'll not let be, then join me."

With a snort of disapproval, she clambered up the rock to squat at his side, groaning a little as her hipbones popped and creaked. He shifted to make room for her, digging into the worn pouch that hung at his waist and passing her a pinch of *gamal*. Her jaws worked, softening the dried fibers, working her mouth's moisture into them. Eighty-three years old, and her teeth still strong, working the *gamal* into a moist wad to tuck into her cheek.

Side by side, they squatted and watched the stars.

Especially the red one low on the western horizon.

Her voice, when she spoke, was sombre. "It's the choosing-time, isn't it?"

He nodded. "Coming fast."

"The poor boy." She shook her head. "Poor boy! There's no fairness in it. He's not fit to make such a choice. Who is?"

He shrugged. "Doesn't stop it from coming."

She eyed him acerbically. "And how would you choose, old one?"

"Me?" He turned his hands over, examining his palms. Paler than the rest of his skin, they were leathery and creased, tanned like an old hide. Age had marked them, and wear, and the lines of mortality. Nothing else. "It's not mine to choose."

"I know," she whispered. "Poor boy! I pray he chooses aright."

The old man squatted and listened to the sounds of the desert, while the stars wheeled slowly overhead. He felt the slow, steady beat of his heart, winding down to its inevitable faltering, the blood coursing through his veins, as water coursed through the earth far, far below them. In the heart of the Unknown Desert, there was water, water from the deepest place, the oldest place.

Birru-Uru-Alat, the Navel, the Well of the World.

It had been forgotten by all save the Yarru, who had cause to remember. Long ago, Haomane's Wrath had driven them beneath the earth, where they fled for shelter and in turn were given a trust. The Elders had kept the wisdom of Uru-Alat. When the boy was born with the markings on his hands, they had known. He was the Bearer, one who could carry the Water of Life, though it weighed heavier than stone or steel, as heavy as the burden of choice itself.

The Water of Life, which could extinguish the marrow-fire.

It would not be forgotten forever. A red star had risen and the Bearer was nearing manhood. The choosing-time would be upon him.

It was coming.

TANAROS CHOKED BACK A GASP as he emerged in the Chamber of the Marasoumië beneath Darkhaven, his heart constricting with a sharp pain as the node-point closed, hurling his form back into the framework of mortality, stumbling and shaken, his senses blurred with the speed of his passage.

"Steady, cousin." Vorax's deep voice reassured him, a solid hand on his elbow, anchoring him in time and place. Tanaros blinked, waiting for his vision to clear, every bone in his body aching at the abrupt transition. The world seemed preternaturally *slow* after traveling the Ways. He stared at the Staccian's beard, feeling he could number each auburn hair of it while the fleshy lips formed their next sentence. "Did the Sorceress consent?"

"Aye." Seizing upon the question, he managed an answer. His chest loosened, normal breathing returning. "The lady and the dragon consented alike."

"Well done." Forgetting himself, Vorax thumped his shoulder with a proud grin. "Well done, indeed! His Lordship will be pleased."

Tanaros winced as the edge of his spaulder bruised his flesh. "My thanks. What has transpired here, cousin?"

"General." A Fjeltroll stepped forward, yellow-eyed in the pulsing light of the chamber. One of the Kaldjager, the Cold Hunters, who patrolled the vast network of tunnels. "We have scouted passage to Lindanen Dale. We may pass below the Aven River. An entrance lies less than a league to the north. Kaldjager hold it secure. We took pains not to be seen."

"Good." Tanaros collected his wits, which were beginning to function once more. "Good. And Vorax, on your end?"

The Staccian shrugged. "I am in readiness. A chamber has been prepared, fit for a Queen. As for the rest, there's a fast ship awaiting in Harrington Bay, and a company of my lads ready to outrace the Ellylon to it, posing as Beshtanagi in disguise."

"Good," Tanaros repeated. "And the Dreamspinner? Did he succeed?"

"Well . . . don't go a-walking in the wood, cousin." Vorax grinned. "Does that answer it for you?"

It did.

IT WAS A PLAN, A simple plan.

Tanaros considered it as he lay in his bath.

The difficulty lay in gaining access, for the full might of the Rivenlost would be turned out to safeguard this wedding; aye, and the Borderguard of Curonan, too. And unless Tanaros missed his guess, the Duke of Seahold would have a contingent present as well. Every inch of ground within a dozen leagues of Lindanen Dale would have been scouted and secured.

Except the tunnels.

It was a pity they could not make use of the Marasoumië, but that would come later. Merely to hold the Ways open for so many would require two of the Three, taxing them to their utmost, and Ushahin was needed for this plan. The tunnels would be slower, but they would suffice.

It was a pity, a grave pity, that he could not bring the entire army through them with sufficient time to assemble. That would put an end to it. The army of Darkhaven was not so vast as Men believed it; that was Ushahin Dreamspinner's work, who walked in the dreams of Men and magnified their fears, playing them into nightmares. But it was vast enough, Tanaros thought, to win in a pitched battle. Under Lord Satoris' protection, the numbers of the Fjel had grown steadily throughout the centuries. Not enough to rival Men, who held nearly the whole of Urulat as their domain, but enough. And Tanaros had trained them.

On level ground, on the open field . . . ah, but the Ellylon and the sons of Altorus were too clever for that gambit. Once, it had worked. Long ago, on the plains of Curonan. He had donned the Helm of Shadows, and led the army of Darkhaven against the forces of Altoria, bringing down a nation, securing a buffer zone.

Altoria had had a Queen, then. He had never met her, never seen her. He wondered, sometimes, if she had resembled his wife. In the adamance of her pride, at the urging of her advisors, she had poured all the resources of her realm into that war, until nothing was left. In the end, Altoria lost Curonan and the throne, leaving the remnants of the sons of Altorus to patrol the verges of the lost plains.

Now, it was different. They needed to draw their Enemy out into the open. And they needed bait to do it. That was where the tunnels came into play, and Beshtanag, and above all, the Were that Ushahin had brought to Darkhaven.

The bath-water was growing cool. Tanaros stood, dripping.

"Here, Lord General."

Meara, the madling, slunk around the entrance to his bathing-chamber, proffering a length of clean linen toweling and eyeing him through her tangled hair. She had never done such before.

"Thank you, Meara." He dried himself, self-conscious for the first time in many decades. Physically, his body was unchanged. Save for the mark of his branding, it was little different than it had been on his wedding night, strong and lean and serviceable. Only the puckered, silvery scar on his breast gave evidence of his nature; that, and the deep ache of years.

"Does it hurt?" She pointed at his chest.

"Yes." He touched the scar with his fingertips, feeling the ridged flesh, remembering the searing ecstasy he'd felt when his Lord took Godslayer from the blazing marrow-fire and branded him with it, using the force of the Souma to stretch the Chain of Being to its limits to encompass him. "It hurts."

Meara nodded. "I thought so." She watched him don his robe. "What was she like, Lord General?"

"She?" He paused.

Her eyes glittered. "The Sorceress."

"She was . . . courteous."

"Was she prettier than me?" she asked plaintively.

"Prettier?" Tanaros gazed at the madling, who squirmed away from his scrutiny. He thought about Lilias, whose imperious beauty softened only in the presence of the dragon. "No, Meara. Not prettier."

She followed him as he left the bathing-chamber, tossing back her hair and glaring. "Another one is coming, you know. Coming *here*."

"Another one?"

"A *lady*." She spat the word. "An *Ellyl* lady."

"Yes." He wondered how she knew, if they all knew. "Such is the plan."

"It is a mistake," Meara said darkly.

"Meara." Tanaros rumpled his hair, damp from the bath. He remembered the Sorceress, and how the wind on the mountainside had tugged at her hair, that had otherwise fallen dark and shining, bound by the circlet, the red Soumanië vivid against her pale brow. He wondered what the other would be like, and if it were a mistake to bring her here. "The lady is to be under our Lord's protection."

The madling shuddered, turned and fled.

Bewildered, Tanaros watched her go.

THERE WAS NEVER ENOUGH TIME to prepare, when it came to it.

The Warchamber was packed with representatives of three of the races of Lesser Shapers, all crowded around the map-table and listening intently to the Commander General of the Army of Darkhaven. It was a simple plan. Tanaros wished he liked it better. Nonetheless, it was his Lord's will, and he continued, carrying it out to the letter. "And here,"—he pointed at the map—"is the mouth of the tunnel. Here, and here and here, there will be sentries posted, guarding the perimeter of Lindanen Dale. Those,"—Tanaros glanced at the Were Brethren—"will be yours to dispatch, as we agreed."

A flat voice spoke, passionless and grey. "And here they plight their troth?"

"Aye." The skin at the back of his neck prickled. With an effort, Tanaros made himself meet the gaze of Sorash, the Grey Dam of the Were, who rested one clawed forefinger upon the heart of Lindanen Dale. "That is where you will strike, honored one, if you be willing."

The Grey Dam gave him a terrible smile. "I am willing."

There was no telling her age. The Were had used the strange magics bequeathed them by Oronin Last-Born to circumvent the very Chain of Being, at least for the Grey Dam. Tanaros knew only that she was ancient. Ushahin Dreamspinner had been a boy when Faranol, Crown Prince of Altoria, had slain the Grey Dam's cubs and her mate in a hunting excursion, heaping glory upon his kindred during a state visit to Pelmar.

"You are brave, honored one," Tanaros said.

The ancient Were shook her head. "My successor is chosen."

Grey her voice, grey her name, grey her being. One year of their lives, that was what each of the Were surrendered that the Grey Dam might endure. So it had been, in the beginning; now, it was more, for their numbers had dwindled. Five years, ten, or more. Tanaros knew naught of what such ceremonies might entail, how it was enacted. Only that the Grey Dam endured, until the mantle was passed, and endured anew.

It had been many centuries since that had happened.

"You know you will die, old mother?"

Ushahin's voice, raw and aching. It was not the first time he had asked it.

"Little Man-cub, little son." The old Were's amber gaze softened, and she patted his misshapen cheek with her padded, hairy palm. "You have assuaged my pain these many years, but the time has come to make an end. It is a good way to die. If the Glad Hunter wills it, my teeth will meet in the flesh of an Altorus before the finish."

He bowed his head. The Were Brethren growled softly.

Tanaros cleared his throat. "Then you will strike here, honored one, and your Brethren will clear the way. In the confusion, we will make our move, here." He traced a pathway on the map. "Under my command, a company of Lord Vorax's men will seize Cerelinde of the Rivenlost, and fall back to the meeting point, where the switch will be made. From thence, they will flee east, with the decoy. Lord Ushahin, weave what visions you may. The remaining men and I will hold them as long as we dare, before we retreat to the tunnels and the Kaldjager Fjel hide our passage."

And there it was, the first phase of it, in all its risky totality.

"General." Hyrgolf's shrewd eyes met his with a soldier's frankness. "The Fjel are ready to serve. It would be better if you did not command the raid yourself."

"It must be," Tanaros said bluntly. "It is his Lordship's will, and there is no room for error. Hyrgolf, I would trust you to lead it, and I would trust any lieutenant of your appointing. But if we are to convince the Ellylon and the Altorians that this raid originated in Beshtanag, there can be no hint of the presence of Fjeltroll."

"Cousin, I would command my own—" began Vorax.

Ushahin cut short his words, his tone light and bitter. "You can't, fat one. Your bulk can't be concealed under Pelmaran armor, as can the rest of your beard-shorn Staccians, and Tanaros, too." With a twisted smile, he raised his crippled hands that could grip nothing heavier than a dagger. "I would do it myself, if I could. But I think my skills do not avail in this instance."

"Enough!" Tanaros raised his voice. "It is mine to do." For a moment, he thought they would quarrel; then they settled, acceding to his command. He leaned over the map-table, resting his hands on the edges, the southwestern quadrant of Urulat framed between his braced arms. "Are we in accord?"

"We are, brother," whispered the Grey Dam. "We are."

No one disagreed.

HIS DREAMS, WHEN HE HAD them, were restless.

Tanaros slept, and awoke, restless, tossing in his bed-sheets, and slept only to dream anew, and twist and wind himself into shrouds in his dreaming.

Blood.

He dreamed of blood.

An ocean of it.

It ran like a red skein through his dreams, wet and dripping. Red, like the Souma, like Godslayer, like the star that had arisen in the west and the one that adorned the Sorceress' brow. It dripped like a veil over the features of his wife, long-slain, and over his own hands as he looked down in horror, seeing them relinquish the hilt of his sword, the blade protruding from his King's chest.

Tanaros tossed, and groaned.

It went back, further back, the trail of blood; far, so far. All the way back through the ages of the Sundered World, blood, soaking into the earth of a thousand battlefields, clots of gore. Back and back and back, until the beginning, when a great cry rent the fabric of Urulat, a mighty blow parted the world, and the Sundering Seas rushed in to fill the void, warm and salty as blood.

Tanaros awoke, the mark of his brand aching in summons.

He dressed himself and went to answer it.

Downward he went, through one of the three-fold doors and down the spiraling stairs that led to the Chamber of the Font, down the winding way where the walls shone like onyx, and the veins of marrow-fire were buried deep and strong. At the base of the spiral stair a blast of heat greeted him.

"My Lord."

Some distance from the center of the chamber, in a ringed pit, the marrow-fire rose from its unseen Source to surge like a fountain through a narrow aperture, blue-white fire rising up in a column, falling, coruscating. And in the heart of it—ah! Tanaros closed his eyes briefly. There in midair hung the dagger Godslayer, that burned and was not consumed, beating like a heart. Its edges were as sharp and jagged as the day it had been splintered from the Souma, reflecting and refracting the marrow-fire from its ruby facets.

"Tanaros." The Shaper stood before the Font, a massive form, hands laced behind his back. The blazing light played over his calm features, the broad brow, the shadowed eyes that reflected the red gleam of the Souma in pinpricks. "Tomorrow it begins."

He knew not what to say. "Yes, my Lord."

"War," mused the Shaper, taking a step forward to gaze at the Font. The preternatural light shone on the seeping trail of ichor that glistened on his thigh, and the marrow-fire took on an edge of creeping blackness, like shadow made flame. "My Elder Brother gives me no peace, and this time he wagers all. Do you understand why this must be, Tanaros? Do you understand that this is *your* time?"

"Yes, my Lord." His teeth chattered, his chest ached and blazed.

"I was stabbed with this dagger." Lord Satoris reached out a hand, penetrating the blue-white fountain, and the flames grew tinged with darkness. "Thus." His forefinger touched the crudely rounded knob that formed Godslayer's hilt. Tanaros hissed through his teeth as the dagger's light convulsed and the scar of his branding constricted. "To this day, the pain endures. And yet it is not so great as the pain of my siblings' betrayal."

"My Lord." Tanaros drew a deep breath against the tightness in his chest. On the eve of war, he asked the question none of the Three had voiced. "Why did you refuse Haomane's request?"

"Brave Tanaros." The Shaper smiled without mirth. "There is danger in conversing with dragons. I saw too clearly the Shape of what-would-be if my Gift were withdrawn from Men, uncoupled forever from the Gift of thought. Out of knowledge, I refused; and out of love, love for Arahila, my Sister. Still." He paused. "What did Haomane see, I wonder? Why did he refuse my Gift for his Children? Was it pride, or something more?"

"I know not, my Lord," Tanaros said humbly.

"No." Considering, Lord Satoris shook his head. "I think not. My Elder Brother was ever proud. And it matters not, now." His hand tightened on Godslayer's hilt. "Only this. Haomane seeks it, my General. That is what it comes to, in the end. Blood, and more blood, ending in mine—or his."

"My Lord!" Tanaros gasped, tearing at his chest.

"Forgive me." The Shaper withdrew from the marrow-fire, his hands closing on Tanaros' upper arms. The power in them made Tanaros' skin prickle. "Would you know what is in my heart?" he asked in a low voice. "I did not choose this, Tanaros Blacksword. But I will not go gently, either. Any of them . . . *any* of them!" He loosed his hold and turned away. "Any of them could cross the divide," he said, softly. "Any of the Six. It is theirs to do, to defy Haomane's will, to risk mortality. If they did . . ." He smiled sadly. "Oh, Arahila! Sister, together, you and I . . ."

Catching his breath, Tanaros bowed, not knowing what else to do before such immeasurable sorrow. "My Lord, we will do our best to deliver you Urulat."

"Urulat." The Shaper gathered himself. "Yes. Urulat. If I held Urulat in my palm, would it be enough to challenge Haomane's sovereignty?" His laughter was harsh and empty. "Perhaps. I would like to find out."

"It shall be yours, my Lord!" Tanaros said fiercely, believing it, his heart blazing within him like the marrow-fire. "I will make it so!"

Blood yet unshed dripped between them.

"Tanaros." His name, nothing more; everything. The touch of the Shaper's lips on his brow, chaste and burning. It had been his Gift, once. The quickening of the flesh, joyful blood leaping in the loins. A crude Gift, but his, cut short by Godslayer's thrust. "May it be so."

"My Lord," Tanaros whispered, and knew himself dismissed.

As he took his leave, Lord Satoris turned back to the marrow-fire, gazing at it as if to find answers hidden in the ruby shard. The Shaper's features were shadowed with unease, a fearful sight of itself. "Where is your weapon Malthus, Brother, and what does he plot?" he murmured. "Why must you force my hand? I did not Sunder the world. And yet I have become what you named me. Is that truly what must come to pass, or is there another way?" He sighed, the sound echoing in the Chamber. "If there is, I cannot see it. Your wrath has been raised against me too long. All things must be as they must."

Tanaros withdrew quietly, not swiftly enough to avoid hearing the anguish in the Shaper's final words.

"Uru-Alat!" Lord Satoris whispered. "I would this role had fallen to another."

SIX

❖

"COUNSELOR, FORGIVE ME," THE ARDUAN croaked, falling to her knees.

The Company of Malthus halted beneath the hammer of the sun, a merciless, white-hot blaze in the vivid blue sky. All around them, the scorched landscape extended farther than the eye could see in any direction, red earth baked and cracking, broken only by the strange, towering structures of anthills.

"I told you it was no journey for a woman." Although his face was drawn beneath beard-stubble, the former Commander of the Borderguard kept his feet, wavering only slightly. "We should have sent her back."

"Peace, Blaise." Even Malthus' voice was cracked and weary. "Fianna is the Archer of Arduan. It is as it must be. None of us can go much farther." Drawing back his sheltering hood, the Counselor bowed his head and took the Soumanië from its place of concealment beneath his robes, chanting softly and steadily in the Shaper's tongue. The gem shone like a red star between his hands.

Ants scurried on the cracked earth as it stirred beneath them, departing in black rivulets. Dry spikes of thorn-brush rattled, trembling.

"Look!" It was the young Vedasian, Hobard, who saw it first, pointing. A green tendril of life emerging from the cracks in the desert floor, questing in the open air. "A drought-eater! Yrinna be blessed!"

It grew beneath the Counselor's fraying chant, the green stalk thickening, branches springing from the trunk with a thick succulent's leaves; grew, and withered, even as flowers blossomed and fruited, seeds swelling to ripe globes. A drought-eater, capable of absorbing every drop of moisture within an acre of land and producing fruit that was almost wholly water. Water, held within a tough greenish rind.

They fell upon it, ripping the fruit from its stems even as the branches shriveled. Hobard split his with both thumbs, sucking at the pulpy interior. Blaise Caveros, for all his harsh words, had a care with the Arduan woman, cutting the fruit and feeding it to her piece by dripping piece. Malthus the Counselor leaned wearily on his walking-staff and watched them, and among all his Company only Peldras of the Rivenlost, whose light step left no tracks on the red, dusty soil, waited his turn until the rest were sated.

Thirst could not kill Haomane's Children; only steel.

Peldras shaded his eyes, gazing at the endless vista of baked red earth. If the Counselor's wisdom were true, they should have found the ones they sought long before; the Charred Ones, who had hidden from the scorching fire of Haomane's wrath.

"What do you see, my long-sighted friend?" Malthus asked in a low tone.

The Ellyl shook his head. "Nothing."

"HUSH."

Staring at the vine-curtained opening, Tanaros lifted a hand for silence. To a fellow, Men and Fjel obeyed him alike. No need to caution the Were, who were silence itself. Only the shuffle and stamp of the horses disturbed the quiet, and even that was minimal. Green light filtered into the tunnel, and beyond the opening he could hear birdsong.

"Go." He motioned to the Were brethren. "Clear the perimeter, and report."

They went, both of them, like arrows shot from the bow, low to the ground and sleek, traveling at an inhuman gait, muzzles pointed forward, ears pricked and wary.

"Good hunting, brothers," the Grey Dam murmured.

Tanaros repressed a shudder.

Always, the waiting was the hardest. He felt awkward in the unfamiliar Pelmaran armor; steel plates laced onto boiled leather, and an ill-disguised conical helmet. Their arms had been chosen with care, to give a semblance of Beshtanagi troops in disguise. Tanaros rolled his shoulders, loosened his sword in its sheath. A borrowed sword, not his own, with a Pelmaran grip.

Behind him, Vorax's Staccians whispered in excitement. This was their moment, the role only they could play. Among them, Vorax had chosen the youngest, the fiercest, the swiftest. They had trained hard, and rehearsed their roles to perfection. They had shaved their beards and stained their skin with walnut dye. Tanaros turned in the saddle to survey them, feeling the battle-calm settle over him.

Their lieutenant met his eye; Carfax, a steady fellow. They exchanged nods. And there, in the vanguard, Turin, the yellow-haired decoy, swallowing hard. *Choose one who is fair,* his Lordship had said, *fair as morning's first star.* He was a youth, still beardless, his skin undyed and pale, clad in bridal silks. The troops had laughed, to see him thus. Now, none laughed.

"We strike a blow this day, brothers," Tanaros said in a soft, carrying voice, jostling his mount to face them. "A mighty blow! Are you ready?"

They gave a whispered cheer.

"Field marshal." His gaze roamed past the Staccians, falling upon Hyrgolf, who stood with the massed Fjeltroll at the rear. "Are you ready?"

Hyrgolf of the Tungskulder Fjel stood like a boulder, stolid and dependable. "We are ready, General," he rumbled. "Bring us the El-lyl lady, and we will conduct her in all speed to Darkhaven."

"Dreamspinner." Tanaros bent his gaze upon the half-breed, who crouched at the entrance to the tunnels, holding the Helm of Shadows in his trembling hands. "Are you ready, cousin?"

"I am ready." Ushahin bared his teeth, the enlarged pupil in one eye glittering. In the green light, his face looked ghastly. The thing in his hands throbbed with a darkness that ached like a wound, unbearable to behold. "Upon your command!"

As if summoned by his words, one of the Were brethren dashed through the hanging vines that curtained the entrance, eyes glowing amber, bloodstains upon his muzzle. "The way is clear," he said, the words thick and guttural in his throat. Sharp white teeth showed as he licked blood from his chops. "Why do you wait? In the Dale, they wed. Go now, now!"

Sorash the Grey Dam lifted her muzzle and keened a lament for her long-slain cubs.

The moment had come.

Tanaros drew his sword, and though it was not his, still it sang as it cleared the scabbard, a high, piercing sound that echoed inside his head. "Go!" he shouted, digging his heels into his mount's sides, feeling the surge of muscle as the black horse lunged up the sloping tunnel for the entrance. "Go, go, go!"

Lashed by green vines, Tanaros burst through the tunnel entrance, bounding into a forest in the full foliage of spring. A grey form hurtled past him, bound at speed for Lindanen Dale.

Altorus!

The word was a battle-paean in his head, igniting the ancient hurt, the ancient hatred. Altorus! He took a deep breath, filling his lungs with it. Rage, cleansing rage. Tanaros wheeled the black horse, his mind clear and sharp. There, the Staccians, emerging in formation. There, the dim figures of the Kaldjager Fjel, slipping through the trees. There, by the opening, Ushahin Dreamspinner, lowering the Helm of Shadows onto his head.

"Ride!" Tanaros shouted. "Men, *ride!*"

They rode, pounding through the oak wood, the ancient holdings of Altoria, and the mounts they rode were the horses of Darkhaven, swift-hooved and high-spirited, their glossy coats disguised with mud and burrs. They rode, and the trees passed in a blur, and behind them slid Fjeltroll with yellow eyes and sharp axes, laying a trap for those who would follow—and there four of their number paused, waiting. Here and there lay corpses, Ellylon and Men alike, sentries who grinned in death at the innocent spring leaves. They rode, and death ran before them, Oronin's Children, grey and implacable.

A league, a league, less than a league.

Ahead, the trees thinned, bright sunlight shining on Lindanen Dale. Tanaros glanced left and right, wind-sprung tears blurring his vision. In the periphery of his gaze, he could see the Staccians following, falling into a wedge formation. The Were had vanished. Let them be there, he thought, a desperate prayer. Oh my Lord, let them be there! Drawing his sword, he loosed a wordless cry as they emerged into the Dale.

Greensward, and flowers hidden in the grass.

Silk tents, with pennants fluttering.

And the host, the nuptial host, milling on the lawn, chaos sown in their midst, with rent garments and blood flowing freely. A harpist, moaning and pale, cradled a torn forearm; others lay unmoving, and their blood spread on the grass, darkening. This, they had not expected. Not the grey hunters of the Were, not Oronin's Children, who could penetrate any defense not raised behind walls. Ah, and even so! So many, so many of Haomane's Allies, gathered in one place. Lindanen Dale seethed like a kicked anthill. Unready and unmounted they might be, but they had not come unarmed. Already, the soldiers were gathering their wits. There was one of the Were brethren, dying, his hairy belly slit, entrails dragging on the greensward. And there, the other, brought to bay by the Duke of Seahold's men, closing in with spears.

Tanaros thundered past, ignoring them.

There . . . *there*.

Before the bower, wrought with Ellylon craftsmanship, enwrapped with flowers—*there*. A man, bare-headed, danced with death in a bridegroom's finery, and the sunlight gleamed on his red-gold hair and the naked steel of his blade. A grey, shadowy figure lunged at his throat, teeth snapping in a hunger that had honed itself for centuries. Around and around they went in a deadly pavane. After a thousand years, the Grey Dam of the Were sought to avenge the deaths of her mate and cubs. And all around them, the Altorians stood in a ring, the Borderguard of Curonan, holding their blades for fear of striking awry, shouting fierce encouragement to their king-in-exile, so grievously assaulted on his wedding day.

Not there. No.

To the left, where an Ellyl woman stood, clad in bridal silks. There was fear in her face, and pride. Oh yes, Haomane knew, there was pride! She shone like a flame, lending courage to the women who attended her and cowered at her side, strengthening the hearts of her Rivenlost guards who bristled about her, swords and spears at the ready.

It took all his strength not to howl his Lord's name, betraying the origin of their attack; though in truth, it would not have mattered if he did, for at that moment the Dreamspinner's subtle influence began to manifest, warping sight and sound, and Men turned in confusion toward imagined attackers where there were none. Such was Ushahin's illusion, augmented by the Helm of Shadows, that even the Ellylon believed with utter certitude that an involuntary Beshtanagi warcry was uttered in the mêlée.

"Now!" Tanaros shouted to his men. "Now!"

They followed as he led them in a charge against the personal guard of Cerelinde, granddaughter of Elterrion the Bold, Lord of the Rivenlost. Young men—boys, some of them—sworn to fat Vorax. Why? He didn't dare ask, but must trust them to be there, fighting on horseback at his side as his sword rose and fell, rose and fell, dripping with Ellyl blood. The cries of the dying rang in his ears, his and theirs. Proud Ellyl faces, eyes bright with Haomane's favor, swam in his vision; he cut them down, cleaving a path through them, again and again and again, until his sword-arm grew tired.

And then . . .

Only fear, in her beautiful face; fear and disbelief.

"Lady, come!" he gasped, discarding his buckler and hauling her across his pommel with one strong arm.

The weight of her—oh Lord, oh my Lord Satoris!

Tanaros gritted his teeth, feeling her struggle, her flesh against his; Ellyl flesh, a woman's flesh, warm and living. Her hair spilled like gleaming silk over his left knee, tangling in his Pelmaran greaves, his stirrup. Pale, her hair, like cornsilk. The surviving Staccians closed around him, swords flashing as they fought, checking their mounts broadside into the bodies of her defenders. Across the Dale, cavalry units scrambled to assemble and an Ellyl horn blew, a sound of silvery defiance, summoning the Host.

"Lady, forgive me," Tanaros muttered and, raising his sword, brought the hilt down sharply on the base of her skull. Her weight went still and limp, quiescent.

A cry of rage and fury shattered the air.

"*Cerelinde! CERELINDE!*"

Tanaros turned his head and met Aracus Altorus' gaze.

In that instant, the Grey Dam of the Were made her final lunge; one last, desperate attack, carrying the onus of the battle to her opponent, spending her life upon it. Altorus' sword came up between them, spitting her, and he wept with futile anger as her weight bore him down, jaws seeking his throat even as her eyes filmed.

"Go!" Tanaros shouted, wheeling the black. "*Go!*"

TANAROS CLUNG TO HIS MOUNT like grim death, one hand on the reins, one clutching the limp burden athwart his pommel, the Staccians surrounding him as they raced for the treeline. The greensward of Lindanen Dale was churned to mud beneath the pounding hooves of the horses of Darkhaven.

And behind them, Haomane's allies were closing fast, astride and racing, and in the vanguard was the cavalry of Ingolin the Wise, Lord of the Rivenlost, moved to hot-blooded wrath for the first time in centuries; and close at their heels were the Borderguard of Curonan in their dun-colored cloaks. Thirty paces to the forest, twenty . . .

With Cerelinde to carry, he couldn't outrun them.

"Now, Dreamspinner," Tanaros whispered under his breath. "Now!"

Madness broke.

Like a wave, a vast black wave, it crashed down upon them, and the sound in his skull was an atonal howl of grief, as if the whole of Oronin's Children mourned at once, as if every Were in Urulat opened throat in lament. And so it was, in a fashion, for Ushahin Dreamspinner unleashed the full force of his power and gave voice to the grief of them all, and the form of his grief was madness, given shape by the Helm of Shadows.

It halted the armies of Haomane; horses balking, throwing riders, Men clapping hands over ears and falling to writhe on the ground, while the Ellylon sought in vain to control mortal steeds that plunged and pitched in terror. Only the horses of Darkhaven, tended from their foaling by the hands of madlings, were untouched by it.

"Ride, damn you!" Carfax, the Staccian lieutenant, exhorted his troops, almost weeping. "Ride, you sons of whores!"

A flurry of ravens arose as they entered the forest.

Branches, breaking at their passage. Tanaros bent low over the black stallion's neck, clinging with his knees, concentrating on the limp form of the Ellyl woman. The horse's mane stung his eyes. Oh, brave heart! Hooves pounded the loam, massive trunks rushed past them. How long, until Haomane's Allies gathered themselves to follow?

A league, less than a league to the meeting place.

In a dappled glade surrounded by dense thickets and tall oaks, he drew rein, sawing at the black's lathered neck. Turin the decoy was there waiting, and three others, helping as he dismounted, easing the Ellyl noblewoman to the ground. She moaned faintly, stirring against the loam. Tanaros reached down, unclasping her outer garment; a cloak of white silk, embroidered in gold thread and rubies with an interlacing pattern of crown and Souma. It came loose with surprising ease, and he straightened with it.

"That would be for me, Lord General." The young Staccian settled the cloak over his shoulders and fastened the clasp, tossing his yellow locks back. He nodded at a round Pelmaran buckler propped against a rock. "In thanks, I give you my shield."

Tanaros clasped his hand. "Lord Satoris' blessing on you, Turin."

The Staccian spared him a brief grin. "And you, General. Buy us time."

With that, he turned away, and one of his comrades, astride a black horse, gave him a hand, slinging him across the pommel where he landed with a grunt. The decoy was in place.

"Lord General!" Carfax saluted.

"Go," Tanaros said softly. "We'll hold them long enough for you to cross the Aven. Cut the bridges if you can. After that, you're on your own. Lord Vorax's ship awaits you in Harrington Bay."

Carfax smiled. "We'll see you in Beshtanag."

With that, he gave the command, wheeling; the bulk of the Staccians thundered with him, heading eastward through the forest, toward the River Aven, Turin the decoy jouncing athwart the pommel of one.

"General," a deep voice rumbled, as Hyrgolf stepped between the trees, massive and deliberate. Lowering his thick head, he stared under his brow-ridges at the inert form of the Ellyl woman. "This is her?"

"Aye."

"Well, then." The Fjeltroll stooped, gathering Cerelinde of the Ellylon in his thick-hided arms. Her body sagged, pale hair trailing earthward on one end, slipper-shod feet twitching at the other. "Poor lass," Hyrgolf murmured.

"Take her to Darkhaven!" Tanaros snapped, swinging astride his mount.

"Aye, General." The Fjel's tone was mild as he turned away, bearing his burden. "We will do that," he said over his shoulder. "Hold the glade, as long as you dare. The Kaldjager are ready with their axes. Do not wait too long."

Tanaros nodded and settled Turin's buckler on his left arm.

He was ready.

THEY WERE FEW, SO FEW.

Tanaros did not count the losses; he did not dare. Even now, after so many, it hurt to number them. He merely waited, with Vorax's Staccians, and knew that a dozen were left to him. Bold lads, to a man. Their teeth gleamed white against their dyed skin as they awaited the onslaught. This time, there would be no help from the Dreamspinner; Ushahin was spent. Only them, with mortal steel against innumerable odds.

It came quickly.

The passage into the glade was narrow. Tanaros took the lead position, with a soldier a pace behind him on either side, the rest arrayed in ranks of three behind them, ready to move up should any fall. The forest resounded with the sound of enemy pursuit. Through the trees, he saw them coming, and a lord of the Ellylon led the charge, checking when he saw the narrow gap with its defenders. Horns blew, ordering a halt, but even so Haomane's Allies continued to come by the hundred; the Borderguard of Curonan, blue-clad men of Seahold, massed behind the Ellylon.

"Yield, defiler." The Ellyl lord's voice was implacable. "Return the lady."

Tanaros shook his head.

The Ellyl drew his sword, and dappled sunlight shone silver on it; silver was his armor, and worked on his shield a thistle-blossom, marking him of the House of Núrilin. "Then you will die."

Nudging his mount forward, Tanaros drew his Pelmaran sword in salute.

They engaged.

The Núrilin's first blow reeled him in the saddle, nearly cracking the borrowed buckler with its force. This was no mere guardsman taken unaware and on foot, but a lord of the Ellylon fighting on horseback, equal to equal. Tanaros' shield-arm went numb to the shoulder. Anger rose in him like a tide. With a wordless shout, he pressed the attack, driving the Ellyl back by main force. The heaving sides of their mounts jostled one another as they grappled, too close for either to get a solid blow. On the left and right, the sounds of battle arose.

"You're too few," the Núrilin lord said. "Surrender, and be spared."

Tanaros gritted his teeth and raised his aching shield-arm, shoving the buckler hard into the Ellyl's body, gaining a few inches of space. Obedient to the command of his knees, the black horse wheeled and Tanaros brought his sword around in a flashing arc, landing a solid blow to the helm. The Núrilin retreated a pace, shaking his head, but to his left, one of the Staccians cried out and fell back, wounded. Even as another struggled to take his comrade's place, battle surged, pressing toward the glade. Tanaros cut across, driving them back, gasping as the tip of a blade scored his unprotected side, piercing the leather seam of his armor. Blood trickled down his ribcage.

"How long, defiler?" the Núrilin lord called. "Until all your men are dead?"

From the corner of his eyes, Tanaros could see movement in the massed ranks behind the Ellylon. Dun-colored cloaks, moving through the trees. He swore under his breath. The Borderguard of Curonan was spreading out, seeking another passage, trying to come around and flank them. It was what he would have ordered.

They would do it, in time; and worse, they would find the decoy's trail, too soon.

"How long, General?" one of the Staccians muttered behind him as the onslaught redoubled its efforts, forcing them back another pace.

Tanaros pressed his elbow against his bleeding side. "We will—"

At the rear of the massed Allies, something stirred, the troops of the Duke of Seahold parting to admit a handful of men, spearheaded by one who uttered a single cry. "*Curonan!*"

In the woods, the dun-colored cloaks turned back in answer.

The Ellylon halted their attack, waiting.

In the gap, the Staccians held, panting, Tanaros at their head. One was dead, two direly wounded. Tanaros pressed his wound and watched as Aracus Altorus made his way through the ranks. Pride, he thought, as Aracus drew nearer. Always pride. His armor had been donned in haste, flung over his bridegroom's finery. He held his helmet under one arm, and his wide-set eyes were filled with fury.

"Now," Tanaros whispered.

His blow caught the Núrilin lord unaware, the sword finding a gap in the Ellyl's armor. With cries of wrath, the Ellylon surged to the attack. Everywhere, silvered armor, fair Ellyl faces, eyes bright and fierce behind visors, horseflesh churning as they pressed through the gap, forcing the Staccians backward. Aracus Altorus and the Borderguard of Curonan were lost in the center of the mêlée.

One more step, Tanaros thought, wielding his Pelmaran sword with desperate energy, guarding their retreat and trying to save as many of Vorax's men as he might. The Ellylon were fearful in their wrath, and he could feel the Staccians' courage ebbing, turning to terror. It was why he had needed to lead the raid himself. Battle-trained, the black horse retreated, obedient to his commands, turning this way and that to allow him room to swing his blade.

One more step, one . . . more . . . step . . .

With a sound like cracking thunder, trees began to fall; ancient trees, mighty oaks, the sentinels of Lindanen Wood. And the first to fall toppled like a giant across the gap, smashing the enemy vanguard, shattering bone and crushing flesh, the earth shuddering at its impact. The way was blocked, for now, and above the moans of the enemy rose the screaming of injured horses.

The Kaldjager Fjeltroll had done their job.

Weary and sore, Tanaros turned his mount and ordered his Men back to the tunnels. There should have been joy in the victory, and yet there was none. Once, he would have been on the other side of this battle, defending his liege-lord. Those days were long gone, and yet. . . . Destroying the happiness of one Son of Altorus did not bring back the love Tanaros had lost, the life that had once been his. Nothing would, ever. With his own hands, he had destroyed it, and chosen Lord Satoris' dark truth over the bright lie of love that he had once cherished.

If it had been true before, it was true twice over this day. He had sealed that path as surely as the Kaldjager Fjel had blocked their retreat. There was no merit in regretting what was done, and no choice but to continue onward.

Darkhaven was all that was left to him.

SEVEN

❖❖

CERELINDE OPENED HER EYES ONTO a nightmare.

Fjeltroll.

She was the Lady of the Ellylon and, to her credit, she did not cry aloud, though the face that hovered over hers was immense and hideously ugly, covered in a thick, grey-green hide. It was so close she could smell its musk, feel its breath on her skin. Its nostrils were the size of wine goblets. Tiny eyes squinted down at her beneath the bulge of an overhanging brow. A broad mouth stretched its width, yellowing tusks protruding above and below the leathery lips.

Even as she blinked in uncomprehending fear, its maw opened. A voice emerged, deep and rumbling, speaking in the common tongue. "The Lady wakes."

Cerelinde sat up, seeking to scramble backward. A sharp pain lanced her skull, and a wave of sickness clutched her stomach.

"Peace, lass." The squatting Fjeltroll held up one enormous hand. The hide was thick and horny, the dangerous talons grimy. It was not a reassuring sight. "You will come to no harm here."

"No harm?" With an effort of will, she quelled the sensation of sickness. Memories of Lindanen Dale rose in its place and overwhelmed her; the grey Were in their midst, her kinsmen slain and Aracus fighting for his life, the mounted figure in Pelmaran armor bearing down upon her, blood dripping from his blade. "Ah, Haomane! There is naught but harm in this day!"

"As you say, lass." The vast shoulders moved in a shrug. "It is Haomane's Prophecy you sought to fulfill this day. Still, I tell you, you will not be harmed by my Lordship's hand."

"Your Lordship." Cerelinde glanced at her surroundings. She was underground in a vast tunnel, tall and wide. A handful of Fjel carrying heavy packs squatted in waiting, their fearsome features further distorted by wavering torchlight. She repressed a shudder. Beyond them, another figure stood, dismounted beside a restless horse, a bundle under one arm. His head was bowed, his face in shadow. The torchlight glinted on his pale hair, which shone like that of her own people. Through the anguish in her heart and the throbbing pain in her head, slow realization of her plight dawned. It was not Beshtanagi who had attacked her wedding. It was worse, far worse. "Who are you?" she asked, already fearing the answer. "What is this place?"

The Fjeltroll smiled with hideous gentleness. "Lady, I am Hyrgolf of the Tungskulder Fjel, field marshal of the Army of Darkhaven," he said. "And this place is merely a waystation."

"Darkhaven," she whispered. "*Why?*"

He looked at her a moment before speaking. "Surely you must know."

Cerelinde closed her eyes briefly. "Your master seeks to destroy us."

"Destroy?" The Fjeltroll gave a rumbling snort. "Haomane's Wrath brings destruction upon us. His Lordship wishes to survive it." He rose, extending one horny hand. "Come, lass. Can you travel? I will bear you if you cannot."

"I pray you, Marshal Hyrgolf, do not." Cerelinde took a shallow breath, conscious of the limited air, of the weight of the earth pressing above them. It was a sickening sensation. Her head ached and her heart felt battered within her breast. Her flesh retained a vague, horrible memory of being borne in the Fjeltroll's arms. She had been right; there was risk, too much risk.

Lindanen Dale had been a mistake.

"It is no hardship," Hyrgolf said, misunderstanding her hesitation. His talons brushed her fingertips.

"*No!*" Cerelinde shrank from his touch. She found the wall of the tunnel at her back and levered herself upright. "If I must walk," she said, summoning her dignity and gathering it around her, "I shall walk."

"Lady." Hyrgolf uttered a few words in the guttural Fjel tongue, and the others shook off their apparent torpor. The light of their torches receded as they began to trot down the tunnel at a steady pace. The other figure, beside the horse, stood unmoving. Hyrgolf gestured for her to precede him. "As you will."

The rocky floor of the tunnel was harsh beneath her feet, clad in the embroidered slippers of her wedding finery. As they passed the motionless figure with the pale hair, she glanced sidelong.

Ushahin the Misbegotten raised his head, his mismatched eyes glittering with unshed tears and hatred. His combined heritage was stamped on his face, as clearly as the marks of violence left by those who had sought to erase his existence.

"Ah, Haomane!" She breathed the word like a prayer, faltering.

"Come, Lady," Hyrgolf said low in his throat. His talons were on her arm, hurrying her past. "Leave the Dreamspinner to his grief."

She went without arguing.

Behind them, she heard the sound of hooves shuffling and stamping, a horse's snort. And then hoofbeats, following in their wake. When she dared glance behind once more, he was there, riding astride with the leather case in his lap. He stared hard at her, his twisted face a parody of Haomane's Children, of almost all she held dear.

And there were no more tears in his eyes, only hatred.

She was alone among the Sunderer's minions.

The Fjel were not swift, but they were steady and tireless. They spoke little, keeping to their pace, and the Misbegotten spoke not at all. Cerelinde walked among them for hours, feeling Ushahin's hatred at her back, as palpable as the heat of a blazing hearth. The tunnel sloped downward, and with each step she felt herself taken further from the surface, from Aracus and her kinfolk, from clean air and the light of Haomane's blessed, life-giving sun. The air within the tunnels was dank and close, growing ever more so the further they went. Only a handful of shafts pierced the stifling darkness, providing barely enough air to keep them alive, to keep the torches alight.

Within the first hour, they passed beneath the Aven River.

The sound, a deep, muffled rushing sound, announced it. The walls of the tunnel thrummed and groaned. Cerelinde started in terror even as the Fjel tramped onward, unperturbed.

"Peace, lass," Hyrgolf rumbled. "It is only the river above us."

"Above us?" Cerelinde echoed the words, feeling ill. The weight of all that water, rushing overhead, was incomprehensible. She knew the river well. Some leagues to the south, Meronil, the white city, sat on its banks.

"Aye, far above." Hyrgolf regarded her. "The Fjel know tunnels, lass. You're safe with us. You've no need to fear."

"Lass!" A despairing laugh escaped her. "Ah, Marshal! So you call me, and yet I have lived long enough for ten score of your generations to toil and die in the Sunderer's name. Have you any idea what it is you do here?"

He gave another shrug, as though her words glanced off his impervious hide. "As you will, Lady. Can you continue?"

"Yes," Cerelinde whispered.

Onward they tramped, and the sound of the Aven River grew louder and more terrifying, then faded and vanished. Cerelinde thought of Meronil, of her home, passing steadily beyond her reach, and fought against despair.

After many hours, they reached a vast, open cavern where Hyrgolf called a halt. Cerelinde stood on battered and aching feet, watching as his Fjel made camp, dispersing the supplies they bore. There were food and water, as well as bedrolls and fodder for horses. Others, it seemed, were anticipated. Only the Misbegotten took no part in the preparations, retreating to a dark alcove and crouching in misery, arms wrapped around the case he carried.

Cerelinde was too weary to care. Whatever ailed him, there was no room in her heart for compassion, save for those she had left behind. When Hyrgolf pointed to a hide tent his Fjel had erected for her, pounding tent-pegs into rock with sheer might, she crawled into it without a word, drawing the flap closed behind her. There she lay, staring open-eyed at the tent's peak, and reliving the bloody memories of Lindanen Dale.

Hours passed.

The hoofbeats, when they came, were weary and slow. Cerelinde lay tense and quiet, listening to the sounds of the camp. There was a Man's voice speaking in the common tongue, tired, yet filled with command. "How is she?"

"Quiet, Lord General," answered Hyrgolf's deep tone.

The voice spoke in Staccian, giving orders. For a moment, Cerelinde relaxed; then came the sound of booted feet drawing near her tent.

"Lady," the Man's voice said. "I bring you greetings from my Lord Satoris."

Her fingers trembled as she drew back the tent's flap. He averted his gaze as she emerged, allowing her to study him. The sight made her stomach clench. His was the face she had seen through the opening of a Pelmaran helm, bearing down upon her, a bloody sword in his fist.

Not until she stood did he meet her eyes, and she knew, then, that she had seen his likeness elsewhere, in the shadow of features worn by his distant kinsman. The dark hair was the same, falling over his brow; the stern mouth, the face, austere and handsome by the standards of Men. Only the eyes were different, weary with the knowledge of centuries beyond mortal telling.

Her voice shook. "*You!*"

"Lady." He bowed, correct and exacting. "I am General Tanaros of Darkhaven, and I mean you no harm."

"Harm!" Cerelinde passed her hands over her face, another wild laugh threatening to choke her. "O blessed Haomane, Arahila the Fair, what does such a word *mean* to you people? I know you, Tanaros Kingslayer, Banewreaker's Servant."

"So you name me." A muscle in his jaw twitched. "I did not choose such names, Lady. Is this how you return a greeting fairly given?"

"You cut down my guardsmen where they stood, sent one of Oronin's Hunters against my husband-to-be, unarmed in his wedding bower. How can you say you mean me no harm?" Anger set her words ablaze. "What happens to me matters naught, Kingslayer. I am resolved to die. But do not slay my kinsmen and tell me you mean no harm! In cold blood, unprovoked—"

Tanaros interrupted her. "Why did you agree to wed him?"

Cerelinde looked away, gazing past him, through the impenetrable cavern walls.

"*Why?*"

She flinched at his tone; the granddaughter of Elterrion the Bold. Yet there was steel in her—courage, and heart. Oh yes, Haomane's Children had heart. It had been Arahila's Gift to them, the only one Haomane had permitted. "You need to ask?" Her backbone rigid, she stood straight and tall. "There is valor in him, and a noble spirit. I am a woman, Tanaros Kingslayer, Ellyl or no." Color flushed her cheekbones. "And there is naught in him a woman would not—"

He cut her short. "You sought to fulfill the Prophecy."

Cerelinde opened her mouth, then closed it.

Tanaros laughed, a dry sound. "You sought to fulfill the Prophecy. Make no mistake. It was an act of war."

"I seek to preserve the lives of my people, Tanaros Blacksword." Her grey eyes were somber. "Can you say the same?"

"Aye, I can and do. You are a pawn, Lady, in a war of Haomane First-Born's devising." He raked a hand through his hair; it was greasy, after days under a helm. "Who talked you into the wedding? Ingolin the Wise? Malthus the Counselor, Haomane's Servant and Weapon?" Tanaros gave a bitter smile at her expression. "See how their wisdom availed them! Well, now I have taken you, and you are Lord Satoris' pawn. At least he is honest about it. And as his emissary, I tell you this: He means you no harm."

"I have been abducted." Cerelinde's voice trembled, with anger and the effort of holding her fear at bay. "Abducted by force, brought here against my will, held captive by—" Catching sight of Ushahin huddled against the far wall, she pointed with a shaking finger. "By *creatures,* by Fjeltroll and that foul Misbegotten—"

"Enough!" Tanaros struck her hand down, a sharp, shocking blow.

Too close for comfort, they stared at one another.

"Your people abandoned Ushahin, Lady," Tanaros said to her. "Remember that. Such as he is, your own children would have been, had you wed Aracus Altorus."

"Never!" She flung the denial out in defiance, his words touching on her darkest fear. "They will be conceived in love, in accordance with Haomane's Prophecy." Cerelinde shook her head. "It is not the same, not the same at all. Why do you think we name him thusly? It is not for the mixing of the races. Ushahin the Misbegotten was conceived in lust, in base desire." She pronounced the words with distaste. "The Sunderer's *Gift,* not fair Arahila's."

Tanaros raised his brows. "Thus you hold him accountable for his birth?"

"Not his birth, but what he has made of the ill-conceived life he was given," Cerelinde said evenly. "And my folk gave him into the care of yours, Tanaros Kingslayer. We are not to blame for the cruelty wrought by the children of Men."

"No." He looked away from her, gazing at Ushahin. "And yet you were quicker to abandon him than the children of Men were to assail him. Only Oronin's Children rose above such pettiness. The Were took him in when none other would." His gaze returned to hers. "Leave him be. He lost more than any of us in Lindanen Dale."

She remembered the grey forms in their midst, Aracus engaged in combat. Her breath was quick and shallow. "The one who attacked my betrothed . . ."

"The Dreamspinner called her 'mother,'" Tanaros said quietly. "Remember that, when you condemn us in Haomane's name, Lady. You have my word as surety: No harm will come to you here."

Bowing stiffly, he took his leave.

Cerelinde watched him go. A part of her heart soared, for if his words were true, it meant that Aracus lived. As dire as her prospects appeared, while they both drew breath, hope must not be abandoned. Haomane's Prophecy might yet be fulfilled, and Satoris Banewreaker destroyed through his own folly.

And yet she was troubled.

Tanaros moved through the encampment, greeting the Fjel, checking on his injured Men, making his way to Ushahin's side. There he squatted on his heels, speaking in low tones, one hand on the Misbegotten's shoulder.

He was her enemy, one of the Three. He had killed his wife and slain his King. He was the servant of Satoris Banewreaker.

He was not at all what she had expected.

THE WHITE SLIVER OF THE new moon was bright enough to cast shadows.

The old man shook his head, watching the strangers stumble into the Stone Grove. Half dead, most of them, past caring that they entered a sacred place. One crumpled, unable to walk another step; another knelt beside her, breathing hard through his mouth. Foolish, wasting his breath's moisture in the desert, but what else were they to do with those tiny nostrils?

One stayed upright through sheer will, glancing at the tall rocks surrounding the empty circle, eyes suspicious by moonlight. The old man smiled. Stubborn, that one. He must be the appointed guardian. And the others . . .

"Ngurra!" His wife's whisper tickled his ear with delight. "Look! One of the Haomane-gaali."

And so it was, tall and fair, wrought with such grace that thirst and hunger only stripped him to a translucent beauty, his Shaper's intended essence. Ngurra clicked his tongue. Fair, yes, but could Haomane's Children find water in the desert? No.

One of the strangers could, though; their old one—or at least, where he could not find it, he could compel it. And he'd done so, the old wizard. From Dry Basin to Lizard Rock, across the Basking Flats, he'd done it, calling drought-eaters from barren sand. The desert was leached where they had passed, struggling for survival. The old man felt it, himself; there, above his third rib, a dull ache where Thornbrake Bore had run dry.

"Did you see—?" his wife whispered.

"Shhh." He hushed her. "Watch. They have found it."

It was their old one, their wizard. He leaned on his staff, bowing his head. One hand fumbled beneath the moonlit spill of his beard, drawing forth the Soumanië. It shone like a red star in his hand. The wizard raised his head, gazing at the pile of rocks in the center of the Stone Grove. "It is here," he said softly. "Ah, Haomane! The Unknown made Known. Blaise, Peldras, come."

Together, they clambered over the rocks. What they found there, every member of the Yarru knew full well. A cleft, ringed round with rocks, opening onto unfathomable depths, and from it emerging a breath of water, heavy, with a strong mineral tang. A battered tin bucket, sitting atop an endless coil of rope. A faint sigh whispered around the Stone Grove.

"Is it . . . ?" asked the one called Blaise.

"It is the Well of the World and the Navel of Uru-Alat." The wizard's voice held awe. "*Try though they may, one and all, by no hand save the appointed Bearer . . .*" He halted his recitation. "Let us try, then, and see."

Among the rocks surrounding Stone Grove, the Yarru chuckled, a soft, soughing sound, like the shifting of desert sands. Ngurra rested on his haunches, watching as the strangers fed the tin bucket into Birru-Uru-Alat, the hole at the center of the world. Down and down and down it went, on a coiling rope of thukka-vine. He counted the heartbeats, waiting as the rope uncoiled.

Down . . .

Down . . .

Down.

Almost, the strangers gave up after long minutes, for there seemed no end to the coiling rope. Ngurra knew how long it was. He had measured it, cubit by cubit, all the days of his life. That was his charge, as chieftain of the Stone Grove Clan. His grandmother, who had been chieftainess before him, had passed it to him, along with her knowledge. Maintain the rope, inch by inch. It was one of his charges.

A faint splash in the night.

"Water," said Peldras the Haomane-gaali, lying prone above the opening. His ears were sharper than those of Men. "The bucket has struck water, Counselor."

One after another, they tried it. Blaise, the appointed guardian, tried it first, grunting in the moonlight, muscles straining as he sought to raise the bucket. Then the Haomane-gaali Peldras tried, and fared no better. The wizard tried, too, muttering spells that availed him naught, but earned a silent chuckle from the watching

Yarru. In the end, they all tried, the whole of Malthus' Company, even the thirsting Archer and the bone-weary Knight, laying hands on the rope together and hauling as one. Yet, even as a whole, bone and muscle and sinew cracking, they failed.

The laden bucket was too heavy to raise.

"Enough," whispered their old one, their wizard. "We have tried, one and all, and fulfilled the letter of the Prophecy." Laying down his staff, he cupped the Soumanië in both hands. His voice grew strong as he spoke the words of the choosing, and the ruddy glow of the chip of the Souma grew, spilling from between his cupped hands to illuminate the Stone Grove. "Yarru-yami! Charred Ones! Children of Haomane's wrath! I call upon you now in his name. Lend us your aid!"

"Time and gone he asked," Warabi muttered.

"Hush, old woman!" Ngurra glared at her. She wouldn't understand the common tongue if he hadn't taught it to her himself. "Kindle the torch."

Still muttering, she obeyed, striking flint to iron. The oil-rich fibers of the bugy-stick sputtered and lit, sending a signal. All around the perimeter of the Stone Grove, bugy-stick torches caught and kindled as, one by one, members of the Six Clans of the Yarru revealed themselves.

Ngurra stepped before the torches, gazing down at the small figures gathered around the Birru-Uru-Alat, their shadows stark on the sand. "The Yarru are here," he called in the common tongue, the language his grandmother had taught him. "As we have always been, since before the earth was scorched. What do you seek?"

Malthus the Counselor opened his arms, showing himself weaponless, offering himself as surety. The Soumanië shone like a red star upon his breast. "Speaker of the Yarru, I greet you. We come seeking the Bearer."

In the night, someone gasped.

FOR TWO MORE DAYS, THEY traveled through the tunnels.

Truth be told, Tanaros had never been comfortable in them. They reminded him, too acutely, that Urulat was old, older than his lifespan, unnatural as it was, could reckon. Dragons had carved them, it was said; whether or not it was true, dragons did not acknowledge. Still, they served their purpose for the armies of Darkhaven.

It was harder, with the Lady of the Ellylon.

Vast as they were—broad enough at all times for two horses to ride abreast, and sometimes three—the tunnels were dark and stifling, a mass of earth pressing above at all times. At times, when it was far between vents, the air grew thick and the torches guttered, burning low. Then it was worse, and even Tanaros fought panic, his chest working to draw air into his lungs.

The Fjel, rock-delvers by nature of their Shaping, were untroubled. Their eyes were well suited to darkness and they could slow the very beat of their hearts at need, breathing slow and deep, moving unhurried at a steady pace, carrying heavy packs of supplies. Brute wisdom, mindless and physical, attuned to survival. Even the horses, bred in the Vale of Gorgantum to fear no darkness, endured without panic.

It was different for Men, who thought overmuch.

It was worst of all for the Ellyl.

Tanaros saw, and sympathized against his will. It was simpler, much simpler, to despise her. Ushahin Dreamspinner managed it without effort, his face twisted with pure and absolute despite when he deigned glance her way. By all rights, the Dreamspinner should have hated the tunnels, being human and Ellyl, a creature of open skies. But he was a child of the Were as well, and at home underground.

Not so the Lady Cerelinde.

Her face, by torchlight, was pale, too pale. Skin stretched taut over bones Shaped like lines of poetry, searing and gorgeous. Haomane's Child. Even here, her beauty made the heart ache. Her eyes were wide, swallowed up by darkness. From time to time her pale fingers scrabbled at her throat, seeking to loosen the clasp of a rough-spun wool cloak someone had loaned her on the first day; Hyrgolf, at a guess.

On the second day, Tanaros could bear it no longer.

An escort of marching Fjel surrounded her as she rode, seated on one of the fallen Staccian's mounts. Tungskulder Fjel, Hyrgolf's best lads, their horny heads at a level with her shoulder even as she rode astride. She bore it well, Cerelinde of the Ellylon, only a faint tremor giving evidence to her fear, until the air grew thick once more and she clutched her throat, gasping.

"Give way," Tanaros murmured to the rearguard.

"General!" A Fjeltroll grinned and saluted, dropping back.

He made his way to her side, maneuvering the black horse. "Lady," he said, and her stricken gaze met his. "All is well. There is air, see?" He inhaled deeply, his chest swelling, detecting a waft of fresh air from an unseen vent. His brand pulsed like bands of marrow-fire around his heart. "We will survive, and endure."

"I am afraid." Her frightened eyes were like stars.

Once, Calista had said that to him; his wife. He hadn't know, then, what she meant. Hadn't known of her past-dawning attraction to his blood-sworn kinsman, his king, Roscus Altorus, or the affair it had engendered. He had laughed at her fears, laughed and embraced her, protecting the child that grew in her belly with his own strong arms, believing them strong enough to fend off aught that might harm them.

Now, he didn't laugh.

"I know," he said instead, somber. "Tomorrow we ride above-ground."

Cerelinde of the Ellylon shuddered with relief. "You might die, Kingslayer," she said in her low, musical voice. "If the tunnel fell, deprived of air, you would die and your comrades with you. It would be terrible, but swift. My death would be slow, for such is Haomane's Gift. I would die by inches, and my mind last of all. Though my body held the semblance of death, I would endure. Days, or weeks, alive in the crushing darkness, aware. Think on that, before you name me a coward."

"I would not." He felt embarrassed. "I would not say such a thing."

Her gaze slid sideways, touching him. "What of him?" She indicated the Dreamspinner, who rode before them in the vanguard, trailing the Cold Hunters, the Kaldjager Fjel, who scouted before them to ensure the way was secure. "The blood of Men and Ellylon runs in his veins, yet he knows no fear."

"There is little Ushahin Dreamspinner fears."

"He is mad."

"Yes and no." Tanaros regarded her. "He has reason to hate your kind, Lady. And mine. If it is madness that warps him, it is of our people's devising."

She looked away, showing her profile, clear-cut as a cameo. "So you have said," she said quietly. "And yet, did he come to us, Malthus would heal him. He is wounded in body and mind. It could be done, by one who knew how to wield the Soumanië. Such is the power of the Souma, to Shape and make whole. Even in the merest chip, it abides. In the dagger Godslayer, it abides tenfold. Satoris Banewreaker is cruel to deny him."

"Deny?" Tanaros laughed aloud.

"You are quick to speak of his pain!" Cerelinde's voice rose with her temper. "And the Sunderer was quick to turn it to his ends. Did you never think that Ushahin the Misbegotten might be better served by kindness?"

"Kindness?" Tanaros drew rein, halting their progression. Behind them, the Fjel chuckled, amused by their exchange. "Lady, my Lord Satoris has offered healing to the Dreamspinner more times than I can number." He smiled grimly at her reaction. "Aye, indeed. Do you think the Lord of Darkhaven does not know how to wield Godslayer? He is a Shaper, one of Seven, no matter that Haomane abjures him. It is Ushahin's choice, to wear this broken face, these crippled hands. He was not denied. He chose to keep his pain, his madness. Again and again, he has chosen."

"It is not right." She was shaken.

"Why? Because you say so?" Tanaros shook his head, nudging his mount to a walk. "You understand nothing."

"Tanaros." The fear in her voice and the fact that she spoke his name made him turn in the saddle. Her face was pale against the darkness of the tunnel, and her upraised chin trembled. "What does he want of me, the Sunderer? Why was I taken and yet not slain? It makes no sense. When you attacked . . ." Cerelinde closed her eyes briefly. "When you attacked, I thought you were Beshtanagi in disguise. Haomane help me, I would have sworn to it. Then I awoke, surrounded by Fjeltroll . . ." She shuddered, swallowing. "Why?"

Pity stirred in his heart, a dangerous thing. "Lady, I cannot say. Only trust that you will be unharmed. My Lord has sworn it."

There was despair in her face, and disbelief.

"Be we moving or no, Lord General?" Hyrgolf's rumbling voice called.

"Aye!" Tanaros tore his gaze away and dug his heels smartly into the black's sides. It snorted, moving at a trot through the ranks of the Fjel, who offered good-natured salutes. "Call the march, Field Marshal!"

"March!" Hyrgolf shouted.

Onward they marched. Tanaros let them pass, falling in beside Ushahin Dreamspinner, who regarded him with an unreadable gaze. "You play a dangerous game, cousin," he said.

Tanaros shook his head. "There is no game here."

Ushahin, still clutching the case containing the Helm of Shadows to his belly, shrugged his crooked shoulders. "As you say. Were the choice mine, I would waste no time in killing her."

"The choice is his Lordship's." Tanaros' voice hardened. "Would you strip all honor from him?"

"In favor of survival?" Ushahin looked bleak. "Aye, I would."

Tanaros reached over to touch his crippled hand where it rested on the case. "Forgive me, cousin," he said. "The Grey Dam of the Were is due all honor. She spent her life as she chose and died with her eyeteeth seeking her enemy's throat."

"Aye." Ushahin drew a deep breath. "I know it." In the torchlit tunnel, his mismatched eyes glittered. "Do you know, cousin, my dam afforded you a gift? Even as she died. You will know it ere the end."

"As you say, cousin." Tanaros withdrew his hand, frowning in perplexity. Perhaps, after all, the Dreamspinner's grief had worsened his madness. "Her life was gift enough."

Ushahin bared his teeth in a grimace. "It was for me."

THE SIX CLANS OF THE Yarru-yami, the Charred Ones, Children of Haomane's Wrath, debated the matter for two days. In the cool hours of the early morning and the blue hours of dusk they debated, each member given his or her allotted length of time to speak in the center of the Stone Grove, atop the rocks that marked the Well of the World.

The debate hinged on a single Yarru, the one who must choose.

He was young, the Bearer, still a youth. Of average height for one of his folk, his head scarce reached the Counselor's shoulder, with coarse black hair falling to his shoulders and liquid-dark eyes in an open, trusting face, struggling manfully to listen and weigh all that was said. He was quick and agile, as the Yarru were, with bare feet calloused by the desert floor, and brown-black skin. It was the mark of his people, the Charred Ones, unwitting victims of Haomane's wrath—save his palms, that were pinkish tan, creased with deep-etched lines.

And when he pressed them together and made a cup of his hands, those lines met at the precise base of the hollow to form a radiant star, for such was the sign of the Bearer.

He was seventeen years old and his name was Dani.

"Can he hoist the bucket?" Blaise Caveros had asked bluntly.

"Yes, Guardian." The old man Ngurra had shifted a wad of *gamal* into the pocket of his cheek, regarding the Altorian. "He is the Bearer. It is what he was born to do, to carry the water of Birru-Uru-Alat, that weighs as heavy as life. But whether or not he does is his choosing."

And so there was debate.

It began with Malthus the Counselor. "Dani of the Yarru," he said, leaning upon his staff. "You have seen the red star, the signal of war. In the west, the Sunderer's army grows, legion upon legion of Fjeltroll streaming to join him. Soon he will move against us like a mighty tide, for it is his will to lay claim to the whole of Urulat and challenge his brother, Haomane First-Born, Lord-of-Thought, the Will of Uru-Alat." The Counselor scowled, his bushy eyebrows fierce. "We can fight, and die, we who are loyal to Haomane and the light of the Souma, who would see Urulat made whole. We *will* fight, and die. But in the end, only one thing can halt Satoris Banewreaker."

With his staff he pointed to the rock-pile in the center of the Stone Grove. "Therein," he said, "lies the Water of Life. It alone can quench the marrow-fire that wards the dagger Godslayer. And you alone can draw it, Dani of the Yarru. You alone can carry it. You are the vessel, a part of the Prophecy of Haomane, the Unknown made Known." The Counselor opened his arms. The Soumanië gleamed red upon his breast, nestled amid his beard. "It is a grave matter," he said. "To bear the Water of Life into the Vale of Gorgantum, inside the walls of Darkhaven itself, and extinguish the marrow-fire. We who stand here before you, the Company of Malthus, are pledged to aid you in every step of the way. Yet in the end, the fate of Urulat rests in your hands, Bearer. Choose."

Such was the beginning.

Many others spoke, and among the Company of Malthus, only the Counselor understood the tongue of the Yarru; for many years had he studied it in his quest to unravel the Prophecy. And what he understood, he kept to himself over the days that followed.

When all was said, Dani the Bearer chose.

EIGHT

❖

"YES?" LILIAS RECLINED ON SILK cushions, raising her brows at the page.

"My lady," he said and gulped, glancing sidelong at pretty Sarika in her scanty attire, kneeling at her mistress' side and wafting a fan against the unseasonal heat of a late Pelmaran spring. "My lady . . . there is an ambassador to see you. From the Were."

"Well?" Lilias arched her carefully plucked eyebrows a fraction higher, watching the page stutter. "Are the Were not our allies? See him in!"

He left in a rush. Sarika ceased her fanning. "You should bind him to you, my lady," she murmured, lowering her head to press her lips to the inside of Lilias' wrist. "He would be quicker to serve."

"I've no need of fools and imbeciles, dear one." She stroked the girl's hair. "Enough surround me without binding."

Head bent, Sarika smiled.

Calandor?

Abide, little sister.

The Were ambassador, when he came, entered the room like grey smoke, flowing around corners, low to the ground. Only when he stood and bowed did his form become fixed in the mind's eye. Sarika let out a squeak, huddling close to her mistress' couch. "Sorceress of the East." The Were dipped his muzzle in acknowledgment. "I am Phraotes. I bring you greetings from the Grey Dam of the Were."

Lilias frowned. "Where is Kurush to whom I spoke a fortnight ago? Has he fallen out of favor with the Grey Dam Sorash?"

Phraotes grimaced, lips curling back to show his sharp teeth. "The Grey Dam is dead. The Grey Dam lives. Vashuka is the Grey Dam of the Were."

"Ahhh." A pang ran through her. For as long as Lilias had lived—far longer than the allotment of Arahila's Children—Sorash had been the Grey Dam. "I grieve for your loss, Phraotes," she said in formal response, rising from her couch and extending her hand. "I give greetings to the Grey Dam Vashuka, and recognize the ancient ties of alliance. Thy enemies shall be mine, and my enemies shall be thine."

"Sorceress." He bowed his head, but his amber eyes glowed uneasily at her. "The Grey Dam values the friendship of Beshtanag."

The words were a blow. "Friendship." Lilias withdrew her outstretched hand, regarding Phraotes. "Not alliance."

The ambassador's keen, pointed ears tightened against his head. "War comes to Beshtanag. We do not desire war. Only to hunt, and live."

"You helped to set these forces in motion, Phraotes."

"Yes." His muzzle dipped in a nod. "The Grey Dam Sorash had cause for vengeance. Two Brethren accompanied her. All are dead. The debt is paid. The Grey Dam Vashuka does not desire war."

"Why?" she asked him.

His lip curled. "Once was enough, Sorceress."

Lilias paced her drawing-room, ignoring the clatter of Gergon's wardsmen arriving in a panic, waving them back when they sought to enter the room. Phraotes watched her with wary patience. "You prevailed in that war, Phraotes."

The Were shook his head. "We won our battle, Sorceress. We lost the war."

It is so, Lilias.

Lilias sighed. "You should have stayed in the west," she said to Phraotes. "The children of Men would not hunt you beneath the Sunderer's protection. He commands a vaster territory than I do."

His amber eyes shone. "Our home is in the east, Sorceress. We are Oronin's Children and it is here he Shaped us."

"Oronin should have better care for his Children," Lilias said sharply.

"No." Phraotes' shoulders moved in a shrug. "He is the Glad Hunter. He Shaped us in joy. The Grey Dam Vashuka believes we were foolish to listen to Satoris Banewreaker, who spoke smooth words and roused our ire against Haomane First-Born for denying us the Gift of cleverness. Only Yrinna's Children were wise."

"The *Dwarfs?*" She laughed. "The Dwarfs are content to till the soil and tend the orchards of arrogant Vedasian nobles, ambassador, accepting humility as their lot. You call that wisdom?"

"No one slaughters their young," said Phraotes. "There is merit in Yrinna's Peace. So the Grey Dam Vashuka believes. I am sorry, Sorceress. You have been a good friend to the Were. In Beshtanag, we have been safe. No longer, if war comes." He paused, then added, "We do not abandon you. The Grey Dam pledges a scouting-pack of yearling Brethren to range the western borders, reporting to you. But we will not join in battle. We are too few."

It is their right, Lilias.

"I know," she said aloud, replying to the dragon. "I know." Reluctantly, Lilias inclined her head to the Were ambassador. "I hear your words, Phraotes. Though I am disappointed, they are fair-spoken. Tell the Grey Dam Vashuka that the Sorceress of the East values her friendship. So long as Beshtanag is under my rule, the Were are welcome in it."

"Sorceress." He bowed with obvious relief, ears pricked at a more confident angle. "You are wise and generous."

In the hallway, one of the warders coughed. Lilias suppressed a surge of annoyance. Her wardsmen enjoyed an easy life, and greater freedom than they might elsewhere in Pelmar, subject to the whims of the Regents. With the aid of the Were, she and Calandor defended the boundaries of Beshtanag. All she had done was to forge a holding where she might live in peace, as she chose.

All she asked was loyalty.

Her indulgences were few. There were her attendants, her pretty ones, but what of it? She liked to be surrounded by beauty, by youth. It was a precious and fleeting thing, that span of time wherein youth attained the outer limits of adulthood and reckoned itself immortal, refusing to acknowledge the Chain of Being. It reminded her of why she had chosen to become what she was, the Sorceress of the East.

Most of them served of their own volition. And the rest . . . well. She tried to choose wisely, but perhaps there were a few exceptions. It was a small Shaping, a minor binding at best. None of them took any harm from it, and Lilias dowered them generously, lads and maids alike, when the freshness of their youth began to fade and she dismissed them from her service to go forth and lead ordinary, mortal lives, shaded by the glamor of being part of a story that had begun before they were born, that would continue after their deaths.

None had any right to complain.

And none of them were wise enough to shudder under the shadow of what had occurred here this day, hearing in Grey Dam Vashuka's stance the echo of what was to transpire in the promise of Haomane's Prophecy. Lilias heard its echo, and knew, once more, the taste of fear.

The Were shall be defeated ere they rise . . .

"Thank you, ambassador," she said. "You have leave to go."

He left, belly low to the ground, flowing like smoke.

"BESHTANAG HAS NEVER DEPENDED ON the Were, little ssissster."

"No." Lilias leaned back against the strong column of the dragon's left foreleg, watching blue dusk deepen in the cavern mouth. "But it's a blow nonetheless. Even if all goes as Tanaros Blacksword claimed, we have to be prepared to keep Haomane's Allies at bay for a day, perhaps longer. Beshtanag won't fall in a day, but it would have helped to have the Were in reserve."

"Yesss."

On the horizon, the red star winked into visibility. "Calandor?"

"Yess, Liliasss?"

"What if he's right?" She craned her neck to look up at him. "What if the Dwarfs *did* choose wisely in choosing Yrinna's Peace? Might we not do the same? Are we wrong to defy the will of Haomane?"

A nictitating membrane flickered over the dragon's left eye. "What is *right*, Liliasss?"

"Right," she said irritably. "That which is not wrong."

"In the beginning," Calandor rumbled, "there was Uru-Alat, and Uru-Alat was all things, and all things were Uru-Alat—"

"—and then came the Beginning-in-End, and the Seven Shapers emerged, and first of all was Haomane, Lord-of-Thought, who was born at the place of the Souma and knew the will of Uru-Alat," Lilias finished. "I *know*. Is it true? Does Haomane speak with the World God's voice? Are we wrong to defy him?"

The dragon bent his sinuous neck, lowering his head. Twin puffs of smoke jetted from his nostrils. "You quote the catechism of your childhood, little ssisster, not mine."

"But is it *true?*"

"No." Calandor lifted his head, sighing a sulfurous gust. "No, Liliasss. You know otherwise. These are things I have shown you. The world began in ending, and it will end in beginning. Thisss, not even Haomane Firsst-Born underssstands. What he grasspss is only a portion of Uru-Alat'ss plan, and his role in it is not as he thinksss. All things mussst be Ssundered to be made whole. It is not finished . . . yet."

"Calandor," she said. "Why did you tell such things to Satoris Third-Born, yet not to Haomane First-Born?"

"Because," the dragon said. "He asssked."

For a long moment, neither spoke. At length, Lilias said, "Is that why Haomane despises him?"

The dragon shifted. "Perhapss, Liliasss. I cannot sssay."

"Between them, they will tear the world asunder anew," she said in a low voice.

"Yesss," Calandor agreed. "One in his pride, one in his defi-ansse. Sso it musst be. All things change and transsmute, even Shapers. They play the roles they mussst."

"Do they know?" she asked.

Calandor blinked once, slowly. "Sssatoriss knows."

In the unseasonal warmth she shivered, wrapping her arms about herself, pressing her body against the scaled forelimb. Even the forge-heat of the dragon's body could not dispel her chill. "Ca-landor, what of us? What happens if we fail?"

"Fail?" There was amusement in the dragon's deep voice. "What is *failure?*"

"RIGHT." THE CAPTAIN OF THE *Ilona's Gull* scratched his stubbled chin, running a calculating eye over Carfax' company. "My bargain was for twenty men, not horses. 'Specially not *these* horses. Reckon they'll wreak right hell in my hold if the crossing's rough, won't they?"

In the bright sunlight of Harrington Bay, the measures taken to disguise the horses of Darkhaven held up poorly. Even with burred manes and ill-kept coats, their eyes gleamed with preternatural in-tellect, muscles gliding like oil under their bunching hides.

"Look, man." Carfax struggled for calm, finding his hand reach-ing for his sword-hilt. Nothing on earth was more frustrating than dealing with the Free Fishers of Harrington Inlet. They owed alle-giance to no mortal ruler, and their independence was legendary. "A bargain was made. My understanding is that it was for passage for my men and their mounts . . . and for the lady. Will you keep it or no?"

A crowd was gathering on the quai, which was to the good.

They wanted witnesses who could testify that a group of armed men, likely Pelmaran, had departed on the *Ilona's Gull,* escorting a woman garbed in a cloak of white silk wrought by Ellylon, the gold-embroidered crowns and ruby Souma glinting in the sunlight.

What they *didn't* want was witnesses who crowded close enough to note that the supposed Pelmarans spoke the common tongue with a Staccian accent, the horses they rode were found nowhere else on earth, and beneath the shadow of her exquisite hood, the Ellyl noblewoman sported blond beard-stubble.

"I might . . ." the captain drawled, winking at his mates. "For a price. A damage tax, y'see."

"Fine," Carfax snapped. If he'd had the luxury of time, he'd have showed the Free Fisherman what it meant to bargain with a disciple of mighty Vorax, whose appetite was matched only by his shrewdness. But somewhere behind them—hours, at best—a host of Haomane's Allies pursued them. "Name your price."

The Free Fisher captain pursed his wind-chapped lips. "I might do it for a pair of those fine steeds you ride, goodman."

"Two horses?" Carfax raised his hand, cutting off a protest from his comrades.

"Two." The captain nodded. "Aye, two will do it. Reckon they'll fetch a good price in Port Calibus." He grinned, revealing strong white teeth. "They do like to cut a fine figure astride, those Vedasian knights."

"Done."

The bargain struck, the planks were laid, and Carfax's company began boarding the *Ilona's Gull*. The horses of Darkhaven permitted themselves to be led down the ramps with wary dignity, eyes rolling as they descended into the ship's hold. Turin in his Ellyl cloak was hustled aboard, surrounded by an escort. Carfax breathed a sigh of relief as he disappeared.

"Lieutenant." One of his men, young Mantuas, tugged at his elbow. "Lieutenant," he hissed in Staccian, "we *can't* part with any of the horses! 'Twill leave a trail pointing straight to Darkhaven!"

"Peace, lad," Carfax muttered out of the side of his mouth. "At least speak in common, if you must. Hey!" he added, shouting at the pressing crowd, affecting a Pelmaran accent rather well, he thought. "You and you, get back! This is important business, and none of yours!"

They withdrew a few paces, the Free Fishers; net-men and fish-wives, curious children with bright eyes. A few paces, no more. Carfax hid a smile. Lord Vorax had a fondness for the Free Fishers of Harrington Inlet, truth be told. Stubborn as they were, they had the pride of their self-interest, unabashed and free—some, like this captain, even willing to strike deals with agents of suspect origin.

But when it came to war, the Free Fishers would side with Haomane's Allies, believing Lord Satoris would strip away their independence. Mantuas was right, of course. They couldn't afford to lose the horses.

If there were more time, Carfax thought, he might try to sway the captain and his crew. They seemed like shrewd men who understood profit and would listen to reason, who could be brought to understand that Lord Satoris offered a greater freedom than they knew existed; freedom from the yolk of Haomane's will, under which they labored unknowing, trudging like a miller's oxen in endless circles.

But given the time constraints, it would be much simpler to kill them at sea.

Carfax hoped he remembered how to sail a ship. It had been a long time since he had summered on the shores of Laefrost Lake with his mother's kin, the clear, ice-blue waters swollen with snowmelt. Well, he thought, crossing the ramp, standing at the railings as the planks were drawn aboard and the mainsail hoisted, the winch grinding as the anchor was raised; we will find out.

The sail bellied full, showing the proud insignia of the Free Fishers of Harrington Inlet, the stone anchor and fishhook. Crewmen scrambled here and there, obeying the captain's shouted orders. A wedge of open water divided them from the shore, growing steadily as the *Ilona's Gull* nudged her prow seaward.

NINE

THEY EMERGED FROM THE TUNNELS in the outskirts of a ruined city.

Once, there had been walls and towers of white onyx, proud spires rising from the plains. Now, the walls were breached and broken, and plain-hawks nested in the toppled towers. Sturdy heart-grass grew in the empty streets, cracking the marble flag-stones, and the wind made a mournful sound in the ruins.

The entrance to the tunnel was partially blocked by great slabs of blue chalcedony, and they picked their way out one by one. Cerelinde, emerging into the cloud-shrouded daylight, reached out from her saddle to touch the cracked walls of the adjacent structure from which slabs of precious stone had slid, revealing the granite beneath. "Ellylon made this."

"Careful, Lady," Tanaros muttered. "It is unstable."

"What is this place?" She shivered. "There is sorrow in its bones."

Hyrgolf glanced backward, his massive head silhouetted against the lowering sky. "Your people called it the City of Long Grass, Lady of the Ellylon," he answered in his guttural voice. "A long time ago."

"Ah, Haomane!" Cerelinde flung herself from her mount's back, kneeling at the base of one chalcedony slab. *"Cuilos Tuillenrad."* Her fingers brushed the moon-blue surface with delicate reverence, revealing lines of Ellylon runes therein engraved. "This city be-longed to Numireth the Fleet," she breathed.

"Yes." Tanaros caught the reins of her mount, glancing around uneasily. The city, or what remained of it, was a desolate place. It had been conquered long ago, in the Third Age of the Sundered

World, when Lord Satoris had led the Fjeltroll out of the fastness of the north and swept westward, driving the Ellylon before him. The plains had reclaimed it since. No one else wanted it. "Lady Cerelinde, we must ride."

"A moment," she whispered, tracing the runes with her fingertips. "I beg you."

He glanced at Hyrgolf, who shrugged. The Fjel were engaged in hauling supplies from the tunnel, assessing what must be ported, what could be left behind. There would be ample grazing now that they were on the open plains. It had been carefully chosen, this site; close enough to Darkhaven to ensure a safe return, far enough to ensure that the Lady of the Ellylon did not guess the extent of the tunnel system that lay beneath Urulat, which led to the door of Darkhaven itself.

And, of course, there was the history, which was supposed to remind her of the folly of opposing Lord Satoris' will. All of these matters were well considered, which did naught to assuage the prickling sensation at the back of Tanaros' neck.

Why had the plains gone wind-still?

"Cousin." Ushahin sidled his mount close to Tanaros. His good eye squinted tight. "I mislike this stillness. Something is wrong."

The Fjel had paused in their labors, broad nostrils sniffing the air. Vorax's Staccians were huddled together, crowding their mounts' flanks. Pressure built all around. At the base of the chalcedony slab, the Lady Cerelinde traced runes, whispering under her breath.

"Dreamspinner!" Tanaros grabbed the half-breed's wrist. "What is she doing?"

"You do not know?" Ushahin's smile was sickly. "This is the crypt where the fallen of the House of Numireth were interred. The tunnels lie beneath it. Where she kneels?" He nodded toward Cerelinde, whose bridal skirts lay spread in a pool. "It is where their kin offered prayers for vengeance against the Sunderer. I imagine she does the same."

Every blade of heart-grass stood motionless, waiting, in the gaps of the walls, the cracked and desolate streets. There was only the whisper of Cerelinde's voice.

Tanaros swore.

"Put on the helm," he said, his fingers tightening hard on the half-breed's wrist. "Dreamspinner! *Don the Helm of Shadows!*"

Too late.

From everywhere and nowhere they came at once; wraiths, the

host of the House of Numireth. Misty riders on misty horses, con-verging from all quarters of the forsaken city. With hollow eyes filled with white flame, the Ellylon dead heeded Cerelinde's prayer, and the clamor of ancient battle rose as they rode, a grief-stricken wail riding above it all.

"Tungskulder Fjel!" Somewhere, Hyrgolf was roaring. "Form a square! Kaldjager! To the hunt!"

Tanaros swore again, having lost his grip on the reins of Cere-linde's mount and on Ushahin. He drew his Pelmaran sword as a ghostly warrior bore down upon him, swinging hard. His blade cleaved only mist, and Ellyl laughter pealed like bells, bright and bitter. Again, and again. The Host of Numireth encircled him, pale mocking in their unsubstantial beauty, riding past to swipe at him with ghostly blades. Filled with unreasoning terror, Tanaros dug his heels into the black's sides, turning him in a tight circle, lashing out with his sword.

Everywhere he turned, the wraiths surrounded him, riding in a ring, swirling into mist when his steel passed through them, only to coalesce unharmed. White fire filled the hollows of their eyes, and death was written in it. Some yards away through the wraith-mist, Ushahin Dreamspinner had fallen writhing to the ground, clutching his twisted hands over his ears. And then one of the riding wraiths brushed close enough to touch him, and Tanaros heard the voices of the dead whispering in his own mind.

. . . *because of you we were slain whom the Lord-of-Thought made deathless, because of you the world was Sundered, because of you we are bound here* . . .

"No!" Tanaros shouted to silence the rising chorus. "It's not true!"

. . . *dwelled in peace until the Enemy came from the north and hordes upon hordes of Fjeltroll tore down our walls and slaughtered our armies* . . .

"It's not true!"

Numireth, Valwe, Nandinor . . . names out of legend, slain before his birth. Tall lords of the Ellylon with eyes of white fire, and on their breastplates the insignia of their House, the swift plains elbok, picked out in sable shadow. Numireth the Fleet, whose silver helm was crowned with wings. They closed around him, wraith-mist touching his living flesh, the tide of their litany rising in his straining mind.

. . . *plains of Curonan ran red with blood and the screams of the dying, and we were driven from our homes, we who are the Rivenlost* . . .

"No." Tanaros shut his eyes against them in desperate denial, putting up his sword. Under his right elbow, he felt the lump of Hyrgolf's *rhios* in its pouch. A familiar rage rose in his heart. "Dwelled in peace, my arse! You marched against him in Neherinach!"

Elsewhere, the sound of battle raged; but the voices fell silent in his mind.

Without daring open his eyes, Tanaros dismounted, letting the reins fall slack. Crawling, he groped his way across the cracked marble and tufted heart-grass toward the sound of Ushahin's agonized keening. There, a few paces from the half-breed, his hands found what he sought—the leather case that held the Helm of Shadows.

"Cousin." He reached out blindly to touch Ushahin. "I'm taking the Helm."

"Tanaros!" A breath hissed through clenched teeth. *"Get them out of my head!"*

"I will try." With fingers stiff from clutching his hilt, Tanaros undid the clasps and withdrew the Helm. It throbbed with pain at his touch and he winced at the ache in his bones. His hands trembled as he removed the Pelmaran helmet and placed the Helm of Shadows on his head, opening his eyes.

Darkness.

Pain.

Darkness like a veil over his vision, casting the plains and the ruined city in shadow; pain, a constant companion. The ghost of a wound throbbed in his groin, deep and searing, pumping a steady trickle of ichor down the inside of his leg. Such was the pain of Satoris, stabbed by Oronin Last-Born before the world was Sundered, and the darkness of the Helm was the darkness in his heart.

Once it had been Haomane's weapon. No longer.

Tanaros rose. Before him, the wraiths of the House of Numireth arrayed themselves in a line, silent warriors on silent horses. In the Helm's shadowed vision they had taken on solidity, and he saw bitter sorrow in their eyes instead of flames, and the marks of their death-wounds upon their ageless flesh.

Across the plains and throughout the city, other battles raged. Westward, the surviving Staccian riders fled in full-blown terror, not even the horses of Darkhaven able to outrun the wraiths. In a deserted plaza where once a fountain had played, Hyrgolf's Fjel fought shadows, their guttural cries hoarse with exhaustion and fear. Here and there in the streets, the stalking Kaldjager waged battle with the dead.

And to the south, a lone rider streaked in flight, unpursued.

"Numireth." Tanaros gazed steadily through the eyeslits of the Helm of Shadows. "I claim this city in the name of Satoris the Shaper. This quarrel is older than your loss, and your shades have no power in Urulat. Begone."

The Lord of Cuilos Tuillenrad, the City of Long Grass, grimaced in the face of the Helm's dark visage; held up one hand, turned away, his figure fading as he rode. One by one, the wraith-host followed, growing insubstantial and vanishing.

"Well done." Breathing hard, Ushahin struggled to his feet. His mouth was twisted in self-deprecation. "My apologies, Blacksword. I've walked in the dreams of the living. I've never had the dead enter mine. It was . . . painful."

"It doesn't matter." Tanaros removed the Helm, blinking at the sudden brightness. The piercing throb in his groin subsided to a vestigial ache. "Can you summon her horse? I've not the skill for it."

"Aye." Donning the Helm of Shadows, Ushahin faced south, sending out a whip-crack of thought. In the distance, the small, fleeting figure of a horse balked. There was a struggle between horse and rider; a brief one. The horses of Darkhaven had strong wills and hard mouths. This one turned in a sweeping loop, heading back for the ruined city at a steady canter, bearing its rider with it.

Tanaros watched long enough to be certain Cerelinde would not throw herself from the saddle, then turned his attention to his company. To the west, the Staccians had regrouped, returning shame-faced at their flight. Singly and in pairs, the Kaldjager loped through the streets, irritable at the false hunt. But Hyrgolf's Fjel . . . ah, no!

They came slowly, carrying one of their number with uncommon care.

"General Tanaros." Hyrgolf's salute was sombre. "I am sorry to report—"

"Jei morderran!" It was a young Tungskulder Fjel, one of the new recruits, who interrupted, hurling himself prone on the cracked marble, offering his bloodstained axe with both hands. "Gojdta mahk åxrekke—"

"Field marshal!" Tanaros cut the lad short. "Report."

"Aye, General." Hyrgolf met his gaze. "Bogvar is wounded. I do not think he will live. Thorun asks you to take his axe-hand in penance."

"He asks *what?* No, never mind." Tanaros turned his attention to the injured Fjeltroll, laid gently on the ground by the four comrades who carried him. "Bogvar, can you hear me?"

"Lord . . . General." Bogvar's leathery lips parted, flecked with blood. One of his eyetusks was chipped. A dreadful gash opened his massive chest, and air whistled in it as he struggled for breath, blood bubbling in the opening, gurgling as he spoke. "You . . . were . . . right." The claws on his left hand flexed, and he forced his lips into a horrible smile. "Should have held . . . my shield higher."

"Ah, curse it, Bogvar!" Kneeling beside him, Tanaros pressed both hands hard over the gash. "Someone bring a—ah, no!" A rush of blood welled in the Fjel's open mouth, dribbled from one corner. Bogvar of the Tungskulder Fjel lay still, and bled no more. Tanaros sighed and ran a hand through his hair, forgetful of the blood. "You should have held your shield higher," he muttered, clambering wearily to his feet. "The lad Thorun did this?"

"Aye." Hyrgolf's voice came from deep in his chest. "An accident. The dead came among us, and some broke ranks. Thorun was one. He thought he struck a blow at an Ellyl wraith. My fault, General. I reckoned him ready."

"Gojdta mahk åxrekke . . . " The young Fjel struggled to his knees, holding his right arm extended and trembling, clawed fist clenched. "Take my axe-hand," he said thickly in the common tongue. "I kill him. I pay."

"No." Tanaros glanced round at the watchful Fjeltroll, the chagrined Staccians straggling back on their wind-blown mounts. "The first fault was mine. I chose this place without knowing its dangers. Let it be a lesson learned, a bitter one. We are at war. There are no safe places left in the world, and our survival depends on discipline." He bent and retrieved Thorun's axe, proffering it haft-first. "Hold ranks," he said grimly. "Follow orders. And keep your shields up. Is this understood?"

"General!" Hyrgolf saluted, the others following suit.

The young Fjel Thorun accepted his axe.

THE TASTE OF FREEDOM WAS sweet; as sweet as the Long Grass in blossom, and as fleeting. She felt the Host of Numireth disperse, its bright presence fading. She felt the Misbegotten's thought flung out across the plains, a thread of will spun by an unwholesome spider of a mind.

If he had reached for her, Cerelinde might have resisted. Even with the Helm of Shadows, he was weak from the ordeal and here, on the threshold of Cuilos Tuillenrad, she was strong. The old Elly-lon magics had not vanished altogether.

But no, he was cunning. He turned her mount instead.

She had dared to hope when it had raced willingly at her urging; another of Haomane's Children's ancient charms, the ability to sooth the minds of lesser beasts. But the horses of Darkhaven were willful and warped by the Sunderer's Shaping, with great strength in their limbs and malice in their hearts. It fought against her charm and the bit alike, its eyes roiling with vile amusement as it turned in a vast circle to answer the Misbegotten's call.

She let it carry her back to the ruined city, its path carving a wake through the long grass. There Tanaros stood, watching and awaiting her return. Her dark-dappled mount bore her unerringly to him then stopped, motionless and quiescent.

"Lady," Tanaros said, bowing to her. "A noble effort. Bravely done."

Cerelinde searched his face for mockery, finding none. "Would you have done otherwise?" she asked.

"No," he said simply. "I would not."

Behind him, grunting Fjel wielded their maces with mighty blows, breaking the chalcedony slabs into rubble, demolishing forever the inscriptions upon them. They were porting massive chunks of moon-blue stone and heaping them atop a fallen comrade to form a cairn. Cerelinde felt herself turn pale at the sight. "They are destroying the resting-place of my ancestors!" Her voice shook. "Ah, Haomane! Is it not enough the city was destroyed long ago? Must you permit this desecration?"

Tanaros' expression hardened. "Lady," he said, "Your *ancestors* marched against theirs long before the City of Long Grass fell. Marched into Neherinach, and took arms against Neheris' Children in the high mountains. Do you blame them?"

Two spots of color rose on her cheeks. "They chose to shelter the Sunderer!"

"Yes." He held her gaze. "They did."

Cerelinde shook her head. "I do not understand you," she said in a low tone. "I will never understand. Why do you serve one such as Satoris Banewreaker, who exists only to destroy such beauty?"

Tanaros sighed. "Lady, these ruins have stood untouched for centuries. It was you who sought to make a weapon of them," he reminded her. "For that, I do not blame you. Do me the courtesy of understanding that I must now destroy them in turn."

Though his words were just, her heart ached within her breast.

The Fjel maces swung onward, breaking and smashing, each blow further diminishing the presence of the Rivenlost in the Sundered World. Never again would the wraiths of the valiant dead of the House of Numireth ride the plains of Curonan. "You did not have to choose this," Cerelinde whispered. "My paltry effort caused you no harm."

"No harm?" Tanaros stared at her. "Lady Cerelinde, I do not begrudge you either your valor or your vengeance, but I pray you, spare me your hypocrisy. One of my lads lies dead, and that is harm aplenty." Contempt laced his voice. "Unless that is not what such a word *means* to your people."

Without another word, he walked away.

Cerelinde bowed her head, weary and defeated. It was true, she had forgotten about the slain Fjeltroll. Until this moment, she had not known it was possible for a Man to mourn the passing of such a creature.

It seemed it was.

She did not understand.

Ushahin Dreamspinner slept, and dreamed.

On the plains of Curonan, the wind blew low and steady, soughing through the heart-grass. The city of Cuilos Tuillenrad lay three leagues to the south, and the dead lay quiet in it, including Bogvar of the Tungskulder Fjel, who slept the sleep of the dead beneath a cairn of Ellylon rubble.

On the plains, the Cold Hunters stood sentry, watching the grass bow in the wind through yellow eyes that could see in the dark. Even so, Field Marshal Hyrgolf walked the perimeter with heavy steps, peering into the night. No Fjel were to have died on this mission, and his heart was uneasy.

General Tanaros slept, fitful in his bedroll.

In a simple hide tent, Cerelinde of the Ellylon did not sleep, and her eyes were open and wakeful onto the world.

These, the Dreamspinner passed over.

Over and over, ranging far afield. Outside the warded valley of Meronil, he sifted through the sleeping thoughts of Altorian warriors, flinching at their violence as they dreamed of a council of war in the halls of the Rivenlost. On the rocking waters of Harrington Bay, he brushed the mind of a dozing Staccian lieutenant, filled with reef-knots and mainsails and a dagger stuck in a Free Fisherman's throat.

Further.

Further.

A dry land, so dry the ravens feared it.

There, he found seven minds sheltered, warded against incursions in one manner or another. One, that shone like a red star, he avoided like plague. One was Ellyl, and made him shudder. One was wary, bound with suspicion. One dreamed only of the bow's tension, the drawn string quivering, the arrow's quick release.

One dreamed of water, following the veins of the earth, carrying a digging-stick.

One dreamed of marrow-fire and clutched his throat.

But one; ah! One seethed with resentment and dreamed of what displeased him, and his envy made brittle the wardings that protected him until his thoughts trickled through the cracks and he might be known, his place located and found upon the face of Urulat, his destination discerned. Hobard of Malumdoorn was his name, and he was Vedasian. A young knight, given his spurs only because of his family's long association with the Dwarfs and the secret they guarded. Were it not for that, he would never have been knighted, never sent to Meronil to confer with the wise.

Never chosen for the Company of Malthus.

In the darkness, Ushahin smiled, and woke.

Sitting cross-legged, he summoned the ravens of Darkhaven.

TEN

Sunlight flooded the great hall of Meronil, streaming through the tall windows. The slender panes of translucent blue flanking the clear expanses of glass laid bars of sapphire light across the polished wood of the long table.

Ingolin the Wise surveyed those assembled.

"There are tidings," he said to them. "Good and ill."

"Give us the bad news." It was Aracus Altorus who spoke. The loss of Cerelinde had struck him hard, etching lines of sorrow and self-blame into his features. No longer did the ageless Ellylon behold the Altorian king-in-exile and reckon him young for one of his kind.

"The Lady Cerelinde's abductors elude us," Ingolin said. "Even now, we pursue them across the waters. But hope dwindles."

"Why?" Aracus' voice was grim. "Do our allies fail us?"

Duke Bornin of Seahold cleared his throat. "Kinsman, I have bargained with the Council of Harrington Bay on our behalf, and all aid they have given us. This much is known. The miscreants booked passage to Port Calibus aboard the *Ilona's Gull*. Witnesses in the harbor attest to the fact that the Lady Cerelinde was with them, and seemingly unharmed. But," he said somberly, "ships returning from Vedasia report passing no such vessel en route. I fear they changed their course at sea."

There was silence in the great hall.

"So we have lost them?" A single frown-line knit the perfect brow of the Lady Nerinil, who spoke for the surviving members of the House of Numireth.

"Yes." Ingolin bowed his head to her. "For now. If they are bound for Port Calibus, we will intercept them there. If not—"

"Lord Ingolin, we know where they are bound. All signs point to Beshtanag." Aracus Altorus flattened his hands in a patch of blue light atop the table. "The question is whether or not the Rivenlost and our allies dare to challenge the Sorceress of the East." His face was hard with resolve. "Ingolin, I fear the Sorceress and the Soumanië she wields, that we must face without the aid of Malthus the Counselor. I fear the Dragon of Beshtanag in his ancient lair. But I fear more hearing you say, 'hope dwindles.'" He raised his chin an inch, sunlight making a brightness of his red-gold hair. "Cerelinde lives, Ingolin. The Prophecy lives, and where there is life, there is hope. The Borderguard of Curonan will *not* despair."

"Nor do I suggest it," Ingolin said gently. "Son of Altorus, did I not say there were glad tidings among the sorrowful?" Turning in his chair, the Lord of the Rivenlost beckoned to an attendant, who came forward to set a gilded coffer on the table before him. It was inlaid with gems, worked with the device of the Crown and Souma.

"That is the casket Elterrion the Bold gave to Ardrath, Haomane's Counselor, is it not?" the Lady Nerinil inquired."

"Yes." Ingolin nodded. "And it passed to Malthus, who gave it to me. 'Ward it well, old friend,' he told me, 'for I have attuned the humble stone within it to the Gem I bear. If it kindles, you may know we have succeeded.'"

And so saying, he opened the casket.

It blazed.

It blazed with light, a rough shard of tourmaline, spilling pale blue light across the polished surface of the table like water in the desert. Incontrovertible and undeniable, the signal of Malthus the Counselor shone like a beacon.

"The Unknown," said Ingolin, "is made Known."

And he told them of the Water of Life.

STRIPPED TO THEIR BREECHES AND sweating, the riders straggled along the riverbank, each picking his path through sedge grass. Insects rose in buzzing clouds at their passage, and even the horses of Darkhaven shuddered, flicking their tails without cease. Little else lived along the lower reaches of the Verdine River, which flowed torpid and sluggish out of the stagnant heart of the Delta itself.

"Sweet Arahila have mercy! I'd give my left stone for a good, hard frost."

Snicker, snicker. "Might as well, Vilbar. It's no use to *you*."

"A sodding lot you know! I've had girls wouldn't give you a drink in the desert."

"Wishing don't make it so."

"Wish we *were* in the desert. At least it would be dry."

"Wish I had a girl right now. This heat makes me pricklish."

"Have a go at Turin, why don't you? He's near pretty enough."

"Sod you all!"

"Quiet!" At the head of their ragged column, Carfax turned to glare at his men. They drew rein and fell into muttering silence. "Right," he said. "It's going to get worse before it gets better. If you think this is bad, wait until we get into the Delta. In the meantime, save your breath and keep your flapping jaws *shut*."

"Who's going to hear us out here, lieutenant?" Mantuas gestured, indicating the broad expanse of sedge grass, the open sky. "The local frog-hunters? There's not a living soul in shouting distance! Vedasian patrols wouldn't bother getting their gear muddy this close to the stinking Verdine. Look around you, there's . . . " He stopped, staring.

To the west, three specks in the sky.

"Ravens," someone breathed.

"Hey!" Turin dragged the Lady Cerelinde's cloak from his saddlebag, waving it in the air. "The Dreamspinner must have sent them to find us, lieutenant. Mayhap they carry a message. Here!" he shouted, waving the white cloak. Gilt embroidery and tiny rubies flashed in the sun. "We're over here!"

High above, a half league to the west, the ravens paused, circling.

"Over here!" Turin shouted. "Here!"

"Idiot!" Carfax jammed his heels into his mount's sides, plowing through the sedge grass to snatch the cloak away. "They're not looking for us."

"Then what—" Turin shoved his fist against his teeth. "Ah, no!"

A faint streak, tipped with a spark of sunlit steel; one, two, three. Arrows, shot into the sky, arcing impossibly high, impossibly accurate. A burst of feathers, small bundles of darkness plummeting; one, two, three.

"Haomane's Allies." Mantuas swallowed. "You think they found the ship, lieutenant? Are they after us?"

"They couldn't have found the damned ship." It had been near

dusk on the second day at sea when Carfax had dispatched the
captain of the *Ilona's Gull,* planting a dagger in the side of his
throat. An ignoble death, but a swift one. His men had seen to the
crew, and together, under cover of darkness, they'd gotten the ship
headed north, making landfall the next day at the fetid, uninhab-
ited mouth of the Verdine. "Why would they look there?"

Turin retrieved the Ellyl cloak and folded it away, not meeting
his eyes. "We were seen crossing the Traders' Road, lieutenant."

"We were *supposed* to be seen. Heading north, overland to Pelmar." Carfax passed a hand over his face, found it oily with sweat.
If he looked anything like his men, he looked a mess, the walnut
dye darkening his skin to a Pelmaran hue streaking in the humid
heat. That had been the last effort of their pretense, crossing the
old overland trade route that ran between Seahold and Vedasia.
Since then, they'd seen no other travelers and had let their guises
fail. "We've made good time. They couldn't have followed that
quickly."

"Well, someone did."

They watched him, waiting; waiting on *him,* Carfax of Staccia.
His comrades, his countrymen. There was no one else in command
in this desolate, humid wasteland. What, Carfax thought, would
General Tanaros do if he were here?

"Right," he said smartly. "Someone did. Let's find out who."

THEY HAD REACHED THE DEFILE'S Maw.

It was aptly named, a dark, gaping mouth in the center of the
jagged peaks that reared out of the plains, surrounding and protecting the Vale of Gorgantum. They looked to have been forced
out of the raw earth by violent hands, those mountains; in a sense,
it was true, for Lord Satoris had raised them. It was his last mighty
act as a Shaper, drawing on the power of Godslayer before he
placed the shard of the Souma in the flames of the marrow-fire. It
had nearly taken the last reserves of his strength, but it had made
Darkhaven into an unassailable fortress.

Tanaros breathed deep, filling his lungs with the air of home.
All around him, he saw the Fjel do the same, hideous faces break-
ing into smiles. The Staccians relaxed, sitting easier in the saddle.
Even Ushahin Dreamspinner gave a crooked smile.

"We are bound *there?*"

He studied the Lady Cerelinde, noting the apprehension in her
wide-set eyes. They were not grey, exactly. Hidden colors whis-

pered at the edges of her pleated irises; a misty violet, luminous as the inner edge of a rainbow. "It is safe, Lady. Hyrgolf's Fjel will not let us fall."

She clutched the neck of her rough-spun cloak and made no answer.

Kaldjager Fjel ran ahead up the narrow path, bodies canted forward and loping on knuckled forelimbs, pausing to raise their heads and sniff the wind with broad nostrils. They climbed the steep path effortlessly, beckoning for their comrades to follow.

"Lady," Hyrgolf rumbled, gesturing.

One by one, they followed, alternating Fjel and riders. The horses of Darkhaven picked their way with care, untroubled by the sheer drops, the steep precipice that bordered the pathway. Below them, growing more distant at each step, lay the empty bed of the Gorgantus River. Only a trickle of water coursed its bottom, acrid and tainted.

At the top of the first bend, one of the Kaldjager gave a sharp, guttural call.

A pause, and it was answered.

It came from the highest peaks, a wordless roar, deep and deafening. Thunder might make such a sound, or rocks, cascading in avalanche. It rattled bones and thrummed in the pits of bellies, and Tanaros laughed aloud to hear it.

"Tordenstem Fjel," he shouted in response to the panicked glance Cerelinde threw him over her shoulder. "Have no fear! They are friends!"

She did fear, though; he supposed he couldn't blame her. It had taken him hard, a thousand and more years gone by. A Man in his prime, with blood on his hands and a heart full of fury and despair, riding in answer to a summons he barely understood.

Bring your hatred and your hurt and serve me . . .

Then, he had shouted in reply; had faced the Tordenstem as it crouched atop the peak with its barrel chest and mouth like a howling tunnel, and shouted his own defiant reply, filled with the fearless rage of a Man to whom death would be a welcome end. And the Tordenstem, the Thunder Voice Fjel, had laughed, barrel chest heaving, ho! ho! ho! Maybe you are the one his Lordship seeks, scrawny pup!

And it had been so, for he was; one of the Three, and the Tordenstem had led him along the treacherous passage to Darkhaven, where he pledged his life to Lord Satoris, who had withdrawn Godslayer from the marrow-fire and branded him with its hilt, circumscribing his aching heart. A haven, a haven in truth, sanctuary for his wounded soul . . .

"What?" Echoing words penetrated his reverie; the Tordenstem sentry—kinsman, perhaps, of the long-dead Fjel who had intercepted him, was shouting a message, incomprehensible syllables crashing like boulders. Tanaros shook himself, frowning, and called to his field marshal. "What did he say?"

"General." Hyrgolf trudged back to his side, stolidly unafraid of the heights. "Ulfreg says they captured a Man in the Defile, two days past. One of your kind, they think. He made it as far as the Weavers' Gulch. They took him to the dungeons."

"Aracus!" Cerelinde breathed, her face lighting with hope.

It struck him like a blow; he hadn't believed, before now, that the Lady of the Ellylon could love a Son of Altorus. "Not likely," Tanaros said sourly, watching the light die in her lovely face. "He'd have been killed thrice over. Dreamspinner?"

Ushahin, huddled out of the wind with his mount's flank pressed to the cliff wall, shrugged. "Not one of mine, cousin. I alert the sentries when a madling comes. Those with wits to seek shelter have already fled the coming storm." He touched the case that held the Helm of Shadows with delicate, crooked fingers. "Do you want me to scry his thoughts?"

"No." Tanaros shook his head. "Time enough in Darkhaven."

Onward they continued, winding through the Defile. After the first peak, the path widened. The Kaldjager continued to lope ahead, scouting. Periodically, one would depart from the path to scale a crag, jamming sharp talons on fist and foot into sheer rock, scrambling with four-limbed ease. There they would perch, yellow eyes glinting, exchanging calls of greeting with the Tordenstem sentries, who replied in booming tones.

Hyrgolf explained it to Cerelinde with Fjel patience.

". . . worked together, you see, Lady. Used to be the Tordenstem—Thunder Voices, you call them—would herd game for the Cold Hunters, driving them to the kill. They'd flee the sound, you see, and there would be plenty for all. When your folk invaded the Midlands, they did the same. It worked, too."

Her face was pinched. "You herded my people to slaughter."

"Well." Hyrgolf scratched the thick hide on his neck, nonplussed. "Aye, Lady. You could see it as such. The Battle of Neherinach. But your folk, your grandsire's sons and the like, were the ones brought the swords."

"You sheltered the Sunderer!"

Cerelinde's voice, raised, bounced off the walls of the Defile, clear and anguished. A sound like bells chiming, an Ellylon voice, such as had not been heard within a league of Darkhaven for ten centuries and more. The Kaldjager crouched yellow-eyed in the heights, and the Tordenstem were silent.

"Aye, Lady," Hyrgolf said simply, nodding. "We did. We gave shelter to Lord Satoris. He was a Shaper, and he asked our aid. We made a promise and kept it."

He left her, then, trudging to the head of the line, a broad figure moving on a narrow path, pausing here and there to exchange a word with his Fjel. Tanaros, who had listened, waited until they rounded a bend, bringing his mount alongside hers when there was room enough for two to ride abreast. Side by side they rode, bits and stirrups jangling faintly. The horses of Darkhaven exchanged wary glances, snuffled nostrils, and continued. The Lady Cerelinde sat upright in the saddle and stared straight ahead, her profile like a cut gem.

"I do not understand," she said at length, stiffly.

"Cerelinde." Tanaros tasted her name. "Every story has two sides. Yours the world knows, for the Ellylon are poets and singers unsurpassed, and their story endures. Who in Urulat has ever listened to the Fjeltroll's side of the tale?"

"You blame us." Cerelinde glanced at him, incredulous. "You blame us! Look at them, Tanaros. Look at *him*." She pointed at the Fjel Thorun, marching in front of them in stoic silence. He had spoken seldom since Bogvar's death. His broad, horny feet spread with each step, talons digging into the stony pathway. The pack he bore on his wide shoulders, battle-axe lashed across it, would have foundered an ox. "Look." She opened her delicate hands, palm-upward. "How were we to stand against *that?*"

Ahead, the path veered left, an outcropping of rock jutting into the Defile. Thorun lingered, pausing to lead first Cerelinde's mount, then Tanaros', around the bend. Though he kept his eyes lowered, watching the horses' hooves, unsuited for the mountainous terrain, his hand was gentle on the bridle.

"He speaks Common, you know," Tanaros said.

The Lady of the Ellylon had the grace to blush. "You know what I mean!"

"Aye." Tanaros touched the *rhios* in its pouch. "Neheris-of-the-Leaping-Waters Shaped the Fjel, Lady. Fourth-Born among Shapers, she Shaped them to match the place of her birth; with talons to scale mountains, strong enough . . . " he smiled wryly, " . . . to carry sheep across their shoulders, enough to lay up meat to stock a larder against a long winter."

"Strong enough," she retorted, "to tear down walls, General. You saw Cuilos Tuillenrad! Do you deny the dead their due?"

"No." He shook his head. "Only their version of truth, Lady." He nodded at the axe that jounced against Thorun's pack. "You see that weapon? Until the Battle of Neherinach, it was unknown among the Fjel. We taught them that, Cerelinde. Your people, and mine."

Her face was pale. "Satoris Banewreaker armed the Fjel."

"It is what your people claim," Tanaros said. "Mine too, come to it. But I have learned better in a thousand years, Lady. My Lord armed them, yes; after the Battle of Neherinach, after hundreds of their number fell defending him with tusk and talon. Yes, he taught them to smelt ore, and gave them weapons of steel. And I, I have done my part, Cerelinde. I taught them to use those weapons and such gifts as Neheris gave them in the service of war. Why?" He touched one forefinger to his temple. "Because I have the gift of intellect. Haomane's Gift, that he gave only to his children, and Arahila's. And that, Lady, is the Gift the Fjel were denied."

Cerelinde raised her chin. "Was their lot so terrible? You said it yourself, General. The Fjel were content, in their mountains, until Satoris Banewreaker convinced them otherwise."

"So they should have remained content with their lot?"

"They *were* content." Her gaze was unwavering. "Haomane First-Born is Chief among Shapers, Lord of the Souma. Satoris defied him, and Sundered the world with his betrayal. He fled to Neherinach in fear of Haomane's wrath, and there he enlisted the Fjel, swaying them to his cause, that he might avoid the cost of his betrayal. Did he reckon the cost to *them?*"

Beneath her horse's hooves, the edge of the path crumbled, sending stones tumbling into the Defile. Tanaros checked his black violently, and it shied against the cliff wall. Ahead of them, Thorun whirled into action, spinning to grab at Cerelinde's bridle, wedging his bulk between her and the sheer drop. Pebbles gave way as his taloned toes gripped the verge of the path and his eyetusks showed in a grimace as he urged her mount to solid ground by main force, shoving his shoulder against its flank, hauling himself after it.

"My thanks," Cerelinde gasped.

Thorun grunted, nodding, and resumed his plodding pace.

For a time, then, Tanaros rode behind her, watching the shine of her hair, that hung like an Ellyl banner down her spine. Downward wound the path, then upward, winding around another peak. And down again, where the river-basin broadened. Soon they would enter the Weavers' Gulch. He dug his heels into the black's sides, jogged his mount alongside hers.

"How does it feel, then, to owe your life to a Fjeltroll?" he asked her.

Cerelinde did not spare him a glance. "You brought me here, Tanaros."

"Of course." He bowed from the saddle, mocking. "Proud Haomane will suffer no rivals. Like the Fjel, my Lord Satoris should have remained *content* with his lot."

Ahead, the low river-bottom opened onto a narrow gorge. It was flat, as flat as anything might be in the Defile. The dank trickle of water intensified. This was water tainted by the ichor of Satoris the Shaper, seeping slow and dark. It reeked of blood, only sweeter. The walls of the gorge loomed high on either side, strung across with webs like sticky veils.

One by one, the Kaldjager Fjel parted the veils and entered. Ushahin Dreamspinner passed into the gorge, seemingly unperturbed. At the rear of the company, the Staccians mingled with Hyrgolf's Tungskulder Fjel and made uneasy jests in their own tongue, awaiting their turn.

"What is this place?" Cerelinde asked, her voice low.

"It is the Weavers' Gulch." Tanaros shrugged. "There are creatures in Urulat upon whom the Shapers have not laid hands, Lady. In these, my Lord is interested. Do you fear them? They will do us no harm if we leave them undisturbed."

At the entrance, Thorun waited for them, holding back the skeins of sticky filament so they might pass untouched. A small grey spider scuttled over the gnarled knuckles of his hand. Another descended on a single thread, hovering inches above his head, minute legs wriggling.

Cerelinde looked at what lay beyond and closed her eyes. "I cannot do this."

"I'm sorry, Lady." It had turned his stomach, too, the first time. Tanaros touched his sword-hilt. "But willing or unwilling, you will go."

At the threat, she opened her eyes to regard him. She was Ellylon, and the fineness of her features, the clear luminosity of her skin, were a silent reproach, a reminder that he aspired to that which was beyond him.

Tanaros clenched his teeth. "Go!"

Drawing her hood, the Lady Cerelinde entered the Weavers' Gulch.

ELEVEN

❖

"HERE'S A GOOD SPOT, LIEUTENANT."

Crawling on his belly, Carfax made his way to Hunric's side. Saw-toothed blades of sedge grass caught at him, sweat trickled into his eyes and midges buzzed in his ears. He fought the urge to swat at them.

"Hear that, sir?" The tracker laid his ear flat to the ground. "They'll be along presently. It's a small company, I'm thinking."

Carfax rubbed at the sweat on his brow with the heel of his hand, leaving a grimy streak. "As long as they can't see us."

"Not here." Hunric glanced at him. "Long as we stay quiet. It's tall grass, and we've a clear sight-line to the verge, there. Lay low and you'll see, Lieutenant."

Overhead, the sun was relentless. One forgot, in Darkhaven, how bright it could be—and how hot. It had made him squint at first and, despite many days on the road, he had not fully adjusted to it. A moist heat arose from the earth, smelling of roots. Carfax was aware of his own odor, too, rank as a badger, and Hunric no better. A good tracker, though, the best in the company. In Staccia, he could track a snow-fox through a blizzard. Pity there wasn't a blizzard here. The place could use one. Or a good hard frost, like Vilbar had said. It wouldn't be so bad, hoar-frost glistening on the sedge grass, every blade frozen . . .

"Sssst!"

Hoofbeats, and a single voice raised in tuneless song, the words unfamiliar. Plastered to the earth, Carfax squinted through the tall grass and caught himself before he whistled in amazement.

"What the sodding hell?" Hunric whispered.

Seven strangers, traveling in company, led by a bearded old man in scholars' robes, astride what was clearly the best horse in the lot. An Ellyl, who traveled on foot, stepping lightly, with that annoying air of his kind. A young man sweltering in the armor of a Vedasian knight, ill-fitting and much-mended. Another, older, dun-cloaked and watchful.

"Borderguard," Carfax muttered. "That one's from Curonan."

"Blaise Caveros?" Hunric's eyes widened. Everyone in Dark-haven knew that General Tanaros' distant kinsman was second-in-command among the Borderguard.

"Could be."

"Then that's—"

"Malthus' Company." Carfax studied the remaining three. One, to his surprise, was a woman; clad in leathers, a quiver and an un-strung bow at her back. An Archer of Arduan. And good, too. She would have to be. The carcasses of three ravens dangled from her saddle, tied by their feet, a sad bundle of black feathers. But the others . . . he frowned.

"Charred Folk," Hunric murmured. "Heard tell of those, Lieu-tenant."

Indeed they were, their skins a scorched shade of brown. It was one of the two who was singing tunelessly, riding astride a pack mule, clad only in a threadbare breechclout. From time to time he patted his brown, swelling gut, punctuating his song. Car-fax, listening to the incomprehensible words, found himself think-ing of water, flowing the hidden pathways of Urulat, coursing like blood in the veins, racing from the leaping snowmelt of a swollen Staccian river to sink torpid in the Delta, bearing life in all its forms . . .

"One's scarce more'n a boy," Hunric observed.

Last among them, a wide-eyed youth, wiry and dark as sin, perched uneasily atop a pony. Something hung about his throat; a flask of fired clay, strung on corded vine. He was the one the Bor-derguardsman shadowed, unobtrusively wary in his dun cloak.

Small hairs stirred at the back of Carfax's neck.

He felt a chill, like a wish granted.

"Hunric," he whispered, his mouth dry. "They're not following us, and they didn't come from the Traders' Road. Or if they did, it was only long enough to buy mounts. They came from the Un-known. This is the Prophecy at work. And whoever sent the ravens, whether it was the Dreamspinner or Lord Satoris, they failed."

Side by side in the sedge grass, they stared at one another.

"What do we do, Lieutenant?"

It was a gift, an unlooked-for blessing. Malthus' Company, crossing their path unaware. Three dead ravens, tied by their feet; it meant no one in Darkhaven knew anything of this. Carfax licked his dry lips. There were only seven of them, and two, surely, were no warriors. What about the Counselor? Malthus had fought at the Battle of Curonan, had nearly slain Lord Satoris himself. If the news of Dergail's fall had not caused the armies of Men to falter, he might even have prevailed.

But he had borne the Spear of Light, then.

He wasn't carrying it now.

And where was the Soumanië? Mayhap he didn't bear it, either. It would be foolish, after all, to risk such a treasure on an ill-protected journey. Mayhap, Carfax thought, Malthus had entrusted the Soumanië to the keeping of Ingolin the Wise, who would keep it safe in Meronil. After all, this mission was undertaken in secrecy. And if it were so . . .

"Regroup!" he hissed to Hunric. "We need to plan an attack!"

USHAHIN DREAMSPINNER GAZED ABOUT HIM as he rode.

It was a wondrous place, the Weavers' Gulch, though few appreciated it. Everywhere he looked, gossamer filaments were strung, filtering the few rays of cloud-muted sunlight that pierced the gulch with its inward-leaning cliff walls.

And the patterns, ah!

Intricate, they were; and vast. Some, incomprehensibly so. He watched the grey spiders shuttle to and fro, the weavers at their loom. How long did it take for a single spider to spin a web that crossed the Defile? One lifetime? Generations? With delicate thread that broke at a hand's careless wave. But it was strong, too. Given time, Satoris' weavers could spin a cocoon that would render a strong man immobile. And small though they were, their sting was paralyzing.

It could be done, in time.

No wonder Satoris was interested in them.

It saddened him, that so few people understood this. There was a pattern at work in the Sundering of Urulat, one would take many ages to come to fruition. Ushahin, born unwanted to two races of the Lesser Shapers, raised by a third, understood this in his ill-mended bones. He wished that Tanaros understood it, too. It would have been good if he had. But Tanaros, when all was said and done, was a Man, burdened with the short sight of his race. Even now, after so long.

Among all the Lesser Shapers, only Men had found no way to make provision for the shortness of memory. Oronin's Children had done so. What the Grey Dam had known, the Grey Dam knew, and it encapsulated all that every predecessor before her had known. So it was among the Fjel, who passed their memory into the bone and bred it among their descendants. It was why they had remained loyal to Lord Satoris after so many generations, remembering that first promise.

A single thread, Ushahin thought, descending through time.

A pity, after all, that they lacked the scope—the *wit*—to discern the pattern. That was what Haomane had denied them. A single spider, shuttling on the loom of Weavers' Gulch, had more perspective.

Of course, no one had Shaped them.

Tanaros *should* have seen it. After so many centuries in Darkhaven, he had learned to see its underlying beauty. Was that not enough? Ah, but he was a Man, and ruled by his heart. Arahila's Child, in whom love and hatred grew intertwined. Look at him now, solicitous of the Lady of the Rivenlost. Haomane's Child, whose people had no need of a remembrance born in the flesh, for their flesh was untouched by time. Of their fallen, they told *stories,* shaping history in their image. And the Children of Men, who emulated them in all things, learned to do the same though their lives were as the passage of shooting stars measured against the span of the Ellylon.

Yet their numbers increased, while the Ellylon dwindled.

The Lady Cerelinde gave a choked cry, beating at her cloak. Ushahin watched with a cynical gaze as Tanaros aided her, brushing hurriedly at the woolen fabric with his gauntleted hands. Small grey figures dropped, scuttling on the rocks. One of the Tungskulder Fjel stamped after them, squashing them beneath the impervious hide of his feet. It wouldn't do to have their prize arrive in a state of paralysis.

"This land breeds foulness!" The Lady was pale. "It is the taint of the Sunderer!"

Foul is as foul does, Ushahin thought in silence. What harm did the weavers do before you blundered through their webs? If they did not feed, we would have a pestilence of flies in Darkhaven, because yes, Lady, this land is tainted with Lord Satoris' blood, which has seeped into the very ground, which taints the waters we drink.

He bleeds and bleeds anon, for the wound that was dealt him with the Godslayer, the wound that destroyed his Gift, is unhealing.

And why was he wounded?

Smiling to himself, Ushahin gazed at the delicate spans of webbing. Hanging veils, swags of filament, finespun and milk-white. The vast network filled him with delight. What architect could have wrought such a thing? A tendril of thread, flung out into empty space, meets another. Is it chance, or destiny? Will the weavers defend their territory in jealous battle, or will they knit their threads together to span the void?

The Ellylon would dwindle, while Men increased.

Lord Satoris was wounded because he defied Haomane's will.

He had refused to withdraw his Gift from Men.

And Ushahin was one of the Three and madness was his moiety, because he had his roots in three worlds and saw too clearly that which none of the Lesser Shapers were meant to know. What sanity he possessed was instilled in a thin strand of pain; the ache of bones ill-set and ill-mended, the sharp pang of light piercing his skull through a pupil unable to contract. Walking this fine-spun thread of pain, Ushahin knew himself sane in his madness.

Not even Lord Satoris, who would have healed him, who had kindled in his soul a fierce ache of love and pride, understood that part.

It didn't matter, though.

Ahead, a narrow aperture, marking the end of the Weavers' Gulch. The Kaldjager scrambled around it, drawing back the hanging veils of webbing with unexpected care. They, at least, understood that the little weavers were as much a part of the defense of Darkhaven as the strong walls beyond; not for nothing were they called the Cold Hunters. Ushahin, passing through, approved. Of all the Fjel, he understood them best, for they were most like the Were who had raised him.

The thought was accompanied by pain.

Oh, Mother!

She had died well, her jaws snapping at her enemy's throat, Ushahin reminded himself for the hundredth time. It was what she had chosen. And if he could not inherit her memories, still, he would carry the memory of her in his heart. Of the gentleness she had shown, finding him in the Pelmaran forest where he had crawled in blind agony. Of the touch of her rough-padded hands as she cradled his child's body, protecting his broken face, his shattered hands. Of her harsh grey pelt warm against his skin as she carried him to safety, grieving for her own lost ones.

The Grey Dam is dead. The Grey Dam lives.

Beyond the aperture, the Defile opened onto the Vale of Gorgantum. Ushahin, who passed this way more often than most, was inured to it. He heard a gasp as the Lady Cerelinde beheld it for the first time: the rearing towers that flanked the Defile Gate, the vast wall winding league upon league up the low mountains, the massive edifice of Darkhaven itself.

Marvel at it, Ellyl bitch, he thought; marvel at it and fear. Your visit here has been paid for in blood, with the life of one I held dear. What do you know of kindness and compassion? Your kinfolk left me to die, for I was a shame to them, a reminder of the dark underbelly of the Gift they were denied; Lord Satoris' Gift, which Haomane spurned. And yet he seeks it now, on his own terms. Do you truly believe your offspring would be so different from me? I would be otherwise had your people embraced me.

Atop a high peak, one of the Tordenstem Fjel crouched. As the last of the company emerged from the Weavers' Gorge, he announced them, filling his mighty lungs to bursting and hurling words aloft in his thunderous voice. Boulders shuddered in their stony sockets. Shouts of greeting answered from the sentry-towers, and Tanaros rode forward to salute them and give the password.

The Defile Gate was wrought of black granite, carved with scenes from the Battle of Neherinach. The central panel showed the death of Eldarran and Elduril; the sons of Elterrion the Bold, Cerelinde's uncles. Once the bar was lifted, it took two teams of four Fjel each to shift the massive doors, and it creaked as it opened.

Darkhaven stood open for their victorious entry.

"Dreamspinner." It was one of the Kaldjager, yellow-eyed, who pointed to the specks of darkness circling the spires. "The ravens are restless."

Victorious cries rained down from the sentry-towers and the walls as they entered Darkhaven. The Lady Cerelinde kept her chin aloft, refusing to show the terror that must be coursing her veins. She had courage, Ushahin had to give her that. Tanaros stuck close by her side, clearly torn between reveling in his triumph and protecting his trophy. How not? If he'd had the heart for it, Ushahin would have appreciated the irony. The Lady of the Rivenlost had given her love to a Son of Altorus, even as Tanaros' wife had done so long ago. It must gall the mighty General.

Poor Tanaros.

They must be something, those Sons of Altorus, to command such passion.

Being a portion of the Prophecy and bespeaking as it did the union of Men and Ellylon, it would have interested Ushahin more had the ravens of Darkhaven not been circling. As the cheers rained down, he clutched the case that held the Helm of Shadows close to him, longing only for a quiet place where he could free his mind to roam the length and breadth of Urulat.

If victory was theirs, why were the ravens restless?

"SO THIS IS IT." LILIAS held the mirror in both hands. It was small and tarnished, reflecting dimly in the low-burning torchlight that augmented the diffuse light of dawn. The dragon did not like any fire save his own to illuminate his lair. "We do it now?"

"It is time, Liliasss." Calandor's claws flexed, sifting through gold coins, jeweled goblets. High above her, his eyes winked like emeralds in the torchlight. "Elterrion's granddaughter has arrived in Darkhaven."

"How can you be sure?"

The emerald eyes stared unwinking. "I am sure."

Outside the mouth of the cavern, a troop of Gergon's wardsmen and her personal attendants huddled, waiting. What Lilias attempted this morning would draw strength from her, even with the aid of the Soumanië. It was Ellylon magic, and not meant to be undertaken by a Daughter of Men. "If we used only the eyes, if we watched them longer, we might learn more of their plans."

Calandor snorted smoke in a laugh. "Can you read the speech of their lipsss, little ssissster? Neither can I."

"I know." Lilias flicked the mirror with a fingernail in annoyance. "Haergan the Craftsman should have crafted ears onto his creation, instead of eyes and a mouth. It would have been more useful."

"Indeed." A nictitating membrane blinked over the dragon's eyes. "I might not have eaten him if he had been more ussseful."

"I would feel better if Lord Satoris' decoy had arrived in Beshtanag."

"Sso would I, little ssissster." Calandor sounded regretful. "But there is risssk in waiting. I would have gone, if you wished, to sssseek them."

"No." Lilias covered the mirror with her palm. On that point she had been adamant. Calandor was one of the last of his kind, the last known to the Lesser Shapers. In the Shapers' War, scores of dragons had died defending Satoris from his kin; after the Sundering, the Ellylon had hunted them mercilessly, slaying the weak and wounded. She would not allow Calandor to risk himself for a Shaper's machinations. "My spies have laid a trail of rumor from Pelmar to Vedasia, swearing the Dragon of Beshtanag was seen aloft and heading south. It is enough."

"Then it is enough," the dragon said gently. "Haomane's Allies will believe I ferried the Lady here on dragonback. If you ssspeak now, they will be ssertain of it. If you delay, it may be proved a lie."

"All right." Lilias sighed again. "It's time, it's time. I understand. I'll do it."

"You know the way . . . ?"

"Yes," she said shortly. "I know it."

She knew it because Calandor had showed her, as he had done so many times before. What the dragon consumed, he consumed wholly, knowledge and all. And long ago, in the First Age of the Sundered World, he had consumed Haergan the Craftsman, who had built a folly into the great hall of Meronil.

It was a head, the head of Meronin Fifth-Born, Lord of the Seas; Haomane's brother and chiefest ally, patron of Meronil. And it adorned a marble pediment atop the doorway into the great hall, his hair wrought into white-capped waves. When the world was Sundered, Meronin had brought the seas to divide the body of Uru-lat from Torath, the Souma-crowned head of the world.

But truth be told, there was precious little to be seen in the great hall of Meronil. Lilias knew, having looked into the mirror, Haergan's mirror, through the sculpture's eyes. Ingolin the Wise convened his assembly, day in and day out. One day, he brought forth a stone in a casket. It blazed with a pale blue light, which seemed to impress those assembled. Well and good; what did it mean?

"I know not," Calandor had said, though he sounded uneasy, for a dragon. "But it is nothing to do with Beshtanag. This I ssswear, Liliasss."

She believed him, because she had no choice. If Calandor was false . . . ah, no. Best not to think of such things, for she would sooner die than believe it. Lilias gripped the mirror, letting her vision diffuse, sinking into its tarnished surface, sensing the marble eyes wrought by Haergan the Craftsman open.

There.

There.

A skewed view, seen from the pediment. Ingolin the Wise, Lord of the Rivenlost, presiding over the argumentative assembly. Had it ever been otherwise? There, Bornin of Seahold, stout in his blue livery. There, Lord Cynifrid of Port Calibus, pounding the table with his gauntleted fist. There, two representatives of the Free Fishers of Harrington Bay, clad in homespun. And there, Aracus Altorus, taut with energy, willing the Council of War onward.

So few women, Lilias thought, gazing through the marbled eyes. So few!

"Liliassss."

"I know. I know." Drawing on the power of the Soumanië, feeling the fillet tighten on her brow, and speaking the words of invocation set forth by Haergon the Craftsman, who had left his knowledge in a dragon's belly.

In Meronil, Haomane's Allies gaped.

It was hard, at such a distance. Her flesh was mortal, and not meant to wield a Shaper's power nor Ellylon magics. Lilias closed her eyes and willed the marble lips to speak, stiff as stone, forming words that boomed in the distant hall.

"GREETINGS . . . TO . . . HAOMANE'S . . . ALLIES!"

Her face felt rigid and unfamiliar, inhabiting the sculpted relief more thoroughly than ever she had dared. She forced open the dense marble lids of her eyes, gazing down at the assembly. They were all on their feet, staring upward at the pediment, giving her a sense of vertigo.

"YOU   SEEK . . . THE   LADY . . . CERELINDE.   SHE   IS . . . SAFE . . . IN BESHTANAG." The words made a knot in her belly. It was the end of deniability, the beginning of blame. "SHE WILL BE RESTORED TO YOU . . . FOR A PRICE."

There was squabbling, then, in the great hall of Meronil. Lilias watched them through marble eyes, dimly aware that in a Beshtanagi cavern, the edges of a small mirror bit into her clutching palms. Some were shouting as if she could hear them. She watched and waited, and wished again that Haergan the Craftsman had given ears to his creation.

One knew better.

Ingolin the Wise, Lord of the Rivenlost. Ignoring the chaos, he approached to stand beneath the pediment, his ageless face tilted upward.

Among the Ellylon, the best and brightest had stood nearest to the Souma. When the world was Sundered and the seas rushed in to fill the divide, they remained upon the isle Torath, and there they dwelt, singing the praises of Haomane and the Six Shapers. It was only those who dwelt upon the body of Urulat who were stranded, separated forever from Haomane First-Born who Shaped them.

They were the Rivenlost.

And Elterrion the Bold had been their Lord, once; but he was dead, and with him Cerion the Navigator and Numireth the Fleet, who were also Lords of the Rivenlost. Only Ingolin was left, who was called the Wise.

Lilias gazed down upon him and felt pity, which she had not expected. A simple fillet of gold bound his shining hair and his brow was marked with worry. His eyes were grey as a storm, and deep with sorrow. How not, when they bore the shadows of centuries unnumbered? Urulat had not been Sundered when Ingolin first walked the earth. Perhaps, if he had been Lord of the Rivenlost in the First Age of the Sundered World and not Elterrion the Bold, it might have been different. Ingolin the Wise spread his arms, his lips shaping words clear enough for her to read: What do you want?

Her marble lips moved, forming the answer.

"I WANT MALTHUS . . . AND HIS SOUMANIË. BRING THEM TO BESHTANAG." Chaos followed on the heels of her words. How they quarreled, the Sons of Men! Lilias kept her stone eyes fixed on the Lord of the Rivenlost. "THE LADY IS YOURS IN TRADE."

A flash of red-gold, caught in periphery. Aracus Altorus had leapt upon the table, his boot-heels scarring the polished wood, his sword-arm cocked. His face was lit with fury and in his hand he held the haft of a standard, snatched from a wall. With a soundless cry, he hurled it at her like a javelin.

A pennant fluttered in midflight. An argent scroll, half open upon a field of sage; the device of the House of Ingolin.

So much and no more did Lilias see before the pointed iron finial that tipped the standard struck, marble shattering at the force of the blow. She cried out loud, feeling her brow-bone splinter at the bridge of her nose, clapping both hands over her face.

"Aaahhhh!"

The pain was unspeakable. Dimly, Lilias was aware that in the great hall of Meronil, blow after blow was struck at the pediment, gouging chunks of marble, destroying forever the head of Meronin, Haergan's creation. For the most part, she was aware only of agony, of splintered bones piercing her flesh as she writhed on the floor of the dragon's cavern, the bronze mirror forgotten beside her.

"My lady, my lady!" It was Gergon's voice, uncharacteristically terrified. Her Ward Commander's strong hands covered hers, trying to draw them away from her face. "Are you injured? Lady, let me see!"

"Hurts," Lilias managed to whisper. "Oh blessed Haomane, it hurts!"

Lilias. Lilias, it is only an illusion.

"Calandor, help me!"

The dragon's bulk shifted, rasping on the stony floor. One mighty claw reached, talons closing delicately on the round mirror. "Ssstand back, Ssson of Man!"

Gergon scrambled backward, holding her against his chest with one strong arm. With pain-slitted eyes, Lilias peered through her fingers as the dragon bent his sinuous neck. Scales glinted dully as he lowered his head to the object he held in the talons of one up-lifted claw. The pale armor of his underbelly expanded as he drew breath.

The dragon roared.

Fire shot from Calandor's gaping jaws; blue-hot at its core, the flames a fierce orange shading to yellow. Gripped in his talons, Haergan's mirror *melted,* droplets of bronze falling molten and sizzling to the cavern floor.

The connection was broken.

The pain stopped.

Cautiously, Lilias felt at her face. It was whole and intact, no bone-splinters piercing her smooth skin. No pain, only the ghost of its memory. There, on her brow, was the Soumanië, nearly lifeless. "Calandor?"

"Forgive me, Liliasss." The dragon sounded contrite. "I did not . . . antisssipate . . . such violence."

"You're all right then, my lady?" Gergon asked with gruff solicitude.

"My lady!" Pietre burst into the cavern, flinging himself to his knees. There were tears in his eyes. "I thought you were killed!"

"Not yet, sweetling." She smiled at him through deep-rooted exhaustion. They were there, they were all there, her pretty ones, crowding behind Pietre. Not wholly willing, not all of them, no, she had not always chosen wisely—there was Radovan, scowling, near time to release him, and sullen Marija—but there was worried

Stepan, dusky-eyed Anna, and dear Sarika biting her trembling lip. "Only tired, now."

"I'll take you to your quarters, my lady." Without waiting for permission, Pietre scooped her into his arms and stood. To his credit, he only shivered a little at the dragon's amused regard.

Too weary to object, Lilias allowed it. Gergon snapped orders, his wardsmen falling in around them. It was a frightening thing, to be this weak, even with a Soumanië in her possession. Now, more than ever, Beshtanag needed her.

Rest, Lilias. Recover.

She nodded in silent answer, knowing the dragon understood. Beneath her cheek, the bare skin of Pietre's chest was warm and resilient. Such a heady elixir, youth! Lilias felt her thousand years of age. It came at a price, cheating death. If her flesh did not show it, still, she felt it in her bones, now as never before. Had she invoked Haomane's name in her agony? Yes, and there was something fearful in it. Pietre murmured endearments under his breath, walking as though he held something precious in his arms. I should let him go, Lilias thought. I should let them all go, before danger comes. But I am old, and I am afraid of being alone.

Calandor?

I am here, Lilias.

It was enough. It had to be enough. It was the bargain she had made, a thousand years ago. And it had always, always endured. As long as it did, nothing else mattered. The thing was done, the die cast. Why, then, this foreboding?

Calandor?

Lilias, you must rest.

Calandor, where are Lord Satoris' men?

"RIGHT." CARFAX SURVEYED HIS MEN with a sharp eye. "Vilbar, scrub your face again. Use marsh-root if you have to. You're still spatch-cocked with dye."

"That river water stinks, Lieutenant!"

"I don't care," he said ruthlessly. "Scrub it! Turin, Mantuas, Hunric—you understand your mission?" There was silence in answer. Mantuas, holding his mount's reins, kicked stubbornly at a clump of sedge grass. "You understand?"

"Don't worry, sir." Hunric leaned on his pommel. "I'll see 'em through the Delta and on to Beshtanag."

"Good. With luck, we'll be no more than a day behind you. But whatever happens here, you need to report what we've seen to the Sorceress of the East. Now,"—Carfax drew a deep breath—"are the rest of you ready?"

They shouted a resounding yes. With the last remnants of dye washed from their skin, and beards beginning to grow, they looked more like Staccians, members of the boldest nation on earth; Fjel-friends, frost-warriors, allies of the Banewreaker himself. Had they not slain scores of the enemy at Lindanen Dale? And if they could do this thing, if they could capture Malthus' Company and prevent the Prophecy from being fulfilled . . .

A grin stretched Carfax's face. Lord Satoris would be pleased, mightily pleased. Mayhap pleased enough to consider making the Three into Four. Immortality would be a fine thing, indeed.

He drew his sword. "For the honor of Darkhaven!"

TWELVE

❖

THE GARRISON HAD TURNED OUT for their return, rank upon rank of Fjel flanking the approach to Darkhaven, holding formation with military discipline, issuing crisp salutes.

It was an imposing sight. It was meant to be.

All the tribes were represented; Tungskulder, Mørkhar, Gulnagel, Tordenstem, Nåltannen, Kaldjager. Tanaros gazed over a sea of Fjel, with thick hides of smooth grey, of a pebbled greenish-brown, or black with bristles. His troops, his men. They wore their armor with pride, pounding the butts of their spears in steady rhythm. They kept their shields raised.

"So many!" Cerelinde whispered.

Tanaros bowed from the saddle. "Welcome to Darkhaven, Lady."

Before them loomed the edifice itself, twin towers rearing against an overcast sky, dwarfing the entrance until they drew near enough to see that the portal itself was massive; thrice the height of any Fjel. The bar had been raised and the brass-bound inner doors flung open.

In the entrance stood Vorax of Staccia, gleaming in ceremonial armor.

"Lady Cerelinde of the Rivenlost!" he called. "Lord Satoris welcomes you."

At his words, a stream of madlings spewed forth from the interior of the fortress, surging into their midst to lay hands on the bridles of their horses. Tanaros dismounted, and helped the Lady down. He felt her trembling underneath his touch.

Her gaze was locked with the Staccian's. "This hospitality is a gift unwanted, Lord Glutton."

Vorax shrugged. "It is a gift nonetheless, Lady. Do not disdain it. Hey! Dreamspinner!" He clapped Ushahin on the shoulder. "Still sky-gazing? I hear you did well in the Dale, wielding the Helm of Shadows."

The half-breed muttered some reply, moving away from the Staccian's touch, the helm's case clutched under his arm. Tanaros frowned. Why were the ravens circling? He spared a thought for Fetch as he approached the entrance, hoping the scapegrace was unharmed.

"Blacksword." The Staccian clasped his forearm.

"Vorax. Your men did well. Commend them for me."

"I'll do that." Vorax paused, lowering his voice. "His Lordship awaits you, Blacksword; you and the Ellyl. Come see me when he's done."

"The captive?"

"Aye."

"I'll be there." An escort of Mørkhar Fjel stood waiting just inside the vast doors; four brethren all of a height, the silver inlay on their weapons-harnesses contrasting with their dark, bristling hides. "Dreamspinner?"

"You go, cousin." Ushahin thrust the helm's case into his unready arms. "You took the risks, not I. Tell Lord Satoris . . . tell him I am in the rookery. I will make my report anon."

"All right." Tanaros frowned again. It should have been a glorious homecoming, this moment; it *was* a glorious homecoming. The Prophecy had been averted, and the Lady of the Ellylon was theirs. She didn't look it, though. As frightened as Cerelinde was—and she *was* frightened, he'd felt it in his fingertips—she held herself with dignity. "Lady. Are you ready?"

Wide, her eyes; wide and grey, luminous as mist. "I do not fear the Sunderer."

"Then come," Tanaros said grimly, "and meet him."

THE SEDGE GRASS APPEARED TO bow at their approach, flattening as if a great wind preceded them. Carfax, sword in hand, found a Staccian battle-song on his lips as he rode. He sang it aloud, heard other voices echoing the words.

To battle, to battle, to battle! What a glorious thing it was! The horses of Darkhaven, who had borne them so faithfully, were bred to this purpose. His mount sensed it, nostrils flaring, the broad chest swelling with air as its hooves battered the marshy plains.

And there, ahead: The Enemy.

Malthus' Company had heard their approach, the hooves drumming like thunder. They prepared, as best they could, making a stand on the open sedge. Carfax watched them encircle the Charred Ones, back to back to back.

"Fan out!" he cried, seeking to pick his target.

The Staccian riders divided, two wings opening to encompass the tight-knit company, which they outnumbered nearly three to one. Which one, which one? The old Counselor, staff in hand? The Vedasian, glaring defiance? The Archer, coolly nocking arrows? The Ellyl lordling with his bright eyes, sword braced over his shoulder?

Ah, no, Carfax thought. You, Borderguardsman. You, in your dun cloak and false modesty. Unless I am much mistaken, I think you are charged with the protection of this Company, Blaise Caveros, my General's kinsman. We are of an age, you and I; but I am Tanaros' disciple, and you are Altorus' dog. Let us cross steel, shall we?

He swung close, close enough to exchange blows. His round Pelmaran shield rang with the force of the Borderguard's strength; rang, and held true. Carfax kneed his mount and swung away, exultant. In the center of their circle, the Charred lad looked wild-eyed, clutching a flask at his throat. Only his kinsman, the fat one, stood at his side, wielding a digging-stick like a quarterstaff, huffing as he did.

Carfax laughed aloud.

Thrum, thrum, thrum.

Arrows, flying level as a bee to clover. Two Staccians cried out, fell. The Archer of Arduan had dismounted, kneeling on the marshy soil; the Vedasian knight protected her, swinging his father's sword with ferocious blows.

"Take the Archer!" Carfax cried, readying for another pass at the Borderguard.

He was aware, distantly, of his men closing in on Malthus' Company, overwhelming them by sheer force; surging past the old Counselor, peeling the Vedasian away from the Archer and surrounding her, penetrating the silvery circle of defense the Ellyl wove with the point of his blade. A surprise, there on the inside, how deftly the fat one wielded his digging-stick, protecting his young kinsman.

It didn't matter, though. They were too few, and Carfax's men too many. He watched Blaise Caveros angle for position, setting his sword a touch too high. A good trick, that, good for luring in an overconfident enemy. General Tanaros had devised it a thousand years ago and taught it to his troops, as well as how to evade it.

All those hours on the practice-field paid a reward.

Carfax shifted his grip on his sword, digging his heels into his mount's sides. Let him believe, he thought, bearing down on his dun-cloaked opponent. Let him believe I have taken the gambit, and at the last moment, I shall strike high where he looks for low . . .

"Enough!"

It was Malthus who spoke, and the Counselor spread his arms, his staff in his right hand. There, gleaming through the parted strands of his beard, was the Soumanië. Red, it was, like a star, and it shone upon his breast, until no one could look away. A ruddy glow rippled in the air and a force struck like a hammer.

And the world . . . changed.

Carfax felt it, felt his mount's knees buckle beneath him, shifting and . . . *changing*. He hit the ground, hard, flung from the saddle. Like a vast wave, the might of the Souma overtook them all. Horses fell, and Men. The Counselor closed his eyes as if in pain, wielding the Soumanië. In the space of a shrieked breath, Staccian and equine flesh crumbled to loam, fingers sprouted tendrils and strands of hair sank rootlets into the earth. Shaped from their bodies, hummocks arose on the flat marshes, marking the territory forevermore.

Where they fell, sedge grass grew.

Except for Carfax.

He tried to move, the cheek-plates of his Pelmaran helmet scraping the rich loam. No more could he do; the strength had left his limbs. Only his senses worked. Through helpless eyes, he watched as the Borderguardsman's booted feet approached. Ungentle hands rolled him onto his back and patted him down, taking his belt-knife. His sword had been lost when he fell. Lying on his back, Carfax stared helpless at a circle of empty sky.

"Is he . . . dead?" A soft voice, an unplaceable accent.

"No."

A face hovered above him; young and dark, rough-hewn, with wide-set eyes. Sunlight made a nimbus of his coarse black hair and an earthenware flask dangled around his neck, swinging in the air above Carfax.

"Stand back, Dani." It was a weary shadow of the Counselor's voice. "It may yet be a trap."

The face withdrew. A boot-tip prodded his side. "Shall I finish him?"

"No." Unseen, Malthus the Counselor drew a deep breath. "We'll bring him with us. Let me regain a measure of strength, and I'll place a binding upon him. There may be aught to learn from this one."

Unable even to blink, Carfax knew despair.

MADLINGS SKITTERED ALONG THE HALLS of Darkhaven, their soft voices echoing in counterpoint to the steady tramp of the Fjel escort's feet. Old and young, male and female, they crept almost near enough to touch the hem of the Lady Cerelinde's cloak before dashing away in an ecstasy of terror.

It had been a long time, Tanaros realized, since he'd seen Darkhaven through an outsider's eyes. It must seem strange and fearful.

Inward and inward wound their course, through hallways that spiraled like the inner workings of a nautilus shell. There were other passageways, of course; secret ones, doors hidden in alcoves, behind tapestries, in cunning reliefs. Some were in common usage, like those that led to the kitchens. Some were half-forgotten, and others existed only as rumor. Madlings used many, of course, taking care not to be seen. Vorax disdained them, and Ushahin preferred them. Tanaros used them at need. The Fjel used them not at all, for the passages were too winding and narrow to admit them. No one knew all their secrets.

Only Lord Satoris, who conceived them—or their beginnings.

And so the main halls spiraled, vast curving expanses of polished black marble, lit only by the veins of marrow-fire along the walls. It was a winding trap for would-be invaders, Fjel guards posted at regular intervals like hideous statues. It should have awed even the Lady of the Ellylon.

Tanaros stole a sidelong glance at her to see if it did.

There were tears in her luminous eyes. "So many!" she whispered, and he thought she meant the Fjel again; then he saw how her gaze fell on the madlings. She paused, one hand extended, letting them draw near enough to touch and turning a reproachful look upon him. "Merciful Arahila! What manner of cruelty is this, Tanaros? What has been done to these folk?"

"Done?" He stared at her. "They sought sanctuary here."

"Sanctuary?" Her brows, shaped like birds' wings, rose. "From *what?*"

"From the world's cruelty, which drove them to madness." Tanaros reached out, grabbing the arm of the nearest madling; by chance, it was one he knew. A woman, young when she came to Darkhaven, elderly now, with a birthmark like a dark stain that covered half her wrinkled face. "This, my Lady, is Sharit. Her parents sold her into marriage to a man who was ashamed of her, and beat her for his shame. Do you see, here?" He touched her skull beneath wispy hair, tracing a dent. "He flung her against a door-jamb. Here, no one will harm her, on pain of death. Is that *cruelty?*"

"You're frightening her," Cerelinde said softly.

It was true. Repentant, he released the madling. Sharit keened, creeping to crouch at Cerelinde's skirts, fingers plucking. The Mørkhar escort waited, eyeing Tanaros. "I didn't mean to," he said.

"I know." She smiled kindly at the madling, laying a gentle hand on the withered cheek, then glanced at Tanaros. "Very well. I do not deny the world's cruelty, General. But your Lord, were he compassionate, could have healed her suffering. You said as much; he offered to heal the half-breed." Her delicate fingers stroked Sharit's birthmark, and the madling leaned into her touch. "He could have made her beautiful."

"Like you?" Tanaros asked quietly.

Cerelinde's hands fell still. "No," she said. "Like *you.*"

"Like Arahila's Children. Not Haomane's." Shifting the Helm of Shadows under one arm, Tanaros stooped, meeting the old woman's eyes. They were milky with cataracts, blinking under his regard. "You don't understand," he said to Cerelinde, gazing at Sharit. "To Lord Satoris, she *is* beautiful."

There was magic in the words, enough to summon a smile that broke like dawn across the withered face. Taking his hand, she rose, proceeding down the hall with upright dignity.

Tanaros bowed to Cerelinde.

Her chin lifted a notch. "It would still be kinder to heal her. Do you deny it?"

"You have charged my Lord with Sundering the world," he said. "Will you charge him now with healing it?"

One of the Mørkhar shifted position, coughing conspicuously into a taloned fist.

"It's in his power, Tanaros." Passion and a light like hope lit

Cerelinde's eyes. "It *is,* you know! Did he but surrender to Haomane and abide his will—"

Tanaros laughed aloud. "And Haomane's Children accuse his Lordship of pride! Be sure to tell him that, Lady."

She drew her cloak around her. "I shall."

USHAHIN DREAMSPINNER STEPPED AS LIGHTLY as any Ellyl under the canopy of beech leaves, grown thicker and darker with the advent of summer. Setting loose his awareness, he let it float amid the trunks and branches, using the ancient magic the Grey Dam Sorash had taught him so long ago.

Ah, mother!

Tiny sparks of mind were caught in his net; feathered thoughts, bright-eyed and darting. One, two, three . . . five. Folding his legs, Ushahin sat in the beech loam, asking and waiting. What is it, little brothers? What has befallen your kin?

A raven landed on a nearby branch, wiped its beak twice.

Another sidled close.

Three perched on the verge of an abandoned nest.

Thoughts, passed from mind to mind, flickered through his awareness. Not a thing seen, no; none who had *seen* lived to show what had happened in the dark shimmering of the Ravensmirror. Only these traces remained, drifting like down in the flock's awareness. Marshes, an endless plain of sedge grass. A high draft, warm under outspread wings. A target found, a goal attained. One two three four seven, circling lower, a good draft, good to catch, wings tilting, still high, so high, only close enough to see—

Arrow!

Arrow!

Arrow!

And death, sharp-pointed and shining, arcing from an impossible distance; the *thump* of death, a sharp blow to the breast, a shaft transfixed, wings failing, a useless plummet, down and down and down, blue sky fading to darkness, down and down and down—

Earthward.

Death.

The memory of the impact made his bones ache. Ushahin opened his eyes. The living ravens watched him, carrying the memories of their fallen brethren, waiting and wondering. I am sorry, little ones. It was dangerous, more dangerous than I reckoned. Malthus was clever to bring an Archer.

What was the Company of Malthus doing in the Vedasian marshes?

Ushahin stared at the cloud-heavy sky, seen in glimpses through the beech canopy. It was early yet, too early for the dreams of Men to be abroad. He sighed, flexing his crippled hands. Tonight, then. When the moon rode high over the Vale of Gorgantum, darkness would be encroaching on the marshes.

Time to walk in their dreams.

THE DOORS TO THE THRONE Hall stood three times higher than a tall man, wrought of hammered iron. On them was depicted the War of the Shapers.

The left-hand door bore the Six: Haomane, chiefest of all; Arahila, his gentle sister; Meronin, lord of the seas; Neheris of the north; Yrinna the fruitful; and Oronin, the Glad Hunter. Haomane had raised his hand in wrath, and before him was the Souma—an uncut ruby as big as a sheep's heart, glinting dully in a rough iron bezel.

On the right-hand door were Lord Satoris, and dragons. And they were glorious, the dragons depicted in lengths of coiling scales, necks arching, vaned wings outreaching, the mighty jaws parted to issue gouts of sculpted flame. At the center of it all stood the wounded Satoris, a glittering fragment of ruby representing Godslayer held in both hands like a prayer-offering.

"General!" The Fjeltroll on guard saluted. "His Lordship awaits."

"Krognar. You may admit us."

As ever, Tanaros' heart constricted as the massive doors were opened, parting Torath from Urulat, mimicking the Sundering itself; constricted, then blazed with pride. Beyond was his Lord, who had given him reason to live. The Throne Hall lay open before them, a vast expanse. Unnatural torches burned on the walls—marrow-fire, tamed to the Shaper's whim, casting long, crisscrossing shadows across the polished floor. A carpet of deepest black ran the length of the Hall, a tongue of shadow stretching from the open maw of the iron doors to the base of the Throne. It was carved of a massive carnelian, that Throne, the blood-red stone muted in the monochromatic light.

There, enthroned, sat a being Shaped of darkness with glowing eyes.

"Tanaros." Cerelinde's voice, small and dry.

"Don't be afraid." There was more, so much more he wanted to tell her, but words fell short and his heart burned within him, drowning out thought. Settling the Helm of Shadows under his left arm, he offered the right in a gesture half-remembered from the Altorian courts. "Come, Lady. Lord Satoris awaits us."

How long? Ten paces, twenty, fifty.

Thrice a hundred.

The torches burned brighter as they traversed the hall, gouts of blue-white flame reaching upward. The Mørkhar Fjel paced two by two on either side of them, splendid in their inlaid weapons-harnesses that glittered like quicksilver.

Always, the Throne, looming larger as they drew near, Darkness seated in it. Fair, once; passing fair. No longer. A smell in the air, the thick coppery reek of blood, only *sweeter*. The brand that circumscribed Tanaros' heart blazed; Cerelinde's fingertips trembled on his forearm, setting his nerves ablaze. Directly beneath the Throne Hall lay the Chamber of the Font, and below it, the Source itself. In the dazzling light, she might have been carved of ivory.

"Tanaros."

He drew a deep breath, feeling his tight-strung nerves ease at the Shaper's rumbling voice. Home. "My Lord Satoris!" The bow came easily, smoothly, a pleasing obeisance. He relinquished Cerelinde's arm, placing the Helm's case atop the dais. "Victory is ours. I restore to you the Helm of Shadows, and present the Lady Cerelinde of the Rivenlost, the betrothed of Aracus Altorus."

Gleaming eyes blinked, once, in the darkness of the Shaper's face; one massive hand shifted on the arm of the Throne. His voice emerged, deep and silken-soft. "Be welcome to Darkhaven, Elterrion's granddaughter, daughter of Erilonde. Your mother was known to me."

Her chin jerked; whatever Cerelinde had expected, it was not that. "Lord Satoris, I think it is not so. Your hospitality has been forced upon me at the point of a sword, and as for my mother . . . my mother died in the bearing of me."

"Yes." A single word, solemn and bone-tremblingly deep. "Erilonde, daughter of Elterrion, wife of Celendril. I recall it well, Cerelinde. In the First Age of the Sundered World, she died. She prayed to me ere her death. It is how I knew her."

"No." Delicate hands, clenched into fists. "I will not be tricked, Sunderer!"

Laughter, booming and sardonic. The rafters of the Throne Hall rattled. The Mørkhar Fjel eyed them with pragmatic wariness. "Is it so hard to believe, Haomane's Child? After all, it was my Gift . . . once. The quickening of the flesh. Generation." The air thickened, rife with the sweet scent of blood, of desire. Satoris' eyes shone like spear-points. "Do you blame her? Many women have prayed to me in childbirth. I would have saved her if I could."

"Then why didn't you?"

The words were flung, an accusation. Tanaros shifted uneasily between his beloved Lord and his hostage. The Shaper merely sighed, disturbing the shadows.

"My Gift was torn from me, pierced to the heart by Oronin Last-Born, who drove a shard of the Souma into my thigh. I had nothing to offer your mother. I am sorry. If Haomane had not disdained my Gift when I had it, it might have been otherwise. I grieve that it was not. Your people will dwindle for it, and die, until you pass forevermore from Urulat's memory."

Cerelinde eyed him uncertainly. "You lie, Lord Sunderer."

"Do the Ellylon not dwindle in number?"

"Yes." She held his gaze, a thing few mortals could do unflinching. "And so we shall, until you relent or the Prophecy is fulfilled. Haomane has pledged it."

"Haomane," the Shaper mused, plucking the case that held the Helm of Shadows from the dais. "My Elder Brother, the Lord-of-Thought. Do you not find him an absent parent to his children, Lady Cerelinde?"

"No." She stared, transfixed, as his dark fingers undid the case's clasps.

"This was his weapon, once." Satoris lifted the Helm and held it before him, its empty eye-sockets gazing the length of the hall. "It contained in its visage the darkness of Haomane's absence, the darkness that lies in the deepest cracks of the shattered Souma, those things which all the Children of Uru-Alat fear most to look upon. To Ardrath the Counselor my Elder Brother gave it, and Ardrath called me out upon the plains of war." He smiled, caressing the worn, pitted bronze of the Helm. "I prevailed, and now it is *mine*. And I have Shaped into it my own darkness, of truth twisted and the shadow cast by a bright, shining lie, of flesh charred to blackness by the wrath of merciless light. Will you gaze upon it, Haomane's Child?"

So saying, he placed the Helm upon his head.

Cerelinde cried out and looked away.

"My Lord," Tanaros whispered, stretching his hands helplessly toward the Throne. Pain, so much pain! "Oh, my Lord!"

"It is enough." Satoris removed the Helm and regarded it. "Send for Lord Vorax," he said to the Mørkhar Fjel, "that he might conduct the Lady to the quarters prepared for her. I will speak more with her anon. General Tanaros." The gleaming eyes fixed him. "Tell me of Lindanen Dale, and what transpired thereafter."

A SULLEN CAMPFIRE BURNED. ARMFULS of dried sedge grass were thrown upon it, sending sparks into the starry skies. Carfax watched them rise. He was able, now, to move his eyes. He could move his limbs, too, so long as he did not contemplate violence against his companions. The mere thought of it brought retching nausea.

"You are safe, here." It was the Counselor who spoke, his voice calm and soothing. He pointed around the perimeter of an invisible circle with the butt-end of his staff. "Inside this ring, nothing can harm you; not even Lord Satoris. Do you understand?"

He did. All too well, he understood. He had failed.

"It is dangerous to keep him." Firelight played over Blaise Caveros' face; spare features, like the General's, yet somehow stirring.

"He is no danger to us now."

It was true. Carfax's tongue was sealed, stuck to the roof of his mouth by force of will and the oath he had sworn. Silence was his only protection, his only weapon. His hands lay limp, upturned upon his thighs. Yet if he had the chance . . .

"Who are you? Why were you sent?"

He could have laughed; he would have laughed, if the binding had permitted it. Faces, arrayed around the campfire. Such a tiny company, to threaten the foundations of Darkhaven! He knew their names, now. Not just the Counselor and the Borderguardsman, but the others. Fianna, the Archer; a tenderness there despite the lean sinews of her arms. He saw it when she looked at Blaise. Peldras, the Ellyl; of the Rivenlost, Ingolin's kindred, young and ancient at once. Hobard, proud and angry in his hand-me-down armor, his every thought writ on his face.

You were the one, weren't you? The Dreamspinner found you and sent his ravens . . .

But not the boy, ah, Arahila! What was his role? Fingering the flask that hung about his neck on corded twine. Dani, they called him. A cruel fate, to summon one so young. If he'd been Staccian, Carfax would have sent him back to gain another summer's age. Small wonder his uncle had accompanied him. Thulu, that one was called. Unkempt black hair, thick and coarse. A broad belly, spilling over his crude breechclout. Lord Vorax would have understood this one, whose eyes were like raisins in the dark pudding of his face.

"Why were you sent?"

Why? Why, indeed? To secure the world against your machinations, Haomane's tool! Carfax suffocated his laughter, biting his tongue. Red foam spilled from the corners of his mouth. Why? Why are you *here,* in these Shaper-forsaken marshes? What do you want in Vedasia? What does the boy Dani carry in his flask, that you guard so fearfully?

"Why doesn't he answer?"

"He is afraid, Dani." It was Peldras the Ellyl who answered in gentle tones. "He has served a cruel master. Give him time, and he will come to see we mean him no harm."

"Can you not compel him, wizard?" Hobard challenged the Counselor.

"No." Malthus shook his head wearily, taking a seat on a grassy tussock. "Satoris' minions swear an oath bound by the force of Godslayer itself. I can compel his flesh, but not his loyalty. Not even the Soumanië can undo that which is bound to a shard of the Souma." His deep-set gaze rested on Carfax. "That, he must choose himself."

"He's bleeding." The boy poured water from a skin into a tin cup, approaching Carfax and squatting to proffer the cup. In the firelight, the tin shone like a ruddy star between his palms. "Would you like a drink to rinse your mouth?" he asked.

Carfax reached for it with both hands.

"Dani," Blaise cautioned. "Don't go near him."

"Let him be, swordsman." Fat Thulu spun his digging-stick with deceptive ease. "'He's the Bearer, and that's water he bears. Let him do it."

Cool tin, sweet water. It stung his tongue and turned salty in his mouth. Carfax spat pink-tinged water onto the marshy soil, then drank, his throat working. Water, cool and soothing, tasting of minerals and hidden places deep in the earth. "Thank you," he whispered, returning the cup.

The boy smiled, an unexpected slice of white in his dark face.

"Malthus." Blaise raised his brows.

The Counselor, watching, shook his head. "Thulu is right, Blaise. Whether he knows it or not, the boy does Haomane's work in ways deeper than we may fathom. Let it abide. Mayhap his kindness will accomplish what the Soumanië cannot. Any mind, I have spent too deeply of myself to pursue it further this night." Yawning with weariness, he let his chin sink onto his chest, mumbling through his beard. "In the morning, we will continue on toward Malumdoorn. Peldras, the first watch is yours."

Overhead, the stars wheeled through their courses.

One wouldn't expect a wizard to snore, but he did. One might expect it to loosen his bindings, but it didn't. Carfax struggled against them, testing of his circumscribed thoughts and constrained flesh. The Ellyl watched him, not without pity, an unsheathed blade across his knees. All around them, starlight shone on the hummocks and knolls that had been Carfax's companions when dawn had risen on that day. Now it was night and they were earth and grass, nourished by his bloody spittle, glimmering beneath the stars and a crescent moon.

"She Shaped them, you know." The Ellyl tilted his perfect chin, gazing at the night sky. "Arahila the Merciful took pity on night's blackness and beseeched Haomane to allow her to lay hands upon the Souma, the Eye of Uru-Alat that she might Shape a lesser light to illume the darkness." He smiled compassionately at Carfax's struggle. "It is said among the Rivenlost that there is no sin so great that Arahila will not forgive it."

It was dangerous to match words with an Ellyl; nonetheless, Carfax left off his efforts and replied, the words grating in his throat. "Will she forgive Malthus what he did to my men?"

"It does not please him to do so, Staccian." The Ellyl's voice held sorrow. "Malthus the Wise Counselor would harm no living thing by his own choice. You sought to slay us out of hand."

"What do you seek, Rivenlost?"

"Life." The Ellyl's hands rested lightly on his naked blade. "Hope."

Carfax bared his bloodstained teeth. "And Lord Satoris' death."

Peldras regarded the stars. "We are Haomane's Children, Staccian. It is the Sunderer's choice to oppose him and it is the Rivenlost, above all, who will die for this choice if we do not take it from him." He looked back at Carfax, his gaze bright and direct. "Torath is lost to us and, without the Souma to sustain us, we diminish. Our numbers lessen, our magics fading. If Satoris

Banewreaker conquers Urulat, it will be our end. What would you have us do?"

Dangerous, indeed, to match words with an Ellyl. This time, Carfax held his bitten tongue. Better to keep silent and hope against hope for rescue or a clean death that would place him beyond his enemies' reach.

If either could find him here.

On and on the night sank into darkness, the fire settling to embers. Carfax dozed in exhaustion. A mind, borne on dark wings, beat desperately at the outskirts of the Counselor's circle; beat and beat, skittering helpless away. The Vedasian groaned in his sleep, untouchable. In the sedge grass, a saddle sat empty, three dead ravens tied by their feet. Waking, dimly aware, Carfax strained against the Counselor's binding.

Dreamspinner, I am here, here!

Nothing.

THIRTEEN

"It took you long enough, cousin." Standing before the dungeon stair with a smoldering torch in one hand, Vorax raised his bushy red brows. "Was it a hard reckoning?"

"No harder than it ought to be," Tanaros said. "His Lordship wanted the details."

"Twenty-three lost in Lindanen Dale."

"Aye. Yours." He met Vorax's gaze. "Good men. I'm sorry for it."

The Staccian shrugged. "They knew the price, cousin. Battle-glory, and fair recompense for the fallen. The couriers will leave on the morrow, bearing purses. At least every man's widow, every man's bereaved mother, will know the cost to a coin of her husband or son's life."

Tanaros touched the pouch where Hyrgolf's *rhios* hung, thinking on the death of Bogvar in the City of Long Grass, and how Thorun had begged him take his axe-hand. "Do they reckon it enough, in Staccia?"

"They reckon it a fairer trade than any Haomane offered." Vorax raised the torch, peering. Light glittered on the rings that adorned his thick fingers; topaz, ruby, emerald. "Cousin, this can wait until you're rested."

"No." Tanaros gathered himself with an effort. "I want to see the prisoner."

Keys rattled as Vorax sought the proper one to open the door to the lower depths. Tanaros held the torch while he fumbled. The Fjel guard stood at attention. Dank air wafted from the open door, smelling of mold and decay. Below, it was black as pitch. No marrow-fire threaded the veins of the dungeon's stone.

"Phaugh!" Tanaros raised the torch. "I forget how it stinks."

"No point in a pleasant prison," Vorax said pragmatically.

Stepping onto the first stair, Tanaros paused. "You didn't put the Lady Cerelinde in such a place, I hope."

"No." Torchlight made a bearded mask of the Staccian's face. "She's our *guest,* cousin, or so his Lordship would have it. Her quarters are as fine as my own; more so, if your taste runs to Elly-lon gewgaws."

"Good," Tanaros said shortly. The winding stairs were slippery and he took them with care, one at a time. It would be a bitter irony indeed if he slipped and broke his neck here and now, in the safe confines of Darkhaven. Something moved in the reeking dark-ness below; there was a sound of chains rattling, a phlegmy cough. "Tell me of the prisoner. He was captured in the Weavers' Gulch?"

Behind him, Vorax wheezed with the effort of descending. "Trussed like a goose in spider-silk and glaring mad at it. He bolted like a rabbit when the Thunder Voice challenged him at the Maw. They let him go to see how far he'd get."

In the darkness, Tanaros smiled. "You put him to the question-ing?"

"Aye." Vorax bent over, resting his meaty hands on his knees. "Some of Hyrgolf's lads gave him a few love-taps when he strug-gled. Otherwise, we held his feet to the fire." Seeing Tanaros' ex-pression, he straightened. "Only the usual, not enough to cripple. He might be missing a few fingernails."

"And?" Tanaros waited mid-stair.

"Nothing." The Staccian shrugged. "Says he's a Midlander, a horse-thief. Says he's here to offer his service. Doesn't appear to be mad. We waited for you, otherwise."

"My thanks, cousin." Descending the final steps, his boots squelched in the damp. There must have been an inch of standing water on the floor, seeping through the dungeon's foundation. Tanaros crossed the cell and thrust the torch into a waiting sconce. "Let's see what we have."

It took a moment for his eyes to adjust. Wavering torchlight re-flected on the standing water and the dark, moisture-slick walls. On the far wall, a single prisoner hung, knees sagging, resting his weight on the chains that held his arms upraised. Under Tanaros' regard, he hauled himself upright, his blistered feet disturbing the stagnant water. "General Tanaros Blacksword." A broad Midlander accent placed his origin in the fertile territories south of Curonan. He was young, not out of his twenties, with light brown hair falling matted and greasy over his brow. "A fine welcome you give those who would serve you."

"Count yourself lucky for it, boyo," Vorax muttered, making his way to the bottom of the stair, one hand on the wall for balance. "The Tordenstem Fjel could have killed you as easily as not."

"Lucky me." The prisoner smiled crookedly. His lips were split and swollen, one of his front teeth a ragged stump, broken by a Fjel love-tap. "What do you say, General? Could you use one such as me?"

Tanaros folded his arms. "Who are you?"

"Speros of Haimhault. I'd make a proper bow, Lord General, but . . ." The prisoner twitched his hands, dangling limp in their iron manacles. His fourth and fifth fingers ended in raw wounds. "Well, you see."

"And you seek to offer your service?" Tanaros raised his brows. "Others in your position might complain of such treatment."

The prisoner Speros shrugged, causing his chains to rattle. "I came unannounced. Darkhaven has cause for suspicion. Shall we say as much and begin anew?"

Vorax stifled a yawn and settled his bulk on a three-legged stool left by the prisoner's questioners. Tanaros ignored him, eyeing the young man. "Lord Vorax says you claim to be a horse-thief."

"I have done." Brown eyes glinted through matted hair. "Stole a Seaholder lordling's mount, once, when I was employed at a black-smith's forge. Cut purses, wooed women I'd no intent to wed. Served as second-in-command to the volunteer militia of Haimhault, for a time. I've done lots of things, Lord General. I've lots of ideas, too. I'm chock full of ideas."

"Have you shed innocent blood?" Tanaros asked brusquely.

There was a pause, then, punctuated only by another stifled Staccian yawn.

"Aye." The prisoner's voice was soft. "That, too."

Tanaros paced the narrow cell, his boot-heels splashing in the standing water. In the wavering torchlight, Vorax watched him without offering comment. As it was, as it should be. It was true, this was one of his, one of his own. He fetched up before the prisoner, peering at his bruised face. "You do know where you are? This is Darkhaven, lad. Beyond the wall, the world is our enemy. If you swear loyalty to Lord Satoris—for it is him you will serve, and not me—it will be your enemy, too. Your name will become poison, a symbol of the worst betrayal a man may commit."

"Aye, Lord General." Speros straightened in his chains. "I know."

"Then why?"

An inch could have closed the space between them; even in chains, Speros could have flinched. He didn't, clenching his mana-cled fists instead. Blood fell, drop by drop, from his wounded fin-gertips. It made a faint splashing sound as it struck the water. "You need to ask?"

Tanaros nodded. He could smell the prisoner's suppurating wounds. "I do."

"I'm tired of paying for my sins." Speros smiled, taut and bitter. "I never set out to become a thief and a killer, but it's funny the way things go. You make enough mistakes, comes a day when no one will take a chance on you. Arahila may forgive, General Blacksword, but her Children do not. I am weary to the bone of courting their forgiveness. Lord Satoris accepted your service. Why not mine?"

Had he been that young, that defiant, twelve hundred years ago? Yes, Tanaros thought; he had been. Twenty-and-eight years of age, hunted and despised throughout the realm. Kingslayer, they had called him. Wifeslayer, some had whispered. Cuckold. Mur-derer. He had yearned for death, fought for life. A summons tick-ling his fevered brain had led him to Darkhaven.

Still, he shook his head. "You're young and angry at the world. It will pass."

The brown eyes glinted. "As yours did?"

Tanaros awarded him a slight smile. "Anger is only the begin-ning, Midlander. It does not suffice unto itself."

"What, then?" Speros shifted in his chains, but his gaze never left Tanaros' face. "Tell me, General, and I will answer. Why do *you* serve him? For gold and glory, like the Staccians? Out of mind-less loyalty, like the Fjeltroll?"

On his stool, Vorax coughed. Tanaros glanced at him.

"The Staccians' bargain grants peace and prosperity to the many at a cost to the few," he said. "And the Fjel are not so mind-less as you think."

"Yet that is not an answer," Speros said. "Not your answer."

"No." Tanaros faced him. "I serve my Lord Satoris because, in my heart, I have declared myself the enemy of his enemies. Be-cause I despise the hypocrisy and cowardice of the Six Shapers who oppose him. Because I despise the tyranny of certitude with which Haomane First-Born seeks to rule over the world, placing his Children above all others." His voice grew stern. "Make no mistake, lad. For many years, his Lordship sought nothing more than to live unmolested, but great deeds are beginning to unfold. I tell you this, here and now; if you swear yourself to Lord Satoris' service, you are declaring yourself an enemy of the Lord-of-Thought himself, and a participant in a battle to Shape the world anew."

The prisoner grinned with his split, swollen lips. "I am not fond of the world as I have found it, General. You name a cause in which I would gladly believe."

"Haomane's Wrath is a fearsome thing," Tanaros warned him.

Speros shrugged. "So was my Da's."

It was a boy's comment, not a Man's; and yet, the glint in the lad's eyes suggested it was deliberate, issued as a reckless dare. Against his better judgement, Tanaros laughed. He had found fulfillment and purpose in service to Lord Satoris, in seizing his own warped destiny and pitting himself against the will of an overwhelming enemy. If it afforded him the chance to play a role in Shaping the world that had betrayed him, so much the better.

Did the lad deserve less?

"Vorax," Tanaros said decisively. "Strike his chains."

THE LAMPS BURNED LOW IN her quarters.

There was a veneer of delicacy overlaying the appearance of the rooms to which she had been led. Tapestries in shades of rose, celadon and dove-grey hid the black stone walls; fretted lamps hung from the buttresses, their guttering light casting a patterned glow. These elements had been added, tacked atop the solid bulwark of the fortress in an effort to disguise the brooding mass of Darkhaven.

Cerelinde was not fooled.

This prison had been made for her.

She paced it, room by room, her feet sinking deep into the cloud-soft carpets that concealed the polished floor. What halls had they adorned? Cuilos Tuillenrad? A faint scent arose at her passage. Heart-grass, bruised and crushed by her feet. Oh, this was Ellylon craftsmanship, to be sure! Her kinfolk had woven it in ages past, with fingers more nimble than any son or daughter of Man could hope to emulate. The wool would have been culled from the first coats of yearling lamb, washed with an effusion of the delicate flowers of heart-grass that bloomed for three days only in the spring. Journeymen would have carded it, singing under the open skies, but the spinning, ah! That would have been done by Ellylon noblewomen, for they alone had the nicety of touch to spin wool thread as fine as silk.

Her own mother might have touched it . . .

Your mother was known to me.

Cerelinde closed her eyes. Unfair; oh, unfair!

It was not true. It could *not* be true. Time and time again, Malthus had said it: Satoris Banewreaker is cunning, he Shapes truth itself to his own ends. Her father . . . her father Celendril, she remembered well, for he had died in the Fourth Age of the Sundered World, slain upon the plains of Curonan amid the host of Numireth.

And left her alone.

No. That, too, was a lie; this place bred them like flies. Lord Ingolin had opened the gates of Meronil to all the Rivenlost who had fled the Sunderer's wrath. Always her place there had been one of honor, even during the long centuries she had refused to hear their arguments. Malthus had been the first to say it, his wise old eyes heavy with grief at the death of his comrades. It is your duty and destiny, Cerelinde.

When a daughter of Elterrion weds a son of Altorus . . .

What a bitter irony it was!

At first, she had refused out of anger. It was a son of Altorus who had cost them dear on the plains of Curonan; Trachan Altorus, who received the news of Dergail's defeat, who saw Ardrath the Counselor fall. Too soon he had sounded the retreat, and in that moment Satoris Banewreaker regained the dagger Godslayer and fled.

Long years it had taken for her people to overcome the bitterness of that blow and the ill-will it engendered between their races. Indeed, there were many among the Rivenlost who blamed Men for all the woes of their people; jealous, short-lived Men, who had long ago made war upon the Ellylon, coveting the secret of immortality. None of the House of Altorus, no, but others. And the ill-will flowed both ways, for the descendents of those Men who had kept faith with the Ellylon blamed them for repaying loyalty by drawing them into dire war against the Sunderer.

It was not their fault, not entirely. The lives of Men were brief, flickering like candles and snuffed in a handful of years. How could they hope to compass the scope of the Sunderer's ambition when Satoris Banewreaker was content to wait ages for his plan to unfold? It was the second reason Cerelinde had refused to hear the arguments of Malthus and Lord Ingolin. Though she was young by Ellylon reckoning, she remembered ages preserved only in the dusty memories of parchment for the sons and daughters of Men.

How would it be, to wed one whose life passed in an eye-blink? One in whose flesh the seeds of death already took root? For century upon century, Cerelinde had never contemplated it with aught but a sense of creeping horror.

And then Aracus had come.

Oh, it was a bitter irony, indeed.

What lie, she wondered, would the Sunderer make of it? The truth was simple: He had won her heart. Aracus Altorus, a King without a kingdom, had ridden into Meronil with only a handful of the Borderguard to attend him. By the time he left, she had agreed to wed him.

Now she knew better the machinations behind that meeting, the long planning that had gone into it. By whatever tokens and ar-cane knowledge he used to determine the mind of Haomane, the Wise Counselor had divined that the time of reckoning was coming and Aracus Altorus, last-born scion in a line that had endured for five thousand years, must be the one to fulfill the Prophecy. Malthus had begun laying the groundwork for it when Aracus was but a child, visiting the boy in the guise of an aged uncle, filling his ears with portents.

With one wary eye on Darkhaven, for nearly thirty years he had exerted his subtle influence, laying seeds of thought and ambi-tion in the boy that came to fruition in the man. And he had done his work well, Cerelinde thought with rue. The Wise Counselor had set out to Shape a hero.

He had done so.

For all the dignitaries assembled in the Hall of Meronil, they might have been alone, they two. It had passed between them, a thing understood, undetermined by the counsels of the wise. He reached out to grasp his destiny like a man grasping a burning brand. He would love her with all the fierce passion of his mortal heart. And she, she would love him in turn, in a tempestuous blaze. There was sorrow in it, yes, and grief, but not horror. Love, fair Arahila's Gift, changed all.

And while it lasted, the fate that overshadowed them would be held at bay. Oh, the price would be high! They knew it, both of them. Death would come hard on its heels, whether by sickness or age or the point of a sword. Oronin Last-Born, the Glad Hunter, would blow his horn, summoning the hero home. And Cerelinde would be left to endure in her grief. Even in victory, if the Sunderer were defeated at last and Urulat healed, her grief would endure. But their children; ah, Haomane! Mortal through their father's

blood, still they would be half-Ellylon, granted a length of days uncommon to Men, able to reckon the vast span of time as no mortals
among the Lesser Shapers had done before them. Their children
would carry on that flame of hope and passion, uniting their races
at last in a world made whole.

The image of the half-breed's crooked face rose unbidden in
her memory, Tanaros' words echoing dryly. *Such as he is, your
own children would have been . . .*

A lie; another lie. Surely children conceived in love would be
different, would be accepted by both races. Was that not the intent
of Haomane's Prophecy? Cerelinde sat upon the immense bed that
had been prepared for her, covering her face with both hands. If
she could have wept, she would have, but Ellylon could only shed
tears for the sorrow of others. A storm of terror raged in her heart
and mind. After five thousand years of resistance, she had relented,
had accepted her fate. A moment of joy; an eternity of grief. It was
enough; merciful Arahila, was it not enough?

This was not supposed to happen.

"Aracus," she whispered.

DAWN ROSE ON THE DELTA, and with the return of the light came
swarms of gnats. They were merciless, descending in dark clouds,
settling on sweat-slick skin already prickling in the heat, taking
their measure of blood and leaving itching welts in trade. Turin
waved his arms futilely and swore.

It didn't matter.

Nothing mattered. Mantuas, quick-witted, loud-mouthed Mantuas, was dead, drowned in a sucking mudpool. It happened so
fast. Even Hunric, who could track his way through a Staccian blizzard, hadn't seen it coming. There hadn't been a thing they could
do. Slithering on their bellies, poking branches; Mantuas, take hold,
take hold! He couldn't free his arms from the muck, could only
blink, desperately, as it covered his nostrils. He sank fast. Turin had
turned away when the mud reached his eyes. By the time he dared
look, only a few locks of hair lay atop the burbling muck.

Farewell, Mantuas.

A good job they'd turned the horses loose.

Lord Satoris might be wroth, but Lord Satoris should have
known. This was the place that had engendered him. Had it been
fair, once? Hunric said old trackers' tales claimed as much. Well, it

was foul, now. All the muck and foetor that fouled the Verdine River crawled straight from the stinking heart of the Delta.

"Hold." Ahead of him, Hunric paused, probing the watery passage with a long stick he'd cut from a mangrove tree. "All right. Slide along here."

"I'm coming." Turin followed his lead, slogging through waist-deep water along the edge of a clump of mangroves. His water-logged boots were like lead weights on his feet, slipping on the slick, knotted roots that rose above the swamp. Only fear of snakes kept him from removing them. A few feet away, a basking lizard blinked at him and slithered rapidly in his direction, flicking a blue tongue. "Gah!" Turin recoiled, flailing his arms as the heavy pack strapped across his shoulders overbalanced him.

"Steady!" Hunric caught his flailing wrist, bracing him. "It's just a lizard, lad. It won't harm you."

"All right, all right, I'm all right!" Turin fought down his panic and shook off the tracker's hand. Was his gear secure? Yes, there was his sword, lashed sideways atop his pack. He reached behind him, felt the reassuring bulk of the supplies he carried. There was gold coin there, Lord Vorax's gift, useless in this place. Arahila willing, the bannock-cakes were secure in their oilcloth wrappings and they would not starve just yet. "All right. Let's go."

"Here." Hunric scooped a handful of muck from the bottom of the swamp. "Plaster it on your skin. It will help keep the gnats off."

He pushed away the proffered hand, dripping mud. "I don't want it on me."

"Turin." There was a despairing note in the tracker's voice. "Don't make it harder. I'm sorry about Mantuas, truly. I don't know the terrain and the Delta is harder than I thought. I'm doing my best."

"Hunric?"

"Aye?"

"They're not coming, are they?" Turin swallowed, hard. The words were hard to say. "Lieutenant Carfax, the others . . . you've been scoring trees, marking the safest route, ever since Mantuas died. I've watched you. If they were following, we'd have heard them by now."

"Mayhap." The tracker's eyes were shuttered in the mask of drying mud that coated his face. "If they captured Malthus' Company . . . if they did, lad, it may be that they found more pressing business lay elsewhere. Mayhap they seek to catch the Dreamspinner's thoughts, aye, or his ravens, to make a report to General Tanaros, aye, or Lord Satoris himself."

"Mayhap." Waist-deep in water, Turin tilted his chin and gazed at the sky, a heated blue against the green leaves of the mangroves. Birds roosted in the treetops, but only the kind that were born to this place. High above, the sun blazed like a hammer. Haomane's Wrath, beating down incessantly on the birthplace of Satoris Third-Born, who had defied his will. Banewreaker, the world named him, but he had always honored his word with Staccia, ever since Lord Vorax struck his bargain over a thousand years ago. What other Shaper had done as much since the world was Sundered? If matters went awry now, it meant something had gone grievously wrong. And Turin had a bad feeling that it had. "I don't think so, Hunric."

Water splashed as the Staccian tracker shifted, settling his own pack on his shoulders. "Well, then," he said, his voice hardening. "We'll have to press on, won't we?"

FOURTEEN

A HUNDRED BANNERS FLEW IN Seahold.

There was the trident of Duke Bornin, of course, argent on a sea-blue field. And there were others; a dozen of his liege-lords, the barons and earls who held fiefdoms in the Midlands. There was the spreading oak of Quercas, the gilded stag of Tilodan, the harrow of Sarthac, all declaring their allegiance with pride. All had been seen in the city of Seahold, though never at once.

Not the Host of the Ellylon.

It had been a long time, since the Fourth Age of the Sundered World. Altoria had reigned and the Duke of Seahold had sworn fealty to its Kings when last these banners had been seen in the city.

It was a glorious sight.

Pennants and oriflammes hung from every turret, overhung every door of Castle Seahold. In the marketplaces, merchants displayed them with pride, hoping to stake some claim by virtue of symbolism to Ellyl patrons. In the streets, companies of Ellylon passed, carrying their standards with sombre pride. There was the argent scroll of Ingolin, the thistle-blossom of Núrilin, the gilded bee of Valmaré, the sable elbok of Numireth, the shipwright's wheel of Cerion . . . all of these and more, many more, representing the Houses of the Rivenlost, personified by their living scions and grieving kin alike.

Above them all hung the Crown and Souma of Elterrion the Bold.

No company dared bear this standard, no merchant dared display it. It hung limp in the summer's heat from the highest turret of

Castle Seahold, gilt and ruby on a field of virgin white, a dire reminder of what was at stake.

Cerelinde.

And one other standard flew, plain and unadorned, taking
place of precedence above the Duke of Seahold. It was dun-grey,
this banner; a blank field empty of arms. From time to time, the
summer breezes lofted its fabric. It unfurled, revealing . . . nothing.
Only dun, the dull-yellow color of the cloaks of the Borderguard of
Curonan, designed to blend with the endless plains of heart-grass.

Once, Altoria had reigned; once, the King of Altoria had born
different arms. A sword, a gilt sword on a field of sable, its quillons
curved to the shape of eyes. It was the insignia of Altorus Farseer,
who had been called friend by the Ellylon and risen to rule a nation
in the Sundered World of Urulat.

No more.

Aracus Altorus had sworn it. Not until his Borderguard opposed
Satoris Banewreaker himself would he take up the ancient banner
of his forefathers. But he did not doubt—did not doubt for an instant—that the Sunderer was behind the Sorceress' actions. Once
Cerelinde was restored, he would turn his far-seeing gaze on their
true Enemy.

Rumor ran through the city. Citizens and merchants and free-
holders assembled in Seaholder Square, gazing up at the Castle,
waiting and murmuring. Opportunistic peddlers did a good trade in
meat-pies wrapped in pastry; winesellers prospered, too. At noon,
Duke Bornin of Seahold appeared on the balcony and addressed
them. Possessed of a good set of lungs, he spoke with volume and
at length.

It was true, all true.

The Prophecy, the wedding-that-would-have-been, the raid on
Lindanen Dale. Oronin's Children, the Were at hunt. An abduction;
the Lady of the Ellylon. Pelmaran soldiers in guise, falling trees. A
message, an impossible ransom, delivered at a magical distance;
rumors of the Dragon of Beshtanag, seen aloft.

Oh, it was all true, and the Sorceress of the East had overreached.

There was cheering when Duke Bornin finished; cheering, rising en masse. He had ruled long enough to be clever. He waited
for it to end. And when it was done, he introduced to them Aracus
Altorus, naming him warleader of the Allied forces of the West.

Primed for it, they cheered all the louder.

War was declared on Beshtanag.

❖

WASHED, SALVED AND RESTED, CLAD in the armor of slain a Staccian warrior, Speros of Haimhault looked much improved by daylight. Despite his travail, his eyes were clear and alert and he moved as smoothly as his bandaged wounds allowed, a testament to the resilience of youth.

He hadn't lied, either; he knew how to handle a sword. At his insistence, Tanaros tested the former prisoner himself on the training-field of Darkhaven. Hyrgolf brought a squadron of Tungskulder Fjel to watch, forming a loose circle and leaning casually on their spears.

Inside the circle of onlookers, they fought.

Speros saluted him in the old manner; a clenched fist to the heart, then extended with an open palm. *Brother, let us spar. I trust my life unto your hands.* The old traditions died hard in the Midlands. How many times had he and Roscus Altorus saluted each other thusly in their Altorian boyhood?

Too many to count, and the memories were fond enough to hurt.

Tanaros returned the salute and drew his sword. Speros wasted only one glance upon it, briefly disappointed to see that it was not the General's infamous black sword, but merely an ordinary weapon. As well for him, since the black sword could shear through steel like flesh. Afterward, he ignored it, fixing his gaze on Tanaros himself, watching the subtle shifts in his face, in the musculature of his chest, in the set of his shield, that betokened a shift in his attack.

Flick, flick, flick, their blades darted and crossed, rang on the bosses of their shields. It made a prodigious sound on the training-field. Back and forth they went, churning the ground beneath their boots. Such was the swordplay of his youth, drilled into him a thousand years ago by a grizzled master-of-arms, sharp-tongued and relentless, always on the lookout for a pupil of promise.

"Not bad, horse-thief." Tanaros found himself smiling. "Not bad at all!"

"I do better . . . " Speros essayed a thrust and stumbled, wincing, forced to make a desperate parry. "I do better," he gasped, "when I've not been clamped in chains and had hot pokers held to my feet, Lord General."

"You do well enough." Putting an end to it, Tanaros stepped inside the young man's guard, catching his ill-timed swing on the edge of his shield. The point of his sword came to rest in the hollow of the lad's throat. "I am not displeased."

Speros, with commendable poise, held himself still, although his brown eyes nearly crossed in an effort to look down at Tanaros' sword. "I concede, my lord. You have the better of me."

"Well, then." Tanaros put up his sword. "We have each other's measure."

Deep, booming laughter ensued; Hyrgolf, who stepped forward to clap a massive hand on Speros' shoulder. It rested there, heavy as a stone, talons dangling. "Give the lad a dram of *svartblod*," he rumbled, beckoning to one of his soldiers with his free hand. "He's earned it."

To his credit, Speros grinned with gap-toothed fearlessness at the Fjel, sheathing his sword and hoisting the skin one of the Tungskulder proffered. It was a foul liquor, black as pitch, fermented from the blood of sheep that drank the tainted waters of the Gorgantus River, and Speros sputtered as he drank, dark liquid running in rivulets from the corners of his mouth. He shook himself like a wet dog, spattering droplets of *svartblod*.

The Fjel, who adored the foul stuff, laughed uproariously.

Tanaros touched the carved *rhios* that hung from his belt. "Take him in hand, Hyrgolf," he said to his field marshal. "Show him what there is to be seen in Darkhaven, and let him have a look at the forges. He may be worth keeping, this one."

"General." Hyrgolf inclined his head. There was a shrewdness in his small boar's eyes. Fjeltroll he might be, Tungskulder Fjel, broadest and strongest of his mighty race, but he was a father, too, and there were things he knew that Tanaros did not. "Aye, General."

"Good." It was a relief, after all, to strip the practice helmet from his head, to raise two fingers to his lips and give the shrill whistle of command that summoned the black horse. Tanaros mounted, gazing down at Hyrgolf. "The Dreamspinner has requested my counsel. We'll resume drills in two days' time. See that the Midlander's taught the rudiments of battle formations and the proper commands. I could use a subordinate on the field."

"Aye, General." The tips of Hyrgolf's eyetusks showed as he smiled.

Under his thighs, the black's hide rippled. Tanaros raised his hand. "Speros of Haimhault!" he called. "I'm leaving you to the untender mercies of Field Marshal Hyrgolf, who will teach you to be a soldier of Darkhaven. Can you handle it, lad?"

"Aye, Lord General!" Surrounded by Fjel, the former prisoner gave his gap-toothed grin and a cheerful salute. Clearly, Speros found himself at home here, unabashed by the rough camaraderie of the Fjel. "Can I have one of those horses to ride if I do?"

Tanaros rode toward the rookery, a lingering smile on his lips. How long had it been, since one of his countrymen had served Darkhaven? Too long. Loathe though he was to admit it, he'd missed it.

At the outskirts of the beech wood, he turned his mount loose and proceeded on foot, boots sinking deep into the soft mast, his shield slung over his back. Truly, he thought, the lad had fought well. It was no easy chore, to spar when one's every step was a waking agony. It must be so, with the searing wounds Speros had endured. A good thing Vorax's own physician had attended him. Though it had done no permanent harm, it had been an ungentle questioning.

Tanaros' own arrival had differed. He was one of the Three, and Lord Satoris himself had sensed his broken heart and his wounded pride, had used the Helm of Shadows to summon him. And in all the wildness of his despair, Tanaros had answered the summons, had out-faced and out-shouted the Thunder Voice Fjel, and made his way through the Defile unaided and undeterred.

And presented himself to the Sunderer, who had asked his aid.

Even now, after so long, he shuddered in remembered ecstasy. The knot of scarred flesh that circumscribed his heart constricted at the memory of his branding, of how the hilt of Godslayer, laid against his skin, had *stretched* the chains of his mortality. Even now, when his aching joints remembered their endless sojourn, it moved him.

He had spoken the truth to Speros. In the beginning, there had been only rage. It had driven him to Darkhaven in fury and despair, and he had laid it at the feet of Lord Satoris, willing to serve evil itself if it would purge his furious heart. Since then he had come to understand that the world was not as he had believed it in his youth. He had come to love Lord Satoris, who clung to his defiance in the face of the overwhelming tyranny of Haomane's will, wounded and bereft though he was. Haomane's Wrath had scorched the very earth in pursuit of Satoris. Were it not for Arahila's merciful intervention, the Lord-of-Thought might have destroyed Urulat itself.

Tanaros wondered if Haomane would have reckoned it worth the cost. After all, it would enable him to Shape the world anew, the better to suit his desires. It was the will of Uru-Alat, Haomane claimed, that he should reign supreme among Shapers; and yet, each of them held a different Gift. Was the Gift of thought superior to all others? Once, Tanaros had believed it to be so; until the courage and loyalty of the Fjel humbled him.

It was a pity Haomane First-Born had never known humility. Perhaps he would not be so jealous of his station, so quick to wrath, if he were humbled. Perhaps, after all, it was Lord Satoris' destiny to do so.

He wondered how he could ever have believed in Haomane's benevolence. Surely it must be the power of the Souma. But as long as Lord Satoris opposed him with Godslayer in his possession, Haomane could not wield its full might. And Tanaros meant to do all in his power to aid his Lordship. Perhaps, one day, he might be healed, and Urulat with him.

O my Lord, he thought, my Lord! Let me be worthy of your choosing.

"Blacksword."

A dry voice, dry as the Unknown Desert. Ushahin Dreamspinner, seated cross-legged under a beech tree, still as the forest. Lids parted, mismatched eyes cracked open. Sticky lashes, parched lips.

"Cousin," Tanaros said. "You wished to see me?"

"Aye." Dry lips withdrew from teeth. "Did you see the ravens?"

"Ravens?" Tanaros glanced about with alarm. The rookery was sparsely populated, but that was not unusual. It was more seldom than not that he espied his tufted friend. "Is it Fetch? Has something happened to him?"

"No." The half-breed rested his head against a beech bole. "Your feathered friend is safe, for the nonce. He keeps watch, with others, on Haomane's Allies as they make ready to depart for Pelmar. But something has happened."

Tanaros seated himself opposite the Dreamspinner, frowning. "What is it?"

"I don't know." Ushahin grimaced, raising crooked fingers to his temples. "Therein lies the problem, cousin. All I can do is put a name to it."

"And the name?" A chill tickled Tanaros' spine.

"Malthus."

One word; no more, and no less. They gazed at one another, knowing as did few on Urulat what it betokened. Malthus the Counselor was Haomane's weapon, and where he went, ill followed for those who opposed him.

"How so?" Tanaros asked softly.

Ushahin gave his hunch-shouldered shrug. "If I knew, cousin, I would tell you, and his Lordship, too. All I know is that Malthus' Company entered the Unknown Desert. Some days past, they emerged. And they brought someone—and something—with them."

"Bound for Darkhaven?"

"No." Ushahin shook his head. "They went east. That's what worries me."

"Toward Pelmar?" Tanaros relaxed. "Then Malthus himself has bought our gambit, and there is no cause for fear—"

"Not Pelmar." The half-breed tilted his head, the dim, patterned shadow of beech leaves marking his misshapen face. "Malthus' Company is bound for Vedasia."

There was a pause, then.

"Send your ravens," Tanaros suggested.

Ushahin spared him a contemptuous glance. "I *did*. Three I sent, and three are dead, strung by their feet from an Arduan saddlebag. And now, the circle has closed tight around Malthus' Company, and there is no mind open to me. I cannot find them. I do not like it. Who and what did Malthus bring out of the Unknown Desert?"

Both of them thought, without saying it, of the Prophecy.

"Does his Lordship know?" Tanaros asked.

Dabbling his fingers in the beech mast, Ushahin frowned. "What he fears, he does not name. And yet I think some part of it is unknown to him, for the desert was much changed by Haomane's Wrath."

"It doesn't matter, does it?" Sitting on the soft ground, Tanaros squared his shoulders. "We've already thwarted the first part. The daughter of Elterrion's line is in our keeping, and the son—" his voice grew hard, "—the son of Altorus' line is bound for Pelmar at the head of a doomed army."

Crooked lips smiled without humor. "Then why is Malthus bound for Vedasia?"

"Would that I knew. But I am a military strategist, not a spymaster, cousin." Tanaros unfolded his legs and stood, placing a hand in the small of his back, feeling stiff joints pop. Sparring with the young Midlander had taken its toll. "What, then, does his Lordship say?"

"Watch," Ushahin said flatly, "and wait. Report."

"Well, then." Tanaros nodded, half to himself, gazing about the rookery. Haphazard nests rested in the crooks of trees, a dark flurry of twigs protruding. Which one, he wondered, belonged to Fetch? "I can advise you no better, Dreamspinner. Watch, and wait. Learn what you may. In the meantime, I must bring our forces to readiness and plot our course through the Marasoumië. When your knowledge impinges on the disposition of the army, alert me."

Two strides he took; three, four, before Ushahin's voice halted him.

"Tanaros?"

He looked small, seated under a beech tree; small and afraid.

"Aye, cousin?"

"He should kill her, you know." Muscles worked in the half-breed's throat as he swallowed. "Nothing's done, nothing's averted, while she lives."

It was true. True and true and true, and Tanaros knew it.

Cerelinde.

"He won't," he whispered.

"I know." Unexpected tears shimmered in the mismatched eyes. "There is hope in him; a Shaper's hope, that would recreate the world in his image. If it comes to it . . . could you do it, Tanaros?"

On a branch, a raven perched. Twigs, protruding from a rough-hewn nest. The bird bent low, his head obscured by gaping beaks, coughed up sustenance from his craw. What manner was it? Earthworms, insects, carrion. Even here, life endured; regenerated and endured, life to life, earth to earth, flesh to flesh.

Cerelinde.

"I don't know."

THE WEATHER WAS BALMY IN Vedasia.

It was the thing, Carfax thought, that one noticed first; at least, one did if one was Staccian. Summer was a golden time in Staccia, with the goldenrod blooming around the shores of inland lakes and coating the harsh countryside in yellow pollen. It was nothing to this. This, this was sunlight dripping like honey, drenching field and orchard and olive grove in a golden glow, coaxing all to surrender their bounty. Fields of wheat bowed their gold-whiskered heads, melons ripened on the vine, the silvery-green leaves of olive trees rustled and boughs bent low with the weight of swelling globes of apple and pear. This was the demesne of Yrinna-of-the-Fruits, Sixth-Born among Shapers.

They had gained the Traders' Route shortly after entering Vedasia proper and Carfax's skin prickled as they rode, knowing himself deep in enemy territory. It was a wonder, though, how few folk noted aught awry. Children, mostly. They stared wide-eyed, peering from behind their mothers' skirts, from the backboards of passing wagons. They pointed and whispered; at the Charred Folk, mostly, but also at the others.

What, he wondered, did they see?

A grey-beard in scholar's robes, whose eyes twinkled beneath his fiercesome brows; Malthus, it seemed, had a kindness for children. A frowning Borderguardsman in a dun cloak. An Ellyl lordling, whose light step left no trace on the dusty road. An Arduan woman in men's attire, her longbow unstrung at her side. A young knight sweating in full Vedasian armor.

A man with nut-brown skin and a rounded belly.

A nut-brown boy with wide dark eyes and a flask about his neck.

They sang as they traveled, the Charred Folk. Monotonously, incessantly. Thulu, the fat one, sang in a bass rumble. Sometimes Carfax listened, and heard in it the deep tones of water passing through subterranean places, of hidden rivers and aquifers feeding the farthest-reaching roots of the oldest trees. The boy Dani sang too, his voice high and true. It was most audible when running water was near. Then his voice rose, bright and warbling. Like rivers, like streams, bubbling over rocks.

Children noticed.

Malthus the Counselor noticed, too, his keen ears and eyes missing little. He nodded to himself, exchanged glances with Blaise of the Borderguard, with Peldras the Ellyl, nodding with satisfaction and fingering the ruby-red Soumanië hidden beneath his beard. Everything, it seemed, went according to Malthus' plan.

Old man, Carfax thought, I hate you.

And since there was nothing else for him to do, his flesh and his will bound and circumscribed by the Counselor's Soumanië, Carfax rode alongside them, ate and slept and breathed road-dust, keeping the silence that was his only protection, watching and hating, willing them harm. Sometimes, the children stared at him. What did they see? A man, dusty and bedraggled, his tongue cleft to the roof of his mouth. Deaf and dumb, they thought him. Betimes, there were taunts. Carfax endured them as his due.

What folly, to think Malthus would have surrendered his Soumanië!

Sometimes there were couriers, royal couriers, carrying the

standard of Port Calibus. They traveled in pairs. One would sound the silvery horn, hoisting the standard high to display a pennant bearing an argent tower on a mist-blue field. Other sojourners cleared the well-kept road in a hurry at the sight of it, including Malthus' Company. The old wizard would stand with his head bowed, one hand clutching beneath his beard, muttering under his breath. Whatever charm it was, it worked. The Vedasian couriers took no notice of them.

Within days of their arrival, they began to see companies of knights headed east on the Traders' Route. Twenty, forty at a time, riding in orderly formations, baggage trains following. More and more frequently couriers appeared, stitching back and forth the length of the country, horns blowing an urgent warning. Commitments were asked and given, numbers were tallied, supplies were rerouted. The rumors were spoken in a whisper, became news, stated aloud.

Vedasia was committing its knights to war.

Stories were passed from mouth to ear along the Traders' Route. The Sorceress of the East had made an unholy pact with the Sunderer himself, who had promised to make her his Queen in exchange for the head of Malthus the Counselor. She had sent her dragon to abduct the Lady of the Rivenlost and offered a dreadful bargain.

Haomane's Allies had chosen war instead.

Not all of them, no, but already a mighty force was on the march, moving from Seahold to Harrington Bay, where the Free Fishers had agreed to carry them to Port Calibus. There, a fleet of Vedasian ships would ferry them around the lower tip of Dwarfhorn and on to Port Eurus to unite with a Vedasian company under the command of Duke Quentin, the King's nephew. Two of the Five Regents of Pelmar had given pledges of war, and the another was expected to agree soon. It was a force the likes of which had not been seen since the Fourth Age of the Sundered World. The Sorceress of the East, all agreed, had overreached.

These were the stories heard along the Traders' Route, until they turned south onto a lesser road that led unto the heart of the Dwarfhorn.

"Why do you smile?"

It was Blaise of the Borderguard who asked the question one evening, pausing in the process of skinning a rabbit the archer Fianna had shot for the supper-pot. She was some distance away, motionless in the uncultivated field, bow drawn, tracking some un-

seen movement. Malthus had vanished; communing with Haomane, perhaps. Hobard was gathering firewood, while Peldras
knelt in serene concentration, stacking kindling in an intricate
structure. Nothing burned hotter and cleaner than an Ellylon-laid
campfire, constructed in tiers which collapsed in on themselves
with a delicate shower of sparks, laying a bed of immaculate embers. At his side, Dani squatted and watched in fascination, while
his fat uncle Thulu went in search of running water.

On alert, Carfax regarded the Borderguardsman in wary silence.

"You smile." Blaise's hands resumed their movement, parting
the rabbit's skin from its flesh. His gaze remained fixed on Carfax.
In the deepening twilight he looked much akin to General Tanaros,
with the same unthinking competence. "Watching the knights pass.
I've seen it. Why?"

A thrill of fear shot through him. Had he smiled? Yes, probably.
It was the one bitter pleasure left to him, watching Haomane's Allies dance unwitting to a tune of Lord Satoris' piping, marshaling
their forces eastward.

"You're afraid," Blaise said softly, plying his knife.

To speak or not to speak? There was no safety in silence, if his
face betrayed him. Carfax met the Borderguardsman's gaze.
"Afraid, aye." His voice was rusty with disuse. "You want me dead."

"Aye." A brusque nod, brows rising a fraction to hear him
speak. "You're a liability, I reckon. You'd do the same if it was your
command. But I swore to obey the Counselor's wisdom, and he
wants you alive. So why do you smile?"

"Why does Malthus hide from Haomane's Allies?" Carfax asked
instead of answering. "Why have we turned south, when the war
lies north? What does the boy Dani carry in that flask about his
neck?"

"You're stubborn, I'll give you that much." The Borderguardsman set aside the skinned carcass with a speculative look in his
eye. "What's your name, Staccian?"

Carfax shook his head.

Blaise wiped his skinning-knife on a tuft of grass. "You know
mine."

"Yes." He swallowed.

"Do you serve under his command?" Dark eyes, steady and
calm. "You know of whom I speak. He who caused my family
name to live in infamy."

Carfax looked away. "General Tanaros Blacksword."

"The Kingslayer." Blaise's voice was flat. "You do, don't you?"

He waited, but Carfax kept his silence. "He strangled his wife, Staccian. He put his hands around her neck and he throttled her dead. He walked up to his sovereign lord, a man who was nearly a brother to him, and plunged his sword into his guts. And then he rode to Darkhaven and pledged his life to the Sunderer in exchange for immortality. Are you proud to serve under his command?"

"Who should I serve, then?" He dared a glance. "You?"

"You could do worse."

Carfax laughed in despair.

"What manner of man do you wish to be?" The Borderguardsman watched him keenly. "You have a choice, Staccian. I've heard it said your folk made allegiance with Satoris Banewreaker to preserve peace and prosperity in your country. No one in Urulat would condemn you for deciding the cost was too high."

Peace and prosperity, Carfax thought. Yes. Those were not small things to a people who dwelled in a stony land, to a people whose nation bordered on the territory of the Fjel, who made for ungentle neighbors were there enmity between them. Whatever was said of him, Lord Satoris kept his bargains. And whatever General Tanaros had done a thousand years ago, he treated his Men with honor. Carfax had sworn an oath of loyalty, and they had given him no cause to break it.

Without honor, a Man might as well be dead. Indeed, it was better to die with honor than to live without it. But he hadn't expected it to come so soon.

Across the field, the Arduan archer Fianna stood like a statue in the lowering twilight, longbow drawn in a strained arch, holding the taut string close to her ear. Her figure had an unearthly beauty in the gloaming. Carfax stared at her, thinking of girls he had known, of one he had hoped to wed, long ago. Of how she had laughed and wrinkled her freckled nose when he brushed it with the tip of a goldenrod in full bloom, dusting her skin with pollen. What would he have done, had he known he had so little time? The Archer released her string and her bow hummed. Somewhere unseen, a rabbit squealed, the sound cut short.

Blaise repeated the question, still watching him. "Why do you smile, Staccian?"

"To make a friend of death," Carfax answered.

FIFTEEN

❖

"THEY'RE COMING."

Lilias frowned at her Ward Commander. "How soon?"

"Thirty days." He paused. "Less, if the winds blow fair from Port Eurus."

The weight of the Soumanië made her head ache. Strange, how something so light could weigh so heavy! And yet, how not, when she had had been shifting a mountain with it. Lilias grimaced, pressing her fingertips to her temples. The Beshtanagi sunlight seemed cursedly bright. "And the Pelmarans?"

"Assembling at Kranac, to await the Allies' arrival." Gergon cleared his throat. "Regent Heurich has agreed to send a force."

"How long can we hold them?"

"It depends upon their numbers, among other things." He nodded at the southernmost passage, where workers piled boulders on either side of the opening. "How fast can you seal that breach, my lady?"

Lilias considered the gap in the high granite wall that enfolded the base of Beshtanag Mountain. Beyond lay the forest, spreading its dense apron of dark green. It was through those trees that her enemies would come, in greater numbers than she had reckoned. "Can we not seal it now and be done with it?"

"No." Gergon looked regretful. "We've too many men to feed and water, and too few resources on the mountain. Our stores would not last. After ten days' time, we would begin to starve. If the . . . " He cleared his throat again. " . . . if the Were give ample warning, you will have a day's notice."

"They will," Lilias said, pacing a length of the Soumanië-erected wall, her fingertips trailing along its smooth surface. "And I will. What the Were do not tell me, Calandor will. We are prepared, Ward Commander. If the raw materials are there, the breaches will be sealed, the gaps closed. In the space of a day, no less. So how long, Gergon, will this wall hold off Haomane's Allies?"

He squinted at the fortress, perched atop the mountain. "Three days."

"Three *days?*" She stared at him.

"My lady." Gergon shrugged, spreading his hands. "You have always demanded truth. So my father said, and his father's father before him. We are speaking of the concerted might of over half of Pelmar, augmented by Vedasian knights, the Host of the Ellylon and Midlander troops under the command of the last scion of Altorus. If we cannot hold the forest—and we cannot, without the Were—they will come against the wall. And they will ransack the forest and build ladders and siege engines, and they *will* breach the wall."

"No." Lilias set her jaw, ignoring the ache in her head. "They will *not* breach it, Ward Commander. I have Shaped this wall myself from the raw stone of Beshtanag, and it will hold against their siege engines. I shall will it so." ·

Gergon sighed. "Then they'll come over the top, my lady. They've no shortage of men, nor of wood for ladders and towers, unless you can close the very forest itself to them."

"No." She shook her head, gazing at the dark carpet of pines. "Not for so many. It is harder to shift forest than stone, and we must leave an avenue open for Lord Satoris' troops. Order more stone brought, and I will raise the wall higher. A foot or more."

"As you wish." He bowed, his eyes wary. "It will delay them, by a few hours. Our enemies will still have ample resources if it comes to it."

"All right. Three days," she repeated, gesturing at the grey expanse of loose scree at the mountain's base. "Let us say it is so, Gergon. And then, if it came to it, we would engage them here?"

"Will it come to it, my lady?"

She met his honest gaze. "No. But we must plan as if it would. So what happens, if we engage them here?"

"It's poor footing." Gergon sucked his teeth, considering. "Knights a-horse would be at a disadvantage, here. They'll come in with infantry. I'd place archers there," he said, pointing to overhangs, "there and there, to cover our retreat."

"Retreat?" Lilias raised her brows.

"Aye." Her Ward Commander nodded his grizzled head. "Once the wall is surmounted, my lady, we've nothing to fall back upon but Beshtanag itself."

"They *will* come, Gergon." Lilias held his gaze. "It won't come to it."

"As you say, my lady." He glanced at the Soumanië on her brow, and some of the tension left his stocky frame. He nodded again, smiling. "As you say! I'll have the lads in the quarry work overtime. You'll have as much stone as you need, and more."

"I *will* hold the wall, Gergon."

"You will." He nodded at her brow, smiled. "Yes, you will, my lady."

Lilias sighed as he left on his errand, her skin itching beneath her clothes in the heat. Where was Pietre with the cool sponge to soothe her temples? He should have been here by now. There he was, hurrying down the pathway from the fortress and lugging a bucket of well-water, Sarika behind him struggling with a half-opened parasol. The collars of their servitude glinted in the Beshtanagi sunlight, evoking an echoing throb from the Soumanië. Her mouth curved in a tender smile. So sweet, her pretty ones!

She wondered if they understood what was at stake.

She wondered if she did.

Calandor?

Yes, Lilias?

Satoris will *keep his word, won't he?*

There was a silence, then, a longer pause than she cared to endure.

Yes, Lilias, the dragon said, and there was sorrow in it. *He will.*

Why sorrow? She did not know, and her blood ran cold at it. Teams of grunting men moved boulders into place. Granite, the grey granite of Beshtanag, mica-flecked and solid. The raw bones of the mountain; her home for so many long years, the bulwark that sheltered her people. Now that events had been set irrevocably in motion, the thought of risking Beshtanag made her want to weep for the folly of it.

Beshtanag was her haven, and she was responsible for preserving it, and for the safety of her people. All she could do was pledge everything to its defense. Lilias closed her eyes, entered the raw stone and *Shaped* it, feeling granite flow like water. Upward, upward it flowed, melding with its kinstone. A handspan of wall— two handspans, five—rose another foot, settled into smoothness.

Doubling over, Lilias panted. Despite the patting sponge, the

Soumanië was like a boulder on her brow, and there was so much, so much to be done!

And where were Lord Satoris' messengers?

THE TRACKER WAS RIGHT, TURIN discovered when he relented. The mud *did* help. It itched as it dried, though, forming a crackling veneer on his face and arms. Best to keep it wet, easily enough done as they slogged through water ankle-deep at the best of times, and waist-deep more often than not. Easiest to strip to the skin to do it, and more comfortable in the Delta's heat. Turin kept his short-breeches for modesty's sake. Little else, save the pack on his back and his waterlogged boots. At night, whether they perched in mangrove branches or found a dry hummock of land, he had to peel the soft, slick leather from his calves and feet, fearful of what rot festered inside.

It stank, of mud and sweat and rotting vegetation.

And the worst of it . . . the worst of it was the *desire.*

It made no sense, no sense at all. Why here, amid the muck and squalor? And yet, there it was. Desire, fecund and insistent. It beat in his pulse like a drum, it swelled and hardened his flesh, it made the hair at the back of his neck tingle.

"This is *his* birthing-place." Hunric turned back to him and grinned, his teeth very white in the mud-smeared mask of his face. He spread his arms wide. "Do you feel it, Turin? His Gift lingers, here!"

"You've swamp-fever, man." Turin shoved his hair back from his brow, streaking it with muck. "Lord Satoris' Gift was lost when Oronin Last-Born plunged Godslayer into his thigh."

"Was it?" The tracker turned slowly, arms outspread. "This was the place, Turin. It all began here! Look." His voice dropped to a whisper and he reached for his crude spear with the tip hardened by fire. "A slow-lizard."

Turin watched, fighting despair and desire as Hunric the tracker stalked and killed one of the meaty, slow-moving denizens of the Delta. They were good eating, the slow-lizards. Mantuas, whooping and shouting in the chase, had been the first to suggest it, roasting the white meat over a fire that had taken ages to kindle. It was all different, now.

"What?" Hunric, gnawing at his prey, stared at him.

"Beshtanag," Turin whispered. "Hunric, we have to get to Beshtanag!"

"Do we?" For a moment, the tracker looked confused. "Oh, right!" The febrile light in his eyes cleared and he lowered the slow-lizard's carcass, blinking. "Beshtanag. It lies east, northward and east. We're on the route, Turin."

"Good." Turin nodded. "We have a message to deliver. Remember, Hunric?"

"A message, right." Hunric grinned, showing bloodstained teeth. "We won, didn't we? Got the princess, the Lady of the Ellylon. Did you see her, Turin? You're a poor substitute! Limbs like alabaster, throat like a swan. I could swallow her whole!"

"Don't say that." Turin shook himself. "The other message, Hunric! About Malthus' Company?"

"Malthus." It settled the tracker, and he pointed. "We need to go that way."

"Good." Turin sloshed alongside him. "Hunric," he said, grasping the tracker's forearm. "It's important. We need to deliver this news to the Sorceress of the East. You do remember, don't you?"

"Of course." The tracker blinked. "It's that way."

He hoped so. He fervently hoped so. Because it was obvious, now, that no one had entered the Delta after them. No doubt lingered. They'd been here too long for it.

They'd been here altogether too long.

Turin was no tracker, to hold a place in his mind and chart a path through it unerring, but he'd seen a map of the Delta in Lord Satoris' Warchamber. It wasn't that large. Even on foot, even at this pace, they should have reached the far edge. Following Hunric, he counted on his fingers. How many days had it been? At least eight since Mantuas had died.

That was too many.

Had they been walking in circles? It was hard to tell, here. One had to follow the waterways, winding around mangroves. It was impossible to keep in a fixed location relative to the sun's course, and there were no landmarks by which to chart one's progress, only endless swamp. Hunric was the best, of course. But Hunric . . . Hunric was *changed,* and Turin was afraid. Reaching behind him, he groped at his pack, feeling for the pouch containing Lord Vorax's gold coins. Still there, solid and real. It was enough to buy them lodging in Pelmar, enough to purchase a pair of swift horses, enough to bribe their way to Beshtanag if need be.

All they had to do was make their way out of this cursed swamp.

A bright-green snake looped along a branch lifted its head to stare at him with lidless eyes. Turin fought down a rush of fear, splashing doggedly past it. By all the Shapers, it stank here! Ahead of him, Hunric hummed, deep and tuneless. The sound worked on his nerves. There was a leech clinging to his thigh and his sodden short-breeches chafed. Why this desire? If he'd had a woman, any woman, he would have coupled in the muck with her. Even the thought of it filled his mouth with a salty rush of taste. Any woman. One of Vorax's handmaids or the withered flesh of the Dreamspinner's oldest madling, it didn't matter.

Or his own sister, Turin thought, remembering how he had seen her last, yellow braids pinned in a coronet, bidding him farewell. Or—oh, Haomane help him!—the Lady of the Ellylon. Ah, Shapers! Slung over the General's pommel, her pale hair trailing. Sprawled on the greensward, helpless and unaware, her white limbs stirring as the General removed her cloak. He had worn that cloak himself, still warm and scented by her body.

Unable to suppress himself, Turin groaned aloud.

"You feel it." Hunric glanced over his shoulder, eyes shining. "We're near the heart of it, Turin. The heart of the Delta! I told you Lord Satoris' Gift lived in this place."

"No." He swallowed with an effort. His tongue felt thick. "This isn't right. It's *tainted*. It shouldn't be like this."

The tracker shrugged. "Oh, there's death in it, all right. What do you expect? Godslayer struck him to the quick. Nothing could be the same. But it's still *here*."

"Hunric." Turin, itching and aching and scared, tightened his throat at the sudden sting of tears. "I don't care, do you understand? If there were power in this place that Lord Satoris could use, he would be here, not in Darkhaven. I'm tired, sodden and miserable. All I want to do is find a dry place to make camp, and press on to Pelmar."

All around them, the lowering sun washed the Delta with ruddy gold, glimmering on the standing water. Hunric watched it with awe, fingering his handmade spear. Where was his sword? "Beautiful, isn't it?" he asked softly.

"Hunric!" It was all he could do not to cry.

"All right." The tracker smiled at him. "But you're wrong, you know. There *is* power here. Rebirth, generation. It's all here, Turin. Here, at the beginning. Lord Satoris thinks too much on his brother Haomane, and not enough on his own origin. The Souma is not the only power on Urulat, you know."

Shadows lengthened, cast eastward across the swamp. Turin let out his breath in a final plea. "Hunric . . . "

"There." The tracker turned, pointing north. Through the dense mangroves, something was visible in the distance; a vast hummock rising above the stagnant waters under the spreading shelter of a tall palodus tree. "Do you see it? Dry land, Turin, here at the heart of the Delta. We'll camp there tonight, and make for the border in the morning. Does that please you?"

Dry land, a chance to build a fire, eat roasted slow-lizard, nibble the last crumbs of bannock-cake, to remove his rotting footwear and pluck the leeches from his legs. Turin gauged the distance as no more than an hour's slog and sighed.

"Yes."

"MY LADY?" TANAROS PAUSED, HIS fist poised to knock again, when the door was flung open. Meara.

The madling tossed her tangled hair and sized him up and down. "What brings *you* here, Lord General?"

"Meara," he said politely. "I'm glad to see you well. I've come to invite the Lady Cerelinde to view the moon-garden."

Her mouth stretched into a grimace. "Oh, you *have*, have you?"

"Meara?" A voice from another room, silvery and clear. "What is it? Does Lord Satoris summon me again?"

Tanaros shifted uncomfortably, tugging at his collar as Cerelinde entered the foyer. "My lady. Arahila's moon shines full this evening. I thought it might please you to view the garden of Darkhaven."

"At night?" Her fine brows rose a fraction.

"It is a moon-garden, my lady." A slight flush warmed his face.

"Ah." She regarded him, grave and beautiful, clad in a robe of pale blue. "So you would permit me a glimpse of sky."

"I would."

"Thank you." Cerelinde inclined her head. "I would like that."

Meara hissed through her teeth, stamping into the quarters beyond and returning with a pearl-white shawl, woven fine as gossamer. "Here," she muttered, thrusting it at Cerelinde. "You'll take a chill, Lady."

"Thank you, Meara." The Lady of the Ellylon smiled at the madling.

"Don't." She bit her lip, drawing a bead of blood, then whirled on Tanaros. "I told you it was a mistake to bring her, with all her beauty and kindness! Did you not think it would make it that much harder for the rest of us to endure ourselves?"

He blinked in perplexity, watching her storm away, doors slamming in her wake. "I thought she had taken kindly to you, my lady."

"You don't understand, do you?" Cerelinde glanced at him with pity.

"No." Tanaros shook his head, extending his arm. "I don't."

He led her through the gleaming halls of Darkhaven, acutely aware of her white fingers resting on his forearm, of the hem of her silk robe sweeping along the black marble floors. There were shadows beneath her luminous eyes, but captivity had only refined her beauty, leavening it with sorrow. Haomane's Child. The Havenguard on duty saluted as they passed, faces impassive, keeping their thoughts to themselves.

"Here, my lady." A narrow hallway, ending in a wooden door polished smooth as silk, with hinges and locks of tarnished silver. Tanaros unlocked the door and pushed it ajar, admitting a waft of subtle fragrances. He stepped back, bowing. "The garden."

Cerelinde passed him.

"Oh, *Haomane!*"

The mingled joy and grief in her tone made a knot in his belly. Tanaros entered the garden, closing the door carefully behind him. Only then did he dare look at her. The Lady of the Ellylon stood very still, and there were no words in the common tongue to describe her expression. The air was warm and balmy, rich with the scent of strange blossoms. Overhead, Arahila's moon hung full and bright off the left side of the Tower of Ravens, drenching the garden in silvery light.

It was very beautiful.

She hadn't expected that, Tanaros thought.

Tainted water, feeding tainted earth, saturated with the seeping ichor of Lord Satoris' wound. Such was the garden of Darkhaven, and such flowers as grew here grew nowhere else on Urulat. By daylight, they shrank. Only at night did they bloom, stretching tendrils and leaves toward the kindly light of Arahila's moon and stars, extending pale blossoms.

Cerelinde wandered, the hem of her robe leaving a dark trail where it disturbed the dewy grass. "What is this called?" She paused beneath the graceful, drooping branches of a flowering tree, its delicate blossoms, pale-pink as a bloodshot eye, weeping clear drops upon the ground.

"A mourning-tree." Tanaros watched her. "It grieves for the slain."

"And these?" She examined a vine twining round the trunk, bearing waxy, trumpet-shaped flowers that emitted a pallid glow.

"Corpse-flowers, my lady." He saw her lift her head, startled. "At the dark of the moon, they utter the cries of the dead, or so it is said."

Cerelinde shuddered, stepping back from the vines. "This is a dire beauty, General Tanaros."

"Yes," Tanaros said simply, taking her arm. Stars winked overhead like a thousand eyes as he led her to another bed, where blossoms opened like eyes underfoot, five-pointed petals streaked with pale violet. "Have you seen these?" A faint, sweet fragrance hung in the air, tantalizing. His eyes, unbidden, filled with tears.

. . . her face, his wife Calista, her eyes huge and fearful as she lay upon the birthing-bed, watching him hold the infant in his arms . . .

"No!" Cerelinde struggled out of his grip, eyeing him and breathing hard. "What manner of flower is this, Tanaros?"

"Vulnus-blossom." His smile was taut. "What did you see?"

"You," she said softly. "I saw you, in Lindanen Dale, your sword stained with my kinsmen's blood."

Tanaros nodded, once. "Their scent evokes memory. Painful memory."

Cerelinde closed her eyes. "What do you see, Tanaros?"

"I see my wife." The words came harsher than he intended. He watched her eyelids, raising like shutters, the sweep of lashes lifting to reveal the luminous grey.

"Poor Tanaros," she murmured.

"Come." He dragged at her arm, hauled her to another flowerbed, where bell-shaped blossoms bent on slender stalks, shivering in the moonlight with a pale, fretful sound. "Do you know what these are?"

She shook her head.

"Clamitus atroxis," Tanaros said shortly. "Sorrow-bells. They sound for every senseless act of cruelty that takes place in the Sundered World. Do you wonder that they are seldom silent?"

"No." Tears clung to her lashes. "Why, Tanaros?"

"Look." He fell to his knees, parting the dense, green leaves of the clamitus. Another flower blossomed there, low to the ground, pure white and starry, shimmering in its bed of shadows. "Touch it."

She did, kneeling beside him, stroking the petals with one fingertip.

The flower shuddered, its petals folding into limpness.

"What have I done?" Cerelinde's expression was perturbed.

"Nothing." Tanaros shook his head. "It is the mortexigus, Lady; the little-death flower. That is its nature, to mimic death at a touch. Thus does it loose its pollen."

Cerelinde knelt, head bowed, watching the plant stir. "Why do you show this to me, Tanaros?" she asked quietly.

A soft breeze blew in the garden, redolent with the odor of memory, making the clamitus sound their fitful chimes. Tanaros stood, his knees popping. He walked some distance from her. "Lord Satoris has summoned you to speak with him."

"Yes." She did not move.

"What does he say?"

"Many things." Cerelinde watched him. "He says that the Prophecy is a lie."

"Do you believe him?" Tanaros turned back to her.

"No." A simple truth, simply spoken.

"You should." A harsh note entered his voice. "He speaks the truth, you know."

Her face was calm. "Then why do you fear it, Tanaros? Why am I here, if the Prophecy is a lie? Why not let me wed Aracus Altorus in peace?"

"Is that what you would bring us here in Darkhaven?" he asked her. "Peace?"

At that, she looked away. "The Lord-of-Thought knows the will of Uru-Alat."

"No!" Tanaros clenched his fist against his thigh, forced himself to breathe evenly. "No, he doesn't. Haomane knows the power of thought, that's all. The leap of water in the stream, of blood in the vein, of seed in the loins . . . these things are Uru-Alat too, and these things Haomane First-Born knows not. That is the core of truth he has Shaped into the lie of the Prophecy."

Cerelinde composed herself. "The other Shapers disagree, General."

"Do they?" Tanaros caught a bitter laugh in his throat and pointed to the moon. "See there, my lady. Arahila's moon sheds its blessing on Lord Satoris' garden."

Her gaze was filled with compassion. "What would you have me say? Arahila the Fair is a Shaper, Tanaros. Not even the Sunderer is beyond redemption in her eyes."

"No." He shook his head. "Oh, Cerelinde! Don't you understand? Any of the Shapers, any of the Six, could leave Torath and cross the Sundered divide. They will not." He raised his chin, gazing at the stars. "They will not," he said, "because they fear. They fear Haomane's wrath, and they fear their own mortality. Even Shapers can die, Cerelinde. And they fear to tread the same earth where Godslayer abides."

"Is that the lesson of the garden?" Her grey eyes were cool, disbelieving.

"No." Tanaros pointed to the mortexigus flower. "That is. Lady, any Son of Man would do to serve your need. In our very mortality, we hold the keys to life. We hold the Gift Lord Satoris can no longer bestow, the key to the survival of the Rivenlost. Your people and mine conjoined. That is the truth of the Prophecy, the deeper truth."

She frowned and it was as though a cloud passed over the moon's bright face. "I do not understand."

"Do the numbers of the Ellylon not dwindle while those of Men increase?" he asked her. "So it has been since the world was Shaped. Without Lord Satoris' Gift, in time the Ellylon will vanish from the face of Urulat."

"Now it is you who lies," Cerelinde said softly. "For the Lord-of-Thought would not allow his Children to be subsumed, not even by fair Arahila's."

Tanaros held her gaze. "Why, then, does Haomane's Prophecy bid you to wed one?"

Her winged brows rose. "To unite our people in peace, Tanaros. Aracus Altorus is no ordinary Man."

"Aye, Cerelinde, he is. As I am." Tanaros sighed, and the sorrow-bells murmured in mournful reply. "The difference is that the House of Altorus has never faltered in its loyalty to Haomane First-Born."

She stood and touched his face with light fingertips, a touch that burned like cool fire. "A vast difference, Tanaros. And yet it is not too late for you."

He shuddered, removing her hand. "Believe as you will, Lady, but the sons of Altorus Farseer were chosen to fulfill Haomane's Prophecy that in their loyalty they might bring down Lord Satoris. The truth is otherwise. It need not be a daughter of Elterrion, nor a son of Altorus. You and I would serve. Our seed holds the key to your perpetuation."

"You!" She recoiled, a little.

"Our people. Any two of us. We hold within ourselves the Gifts of all the Seven Shapers and the ability to Shape a world of our choosing." He spread his hands. "That's all, Cerelinde, no more."

"No." She was silent a moment. "No, it is another of the Sunderer's lies, Tanaros. If it were so simple, why would Haomane not so bid us?"

"Because he requires the Prophecy to destroy Lord Satoris," he said. "We are all pawns in the Shapers' War, Cerelinde. The difference is that some of us know it, and some do not." Something in his heart ached at the naked disbelief on her face. "Forgive me, Lady. I had no intent of troubling you. I thought you would like the garden."

"I do. And I am grateful for a glimpse of sky." She drew Meara's shawl tighter around her shoulders. "Tanaros. I am sorry for your pain, and I do not doubt that you have taken the Sunderer's lies for truths. But Haomane First-Born is chief among Shapers, and I am his child. Your Lord need only bow to His will, and the Sundered World will be made whole. Can you ask me to believe aught else?"

"Yes," Tanaros said helplessly.

Her voice was gentle. "I cannot."

SIXTEEN

❖

DWARFS CAME OUT OF THE gloaming.

It happened a few leagues west of Malumdoorn, the young knight Hobard's ancestral estate. As twilight fell over their kindling campfire, the shadows moved, twining like roots. Four figures, waist-high to a tall man, with gnarled faces and knotted muscles, spatulate hands engrained with soil.

"Yrinna's Children." Malthus the Counselor stood to greet them, bowing in his scholar's robes. "Hail and well met."

"Haomane's Counselor." One of the dwarfs acknowledged him in a deep, calm voice, then turned to Hobard. "Son of Malumdoorn. You have broken Yrinna's Peace, bringing them here."

"I had cause, Earth-Tender."

The Vedasian's voice was strung tight, Carfax noted. He sat quiet with his arms wrapped around his knees, watching with wonder. Dwarfs! Yrinna's Children had not been seen west of Vedasia for long ages.

"It must be a mighty cause to break Yrinna's Peace."

"It is." Malthus took a step forward, touching the Soumanië on his breast. "You have an item in your possession that does not belong to you."

There was a pause then, a long one.

"It may be," the Dwarf leader allowed, his deep-set gaze scanning the small company. "Haomane's Child. Do the Rivenlost venture in search of this thing?"

"We do, Earth-Tender." Peldras the Ellyl bowed, light and graceful. "Will you not hear our plea?"

A hushed conference, then, among the four visitors. Carfax

strained his hearing to no avail. "*Uru-Alat!*" A soft whisper sounded at his ear. "They're so *small!* Are they Men, or children?" It was the boy, Dani, squatting fearless at his side, his dark eyes wide in the firelight. They tell him no more than they do me, Carfax thought, pitying the boy. What was Malthus thinking, to venture into the Unknown and drag the boy from his home, keeping him in ignorance? At least in Darkhaven, one knew the price of one's bargain.

"No," he said. "They are Dwarfs, Dani. A long time ago, they withdrew from the affairs of Men."

One dark hand rose to clasp the flask at his throat, dark eyes bewildered. "What is it Malthus thinks they have?"

"I don't know." He wished he did.

A decision was made, and the Dwarf leader stepped forward. "There will be a hearing on the morrow," he said. "In the orchards of Malumdoorn. Come in peace, or not at all."

"It will be so," Malthus said with dignity.

NIGHT.

It fell hard and fast in the swamps of the Delta. Turin hurried after the fleeting form of Hunric the tracker, falling and splashing and cursing his speed. Before them, the hummock of dry land loomed, elusive and retreating in the fading light. A last, dying spear of light lit the palodus tree that stood sentry over it.

"Come on!" Hunric shouted, scrambling up the hummock ahead of him, the slow-lizard's carcass tied to a string about his waist. "Come *on!*"

Waist-deep in water at the foot of the hummock, Turin set his teeth and grabbed for a handhold. Shale rock, plates as broad as both his hands, slick and overgrown with moss. There would be nothing edible growing on this island. By main force he hauled himself, hand over hand, up the steep incline, his breath searing his lungs.

At the top, he bent double, panting.

"Look!" Hunric was grinning, arms open wide. "The heart of the Delta. Is it not a glorious thing?"

Turin could have wept.

There was nothing, nothing atop the hummock, only moss-covered black shale in articulated ridges that hurt his sodden feet, and a few fallen branches of palodus wood. He was tired and soaked and footsore, and his loins ached with gnawing desire.

"A freshwater spring would have been nice," he said wearily, sitting down and removing his pack, beginning the tiresome process of peeling off his boots. "You're sure this is the way *out?*"

"The way in is the way out." The tracker eyed him, then began gathering branches. "You're done in. Sit, then. I'll do it."

He sat, rubbing his aching feet. No need for a fire, really. The shale was warm, retaining the sun's heat like a forge. He could almost smell the sulfur. It would be nice, though, to have fresh-roasted meat, even if the kill was a day old. Meat went off fast in the heat; no wonder Hunric was minded to eat it raw.

So warm, here. So warm.

It made his aching flesh prickle.

"This is his place." At the crest of the hummock, Hunric had stacked branches into a neat structure and knelt reverently over them. "*His* place!" he repeated fervently, striking a spark and blowing. An ember kindled, tiny flames flickering.

"His place," Turin echoed dully. In the dark swamp beyond, an ember of yellow-green kindled. "And tomorrow, we head straight for Pelmar, yes?"

"Pelmar." Hunric, kneeling, grinned at him. "Oh, yes."

Something in the air throbbed, echoing the throbbing in his loins. He thought again of the white limbs of the Lady of the Ellylon, gritted his teeth and thrust the thought from his mind. In the air? No. It was the very rock beneath him that throbbed, slow and steady, warm as a pulsing heart.

An ember of yellow-green, lifting.

"Hunric." His voice was frozen in his throat. "Hunric!" A shape, moving, impossibly large. Roots ripped, dripping, from the swamp itself. Slow, so slow! An ember of yellow-green. A lidded eye, a dripping chin. "Hunric . . ." he whispered.

"What?" The tracker sounded almost friendly as he gauged the coals, skewering the slow-lizard and thrusting it into the flames. "Pelmar, yes. I remember. We'll leave on the morrow. Is that what troubles you?"

Unable to speak, Turin pointed.

"*What?*" The tracker squinted into the swamp.

When it struck, it moved fast. A wedge of darkness blotting out the emerging stars, swinging on a sinuous neck. Its hinged jaws opened wide, rows of teeth glistening like ivory daggers. The ground beneath Turin *lurched,* surging with the motion of the strike as, somewhere in the swamp, anchored talons gripped and heaved. He saw the lidded eye as it swung past him, the open maw snapping.

A strangled sound cut short, and the embers of the campfire scattered.

Hunric.

Turin gibbered with fear, scuttling backward crab-wise. Plates of shale beneath his hands and feet, the edges cutting his flesh. Not shale, no; *scales,* ancient and encrusted, dark as iron. Before him, the long neck stretched high, lifting the massive head to the top of the palodus tree while the throat worked in gulps.

It didn't take long. Not long enough.

"Please," Turin whispered as the terrible head swung back his way, arching over its own back, bearded and dripping with moss. "Oh, *please!*"

A nictitating lid blinked over the yellow-green eye. "Who assssksss?"

"Turin of Staccia." His voice emerged in a squeak. "I am here in the service of Lord Satoris."

"Sssatorisss . . ."

"Third-Born among Shapers." Summoning a reserve of courage he hadn't known he possessed, Turin found his feet, confronting the hovering head, fighting his chattering teeth. "This is his place, Lord Dragon, and he sent me here!"

"Yessss." The yellow-green eye blinked. "Your companion was . . . tassssssty."

"Lord Dragon!" Terror threatened to loosen his bowels. "My Lord was a friend to your kind!"

"A friend," the dragon mused. "Yesss, onssse."

"Once, and always." Breathing hard, Turin wrestled his sword free of his pack and held it aloft. Its steel length glinted greenish in the light of the dragon's eye. "I carry a message for the Sorceress of the East and the Dragon of Beshtanag. Will you not let me pass?"

"I grieve for my brother." There was something resembling sorrow in the dragon's fearful mien. "He has chosen his path. There is power in thissss plassse, Sson of Man. It might even have healed Sssatoriss the Ssssower, onssse, but Haomane's Wrath ssscorched his thoughtss to madnesss, and he fled north to the cooling sssnows. It is too late for the Sssower. Now this is *my* plassse, and I mussst abide."

"Who are you?" Turin whispered.

"Calanthrag," the answer was hissed. "The Eldessst."

Swift came the attack, the massive head darting. Turin dodged once, striking with his sword, aiming for the glinting eye. He missed, his blade clattering against impervious scales. This, he thought in an ecstasy of terror, is the end. The dragon's head reared back and swayed atop its sinuous neck, blocking out the sky. Turin's hand loosened on his sword-hilt. He stood on a dragon back, feeling the warmth under his bare, lacerated soles, and thought of the vows he had taken, the women he had known. A smell of rot hung in the air. The dragon's eye roiled, yellow-green. Old, so old!

Older than the Delta.

There were things he knew before the end, Turin of Staccia, things he read in the dragon's roiling eye. Of a knowledge older than Time itself, older than the Chain of Being. Of the birth of dragons, born of the bones of Uru-Alat; first-born, Eldest. Of warring Shapers, and how they had Sundered the earth. Of their Children and their wars, their endless hierarchies and vengeances. Of Lord Satoris, who spoke to dragons; of dragons, who aided him. Of dragons dying by steel borne by Haomane's Children, by Arahila's. Of Calanthrag the Eldest, hidden in the Delta.

All these things, and the whole more than the sum of its parts. This was the knowledge vouchsafed to Turin of Staccia, whose yellow hair was caked with mud, who stood barefooted on a dragon's back, with a useless sword in his limp hand, bannock-crumbs and gold coins at the bottom of his pack.

He was a long way from home.

Oh mother! he thought at the last.

It was fast, the dragon's head striking like a snake, low and sure and swift. Massive jaws stretched wide, breathing sulfur fumes. A snap! A gulp and a swallow, the impossibly long gullet working, neck stretched skyward. In the swamp of the Delta, the tall palodus tree stood unmoving, while small creatures keened in distress.

Inch by inch, Calanthrag the Eldest settled.

An insect chirruped.

Stillness settled over the Delta, ordinary stillness. Lizards crept, and snakes stirred their coils. Gnats whined, protesting the fall of darkness. A dragon's talons relaxed their purchase in the mire. Straining wings eased their vanes. A long neck settled, chin sinking into muck. Membranes closed over glowing eyes to the lullaby of the Delta. In the moonlight, a hummock, black as slate, encrusted with moss, loomed above the swamp.

Calanthrag the Eldest slept.

GREEN. GREEN AND GREEN AND green.

It whirled in the Ravensmirror, reflected in the sheen of glimmering feathers. Green leaves, palodus and mangrove, a dense canopy. Dark green, pine green, the forests of Pelmar. Softer green, new vines and cedars, wings veering in fear from Vedasia, where death lurked, arrow-tipped.

"ENOUGH!"

Ushahin Dreamspinner pressed his fingertips to his crooked temples, his head aching at Lord Satoris' roar.

The Ravensmirror shattered, bursting into feathered bits, heads tucked under wings in fearful disarray.

Back and forth he stormed, red eyes glowing like coals. The tower trembled beneath his tread. A smell in the air like blood, only sweeter. "What," Lord Satoris asked with deceptive gentleness, "is Malthus *doing?*"

"I don't know, my Lord," Ushahin whispered.

"My Lord." Tanaros executed a crisp bow. "Whatever the Counselor attempts, it matters naught. Our plans proceed apace, and your army stands in readiness. Our course through the Marasoumië is plotted, and Lord Vorax has seen to our lines of supply. Haomane's Allies walk into a trap unwitting. We are prepared."

The glowing red gaze slewed his way. "I mislike it."

"My Lord." Ushahin cleared his throat. "There is one way."

"What?"

He flinched under the Shaper's regard. "Ask the Ellyl. Put her to questioning. I cannot breach Malthus' defenses, my Lord. I have tried. It may be she knows his plans."

Tanaros shifted, disturbed.

"No." The Shaper shook his head. Deep in their throats, ravens muttered. "I am a Shaper, one of the Seven. Let my Elder Brother name me what he will; I will not play into his hands by accepting the role he has allotted me. He holds his pride dearer than I, yet I am not without honor. Would you see it stripped from me? My Elder Brother has made a move, and I have countered it. I will not become the monster he has named me."

Frustration surfaced in Ushahin's crooked gaze. "It is better to live a monster than to die with honor, my Lord!"

"No." There was finality in Lord Satoris' deep voice. "She is a guest, Dreamspinner, and to be treated as such. I will not allow aught else."

"My Lord . . ."

"I said no."

SEVENTEEN

❖

SUNLIGHT SLANTED THROUGH THE APPLE trees in the orchards of Malumdoorn.

It was an unlikely setting for a meeting of such moment. Carfax only wished he knew what it was about. The Dwarfs had assembled en masse, awaiting them, standing in wary ranks amid the gnarled apple trees.

Hobard, they greeted with respect, giving evidence of a long-standing agreement between their folk and the scions of Malumdoorn. The surly young knight glowed at the attention, in his element.

Yrinna's Peace, Carfax thought. It was the bargain the Dwarfs had made, taking no part in the battles that divided the Lesser Shapers. Eschewing Lord Satoris' Gift, they were parsimonious with carnal pleasure, and bore only enough children to ensure their own continuance. In turn, they asked only the freedom to tend the land, making it fruitful as Yrinna Sixth-Born had willed it.

This was the bargain old Vedasian families such as Hobard's had struck, offering protection and noninterference for the goodwill of Yrinna's Children, who made their orchards fruitful.

What now threatened it?

"Earth-Tenders." Malthus' voice was soft and soothing: he spread his arms, indicating he held naught but his staff. "You know who I am. And you know what I have come for."

The Dwarfs murmured, a low sound like the wind through apple leaves.

"We know." A Dwarf elder stumped forward, thrusting out his

stubborn chin. Tangled beard, aggressive eyes, honest dirt in-grained in his hands. "You bring war, Counselor. You breach Yrinna's Peace. Why? Why should we heed you?"

"Because Satoris Banewreaker will hold sway over the whole of Urulat if you do not," Malthus said steadily. "Is that your wish, Earth-Tender Haldol? To see the soil of Yrinna's bosom poisoned with his dripping venom? It shall come to pass, and no seed may grow untainted, no blossom bear fruit."

It was not true. In the long years that Staccia had held an alle-giance with Lord Satoris, its lands had come to no harm. His Lord-ship sought only to live unmolested by Haomane's Wrath. Carfax opened his mouth in protest, found his tongue hopelessly stilled, useless as a dried root. Bright sparks burned in the Elder Haldol's eyes, doubt nurtured by the Counselor.

"We do not take part in the Shapers' War," the Dwarf said.

"Oh, but you do." Malthus the Counselor's voice was soft, sweet and cunning. "Yrinna's Children deny it, yes. But you have withheld that which is not yours, and so doing, you aid the Enemy. Our greatest Enemy, he who would scorch the earth."

"So you say." The Dwarf Elder rubbed his chin. "So you say. We have a test, Counselor, for those who would claim Yrinna's fa-vor. Is your Company willing to attempt the Greening?"

"It is," Malthus said steadily.

There was a stirring among the Dwarfs, a parting of the ranks. From the rear of the gathering, two approached, bearing an object with reverence. Male and female, they were, gnarled as roots, with eyes that shone at the sanctity of their office. Carfax craned his head to see what they carried.

A staff, like unto Malthus' own, but untrimmed—a dead branch wrenched whole from the tree. Twigs it sprouted, and a few desic-cated leaves, shriveled and brown. Haldol the Elder received it with both hands, raised it to touch his lips to the rough bark before planting it like a spear in the orchard soil of Malumdoorn, driving the butt-end into the earth.

It stood like a standard, brittle and ash-grey.

"The challenge of the Greening is begun," said Haldol.

"So mote it be." Malthus bowed his head and grasped the Soumanië.

"*No.*" The Dwarf's voice was sharp. "You are Haomane's weapon, Counselor, and bear his tools. What the Souma may ac-complish, we know too well. It is Yrinna's will the Greening seeks to divine. We shall choose among your Company who shall attempt it." His deepset gaze roamed over the Company. "You," he said abruptly, pointing a thick finger at Dani. "The least among them. Let us see if Yrinna favors *you*."

"Earth-Tender—" Malthus glowered, the Soumanië flickering.

"It is as it shall be." The Dwarf Haldol crossed his arms, backed by his people. "Do you gainsay it, Counselor? Son of Malumdoorn, what say you, who brought them here?"

Hobard of Malumdoorn cast a bitter sidelong glance at the young Yarru-yami. "Malthus, I came in faith to Meronil to bring you these tidings, but as I am Vedasian, my sworn oaths are to Yrinna's Children. I abide by their demands. You drove us into the Unknown to secure the Charred lad, risking all our lives to find him. Let him answer for it, if it is their will."

Ranked behind the dead branch thrust like a challenge into the earth, the Dwarfs waited. Malthus' Company shifted, awaiting the Counselor's decision. Carfax watched them all. Blaise Caveros was tense, small muscles moving along his clenched jaw. The Ellyl, Peldras, was at once watchful and tranquil. There was hunger in the eyes of Fianna the Archer, desperate and keen.

Why, Carfax wondered?

As for the Yarru, they whispered together, fat uncle Thulu bending his head to the boy's ear, lips moving. What was he saying? Why was the boy smiling? Did he not realize, Carfax thought in frustration, he was naught but a pawn?

"*So be it!*" Malthus' voice cracked like thunder, then softened. "Dani. Try. You can but try, lad."

That he did, Dani of the Yarru, earnest of face, approaching the dead branch in all seriousness. He reminded Carfax, unexpectedly, of Turin, the young Staccian in his command. He'd taken his duties thus seriously, Turin had, given the difficult task of impersonating an Ellyl maiden. It had galled him to be left out of their ill-fated attack on the Company of Malthus. Remembering the barrows of grass where his comrades had fallen, Carfax was glad he'd spared the lad. He wondered if the young Staccian and his two companions had made it safely to Beshtanag, and hoped they had. In the silence of his locked tongue Carfax hoped, very much, that Lord Satoris' plans were uncompromised.

Dani squatted before the branch, laying hands upon it.

Pale and weathered and grey, the dead wood; the boy's palms were pale too, lined and weathered. He cupped them together, and the radiating lines met to form a star in the hollow of his palms. He bowed his ragged head as if listening, and his uncle, his fat uncle, chanted low under his breath, grinning. Blaise raised an eyebrow. The Archer bit her lip. In the orchard, with the sweet smell of sun-warmed apples in the air, the Dwarfs gathered close, watching.

Dani uncorked the vial at his neck.

One drop; one drop of water he let gather at the lip of the vial. One drop. And it smelled—*oh, Shapers!* Carfax inhaled deeply, unable to help himself. It smelled . . . like water. Like life, dense and condensed, mineral-rich. It swelled, gathering roundness, shining bright as steel. Swelled, rounded . . .

. . . dropped.

Greenness, dizzying and sudden, as the earth rang like a struck bell. Urgent leaves burst from the dead wood, a riot of green. Twigs sprouted and grew buds, blossoms opened, releasing sweet fragrance. Pierced by plunging roots, the very soil buckled, even as the branch thickened into a sapling's trunk.

"Aiee!" Dani leapt back, wide-eyed, clutching his flask. "I did that?"

"You did." Malthus smiled, laying a hand on the little Yarru-yami's shoulder. There was approval in his grave features, and at his breast, the Soumanië lay quiescent and dark; a red gem, nothing more. "You did, Dani."

Gazing at the tree, the assembled Dwarfs murmured in awe.

"The Water of Life," the Elder Haldol said. "That is what he carries."

"Yes." Malthus inclined his head, one hand still resting on Dani's shoulder. "The lifeblood of Uru-Alat. He is the Bearer. Has he met your challenge, Earth-Tender?"

In the silence that followed, Haldol of the Dwarfs sighed, and the weight of the world was in that sigh, his broad, sturdy shoulders slumping. "Yrinna's Peace is ended," he whispered, then straightened, a terrible dignity in his features. "So be it. Counselor, that which you sought shall be yours."

"It was not yours to keep, Elder," Malthus said gently.

"No." The Dwarf lifted his chin and met his gaze. "But we kept it well, Wise Counselor. It has never been used, for unlike other of Haomane's weapons, it may be used only once, and the Counselor Dergail held his hand. I pray you use it well."

A bright spark wove its way through the ranks of Dwarfs, who shrank at its passage. One more came, wizened and old, eyes closed against the brightness he bore. Even in daylight, it trailed flame. Fianna the Archer stepped forward, her mouth forming a soundless O, hands reaching unthinking.

"Behold," Haldol said. "Oronin's Bow, and the Arrow of Fire."

"They are yours," Malthus said to the Archer.

Her hand closed on the haft of the bow; black horn, with an immense draw. Kneeling, she set the bottom tip, fingers curling, seeking the string unthinking and drawing it to her cheek. A shaft of white fire tinged with gold, the Arrow flamed, illuminating her cheek, the tendrils of hair curling at her temple. "Oh," she said, her tone amazed. "Oh!"

Carfax, watching, shivered to the bone.

When the unknown is made known, when the lost weapon is found . . .

The Prophecy was being fulfilled.

BESIDE THE SWELTERING FURNACE, THE flow of the Gorgantus River, diverted by Lord Satoris himself, powered a wooden waterwheel. From it led a welter of rods and cranks, turning and clanking. Levered weights rose and fell, pressing down on the springboards that powered the bellows, which opened and closed on their leather hinges, blowing strong drafts. Teams of Fjeltroll worked steadily, feeding coal and ore into the endless maw of the furnace.

It was hotter than before, so hot Tanaros could feel the skin of his face tightening. And the metal that emerged was glowing and molten, pure iron, collected in molds to cool. No longer did the Fjel need to beat the impurities from it before it was fit for the forge.

"You see?" Speros, soot-darkened, was grinning. He shouted above the clamor of the smelting furnace. "We use the force of the river to drive the bellows, providing more heat than even the Fjel can muster!"

"I see." Tanaros had to raise his own voice to be heard. "A commendable innovation! Is it done thus in the Midlands now?"

"No." Speros shrugged, his restless gaze surveying his efforts. "Only to grind grain, but I thought it might serve. No one ever gave me the means to try it, before. I reckon it will help. No small task, to equip such an army." He settled his gaze on Tanaros. "We *are* going to war, are we not, Lord General?"

"Yes." Tanaros beckoned, leading him a distance from the furnace. Outside, the grass was parched and a reeking cloud of smoke and sulfurous gases hung heavy under the lowering sky, but at least the air did not sear his lungs. "Some of us are, Midlander."

"I want to ride with you," Speros of Haimhault said, direct and sure. "You promised me a horse; one such as *you* ride, General. Have I not done all I promised, and more?"

Of a surety, the lad had done so. His innovations had increased productivity. With the aid of his waterwheel, the forges of Darkhaven smelted iron at twice their usual rate. This was the first chance Tanaros had had to inspect them, but it was said Lord Satoris himself was pleased.

"Aye." Tanaros ignored his own misgivings, clapping a hand to the young man's shoulder. "You have. You'll have your mount, boy, and your place in the ranks."

Speros smiled with fierce, unadulterated joy.

It was not that his trust had proved ill-placed, for it had not. In a short time, Speros of Haimhault had proven himself in Darkhaven. The Fjel trusted him. Hyrgolf spoke well of him, and Tanaros valued his field marshal's opinion above all others. The young man's energies and ambitions, that had found too narrow an outlet in the Midlands, flourished in Darkhaven. He bore no resentment for the harsh treatment he had received at the outset, reckoning it worth the price. Against his better judgement, Tanaros liked the young man.

That was the problem.

How long had it been since Tanaros had donned the Helm of Shadows and led the forces that destroyed Altoria? Eight hundred years, perhaps. Even so, he had not forgotten how, beneath the blaze of hatred in his heart, there had been a twinge of sorrow. For as much as he had been wounded and betrayed, hated and hounded, they had been his people. And he had destroyed them, bringing down a realm and reducing a dynasty to a shade of its former self.

"You may have kin among the enemy, you know," he told Speros. "It may be a cousin or a brother you face in battle. And this war will not be one such as the poets sing. We fall upon them from behind, and allow no quarter until the threat is eliminated. There is no glory in it."

Regarding his furnace with pride, the Midlander shrugged. "You have outwitted them, General. Is that not glory enough?"

"We do not do this for glory. Only for victory."

"Victory." Speros ran a hand through his brown hair, sooty and disheveled. "A Sundered World in which Lord Satoris reigns victorious. What will happen then?"

"Then," Tanaros said slowly, fingering the *rhios* in his pocket, "it may be that the Six Shapers will capitulate and make peace. Or it may be that they will not. Either way, Urulat will be in Lord Satoris' possession, as will Godslayer and two of the three Soumanië. And it may be that the third, Dergail's Soumanië, is not beyond reach."

Speros' eager, indrawn breath hissed between his teeth, and his eyes glowed at the possibilities. "With those things, he could challenge Haomane himself!"

"Yes," Tanaros said. "He could."

"And if he won?" Speros asked. "Would he slay the Six?"

"No." Tanaros shook his head. "I think not. He loved his sister Arahila well, once; I believe he loves her still. Though she sided with Haomane against him, it was she who stayed the Lord-of-Thought's hand when his Wrath scorched the earth, and she who raised the red star in warning. Lord Satoris cares for his honor. It may be that she would persuade him to mercy."

Speros glanced westward. "What manner of world do you suppose his Lordship would Shape?"

"Only his Lordship knows for certain," Tanaros said. "Yet I imagine a world in which the tyranny of one Shaper's will did not hold sway over all. And that," he added, "is enough for me."

"It's a beginning," Speros agreed. He looked curiously at Tanaros. "What would you do in such a world, Lord General?"

Unaccountably, Tanaros pictured Cerelinde's face. "I don't know," he murmured. "Yet I would like to find out. Perhaps I would become a better Man than I have been in this one." He gathered himself with a shake, ignoring the Midlander's quizzical expression. "Come on, lad. Let's choose a horse for you."

Perplexity gave way to a grin. "Aye, General!"

In the Chamber of the Font, the marrow-fire burned unceasing, a column of blue-white flame rising from its pit, so bright it hurt the eye. And in the center the shard of Godslayer hung, pulsing like a heart to an unseen rhythm.

"My Lord." Cerelinde of the Ellylon clasped her hands in front of her to hide their trembling. Valiant as she was, the fear came upon her every time the tapestry in her quarters twitched at the opening of the secret door, a wary madling emerging to beckon her through the winding passages behind the walls to the three-fold door and the spiral stair, to answer the summons of the Lord of Darkhaven. "You sent for me?"

"Yes." The Shaper's voice was gentle. He moved in the shadows at the outskirts of the room, his massive figure blending into darkness. Only the red, glowing eyes showed clearly. "Be at your ease, Lady."

Cerelinde sat in the chair he indicated, stiff-backed and fearful.

His deep laugh rumbled. "You have been my guest these weeks now. Do you still think I mean you harm?"

"You hold me against my will." She fixed her gaze on the beating heart of Godslayer within the marrow-fire. "Is that not harm, my Lord?"

"Will," Satoris mused, and the stones of Darkhaven shivered under his mighty, soundless tread. A reek of ichor in the air grew stronger at his approach, sweet and coppery. "What do you know of will, little Ellyl?"

"I know it is mine to defy you." The words came hard, harder than she could have imagined. It was hard, in this place, to cling to all that she knew was true.

Fingers brushed her hair. "What if I offered you a kingdom?"

Closing her eyes, Cerelinde shuddered at the touch of a Shaper's power. With Godslayer to hand, he could remake her very flesh if he willed it. "You would not, my Lord Sunderer," she said. "While I live, I am a threat to you, and I do not believe that you will let me live for long, let alone offer me power. I am not a fool, my Lord. I have made my peace with it. I am not afraid to die."

"No." The Shaper withdrew, his voice contemptuous. "Only to *live*. Will you cling to this Prophecy with which my brother Haomane Shapes the world? I tell you this: You are not the only one, you know, daughter of Erilonde."

"What?" Cerelinde opened her eyes. "*What* do you say?"

"Oh, yes." Lord Satoris smiled, a fearful thing. "Elterrion the Bold had a second daughter, gotten of an illicit union. Somewhere among the Rivenlost, your line continues. Do you suppose such things never happen among the Ellylon?"

"They do not." Cerelinde drew herself up taut.

"They do upon very rare occasion." The Shaper's eyes glittered with red malice. "It is a pity your people dare not acknowledge it, Lady. The weight of the world might not rest upon your shoulders if they did."

"You lie," Cerelinde whispered.

Lord Satoris shrugged, the movement disturbing the shadows. "More seldom than you might imagine, Lady," he said, regret in his tone. "These things lie within the purview of the Gift that was mine, and they are mine alone to know. Although the Ellylon themselves do not know it, I tell you: There is another."

"Who?" Cerelinde leaned forward, forgetting herself. "*Who, my Lord?*"

He eyed her, slow and thoughtful. "I will tell you, in exchange for knowledge freely given. The Three would see you put to questioning. I, I merely ask, Lady. What is the purpose of Malthus the Counselor?"

He would ask that; he *would*. Cerelinde hid her face in her hands, wishing she knew the answer. Whether she gave it or not, at least it would be a bargaining chip. With a bitter sense of irony, she remembered Aracus' words in Lindanen Dale. *It is for a short time only, my lady. Malthus knows what he is about.* She wondered if the Wise Counselor had known what would befall her, and prayed it were not so. It was too cruel to contemplate.

Surely, Aracus had not.

"I don't know," she murmured through her fingers. "I don't."

Satoris waited until she raised her head to look at him. Reading the truth written in her face, he nodded once. "I told them as much. Very well, you may go. We will speak anon, Lady."

"All three?" Cerelinde swallowed. "All of the Three would see me questioned?"

For a long time, he did not answer. The marrow-fire burned soundless, shedding brightness throughout the Chamber of the Font; in its midst, Godslayer hung like a suspended wail, pulsing. Darkness gathered around the Shaper like stormclouds and his eyes sparked a slow, inexorable red.

"No," he said at last. "Not all. Not Tanaros."

It gladdened her heart to hear it in a manner that filled her with uneasiness. How far had she fallen, how deeply had this touched her, that the kindness of Tanaros Kingslayer could make her glad? The Sunderer's lies undermined the foundation of her certainty. Could there be another capable of bringing the Prophecy to fruition, another daughter of the House of Elterrion? Malthus kept his counsel close . . .

No. No. To believe as much was to open a door onto despair. Satoris Banewreaker was the Prince of Lies, and behind the courtly courtesies General Tanaros extended was a man who had throttled his wife and slain his sovereign. There were no other truths that mattered.

In the garden, a mortexigus flower shivered untouched and loosed its pollen.

Oh, Aracus! Cerelinde thought in despair. *I need you!*

EIGHTEEN

❖

THANKS TO MERONIN FIFTH-BORN, Lord of the Seas, the winds blew fair from Port Eurus and Haomane's Allies arrived safe on Pelmaran soil, where they were met by a deposition from Regent Martinek. Borderguard, Seaholders, Midlanders and Vedasians, not to mention the Host of the Ellylon—it was a difficult thing, establishing preeminence among them.

Out of necessity, all bowed to the Pelmaran regent.

"We need him," shrewd Duke Bornin murmured to Aracus Altorus. "We need all of them, else we will not prevail against the Sorceress."

So it was that Aracus, the last scion of House Altorus and king-in-exile of the West, bent his red-gold head in courteous acknowledgment, and all who followed him followed suit save only the Rivenlost, those of the Host of the Ellylon, who held themselves second in stature to none of the Lesser Shapers.

"Right." Martinek's captain, whose name was Rikard, rode up and down the lists, surveying them with a keen eye. "We're bound for Kranac, then. Is there anyone among you who has trouble acknowledging his honor's sovereignty in the third district of Pelmar?"

He halted his mount before Aracus Altorus, raising dark brows.

"Captain." Aracus' voice was steady. "I am here for one reason only: To assure the safe return of my Lady Cerelinde. All else is naught to me."

"And you?" Rikard paused before Lorenlasse of Valmaré, who commanded the Host of the Ellylon. "What of you, my fine Ellyl lord?"

Now the Ellyl did bow, and the gesture was smooth and dismissive, the gilded bee of his House gleaming at the closure of his cloak, its wings wrought of purest crystal. His arms were immaculate, his face beautiful and impassive. Only his luminous eyes gave evidence of his passion, keen and glittering. "We follow Aracus Altorus, Captain. Our kinswoman and his bride has been lost. All else is as naught."

Rikard grunted. "See that it is so." Raising one arm, he summoned the Regent Martinek's forces, scores of Pelmarans in leather armor augmented with steel rings, keen and ready. "You hear it, lads! We ride to Kranac! The Sorceress' days are numbered!"

Out of port they rode, and into the dark forests of Pelmar.

It was a swift ship.

If he'd had to guess, Carfax would not have supposed the Dwarfs would make good seafarers. He would have been wrong. It was choice, and not necessity, that kept them primarily land-bound.

Their ship sailed from Dwarfhorn, making good time under a steady wind. The crew was polite and competent, unapologetic for the inconveniences of tall folk on a Dwarf ship. Whatever it was that had transpired with the Greening of the branch in the orchards of Malumdoorn, it had won the aid of Yrinna's Children, if not their goodwill.

Most of Malthus' Company spent their time belowdecks, closeted in close council. For the nonce, Carfax was forgotten, reckoned harmless. Only Malthus' binding held him, circumferencing his mind even as it loosened his tongue.

Fat Thulu stood in the prow, holding his digging-stick and keening exuberant songs. It got on Carfax's nerves.

"What does he *do?*" he snapped at Dani.

"He charts the ways." The young Yarru was surprised. "The ways of water, fresh water, as it flows beneath the sea's floor. Do your people not do the same?"

"No, they don't." Carfax thought of home, of Staccia, where the leaping rivers of Neheris ran silver-bright and a thousand blue lakes reflected the summer sky. No need, there, to chart abundance. "Dani, why are you here?"

"To save the world." Gravely, Dani touched the flask at his throat. "It is necessary. Malthus said so."

"He said so." Carfax regarded him. "Then why does he not invite you belowdecks, to take part in his counsel? Why does he withhold his plan from you?"

There was doubt in the boy's eyes, a faint shadow of it. "He says there are things it is better I do not know. That a choice comes I must make untainted. Malthus is one of the Wise, Carfax. Even my elders said so. He would not lie to me. I must trust him."

"Oh, Dani!" He laughed; he couldn't help it. Bitter laughter, bitter tears. Carfax wiped his stinging eyes. "Oh, Dani, do you think so? Malthus uses you, boy; uses you unwitting. This water—" Reaching out, he grasped the flask threaded around the boy's neck and found it heavy, impossibly heavy, wrenching his wrist and driving him to his knees on the planked deck. "Dani!"

"Let it go!" Hobard of Malumdoorn strode across the deck to strike his hand away, lip curling. "Have you learned nothing, Staccian?"

"Oh, but I have." Cradling his aching hand, Carfax looked from one to the other. "It's the Water of Life the boy bears, isn't it? And no one else can carry it." Laughing and hiccoughing, he fought to catch his breath. "Why else would you bring him?" he gasped. "What virtues does it have, I wonder? No, no, let me guess!"

A dark shadow loomed over the deck.

"Staccian," a deep, accented voice rumbled.

Craning his neck, Carfax saw fat Thulu's face blotting out the sun, his broad belly casting shade. One large hand clasped his digging-stick, and sweat glistened oily on his wide nose. "You." Carfax pointed at him. "You're just here on sufferance, aren't you? A package deal, your presence endured for the boy's cooperation. You're a laughingstock, fat one! The Wise would sooner invite a donkey into their counsels than you!"

"It may be," Thulu said calmly, squatting on his massive hams.

Carfax stared at him. Throwing up his hands in disgust, Hobard of Malumdoorn stalked away. The Dwarf crew whispered and shrugged among themselves, going about their business with disinterested competence. Dani hovered behind his uncle's shoulder, a frown of concentration on his brow. "And you don't care?" Carfax said at last. "You don't *care* that they disdain you? You don't care, in all their wisdom, that they may be *wrong?*"

"Does it matter?" Propping chin on fist, Thulu regarded him. "There is wisdom, and there is wisdom. Dani is the Bearer, and his choice is his own. I am here to safeguard it. That is all."

Sunlight glinted dully on the clay flask that hung about the boy's neck.

Water.

It was the Water of Life, and it could make a dead branch burst into green leaf like a sapling. What else could it do?

When the unknown is made known, when the lost weapon is found, when the marrow-fire is quenched . . .

Ushahin! Dreamspinner! Alone and untutored in the ways of magic, Carfax flung his desperate thoughts out onto the wind. Encountering the circumference of Malthus' will, his call rebounded, echoing in his aching skull like thunder in an empty gorge, only the seagulls answering with raucous, hollow cries.

Huddled on the deck, he clutched his head and wept.

SORCERESS.

A whisper of thought along the ancient Ways of the Marasoumië.

Lilias waited in the cavern, composed and steady, watching the node-light surge, fitful and red, answering pulses traveling eastward along the branching Ways. One was coming, one of the Branded.

This time, she was ready.

Beshtanag was ready.

A wall of stone encompassed the mountain's base; granite, seamless and polished. And though she was exhausted in limb and spirit, the wall stood. Only the narrowest gap remained, and the raw stone was heaped in piles, awaiting her mind's touch to close the gap. The cisterns were full, the storerooms stocked.

There came a figure, blurred—lurching, uneven, an impression of limbs frozen in motion, too swift across Time to register; of pale, shining hair and mismatched eyes. A crooked grimace, caught redly in the node-light's sudden flare.

"Dreamer." Lilias inclined her head.

"Sorceress." For all his body was damaged, he emerged from the Ways with an odd, hunch-shouldered grace, inclining his head. When all was said and done, although he spoke Pelmaran with an accent undistinguishable from her own, he was still half-Ellyl. "I bring you greetings from Darkhaven."

"Is there news?" Raising her brows, she felt the weight of the Soumanië.

"Yes, and no." Ushahin drew a deep breath. "Lady, let us confer."

He followed her through the tunnels into the fasthold of Beshtanag, into the rose-and-amber luxury of her drawing-room, where Sarika knelt waiting to serve them. He spared one glance at the girl, and took sparingly of the offered refreshments.

"The Ways do not tax you as they do the General," Lilias observed.

"No." Ushahin took a sip of water, cool from the cistern. "Tanaros wields a mighty sword, and a mighty command of battle. I have . . . other skills. It is why I am here. Lady Sorceress, what news of Haomane's Allies?"

"They converge upon Kranac." Nervous, Lilias ran a finger underneath Sarika's collar of Beshtanagi silver, wrought in fine links, felt the girl lean adoringly against her knee, offering her soft throat. Calandor had showed her how to bind them to the Soumanië, to her will. "Is that not in accordance with your Lordship's plan?"

"Yes." The half-breed's eyes uneven pupils shone. "What of *Malthus?*"

"Malthus the Counselor?" Lilias blinked. "There is no news. Why?"

The Dreamer turned his head, considering the unused spinning-wheel collecting dust in the corner. "Because I have no news of him either," he said softly. "Sorceress, is Beshtanag ready for assault?"

"It is," Lilias said grimly, straightening. "Do you say the plan has changed?"

"No." After a pause, Ushahin shook his head with a susurrus of shimmering hair. "No," he said, strongly. "I leave you to travel the Ways to Jakar, on the outskirts of Pelmar. There, where the forest of Pelmar abuts the Unknown Desert, is a node, a portal of the Marasoumië. There, two units of mounted Rukhari tribesmen await the arrival of our troops. Lord Vorax has sworn it is so. Do you doubt?"

"No," Lilias whispered, asking silently, *Calandor?*

It is so, Lilias, the dragon affirmed.

"Good," Ushahin said. "There, in Jakar, I will open the portal of the Marasoumië—open it, and hold it. In Darkhaven, Lord Vorax will hold open the other end, and General Tanaros will bring the army through the Ways."

"Can this be done?" she asked him.

"Yes." He gave her a twisted smile. "Not without strain. But with Lord Satoris' aid, Vorax and I will bear the cost of it. Tanaros and his army will be untouched by it. In Jakar, they will rally and prepare to fall on the rearguard of Haomane's Allies."

Lilias looked away. "Jakar is far from Beshtanag, Dreamer. Too far."

The half-breed shrugged. "It is far enough to be safe, Lady.

There is nowhere within the boundaries of Pelmar that the army of Darkhaven can assemble unseen, and it is the element of surprise that assures our victory."

"It seems to me it would be a considerable surprise for Haomane's Allies to find them *here,*" Lilias said in a dry tone. "There is, after all, a node of the Marasoumië here in Beshtanag."

"Yes." Ushahin looked at her with something like regret. "There is. And there is a wall to pen us in Beshtanag, and the forest of Pelmar dense around it. A trap must close at both ends, Lady. If we awaited them here, we would have no means of surrounding them, nor of sealing the avenue of their retreat. Do not fear. Jakar is near enough, and General Tanaros' army is capable of traveling at great speed. The path they follow will already have been blazed by the enemy. It will take three days, no more."

She bit her lip. Yesterday, one of the Were Brethren had come—a grey shadow of a yearling, thin-shanked and wary, making his report as the Grey Dam Vashuka had pledged. "Haomane's Allies assemble at Kranac. In five days, they will be here, mounting a siege on Beshtanag." She looked directly at him. "Where will your army be then, Dreamer?"

"On their heels." He returned her gaze unblinking. "One day, or two. Such was the nature of your bargain, Sorceress. Can you hold?"

"What do you think?" Lilias asked grimly. Rising from her cushioned couch, she strode past the kneeling Sarika to the balcony doors, thrusting back the heavy silk curtains that veiled them. "Look and see."

He stepped through the doors and onto the balcony. His crippled fingers rested on the marble railing as he looked down at the mighty wall that encircled Beshtanag Mountain. Gauging by the figures that moved in its shadow, the wall stood three times as high as a tall man. There were no hewn blocks, no mortar—only smooth and polished granite, flecks of mica glinting in the sun.

"Such is the power of the Soumanië?" Ushahin glanced at her.

"Yes."

In daylight, the ravages wrought on his body were more evident. Whatever other gifts the Were possessed, healing was not one. How many bones, Lilias wondered, had been broken? There was a Pelmaran children's counting rhyme that gave the litany, all the way from one left eye-socket to each of his ten fingers. It was told as a heroic act in Pelmar, that beating, a blow struck against the Misbegotten, minion of the Sunderer himself. The stories failed to take into account the fact that it was a child beaten, a child's bones broken. Ill-knit, all of them, from his knotted cheekbone to his skewed torso.

On her brow, the Soumanië flickered into life.

Birds rode the currents of wind above Beshtanag, calling out inconsequential news. Lilias touched the half-breed's arm with her fingertips, watching his knuckles whiten on the railing. It would be easy, so *easy,* to Shape his bones, to straighten what was crooked, smooth what was rough. Easier than Shaping granite, to mold flesh and bone like clay. And he would be beautiful, oh! Prettier than her pretty ones, were he healed.

"Sorceress." Ushahin's mismatched eyes glittered. "Do not think it."

And then he was there, in her thoughts, peeling away her defenses to lay bare her deepest fear—there, alone and defeated, the Soumanië stripped from her brow, leaving her naked and defenseless, *alone.* The Chain of Being reclaimed her, mortality, age sinking its claws into her, withering flesh, wrinkling skin, and at the end of it Oronin the Glad Hunter sounding his horn, for her, for her . . .

"Stop it!" Lilias cried aloud.

"So be it." He turned away, watching the birds soaring on the air. "Leave me my pain, Sorceress, and I will leave you your vanity."

"Is it vanity to cling to life?" she whispered.

The half-breed ignored her and closed his eyes. His long, pale lashes curled like waves against the uneven shoals of his sockets. One of the soaring birds broke loose from its broad spiral, a sturdy-winged raven with a rakish tuft of feathers protruding from his gleaming head. Circling tight, he cawed and chattered at the Dreamer. Frown lines appeared between Ushahin's brows.

"Gulls carry rumors," he said, opening his eyes. "And ravens hear them. Lady, what do you know of a ship sailing from Dwarfhorn?"

Lilias stared at him. "*Dwarfhorn?*"

"I am uneasy." Ushahin made a gesture at the raven, which made a sharp sound and winged off southward, in the direction of the southern coast of Pelmar. "Lady Sorceress, I would speak with the Dragon of Beshtanag."

Calandor? she asked.

Bring him.

She escorted him to the guarded exit at the rear of the fortress, where a doubled guard of ward-soldiers saluted her, eyeing the

Dreamer askance with unconcealed fear. Outside, he did not wait
for her lead, but climbed steadily up the winding mountain path.
Lilias followed, a shadow of fear lying over her thoughts. Ushahin
the Misbegotten, who could walk in the darkest places of the mortal mind. It was said he could drive Men mad with a glance. And
she had thought, in her folly, that he would be less dangerous, less
strange, than Tanaros Kingslayer.

Lilias, little sister.

Ahead on the ledge, a massive brightness shone, bronze scales
gleaming in the sun. Calandor awaited them. At the sight of him,
her heart lifted, the darkness clearing. "Calandor!"

"Liliasss." The dragon bent his sinuous neck so she could press
her cheek to the scale-plated warmth of his. Lifting his head, he
fixed his slitted green stare on the half-breed. "Child of three
rassses, ssson of none. What is it you ssseek?"

Ushahin stood unflinching. "Knowledge, Lord Calandor."

A nictitating blink, the dragon's slow smile. "You ssseek the
Counsselor."

"Yes."

"He chasses the Prophesssy, Dreamsspinner."

"I know that." A muscle twitched along Ushahin's jaw.
"*Where?*"

"I do not know, Dreamssspinner." Raising his head to its full
height, Calandor gazed out over the dark green forests of Pelmar.
"Uru-Alat is Sssundered, and Malthus the Counssselor was Shaped
on the far ssside of that ssschism. Him, I cannot ssssee, nor any
weapon Shaped there. Only the effectss of their actions."

"What actions?" His voice was taut. "Where?"

"In the desert of Haomane's Wrath." The dragon sounded
amused and regretful. "Sssuch a sssmall choissse, on which to
hinge ssso much. A boy and a bucket of water. Is that what you
ssseek to know, ssson of no one?"

Ushahin, pale as death, nodded. "Yes."

NINETEEN

❖

DARKHAVEN SHOOK WITH LORD SATORIS' fury.

The very foundations trembled at the Shaper's roar. Torches rattled in their sconces, flames casting wavering shadows against the black, marble walls. Overhead, storm clouds gathered and roiled, shot through with smoldering bolts of lightning. In the Chamber of the Font, the marrow-fire surged in blinding gouts and Godslayer pulsed, quick and erratic.

"Where?" the Shaper raged. "*Where are they?*"

Tanaros closed his eyes and touched the *rhios* in his pocket. "I do not know, my Lord Satoris," he whispered.

"The Dreamspinner didn't know, Lordship. Said the dragon couldn't say." Vorax tugged at one ear and scratched his beard. "Only it wasn't heading here, like you'd think. Vedasia, he thought." The Staccian shrugged. "Something about birds and Dwarfs."

"It's what the ravens saw, those who were shot." Tanaros cleared his throat, summoning the will to meet the Shaper's furious red stare. "Did Ushahin not speak to you of it, my Lord?"

"Yes." It was a low growl, rising as he continued. "Of Malthus and deserts and ravens and Vedasia. *Not* of the *Water of Life!*"

Tanaros winced at the volume. "He didn't know, my Lord."

"So this Water of Life, it can put out the marrow-fire itself?" Vorax cast a dubious glance at the surging blue-white column of the Font, which was the merest manifestation of the Source below. "Take a river's worth, I reckon. No need to fear, my Lord, unless Neheris Fourth-Born herself plans to cross the divide and Shape the rivers."

"No." The Shaper sounded weary. "You misunderstand, Staccian. The Water of Life is the very essence of water, drawn from the navel of Uru-Alat itself. It would take no more than a mouthful to extinguish the marrow-fire. And I . . . I did not know any lived who could draw it forth from the earth."

There was a profound silence.

"Well," Vorax said. "Why would sodding Malthus take it to Vedasia?"

Lord Satoris glared at him, raising his voice to rattle the rafters. "*I don't know!*"

"My Lord," Tanaros said carefully, pressing his fingertips to his temples to still the echoes. "Whatever else is true, it seems certain that he did. Malthus' Company was seen in the marshes, and Carfax's men vanished there. Ushahin said . . . " He cleared his throat again " . . . Ushahin said seagulls bore rumors of a ship, sailing from Dwarfhorn. If it is so, then they are bound for Pelmar to unite with Haomane's Allies."

"Seagulls." The Shaper's glare turned his way. "*Seagulls!*"

"My Lord Satoris." Tanaros spread his hands helplessly. "It is what he said."

The Shaper brooded, pacing the Chamber of the Font. Shadows swirled in his wake, and his eyes were like two red embers. "Ushahin Dreamspinner waits in Jakar," he growled. "Haomane's Allies march toward Beshtanag. The trap lies baited and ready. If my brother Haomane thinks I will fold my hand at this new threat, he is very much mistaken." He halted, pointing at Vorax. "Lord Vorax. With two things, I charge you. You will use the Marasoumië to communicate my will to Ushahin. He is to summon the Grey Dam of the Were. Oronin's Children do not wish to be drawn into war; very well. But this thing, they will do." He smiled, and his smile was grim. "On pain of my wrath, they will hunt Malthus' Company, and slay them. All of them, and most especially this . . . *boy* . . . from the Unknown Desert. The Water of Life, they will spill where they find it."

"My Lord." Vorax bowed, his rings glittering. "And the second thing?"

"I charge you with the defense of Darkhaven. To that end, I lend the Helm of Shadows into your usage." Lord Satoris glanced at Tanaros, and his voice softened. "Forgive me, my general. You have born it nobly in my service. But I dare not leave Darkhaven without a safeguard."

"My Lord Satoris." Tanaros touched the hilt of the black sword at his waist. "This is all I need. This is all I have ever needed."

OVERHEAD, THE STARS CONTINUED THEIR slow, inevitable movement.

In the desert, Ngurra raised his voice. "I hear you, old woman!"

She made an irritated noise, emerging from the spindly shadows of the thorn-brush to join him on the cooling rock. "You've ears like a bat, old man!"

He worked a wad of *gamal* into his cheek, smiling into his beard. "Bats hear much that is hidden from other ears."

The red star had risen on the western horizon, riding higher than before. Warabi settled herself beside him, joints creaking. Together, they watched the stars revolve around the basin of Birru-Uru-Alat and the cleft rock-pile in its center. Alone among the old ones gathered at the Stone Grove, they kept the watch. As for the rest of the Yarru-yami, they were dispersed among the Six Clans. At Dry Gulch and Owl Springs, at Blacksnake Bore, Ant Plains and Lizard Rock, the Yarru had gone to earth.

"So it comes," she said with sorrow.

"It comes." He nodded, shifted the *gamal* wad into his other cheek. It fit neatly into a pocket there alongside his gums, teeth and tongue teasing out the bittersweet juices that sharpened the mind. "They have a choice, old woman. They all have a choice. Even the one who comes with a sword."

"I know." Her voice was muffled, gnarled fingers covering her face. "Ah, Ngurra! It is such a short time we have."

"Old woman!" His hands encircled her wrists, swollen by a lifetime of digging and labor. "Warabi," he said, and his voice was gentle. "An eternity would not be enough time to spend with you. But it has been a *good* time."

Lowering her hands, she looked at him. "It has."

"The children," he said, "are safe."

"But who will teach them if we perish?" Her eyes glimmered in the starlight. "Ah, Ngurra! I know what must be. I know we must offer the choice. Still, I fear."

He patted her hands. "I too, old woman. I too."

She stared at the stars. "The poor boy. Where do you think he is tonight?"

He shook his head. "The Bearer's path is his own, old woman.

I cannot guess. He has chosen, and must choose again and again, until his path finds its end."

THE DWARF SHIP DOCKED AT Port Delian, on the southern coast of Pelmar.

Carfax had the impression that the Dwarfs were glad to be rid of them, for which he did not blame them. Malthus' Company had breached Yrinna's Peace, destroying it irrevocably. As a war-proud Staccian in the service of Lord Satoris, he'd never had much use for peace.

Captivity had begun to change his perspective.

Peace, he thought, did not seem such an undesirable thing. Mayhap it would quench the killing urge he saw in the young knight Hobard's eyes whenever the Vedasian glanced at him, or the cold calculation in the eyes of Blaise Caveros, who still considered him an unwelcome threat.

Mayhap he would know himself deserving of the kindness that Dani and his uncle Thulu extended to him, of the burdensome compassion of Peldras the Ellyl, of the patient regard of Malthus the Counselor. And mayhap, mayhap, Fianna of Arduan would have some tenderness to spare for him, and cast a few of the yearning glances she saved for Blaise in his direction.

Would that be so wrong?

I am confused, Carfax thought as the Company departed Port Delian, I am heartsick and confused. His hands held the reins, directing his newly purchased gelding in a steady line, following on the haunches of Blaise's mount. It was so much easier to follow, to obey unquestioning. What merit was there in fruitless resistance? He had tried and tried and tried, to no avail.

Malthus knew it. He saw it in the Counselor's gaze, gentle and wise.

What if Malthus were a match for Lord Satoris?

It was heresy, the deepest kind of heresy. It froze his blood to think on it; yet think on it he must. What if it were so? Step by step, the Prophecy was being fulfilled. And they did not seem, after all, so evil. They believed in the *rightness* of what they did, in the quest to render the Sundered World whole.

Was it wrong?

Would Urulat be the worse if they succeeded?

Searching his mind, Carfax found no answers. And so he rode among them as they entered the depths of the Pelmaran forests, his dreams of vengeance giving way to vague thoughts of escape and warning. And he found himself seeking, unwitting, to win their approval, gathering firewood and making himself useful. *Ushahin!* he whimpered in his thoughts from time to time, but there was no answer, for Malthus' binding held, more gentle but no less firm.

And Fianna smiled at him when he gathered pine rosin for her bow, the ordinary Arduan bow she used for shooting game, and her smile echoed the smile of another girl long ago in Staccia. Goldenrod pollen, and freckles on the bridge of her nose.

Oh, my Lord! Carfax prayed. *Forgive me. I know not what I do.*

ALTHOUGH IT HAD STOOD FOR many years, Jakar remained a desert encampment, a few sandstone buildings erected around a scrubby oasis, the rest of it a city of tents. From time out of mind, Rukhari traders had used it as a last stopping-place before entering the trade routes that cut into the forests of Pelmar. Now the traders had fled, making way for fierce warriors with sun-scorched faces and black mustaches, who raced their swift desert ponies between the lines of tents with ululating cries.

It was a good bargain Vorax had offered them.

A half league to the west, a stony ridge sprawled across the landscape, ruddy and ominous in the light of the setting sun. It was haunted, the Rukhari said; riddled with caverns and haunted by bloodthirsty spirits of the unavenged dead. Small wonder, for it held a node of the Marasoumië, which was death to the unwary traveler.

A half league to the east, the Pelmaran forest began, a dark and ragged fringe looming over the barren plains of Rukhar. Beyond the verge was a darkness even the slanting rays of the sun could not penetrate, where Oronin's Children might lurk in the shadows a stone's throw from the trodden path.

Between the two was Ushahin, cross-legged before his tent. He was Satoris' emissary and one of the Three; he could have had the finest lodging Jakar had to offer, had he wished it. He had chosen otherwise. It was a cruel task his Lord had set him; the cruelest he had known. Still, he understood what was at stake. It was that and that alone that had decided him, that had set his course. Borrowing a pony from Makneen, the Rukhari commander, he had ridden to the verge of the Pelmaran forest and beyond, into the shadows. There, he had given the summons.

Ravens would carry it and Were would answer. The Grey Dam

herself would answer. Of that, he had no doubt. It was a rare gift, a rare trust, that Sorash had given her adopted son before she died. Her successor Vashuka had no choice but to honor it.

Oh, Mother!

His eyes stung, remembering. No one's son, the dragon had called him, but he had loved her like a son; loved her enough to know he could not stay among the Were. For the great sacrifice Lord Satoris had asked of her, he had gone as a supplicant. He had asked, praying all the while she would refuse. But she had not, had chosen to find an honorable death in the request, though his heart grieved at it.

In this, there was no honor.

The sun sank below the stony ridge, and shadows crept across the ground. Near the oasis, cooking-fires were lit and the smell of lamb roasted on the grill wafted in the air. Dry, warm air; it made his bones ache less. Lamps were kindled as Ushahin watched, tallow candles lit inside lacquered bladders and hung from the openings of tents. By the shouting and raucous bursts of song, the Rukhari might have been on holiday, awaiting the arrival of the army of Darkhaven. Having walked in their dreams, he knew what a harsh and difficult living there was to be eked out on the skirts of the Unknown Desert, in what fearful contempt the Pelmarans held them, what potential lay in the promise of a Staccian alliance.

Hoofbeats clattered between the tents, and lamplight gleamed on polished horseflesh as a pony rounded the tent, muscles surging as it was drawn up short in a scatter of pebbles. A swarthy face; Zaki, Makneen's second-in-command, peered down at his feet, studiously avoiding eye contact.

"Meat ready, Dream-stalker," the Rukhar offered in broken common. "You eat?"

"No." Sitting straight-backed, Ushahin did not rise. "Thank you, Zaki."

After a moment, the Rukhar shrugged. "Makneen offer. Is good, yes? You are pleased? Not to trouble sleep?"

"It is well done, Zaki. We are allies. I will not trouble your dreams." Ushahin watched as the Rukhar shrugged again, then lashed his pony's rump with trailing reins, startling it into a galloping spurt. The Rukhari feared him. Well and good; they should. He resumed his vigil, watching the darkening verge of the forest.

Time passed.

A half moon rose and the stars emerged, and brightest of them was the red one, high above the horizon.

"Brother."

A grey voice, emerging from darkness. It named him in the tongue of Oronin's Children, which he had spoken seldom since childhood. Ushahin rose, straightening his stiffening joints and inclining his head. "Brother," he replied in kind. "Well met by moonlight."

There was a gleam, as of bared teeth. "I do not think so. Follow."

Follow he did, leaving the illuminated tents behind, traveling on foot over the stony soil. Ahead of him, a grey shadow moved low to the ground, silent but for the occasional click of claw on stone. On and onward they traveled, until the lamps of Jakar were distant sparks and the forest enveloped them.

Into the tall pines his guide led him, leaving behind the beaten paths and treading on soft pine mast, to a glade where moonlight spilled on silvery fur, and one awaited in a circle of many. By this alone, by the honor the pack accorded her, he knew her.

"Old mother." Ushahin bowed low. "I give you honor."

"Son of my self." Ritual words, devoid of affection. Vashuka the Grey Dam stood upright and her amber eyes were narrowed in the moonlight. A score of dim figures crouched around her, hackled and wary. "The Grey Dam Sorash gave you a sacred trust. Why have you used it to summon me here, so near to a place of Men?"

"Honored one, forgive me." He felt sick, the brand on his chest a searing pain. "Oronin's Children are my kin, but I have sworn a deeper oath."

Her lip wrinkled, exposing her canines, still white. "Satoris."

"To my Lord Satoris, yes." Ushahin drew a deep breath, trying to loosen his chest. Where were the ravens? The trees should be full of them; were empty instead. He reached out with his thoughts, and a low, concerted growl came from the crouching circle of Were. "Brethren! Has it come to this?"

Vashuka raised a clenched, clawed hand, and the circle fell silent. Her gaze never left him. "Tell us, Ushahin-who-walks-between-dusk-and-dawn. What *has* it come to?"

"A favor." It was harder than he had imagined to hold his ground before her. His very flesh was vulnerable. For all that he was one of the Three, he was no warrior like Tanaros or Vorax. His crippled hands could scarce grip a sword, and such powers as he had would avail him little against the Were, who were themselves the stuff of which Men's nightmares were made. "Death."

"War!" she growled, and the pack echoed her.

"No." Ushahin shook his head. "You have refused to commit

Oronin's Children to war, honored one, and Satoris Third-Born respects this. It is death he asks of you; a hunt, far from the battlefield. There is a company, a small company, that enters the forests of Pelmar. These, my Lord wishes slain."

"Wishes." The Grey Dam's voice was dry. "Asks. Who are we to slay?"

"Malthus the Counselor," he whispered. "And all who accompany him."

At that, she threw back her head, loosing a howl. It echoed forlorn throughout the forest, and the Were who accompanied her crouched and quivered.

"Old mother," Ushahin said to her. "Has Malthus the Counselor been a friend to our kind? Have the Sons of Men? Have the Ellylon? No! Only Lord Satoris. Seven deaths is not so much to ask."

Closing her jaws with a snap, Vashuka snarled. "Have we not given as much?" She jerked her chin toward the red star above the tree-line of the glade. "There, Ushahin-who-walks-between-dusk-and-dawn! The Counselor Dergail's Soumanië, that we wrested from him! For this, Men and Ellylon name us enemy and hunt us without mercy." She folded her arms across her gaunt bosom. "I am the Grey Dam; I remember. I am the Grey Dam; I say, no more."

"And I say," Ushahin said softly, with infinite regret, "that do you refuse, Lord Satoris will name you his enemy. And there is an army coming, old mother. An army of Fjeltroll with hides like leather and the strength to move mountains, commanded by General Tanaros Blacksword himself. Right now, there is a force—" he pointed, "—of two hundred Rukhari warriors on that plain, and their swords are whetted. Who will you turn to if Lord Satoris turns against you? The Pelmaran Regents, who have sought to stamp out your kind? Aracus Altorus?" He shook his head. "I do not think so. My mother-who-was spent her life's last blood seeking Altorus' throat. He will not be quick to forgive."

She snarled again, and the moonlight glittered on her sharp teeth. "*Ask!* You ask nothing and demand everything!"

Heavy with sorrow, he nodded. "Yes, old mother. Childhood must end, even for immortals. Will you abide or refuse?"

Lifting her muzzle, the Grey Dam gazed at the night sky. "If I refuse," she mused aloud, "who will obey? The Counselor Malthus wields the Soumanië. Who among you can look upon it? Oronin's Children alone can withstand it, we whom the Glad Hunter Shaped, we who can veil our eyes and hunt by scent alone."

"Yes," he said. "It is so. But Oronin's Children are few, and Lord

Satoris' armies are many." Thinking of the raging storm of fury emanating from Darkhaven, Ushahin shuddered. In the depths of his
shattered bones, it was a madness he understood. "Make no mistake, old mother. One way or another, he will triumph. And if you
refuse him, he will have his vengeance."

"*Aaaarrhhhh!*" A raw cry, half howl. Her furred hands rose to
cover her face, and the Were Brethren surrounding her keened.
"Selves of myself," she whispered to her predecessors' memories,
"why did you make an ally of he who Sundered the world?" Lowering clenched hands, she hardened her voice. "So be it." The Grey
Dam spun, pointing. "You," she said harshly. "You. You and you,
you, you and you! Seven Brethren for seven deaths." Her amber
eyes shone hard and cold, and her voice imparted hatred to her
words. "Will it suffice, son of my self?"

"Yes, honored one." Ushahin bowed low. "It will."

She turned her back to him, speaking over her shoulder. "Show
them."

This he did, opening his mind to them in the ancient tradition
of the Were, showing them in pictures the Company as he had witnessed it upon the marshlands of Vedasia: The Counselor, the Ellyl,
the Borderguardsman, the Archer, the Vedasian, the Yarru boy and
his guardian uncle. He showed them the death that must be, the
rent flesh and life's blood seeping into the forest's floor, the red
gem of the Soumanië to be kept for Lord Satoris, the clay flask containing the Water of Life that must be broken and spilled. And he
showed them the pictures that had filtered through the fractured
shards of the Ravensmirror, the rumor of gulls and a ship setting
anchor on Pelmaran soil.

"There," he whispered. "Find them and slay them."

In their minds there opened a dry gully of thirst that only red
blood could slake. As one, the seven Brethren bowed, obedient to
the will of the Grey Dam, and death was their every thought. As
one, they crouched low and sprang into motion, seven shadows
moving swift and grey through the Pelmaran forests. Only the
barest rustle of pine needles marked their passing. Oronin's Children, direst of hunters.

"Go." It was the Were who had guided him who spoke, rising
from the shadows to stand upright, his voice harsh and choked.
"Go now, no one's son!"

"Old mother . . . " Helpless, Ushahin reached out a hand toward the motionless figure of the Grey Dam, remembering Sorash-
who-was, remembering the touch of her rough pelt as she cradled

his broken limbs. His boyhood self, and the only mother he had ever known. *The Grey Dam is dead. The Grey Dam lives.* The keen wire of pain that defined him grew tighter, madness pressing in close and a sound rising in his mind, rising and rising, a howl un-uttered in his branded chest. "Oh, mother! I am sorry . . . "

"*Go!*"

TWENTY

❖

"Lady." Tanaros caught his breath at the sight of her. In the confines of her chambers, clad in the robes of her ancestors, she shone like a candle-flame. It made his heart ache, and he bowed low. "I come to bid you farewell."

Cerelinde's hand rose unbidden to her throat. "You depart?"

"On the morrow." He straightened. "I will return."

"You will kill him," she whispered, eyes wide and fearful. "Aracus."

For a long time he did not answer, remembering the battle in Lindanen Dale and Aracus Altorus struggling with the Grey Dam of the Were on the end of his blade; remembering another, Roscus. His king, his foster-brother. A ready grin, an extended hand. A babe with red-gold hair, and his wife's guilt-ridden gaze. At the end, Roscus had looked surprised. It would end, with Aracus. It would be done.

"Yes," he said. "I am sorry."

She turned her back to him, her pale hair a shining river. "Go," she said, her voice taut and shaking. "*Go!* Go then, and kill, Tanaros Blacksword! It is what you do. It is all you are good for!"

"Lady." He took a step forward, yearning to comfort her and angry at it. "Do you understand so little, even now? Haomane has declared war upon us. We are fighting for our lives here!"

"I understand only grief." Turning, she gazed at him. "Must it be so, Tanaros? Must it truly be so? Is there no room for *compassion* in your understanding of the world? Haomane would forgive, if you relented."

"Would he?" he asked, taking another step. "Would *you?*"

Cerelinde shrank from his approach.

"You see." He felt his lips move in a grim smile. "Limits, always limits. You would forgive us, if we kept to our place. Ah, my Lady. I did keep to my place, once upon a time. I was Tanaros Caveros, Commander of the King's Guard in Altoria. I honored my liege-lord and served him well; I honored my wife and loved her well." He opened his arms. "You see, do you not, what it earned me?"

She did not answer, only looked at his spread hands and trembled.

He had throttled his wife with those hands.

"So be it." Gathering himself, Tanaros executed one last bow, crisp and correct. "Lady, you will be well cared for in my absence. I have sworn it so. I bid you farewell." Spinning on his heel, he took his leave of her. No matter that her luminous eyes haunted him; it was satisfying, hearing the door slam upon his departure.

She did not know.

She did not understand.

Cerelinde was Haomane's Child, Shaped of rational thought. She would never understand the passion with which he had loved his wife and his liege-lord alike, and how deeply their betrayal had wounded him. No more could she comprehend Lord Satoris, who had dared defy his Elder Brother in order that his Gift should not be wrested from Men, that thought should not be forever uncoupled from desire.

Things were not always as simple as they seemed.

But Haomane's Children could not think in shades of grey.

Even now, with the old rage still simmering in his heart, it grieved Tanaros to think upon all he had lost, all he had cast aside. How much more so, he wondered, must it grieve his Lordship? And yet Cerelinde refused to see it.

Though he wished that she would.

With an effort, he thrust the thought away. A door closed; well and good. Nothing left, then, but what lay ahead. It had come down to it. All the variables, the plans within plans; what were they to him? Nothing. There was a war. War, he understood. At every corner, Tanaros passed sentries standing guard. Hulking shadows, armed to the eyetusks. They saluted him, each and every one, acknowledging the Commander General of Darkhaven.

Yes. These were his people.

"Admit no one," he told the Fjel on guard outside his door. "I will rest."

In his quarters, everything was immaculate. The lamps had

been trimmed, the bed-linens were crisp and clean. There were madlings who never left the laundry, taking a remorseless joy in toiling over boiling vats of suds and water, expunging filth. His armor of carbon-blackened steel was arrayed on its stand, each piece polished to a menacing gleam. Buckles and straps had been oiled and replaced. It waited for him to fill it, an empty suit, a warrior of shadows. In the corner, the black sword rested propped in its scabbard. Not even a madling would touch it without permission.

His blood, thought Tanaros, *my Lord's blood.*

There was a tray laid unasked-for on the table, steam seeping beneath the covered dish-domes. Peering under one, he found a pair of quail in a honey glaze; another held wild rice, and yet another a mess of stewed greens. For dessert, a plate of cheeses and grapes sat uncovered. Candlelight danced over the table, illuminating the soft, misty bloom on the purple grapes.

Drawing up a chair, Tanaros sat and ate, and tried not to think how lonely, how terribly lonely, his quarters were. He missed Fetch, but the raven was gone, the half-frozen fledgling grown into a full-fledged bird, another daring scout in Ushahin Dreamspinner's strange army. Digging into his pocket, he found Hyrgolf's *rhios* and set it on the table. The sight of it soothed him, the river sprite's face laughing from its rounded curves.

"Is it to your liking, my Lord General?"

Tanaros started at the soft, unfamiliar voice, rising from his chair and half-drawing his dagger. Seeing Meara, he eased. "How did you get in here?"

The madling sidled toward the table, tangled hair hiding her face as she nodded toward his bathing-chamber. "This is Darkhaven. There are ways and ways, Lord General. Is the meal to your liking?"

"Yes," he said gently, pushing away the plate of picked quail bones. "Meara, you should not be here. Is it not our Lord's wish that you attend the Lady Cerelinde?"

"The Lady Cerelinde." Meara sidled closer, her features contorting in a whimper. "It *hurts* to serve her. She pities us, Lord General. And she grieves, in the manner of the Ellylon. She turns her face to the wall, and orders us away. It was never my wish to leave you, Lord Tanaros. Do you not know it?"

Close, so close! In a paroxysm of courage, she reached him.

Touched him, descended on him.

He could smell the heat of her flesh, of her womanhood. Her hands were on him, beneath the collar of his tunic, sliding against the hard flesh of his chest, the raised ridges of his brand. Tanaros gritted his teeth as her weight straddled him. "Meara . . ."

"Oh, my lord, my lord!" Her face, so close to his, eyes wide.

"Meara, no."

"He was the Sower, once." Wide eyes, pupils fixed. Her breath was warm against his skin, unexpectedly sweet. "Do you not *wonder*, Tanaros, do you not *know?* It was his *Gift,* when he had one!"

Her mouth touched his, her teeth nipping at his underlip, the tip of her tongue probing. Her weight, warm and welcome, encompassing him. Jolted by desire, he stood upright, his hands encircling her waist to dump her unceremoniously onto the floor, her skull jolting at the impact.

"Meara, *no!*"

She laughed, then. Limbs akimbo, she laughed, bitter and shrill. "General Tanaros Blacksword! Some hero, some *man* you are, Tanaros Wifeslayer! Did you offer your wife so little satisfaction? No wonder she found cold comfort in your bed! No wonder she turned to the Altorus to quicken her womb!"

"*ENOUGH!*" Stooping, unthinking, he struck her across the face. She whimpered.

"Meara, forgive me." Filled with remorse, Tanaros knelt at her side, dabbing with the hem of his overtunic at a trickle of blood in the corner of her mouth. "Forgive me, I am sorry, I did not mean to hurt you."

"Poor General." Her eyes were curiously limpid, as if the blow had cleared her wits. She touched his hand with gentle fingers, cupping it against her bruised cheek, caressing his knuckles. "Poor Tanaros. Does it hurt so much, even still?"

Her skin was warm and soft and the pity in her eyes terrified him. Withdrawing from her, he straightened. "You should go now."

Gathering her skirts around her, she stood. Not beautiful, no. A woman, not yet old, with tangled hair and skin sallow for lack of sunlight. She would have been pretty, once, in an ordinary, mortal way. Pity in her gaze, and a terrible knowledge. "I warned you, my lord," she said softly. "You should have heeded me. She will break your heart. She will break all our hearts."

"My heart." He shook his head, touching his branded chest. "No, Meara. That lesson, I learned too well. My heart is dedicated to Lord Satoris' service. No other."

"I know," she whispered. "I know."

❖

HAOMANE'S ALLIES ARRIVED EARLY.

Something had happened. The scouting-packs of Were year-lings who were to report on their movements had failed. If not for Calandor's warning, Beshtanag would have been caught unready. As it was, Lilias had closed the last breach in the wall in haste, seal-ing Beshtanag against invasion, and themselves within it.

Her Ward Commander Gergon brought her bits of gossip, gleaned by soldiers shouting back and forth over the granite ex-panse of the wall. A siege, after all, was a tiresome thing and some few had friends and cousins on the other side.

It seemed that, against all odds, Martinek, the Southeastern Re-gent of Pelmar, had taken to Aracus Altorus, the would-be King of the West. The last scion of House Altorus had accorded him the ut-most of respect, convincing even the Host of the Ellylon to bend their stiff necks to Pelmaran authority. Deep in their cups, they had established a rapport; so much so that Martinek had allowed him-self to be swayed by tales of the Borderguard of Curonan, its small, efficient units able to mobilize and maneuver more swiftly than a full-sized army.

Regent Martinek had taken Altorus' advice, and his fellow Re-gents had followed suit. Instead of advancing in a united front, they had restructured their troops into winding columns. No need, then, to forge a broad path through the forest. Unchallenged, Haomane's Allies made good time through the dense terrain. The troops of Aracus Altorus were the first to arrive, sizing up the granite wall that surrounded Beshtanag with cool, measuring glances, retreating out of bowshot to set up an encampment that sprawled through the unguarded forest.

Within the space of a day, the others had arrived.

Pelmaran forces from three of the five sitting Regents, a contin-gent of Vedasian knights, capable Midlanders—and, oh, worst of all was the Host of the Ellylon, the Rivenlost with their piercing beauty and their keen swords. Back and forth they rode, pacing the cir-cumference of the granite wall, needing neither sleep nor nourish-ment to sustain them in their quest.

Only one thing did they require: The Lady Cerelinde.

"I don't like this, Gergon." On her balcony, Lilias regarded the enemy encampment and shivered in the summer's warmth. "There are so many of them."

"We can hold." Her Ward Commander's face was grim. "As long as you hold the wall, my lady. Our stores will last another seven days, if need be."

"Seven days," she echoed. What a paltry amount!

Gergon glanced at her. "The Banewreaker's army should be here in less. They are coming, my lady, are they not?"

"Yes." She made her voice firmer. "Yes. They will be here."

At the base of the mountain, a distant figure stepped forth, clad in shining armor. He was the herald of the Rivenlost and he bore a staff from which flew the standards of both Ingolin the Wise and Elterrion the Bold—the argent scroll and the Crown-and-Souma. As he did three times a day, he lifted an Ellylon horn to his lips and blew, the silvery tone echoing from the sides of Beshtanag Mountain. His voice rang forth, clear and carrying. "*Sorceress! Surrender the Lady Cerelinde, and your people will be spared!*"

"Ellyl arsehole," Gergon muttered, adding, "your pardon, my lady."

Midway down the mountain, a line of kneeling archers loosed their bows, sending a shower of arrows aloft. Sharp shouts came from sentries posted in the trees, and those of Haomane's Allies in reach crouched low, raising their shields above their heads. Arrows arced above the granite wall and fell, clattered uselessly onto warding shields and the loose scree. The Ellyl herald stood contemptuous, watching them fall, before turning to retreat untouched.

"Too far, too high." Gergon shook his head. "Sorry, my lady."

Lilias sighed. "Tell them not to waste their arrows."

"As you wish." He paused. "If it came to it, my lady, there is one weapon they could not withstand."

"No!" Her reply was sharp. "Not Calandor."

"It seems a folly—"

"Hear me, Ward Commander." Lilias fixed him with a steely stare. "This is Shapers' business, and dragonkind is all but vanished because of it. Calandor will not give battle. Put it out of your thoughts."

"My lady." Gergon bowed, unhappy with her answer. "As you order. I will report again at sundown."

It was a relief to have him gone. Lilias watched a pair of ravens circling in the drafts, hoping they made ready to bear word to Darkhaven on urgent wings. While the wall stood, Beshtanag was safe; but there were so many arrayed against them. She touched the Soumanië at her brow, feeling the Shaping force of it pulsing faintly in her veins, in the stone beneath her feet. Faint, so faint!

She was spread too thin. It had taken a great effort to raise the wall, and more to sustain it. Always, it took more effort to create than to destroy. The old linkages were stretched and weak—those incorporating the collars of her pretty ones, binding them to her service; those that bound Beshtanag itself, binding the blood and flesh of her people to loyalty. Even the binding that stretched the great Chain of Being to its limits felt thin and tenuous, and Lilias felt old.

She was old, a thousand years old. Today, she felt it.

Oh, Calandor! she asked silently. *What have we done?*

There was a long pause before the dragon replied, longer than she remembered.

Wait, little sister, and be strong. You must be strong.

There was sorrow in the thought, deeper than she'd known the dragon to evince. Lilias gripped the balustrade with both hands, staring at the mountain's base. There, in the shadow of the forest, a flash of red-gold hair. Aracus Altorus, bare-headed and arrogant, the would-be King of the West. Even at a distance, she saw him pause, his gaze measuring her will and searching the sky for dragon-sign.

And then he turned his back on her, cool and purposeful, ordering his troops as they set about the construction of the implements of war. Ladders of branches, lashed with rope. Siege-towers, capable of holding a dozen men. Entire trunks hewn into battering rams. All of Pelmar's forests provided fodder for his efforts, as if in league with him. Already Haomane's Allies had essayed her wall in a score of places. She could hold it, for now, with the aid of Gergon's wardsmen. What would happen when their stores ran low? What would happen if Malthus arrived to pit himself against her, armed with a Soumanië like her own?

In her deepest self, Lilias knew the answer.

Hurry, she prayed in the direction of Darkhaven; oh, hurry!

TENS OF THOUSANDS OF FJELTROLL were packed into the Chamber of the Marasoumië and the tunnels that underlay Darkhaven. Armor creaked, rough hide jostled hide, horn-calloused feet trod the stony floors. Despite the fact that the ventilation shafts had all been uncovered, the air was stifling with the musky, slightly rank odor of the Fjel. The red node-light was reflected in thousands of eyes, all of them fixed on Tanaros.

Despite it all, they stood patient, adhering to the formations he'd drilled into them and trusting to his leadership. The swift Gulnagel, the ferocious Nåltannen, the dark Mørkhar and the mighty Tungskulder—all his to command, a vast army, divided into dozens of small units, mobile and skilled.

And at his side was Speros of Haimhault, grinning a gap-toothed grin, holding the reins of a pair of the horses of Dark-haven; Tanaros' own black, and a second like enough to be its twin. After much debate, Tanaros had decided to leave the mounted Staccian forces behind. Under Vorax's command, they and the Havenguard would serve to defend Darkhaven. He had made a promise to the young Midlander; let him serve as his equerry.

As for the battle itself; ah! For that, he had his field marshal, and there was no one, Man or Fjel, he trusted more than Hyrgolf. In the suffocating press, their gazes met quietly and Hyrgolf gave a nod, showing his eyetusks in a faint smile.

The Army of Darkhaven was ready.

"My friends." Tanaros raised a hand, and the rustling cavern fell into silence. "Tonight, we go forth to achieve a great good. Tonight, we will travel the ancient Ways of the Marasoumië, that traverse the length and breadth of the Sundered World itself."

There was a murmur; of eagerness, of anxiety.

"Be at ease." He pointed at Vorax, who stood beside the flick-ering node. "There stands Lord Vorax of Staccia, who will open the entrance. At the other end awaits Ushahin Dreamspinner, who will open the egress. Between them, they will hold open the Way, until the last of us has passed. And I, Tanaros Caveros, the Commander General of Darkhaven, will guide you through it."

They were afraid, these mighty warriors, the feared Fjel. It made him fond, and he smiled upon them. "Do not fear, my broth-ers. We are the Three, branded by Godslayer itself. We are the cho-sen of Lord Satoris. We will not fail you."

It braced them like *svartblod*. Tanaros saw it, felt it in his veins. His spirits soared, running high. Within the scarred circle on his chest, his heart beat, strong and steady. This was what he had been born to do. Lord Satoris himself had said it, summoning him to the Chamber of the Font. There, amid the blue-white coruscation of the marrow-fire, Godslayer's pulsing and the sweet reek of ichor, he had spoken words that filled his general's heart to bursting with pride and nameless emotion.

I trust you, Tanaros Blacksword. You will not fail me.

"Brothers!" Tanaros ripped his sword from its sheath, holding it aloft. "Though Haomane First-Born cowers on Torath, for too long his tyranny has held sway over Urulat! In his pride and refusal to relent, he rouses his Children against us, he sends his Counselors to wage war, and looses his Prophecy on us like a hunting dog. Lord Satoris grows weary of being brought to bay like an animal, and I grow weary with him. Have the Fjel not been persecuted by his Wrath, threatened with extinction? I tell you, it need not be so. Our destiny lies within our grasp. Haomane's Allies await us! Shall we make an end to it?"

They roared, then; roared acclaim and battle-readiness, and the sound within the cavern was deafening. Speros dropped the reins he held and clapped his hands over his ears in dismay while the restless horses tossed their heads. Tanaros smiled, letting the sound wash over him in waves, beating against his skin. It was good, this sound. It was a fitting sound to accompany the end of a world; or the beginning of one.

"So be it!" he cried when they had subsided. "By this sword, quenched in the blood of Lord Satoris himself, I do swear it. We will prevail in his name." In a single motion, he sheathed the black sword. "The next blood it tastes will be that of Haomane's Allies, or I am foresworn. We will assemble on the plains of Rukhar. Is all in readiness?"

Hyrgolf turned, repeating the question in the Fjel tongue. Here and there standards rose and dipped, their colors dim in the cavernous light as subcommanders in a sea of Fjel gave answer; yes and yes and yes. The ranks held, the companies were ready. Hyrgolf was smiling broadly as he turned back to his leader, his upper and lower eyetusks gleaming. "They're ready, General," he said in his deep rumble. "For our children and our children's children, shall we make an end to this battle for once and for all?"

"Let's." Tanaros reached out, clasping his field marshal's taloned hand, feeling the stone-roughened hide against his skin. "Let us do that, my brother."

Clearing his throat beside the node-light, Vorax lifted the case that held the Helm of Shadows. "Blacksword," he said softly, red light flickering on the gold inlay of his armor as he summoned Tanaros' attention. "The night is waxing. Are you prepared to depart?"

It was harder than he had reckoned. "You'll keep Darkhaven safe?"

"As immortal fiber can make it." The Staccian smiled into his beard and opened the case, removing the Helm of Shadows. An agony of darkness pulsed between his hands. "Ride forth, cousin. The Dreamspinner is waiting on the other end. Go now, and Lord Satoris' blessings upon you."

So saying, Vorax placed the Helm upon his head and opened the Way. A wash of ruby brilliance filled the Chamber. Squinting against it, Tanaros groped for the reins of his mount, fumbled as Speros handed them to him with tardy alacrity. Swinging himself into the saddle, he set his face toward the open Way and took the first step.

The Army of Darkhaven was on the march.

TWENTY-ONE

❖

DANI SMILED AT HIM IN the twilight. "I'm glad you're staying with us."

Carfax poked at the fire without answering. A knot burst, releasing a crackle of sparks and the fragrance of pine. His muscles ached from the day's hard labor. On the far side of the glade, a dark fissure yawned beneath an overhanging granite shelf, clear at last of the rockfall that had blocked it.

It was there, deep below the earth. A node of the Marasoumië. Alone among Haomane's Allies, Malthus the Counselor knew the secrets of the Ways, and did not fear them.

And he had helped them uncover it.

Wind rustled in the tall pine-tops. Accompanied by the Ellyl, the archer Fianna walked the perimeter of the glade, Oronin's Bow half-drawn. They had seen ravens from afar. At her back, the quiver that held her arrows gleamed with a faint, eldritch light, and one shaft shone a pale silver. It would flame white-gold if she withdrew it.

"Carfax?" Dani prompted him.

"Aye." With an effort, he gathered his thoughts. "Aye, Dani. I'm here."

It had been a near thing. Here, in this glade, their paths would diverge. Malthus the Counselor was leaving them for a time. Alone, he would travel the Ways of the Marasoumië to Beshtanag, where he would confront the Sorceress of the East. Malthus' Company would continue without him, to be reunited in Jakar. Their task— Carfax knew it now—was to shepherd Dani the Bearer and the precious Water of Life to Darkhaven.

To extinguish the marrow-fire and free Godslayer.

There had been quarrels, of course. It had sat ill with the young Vedasian knight Hobard to play nursemaid to a Charred One while his kinsmen gained glory at Beshtanag. Malthus had pointed out the route to the northeast and invited him to depart. In the end, Hobard had elected to stay—but he had argued hard for disposing of Carfax.

The argument had taken hours to resolve.

Dani, soft-hearted Dani, had protested, backed by his uncle. Fat Thulu; not so fat, after their travels. Blaise Caveros stirred, narrowed his eyes, and said nothing. Peldras the Ellyl laced his elegant hands about his knees, thinking abstruse Ellylon thoughts. And Fianna . . . Fianna spoke in a faltering voice on mercy's behalf, her words uncertain.

In the end, of course, it fell to Malthus.

The wizard had fixed him with that keen gaze that seemed to see right through him, eyes bright beneath his fierce brows. And Carfax, to his shame, had trembled. Once upon a time, he had been willing to die for Lord Satoris, filled with a Staccian warrior's pride. No more. He was afraid.

"Yes," Malthus had said with finality. "Let him stay."

So it had been decided, and when it was done, Carfax wished they had killed him after all. It would, at least, be swift. The itch in Blaise's fingers as they strayed over his sword-hilt promised as much. It would put an end to his *knowing*. Malthus the Counselor traveled the Ways into a trap, that much he knew. Carfax thought upon it with guilt and grim satisfaction as he labored to shift rocks on the wizard's behalf. Oh, Malthus might hope to defeat the Sorceress with her Soumanië—but it would take a mighty effort. When General Tanaros and the Army of Darkhaven fell upon Haomane's Allies, the wizard would have naught left to give in their defense.

And yet . . . and yet.

The Company would struggle onward. How doomed were their efforts, if Darkhaven prevailed? It would become a game of cat and mouse, with Lord Satoris' paw poised to strike. He would tell them, if he dared. He would spare them. Not all, no; not the surly Vedasian, nor Blaise Caveros—but the others, yes. Dani, at the least. Poor Dani, who was beginning to feel the weight of his burden, and the cost of protecting it. He belonged in the Unknown Desert, he and his uncle, at peace and unaware of the Shapers' War being waged over Urulat.

Better I should die, Carfax thought, than see this through.

Only I am afraid to die.

And so, alone, he tended the fire and dwelled with his tongue-locked thoughts, while their stores were shared out and everyone ate. And then, in the small hours, Peldras the Ellyl stayed awake with him, with his drawn sword over his knees, watching the moon's course. They had become comrades in these small hours. Even the wizard snored. And as before, it was the Ellyl who spoke first, turning his luminous gaze on the Staccian. "You have given thought to Arahila's mercy, have you not?"

"Mayhap." Carfax kept his gaze fixed on the embers. "Does it matter?"

"It does."

"Why?"

There was a long silence.

"Where to begin?" Peldras sighed, a sound like the wind through pine needles. "I am Rivenlost, Carfax of Staccia. I am one of Haomane's Children; Haomane First-Born, who alone knew the will of Uru-Alat. The world as He Shaped it was a bright and shining thing. I am Ellyl, and I remember. I grieve for what was Sundered from me."

Carfax lifted his head. "Lord Satoris did not—"

"Satoris Banewreaker would cover the world in darkness!" The Ellyl cut him off, his tone grim. "A tide is rising, Staccian. In Dark-haven, it rises. The Fjeltroll are seen in numbers, and the Helm of Shadows has been worn once more. What passes in Beshtanag is merely an opening gambit. Look, there." He pointed to the red star, riding high above the horizon. "There is Dergail's Soumanië, that the Sunderer wrested from him. It is a sign, a challenge. And it is one the Six Shapers cannot answer, for they are trapped beyond the shores of the Sundered World, islanded in their might. It falls to us, Son of Man. We are the last, best hope; each one of us. Do you matter?" He softened his voice. "Yes, Staccian. You matter. You are the twig that may turn a flood. If you choose a path of redemption, who is to say how many will follow?"

"No." Carfax stared aghast at the Ellyl, shaking his head in de-nial. "No! You don't understand! Lord Satoris didn't raise the red star; it was a warning sent by Arahila herself that Haomane First-Born—" Over the Ellyl's shoulder, he glimpsed movement, half-seen shadows moving in the forest's verges, and fear strangled his unspoken words.

Reading his expression, Peldras went motionless. "What is it?"

"There," he whispered, pointing. "Oh, Peldras!"

"The Were are upon us!"

The Ellyl's shout rang clarion in the glade. Already he was on his feet, a naked blade in his hand, his bright gaze piercing the shadows. Already Malthus' Company sprang awake, leaping to the defense. Already it was too late.

From everywhere and nowhere came the attack, for Oronin's Hunters had encircled the glade. Seven hunters for the seven Allies, coming low and fast as they surged from the surrounding darkness. Firecast shadows rippled along their pelts. Oronin Last-Born had Shaped them, and Death rode in his train. Grey and dire, they closed in for the kill with lean ferocity, snarling a song of blood-thirst. Seven throats they sought, and the eighth they ignored, leaving him a helpless witness.

"No," Carfax said dumbly. "Oh, no."

There was Malthus the Counselor in his tattered scholar's robes, the Soumanië blazing in his hand. It lit the glade in a piercing wash of scarlet light; to no avail, for the eyes of the Were were bound with grey cloth. Oronin's Children hunted blind. Their muzzles were raised, nostrils twitching, following scent as keen as sight.

There were the tethered horses, screaming in awful terror. There were the fighters; Peldras, Blaise, Hobard. Back to back to back they fought, forced into a tight knot. They fought better together than Carfax would have guessed, fending off four circling Were. Even the Vedasian proved himself worthy, wielding his father's sword with a ferocity and skill beyond his years.

Still, they were not enough to resist the Were.

Fianna knelt in an archer's stance at the Counselor's feet, drawing the Arrow of Fire with trembling fingers, sighting on shadows as it illuminated her vulnerable face. The black horn of Oronin's Bow seemed to buck in her hands, reluctant to strike against its Shaper's children.

And Dani; oh, Dani!

His eyes were wide, reflecting firelight, his slender fingers closed around the clay flask at his throat. Dani, who had offered him water when he was thirsty. Before him stood Thulu of the Yarru-yami, a bulky figure wielding his digging-stick with grim determination. Already, he was panting and weary, his skin glistening with sweat and the darker sheen of blood where teeth had scored him.

Two of the Were hunters circled him with cunning, twitching nostrils guiding them. One feinted; the other launched past him, a deadly missile, jaws parting to seek Dani's throat.

"*No!*"

Carfax was not conscious of moving, not conscious of grasping the butt-end of a sturdy branch from the fire. Sparks arced through the air as he swung it, interposing himself between the Were and its quarry. There was a thud, the impact jarring his shoulders; a keen whine and the smell of scorched wolf-pelt.

Oh, Brethren, forgive me!

"Dani!" Malthus' voice, strident and urgent. "The cavern! Now! *Now!*"

And the earth . . . *surged.*

Carfax, choking, was flung to the ground. There, scant feet away, was Dani, his face filled with fear and dawning knowledge. Outside the circle of churning earth, the blind hunters gathered to regroup, muzzles raised to quest the air.

"Go," Carfax whispered. "Go!"

He hauled himself to one knee, dimly aware of Thulu grabbing Dani by the collar and racing toward the cavern of the Marasoumië, their retreat warded by Malthus, who caused the very earth to ripple in surging waves, throwing back the attack of the Were.

The Yarru vanished into the cavern.

"Malthus!" Blaise shouted.

At the cavern's mouth, the wizard turned to face the pursuing Were and planted his staff with a sound like thunder. His lips were moving, his ancient face illuminated by the Soumanië that blazed crimson at his breast. Earth roiled, stones cracking like bones. Oronin's Hunters were tossed like jackstraws, howling in anger. Amid the chaos, Malthus shaped words lost in the avalanche of noise, his urgent gaze striving to communicate. ". . . protect . . . Bearer! Beshtanag . . . Jakar . . ."

"What?" Blaise cried. "*What?*"

Taking a step backward, Malthus the Counselor raised his hand. On his breast, the Soumanië surged with brilliance and deep in the cavern, the node-light of the Marasoumië blazed in answer, washing the glade in crimson light and momentarily blinding the onlookers.

When it faded, they were gone.

Unguarded, unprotected, Carfax stood with a smoldering branch in his hand and fought back an awful laugh as he watched his dumbstruck companions stare at the cavern's empty mouth.

Again, yet again, the Were regrouped. One rose onto his rear legs, clawed hands snatching away his blindfold to reveal amber eyes glowing with all the rage of a thwarted hunt. "You rest," the Were leader growled, "die."

A bow spoke in answer; not Oronin's, but an Arduan longbow made of ashwood and sinew, its string singing as shafts buzzed like hornets in the air. Three of the Were fell, silent and stricken, before their Brethren raced for the shadows, howling in wounded anger. "Not yet," Fianna vowed, tears staining her cheeks. "Not yet!"

Then it was Hobard defending her as the surviving Were renewed their attack with doubled stealth and speed, scattering the fire and spoiling the Archer's aim. The young Vedasian fought with all the pride and skill of his knight's upbringing. He swung his sword with a valiant effort, grimacing as one of the Were passed close, fierce teeth scoring his side.

"Blaise!" A silver shout in the smoke-streaked darkness; Peldras had reached the horses. With an Ellyl charm he bound them, horse-flesh shivering in fearful obedience, four sets of equine eyes rolling in terror, four sets of reins tangled in his hands. "'Tis our only chance!"

Blaise of the Borderguard swore, forging a path toward the Ellyl.

Why is it, Carfax wondered, that I am so alone here? What am I doing here? He took a step forward, interposing himself between Fianna and one of the Were, raising his smoldering branch in foolish opposition. A stick, a silly weapon; a few embers and a length of wood. Still, he had done damage with it. The Were halted, dropping to all fours and showing its teeth in uncertainty.

"You were not shown us," it said in guttural common. "You are not prey."

"Yes." Gritting his teeth, Carfax swung the branch at the Were's head. "I am."

The branch connected with a horrible crunch.

There was confusion, then, in the milling darkness; shouts and curses, the high-pitched keen of injured Were. Sparks emblazoned the night and steel flashed, four-legged death dodged and darted with impossible speed, while sharp teeth tore and muzzles were stained with blood. This was battle, and did not need to be understood. Somewhere, Blaise was shouting commands, and Fianna was no longer there. Instead, there were the Were, howling with the fury of betrayal and lunging for his blood, maddened and forgetful of their greater quest. Without thinking, Carfax set his back to Hobard's as to a battle-comrade's and fought, heedless of aught else, until the branch he wielded snapped in two, and he knew his death was upon him.

"Staccian!" The Vedasian gripped his arm. "Go."

Carfax gaped at him.

"Go!" With a curse, Hobard pointed across the glade at the dim figures of mounted riders, horses pitching in barely contained terror. "Go now, and you have a chance! The horses are fresh and the Ellyl can see in the dark."

"Give me your sword!" Carfax thrust out his hand. "Don't be a fool, Vedasian. I've betrayed my loyalties. Either way, I'm a dead man. Let me buy you time. Give me your sword."

"Staccian, if I hadn't argued for killing you, we would not have wasted a day in this place." Hobard jabbed at one of the circling Were. "This is my sword, and my father's before me. I'll not surrender it to the likes of you." In the faint ember-light he gave a grim smile. One cheek was streaming with blood and he no longer looked young. "This is my death. Go."

Carfax hesitated.

"Go!"

He went, racing at full pelt across the darkened glade. Behind him, the three surviving members of Oronin's Hunters gathered, flinging themselves after him like a cast spear. They were swift and deadly, armed with fang and claw, and they could have dropped him like a yearling deer.

But Hobard the Vedasian stood between them.

Once, only once, Carfax glanced behind him, as a terrified Fianna helped him scramble onto horseback. He could scarce make out the figure of Hobard, still on his feet, staggering under the onslaught. Even as Carfax watched, the Vedasian dropped to one knee and the Were closed upon him, a roiling wave of coarse pelts.

It was the last thing he saw as they fled.

He did not know for whom to weep.

SARIKA WAS CARELESS BRAIDING HER hair.

"Let it be!" Lilias slapped the girl's hand in irritation, then sighed as the grey-blue eyes welled with tears, relenting. "Never mind, sweetling. Just don't *pull* so."

"My lady!" she breathed in gratitude. "I will be careful."

After that the girl was careful, her fingers deft and skilled. Lilias watched her in the mirror, winding her braids into an elegant coronet. Her pretty face was a study in concentration. What must it be like to have no greater concern? Even here, in the privacy of her dressing-chamber, the sounds of the siege penetrated, a distant clamor of men and arms, challenges uttered, refuted in jeers. Lilias held the fillet in which the Soumanië was set in both hands. "Sarika?"

"My lady?" The girl met her gaze in the mirror.

"Are you not frightened?"

"No, my lady." Sarika gave her a small, private smile. Around her neck, the silver links of her collar of servitude shone. "You will protect Beshtanag."

Who of us is bound here, Lilias wondered? I thought my pretty ones were bound to my service; now, it seems, I am bound to their protection. She regarded the Soumanië held in her lap. For a thousand years, waking or sleeping, it had never left her touch. Light flickered in its ruby depths, seemingly inexhaustible and endless. Her own energies, like Beshtanag's stores, were nearing their limits. It would be so simple, she thought, to put it down and walk away.

"There!" Sarika tucked a final braid into its coil and beamed.

So simple, so easy.

Instead, Lilias raised the fillet, settling it on her brow. The gold circle gleamed against her dark hair and the Soumanië was crimson against her pale skin. She looked majestic and beautiful. That had seemed important, once.

"My lady." Pietre paused in the doorway, his face frank with adoration above his collar of servitude. "My lady, the Ward Commander is asking for your aid."

A pang of alarm shot through her. "What is it, Pietre?"

He shook his head. "I do not know, my lady."

With their assistance, Lilias robed herself and hurried through the halls, passing servants and wardsmen half-awake in the grey hour that preceded dawn. Everywhere, Beshtanag was feeling the pinch of the siege. Rations had been halved and working shifts had been doubled. An unseasonal chill had caught them unprepared, with a shortage of firewood laid in against the siege and a hard rainfall rendering the fortress dank and cold. The folk of Beshtanag gazed at her with banked resentment as she made her way to her reception hall.

"My lady." Gergon bowed at her arrival.

"Is there a problem, Gergon?" Lilias asked him.

"It's the rain." He looked bleary-eyed and tired, and there were droplets of rain dampening the grey hairs of his brows and beard. "Haomane's Allies have built siege-towers to assail the wall, and moved them into position overnight. We've been firing pots of pitch to keep them at bay, but now the rain aids their cause and the wood will not ignite. They're clearing the wall by the score, and

I'm losing men. If it keeps up, they'll wear us down in a day. Can
you help?"

"Show me," she said.

Outside, it was hard to see in the dim light, and rain fell in cold,
miserable sheets, soaking her hooded woolen cloak in a matter of
minutes. Clinging to Gergon's arm, Lilias picked her way down the
cobbled mountainside road. Her wall stood, a smooth, rain-
darkened expanse of granite, but here and there the framework of
siege-towers scaled it. There were four all told, and Men and Ellylon stood atop the rain-slick platforms, archers armed with short-
bows defending ladders thrust downward into Beshtanag's
fasthold. On the ground, Gergon's archers shot at them, making a
poor job of it firing upward in the pouring rain.

One by one, the ladders descended, and Haomane's Allies
trickled into Beshtanag. All along the wall there were skirmishes
fought in the gloaming.

There, a lone Borderguardsman challenged Gergon's wardsmen.
There, a trio of Midlanders put up a stout defense.

And they fell, fell and died, but for every one that died, two
more waited to follow. There were so many of them, and so few
Beshtanagi. If it became a war of attrition, Beshtanag would lose.

"Short work for a dragon," Gergon said quietly, surveying the
siege-towers.

"No." Lilias drew back her hood, blinking against the rain.
"Ready the catapults with their pitch-pots," she said grimly, watching the wall. "And your archers, Ward Commander. We do not need
a *dragon* to set fire to these vile towers."

He regarded her for a moment before bowing. "As you order."

Lilias watched him stride away and vanish in the dimness,
shouting orders to his wardsmen as he descended the steep incline. Around the base of the wall they obeyed, falling back to regroup around the roofed huts where the warming-fires burned and
pitch was kept bubbling in cauldrons. From the fortress, Pietre
picked his way out to join her, carrying a waxed parasol, which he
raised over her head. Rain dripped off it like silver beads on a
string.

"Are you well, my lady?" he asked anxiously. "You will take a
chill in this rain!"

"Well enough." Lilias smiled humorlessly. "Let us pray a chill is
the worst of it." And so saying, she pressed her fingertips to her
temples, concentrating on the siege-towers and drawing on the

power of the Soumanië, exerting its influence in an effort to *know* the towers and command their substance.

Wood.

Pinewood.

It was fresh-cut, hewn by the axes of Haomane's Allies. Stout trunks formed the supports and slender ones the platforms. Sap oozed from the shorn, splintered ends. At its heart, where new growth was generated, the wood was pink. Pale wood encircled it, layer upon layer, still springy with moisture. Outside was the encompassing bark, dark and tough, shaggy with flakes and boles. Rain, that should have fallen on rich mast to nurture its roots, fell instead on dead bark, rendering it sodden and slippery, penetrating layer upon layer into the green wood.

Water.

Too much water.

Drawing on the Soumanië, Lilias gathered it.

It was an intricate thing Haomane's Allies had wrought; four intricate things. Branch by branch, trunk by trunk, she desiccated the siege-towers. Heartwood died, its pink core turning grey. Outward and outward, pale layers growing ashen. A cloud of fog surrounded the towers as the bark weathered and dried, wrapping their assailants in a veiling mist. The soldiers of Aracus Altorus' army scrambled, disoriented and disorganized. Where booted feet had struggled for purchase on rain-slick wood, brittle bits of bark flaked and fell.

Holding the thought of water in her mind, Lilias *moved* it, until the air roiled with mist and there was none left in the wooden structures. Sharp, cracking sounds emanated beneath enemy boots as branches cracked and splintered under their weight.

The siege-towers had become tinderboxes.

"Now!" Gergon shouted, waving his arm.

Pitch-pots were ignited and catapults thumped, loosing volley after volley. Some missed; most found their targets. Gergon's archers followed with a volley of arrows, trailing fire from oil-soaked rags. Where it struck, the pitch spread its flames, igniting dead-dry wood. Heedless of the pouring rain, the towers burned fiercely, wooden skeletons alight. Here and there, cries of agony arose from those too slow to escape. Gouts of fire towered into the sky as Haomane's Allies retreated, abandoning their siege-engines for the forest's safety. The Beshtanagi defenders shouted at the victory.

Drained, Lilias swayed on her feet.

"This way," Pietre whispered, taking her elbow. "My lady."

Step by stumbling step, she let him lead her back up the mountainside. In the entryway of Beshtanag fortress, another of her pretty ones was on hand to remove her sodden cloak. Radovan, who had pleased her once with his smouldering eyes, rebelling now against the force of her binding, eroding her sapped will. He was one she should have released. Too late, now, to contemplate such niceties.

"Lady." His hands were solicitous, his voice skirted courtesy. There was contempt in his hot gaze. "Yet again, you *protect* us."

Pietre stepped forward, bristling. "Leave her alone, Radovan!"

"No." She laid a hand on Pietre's chest, wearied by their antagonism. The Soumanië was like an iron weight on her brow. Her neck ached at it, and she wanted only to rest, though dawn was scarce breaking. "Let it be, Pietre."

Lilias? They come, little sister. Darkhaven's army travels the Ways.

It was the dragon's voice. Her head rose as a fierce surge of joy sent new strength through her veins. Hope, blessed and welcome. The plan was intact, and all was not lost. "Calandor?" she asked aloud, too tired to scry the Ways. "Where are they?"

ETERNITY BEFORE, ETERNITY BEHIND.

Only the *here* was real, and with each step it was elsewhere.

It was a strange thing, to travel the Ways of the Marasoumië without effort, on horseback. Ahead of him, a tunnel of red light pulsed; behind him, the same. Where he had been, he no longer *was*. Tanaros clamped his thighs hard around the black's barrel, aware of its solid warmth, its hide damp with sweat. No ordinary mount could have endured the strangeness of this journey. Here, and here, and here it placed its hooves, and there were no echoes in the Ways. There became here, here no longer was. How many leagues passed with the fall of each hoof?

He dared not think upon it.

The Way was anchored at either end. In Darkhaven, Vorax held it open; in Jakar, Ushahin Dreamspinner did the same. Lead, Tanaros thought to himself, aware of the press of Fjel at his back, a long, winding horde chary of tunnels they could not delve, of a journey they could not end, of leagues passing between each tramping stride. Of their own accord they would never have attempted such madness. It is enough, he thought. It is your task, General. Lead them, and show no fear.

So he did, step by step, concentrating on the passage, his hands steady on the reins, reassured by the scents of horseflesh and leather. Somewhere, above ground, the stars continued to reel and time passed. In the Ways, there was no time. Only one step further, leading them onward.

It had a taste, this journey, a taste of Vorax, holding open the passage. Gluttony and avarice, aye, but oh! There was the pride, the Staccian pride, that had forged its own path in making this fierce alliance. Tanaros felt the strength that poured forth from the Staccian, the courage and costly dedication, amplified by the Helm of Shadows. He could have wept, for undervaluing his cousin Vorax, whose branding echoed his own.

Staccia has weighed the cost and chosen this.

Lord Satoris had kept his bargain. For a thousand years Staccia had prospered in peace, while elsewhere the nations of Men struggled beneath the absent auspices of Haomane First-Born.

A night's passage, no more. Glancing to his left, Tanaros saw the young Midlander a half pace behind him. In the pulsing red light of the Marasoumië, Speros' face was set and eager, unaware of the dangers that threatened. He was someone's son, someone's brother. Did he even know what he risked?

The power that held open their Way shifted, growing more complex as Jakar drew nigh. There was the taste of Ushahin Dreamspinner, a subtle flavor of terrible power and remorse, of broken things healed awry. *Oh, mother!* It grew stronger as Darkhaven faded behind them. Somewhere, on the desert's edge, the Marasoumië flared into life, the node-points alive and open, rife with regret, loosing it into the open air.

Somewhere, grey dawn beckoned.

One more step, Tanaros thought, urging the black horse, conscious of the weight of the world above them. One more, and one more, and we will be done. And beside him was Speros and behind him was stalwart Hyrgolf and the whole of the Fjel army, and ahead of him lay the end, where all the throbbing crimson lines converged, and there amid the rocks they would emerge, assembling in force . . .

Something happened.

It happened fast, so fast.

There was a flare of scarlet lightning, an impact like a meteor's blow, and the Way . . . *changed.* Another sought to travel them, one with sufficient power to compel the Marasoumië itself. Sundered from its anchors, the Way was strained beyond bearing as the incoming presence sought to occupy the same space as Dark-haven's army. Reality buckled, the very stone warping around them. Amid disembodied cries of dismay, Tanaros fought for control of his now-terrified mount. With a sound like a taut wire snapping, Ushahin Dreamspinner's presence vanished and the Way ahead was severed and gone. There was only *here,* and another inhabited it.

There, stark in the wash of ruddy light, was Malthus the Counselor, with two figures cast in shadow behind him.

Tanaros gaped at him, uncomprehending.

For an instant, the wizard's astonishment was equal to his own.

And then an awful knowledge dawned in Malthus' eyes, quicker to grasp what was happening. He was Haomane's weapon, Shaped for the purpose of defeating Satoris himself, and the might he veiled from mortal sight was formidable indeed. In the dark of underearth, there was a brightness upon him it hurt to behold. The wizard's lips began working, speaking a spell. His beard trailed into his scholar's robes, and on his breast the Soumanië, drawing on Haomane's power, the power of the Souma. Even Sundered, it was enough to command the Ways.

"Turn back!" Tanaros wrenched at the reins left-handed, shouting over his shoulder. "Turn back!"

It was too late. Even as his black mount squealed in fear and ducked its head, sunfishing violently, the Way was collapsing. Terror erupted on every side. Tanaros swore, lurching in the saddle and fighting the black. Behind him there was only chaos as the Fjel broke ranks, milling in an awful press. Speros of Haimhault was caught in the crush, his mount borne along by terrified Fjel.

"General!" Hyrgolf's roar rose above the fray. "Your orders!"

Somewhere, in Darkhaven, Vorax kept a thin, desperate thread of the Way open to retreat, pitting the Helm of Shadows against the awful might of Malthus. Tanaros could feel it, taste it. The Ways shuddered and strained beneath their struggle, threatening to splinter into an infinity of passages, but there was still a chance, an alley. "Retreat!" he shouted, willing the Fjel to hear him. "Field marshal, *retreat!*"

And then the black horse convulsed beneath him, and Tanaros was flung from the saddle. The stony ground rushed up to meet him, striking hard. He covered his head, fearful of stamping hooves. Knowing that the Ways could not destroy him, Tanaros curled around his aching, Souma-branded heart and held himself *here,* knowing there was naught else he could do. Somewhere,

Hyrgolf was roaring, trying to organize his troops, trying to follow the thin thread of hope back to Darkhaven and safety even as the Ways collapsed, flinging them backward in time, sundering their company.

A good general protects his troops.

Everything seemed very quiet, the shouting receding into echo-less silence as Tanaros climbed to his feet to face the Counselor, and drew the black sword. "Malthus," he said, testing the weight of his sword, that was quenched in a Shaper's blood. His circum-scribed heart was unexpectedly light. "Your path ends here."

"Dani," Malthus said, ignoring him. "Trust me."

It was a boy who stepped forth from the Counselor's fearsome shadow and nodded; a boy, dark-skinned and unobtrusive, accom-panied by a wary protector. There was a clay vial at his throat, tied by a crude thong. With a shock, Tanaros recognized it, knew what it must hold. Here, then, was the true enemy, the one who mat-tered. Here was the Bearer of prophecy, who carried the Water of Life, who could extinguish the marrow-fire itself. And it was a boy, a mere boy, a pawn in Haomane's game. Their gazes met, and the boy's was questioning, uncertain.

"No," Tanaros whispered. "*Listen . . .*"

Malthus the Counselor lifted his staff, and light shone between his fingers.

Red light pulsed and the Ways opened.

Light flexed, coruscating.

TWENTY-TWO

❖

IT HAPPENED AS SHE CROSSED the threshold of her reception hall.

One moment she was walking, grateful for Pietre at her elbow, concentrating on keeping her head proudly erect for the watching servants. Relief at the dragon's news made it easier. It didn't matter, now, that the circlet felt too tight around her brow, that the Soumanië lay hot against her flesh, that an unnatural awareness stirred at the base of her skull—those were the harbingers of salvation, signs that the Ways had been opened. Tired as she was, Lilias bore them with gladness.

Between one step and the next, everything changed.

She had been a child, once; a mortal child playing children's games of hide-and-chase in her father's estate in Pelmar. Her younger brother had darted from the ice-house, slamming the heavy stone door in her face. A thousand years later she remembered it; the sound like a thunderclap, the unexpected impact and sudden darkness, and how the air was too tight to breathe.

It was like that, only worse, a hundred times worse. A red light burst behind her eyes as a Way was slammed closed, exploding open elsewhere, splintering into a myriad dwindling passages. By the stinging of her palms, she understood that she had fallen onto the flagstones. Her eyes were open and blind. Somewhere, Pietre was tugging at her arm, begging her to get up. There were tears in his voice. Her brother Tomik had sounded that way, once, when he begged her to abandon the Soumanië after she had descended Beshtanag Mountain to show him. "It's a dragon's gift, Lilias! Put it back!"

Lilias.

"Calandor," she whispered.

I am sorry.

With an effort she dragged herself to kneel in a puddle of her velvet robes, running her hands blindly over her face. There were murmurs all around; of anxiety, of sympathy, of mutiny. None of them mattered. Her little brother was centuries in the grave and her choice had been made a long time ago. "Calandor, what happened in the Marasoumië?"

Malthus.

Lilias blinked. Her vision was clearing. Sarika's face swam before her gaze, tear-stained as she knelt before her mistress, fumbling with a goblet of mulled wine as she sought to press it into her mistress' hands. This was her home, after all. For a thousand years, Beshtanag had been hers. "Calandor." Lilias swallowed, tasting fear. "Is Satoris' army coming?"

No.

SOMEWHERE IN THE NIGHT IT had ceased to matter that they had not begun their journey as comrades. In the headlong flight through the forest there were neither prisoners nor captors, only allies seeking a common cause: Survival.

Hobard had given his life for them. For *him,* Carfax thought, numb and awed. Over and over he saw it; the Vedasian knight going down, the dark wave of fur closing over him. It had bought them time. Not much, but enough. By the time the Were pursued, they were in flight.

Trees, trees and more trees; an endless labyrinth of forest, dampened by skeins of rain. A storm broke, driving their flight with increasing urgency. It lashed their faces, rendering them waterblind. Trunks loomed out of the darkness and branches reached, slashing at unprotected skin, lashing the horses' flanks. They shouldn't have been able to outrun the Were, if not for the Ellyl.

Peldras drew deep on the ancient lore of Haomane's Children, using the Shaper's Gifts to master the horses' fear, mastering all their fear. Such was the skill of the Rivenlost, first among the Lesser Shapers. It lent courage to their hearts, speed to their mounts' heels. Onward and onward they followed him, a slender figure on horseback, lit with a faint silvery luminosity, forging a path through the impossible tangle.

Pursuit came, of course; the Were bounding at their sides, leaping and snapping. Not as many, no; only three. A deadly three. And they came with muzzles red with blood, howling for their slain Brethren, a keening sorrow tinged with the rage of betrayal.

Carfax, unarmed, could only follow blindly in the Ellyl's wake, trying to protect Fianna with the simple bulk of his presence, turning his mount broadside and flailing in the saddle in a vain effort to fend off their attackers. It was Blaise who defended them, who brought up the rear; Blaise of the Borderguard. And he fought with a deadly, tireless efficiency, whirling time and time again to face the onslaught, his sodden hair lashing his cheeks. There was bitterness there, and fury; oh, yes! He was the appointed Protector of Malthus' Company, now shattered. If he had to spend his last breath protecting what remained of it, he would do it. Again and again his sword rose and fell, rain-washed and running with dark fluids, until the clouds broke and the grey light of dawn showed it ruddy, and the four of them alive.

When had Blaise slain the last of the Were?

Carfax could not say. Only that dawn had found them alone.

He sat quiet in the saddle, dripping, marveling at the steady throb of blood in his veins, at his hands on the reins, only his knuckles scratched, listening to their quarreling voices mingle with the rising birdsong while his exhausted mount hung its head low, too weary to lip at the undergrowth.

"But where should we *go?*" Fianna's voice, tired and plaintive. "Blaise?"

"Beshtanag . . . Jakar . . ." The Borderguardsman gave a grim smile. "I cannot guess, Lady Archer. You heard him as well as I did, and as poorly. Peldras?"

Troubled, the Ellyl shook his head. "What I can do, I have done. The ways of the Counselor are the ways of Haomane, cousin, and even I cannot guess at them. It is for you to decide."

"So be it." Blaise drew a harsh breath, laying his sword across his pommel. Red blood dripped from its tip onto the forest floor. "We have lost Malthus—and the Bearer. The Company is broken, and we must go where we will best serve. Staccian?"

Startled, Carfax lifted his head. "My lord?" The words came unbidden.

"Where should we go?"

He averted his face from the Borderguardsman's steady gaze, which said all his words did not. Hobard had given his life. A debt was owed. On a nearby tree a lone raven sat, cocking its head. Carfax swallowed hard and looked back at Blaise. "Beshtanag is a trap."

Was that his voice that had spoken? The words sounded so flat, lacking emotion, nothing to do with his tongue, thick in his mouth. But Blaise Caveros only nodded, as if hearing confirmation of a long-held suspicion.

"Do we have time to warn them?"

"I . . . don't know." Carfax said the words and something in him eased as he met the Borderguardsman's level gaze. "It may be. I don't know."

Blaise nodded again, surveying the remnants of their Company. Fianna straightened in the saddle, one hand reaching to check for Oronin's Bow and the Arrow of Fire. "So be it, then," he said. "To Beshtanag."

On a nearby tree, a raven took wing.

So be it, Carfax thought.

He felt numb. Better to die with honor than to live without it. It was too late, now. It was done. In the space of a few heartbeats, in a few spoken words, he had irrevocably betrayed his oath of loyalty. The words he had exchanged with Blaise long ago rang in his memory. If he could have smiled, he would have, but the corners of his mouth refused to lift. He wanted to weep instead.

There was only one end awaiting him.

Why do you smile, Staccian?

To make a friend of death.

IT WAS A COLD DAWN over the plains of Rukhar.

Ushahin lay curled among the rocks where he had dragged himself, his ill-knit bones aching and his teeth chattering. Behind him, in the cavern of the Marasoumië, the node-lights were as dead and grey as yesterday's ashes. Unable to raise his head, he stared at the pocked face of a sandstone boulder until the rising light made his head ache beyond bearing and he closed his eyes.

He had failed to hold the Way open.

Footsteps sounded, and he squinted through swollen lids. A pair of booted feet came into view; Rukhari work, with soft leather soles and embroidered laces. The toe of one boot prodded his ribs. Childhood memories, half-forgotten, returned in a flood and filled his mouth with a bitter taste.

"Dream-stalker." Above him was Makneen, the Rukhari commander. The rising sun silhouetted his head. "Where is your army?"

"Gone," Ushahin croaked, squinting upward and wincing at the brightness.

The Rukhari nodded in understanding. Somewhere, near, horses stamped and men muttered in their own tongue. Yesterday, they had feared him. Today, they wanted to see him dead. Makneen's hand shifted to the hilt of his curved sword, wrapped in bright copper wire. "So our bargain is broken."

"No." He spat, clearing his mouth of bile. "Wait . . ."

"It is broken." Watching him like a wary hawk, the Rukhari raised one hand, then turned away, speaking over his shoulder with careless aplomb. "Tell the Glutton we kept faith. It is you who failed. Now, we go."

They did, even as he struggled to sit upright, lifting the aching burden of his head. Horseflesh surged on either side of him, urged on with jeering cries. Hooves pounded, sending chips of sandstone flying. Ushahin lifted a hand to shield his face from laceration. Whatever Vorax had promised them, it was all gone, all lost. And there was no satisfaction, none at all, in knowing he had been right.

This was Malthus' doing.

He had felt it, had known the instant the Counselor had entered the Ways, seizing control of the Marasoumië and wresting it to his own ends, severing all of Ushahin's influence in one surge of the Soumanië. And he had known, in that instant, utter helplessness.

It should not have happened.

Something had gone terribly wrong.

Weary and defeated, Ushahin buried his face in his hands, taking solace in the familiar darkness, the misshapen bones beneath his fingertips. *My Lord,* he thought, *I have failed you!* In a moment, in a few moments, he would make the effort that was needful, freeing his mind from the bonds of what Men called sanity to sift through their dreams. Now—

Now was the sound of claws on sandstone.

Seated on barren rock, Ushahin lifted his weary head from his sheltering hands. A grey shadow shifted on the rocks, poking his head into view, muzzle twitching. He was young, this one, sent to bear an unwelcome message. Aching and bone-weary as he was, Ushahin observed the old courtesies, asking in his visitor's tongue, "How fares Oronin's Hunt?"

The young Were howled.

It bounded, clearing the ridge with a single leap to land before him. There was pain in its amber eyes, luminous in the sunlight. One forelimb lashed out, and Ushahin reeled backward as taloned claws raked his misshapen cheek. Groping blindly for power, he drew on the brand that circumscribed his heart, remembering God-slayer and the marrow-fire, and his Lord's long torment. "*Enough!*" he cried harshly, feeling Lord Satoris' strength in his bones. "What of your quest?"

The Were cowered, ears flat against its skull. "Eight," it whimpered in angry protest. "There were eight!"

Eight?

"No," Ushahin whispered. "Malthus' Company . . . Malthus' Company numbered seven."

Baring teeth, the young Brother showed him, putting the pictures in his mind, as the Were had done since Oronin Shaped them. There were eight, and the eighth a Staccian, tall and stricken-faced, a burning brand in his hands. A blow struck when the Brethren expected it not. Sparks against the darkness. A branch, a twig to turn a flood.

"Why?" Ushahin groped for a thread of mortal thought. "*Why?*"

"We have *done*." Emboldened, the young Were reared on its haunches, spat its words, red tongue working in its muzzle. "This says the Grey Dam! No more debts, no one's son. There were eight! We will Hunt for us, only, and fight no more!"

Done.

A slash of talons, a bounding leap. Claws scrabbled on sandstone, and the Were was gone, leaving Ushahin bereft, aching in the cold light of dawn, at last and truly alone.

"Mother." He whispered the word, remembering her scent, her sharp, oily musk. How she let him seek comfort in her form, burying his aching, broken face in her fur. How her hackles raised at any threat, menacing all enemies and affording him safety, a safety he had never known. He had healed in her shadow.

The Grey Dam is dead, the Grey Dam lives.

Not his.

His shoulders shook as he wept. The Ellylon could only weep for the sorrows of others, but Ushahin the Misbegotten was the child of three races and none, and he wept for his own bereavement.

When he was done he gathered himself and stood, and began to make his long way toward Darkhaven, to the only home left to him.

THERE HAD BEEN A CRY, filled with rage and defeat, when the path was severed. A single cry, echoing in Vorax's head, filling his skull like a sounding drum. Through the Helm of Shadows he heard it, filled with an eternity of anguish.

Ah, my Lord Satoris, he thought, forgive us!

It anchored him, that cry, kept his feet solid on the rocky floor of the cavern. It gave him a strength he had not known he possessed and kept him tethered to the Marasoumië. He felt it happen, all of it, as Malthus wielded the Soumanië and wrested control of the Ways from them. And there was only one thing he could do.

Through the eyeslits of the Helm, the node-lights twitched in fitful pain and he saw what he could not see with his naked eyes, the truth no one dared voice. The whole, vast network was dying, aeon by aeon, inch by inch. The Sundering of the world was the slow death of the Marasoumië. Not now, not yet, but over ages, it would happen.

Vorax could not prevent it, any more than he could prevent Malthus from seizing control of the Ways, from closing their egress and sending the army of Darkhaven into flailing chaos. All he could do was hold open his end of the path.

He did.

And he gathered them, scattered like wind-blown leaves through the Ways. It was not his strength, this kind of work, but he made it so. He was one of the Three, and he had sworn to protect his Lord's fortress. What did it matter that his belly rumbled, that the long hours ground him to the bone? He was Vorax of Staccia, he was a colossus. A battle may be lost, but not the war, no. Not on his watch. The army of Darkhaven would endure to fight another day. Like a beacon of darkness, he anchored their retreat, bringing them home.

They surged into the Chamber of the Marasoumië—Fjel, thousand upon thousand of them, stumbling and disoriented, filled with battle-fury and helpless terror. Elsewhere, a struggle continued and he felt the Ways flex and twist under a Soumanië's influence. Malthus remained at large. It didn't matter, that. Only this, only securing the retreat for the tens of thousands of Fjel. Node-points flickered out of his control, slipping from his grasp. It didn't matter. He was the anchor. Wrestling with the portal, he held it open, seeing through the Helm's eyes the fearful incomprehension of the Fjel. So many! It had been easier with Ushahin anchoring the other end.

On and on it went, Fjel streaming past him, until he saw the last, the hulking Tungskulder who was Tanaros' field marshal, who had brought them home to Darkhaven intact. And in Hyrgolf's countenance lay not incomprehension, but a commander's sorrowful understanding of defeat. No Fjel tramped behind him. He was the last.

With relief, Vorax relinquished the last vestiges of his hold and let the Way close. His thick fingers shook with exhaustion as he lifted the Helm from his head, feeling it like an ache between his palms. He needed sleep, needed sustenance—needed to pour an ocean of ale down his gullet, to cram himself full of roasted fowl, slabs of mutton, crackling pork, of handfuls of bread torn from the loaf and stuffed into his mouth, of glazed carrots and sweet crisp peas, of baked tubers and honeyed pastries, of puddings and confits and pears, of anything that would fill the terrible void inside him where Satoris' cry still echoed.

"Marshal Hyrgolf." Was that his voice, that frail husk? He cleared his throat, making the sound resonate in the depths of his barrel chest. "Report."

"We failed," the Fjel rumbled. "Malthus closed the Way."

Vorax nodded. It was what he had known, no more and no less. He wished there was someone else to bear the details of it to Lord Satoris. "And General Tanaros?"

The Fjeltroll shook his massive head. "He stayed to safeguard our retreat from the Counselor. Neheris spare him and grant him a safe path homeward."

Ah, cousin! Vorax spared a pitying thought for him, and another for himself. He was weary to the bone, and starved lean. Sustenance and bed, bed and sustenance. But there would be no rest for him, not this day. Lord Satoris would demand a full accounting, and he was owed it; pray that he did not lash out in rage. Their plans were in ruins, the Three had been riven. Malthus seizing control of the Marasoumië, and Tanaros lost in the Ways, with no telling whether either lived or died, and the Dreamspinner stranded in Rukhar. A vile day, this, and vilest of all for the Sorceress of the East. Beshtanag would pay the price of this day's failure.

At least the army had survived it intact, and there had been no Staccian lives at stake. He ran a practiced eye over the milling ranks of Fjel and frowned, remembering how the army had scattered like wind-blown leaves throughout the Ways, how he had tried to gather them all.

Something was wrong.

Vorax's frown deepened. "Where's the Midlander?"

"WHERE ARE WE?" THERE HAD been a cavern, and an old man with a staff; a terrified crush of flesh. That was when the world had gone away, carried by the General's shouting voice. He remembered the rushing force, the terrible sense of dislocation, and then the fearsome impact. Blinded by the throbbing Marasoumië, jostled and swept away, thrown down and unhorsed, Speros of Haimhault had landed . . . somewhere. He found his feet and staggered, flinging out both arms, hearing his own voice rise in sharp demand. *"Where are we?"*

"Underearth, boss," a Fjel voice rumbled.

There was an arm thrust beneath his own, offering support. Speros grabbed at it, feeling it rocklike beneath bristling hide, as he swayed on his feet. "Where?"

"Don't know."

"Where's the General?"

"Don't know!"

"All right, be quiet." Speros squinted, trying to clear his gaze. They were in a vast space. He could tell that much by the echoes of their voices. Somewhere, water was dripping. Drop by drop, slow and steady, heavy as a falling stone. The mere scent of it made him ache to taste it. "How deep?"

There was a shuffling of horny feet. "Deep," one of the Fjel offered.

It was a pool. Blinking hard, he could see it. A pool of water, deep below the earth. And above it—oh, so far above it!—was open sky. It must be, for there was blue reflected in its depths. Kneeling over it, he made out a dim reflection of his own face; pale, with dilated eyes. "Water," he murmured, dipping a cupped hand into the pool.

The water didn't even ripple. As if he had grasped an ingot of solid lead, his weighted hand sank, tipping him forward. He gasped, his lips breaking the surface of that unnatural water, and he understood death had found him all unlooked-for. How stupid, he thought, trying in vain to draw back from the pool.

One breath and his lungs would fill.

A wet death on dry land.

Then, pressure; a coarse, taloned hand tangled in his hair, yanking his head back and away from the deadly pool. He came up sputtering, his neck wrenched, mouth heavy with water.

"Careful, boss."

They were Gulnagel Fjel; lowlanders, the swift runners, with their grey-brown hides, lean haunches and yellowing talons. They could take down a deer at a dead run, leaping from hill to hill. There were four, and they watched him. Having saved his life, they waited for guidance. Among the races of Lesser Shapers, only Men and Ellylon had received Haomane's Gift, the gift of thought. Speros crouched by the pool, fervently wiping his numb lips, careful to make sure that not a single drop got into his mouth. Thirsting or not, what it might do inside him, he didn't dare guess. One thing was sure, he wouldn't touch that water again.

"All right." He stared at the reflected blue in its depths, then craned his head, squinting. It hurt to look at the sky, even a tiny disk of it. The shaft stretched above him to dizzying heights, and at the top of it lay open skies and freedom. "Up. We need to go up."

It was a despairing thought, here at the bottom of the world. To his surprise, one of the Gulnagel grinned and flexed his yellow talons.

"Not a problem, boss," he said cheerfully. "Up it is."

EVERYWHERE.

Nowhere.

It was dark where he was, and he was not dead. At least he didn't think so. In the darkness, Tanaros flexed his hands. He had hands; he felt them. The fingers of his right hand closed around something hard.

A sword-hilt, he thought.

And, I am lost in the Marasoumië.

What happened to people who got lost in the Ways? Sometimes the Ways spat them out, in some unknowable location, deep beneath the earth. Sometimes the Ways did not. And then they died, of course.

Unless they were immortal.

It was Malthus' doing, may he be cursed with the same fate. In the darkness, Tanaros gave a bitter smile. It had been a near thing at the end. He had hesitated when he saw the boy. He shouldn't have done that. It had given the Counselor time, an instant's time to invoke the Marasoumië's power and send them hurtling away, the boy and his protector, flinging them desperately across the warp and weft of the Ways, enfolded in his enchantments.

A pity, that. But it was all, nearly all, the old wizard had left in him. Tanaros *had* struck, then; had let the rage course through his veins, had swung his sword with all his might at his enemy's neck. Ah, it had felt good! The black blade had bitten deep into the wood of the wizard's staff when Malthus had parried; bitten deep and stuck fast in the spell-bound wood.

He had welcomed the struggle, moving in close to see the fear in the other's eyes, wondering, do you bleed, old one? Of what did Haomane Shape you? Do you breathe, does the blood course warm in your veins? Haomane's Weapon, with my blade so near your throat, do you understand the fragility of your flesh?

And then the Soumanië had flashed, one last time.

The Counselor, it seemed, did not welcome death.

It had cast them both into the oblivion of the Ways. That was his consolation. He had felt it, sensed Malthus spinning adrift, unrooted. Tanaros flexed his hand again, feeling the sword-hilt against his palm, and thought, I am not ready to die either.

There was light, somewhere; a ruddy light, pulsing. So it must seem to a babe in the womb, afloat in blood and darkness. He remembered a birth, his son's birth; the babe he thought his son. How Calista had cried aloud in her travail, her hands closing on his with crushing force as she had expelled the child.

He had been proud, then, terrified and proud. Awe. That was the word. It had filled him with awe, that she would endure this thing; that she could produce such a thing from the depths of her mortal flesh. Life, new life. An infant wholly formed, perfect in every detail, thrust squalling into the light of day. He had cradled the babe, cupping the still-soft skull in his hands, his capable hands, marveling at the shrunken face, the closed eyes. There had been no telling, then, that the eyes behind those rounded lids were blue, blue as a cloudless sky. No telling that the downy hair plastered slick and dark with birthing was the color of ruddy gold.

Oh, my son!

In the darkness, Tanaros groaned. It bit deep, the old betrayal, as deep as his black blade. He remembered the first time he had seen Calista. She had graced Roscus' court with her fresh-faced beauty, her sparkling wit. Their courtship had been filled with passionate banter. Who now would believe Tanaros Blacksword capable of such a thing? Yet he had been, once. He had shouted for joy the day she accepted his marriage proposal. And he had loved her with all the ardor in his heart; as a lover, as a husband, as the father of the child she bore. How had she dared to look at him so? Hollow-eyed and weary, with that deep contentment. Her head on the pillow, the hair arrayed about her shoulders, watching him hold another man's babe.

Once, he had been born again in hatred.

Why not twice?

A node-point was near, very near. Such was the light he perceived behind his lids, the beating red light. His circumscribed heart thumped, responding to its erratic pulse. If he could reach it . . . one, just one. If he could birth himself into the Marasoumië, he would be alive in the world. And where there was one, there was another, in a trail that led him all the way to Darkhaven.

Home.

Tanaros *reached*.

TWENTY-THREE

BESHTANAG ENDURED, HALF-STARVED AND weary.

From her balcony, Lilias watched her enemies, wondering if they knew. Would it matter? Would they act differently? She thought not. They had never known it for a trap. They went about the siege as they had begun it, with determined patience. By late afternoon the skies had cleared, though rain still dripped from the pines. Here and there Aracus Altorus strode, a tiny figure, recognizable by his hair. He wasted no time, ordering construction to begin anew on their siege-engines.

Three days.

That was how long they would have had to wait, if Darkhaven's army had arrived at Jakar as planned. Even now, the Fjeltroll would be on the march, trampling the undergrowth beneath their broad feet, commanded by General Tanaros.

Only they were not coming, would never arrive. Lilias knew. She had gone, alone, to the cavern of the Marasoumië, deep beneath Beshtanag. Had gone and stood, wondering if she dared to flee. The node-lights flickered erratically. Something was wrong, very wrong, in the Ways.

Probing, she had found it. There were not one, but two souls trapped within the Marasoumië; no mere mortals, but beings of power, under whose influence the Ways buckled and flexed. One bore a power equal to her own, a very Soumanië, and only the complete exhaustion of his energies kept him from wielding it. The other was one of the Branded, and the mark of Godslayer and a Shaper's power upon his flesh kept the Marasoumië from devouring him entire. For the rest, it was sheer stubbornness that kept him alive, forcing the Ways to bend to his will.

Either way, it was unsafe to enter.

She had stared at the node-point for a long time. Once, she might have dared it, when she was young enough to be fearless in her abilities. Not now, when she had spent so much of herself, pouring it into the stone and wood of this place. In the end, did it matter? Beshtanag was her home. She didn't know where she would go if she fled it.

So she had stayed.

A hunting-party emerged from the fringe of the forest, whooping in triumph. They carried long poles over their shoulders, a pair of deer between them. Regent Martinek's men, clad in his leather armor overlaid with steel rings. Lilias ground her teeth. Already, they had scoured her smallholders' estates, laying claim to their flocks. Where the armies of Men were camped, the ground was strewn with mutton-bones. Now, they took the bounty of the forest itself while her people went hungry.

"My lady."

It was Gergon, his helmet under his arm. He looked unspeakably tired.

"Ward Commander." Lilias made room for him upon the balcony. "What is it?"

"It is said . . . " He paused, surveying Haomane's Allies. In the waning sunlight, the Ellyl herald was stepping forth to give his third utterance of the day, demanding in a clarion voice the surrender of the Lady Cerelinde. Gergon met her gaze, his features blunt and honest. "You were heard, in the reception hall, where you took ill, my lady. It is said Darkhaven's army is not coming. Is it true?"

Lilias did not answer, watching the Ellyl herald. How could armor shine thusly? It flamed in the slanted rays of sunlight as he turned on his heel, marching back to rejoin the Rivenlost. They held themselves apart from the armies of Men, from the Pelmaran encampment and their feast of bones. Only Aracus Altorus strode between them, stitching together their alliance, Haomane's Children and Arahila's, keeping them united for the sake of the woman he loved; the woman he believed she held captive.

"Is it true?" Gergon's voice was soft and insistent.

What folly, what amazing folly! To think that they had come so far and fought so hard for naught. "No," she said. "It is a lie."

Her Ward Commander gave a sigh from the depths of his being. "Shapers be blessed! Where are they, my lady? How long will it be?"

She met his eyes unflinching. "Three days. They travel from Jakar."

Gergon gave a grim nod and bowed to her. "Then we will hold."

"Good." Lilias bit her lip and swallowed hard. The lie, spoken, seemed to lodge in her throat. And yet what else was there to do? Haomane's Allies might grant merciful terms if she surrendered, but they would take no pity on her. Beshtanag would be dismantled, the Soumanië stripped from her. And Calandor . . . they would slay him if they could. She wanted to weep; for herself, for Gergon, for all of Beshtanag. But it would not do to let Gergon see her weak. Gathering her skirts, Lilias brushed past him. "Carry on, commander."

In her quarters, Sarika startled to her feet, but she shook her head at the girl. Let her get some rest. All her people were hollow-eyed for lack of sleep and hunger. Haomane's Allies had come early; the siege had already endured longer than anticipated. Unattended, Lilias made her way through the fortress, the lie churning in her belly. It would give them hope, for a little while. How long, she could not say.

Her feet trod a familiar path along the stone hallways of Beshtanag, taking her to the tiny egress hidden at the rear of the fortress. For once, it was unguarded; every man who could be spared was on the siege-lines. This too did not matter. No one went this way save her except under duress. Lilias slipped through the door and started up the winding path, heedful of sharp rocks beneath her slippers. After the claustrophobic atmosphere of the fortress, it was good to be outdoors.

The mountain stretched down below her, ringed around with the great wall she had raised. She allowed herself a moment to contemplate it with satisfaction. Even viewed from above, it was a formidable obstacle and, for all their numbers, Haomane's Allies had not breached it yet.

They were trying, though. There, on the eastern side, a group of Altorus' Borderguardsmen had built a roaring fire, seeking to weaken the bindings that held the granite together. Lilias paused, frowning down at them. Tiny figures clustered around a mighty log, a battering ram with its prow sheathed in bronze. Closing her eyes, she probed the section of wall they assailed.

There . . . yes, there. A breach-point, where the smooth stone, annealed by fire, threatened to crack, remembering the composite rocks from which it had been rendered. Faint lines showed on its surface. Drawing on the Soumanië, she Shaped it, restoring it to a seamless whole.

The effort left her weak.

It didn't matter. At the top of the mountain, Calandor was waiting. Gorse bushes caught at her skirts, dragging her back. Lilias tore free, forcing her way upward. Step by weary step, she made her way to the crest of Beshtanag Mountain. When she reached the mouth of the cavern, she was breathless.

He was there, waiting.

"You knew," she panted, the tears coming unbidden. "You *knew!*"

For a long time, the dragon was silent; then he moved, one clawed foot scraping the cavern floor as his mighty head lowered until one green-gold eye was level with hers. "No, Liliasss." A deep voice, laden with sorrow and sulfur fumes. "Only what mussst be. Not when, nor how."

"Why?" Her voice cracked. "*Why?*"

He let her strike him then, her soft fists thudding against his bronze-plated cheeks and jaw. His sinuous neck bent to gather her in a protective coil. "All things musst be as they mussst, little sssis-ster," Calandor murmured, his voice rumbling in his furnace-chest beneath her ear. "All things."

Defeated, she slumped against him. "Must it be *now?*"

The dragon moved, his vanes stirring. "Is it your wish that I carry you, Liliasss? Far away? To Sstaccia, with itss ice and sssnow?"

Uncertain, she drew back. "Is there such a place, where no one could find us?"

"Yesss." The dragon's eyes glowed with regret. "And no. For a time, Liliasss. Only that. In the end, they will always find usss. Is it your wish?"

Walking away, she stood with her back to him, gazing down the mountain. There were dozens of campfires burning at its base. The evening breeze carried the faint strains of revelry and shouting. Inside the wall, Gergon's warders paced the perimeter, or hunkered around braziers and gnawed half-rations, keeping a watchful eye out for assaults. How many, she wondered, would live to see the end of this? They were her people. For generation upon generation, Lilias had bound them to her service. Her actions had brought this fate upon them. It was too late to undo what was done, and yet, if she could do nothing else, at least she would not abandon them.

She would stand or fall with Beshtanag.

It was not much, but it was all she had to offer.

"No," she said. "I will stay."

Even for the Gulnagel, it was difficult.

Throughout the day, Speros watched them with wide-eyed astonishment. Fjel were meant to delve, not to climb.

Still, they managed it. They worked in shifts, shucking the straps of leather armor that held their weapons. One would crouch low beside the pool, bending his back to make a broad surface, boosting up his fellow. And up the other would go, plunging his yellowed talons into the smooth surface of the rocky cistern, forging hand- and footholds by dint of brute strength, stone giving way beneath their blows.

None of them could last more than a few minutes, that was the problem. Their own body weight was too great, threatening to crack their talons the longer they hung suspended. It was Speros who got them to form the base of a pyramid around the pool, arms outstretched to catch their fellows as they made the precarious descent. And they did it. Working without complaint, hour upon hour, they scaled the cistern.

Foot by torturous foot, the Gulnagel forged a ladder.

"Oof!" The last volunteer descended, helped onto solid ground amid the jests of his companions. He rested his hands on his bulging thighs, fighting to catch his breath. "Reckon that's about done it, boss," he said cheerfully, regaining his voice. "Few feet from the lip, any mind. You want to go on up?"

Grabbing a handy shoulder, Speros leaned over the deadly pool and craned his neck, gazing upward. Faint stars twinkled in the distant circle of sky, emerging on a background of twilight. "What's up top?"

Exchanging glances, the Gulnagel shrugged.

"Hot," one said helpfully. "Gets hotter the higher you go."

"Nothing living, don't think," another added. "Quiet, if it is."

"All right." Speros gnawed at thumbnail, thinking. The Gulnagel waited patiently and watched him. In General Tanaros' absence, he was their commander; he was one of Arahila's Children, endowed with Haomane's Gift. A piece of irony, that. He'd been raised on tales of Fjel horrors. In Haimhault, parents threatened to feed misbehaving children to the Fjeltroll; at least his own Ma had done, often enough. Now here he was, with four Fjel patiently awaiting his orders. Well, he'd cast his lot, and he had to live with it. Still, it wasn't so bad, was it? Few mortal men could say they'd had Fjeltroll jump at their command. "Yes, let's try it. Better by night than by day, when we'd be sitting targets emerging. Odrald, will you take the lead?"

"Aye, boss!" The smallest of the Fjel saluted him.

"Good." Speros flexed his muscles, anticipating the climb. "You, give me a boost. The rest of you, follow me."

HE DID NOT SPEAK AFTER he summoned her, not for a long time.

Cerelinde sat in the chair he provided, staring with a fixed gaze at the throbbing image of Godslayer. How could something immersed in the marrow-fire itself retain such a crimson glow? It seemed impossible.

He stalked the outskirts of the chamber.

He was angry; no, he was furious. She felt it on her skin, tasted it in her mouth. A prickling like needles, like an impending storm. A taste of copper, only *sweet*.

"You know what has happened." His voice was a husk, but resonant.

"No." She shook her head, willing her denial to be true. It was true, for the most part. A plan had been made; a plan had failed. That much she knew, and no more. The Fjeltroll had returned. And when she spoke of Tanaros, her maidservant Meara had wailed and fled the room. "I know nothing, Lord Satoris."

"*Malthus was waiting!*"

Unseen rafters rattled at the Shaper's raised voice. Cerelinde winced, and laced her hands together. The light of the marrow-fire cast her raised knuckles in sharp shadow. "Does his Lordship hold me to blame?"

There was a sigh then.

It came from every corner of the room, and it came from him; *him*. And he was before her, then, stooping as a thundercloud might stoop, humbling himself in front of her. The swell of his shoulders blotted out the marrow-fire. His eyes, crimson as Godslayer's beating heart. "No, Cerelinde. I do not blame the blameless. That is my Elder Brother's job."

She shrank back as far as the chair would allow. At close range, the odor was overwhelming; a sweet charnel reek, burned flesh and an undertone of rotting vegetation. It stirred terror in her; mindless terror, and something else, a dark and awful quickening. Trapped and fearful, she lashed out with words. "Your jealousy speaks, Sunderer! What do you *want* of me?"

The Shaper laughed.

It was a hollow sound, filled with bitterness and despair. He bent his head, mighty hands lifting to cover his face. A Shaper's hands, immaculately articulated, for all they were burned black as pitch by Haomane's Wrath. His fingertips dug into the flesh of his brow, pitting the blackened skin.

Somehow, that was the most terrible thing of all.

"*Want?*" His head snapped upright, crimson eyes glaring between his fingers. "Oh, I *want,* Haomane's Child! I want my innocence back, and the happy, happy ignorance that has served your race for so long! I want my Gift back! I want to see my sister Arahila's smile! I want to see my brother Haomane grovel, and his Wise Counselor's head on a pike!"

"I didn't—" she breathed.

"*Who are you to ask me what I want?*"

The Shaper's words ricocheted and echoed in the cavern. The marrow-fire surged in answer, a fierce blue-white light, casting shadows knife-edged and blinding. Cerelinde held herself taut, frozen with terror, fighting the awful tendrils of pity that probed at her heart. "Forgive me," she said softly. "My Lord Satoris."

He rose and turned away from her.

The marrow-fire dwindled. The Shaper's massive shoulders twitched; or was it a trick of the flickering shadows? "You did not know." His voice was rough-edged, pitched to an ordinary tone. "Cerelinde."

She fought back another wave of pity. "I have not lied to you, my Lord."

"No." Again he sighed, filling the chamber, and turned to face her. "Do not take too much hope from this, little Ellyl. What has happened, has happened. If my plans have gone awry, no less have my brother's. And if Tanaros Blacksword is trapped in the Marasoumië, so is the Wise Counselor."

"*Tanaros?*" The word escaped her unwittingly.

Something that might have been a smile shifted the Shaper's ebony features. "My Commander General is resourceful, Cerelinde. Let us hope together, you and I, for his safe return."

She gripped the arms of her chair and steeled her thoughts,

willing them to fix where they belonged. Blue eyes, at once demanding and questioning, met hers in memory. A promise given, a
promise made. It lent a sting to her words. "The Kingslayer has
wrought his own fate, my Lord. What of Aracus Altorus? What of
my betrothed?"

"Your betrothed." The Shaper turned away from her, resuming
his pacing, his shoulders slumping as if beneath a heavy burden.
"Ah, Cerelinde! He may fail, you know. Even in Beshtanag, he may
yet fail."

Her chin rose. "And if he does not?"

From a far corner of the chamber, he regarded her with crimson eyes. "He will destroy something precious," he said softly.
"And the fault will be mine."

She stared at him, uncomprehending.

Satoris Third-Born laughed his awful, hollow laugh. "Ah, Cerelinde! You want me to say he will pursue you in all haste; that he
will come here, seeking you. That Aracus Altorus will lay siege to
Darkhaven itself. Shall I say it? It is true, after all."

Hope and fear warred in her breast. "And what will become of
me, if he does?"

"Do you care so little for what he will destroy?" The Shaper's
voice was wistful. "Will you not even ask what it *is?*"

"My Lord—!"

"Never mind." He turned away from her again, a dark shape in
a dark corner. One hand moved, dismissing her. "Begone from me,
daughter of Erilonde. Your presence does not ease my grief this
night."

She took her leave, then, rising and gathering her skirts. Beyond her the stairwell beckoned, the three-fold door at the top
opening onto the shadowy, twisted passages that led back to her
chambers, to the hidden door behind the tapestry. Hesitating on
the first step, she glanced over her shoulder. He stood yet, motionless, a column of darkness, hands laced behind his back. "My Lord
Satoris . . . "

"*Go!*"

His voice echoed like thunder.

Cerelinde fled. Behind her, the three-fold door closed with a
mighty crash. On the far side, she found herself shaking.

In the thousands of years she had lived, she had never doubted
the nature of truth. Now, uncertainty assailed her; doubt and insid-
ious pity. A thing she had never before grasped had grown clear:

the Sunderer believed his own lies. And in the irregular glimmer of the marrow-fire, a worm of doubt whispered a thought.

What if they were not lies?

"No." Cerelinde said aloud. "It is madness that speaks, not truth."

The words brought a measure of comfort; but only a measure. She made her way slowly through the walls of her prison, the sound of Satoris Banewreaker's terrible, despairing laughter still echoing in her ears.

THREE RAVENS CIRCLED OVERHEAD.

Ushahin watched them, shading his eyes with one hand. The skies above the plains of Rukhar were a merciless blue and the sun's bright light drove a spike of pain through his left eye. It didn't matter. He was used to such pain, and his awareness rode upon it as if borne upward on a warm draught, rising skyward.

Come, little brothers, he thought. What have you seen?

A flurry of images filled his mind in reply; stone, grey and barren. Straggling weeds, bitter ants crawling. There was a paucity of life on the plains, and the ravens did not want to land.

His mouth twisted in a wry smile. For that, he did not blame them.

With Tanaros and Malthus both trapped within them and struggling for mastery, the Ways of the Marasoumië were too dangerous to enter. He had walked out of Jakar; walked a day and a night across the plains, sifting through the dreams of Men as he went, until his ill-knit bones protested at every step. That didn't matter to him either. The only pain that mattered was the one that circumscribed his heart; Godslayer's branding beckoning him *home,* to the only home left to him. But without the Ways, his path was uncertain. To the west lay the Unknown Desert, its blazing sands forbidding. To the north lay the encampments of the Rukhari tribesmen and their scorn. To the east . . . ah, to the east lay Pelmar, where once the Grey Dam had called him her son, and there he did not dare go.

So he had gone south.

You need not land, Ushahin told the ravens. Only tell me what you have seen.

The ravens dipped lower, sunlight glinting violet and green on the edges of their wings as they circled in a narrowing gyre. Flickering images flitted from mind to mind; of the tops of pines like a dark green ocean; of columns of Men and Ellylon winding through the dense forest, amassing at the base of a mountain; of a fortress hunkered on the mountain's swell; of a seamless wall of granite. Of the explosion of sunlight refracting on bronze scales and a sinuous neck lifting a vast-jawed head, amusement in one slitted green eye.

Yes, little brothers, he thought; I know. What of the south?

Their vision skirted the edges of Arduan, where men and women gathered in the marketplaces and exchanged news, waiting; waiting, with longbows close at hand. There the ravens dared not go, remembering the arrows that had felled their brethren. But beyond, the marshes of the Delta unfurled like a rich, grey-green carpet, fecund and plentiful. There, they landed and fed. The shiny carapaces of beetles loomed large in memory, crunching with satisfaction under beaks; small snails, sweet and tasty.

At that, Ushahin smiled.

And further . . . one had flown, only one, following the sluggish path of the Verdine River as it emerged from the marshes. There, where the sharp-toothed sedge grass grew in abundance, three horses grazed. They were tall and strong and clean of limb, with dark, glossy hides and ill-kept manes and tails, tangled from the remnants of a long-abandoned disguise. Whatever had become of the Staccians who had entered the Delta, they had left their mounts behind and no one had succeeded in laying possessive hands on the horses of Darkhaven. One tossed its head as the raven swooped low, nostrils flaring and sharp teeth bared, a preternatural gleam of intelligence in its eyes.

Yes.

Ushahin Dreamspinner laughed. "So, my Lord Satoris," he said aloud. "It seems my path lies through the place of your birth."

Free of his mind's hold, the ravens broke from their tight spiral and soared, winging higher, rising to become specks in the blue sky.

Go, he sent a final thought after them. Go, little brothers, and I will meet you anon!

TWENTY-FOUR

EVEN IN SUMMER, IT WAS cold in the mountains.

It had not seemed so bad when they emerged, though he reckoned that was due to the relief at finding themselves alive. Frightened, yes. He was frightened. One moment, they had been in the Ways of the Marasoumië, under Malthus' protection. He hadn't been afraid, then, after they escaped the Were. Not for himself, only for those they left behind. The Ways were fearful and strange, but Malthus was there.

And then they had encountered the others, with a jolt he still felt in his bones. Thousands and thousands of them, huge and hulking, like creatures from a nightmare. The red light of the Marasoumië illuminated their jutting tusks, their massive talons, the heavy armor that encased their hide-covered bodies. A column of Fjeltroll, an army of Fjeltroll, winding back into the Ways as far as the eye could see.

It was a man on a black horse who led them, and he did not have to be told to know it was one of the Three. The Slayer, who had throttled love with his bare hands. And the sword he bore, the black blade, was forged in the marrow-fire itself and quenched in the blood of Satoris the Sunderer.

Everything the Counselor had said was true.

Whatever Malthus had done with the Soumanië had swept them into the Ways, driving them backward—but not the Slayer. Though he had been unhorsed, the Soumanië's power could not touch him. There was a circle of burning shadow that surrounded and protected him.

He had drawn his black sword, preparing to slay the Counselor.

Trust me, Malthus had said.

And then the world had exploded in a rush of crimson light, and stone had swallowed them whole, sending them hurtling. Away, away, farther than he had dreamed possible. Swallowed them and digested them and spat them out in the cavern in the mountains, so far north that pockets of snow lay in the gulches. And here they had to fight for their survival.

"Dani, you need to eat."

Uncle Thulu's face was worried. He extended a roasted haunch of hare on a spit. It had taken him the better part of a day to catch it.

"Yes, Uncle."

The meat was hot and greasy. Dani picked at it, burning his fingers. It felt slick on his tongue and juices filled his mouth as he chewed. He swallowed, feeling the meat slide down his throat. His belly growled and contracted around it, and he took another bite, suddenly voracious.

Uncle Thulu's dark face creased in a grin. "The Bearer is hungry!"

"Yes." He smiled back around a mouthful of meat. "I am."

"Good."

For a long time, neither of them spoke. There was only the sound of teeth rending meat, the murmurs of gladdened bellies. Between them they picked the bones clean and sucked them. Their little fire crackled merrily. Dani had lit it himself, twirling a sharpened stick between his palms until the pine mast he had gathered caught and glowed, sending a tendril of smoke into the clean air. A good thing, as cold as they were.

When they had done, Uncle Thulu leaned back and patted his belly. "Ah," he sighed. "That's good."

"Uncle." Dani hunched forward, wrapping his arms about his knees, staring at their fire. Afternoon shadows played over his features and the clay vial strung about his neck bumped his bare, bony kneecaps. "Where are we? What has become of us? What has become of Malthus?" He rested his chin on his knees, his expression miserable. "What do I do now, Uncle?"

"I don't know, lad." Uncle Thulu's voice was brusque. Leaning forward he placed another deadfall on the fire. "We're in Staccia, I think. Or Fjeltroll country. North."

"It's cold." Dani shivered.

"Aye." Uncle Thulu watched a shower of sparks rise. "A good job that Blaise bought cloaks for us. Wish I'd taken him up on the boots. Might have, if they'd fit."

Dani regarded his own feet, bare and calloused, broadened by a lifetime of walking on the desert floor. He did not mind the stones, but the beds of his toenails were faintly blue. "It's cold here."

"Aye." Uncle Thulu nodded. "We're in the north, all right."

He lifted his head. "He must have had a plan."

"Malthus?"

Dani nodded.

"I don't know, Dani." His uncle picked at his teeth with a splintered bone, thoughtful and frowning. "I don't think he reckoned on the Sunderer's army being in the tunnels. I think he did his best to protect us, that's all. Sent us as far away as he could. As to what happens next, that's up to you."

"I don't *want* to decide!"

His voice sounded childish. Uncle Thulu gazed at him silently. He sighed and bowed his head, cupping his hands in front of him. The radiating lines that marred his palms conjoined, forming a perfect star. What a simple, silly thing! Why should it mean he, and he alone, could draw the bucket from the well? But it did, and he had. The proof of it was bound on a cord around his neck. Dani swallowed, remembering the words that had first stirred him, spoken by Malthus. *Yet in the end, the fate of Urulat rests in your hands, Bearer.* He had heeded the Counselor's words. He had drawn the Water of Life. He had borne it. In Malumdoorn, it had drawn life out of death. He remembered that, the green leaves springing from dead wood, the surge of joy he had felt at the sight.

"The choice is yours, Dani." Uncle Thulu's voice was gentle. "Always and forever. That is the trust Uru-Alat bequeathed to the Yarru-yami, revealed to us by Haomane's Wrath. We ward the Well of the World. You are the Bearer."

Dani hunched his shoulders. "What if I refuse?"

"Then that is your choice. Do you want to go home?" With the tip of his bone-splinter toothpick, Uncle Thulu pointed southward, to the left of the lowering sun. "It lies that way, Dani. The rivers of Neheris run south. We have but to follow them until they sink beneath the earth and the desert begins."

It was heavy, the vial. It hung about his neck like a stone. The water in it—the Water of Life—could extinguish the very marrow-fire. It had seemed like a glorious destiny at Birru-Uru-Alat. To think he held the power, cupped in his hands, to heal the world! The danger had seemed very far away. Even on the marsh-plains, when they had been attacked, it seemed there was no danger from which Malthus could not protect them. Not any more. Not since the Were had come out of the forest, silent and deadly. Not since he had seen the army of Darkhaven in the Ways in its incomprehensible numbers, led by one of the Three. All that Malthus said; it was true. Satoris the Sunderer had raised a vast legion and he meant to conquer the world.

And the Company that had sworn to protect the Bearer . . .

"Do you think any of them are left alive?" he asked.

"I don't know, Dani," Uncle Thulu said. "It didn't look good."

He turned his head and gazed in the direction of the setting sun, thinking about their companions. Malthus, whom he had believed could do anything. Blaise, steady and competent. The Haomanegaali, Peldras, so gentle and wise. Proud Hobard, whose anger was not really anger, but a thing driven by fear. Fianna, who was kind and beautiful. And Carfax—oh, Carfax! The Staccian had saved him in the end. Tears stung Dani's eyes. A golden wash of light lay over the mountain peaks, casting the valleys in shadow. Already the sun's warmth was fading. He dashed away his tears with the back of one hand and took a deep breath. "How far is it to Darkhaven?"

Uncle Thulu shook his head. "I cannot be sure. A long way."

"Can you find it?"

There was a pause. "Are you sure that's what you want?"

"Yes." Dani laced his fingers about his knees to hide their trembling and met his uncle's somber gaze. "If they died, they died trying to protect me. And if they did not . . . " He swallowed. "I would be ashamed to have them know I failed without trying."

Picking up his digging-stick, his uncle hummed deep in his chest, a reassuring and resonant sound. "Then we will find it, Dani. You are the Bearer, and I have promised the Yarru-yami to remain at your side, to guide your steps no matter how you choose." He turned the stick in his hands, humming absently. "Where water flows beneath the earth, I will chart the ways. When we find the taint of the Shaper's blood, we will follow it to Darkhaven."

"Good." His burden felt lighter for having decided. He edged closer to his uncle. They sat in companionable silence, sharing the warmth of their cloaks, watching blue twilight descend over the mountains. "Uncle?"

"Aye, lad?"

"We're not likely to live through this, are we?"

The deep humming faltered. He looked up to meet his uncle's gaze. "No," Uncle Thulu said quietly. "Venturing into the bowels of Darkhaven? Not likely, lad."

He nodded, remembering the gleam of moonlight on the pelts of the Were, the companions they had abandoned. "That's what I thought."

"I'm sorry, Dani."

"It's all right." Beneath his cloak, Dani fumbled for the vial at his throat, closing his fingers about its strange weight, obscurely comforted by his burden. "Uncle, what do you think he meant?"

"Who?"

He shivered. "The Slayer. The man with the black sword. 'Listen,' he said."

Uncle Thulu gazed at the fire, his hands gone still on his digging-stick. It was dark now, and the flickering light cast shadows in the hollows of his eyes and the crease beside his broad nose. "I don't know, Dani," he murmured. "I am only the guide. You are the Bearer."

"He sought to kill Malthus."

"Aye." His uncle nodded. "Aye, that I believe he did."

He held the vial, pondering its heft. "Well," he said at length. "It is a long way to Darkhaven. We will see."

"Aye," his uncle said softly. "That we will."

THE MARASOUMIË WAS LOOSENING ITS grip on Tanaros.

The terrible will he exerted was only part of it. In truth, he should not have been able to prevail against Malthus; not with the wizard wielding the Soumanië. Once he regained a measure of his depleted strength, Malthus should have been able to wrest himself into the Ways, sealing Tanaros in the Marasoumië.

He hadn't, though. Foolish wizard. It seemed his priorities lay with his Companions. Even now he struggled like a fly caught in amber, sending his strength *elsewhere* to shore up a fading spell, using the dregs of his exhausted power to cast a pall of protection over those who had none. Sensing it, Tanaros grinned without knowing it, the memory of his face shaping a rictus. With his right hand clenched on his sword-hilt, feeling the annealing power of a Shaper's blood temper his will, he fought for mastery of the Ways.

Fought, and won.

It came all of a rush, a node-point opening to his command. Gathering himself and his will, Tanaros scrambled for selfhood, wresting his shape out of the molten *nowhere* of the Marasoumië, reclaiming the mortal form he had worn for more than a thousand years. If there was a hand to grip a sword-hilt, there must be an arm to wield it. If there was a mouth to grin, there must be a face to wear it. If there was a heart to beat, there must be a breast to contain it. Bit by bit, Tanaros gathered himself until he was a man, standing, his feet beneath him.

There.

His lungs opened, drawing in a sobbing breath. Without a second thought, he hurled himself into the Ways, into the constricting passage. One step, two, three; my Lord, I am *coming,* he thought, an ecstatic rush surging into his palm, fueling his veins. The black blade trembled, keening its own song. Stone rushed past him, disorienting.

Crimson light pulsed.

Tanaros stumbled, staggering, into open air.

It was a cavern. That much he saw, as his mastery of the Marasoumië faded. He set his feet and turned slowly in a circle, his sword extended. The sound of his breathing filled the empty space. The node-light went grey and lifeless, and darkness reclaimed the cavern. Somewhere in the Marasoumië, Malthus the Counselor had realized his error and managed to close the Ways at last.

Wherever Tanaros was, he was trapped.

He gave a short laugh at the irony of it. The cavern lay within the Ways, so there must be tunnels—but he was deep, deep below the surface, with no idea in which direction an egress might lie. No food, no water. There was air, for the moment. How long could he endure without them? What would become of his immortal flesh? Tanaros closed his eyes, remembering another journey beneath the earth, and beauty and terror commingled. "Cerelinde," he mused aloud. "Have I found the death you feared?"

His voice echoed in the vaulted space, punctuated by the sound of a drop of water falling; amplified, louder than any drip should be.

Tanaros opened his eyes.

It was dark in the cavern, but not wholly so. And it smelled of water; of the essence of water, of something that was to water as the Shaper's ichor was to mortal blood. Like water, only *sweeter.*

With dark-adjusted eyes he saw it—there, on the far side, a pool of water and a tiny point of light upon it, refracting a distant glitter of sun. Putting up his sword, Tanaros approached it. Deep, that cistern; unknowably deep. A single stalactite overhung it, glistening with gathering moisture. Leaning over the pool and craning his neck, he saw fresh marks gouged into the wall of the cistern. He knew those gouges. Deep and plunging, taking bites from stone as if from a hunk of stale bread; that was the work of a Fjeltroll's talons. A man could climb using those handholds, if he were strong enough to hoist himself up there.

Far, far above was sky, a blue disk no larger than a teacup.

Sheathing his sword, Tanaros reached out into the air above the cistern. The narrow shaft of sunlight illuminated his hand. It was warm on his skin; hot and dry. He rotated his hand. Sunlight lay cupped in his calloused palm. On the underside, the air that kissed his knuckles was cooler and moist, rising from the pool below. He could almost taste it.

"The Well of the World," he whispered.

It seemed impossible . . . and yet. What other water was so still, so motionless? Surely this must be the very navel of Urulat. He crouched beside the pool and watched the motionless water. It was folly to be here, and folly to linger. Still, he could not leave. If it was true, this water was old. It had been old when the world was Sundered; it had been old when the world was Shaped. With the utmost care he extended his arm and dipped the tip of one finger into the water, which didn't even ripple.

It was cool.

It was wet.

It was water, and it was the lifeblood of Urulat; of Uru-Alat, the World-God that was. It was the essence of water, all water, everywhere. Of the snow that fell in the mountains of Staccia, of Meronin's seas that circumscribed dry land. Of rain that fell like mercy on the plains of Curonan, and springs that bubbled in the forests of Pelmar. Of stagnant water standing in the Delta, and swift rivers flowing fresh through the Midlands.

With an effort, Tanaros withdrew his hand.

A single drop of water gathered on the tip of his finger. It was heavy, so heavy! With his free hand, he braced his forearm, watching the drop swell and gather, hanging round and full on his fingertip. It gleamed in the narrow sunbeam, refracting an entire world in its globular walls. Sun and sky, water and stone. As he watched, the drop of water changed shape, its rounded base broadening. Where it touched the pad of his fingertip, there where his skin whorled in tiny ridges, the connection narrowed, becoming a taut band of water, stretching, impossibly thin, until it snapped.

It fell.

A drop of water, falling into the pool. At close range, it rang like a gong in the enclosed space. Slow concentric ripples spread from the center of the pool, measured and perfect. Watching them lap against the edges of the pool and rebound with infinite precision, Tanaros stuck his finger into his mouth and sucked it.

Moisture, the essence of moisture, penetrated his parched tissues.

He hadn't know, until then, how deeply he thirsted. But there was enough life, enough *water,* in the thin film that clung to his skin to revitalize the flesh he had reclaimed from the Marasoumië. Strength, green and young, surged in him; he felt made anew. Every fiber of his being sang with vitality. He had not known such hope and urgency since his wedding night.

That, too, had been a kind of rebirth. A celebration of a mystery, of two becoming one. Of the quickening of desire, the joining of the flesh. A shared breath passed from one mouth to another, hearts beating in rhythm. Calista had laughed aloud in wonder at the discovery; the memory of it still cut like a blade. Tanaros could never have believed, that night, that she would betray their marriage bed.

But she had, and something in him had died. Yet here he was, born anew.

And he had his Lordship's trust, aye, and the loyalty of the Fjel. These things alone sufficed to render life worth the living. Who was to say what else his future held in store? Desire, perhaps; or even love. Not even the Seven Shapers knew the whole of what-might-be.

Tanaros bounded to his feet and laughed. With a standing leap, he caught the lowest tier of holes gouged into the cistern wall, digging his fingers into them. He hung suspended. With an effort he hauled his body upward until his gaze was level with his own knuckles. His armor dragged at him, threatening to dislodge him. Too late to remove it now.

This would be the hard part.

Taking a deep breath, he let go with one hand, reaching upward without hesitation. If he'd swung on Malthus with the same speed at their first encounter, the wizard might have died in the Ways. He shouldn't have hesitated when he saw the boy. Blind and questing, his fingertips found the second tier of handholds; found, and held. Trusting for an instant to his grip, he dangled from one arm. Then he found the second hold with his left hand. His arms strained in their sockets as he hoisted his body upward.

Once more.

In a strange way, it felt good. His muscles quivered in agony at the strain, but it was a simple pain and one he understood. The Water of Life, the lifeblood of Urulat, coursed in his veins and he had never felt more hale or alive. There was no mystery here, only the body's strength, pitted against the sheer rockface. At the third tier of gouges his scrambling feet found purchase. Wedging his booted toes into the lowest holes, Tanaros clung to the cistern wall and caught his breath, letting his legs take his weight.

After that, it was simply a matter of climbing.

It took long hours, and there were times when his fingers ached and his muscles quivered and he could do nothing but press his face to the rock and wait for the trembling to pass, longing only to let go, to let himself fall, plunging into the deep cistern below. Easy, so easy! But he was Tanaros Blacksword, one of the Three, and he would not give up that easily. Inch by inch, he climbed, tenacious as any spider to scale the Defile's walls. Above him, the disk of sunlight broadened, the quality of the light slanting and changing as the sun moved in its circuit westward.

At length his searching hand found no gouge where it reached, only a lip of rough-hewn stone. His fingertips scrabbled, catching a grip. Remembering the taste of the Water of Life in his mouth, Tanaros drew his right leg up beneath him, finding a foothold. Pushing hard and heaving with both arms, he cleared the lip of the well. His head emerged in open air and he shoved hard against the foothold, the rest of his body following as he tumbled over the edge, armor clattering against rock.

"Lord General!" A relieved shout in an unmistakable Midlander accent greeted his arrival. "Am I glad to see *you!*"

Tanaros found his feet and stood.

The setting sun was as red as blood, flooding the desert with a sanguine hue. He stood atop a promontory of rock situated in the center of a dry basin. Arrayed around its perimeter were standing stones, two and three times the height of a man, casting stark shadows on the sand. Within the circle were other figures, human and Fjel alike, set in a strange tableau.

"Speros!" Tanaros shaded his eyes, unreasoningly glad to see the Midlander alive. "How did you come here? Who *are* these people?"

"As to how we got here, I can't say, my lord." Speros picked a path across the basin, carrying his sword unsheathed in one hand and ignoring the motionless figures who sat on their haunches on the cooling sands. A squadron of four Gulnagel Fjel shifted position as he moved, maces at the ready, keeping a watchful eye on the still figures. "The five of us were caught in the Marasoumië, when the wizard came, and here we found ourselves; or underearth,

rather. I'm not one of the Three, to understand the workings of the
Ways. But these—" arriving at the base of the rocks, he nodded
backward at the squatting humans, "—are the Charred Ones, those
whom Haomane's Wrath drove underearth. And unless I miss my
guess, Lord General, these are the ones plotting to extinguish the
marrow-fire."

Tanaros stared at him.

Behind the Midlander, one of the squatting humans rose to his
feet in a painstaking effort, joints creaking. He was old, his dark,
wrinkled face bearing a map of his years. They were all old, all of
them. An elderly woman beside him hissed in disapproval and
tugged at his kneecap, though he paid her no heed. The Gulnagel
moved in a step closer, their hided muscles flexing.

Tanaros held up one hand, halting their movement. "You
would speak, old one?"

"Slayer!" The old man returned his greeting in the common
tongue. Shifting an unseen wad into one cheek, he hawked and
spat onto the sands. "Welcome to Birru-Uru-Alat. We have been expecting you."

"YOU DID A GOOD THING back there, Staccian."

The Borderguardsman's voice was quiet, but it spoke volumes
in praise. Kneeling over the fire, Carfax felt the back of his neck
flush. He concentrated on the fire, feeding it bit by bit, laying
branches in such a way as would build a solid blaze. The silence
lingered between them, growing heavy. "Don't know about that,"
he muttered at length. "I couldn't watch the boy slaughtered, is all."

"Or Fianna," Blaise said softly, so softly the Archer could not
hear.

Carfax looked up sharply, rubbing his palms on his thighs.
"What of her?"

"Nothing." The Borderguardsman shook his head. By firelight
his resemblance to General Tanaros was more apparent; the same
spare, handsome features, the same errant lock of dark hair across
his brow. "You have a good heart, Staccian. Why is it so hard for
you to hear?"

On the far side of the fire, the Ellyl stirred as if to speak, then
thought better of it, rising instead to check on the horses. The gentle whickering sound of their greeting carried in the night air. Carfax watched as Peldras touched them, laying pale hands on their
hides, soothing aching knees, strained hocks. The Ellyl spoke in-

audibly to Fianna, who rummaged through their stores. He could hear her soft laugh of delight at whatever the Ellyl said, and wondered what it must be like to move through the world with such grace that all must acknowledge it. Even so, it was the Borderguardsman she loved. The Ellyl was beyond her reach, a Lesser Shaper of a higher order. It had taken Haomane's Prophecy and a thousand years of refusal before the Lady of the Ellylon would consider a mortal lover. An ordinary woman like Fianna would never dare to dream of such a liaison. What the Ellyl thought, only Haomane knew.

"Staccian?" Blaise prompted him.

"I don't know." Carfax mumbled the words. Shifting, he sat on the pine mast, hiding his face against his knees. "Don't be so quick to speak kindly to me," he said without looking up. "If I had thought deeper, my lord Blaise, I might not have acted. Because of me, the Bearer's quest continues."

"Aye," Blaise said. "Haomane's Allies are in your debt."

Carfax gave a strangled laugh. "I have betrayed my loyalties and all I hold dear."

"No. Only those false loyalties you were taught. It is not the same." Removing a whetstone from a pouch at his belt, Blaise began honing his sword, smoothing away the nicks it had gotten battling the Were. It was a homely sound, stone grinding on metal. "I asked you once what manner of man you wanted to be, Staccian. You have shown me through your actions. A man of honor, willing to risk his life to protect the innocent. I tell you tonight, Aracus Altorus would welcome one such as you into his service."

"Why?" he whispered.

"Because he understands what it means to be King of the West." Fianna had approached him from behind, her steps inaudible on the pine mast. Her hands lit on his shoulders, her face bending down beside his. "Oh, Carfax! You have proved a true companion in this venture when all but the Wise Counselor would have doubted you. Do you think Aracus Altorus will not see it?"

It was hard to think, with her soft breath brushing his cheek. Exhaling hard, he lifted his head and focused on the Borderguardsman. "Why *him*, Blaise? What has he done to win *your* loyalty?"

"Can you not guess?" Blaise Caveros laid his sword across his knees. His dark eyes held Carfax's in a steady gaze. "You, who have served under the Kingslayer? He trusted me, Staccian. Since we were boys. Always." His mouth twisted in a wry smile. "If the Kingslayer's wife had not betrayed him, his blood would run in

Aracus' veins. Instead, Aracus is the last scion of the House of Altorus, while for a thousand years, my family's name has been a by-
word for betrayal. Aracus Altorus measured me by the contents of
my heart and made me his right hand. He gave my family back its
honor, Staccian. Is that not enough? Can you say as much of
Tanaros Blacksword?"

"No," Carfax whispered.

"And Satoris Banewreaker?" Blaise's voice hardened. "How is it
you serve *him*? Has the Sunderer dealt so gently with his Staccian
allies?"

"No." He pressed the heels of his hands against his eyes. "Yes!
I don't know, my lord!" Carfax drew a long, shuddering breath.
"What would you have me say?" he asked miserably, raising his
bloodshot gaze. "He played us fair! Battle-glory and generous recompense for the fallen. That's the bargain Lord Vorax has ever offered on Lord Satoris' behalf, and from time out of mind, we've
taken it. And he has kept his terms! For a thousand years, no enemy has lifted a blade within our borders, and no child has hungered. This, Lord Satoris has done for us. Can any other nation of
Men claim the same? My family dwells in peace and comfort because I serve his Lordship. Is it so wrong?"

"If it keeps the world Sundered, aye." Blaise's tone was surprisingly gentle. "Forgive me, Staccian, but I do believe it."

"You have so much *faith!*" The words burst from his lips. Carfax glared at them; glared at them all, for now the Ellyl had returned and all four were arrayed about the campfire. "How can you
know? How can you be so *sure?*"

They glanced at one another, and at him, pitying.

It was Peldras who answered, lowering himself gracefully to sit
cross-legged beside the fire. "Carfax of Staccia," he said, "let me ask
you this: How is it you cannot?"

Carfax shook his head, unable to articulate a reply.

"My people are dying." The Ellyl tilted his head, regarding the
distant stars. "We are fading, bit by bit. We are Haomane's Children,
and we drew our strength from the Souma. Without it, we are
bereft. We are the Rivenlost. The way home is forbidden us." He
turned the weight of his luminous gaze on Carfax. "We are Haomane's Children, and while we live, we are an affront to the Sunderer, and one he would destroy. Do you deny it?"

"No," he said, miserable. "But—"

"But tomorrow we will be in Beshtanag," Blaise said brusquely.
"Which is a trap. You have said so yourself, Staccian. I mean to give

warning to my lord Aracus Altorus. I spoke the truth, before. You acquitted yourself well. Now I need to know: Do you stand with us or against us? Will you pledge your loyalty to me?"

Carfax blinked, his vision streaked by tears. Why was it that the rest of the world seemed so far away? It felt like a lifetime had passed since he set out from Darkhaven. These people had become his companions, the only ones left to him. He had traveled with them, eaten with them, fought with them back-to-back. One had sacrificed himself to save his worthless life. He remembered Hobard, his father's sword in his hand and urgency straining his bloodstained face, the wave of Were that had swallowed him. *This is my death. Go!*

But . . .

He remembered Turin, Hunric; the men he had left behind, obedient to his orders. He remembered the men he had led and how they had trusted him. How he had led them into battle, singing, sure of victory. They had been good comrades, and true. They had trusted his leadership, and General Tanaros had trusted him to lead them. And he had erred in his folly and the earth had risen to engulf them. He was a traitor, aye. He had saved Dani's life. He had admitted that Beshtanag was a trap, and Lord Satoris' raven had watched him do it. Oh, aye, Carfax of Staccia was a traitor of the first order, but he was man enough still not to profit by it. Not while his own men rotted in barrows beneath the sedge grass.

"I can't." The words came harshly, catching in his throat. The tears were flowing freely, coursing his cheeks. "Forgive me, Blaise, but I can't."

The Borderguardsman nodded with regret.

"Carfax, please!" Fianna's face swam in his vision, and there were tears in her own eyes, shining on her cheeks. How not? Archer or no, she was a woman, and women reckoned the cost. Always, women reckoned the cost. Her hands found his, gripping them tightly. "You saved my life! How can you name yourself aught but a friend?"

"I wasn't prey." He blinked at her, clutching her hands. Soft, so soft, save for the bowstring's calluses. "Do you understand? The Were wouldn't attack me. I might as well have struck an unarmed man."

"As *they* did!" Her voice rose. "You defended Dani, too, who never raised his hand to anyone! Where is the wrong in that?"

Carfax shook his head and looked away, withdrawing from her grasp. "Dani raised his hand against Darkhaven when he drew forth the Water of Life," he murmured. "Malthus knew it, if the boy did not. And the Were knew it, too. I'm sorry, Fianna." Gathering himself, he met Blaise's eyes. "I'll do nothing to thwart your purpose. You have my word on that, my lord. But I cannot pledge you my loyalty." He swallowed against the lump in his throat. "I ride into Beshtanag as your prisoner."

"So be it." The Borderguardsman's gaze was steady. "My hand is extended in friendship, Staccian. It will be there should you wish to take it."

Not trusting himself to speak, Carfax nodded.

TWENTY-FIVE

❖

THE WALL WAS FAILING.

It was simply too much to hold. For three days, Haomane's Allies had assailed it without cease. Day and night, night and day. No one could sleep for the sound of battering rams thudding mercilessly against granite, seeking cracks where Lilias' power weakened.

She had held out longer than she had dreamed possible. It wasn't easy work, Shaping, and she was neither Ellyl nor Counselor, with Haomane's Gifts in her blood to make it easier. Rock and stone fought her will, seeking to return to their original form. Again and again, her bindings loosened. With grim determination, she held them in place, until exhaustion left her weak and dizzy, forgetful of her surroundings.

"Please, my lady! You *must* drink."

The cool rim of a cup touched her lower lip. Raising her head with a jerk, Lilias saw Sarika kneeling before her, eyes pleading. "Sweetling." She steadied the girl's hands with her own, drinking deep. The water forged a cool trail into her empty belly, lending the illusion of fullness. "Our stores endure?"

"Water." Sarika licked her lips involuntarily. "There is water, and quarter-rations of gruel for the wardsmen. As you ordered, my lady."

"Yes." Lilias pressed one hand to her brow, feeling the weight of the Soumanië. "Of course." A hollow boom shook the mountain as a battering ram struck her wall for the hundredth time that morning, and she shuddered. "Where is Gergon?"

"He's coming." It was Radovan's voice that spoke; Radovan, whose smouldering eyes had pleased her once. Now they stared at her with dark hatred, and disdain laced his voice. "My lady." He spat the words like an epithet, running one grimy finger beneath the linked silver collar that bound him to her.

It was folly, of course. She should have freed him before this began; should never have bound them so close. Any of them, her pretty ones. It had never been necessary, not with the good ones. How had it begun? A sop to her mortal vanity; to pride, to desire. What was power good for if not for that? It pleased her to be surrounded by youth in all its fleeting beauty. What was immortality good for without simple pleasures? She was a generous mistress. None of them had ever taken any harm from it, only tales to tell their grandchildren.

Too late, now. As strained as the linkage was, it would take more to sever it than to maintain it. Lilias shoved aside her regrets and shook her head like a fly-stung horse, impatient. "Gergon?"

"There, my lady." Sarika pointed, her voice soothing.

He looked like an ant toiling up the mountainside. They all looked like ants. Her wardsmen, the Warders of Beshtanag, defending the mighty wall. Other ants in bright armor swarmed it, creeping along the top with their siege-towers and ladders, while the battering ram boomed without ceasing. Lilias sat back in her chair, surveying her crumbling empire. She remembered, now. She'd had a high-backed chair of office placed here, on the terrace of Beshtanag Fortress itself, to do just that.

Lilias.

Calandor's voice echoed in her skull. "No," she said aloud. "No."

Her Ward Commander, Gergon, toiled up the mountainside, nodding as he went to archers posted here and there, the last defenders of Beshtanag. It was warm and he was sweating, his greying hair damp beneath his helmet. He took it off to salute her. "My lady Lilias." He tucked his helmet under his arm, regarding her. His face was gaunt and the flesh beneath his eyes hung in bags. He had served her since his birth, as had his father and his father's father before him. "I am here in answer to your summons."

"Gergon." Her fingers curved around the arms of the chair. "How goes the battle?"

He pointed. "As you see, I fear."

Below, the ants scurried, those inside the wall hurrying away under its shadow.

A loud *crr-ackk!* sounded and a web of lines emerged on a portion of the wall, revealing its component elements. Rocks shifted, boulders grinding ominously. Lilias stiffened in her chair, closing her eyes, drawing on the power of the Soumanië. In her mind she saw her wall whole and gleaming; willed it so, Shaped it so, shifting platelike segments of mica, re-forming the crystalline bonds of silica into a tracery of veins running throughout a single, solid structure. What she saw, she Shaped, and held.

There was a pause, and then the sound of the battering ram resumed.

Lilias bent over, gasping. "There!"

"Lady." Gergon gazed down at the siege and mopped the sweat from his brow, breathing a sigh that held no relief. "Forgive me, but it is the third such breach this morning, and I perceive you grow weary." His voice was hoarse. "I am weary. My men are weary. We are hungry, all of us. We will defend Beshtanag unto the death, only . . ." The cords in his weathered throat moved as he swallowed, hale flesh grown slack with privation and exhaustion. "Three days, you said. Today is the fourth. Where are they?"

Lilias, you must tell him.

"I know." She shuddered. "Ah, Calandor! I know."

Before her, Gergon choked on an indrawn breath, a fearful certainty dawning in his hollow-set eyes. He glanced down at his men, his shoulders sagging with defeat, then back at her. "They're not coming," he said. "Are they?"

"No," she said softly. With an effort, Lilias dragged herself upright in her chair and met his gaze, knowing he deserved that much. "I lied. I'm sorry. Something went awry in the Marasoumië. I thought . . . " She bowed her head. "I don't know what I thought. Only that somehow, in the end, it wouldn't come to this. Gergon, I'm sorry. I'm so sorry."

A sound arose; two sounds. They seemed linked, at first—the redoubled sound of the battering ram, Radovan's rising shout. He plunged at her, his smouldering eyes gone quite mad, the paring-knife held high overhead. Somewhere, Sarika's shrill scream echoed against Gergon's belated cry of protest.

Lilias dealt with it unthinking.

The Soumanië on her brow flared into life, casting its crimson glow. Abandoning every tendril of her defense of the wall, she drew upon the Soumanië and hurled every ounce of her remaining strength at him, Shaping the pulse of his life-force as surely as she had Shaped the veins of silica. Radovan stiffened mid-strike, his free hand clutching at his throat; at the silver collar he wore, the token of her will circumscribing his life. Sunlight shone on the edge of the paring-knife, casting a bar of brightness across her face. When had he stolen it? How long had he planned this? She had known, known she should have freed him! If he had only asked, only spoken to her of his resentment . . . but, already, it was too late. Panicked and careless, Lilias forgot all else, concentrating the Soumanië's power upon him, until his heartbeat fluttered and failed.

Lifeless knees buckling, Radovan slumped to earth.

At the base of the mountain, a great shout arose.

The crash resounded across the forests of Pelmar as a portion of her wall crumbled; crumbled, resolving itself irrevocably into shards and chips, rough-hewn boulders. There was a price to be paid for her lapse, for the act of will that had saved her life and taken his. A gap wide enough to drive a team of four through stood open, and Haomane's Allies poured through it. For three days, Aracus Altorus had held his troops at the ready, waiting for such an opening. Now he seized it unhesitating, and a trickle of ants grew to a stream, swelled to a flood. A clangor of battle arose and, all along the wall, defense positions were abandoned as the wardsmen of Beshtanag surged to meet the influx. Siege-ladders thumped against undefended granite. Haomane's Allies scrambled over the wall by the dozen, their numbers growing. On the terrace, her Ward Commander Gergon shouted futile orders.

"No," Lilias said, numb with horror. "No!"

How could it all fall apart so swiftly?

They came and they came, erecting battle-standards on Beshtanag Mountain. Regents of Pelmar, lords of Seahold, ancient families of Vedasia, and oh! The banners of the Ellylon, bright and keen, never seen on Beshtanagi soil. And there, inexorable, moved the standard of Aracus Altorus, the dun-grey banner of the Border-guardsmen of Curonan, unadorned and plain.

"No," Lilias whispered.

Now, Lilias.

"No! Wait!" She reached for the power of the Soumanië; *reached.* And for once, found nothing. After all, when all was said and done, she was mortal still, and her power had found its limits. Radovan lay dead, a paring-knife in his open hand, his heart stopped. The earth would not rise at her command and swallow her enemies; the roots of the dense forest would not drink their blood. The Soumanië was a dead ember on her brow. Somewhere, Sarika was weeping with fear, and it seemed unfair, so unfair. "Calandor, *no!*"

It is time, Lilias.

She had fallen to her knees, unaware. In a rising stillness no one else perceived, something bright flickered atop Beshtanag Mountain. Sunlight, glinting on scales, on talons capable of grasping a full-grown sheep, on the outstretched vanes of mighty wings. No one seemed to notice. At the base of the mountain, Haomane's Allies struggled on the loose scree inside the wall, fighting in knots, surging upward, gaining ground by the yard. Assured of her temporary safety, Ward Commander Gergon, striding down the mountain, shouted at his archers to fall back, fall back and defend. All the brightness in the world, and no one noticed.

"Please don't," Lilias whispered. "Oh, Calandor!"

Atop the mountain, Calandor roared.

It was a sound like no other sound on earth.

It held fire, gouts of fire, issuing forth from the furnace of the dragon's heart. It held all the fury of the predator; of every predator, everywhere. It held the deep tones of dark places, of the bones of the earth, of wisdom rent from their very marrow. It held love; oh yes. It held love, in all its self-aware rue; of the strong for the weak, of the burden of strength and true nature of sacrifice. And it was like trumpets, clarion and defiant, brazen in its knowledge.

"*Calandor,*" Lilias whispered on her knees, and wept.

Haomane's Allies went still, and feared.

Roaring, with sunlight glittering on his scales, on his taloned claws, on the vanes of his wings, rendering pale the gouts of flame that issued from his sinuous throat, the Dragon of Beshtanag launched himself. Below the brightness in the sky, a shadow, a vast shadow, darkened the mountain.

At last, Haomane's Allies knew terror.

Long before they reached Beshtanag they heard the clamor of battle, and another, more fearful sound, a roar that resonated in their very bones and made the blood run cold in their veins. Among the four of them, only the Ellyl had heard such a sound before. Blaise looked at him for confirmation and Peldras nodded, his luminous eyes gone dark and grave.

"It is the dragon."

Blaise looked grim. "Ride!"

For the last time, they charged headlong through the dense Pelmaran forests, matted pine needles churned beneath the hooves of their horses. Half-forgotten, Carfax brought up the rear, wondering and fearing what they would find upon reaching Beshtanag. From the forest's verge they saw the encampment of Haomane's Allies. Above the battlefield, at the foot of the great walled mountain, fire searing the skies.

Blaise Caveros uttered a wordless cry, clapping his heels to his mount's sides. When they reached the point where the treetops were smouldering he streaked into the lead, the other three following as they burst from dense cover. With his bared sword clutched in one fist, he abandoned his company and charged into battle shouting.

"Curonan! *Curonan!*"

Trailing, Carfax halted and watched in awe.

The wall that surrounded the mountain seemed impregnable; seamless granite four times the height of a tall man. And yet it had been breached. A vast gap lay open in the great wall that had surrounded Beshtanag, a gaping hole where the wall crumbled into its component stones. There, Men fought in the rubble, Men and Ellylon, and above it all, a bright shadow circled; circled, and breathed gouts of fire.

His heart caught inexplicably at the sight of it, at the dragon's vaned wings, outstretched to ride the drafts. Such terrible beauty! But where were the others? Where were the Fjel, stalwart and faithful? Where was the company of Rukhari that Lord Vorax had promised? Where was General Tanaros?

Peldras drew rein alongside him. "You did not expect this."

"No." Carfax frowned, following the dragon's flight. "Beshtanag was meant to be a trap. But not like *this*."

"How?" The Ellyl's voice was calm.

Atop her mount, Fianna was trembling. "Oh, Haomane!" The quiver she bore at her back pulsed with light. "Carfax, they are dying. *Dying!*"

It was true. Whatever had transpired before to breach the wall, Haomane's Allies were dying now, by the score. Bodies littered the ground inside the wall, many of them charred beyond recognition. Beshtanag's defenders surged toward the gap, seeking to secure their position and retake the breach, sealing it. And above them all, the dragon circled, casting a vast shadow on the base of the mountain.

"*Curonan!*"

A knot of men answering to the dun-grey standard had forged their way to the forefront. It was to their aid that Blaise had streaked, battling against the tide to reclaim the gap in the wall;

where a handful of men held the gap by dint of sheer valor. Above them the dragon circled, then stooped. The prudent Beshtanagi fell back to regroup on the mountainside. The men of Curonan flung themselves to the ground beneath the dragon's shadow. It passed over them, so low that its scaled belly almost scraped the top of the wall. The mighty jaws opened and gouts of white-hot flame issued forth from the gaping furnace.

One of the Borderguardsmen screamed, rolling. Others cried out and beat at smouldering garments. The smell of burning flesh hung in the air.

"Blaise!" Fianna whispered in anguish.

He was clear, wrenching his horse's reins mercilessly, his mount sidling free of the fire's scorching path. The dragon's wings beat hard, creating a powerful downdraft as its gleaming body banked and rolled. Its scaled tail, tipped with deadly spikes, swept like a cudgel. Blaise's mount danced, avoiding it by a narrow margin.

"Retreat, you idiots!" Watching the battle unfold, Carfax clenched his hands, longing for a blade. "For the love of Urulat, retreat!"

Horns echoed, silvery and clear, sounding a charge.

"My kinsmen!" Peldras' voice held a yearning note.

Beneath the banner of the gilded bee of Valmaré, a squadron of Rivenlost archers advanced in a gleaming line, paused and knelt, bows bent in taut arcs. A flurry of Ellylon arrows split the air, grey shafts arcing. In midair, the dragon turned, effortless as a fish in water, presenting a scaled shoulder. Arrows fell like rain, glancing off that scaled flesh and bouncing harmlessly on the stony ground as the dragon launched itself skyward, ascending out of range. Another horn sounded, Man-wrought, calling the retreat in urgent, brassy tones. Under the cover of Ellylon archers, the Borderguardsmen began a methodical retreat to the siege-lines, flanked by Pelmaran and Midlander soldiers. Blaise wheeled his mount, cantering alongside them. On the slope of the mountain, Beshtanagi wardsmen watched and waited.

"It's all right," Fianna breathed. "That's all right, then."

Peldras shook his head, pointing. "I fear not, Lady Archer."

High overhead the dragon halted its ascent, turning and stooping. There it hung, held aloft by the steady beating of its enormous wings, a glittering speck against the vast expanse of blue. Like a noonday star, Carfax thought, and wondered what had gone wrong. Something had. Something had gone terribly, terribly awry. The Army of Darkhaven had not come, and the Sorceress' power had failed. What else could have caused the wall to fall? He hadn't known every detail of Lord Satoris' plan—only the Three had known—but he was certain that the Dragon of Beshtanag had played no part in it. Not like this. The dragons had aided Lord Satoris once, and most of them had been slain for their role, in the days of old when doughty warriors like Altorus Farseer strode the earth and the Lords of the Ellylon wielded terrible power.

This was one of the last. It should not be here. Not like this.

"Oh, my Lord!" Carfax whispered, numb with horror.

Haomane's Allies halted in their retreat, turning and regrouping, wary of the dragon. They were bunched together; too tight, the ranks too close. Gathering their ragtag forces, the Beshtanagi wardsmen advanced, reclaiming the gap and surging through it, reforming their line in front of the wall.

I should have been there, Carfax thought, among those men. If all had gone as planned, I would be among them. If not for Malthus, I would be. And if the rest had gone as planned, Turin, Mantuas and Hunric *should* be among them, even now. They should have won through to Beshtanag. Have matters gone so terribly wrong that even their mission failed?

He strained his eyes for a glimpse of a familiar Staccian face, and did not know whether to be glad or anxious to see none.

I have no people here, he thought, despite all of Darkhaven's cunning.

Amid the army of Haomane's Allies, Blaise Caveros leaned down from the saddle, clasping hands with one of the Borderguardsman. There were discussion, protest, insistence. Dismounting, Blaise cupped his hands to boost the other into the saddle. Carfax watched as the last living descendent of the first King of Altoria removed his steel helmet, throwing back his head to address his army, words lost in the distance. The sunlight glinted on his red-gold hair. Aracus Altorus, who did not fear to lead men into battle, drew his sword, pointing it at the fortress of Beshtanag. Overhead, the dragon's wings beat steadily, holding it in position, patient as a hawk before it stoops. Aracus Altorus raised his sword aloft like a pennant. A single word tore loose over the din, shouted like a paean, echoed by a thousand throats, Men and Ellylon.

"... *Cerelinde!*"

"They're going to stand," Peldras said somberly. "For the Lady of the Ellylon, they're going to stand their ground."

Something that might have been a laugh or a sob caught in Carfax's throat. He rocked back and forth in the saddle, digging the heels of his hands into his eyes, unable to express the futility of it all. So many assembled, so many dying! And to what purpose? None. There was nothing here but a failed gambit. The agonizing cries of the wounded and dying on both sides of the battlefield scourged his soul. In anguish, Carfax of Staccia committed his final betrayal. "She's not there," he gasped. "She's not even *there!*"

The Ellyl touched his forearm, frowning. "What are you saying?"

"Oh, Haomane!" Fianna cried. "No!"

Too late, too late for everything. Far, far above them all, the dragon folded its wings and dove, dropping like a falling star. Its jaws stretched wide, opening onto an impossible gullet. Smoke trailed from its nostrils. Plated armor covered its breast, a nictitating membrane protected its eyes and its foreclaws were outstretched, each talon like an iron spike, driving earthward.

Whatever resolve Aracus Altorus had instilled in Haomane's Allies shattered.

Crying out in fear, vast numbers of the Pelmaran soldiery fled like leaves blown before a gale, carrying ill-prepared Midlander forces with them. Here and there, pockets of Vedasian knights gathered, seeking to rally around their standards, and the archers of the Rivenlost kept their line intact.

But it was the Borderguard of Curonan that held steadfast in the center.

At the last possible moment, the dragon's wings snapped open, membranes spreading like sails to brake its dive. Arrows and spears clattered from its impervious hide. Its neck wove back and forth like an immense serpent's, fire belching from its open maw as it swept low over the field, cutting a swathe through Haomane's Allies, not discriminating between nations and races. Everywhere, Men and Ellylon gibbered and wept, cowered under shields, died screaming and scorched. The dragon's claws flexed and gathered, and bodies dangled from the clutch of its gleaming talons as it soared upward; dangled, and fell like broken dolls as the talons released.

Somewhere, Aracus Altorus was shouting, and the surviving Borderguard answered with grim determination, gathering tight around him. In the smoke and chaos left in the dragon's wake, the Beshtanagi forces spread out and advanced, closing in on the far-flung edges of their attackers' forces, driving toward the center with desperate urgency.

Their numbers were few—but they outnumbered the Borderguard.

A lone figure stepped forth beneath the dun standard to meet the onslaught.

"Blaise!" Fianna spurred her mount unthinking, guiding it with her legs, her Archer's hands reaching as she sped across the battlefield, dodging around unmounted Beshtanagi wardsmen. Oronin's Bow was in her hand, her hand reaching over her shoulder. Light spilled from her quiver as she grasped an arrow, an ordinary arrow, fitting it to the string. The black horn bow sang a single, deadly note as she loosed it, and a wardsman fell, clutching his chest where an arrow sprouted. "*Blaise!*"

"Fianna!" Starting after her, Carfax felt the Ellyl's grip tighten on his forearm. "Peldras, let me go," he said, trying to pull away. "She's like to get slaughtered out there without armor or a guard!"

"Peace, Arahila's Child. I seek only the truth." The Ellyl's grip was gentle, but surprisingly firm. His deep gaze searched Carfax's face. "Will you withhold it while people die in vain?"

Above the battlefield, the Dragon of Beshtanag circled low, harrying fleeing soldiers and driving them back onto the battlefield as it came in for another pass. Fire roared, and cries of agony rose; a din of chaos and anguish. Somewhere, Oronin's Bow was sounding its single note, over and over. On the outskirts of it all, Carfax met Peldras' gaze. "Can you stop the fighting if I tell you?"

"I don't know, Carfax of Staccia." The Ellyl did not flinch. "I fear it may be too late to sue for a truce. But if the Lady Cerelinde is not here, I will do my best to carry word. Perhaps some lives may be saved, and Fianna the Archer's among them."

It was too late, after all. Too late for everything.

"She's in Darkhaven," Carfax said simply. With those few words, he surrendered the long burden of his loyalty and knew, in doing so, he accepted his death. When all was said and done, it was a relief, an unspeakable relief. He should have died with his men. He wished that he had. There was no honor in a life foresworn. It would be good to have it done. "Your Lady Cerelinde is in Darkhaven. She was never here. It was a trick, all a trick. General Tanaros was supposed to lead the army through the Ways and fall upon you from behind. Something went wrong. I don't know what."

Peldras nodded. "Thank you."

"May I go now?"

The Ellyl removed his hand from the Staccian's arm and drew his sword. Grasping it by the blade, he presented the hilt. "Take my blade, and my blessing. May Arahila the Fair have mercy upon you, Carfax of Staccia."

He grasped the hilt. It felt good in his palm. Firm. He hoisted it. The blade was light in his grip, its edge keen and silver-bright, its balance immaculate. Ellylon craftsmanship. "Thank you, Peldras."

Once more, the Ellyl nodded. "Farewell, my friend."

ON THE BATTLEFIELD, ALL WAS madness.

The Pelmaran forces had been routed to a man. Last to commit, first to flee. Carfax had to dodge them as he rode, his mount's hooves scrabbling on the loose scree at the base of Beshtanag Mountain. Here and there Beshtanagi wardsmen pursued them. It was hard to tell one from the other, clad alike in leather armor with steel rings, colors obscured by veils of smoke.

No matter. He wasn't here to fight anyone's war.

A pall of smoke hung over the battlefield, which reeked of smoke and sulfur, of charred flesh and spilled gore, of the inevitable stench of bowels voided in death. Carfax ignored it, guiding his horse with an expert hand past the dead and the dying, deserters and their pursuers, avoiding them and thinking of other times.

There had been a girl, once, in Staccia. He had brushed her skin with goldenrod pollen, gilding her freckles. And he had thought, oh, he had thought! He had thought to return home a hero, to wipe away the tears his mother had shed when he left, to smile into his girl's eyes and see her a woman grown, and wipe away the remembered traces of pollen from her soft skin.

Blaise had asked him: *Why do you smile, Staccian?*

To make a friend of death.

Thickening smoke made his eyes sting. He squinted, and persevered.

Fianna had smiled at him when he brought her pine rosin for her bow. Her Arduan bow, wrought of ordinary wood and mortal sinew. Not this one, that was made of black horn and strung with . . . strung with what? Hairs from the head of Oronin Last-Born, perhaps, or sinew from the Glad Hunter's first kill, sounding a Shaper's battlecry. It had twisted in her hands when she fought against the Were, refusing to slay its maker's Children.

Not so, here. Oronin's Bow sang in her hands, uttering its single note, naming its victims one by one. She had smiled at him, and he . . . he had made a friend of death. Here, at the end, there was a hand extended in friendship, and it was one he could take at last. A traitor, yes. He was that. Carfax of Staccia would die a traitor.

Still, there was honor of a kind in dying for a woman's smile. If nothing else, there was that.

He found himself singing a Staccian paean as he rode, and the Ellyl's sword was light in his grip as he swung it, forging a path toward the song of Oronin's Bow. Toward the center, the battle was in progress and it was necessary to fight his way through it. With expertise born of long hours on the drill-field, Carfax wielded the Ellylon blade. Left side, right side! On either side of his mount's lathered neck, the silver-bright blade dipped and rose dripping. A man's snarling face appeared at his stirrup and a spearhead gouged a burning path along his right thigh. Carfax bared his teeth in response and made a slashing cut, shearing away a portion of his opponent's face. Friend or foe? Which was which?

No matter.

Peering through the dense smoke, he won through to where the fighting was fiercest. A tight knot of men, hard to see in their dun-grey cloaks. The kneeling line of Ellylon, pausing in their retreat to fire and fire again, the points of their arrows clattering uselessly off their prey. The fine-wrought faces of the Rivenlost were grim. The dragon's body was vast and gleaming, churning the smoke-filled air. Only portions of it were visible at such close range, too vast for the mortal eye to encompass. Despite the whispered incantations of the Ellylon, the terrible courage of the Borderguardsmen, their weapons clattered harmlessly off its hide. Swords shattered, arrows fell to earth.

After all, what could penetrate those scales? This was no mere dragonling, but one of the ancient ones, one of the last. Even Elterrion the Bold would have hesitated to engage the Dragon of Beshtanag in the fullness of its wrath. Under cover of the devastation it wreaked, a desperate wedge of Beshtanagi wardsmen fell upon the enemy. Hand to hand, blade to blade, hollow-eyed and starving, ready to claim victory at the price of death. Some of the outnumbered Borderguard were standing, many were down. A charnel reek hung over them all. It didn't matter. There was only one person for whom Carfax searched. There was only one whose weapon mattered here.

And amidst all the chaos, she stood, calm and ready.

A smoke-wreathed statue, limned in pure light. Her quiver was empty. The Archer of Arduan had drawn her last arrow, *the* arrow, tracking the dragon with it, as calmly as though she were hunting rabbit. Oronin's Bow was in her left hand, the fingers of her right hand curled about the string, drawing it taut to her ear. A shaft of white fire, tinged with gold, illuminated the soft tendrils of hair that curled on her cheek.

The Arrow of Fire, Dergail's lost weapon, was ready to be loosed.

When, Carfax wondered, did she lose her horse?

A vaned pinion passed near overhead, a gout of fire was loosed elsewhere, and his mount squealed in terror, half-rearing and bucking. All unwitting, it took him closer to her, shaking him half-loose in the process. Carfax slid down its back, clutching at its mane with his free hand. He saw her shift at the sound, then gather herself, refusing to relinquish her focus. He saw the body she straddled, protecting it. Blood seeped from a wound on Blaise Caveros' brow, the Borderguardsman's face pale and drawn. He saw the vast, scaled expanse of the dragon's flank sliding past him. He saw a determined squadron of Beshtanagi making for the Archer. Before his thrashing, terrified mount threw him, he heard, somewhere, a voice he knew belonged to Aracus Altorus, shouting futile exhortations.

He saw the stony ground rushing up to meet him and felt it strike him hard.

"Here, dragon! Here, damn you! I'm waiting!"

It was Fianna's voice, rough-edged with despair, strung taut with defiance. Lying on his back, Carfax blinked and lifted his head. He saw tears making clean tracks on Fianna's soot-smudged cheeks. The bow was steady in her hands and the Arrow of Fire trailed flames of white-gold glory as the scaled underbelly of the dragon passed overhead. He groped for the Ellyl's sword and found he held it still, though his knuckles were scraped and raw. He felt at his body and found it intact. Completing its pass, the dragon climbed in the air, gaining altitude. Still alive and standing, Fianna tracked its progress, the Arrow's point blazing like a star. Carfax levered himself to his feet, lurching upright. Wet blood ran down his wounded right thigh, soaking his breeches, squelching in his boot. A reminder of another wound, one that never healed.

Forgive me, my Lord . . .

"The Arrow! The Arrow of Fire!"

It was an Ellyl voice that raised the cry, silvery and unmistakable. It was Men's voices that echoed it, harsh and ragged, forced through throats seared by smoke and fire. They had seen Fianna, seen what she held. With their diminished numbers, the Borderguard of Curonan sought to rally. But no one had expected to find the Archer of Arduan and the lost weapon on the battlefield, and she stood alone, isolated in a tightening circle of Beshtanagi wardsmen, her steady gaze and the Arrow's blazing point tracking the dragon's ascent.

He alone could protect her.

"Time to die," Carfax said aloud.

He took the closest man first. A thrust to the gut, no time wasted. The tip of the Ellyl blade pierced cured leather like butter. His wounded right leg quivered as he withdrew the sword, threatening to give way beneath him. No time for that. He ignored the weakness and made his feet move over the harsh terrain, picking another target, swinging two-handed. Another wardsman fell, and another, clearing a path around Fianna, who hadn't even registered his presence. No matter. It felt good to have a sword in his hands. Better if he had been wearing armor, good Staccian armor. It might have kept him from enduring the myriad strokes that scored his flesh until he bled from a dozen places or more. It might have turned aside the cold blade that ran him through from behind, penetrating something vital. Blood soaked his clothing, mingling with sweat, running down his skin.

Panting, Carfax pivoted on his numb leg and cut down his foremost attacker, and another who followed, and two more after, three more. They came and they came, and he struck and he struck, weaving a circle around her, until his blood-slickened arms had no more feeling in them. Again and again, until he could no longer raise his sword and the battlefield seemed to darken in his vision.

Death is a coin to be spent wisely.

Falling to his knees, he tried to remember who had spoken those words. It sounded like Lord Vorax. It might have been his mother. Oh, there was brightness in the world, for all that it was slipping from his grasp. He thought about blue lakes under a blue summer sky and goldenrod in bloom, a dusting of pollen. A Beshtanagi wardsman loomed out of the smoke, grimacing, a hand-axe held above his head, prepared to deliver the final blow. On his knees, Carfax blinked and thrust upward with both hands, taking the man under the chin. The point of his borrowed sword stuck in the man's brain-pan. "Staccians," he whispered, "die hard."

There was shouting, then, and the clashing of steel. Somewhere, the Borderguard of Curonan claimed ground, driving back the Beshtanagi. Horns were blowing an order to stand, and strain-

ing above them were the clarion sounds of the horns of the Rivenlost in the encampment, pleading a retreat no one heeded. With an
effort, Carfax tried to rise. Instead, the world keeled sideways. He
blinked, realizing his cheek was pillowed on the loose scree of
rocks, and he could no longer feel his body.

So must his men have felt, when they died.

He lay prone, lacking the strength to move. All he could do, he
had done, whether she knew it or not. No matter. He had not done
it for her, but for her smile, and a memory of what might have
been. She was close; so near, so far. The heels of her boots were
inches from his open eyes, cracked and downtrodden. How many
leagues had they traveled together? He could see every shiny
crease worn in the leather. He might have loved her if she had let
him. It would have spread balm on the aching wound of his betrayal. But it was not to be, and all he could do was die for her
sake. It would have to be enough, for there was nothing else left to
him. Between them lay the man she loved and protected. Blaise's
calloused hand was outflung, open, as if to reach in friendship. His
closed lids fluttered and his fingertips twitched.

There was another sound. The dragon's roar.

It hurt Carfax to move his head, but he did. Enough to see the
black horn of Oronin's Bow silhouetted against the sky and the
blazing shaft of the Arrow it held taut. Enough to see the tension in
her body as the stooping dragon began its last dive, growing from
a dwindling speck of brightness to a massive comet. Fianna's legs
were trembling, though she had her feet firmly planted. He saw the
strong muscles of her calves quivering in fear. But she was the
Archer of Arduan and her arms held steady. In the midst of chaos
and battle, she held. Even in the face of the dragon's dive, as its
wings shadowed the sky and its gleaming talons threatened to
gouge the earth.

Even when its jaws gaped wide, revealing the depths of its impossible gullet, and fire spewed from the furnace of its belly. With
tears on her face, she held her ground, shoulders braced, a shaft of
white-gold fire blazing in the arc of horn and hair circumscribed by
her hands. As he watched, her lips shaped a single, desperate
prayer and her fingers released the string.

The Archer of Arduan shot the Arrow of Fire.

Trailing white-gold glory, it flew true between the dragon's
jaws; flew true and pierced the gullet, pierced the mighty furnace
of its belly. There was an explosion, then; a column of fire that
seared the skies, while Men and Ellylon flung themselves to earth,

and from somewhere, a cry, a terrible descant like the sound of a heart breaking asunder.

Dying, the dragon fell.

The impact made the mountain shudder.

Once the tremors faded there was a great deal of activity. Crushed Men screaming, defeated Men surrendering. Hailing shouts, and orders given crisply. Ellylon voices like a choir, intermingled with the sound of horns. A name uttered in a futile paean. None of it had anything to do with him. Carfax closed his eyes, and did not open them for a long time. It would have been better not to know. Still, he looked. Near him, so near him, a massive jaw lay quiescent on the scree, attached to a sinuous neck. Twin spirals of smoke trickled from bronze nostrils, wisping into nothingness in the empty air. The massive body lay beyond the bounds of his vision, broken-winged. Life was fading from a green-gilt eye. "I'm sorry," Carfax said; or tried to say, mouthing the words. There was no strength in his lungs to voice them, and his eardrums were broken. "I'm sorry."

Distant shouting; victory cries.

In a green-gilt eye, a dying light flickered, and a faint voice spoke in his mind. *This battle is not of your making, Arahila's Child. You played your part. Be forgiven.* And then words, three words, wrested forth in an agonizing wrench, one final throe before the end. *Lilias! Forgive me!*

Not for him. No matter. It was enough.

Carfax sighed, and died.

TWENTY-SIX

THE CRASH SHOOK THE VERY foundations of Beshtanag.

Brightness, fading. All the brightness in the world. Kneeling on the terrace, Lilias bent double and clutched at her belly, feeling Calandor's death go through her like a spear. Her throat was raw from the cry his fall had torn from her and her heart ached within her, broken shards grinding one another into dust.

Whatever scant hope remained, his final agonized words destroyed.

Lilias! Forgive me!

Calandor! No!

She clung to the fading contact until his mighty heartbeat slowed and stopped forever. Gone. No more would the sun gleam on his scales, no more would he spread his wings to ride the drafts. Never again would she see a smile in the blink of a green-slitted eye. Her heart was filled with bitter ashes and the Soumanië was a dead ember on her brow, scraping the flagstones as she rocked in her grief, pressing her forehead to the grey stones. For a thousand years he had been her mentor, her friend, her soul's companion. More than she knew. More than she had ever known. "Calandor," she whispered. "Oh, Calandor! Please, no!"

In her mind, only silence answered.

Huddled over the flagstones, the Sorceress of the East grieved.

"My lady." At length a hand touched her shoulder. Lilias raised her tear-streaked face to meet Pietre's worried gaze. He nodded toward the base of the mountain, the linked chains of silver that bound him to her will gleaming around his throat. "They are coming."

They were coming.

Calandor was dead.

On stiff limbs she rose, staggering under the weight of her robes. Pietre's hand beneath her elbow assisted her; nearby, Sarika hovered, her pretty face a study in anguish. At the base of Beshtanag Mountain, her wall lay in ruins. Beyond—no. She could not look beyond the wall, where Calandor's corpse rose like a hillock. Inside the gap, Haomane's Allies were accepting the surrender of her Chief Warder. Even as she looked, Gergon lay his sword at Aracus Altorus' feet and pointed toward the terrace.

"Our archers—" Pietre hissed.

"No." With a weary gesture, Lilias cut him short, touching his cheek. There was courage of a kind in resolve. "Sweetling, it is over. We are defeated. Escort me to my throne room. I will hear their terms there."

They did, one on either side of her, and she was grateful for their assistance, for the necessity their presence imposed. Without it, she could gladly have laid down and died. Step by step, they led her into the grey halls of Beshtanag, past the silent censure of her people, hollow-eyed and hungry. They had trusted her, and she had failed them. Now they awaited salvation from another quarter. Her liveried servants, who wore no collars of servitude, had vanished. Her throne room seemed empty and echoing, and the summer sunlight that slanted through the high, narrow windows felt a mockery.

"How is it, my lady?" Sarika asked anxiously, helping her settle into the throne. It was wrought of a single block of Beshtanagi granite, the curve of the high back set with emeralds from Calandor's hoard. "Are you comfortable? Do you wish water? Wine? There is a keg set aside for your usage. We saw to it, Pietre and I."

"It's fine, sweetling." The effort it took to raise the corners of her mouth in something resembling a smile was considerable. Closing her eyes, Lilias gathered the remnants of her inner resources, the thin trickle of strength restored since Radovan's death. A faint spark lit the Soumanië. It was not much, but enough for what was necessary. She opened her eyes. "Do me a favor, will you? Summon my attendants. All of them, all my pretty ones."

Pietre frowned; Sarika fluttered. In the end, they did her bidding. Marija, Stepan, Anna—all of them stood arrayed before her, their silver collars gleaming. All save Radovan, whose lifeless body lay unmoving on the terrace. So young, all of them! How many had she bent to her will in the course of a thousand years? They were countless.

And now it was over. All over.

"Come here." Lilias beckoned. "I mean to set you free."

"No!" Sarika gasped, both hands rising to clutch her collar.

Sullen Marija ignored her, stepping promptly to the base of the throne. A pretty girl, with the high, broad cheekbones of a Beshtanagi peasant. She should have been freed long ago; Radovan had been a friend of hers. Lilias gazed at her with rue and leaned forward, touching the silver collar with two fingers. Holding a pattern in her mind, she whispered three words that Calandor had taught her and *undid* the pattern the way the dragon had shown her, so many centuries ago.

Silver links parted and slithered to the floor. Eyeing the fallen collar warily, Marija touched her bare throat. With a harsh laugh she turned and fled, her footsteps echoing in the empty hall. Lilias sighed, pressing her temples. "Come," she said wearily. "Who is next?"

No one moved.

"Why?" Pietre whispered. "Why, my lady? Have we not served you well?"

She was a thousand years old, and she wanted to weep. Oh, Uru-Alat, the time had gone quickly! "Yes, sweetling," Lilias said, as gently as she could. "You have. But you see, we are defeated here. And as you are innocent, Haomane's Allies will show mercy, do you submit to it. It is their way."

They protested, of course. It was in their nature, the best of her pretty ones. In the end, she freed them all. Pietre was the hardest. There were tears in his eyes as he knelt before her, blinking. He cried aloud when the collar slipped from his neck.

"Be free of it." Lilias finished the gesture, the *unbinding,* resting the back of her head against her throne. The last connection slid from her grasp, the final severing complete. It was done. On her brow, the Soumanië guttered, and failed for the last time.

She was done.

"Lady." Though his throat was bare, Pietre's hands grasped hers, hard. His throat was bare, and nothing had changed in his steadfast gaze. "A delegation is at the door. Shall I admit them?"

"Yes." Relying on the unyielding granite to keep her upright, Lilias swallowed against the aching lump in her throat. "Thank you, Pietre," she said, her voice hoarse. "I am done here. If you would do me one final service, let them in."

THEY WERE FIVE WHO ENTERED the hall.

The foremost, she knew. She had seen him from afar for too

long not to recognize him. His dun-grey cloak swirled about him as
he strode and sunlight glinted on his red-gold hair. Mortal, yes;
Arahila's Child, with the breath of Oronin's Horn blowing hot on
his neck. Still, there was something more in his fierce, wide-set
gaze, an awareness vouchsafed few of his kind.

Of their kind.

Lilias sat unmoving and watched them come. Over her head,
emeralds winked against the back of her granite throne, ordinary
gems sunk into the very stone. She had wrought it herself when
Calandor first taught her to use the Soumanië to *Shape* elements, almost a thousand years ago. For that long, for ill or for good, had
she ruled Beshtanag from this seat.

The delegation halted before her.

No one bowed, least of all their leader. "Sorceress." His voice
was curt. "I am Aracus Altorus of the Borderguard of Curonan, and
I speak for Haomane's Allies. You know what we have come for. Is
she here?"

Lilias looked past him to the other four. Two of them were
mortal, and one she knew; Martinek, Regent of Southeastern Pelmar, whose face bore a cruel, gloating expression. The other, a
Borderguardsman, seemed unsteady on his feet. There was something vaguely familiar about him; his dark, sombre eyes and the
shock of hair falling over his pale and bandaged brow. The remaining two were Ellylon, their fine-wrought features startling in
her stone halls. One of these too she knew, having seen his standard oft enough; Lorenlasse of Valmaré, gleaming in his armor. The
other Ellyl, in travel-worn garb, she did not recognize. He looked at
her with sorrow.

"No," she said at last; to him, to all of them, letting the word fall
like a stone. Her fingers clutched the throne's arms; there was a bitter satisfaction in the message. "You have assailed us in vain,
would-be King of the West. Beshtanag has committed no crime.
The Lady Cerelinde of the Rivenlost is not here."

Aracus Altorus' sword rasped free of its scabbard. The point of
it came to rest in the hollow of her throat. Lilias sat unflinching. Calandor was dead, Beshtanag had fallen, and she did not care if she
lived or died. He leaned forward, one foot on the throne's base,
pressing hard enough to draw a trickle of blood.

"*Where is she?*"

His breath was hot on her face; well-fed, smelling of heat and
battle-rage, his strength fueled by mutton and deer purloined from

the pastures and forests of Beshtanag. "Aracus," the wounded Man murmured, cautioning. One of the Ellylon spoke to the other in their melodious language. Lilias ignored them and smiled with all the bleak emptiness in her heart.

"Darkhaven," she said, relishing his reaction. "She is in Darkhaven, in the Sunderer's keeping. It is where she has been all along, my lord of the Borderguard. Your people were misled."

He swore, Aracus Altorus did, turning away from her. His shoulders shook, and cords stood out in his neck, taut with anguish. Lilias was glad of it. Let him suffer, then, as she did. Let him know the taste of failure. He had destroyed everything she held dear. And for what? For nothing.

"Son of Altorus." Lorenlasse of Valmaré addressed him in the common tongue, his voice gentle. "Believe me when I tell you that this news is as grievous to the Rivenlost as to you, if not more so. And yet there is another matter at hand."

"Yes." He went still, then turned back to her. "There is."

Despite everything, Lilias found herself shrinking back against the throne. He should have been afraid. He wasn't. His grief, this defeat in the midst of victory, had granted him that much. There was no anger in his face, nor mercy, only a weary nobility for which she despised him. Why should he be appointed to this victory? What accident of birth, what vagary of Haomane's will, vouchsafed him this prize?

Two steps toward her, then three.

He reached out one hand, palm open. "The Soumanië."

It was a dead weight on her brow and it shouldn't have hurt to face its loss. It did. Especially to him, to this one. Lilias gripped the granite arms of her throne until her nails bent and bled. "Will you take it from me, then?" she asked him. "How then, when you have not won it? Do you claim a victory here? I think not, Altorus. This prize belonged to the Dragon of Beshtanag." She laughed, the sound of her laughter high and unstrung. "Do you think Calandor did not see his end, and I with him? Do you think I did not see who wielded Oronin's Bow and the Arrow of Fire? Where is the Archer, son of Altorus? I see no women in your train. Do you fear to give such a prize unto a woman's hand?"

"Sorceress," he said patiently. "The Soumanië."

"No," she whispered. "Martinek! You are Pelmaran. Think what this means. Will you let him claim sovereignty over my lands and yours?"

The Southeastern Regent shifted, adjusting his sword-hilt, setting his mouth in a hard, thin line. He had the decency not to meet her gaze. "I've sworn my allegiance."

"What of you, my lord Valmaré?" In despair, Lilias forced her tone to one of sweet reason, addressing Lorenlasse of Valmaré. "Have matters changed so in Urulat? Do Haomane's Children cede the spoils of victory to Arahila's? This is not a prize for mortal hands to sully. Am I not living proof?"

The Rivenlost Lord frowned, hesitating.

"Lorenlasse." The travel-worn Ellyl spoke the common tongue with soft regret. "Ingolin the Wise himself dared not take on such a burden. Will you gainsay his wisdom, that Malthus the Counselor informed? Let the Son of Aracus claim it. He is the betrothed of the Lady Cerelinde, granddaughter of Elterrion the Bold. Our time ends, and this is his victory. It is his right."

Lorenlasse of Valmaré stepped back, nodding, sorrow and a grave acceptance in his countenance. "So be it," he said. "As I am Haomane's Child, I fulfill his Prophecy. Son of Altorus, the Soumanië is yours."

"Sorceress," Aracus Altorus said simply, extending his hand.

He did not threaten. With a conquering army at his back, he didn't need to.

"Take it, then!" With trembling fingers, Lilias lifted the fillet from her brow. The Soumanië was a dull red stone in its center. For a thousand years it had maintained contact with her unaging flesh. Even now, when she was spent beyond telling, when its power lay beyond her grasp, the Soumanië sustained her, maintaining the bond that stretched the Chain of Being to its uttermost limit. So it had done for a thousand years, since the Dragon of Beshtanag had divulged its secrets to a headstrong Pelmaran girl. Tears burning in her eyes, Lilias placed the fillet in Aracus Altorus' outstretched palm and relinquished it. "Let the Shapers themselves bear witness, I do this against my will."

He closed his hand upon the Soumanië and claimed it.

It was done. The bond was severed, a shock as sudden as icy water, and Lilias dwindled back toward mortality. The confines of her flesh closed in upon her, unexpected and suffocating. Her thoughts, that had extended to the boundaries of Beshtanag, became circumscribed by skin and bone. The dense forests, the harsh mountain crags; lost, all lost. Never again would she *reach* into the world beyond her fingers' touch, not even toward the emptiness of Calandor's absence. It was gone, all gone, and the sands of time that the Soumanië had held at bay began to trickle through the hourglass of her fate. Even now, she felt the slow decay of age creeping. Flesh would wither, bone would grow brittle.

The Sorceress of the East was no more.

In her place sat a mortal woman, a Pelmaran earl's daughter, a vain and foolish woman who had lived beyond her allotted years and brought ruin upon herself and her people. In the face of her conquerors' contempt, Lilias bowed her head, no longer able to meet their eyes. "Calandor," she whispered to the empty space inside her. "Oh Calandor, I miss you!"

Somewhere in the distance, Oronin's Horn was blowing.

STORMCLOUDS GATHERED OVER THE VALE of Gorgantum.

Seated in his deep-cantled saddle atop one of the horses of Darkhaven, Vorax frowned, watching the roiling skies blot out the faint red disk of the sun. The terminal half-light of the Vale grew ominous. Beneath his resplendent armor, the scar that branded his sturdy chest itched and burned. Over plain and forest and rising hills, from the cleft of the Defile to the outermost boundaries of the walls, clouds gathered, dense and heavy. On the training-field, the Fjel broke ranks to glance uneasily at the skies.

"A storm, do you reckon, sir?" Beside him, Hyrgolf squinted at the clouds.

Vorax scratched at his armored chest with absentminded futility. His mount shifted restlessly, stamping a hoof. "I'm not sure." His brand was beginning to sting as if there were a hornet's nest lodged under his armor and there was a distinct *tugging* in the direction of the fortress. "No." He shook his head. "No ordinary storm, anyway. Field marshal, cancel the exercise. Dismiss the troops."

Hyrgolf roared a command in the Fjel tongue, a signal relayed by his bannerman. Pennants dipped and waved under the glowering skies, and a rumble of thunder answered. Thousands of Fjeltroll began to disperse in semi-orderly fashion, forming into winding columns and setting off at a slow, steady jog for their barracks.

Above the looming edifice, clouds built. Layer upon layer they gathered, dark and billowing, echoing the towering structure below. Angry lightning flickered, illuminating the underbellies of the bruise-colored swells. Whatever they contained, it didn't bode well for anyone caught on the field.

"It's his Lordship," Hyrgolf observed. "He's wroth."

"I think you're right." Vorax grimaced and bent over his pommel as pain clutched at his heart like a fist and the tugging sensation intensified. "Field marshal!" The words emerged in a grunt. "Help me. I have to get back there. *Now.*"

"Aye, sir!" Hyrgolf gave a crisp salute and stooped to grasp the reins of Vorax's mount a half a foot below the bit. "Make way!" he bellowed at the retreating backs of his army as he forged a path. "Way for Lord Vorax!"

The columns wavered at his order and parted to create an alley. Through his pain, Vorax was dimly aware of being impressed at the discipline Tanaros had drilled into his troops and at the steady competence of the Tungskulder Fjel who commanded them. Then a bolt of lightning cracked the skies and thunder pealed. His mount, unwontedly skittish, sought to rear, tugging at the reins the Fjeltroll held in an iron grip. With his chest ablaze, it was all Vorax could do to stay upright in the saddle.

Thunder pealed again, sharp and incisive, and the clouds split open to unleash their burden. The rain that spat down was greasy and unclean, reeking of sulfur. Worse, Vorax realized with a shudder, it *burned* like sulfur. It was an unnatural rain, carrying the taint of a Shaper's fury. His flesh prickled beneath his armor, fearful of its touch on his skin, and he was glad his Staccian company wasn't on the field.

"Sir!" Hyrgolf was bawling in his ear, his hideous face looming close. Water dripped from his brow-ridges, carving steaming runnels in his obdurate hide. "Sir, I've called for a Gulnagel escort! It's the fastest way!"

Another seizure clutched at his chest, and his mount trumpeted with pain and fear, flaring its nostrils at the rain's stench. "My thanks!" Vorax managed to gasp; and then the others were there, one on either side, a pair of Gulnagel baring their eyetusks as they leapt to secure his reins.

They set out at a run, ignoring the deluge. The reins stretched taut and his horse followed anxiously in their wake, moving from a trot into a canter, settling into a gallop as the Gulnagel lengthened their strides into swift bounds. Their taloned feet scored deep gouges in the earth as they passed their hurrying brethren. Vorax clutched his deep pommel with both hands, concentrating on keeping his seat. The field was a blur. Corrosive rain sheeted from his Staccian armor and he tucked his chin tight against his chest, letting the visor of his helmet deflect the rain from his face; still, burning droplets pelted his cheeks. His mount squealed, steam arising from its sleek hide. The Fjel yelped and ran onward, leading him at breakneck speed.

At the outermost postern gates, one of Ushahin's madlings was dancing from foot to foot. He held out his hand for the reins in a pleading gesture, heedless of the bleeding scores the rain etched on his face. Still ducking his chin, Vorax struggled to free his feet from the stirrups as the Gulnagel helped him dismount. The madling crooned to his mount, shoulders hunched against the punishing rain.

And then Vorax was on solid ground, screwing his eyes shut as burning moisture seeped under his visor, trickling down his brow. He heard hoofbeats echo on the flagstones as Ushahin's madling led his horse at a run for the shelter of the stables. The obedient Gulnagel gripped his arms, hustling him through the rain toward the inner gate, where the Mørkhar Fjel of the Havenguard granted them passage.

Beneath the tall, heavy ceilings they were safe from the rain. One of the Gulnagel spoke in their guttural tongue, and the Havenguard replied in the same. With deft care, Fjeltroll talons unbuckled straps, removing his armor piece by piece, lifting the helmet from his head. Rainwater dripped and sizzled harmlessly on the stone floor, making the entryway reek of rotten eggs. The Fjel wiped his swordbelt dry, settling it around his waist. Vorax braced his hands on his thighs and took a deep breath against the dizzying pain in his chest. Straightening, he wiped his brow with his sleeve. The fumes made his eyes sting as he opened them and a patch of blisters was rising on his forehead, but he was whole.

"The army?" It was important to ask.

"On their way, boss." One of the Gulnagel pointed past the open door toward the outer gates, where the columns were making their way toward their deep-hewn barracks. He shook himself like a dog, shedding water. Slow, dark blood oozed from pockmarks in his yellowish hide. "This is no good, though, even for Fjel."

"No," Vorax said, wincing at the sight. "It's not." Outside, angry thunder pealed. One of the Mørkhar fingered a carved talisman, leathery lips moving in a whispered prayer. "You, lad," Vorax said to him. Tanaros would have known his name; he didn't. For the first time, he felt bad about the fact. "Take me to his Lordship."

"Aye, Lord Vorax." The Mørkhar stowed his figurine. "This way, sir."

It felt like a long walk, longer than usual. Ushahin's madlings were in hiding, and there were only the empty halls of Darkhaven, veins of marrow-fire pulsing with agitation in the gleaming black walls. Vorax felt his own pulse quicken in accord, his heart constricting. Ah, Neheris-of-the-Leaping-Waters, he thought. Have pity on your Children, and those who have dwelled alongside them! We mean no harm, no, not to you. This is your brother Haomane's quarrel.

There was no answer, of course. For ages beyond counting, no Shaper had ever answered the prayers of mortal kind save Lord Satoris. Distant and remote on Torath, they bent their wills to Haomane's pride, while on the face of Urulat, Lord Satoris fought against a dark tide of pain, and kept his promises to all who honored him.

There was only the journey, and its ending, where the towering iron doors of the Throne Hall had been flung apart, standing open as if onto a vast furnace. The diorama of the Shapers' War was split wide open, separating Lord Satoris from the Six Shapers. Beyond lay a maelstrom of darkness and a throbbing red light, source of the infernal *pull,* beckoning to him like a lodestone.

Godslayer, Vorax thought, his mouth going dry. He's taken it from the Font.

The Havenguard on duty saluted, hands clutched firm on the hafts of their battle-axes. Fjel seldom looked nervous, but these two did. "Lord Vorax," one acknowledged him, deep-set eyes glittering in the light of the marrow-fire. "Be wary. He is wroth."

"I know." Vorax wiped his sweating, blistered brow and sighed. "My thanks, lads," he said, and crossed the threshold. Inside, torches sprang alight with the marrow-fire. He squinted at the blue-white effluence, the shadows of his own body looming in the corners. Fair Arahila, he thought, you've a name for mercy, even his Lordship said so. What wouldn't I give, now, for all that I've taken for granted? A meal fit for a king, a hungry king. A warm bath and a sweet lass to rub oil into my aching shoulders. Is it so much to ask? The red light of Godslayer flared, disrupting his thoughts. Pain seized his chest and hammered him to his knees.

"*Kill them!*" Lord Satoris' voice cracked like thunder, until the very walls creaked and trembled in protest. "*Do you understand? I am giving this order. Kill them. Kill them ALL!*"

"My Lord!" Vorax gasped, floundering on the carpet. His eardrums ached with the pressure and his heart was beating so fast it threatened to burst his chest. I am too old for this, he thought, and too fat. "As you will, it shall be done!"

There was silence, and the pressure abated. "Vorax. My words were meant for another. Tanaros Blacksword lives. He has won free of the Marasoumië."

"Good news, my Lord." Gratefully, he struggled to his feet. He could see, now. The black carpet stretching in front of him and the figure on the Throne, illumed in darkness. Vorax made his feet move. It was not hard, after all. That which compelled him was held in his Lord's hands, a shard of red light pulsing like lifeblood. It reeled him onward as surely as a hook in his heart, and he placed one foot in front of the other until he stood before the Throne and gazed at Satoris' face, hidden behind the aching void of the Helm of Shadows. "You summoned me?"

"My Staccian." The Shaper bent his head. "Yes. Matters have . . . transpired."

"Aye, my Lord." It was hot within the Throne Hall, cursedly hot. The news about Tanaros was welcome. He did not think the rest would be. Vorax watched the dagger throbbing between the Shaper's palms, held like a prayer-offering. The beat of his own scarred heart matched its rhythm. "What matters?"

The shard flared in Satoris' hands. "One of the Eldest has fallen."

Vorax swallowed, hard. "The Dragon of Beshtanag?"

"Yes." Through the eyeslits of the Helm of Shadows, the Shaper stared at him without blinking. "His name was Calandor, and he was old when I first walked the earth; oldest of all, save one. He was my friend, many ages ago."

Dire news, indeed. The Ellylon of old had slain dragons, but never one of the most ancient, the Eldest. Only in the Shapers' War had that come to pass. In the face of the Helm's hollow-eyed stare, Vorax had to look away. "How was it done?" he asked.

Lord Satoris gave a mirthless laugh. "With the Arrow of Fire."

In the sweltering heat of the Throne Hall, his skin turned cold and clammy. Haomane's Prophecy pounded like a litany in his skull. "They did it," Vorax said, forcing the words past a lump of fear in his throat. "Found the lost weapon."

"Yes." The Shaper contemplated the dagger in his hands. God-slayer's flames caressed his fingers, shadows writhing in the Helm's eyeslits. "They did. And they will be coming for us, my Staccian, these Allies of my Brother." His head lifted and his eyes blazed to life. "But what they plan, I have *seen!* I dare what they did not think I would dare! I am not my Brother, to quail in mortality's shadow! I dare to don the Helm, I dare to pluck Godslayer from the marrow-fire and *see!*"

"Right." With a prodigious effort, Vorax filled his lungs, then exhaled. He was tired, his blistered skin stung and his knees ached, but he was one of the Three, and he had sworn his oath a long, long time ago. "What now, my Lord?"

"Vengeance," Satoris said softly, "for one who was a friend, once. Protection, for us. There is something I must do, a grave and dire thing. It is for this, and this alone, that I have taken Godslayer from the marrow-fire. And I have a task for you, Vorax, that will put an end this talk of my Elder Brother's Prophecy."

"Aye, my Lord!" Relief outweighed remorse as Vorax reached for his sword-hilt. To slay a defenseless woman was no welcome chore, but such was the nature of the bargain he had made. Immortality and plenitude for him; peace and prosperity for Staccia. It was the only sensible course, and he was glad his Lordship had seen it at last. One stroke, and the Prophecy would be undone. She would not suffer, he would see to that. It would be swift and merciful, and done in time for supper. "Elterrion's granddaughter will be dead ere dawn, I promise you."

"*No!*"

Vorax winced at the thunderous word, relinquishing his hilt.

"No," the Shaper repeated, leaning forward on the throne. The sweet reek of blood mingled with the distant stench of sulfur, and his eyes burned like red embers through the Helm's dark slits. "I am not my Brother, Staccian. I will play this game with honor, in my own way. I will not let Haomane strip that from me, and force me to become all that he has named me." His voice dripped contempt. "I will not become the thing that I *despise*. I will assail my enemies as they assail me. The Lady Cerelinde—" he lifted one admonishing finger from Godslayer, "—is my guest. She is not to be harmed."

"As you will." Vorax licked his lips. Had his Lordship gone mad? He pushed the thought away, trying not to remember stormclouds piling high over Darkhaven, a foul rain falling, seething flesh. What did it matter if he had? After all, Satoris Third-Born had reason enough for anger. And he, Vorax of Staccia, had sworn an oath, was bound and branded by it, upon a shard of the Souma itself. There was no gainsaying it. To be foresworn was to die. "What, then?"

"Your work lies in the north." Satoris smiled with grim satisfaction. "Malthus erred. He spent his strength shielding his Bearer from my sight, but he cannot conceal the lad's path through the Marasoumië. I know where he lit. The one who would extinguish the marrow-fire is in the north, Vorax. Send a company; Men you trust, and Fjel to aid them. Find the Bearer, and kill him. Let the vial he carries be shattered, and the Water of Life spilled harmless upon the barren earth."

"My Lord." A simple task, after all. Relieved, he bowed. "It will be done."

"Good." Satoris regarded Godslayer, turning the shard in his fingers. "Ushahin comes apace," he mused, forgetting the Staccian's presence, "and Tanaros has his orders, though he likes them not. You must be consigned to the marrow-fire, my bitter friend, for you are too dangerous to be kept elsewhere. But first; ah, first! We have a task to accomplish, you and I."

"My Lord?" Vorax waited, then inquired, uncertain if his services were needed.

The eye slits of the Helm turned his way, filled with all the darkness and agony of a dying world. "It is time to close the Marasoumië," Lord Satoris said. "Now, while Malthus is trapped within it, before he regains his strength."

"Now? Then how will Tanaros and—"

"*Now!*" The Shaper pounded a clenched fist on the arm of the throne. Behind the Helm, his teeth were bared in a rictus. "Understand, Vorax! Aracus Altorus has seized one of the Soumanië! Does he gain mastery over it, with two Soumanië to hand, he and my Elder Brother's Counselor could control the Ways. If I do this thing *now,* then Malthus remains trapped, and the son of Altorus remains ignorant of his counsel. Is that not worth any price?"

There was only one answer, and Vorax gave it. "Aye, my Lord."

"So be it," Satoris said, taking hold of the dagger with both hands. "And you shall bear witness." In his grip, Godslayer's light intensified, bright as a rising sun. "Ah! It burns! Uru-Alat, how it burns!" Rubescent light exploded in the Chamber, and Vorax's branded chest contracted. Struggling for breath, he dropped back to his knees. There he saw Satoris rising triumphant, a vast figure of darkness. Held aloft, Godslayer pulsed in his fist, bleeding light. It was a shard of the Souma itself, filled with the power of the world's birth. Light seemed to illume the Shaper's bones beneath his obdurate flesh, streamed from the wound in his thigh.

"My Lord!" Vorax gasped, wheezing. "Please!"

"Death and death and death," the Shaper whispered, ignoring him. "Oh, Malthus! Haomane's Weapon, my Brother's pawn! Do you think I do not know my true enemy? Do you know what you bring to this world? Do you know how the story ends? Ah, no! So be it, Counselor. I bind you in the web you spun." He tightened his grip on Godslayer and cried aloud, summoning his will in the form of a Shaper's skills, and pouring his strength into the effort. *"Let the Marasoumië be sealed!"*

Attuned to the shard's power, Vorax felt it, and closed his eyes in pain. What he had seen begin through the eyes of the Helm of Shadows came to pass. Deep below the surface of the earth across the vast nation of Urulat, node-points flickered and died, going ashen-grey.

A part of the world, dying, went dead.

"So," Satoris said with vicious satisfaction. "Free yourself from *that,* Counselor!"

TWENTY-SEVEN

◆◆

T_ANAROS' BOOTS CRUNCHED IN THE_ sand as he walked away from the Stone Grove encampment. With every step his scabbard brushed his thigh in reminder, unwanted and unneeded. His Lord's words echoed over and over in his head, and the sun blazing in his face made his ringing head ache.

Kill them. Kill them ALL!

"Lord General?"

"Go away, Speros," he said without looking.

"It's just . . . did Lord Satoris give us orders? Is he going to open the Ways and bring us home? Because I could have the lads back at the node—"

"Go *away*, Speros!"

There was a pause. "Aye, General. We'll be at the campsite when you're ready."

When he was ready; there was a bitter jest! Lifting his head, Tanaros stared at the blinding face of the sun. He remembered how good it had felt in Beshtanag to see the sun's rays gilding the forest after long years of Darkhaven's eternal gloom. Did the sun still shine in Beshtanag? He supposed it did, despite what had befallen there. It seemed closer, here, where Haomane's wrath had scorched the earth in pursuit of Satoris. What was it like, living with this surfeit of light?

Bare feet made no sound on the desert floor. "Slayer."

"Ngurra." Tanaros regarded the sun. "What do you want?"

"Truth." One simple word, spoken in the common tongue. Tanaros sighed and turned. Ngurra squatted on the desert floor, squinting up at him, his brown face a map of wrinkles in the sun's unforgiving light. "It's your choosing-time, isn't it?"

After a day in the Yarru's company, Tanaros didn't bother lying to the old man. "Why?" he asked instead, resting one hand on the black sword's hilt. "Why did you do it? Why did you send this boy, this Bearer—"

"Dani."

"—this *Dani* to extinguish the marrow-fire?" Tanaros' voice rose. "*Why,* Ngurra? Has Haomane been so good to your people? Did he have a care for your welfare when he scorched the earth? Look at this place!" He gestured at the desert. "It's barely enough to sustain life! We would have perished here if you'd not shown us how to survive! For *this,* you seek to thank Haomane First-Born by destroying my Lord?"

"No, Slayer." Ngurra shook his head. "This is Birru-Uru-Alat. Here, where the Well of the World abides, is the center, the choosing-place. We are the Yarru-yami, and that is the trust we preserve."

"*Haomane's* trust," Tanaros said bitterly.

The old man gave a weary chuckle. "When did the Lord-of-Thought ever hold choice to be a sacred trust? No, Slayer. He gave us no choice when he brought the sun's wrath upon us, no more than your Lord Satoris did when he fled to this place. Together, they drove us into hiding. This wisdom comes from the deep places in Uru-Alat, from a time when the world was newly Sundered." He held up his empty hands, palms marked with ordinary, mortal lines. "Such is the burden we carry. That, and the promise that one among us would be born to Bear a greater one."

"Aye." The words came hard, sticking in his throat. "To extinguish the marrow-fire, freeing Godslayer. To fulfill Haomane's Prophecy and destroy my Lord."

Ngurra nodded. "That is one choice."

"It's the choice he *made!*" With an effort, Tanaros controlled his anger. It would do no good to shout at the old man. If nothing else, a day among the Yarru had taught him that much. "Why, Ngurra? Why *that* choice?"

Tilting his head, the old Yarru regarded the sky. "Where were you, to offer another? There are things I could say, Slayer, and the simplest one of all is that it is the choice he was offered. Was Dani's choice right?" He shook his head again. "I do not know. I only know he is the Bearer, and it was his to choose."

Tanaros gritted his teeth. "That's not good enough, old one."

"Isn't it?" Ngurra's eyes shone with sympathy in his wrinkled face. "And yet here you are at the choosing-place." With a grunt he straightened his legs and rose, turning back toward the camp. "Think on it, Slayer," he said over his shoulder. "We are ready. We have been waiting for you. You have a choice to make."

He watched the old man's steady progress across the sand. At the encampment, the Yarru elders hailed his return under the benign gaze of the Gulnagel Fjel on guard. He could hear white-haired Warabi, the old man's wife, scolding him for his folly.

We have been expecting you.

If Ngurra had not greeted him with those words, he might have ordered them slain. Why not? It was true, they were the ones who had sent forth the Bearer to extinguish the marrow-fire. But instead, he had stayed his hand out of curiosity. He had ordered Speros and the Fjel to accept the Yarru's hospitality. And a good thing, too. They would be half dead of thirst if the Yarru hadn't shown them how to find water-holes in the Unknown Desert, how to catch basking lizards, how chewing *gamal* heightened the senses and moistened parched tissues. The Yarru had shown them kindness. Whatever they were, whatever strange beliefs they held, these Charred Ones were not foes.

Old men. Old women.

"I don't want to kill them," Tanaros whispered. Unaccountable tears stung his eyes, and he covered his face with both hands. "Oh, my Lord! Must it be so?"

Distant power flickered as if in answer, and pain seared his scarred breast, so acute it was almost unbearable. So. It had begun as his Lordship had said it would. In the west, in Darkhaven, Satoris was wielding Godslayer with the full might of a Shaper's power, a thing he had not dared since Darkhaven was raised. Tanaros felt his teeth begin to chatter. He dropped to his knees in the sand and pressed his fingertips hard against his temples, willing his flesh to obedience. All across the world, it was as though a thousand doors had been slammed at once. Everywhere, light flared and died, a vast network of connections turning to ash.

The Marasoumië was closed.

That was that, then. The thing was done. His Lordship had no intention of changing his orders. Tanaros waited for his pounding heartbeat to subside, then climbed heavily to his feet and brushed the sand off his knees.

You have a choice to make.

There was no point in waiting. The task was onerous; the journey afterward would be grueling. Trudging across the desert toward the encampment, he drew his sword. It glinted dully in the sun, a length of black steel laying a black bar of shadow on the desert floor. Where would he go if he disobeyed Satoris' orders? What would he do? He was General Tanaros Blacksword, one of the Three, and he had made his choice a long, long time ago.

Speros sprang alert at his approach, whistling for the attention of the Gulnagel. "Lord General! What was that happened just now? Is it time to—" He stopped, eyeing the drawn sword. "What are you doing?"

"They know." Tanaros gestured wearily at the Yarru, who had gathered in a circle. Old men and old women, linked by age-knotted hands clasped tight together. There were tears in the creases of Warabi's dark cheeks as she clung to Ngurra's hand.

"You mean to kill them all?" Speros swallowed, turning pale. "Ah, but Lord General, they're harmless. They're—"

"—old," Tanaros finished for him. "I know." He rubbed his brow with his free hand. "Listen, lads. Beshtanag has fallen, and Lord Satoris has closed the Ways. We're going home the hard way. But we've got business to attend to here first. We're going to bury that cursed well, that no one else may find it. And . . . " he drew a deep breath, pointing his sword at the Yarru, " . . . we leave no survivors to tell of it."

With stoic shrugs, the Gulnagel took up positions around the ring of Yarru elders, who shrank closer together, murmuring in their tongue. Ngurra gently freed his hand from his wife's and stepped forward. There was fear in his face; and courage, too.

"Slayer," he said. "You do not have to choose this."

"Give me a reason, Ngurra." Rage and bleak despair stirred in Tanaros' heart, and he tightened his grip on his sword-hilt, raising it with both hands to strike. "*Give me a reason!* Tell me you're wrong, tell me you're sorry, tell me the Bearer made a bad choice! Send a delegation to bring him back! Can you do that, old man? Is that so much to ask? I didn't ask for this choice! *Give me a reason not to make it!*"

The Yarru elder shook his head, profound regret in his eyes. "I can give you only the choice, Slayer," he said sadly. "Choose."

"So be it," Tanaros whispered. Sick at heart, he swung the blade.

His sword cut clean, cleaving the old man's scrawny chest in a mortal blow. Dark flesh, cleaved by a black blade. There was a single agonized cry from Ngurra's wife, a collective whimper from the other Yarru. The old man went down without a sound, bleeding onto the desert floor as silently as he'd walked upon it. Turning away, Tanaros nodded to Speros and the four Gulnagel Fjel. "See it finished."

Meaty thuds filled the air as the Gulnagel went to work with their maces. There were cries of fear and pain; though not many, no. Hunting Fjel preferred to kill with one blow, and the Gulnagel were swift. Tanaros sat on an outcropping of rock, wiping Ngurra's blood from the black blade. He didn't glance up from his labors until he heard footsteps approaching. "Is it done?"

"Aye, Lord General." It was Speros, looking ill and abashed. "The Fjel have finished." He glanced at the ground, then blurted, "I'm sorry, sir, I couldn't do it. I've got a grandmam at home."

"A grandmam." Tanaros laid his sword across his knees and rubbed his aching temples, not sure whether to laugh or weep. He'd had a grandmother, once. She was long-dead bones, and had died cursing his name. "Ah, Speros of Haimhault! What are you doing here? Why in the name of the Seven Shapers did you come here?"

"Sir?" The Midlander gave him a quizzical look.

"Never mind." He rose to his feet, sheathing his sword. There was a taste of bile in his throat and he knew, with utter and horrible certitude, that he would never remember this day's work without cringing in his soul. "Gather the Fjel, we've got a lot of work to do."

USHAHIN DREAMSPINNER WAS IN ARDUAN when the Marasoumië was sealed.

He was grateful for Lord Satoris' warning. It had been unexpected; the reaching tendrils of Godslayer's power making his scar itch and burn, and suddenly Satoris was *there,* touching his mind, sifting through his thoughts. So it must feel to mortals when he used his Were-taught skills to walk in their dreams.

"I understand, my Lord," he said when the Shaper had finished, bowing to the empty air. A pair of Arduans strolling in the marketplace gave him a wide berth. "I will come as I may."

There was a banyan tree growing on the eastern side of the square. Ushahin found space amid its roots and sat cross-legged in its shade, waiting. He bowed his head, drawing the hood of a cloak he had stolen from a sleeping hunter down to hide his features. It was hot and humid here along the fringe of the Delta; still, better to be uncomfortable than to be recognized.

Arduans were a polite folk, their tiny nation founded on respect for individual rights, including that to privacy. No one would
disturb him if he claimed it; no, not unless he showed his face.
That, he suspected, would invoke the other great passion of Arduan. There was only one misshapen Ellyl half-breed in Urulat.
Even Arduans would require no further justification than his face to
nock an arrow and fire.

Ushahin waited.

A part of the world died.

It hurt. He felt the passing of each node-point as it flared and
died. Little deaths, each and every one, a shock to his flesh where
a shard of the Souma had branded it. He made himself breathe
slowly, enduring it. He wondered if it took Vorax and Tanaros the
same way. He thought about Malthus the Counselor trapped in the
Ways, and smiled through his pain.

It was done.

"Are you all right, mister? Something funny happened just now."

A high voice; a child's voice. Ushahin opened his eyes to see a
young girl stooping under the banyan tree to peer at him. She had
a spray of freckles across the bridge of her nose, and a child's bow
clutched in one grimy hand. The children who had set upon him so
long ago in Pelmar, breaking his bones and rending his flesh, had
been scarce older. Neither had he, then.

"Aye, lass," he said, slipping behind her eyes and into her
thoughts without an effort, *twisting* them to his own ends. "I'm
fine, and so are you. I need to purchase a boat; a skiff, such as fishermen use in the Delta. Surely a clever girl like you would know
where I might find such a thing."

"Oh, aye, you need to see Caitlin's Da!" She beamed with pride,
happy to have an answer. Whatever she had sensed of the death of
the Marasoumië was forgotten. "He's a boatwright, mister. He'll sell
you a skiff!"

"Well done, lass." Ushahin unfolded his legs, rising. He adjusted the hood of his cloak, then extended a hand, suppressing a
smile as she took his crooked fingers into her trusting, grubby grip.
"Take me to him."

SHE HAD NO PRIVACY LEFT.

That was one of the worst aspects of the occupation of Beshtanag. It had been hard to watch when Gergon was led through the
fortress in chains, shooting her an agonized glance of apology and

regret. It had been painful to behold the gratitude with which her Beshtanagi people welcomed the intervention of Haomane's Allies, the alacrity with which they surrendered, eager for a handful of grain, a plate of mutton. Blaise Caveros, Aracus Altorus' second-in-command, took quiet control of the situation. Despite the injury he had sustained on the battlefield, he was calm and competent, seeing to the housing of their troops, ordering supply-trains into the fortress.

Only her Ward Commander and his lieutenants were taken into custody; the rest of her wardsmen were confined to barracks under the eye of Regent Martinek's forces. Members of her household staff were pardoned in exchange for a pledge of loyalty to the Southeastern Pelmaran Regent. A few wept, but what of it? It was only a few. Most helped them search the fortress, scouring it from top to bottom, lest it transpire that the Lady Cerelinde was housed there after all. Haomane's Allies were thorough.

These things, Lilias had expected. The vast numbness that filled her, the void in her heart left by Calandor's death and the Soumanië's loss, insulated her. And in truth, she could not blame her people. She had lied. She had erred. She had failed to protect them. Left to her own devices, she would have begged leave to retire to her chambers, to turn her back upon the world and eschew all sustenance, letting her newly mortal flesh dwindle until Oronin's Horn made good its claim on her spirit. What else was left for her? At least on the far side of death, she might find Calandor's spirit awaiting her.

But Aracus Altorus did not leave her to her own devices.

He didn't know how to use the Soumanië, and there was no one else to tell him. Even the Ellylon shook their heads, saying it was a thing only Ingolin the Wise might know. It afforded her a grim amusement. They were fools to think the Soumanië would be so easily claimed. And so, far from letting her retire in solitude and turn her face to the wall, Aracus kept her at his side, and Lilias kept her silence. He sought to woo her with sweet reason, he bullied her, he chivvied her, he offered her bargains she refused. He would not stoop to torture—there was that much, at least, to be said for Haomane's Allies—but neither would he let her out of his sight. He dragged her into the Cavern of the Marasoumië beneath Beshtanag Mountain, where he made an ill-guided attempt to use the gem to summon Malthus the Counselor.

Even if he had known its secret, he would have failed that day. Lilias had laughed, close to hysteria, as the foundations of the world shifted and the node-point of the Marasoumië turned dull and inert, a dead hunk of grey granite. The bundled fibers of light that had traced the Ways went dead, leaving empty tunnels through solid rock. Aracus had cried aloud in pain, scrabbling at his forehead, removing the fillet from his brow and clutching it in his hand. As the Soumanië shone like a red star in his grasp, answering to the distant power of Godslayer, she knew what it was that the Sunderer had done, and that the Counselor was trapped within the Ways.

"Tell me how to reach him!" Aracus had raged. "Tell me how to *use* this!"

Lilias had shrugged. "Give me the Soumanië."

He didn't, of course; he wasn't a fool. He had merely glared at her, while the Ellylon spoke to him in hushed tones of what had transpired, explaining that not even one of the Soumanië could undo Godslayer's work. If they could not tap the Soumanië's power themselves, still, there were things they knew; things they *understood*, Haomane's Children. A death at the heart of Urulat was one such. They explained it to the would-be King of the West, their perfect faces strained and bone-white. The Ellylon did not love the deep places of the earth.

In the end, they trooped back to her warchamber, where Lilias was not allowed to leave. She was a piece of excess baggage, but one too valuable to discard. Dignity, along with privacy, was a thing from another life. She sat in the corner, covering her face with both hands, while Haomane's Allies spoke in portentous tones of assailing Darkhaven. They let her hear their plans, so little did they fear her. A bitter irony, that.

"My lady," a voice whispered. "Is there aught I can bring you?"

Lilias gazed upward through the lank curtain of her hair. "Pietre!" It was appalling, the gratitude in her acknowledgment. Tears welled in her eyes. "Are you well? Have they treated you kindly?"

"Aye, my lady, well enough. It is as you said, they show us mercy." Stooping on one knee, Pietre offered the tray he held; a silver salver from her own cupboards, laden with cheese and dark Pelmaran bread. There was concern in his gaze. "Will you not eat? A bit of bread, at least? I can ask the cooks to sop it in wine, make a posset . . . "

"No," Lilias began, then paused. "Would you do this for me?"

"Anything."

She told him, whispering, her lips close to his ear. Pietre shook his head vehemently, his brown hair brushing her cheek. Only when one of the Ellylon glanced over in idle curiosity did he relent. Even then, his willingness was fitful. "Are you *sure?*" he asked, begging her with his eyes to say no.

"Yes." Lilias almost smiled. "I am sure."

It gave her reason to live, at least for a little while longer, and that, too, was a bitter irony. She huddled in her corner, arms wrapped around her knees, half-listening to the council of Haomane's Allies while awaiting Pietre's return. In time he came, carrying the silver platter. It made her proud to see the straight line of his back, the pride with which he performed his duties. Aracus Altorus and his peers accepted his service without thinking, reaching for a bite of bread and cheese, a cup of wine. Only Blaise remained on guard, distrustful, making certain Pietre was willing to taste aught he served to Haomane's Allies.

And he was, of course. All save the posset; that was reserved for her.

Pietre knelt to serve it to her, steadying the tray with one hand. There were tears in his eyes now, liquid and shining. "It is what you asked for," he murmured. "Sarika knew where it was kept. But, oh, please my lady! Both of us beg you . . . "

"You have my thanks, Pietre. And my blessing, for what it is worth." Lilias reached eagerly for the cup. Cradling it between her hands, she inhaled deeply of its aroma. Wine and hoarded spices, and an underlying bitterness. It was a fit drink for the occasion. "Both of you," she added. "Are you sure there is enough?"

"Yes, my lady." Swallowing tears, he nodded. "Enough for a whole colony of rats. It will suffice."

Lilias did smile, then, lifting the cup in toast. "You've done a noble deed. Farewell, Pietre."

Bowing his head, he turned away without answering, unable to watch. Still, it gladdened her heart to have him there, loyal to the end. It hadn't all been the Soumanië's power, not all of it. She had loved them well, her pretty ones; as she had loved Beshtanag. Its grey crags, its green forests; hers, all hers. From the sheep grazing in mountain pastures to the Were skulking in the shadow of the pines, she had *known* it, more truly and deeply than anyone else ever would.

And now it was lost to her, all lost. Would it have been different if she had refused Satoris' emissary? A war to prevent a war, she thought, gazing at the cup's contents. So Tanaros Blacksword called it. He had been wrong; but he had been right, too. Ever since Dergail's Soumanië had risen in the West, she had known it; for what Calandor had known, she had shared.

All things must be as they are, little sssisster.

It was a glorious haven they had made in Beshtanag, but the dragon's wisdom held true. Sooner or later, they would have come for her. Better, perhaps, that it was Haomane's Allies than the Lord-of-Thought himself. If Haomane First-Born was coming, Lilias did not intend to wait for him.

"Farewell," she whispered, raising the cup to her lips.

A man's hand dashed it away, hard and swift.

Crockery shattered, and Lilias shrank backward into her corner beneath a sudden shadow. Blaise Caveros stood over her, having shoved Pietre out of his way. "Sorceress." He sighed, rumpling his dark hair. The bandage was gone from his brow and the gash on his temple was knitting cleanly, but he still looked tired and drawn. "Please don't make this difficult."

A wine-sodden piece of bread sat on the stone floor, while dark liquid pooled in the cracks between the flagstones. A pair of flies buzzed, sampling the dregs. As Lilias watched, one twitched in midair and fell. Its wings beat feebly, then went still. "You deny me a clean death," she said in a low voice. "Would you do so if I were a man?"

Blaise nodded at the spilled wine. "Poison? You call that a clean death?"

"It is what is allotted to me!" Lilias shouted, lifting her head. Tears of frustration stung her eyes. "Must I meet you on the battle-field? I'm no warrior, Borderguardsman! I don't *want* to wield a sword! You have won; why can you not let me die?"

Her words rang in a warchamber gone abruptly silent. They were staring, now; all of them, Aracus Altorus and the others, leaving off their poring over maps and plans. She hated them for it. The Ellylon were the worst, with their smug compassion, their eternal condescension toward all things mortal.

No; worst was the Archer, the Arduan woman, who stared aghast and uncomprehending. *She* wouldn't mind dying on a battlefield.

"You," Lilias said to her. "Do you think *you* would be here if you hadn't proved yourself with a sharp, pointy weapon?" Her voice broke as grief rose up to overwhelm her. "Ah, by all the Shapers! Do you even *know* what you destroyed?"

"Sorceress." Blaise moved wearily to block her view, interposing his tall figure between her and the rest of the room. Behind him, the Arduan Archer's voice rose in anxious query, swiftly hushed by others. Haomane's Allies resumed their council in more subdued tones. "We are sorry for your grief. Believe me, we are all of us well acquainted with the emotion. But we cannot allow you to take your life."

Defeated, Lilias let the back of her head rest against the stone wall, gazing up at him. "I have lived too long already, Border-guardsman. If you were truly an honorable man, you'd let me die." A short laugh escaped her. "And if you were a wise one, you'd do the same. I promise you, this is an action you will regret."

"If you were an honorable woman," Blaise said quietly, "you would not have conspired with the Sunderer to deceive and destroy us."

"All I wanted was to be left in peace," Lilias murmured. "To live, unmolested, in Beshtanag, as I have done for so long. Satoris himself in his fortress of Darkhaven desires nothing more. Is it so much to ask? We require so little space upon the face of Urulat. And yet it seems even that is too much for Haomane's pride to endure. Lord Satoris afforded an opportunity, and I seized it. In the end, it is still Haomane's Allies who raised the specter of war. Did you not seek to fulfill his Prophecy?"

Blaise frowned at her, uncomprehending. "We are neither cruel nor unreasonable, Lilias of Beshtanag. If you give us a chance, you may come to see it. If that is not your will . . . You know full well, lady, that you may have your freedom—to do whatever you wish with your life, including end it—for one simple price. Tell us how the powers of the Soumanië may be wielded. Give us the dragon's lore."

Lilias shook her head, aware of the solid wall behind her. Her home, her fortress. Her prison, now. Still, it stood, a testament to what she had achieved. A monument to Calandor's death. The irony in what had passed seemed no longer bitter, but fitting. "No, Borderguardsman. Whatever else you may accuse me of, that is one trust I will never betray, and one death I will never forgive."

He sighed. "Then you remain with us."

TWENTY-EIGHT

"RIGHT HERE, LADS." VORAX TAPPED the map with one thick forefinger. "In the Northern Harrow. There's a node-point in the middle of the range; or was, at any rate. That's where Lord Satoris suspects they landed, based on their trajectory through the Ways."

He glanced up to make sure they were following. Osric and the other Staccians were no worry, but one was never certain with Fjel-troll. A few of them had a look of cheerful incomprehension, or at least one he'd come to recognize as such. For someone unacquainted with their features, it was hard to tell. Still, the one Hyrgolf had recommended to lead their contingent—Skragdal, the young Tungskulder—seemed alert and attentive.

"Now, these are desert folk," Vorax continued. "And bear in mind, they've never been out of their desert before; or at least not that we know of. So they're likely to stick with what they know, which is lowlands. See here, where the Harrow dips." He traced a line on the map. "If they're coming for us, and we have every reason to think they are, they're like to take the valleys, follow the riverbeds."

"Lord Vorax." Osric, bending over the map, met his eyes. The Staccian lieutenant was a man of middle years, solid and reliable. Not the best or boldest of his lads—that had been Carfax, entrusted to lead the decoys—but sensible, a man one could trust. "What if they're *not* coming for us?"

"Well, then we've nothing to worry about, have we?" Vorax grinned through his beard, clapping Osric's shoulder. "Let's say they are, lad. If we're wrong, you retrace your steps. Pick up their trail at the node-point, or what's left of it, and follow them south. Do you see?"

Osric nodded. "Aye, my lord."

"General." Skragdal frowned at the map. "I know the Northern Harrow, though I do not understand how this shape on paper shows it. This I know to be true. Even if we hurry, we will be many days behind their departure. There are valleys and valleys, routes and routes. How do we know which these smallfolk will take?"

"We don't," Vorax said bluntly. "That's why his Lordship wanted Fjel on this mission. See, here." He pointed. "This line is where Fjel territory ends, and Staccia proper begins. That's what it means."

"Neherinach." The Tungskulder's deep voice was sombre. It was a place the Fjel knew well, the ancient battleground where Haomane's Allies had fallen upon them in the First Age of the Sundered World. Their fate had been sealed at Neherinach, for it was there that they had retrieved Godslayer from the hands of the Rivenlost and brought it to Lord Satoris.

"Aye," Vorax said. "Neherinach. If these . . . smallfolk . . . travel southward, Staccians will note their passage. But if they stay to the north, it will be Fjeltroll who track their progress. Either way, they should be easy to mark. They are the Charred Ones, desert folk, dark of skin and unskilled in the ways of mountains." He splayed his hands on the map, gazing at Skragdal. "You may need to divide your forces. That is why I asked both contingents to be present. Hyrgolf said the tribes would give you aid if needed. Is it true, Tungskulder? Does the old oath still stand?"

"Aye, General," the Fjel rumbled. Skragdal's small eyes were grave under the bulging ridge of his brow, the thick hide scarred where Lord Satoris' sulfuric rain had fallen. "We are not like you. Neheris' Children do not forget."

It stung him, though it shouldn't have. "Then you will find aid along the way!" Vorax snapped. "Let the tribes be your guide. I don't care how you find them, Tungskulder, just *find them*. Find them, and kill them, and spill the Water upon barren ground. Do you understand?"

"Aye," the Fjel said softly. "I do."

"General?" Osric cleared his throat. "Lord Vorax, sir? I told my lads there would be hazard pay in this for them."

"Hazard pay." Vorax eyed him wryly. "We're preparing for the whole of Urulat to descend on us, and you want hazard pay for tracking a pair of desert rats through the mountains? This ought to be a pleasure jaunt, my boy."

Osric shrugged. "And we ought to have taken Haomane's Allies at Beshtanag, sir, but we didn't. Instead we lost General Tanaros, and Shapers only know what's become of Carfax and his lot. You say it's just a pair of Charred Folk, but that's just guesswork. What if the Altorian king sent an army to guard them? What if the wizard is with them?"

"It's not *guesswork!*" Vorax brought one fist down hard on the map-table, making his lieutenant jump. "Listen to me, lads. His Lordship took up Godslayer itself, do you hear? What he knows, he *knows.* Haomane's damnable wizard is trapped in the Ways, and like to stay there. The Charred Folk are alone, and as for Tanaros Blacksword, he's about his Lordship's business." He glared at Osric. "Do you think the Three are that easy to kill?"

"No, sir." Osric held his ground. "But mortal men are, Lord Vorax. And we hear the rumors, same as anyone. They say the lost weapon's been found." There was no guile in his grey eyes, only steady honesty and a measure of fear. "A son of Altorus looking to wed a daughter of Elterrion. The lost weapon. Now this Bearer, and you say he's carrying water could put out the marrow-fire. I'm a Staccian, sir, and I'm as true to my word as any lug-headed, leather-hided Fjel. But if I'm going into the teeth of Haomane's Prophecy, I want what I was promised. Battle-glory, and fair recompense for the fallen."

The other Staccians murmured agreement. Vorax blew out his cheeks in a huge sigh, calculating sums in his head. He would be glad beyond words when Tanaros returned. Vorax didn't mind leading a good skirmish, but this business of serving as General was wearying. Bargaining was his strength, not overseeing morale. How could he do one while worrying about the other? Blacksword might be dour company, still mooning over his dead wife's betrayal a thousand years later, but he had the knack of commanding an army. "Fine," he said. "Triple pay. How does that sound, Lieutenant Osric?"

"In advance, sir?"

Vorax stared at the ceiling. "In advance." Lowering his gaze, he fixed it on Skragdal. "What about you, Tungskulder? Are the Fjel-troll afraid of Haomane's Prophecy?"

"Aye, General," Skragdal said simply. "That's why we go."

"Good lad." He clapped a hand on the Fjel's hulking arm, his shoulder being too high to reach. It was like slapping a boulder; ye Shapers, but the lad was huge! "There's nothing wrong with being afraid. His Lordship has powerful enemies, and they'll stop at naught to see him destroyed. They've waited a long time for this. But we haven't exactly been sitting idle, have we, lads? We're ready for them. That's the important thing to remember. Beshtanag may have gone awry, but we *did* succeed at Lindanen Dale, and we'll succeed in this, too." He grinned at them, showing his eyeteeth like a Fjel. "You want to know where our General Tanaros Blacksword is this very moment? His Lordship knows. Our Tanaros is in the heart of the Unknown Desert itself, putting the Charred Folk who sent the Bearer to the sword and silting that cursed well they guard! How do you like *that* news?"

They liked it, well enough to cheer.

"Haomane's Prophecy might be fulfilled someday, lads." Vorax shook his head. "But not today," he said with satisfaction. "Not on *my* watch! And not on yours, damn your eyes. Mark my words, Darkhaven will prevail!"

It braced them like strong drink, and the cheering continued. Vorax grinned some more, slapped a few more sturdy shoulders, ordered a keg of *svartblod* breached and raised a cup to the success of their mission. The Fjeltroll drank deep, roaring toasts in their guttural tongue. Nåltannen, most of them; a few Kaldjager for scouting work, and a pair of Gulnagel from the lowlands. Skragdal was the only Tungskulder, save one. The other Staccians drank the *svartblod* too, gasping and sputtering. It was a matter of pride with them to keep it down.

"Right," Vorax said, gauging the moment. "You have your orders, lads. Report to field marshal Hyrgolf for weapons and supplies, and head out at dawn."

THE DELTA'S WARMTH WAS A GLORIOUS thing.

Against all likelihood, Ushahin found himself humming as he poled the skiff along the waterways. Dip and push; dip and push. It was a soothing motion. The flat-bottomed skiff he'd purchased in Arduan glided effortlessly over the still water. Caitlin's Da, he reflected, was a fine craftsman.

Passing beneath a stand of mangroves there was a green snake, unlooping itself lazily from a limb. Its blunt head quested in the air beside his face, forked tongue flickering.

"Hello, little cousin." Leaning on his pole, Ushahin smiled at the snake. "Good hunting to you, though you may wish to seek smaller prey."

The questing head withdrew and he pushed onward. Dip and push; dip and push. The hot, humid environs of the Delta were kind to his aching, ill-knit bones. For once, his joints felt oiled and smooth. He had not felt such ease in his flesh since he had been a child; indeed, had forgotten it existed. Out of sight of Arduan, he had shed the concealing cloak with its itchy hood. It was good to be unveiled in the open air. Sunlight usually made his head ache, but the dense foliage filtered it to a green dimness gentle to his eyes. That terrible awakening on the plains of Rukhar seemed distant, here.

"*Kaugh!*" Atop the highest branches of a further mangrove, a raven landed and perched there, swaying, its claws clenched on a too-slim branch. It clung there a moment, then launched itself in a flurry of wings, finding a similar perch a few yards to the south. "*Kaugh!*"

"I see you, little brother," Ushahin called to the raven, one of those serving to guide him through the swamp. He thrust strongly on his pole and the skiff turned, edging southward. "I am coming."

Satisfied, the raven pecked at something unseen.

In truth, it would be easy for a man to lose his way in the Delta. And would that be such an ill fate? Pausing to swig from his waterskin, Ushahin pondered the matter. There was something . . . pleasant . . . about the swamp. He felt *good* here. It wasn't merely a question of the moist air being kind to his bones, no. Something else was at work, something *deeper*. There was a pulse beating in his veins that hadn't surged since . . . since when?

Never, perhaps. One half of his blood, after all, was Ellylon. Haomane's Children did not know desire of the flesh, not in the same way other races among the Lesser Shapers did. The Lord-of-Thought had Shaped them, and the Lord-of-Thought had refused Satoris' Gift, that which he freely bestowed on other Shapers' Children.

The other half . . . ah.

Arahila Second-Born, Arahila the Fair. She had accepted his Lordship's Gift for her Children; and Haomane's, too, that which he had withheld from all but his beloved Sister's Children. Thus the race of Men, gifted with thought, quick with desire.

Ushahin had never reveled in the mortal parentage of his father, in his possession of Lord Satoris' Gift. Here, in the Delta, it was different. The songs he crooned under his breath were cradle-songs, sung to him by his mother aeons ago, before his body was beaten, broken and twisted.

"So, Haomane!" Ushahin addressed his words to a cloud of midges that hung in the air before him, standing in lieu of the First-Born among Shapers. "You're afraid, eh? What's the matter? Was Lord Satoris' Gift more powerful than you reckoned?" Pushing hard on his pole, he hummed, watching the midges dance. "Seems to me mayhap it was, Lord-of-Thought. At least in this place."

"Kaugh, kaugh!"

Ravens burst from the tops of the mangroves; one, two; half a dozen. They circled in the dank air above the center of the swamp, and sunlight glinted purple on their wings. Ushahin paused and rested on his pole, gazing upward. Images of a hillock, vast and mossy, flickered through his mind.

"What's this?" he mused aloud. "What do you wish me to see? All right, all right, little brothers! I come apace."

He shoved hard on the pole, anchoring its butt in the sludge beneath the waterways. The skiff answered, gliding over still wa-ters made ruddy by the afternoon sun. In the center of a watery glade stood a single palodus tree, tall and solitary. In the shadow of its spreading canopy arose the mossy hillock he had glimpsed. For no reason he could name, Ushahin's mouth grew dry, and his pulse beat in his loins. It was a strange sensation; so strange it took him long minutes to recognize it as carnal desire.

Such desire! He was tumescent with it. The image, all unbid-den, of the Lady of the Ellylon, slid into his mind. Cerelinde, bent over the saddle, the tips of her fair hair brushing the earth.

"Oh," Ushahin said, grinding his teeth, "I think *not*."

Sluggish bubbles rose in the murky water before him; rose, and burst, carrying the sound of laughter, slow and deep. In the branches, ravens arose in a clatter, yammering. Beneath the surface of the water, a pair of greenish eyes opened, slit with a vertical pupil and covered by the thin film of an inner lid.

Gripped by sudden fear, Ushahin propelled the skiff backward.

Iron-grey and slick with moss, the dragon's head emerged from the water. It was twice the size of the skiff, dripping with muck. Droplets slid down its bearded jaw, plunking into the water, creat-ing circular ripples. It stirred one unseen foreleg, then another, and Ushahin struggled to steady his craft as the swamp surged in re-sponse. The dragon's inner lids blinked with slow amusement as it regarded him, waiting until the waters had quieted and he had regained control of the skiff. Only then did the massive jaws, hung on either side with strands of rotting greenery, part to speak.

"Is thisss desire ssso disstasssteful to you, little brother?"

Ushahin laid the pole across the prow of the skiff and made a careful bow. "Eldest," he said. "Forgive me, Lord Dragon. I did not know you were here."

Overhead, ravens circled and yammered.

The dragon's gaze held, this time unblinking. "You bear Sssatoriss' mark. You are one of his. You have ssseen my brother and know his fate."

"Yes," Ushahin said quietly. "Calandor of Beshtanag is no more."

Turning its head, the dragon sighed. A gout of bluish flame jetted from its dripping nostrils, dancing eerily over the oily waters to set a stand of mangrove alight. A single tree flamed, black and skeletal within a cocoon of fire. The circling ravens squawked and regrouped at a distance. In the skiff, Ushahin scrambled for his pole.

"Peasssse, little brother." The dragon eyed him with sorrow. "I mean you no harm, not yet. Calandor chose his path long ago, thisss I know. We know. We always know." It shuddered, and ripples emanated across the swamp, setting the skiff to rocking upon the waters. "Ssso why come you here?"

"Seeking passage." Emboldened, Ushahin rode out the waves, planting the pole in the mire and gripping it tight in both hands. "Will you grant it, Elder Brother?"

"Brother." Beneath yellow-green eyes, twin spumes of smoke issued forth in a contemptuous snort. "What makesss you think I am your *brother?*"

Ushahin frowned, shifted his grip on his pole. "Did you not name me as much?"

"I named *you.*" The dragon snorted. "Brother!"

"What, then?"

"Would you know?" The nictitating lids flickered. "Guesssss."

A mad courage seized him. What was there to lose, here in the Delta? Whether he would continue onward or die in this place was the dragon's to choose. Craning his neck, Ushahin gazed at the dragon's nearest eye. The yellow-green iris roiled in the immense orb, colors shifting like oily waters. The vertical pupil contracted like a cat's, but vaster, far vaster. Blacker than the Ravensmirror, blacker than a moonless night, it reflected no light, only darkness.

If he hesitated, he would falter; so he didn't. Using the skills taught him long ago by the Grey Dam, Ushahin slid his thoughts into the mind behind that black, black pupil.

It was like stepping into a bottomless pit.

There was nothing *there;* or if there was, it was a thing so huge, so distant, he could not compass it. The way back was gone, the filament that connected him to himself might never have existed. There was only an encompassing, lightless vastness. Deeper and deeper he fell, a tiny star in an immense universe of darkness. There were no boundaries. There would be no end, only an endless falling.

Sundered from himself, Ushahin shaped a soundless cry . . .

. . . and fell . . .

. . . and fell . . .

. . . and fell . . .

Something flickered in the incomprehensible verges of the dragon's mind; something, many somethings. Tiny and urgent and defiant, they came for him like a cloud of midges, a storm of claws. Feathered, frantic thoughts, scrabbling for his. Yellow beech leaves, shiny black beetles, an updraught beneath the wings and the patchwork of the tilting earth glimpsed below.

The ravens of Darkhaven had come for him.

Such were the thoughts they cast out like lifelines to Ushahin Dreamspinner; for they were, after all, ravens. It was enough. Clinging to the filaments of their awareness, Ushahin braked his endless fall and wove of the ravens' thoughts a net, a ladder, and fled the darkness, back to whence he'd come.

Behind him, the dragon's laughter echoed.

The world returned, and he returned to it.

Ushahin opened his eyes and found himself lying on his back in the skiff, half-soaked with bilge water. Hung upon the sinuous length of an arching neck, the dragon's head hovered above him, blotting out a large portion of the sky. Beyond it, he caught sight of the ravens exiting from their frantic ellipse, landing in the high branches of the palodus tree. Though his head ached like a beaten drum, Ushahin sent thoughts of gratitude winging after them. Satisfied, the ravens preened their feathers.

"The wise man," the dragon rumbled, "does not play games with dragons."

With an effort, Ushahin levered himself upward to sit on the bench in the skiff's stern and rested, arms braced on his knees. A strange exhilaration filled him at finding himself alive and whole. He took an experimental breath, conscious of the air filling his lungs, of having lungs to fill with air. "True," he said, finding the experiment a success. "But I am not a man, and I have been accused of being mad, but never wise. Elder Sister . . . " he bowed from the waist, " . . . forgive my folly."

"Ssso." The dragon eyed him with amusement. "It has gained sssome wisdom."

"Some." Ushahin wrapped his arms around his knees and returned the dragon's gaze. "Calanthrag the Eldest, Mother of Dragons. I am a fool, indeed. But tell me, why here, in the heart of the Delta?"

Sulfurous fumes engulfed him as the dragon snorted. "Child of three rasses, ssson of none. Not a Man, yet ssstill a man. You deny your own desire. Do you deny the power here, where Sssatorisss Third-Born arose?"

"No, Mother." Ushahin coughed once, waving away fumes. He shook his head gravely, feeling his lank silver-gilt hair brush his cheeks. "Not the power. Only the desire."

"Why?" The dragon's voice was tender with cunning. "Ansssswer."

She had let him call her mother, had not denied it! No one had done as much since the Grey Dam Sorash, whose heir had castigated him. Ushahin hugged the thought to him and tried to answer honestly. "Because I despise Haomane's Children above all else, for their cowardice in forsaking me and my begetting," he said. "And I will not allow my flesh to become the vehicle by which they receive Lord Satoris' Gift."

"Ssso." The sinuous neck flattened, its spikes lying low as the iron-grey head hovered above him. "You glimpssse the Great Pattern?"

"It may be," Ushahin said humbly. "I do not know."

Smoke puffed from the dragon's nostrils as Calanthrag the Eldest, Mother of Dragons, laughed. "Then tie up your boat," she said, "and I will tell you."

The bark of the palodus tree was silver-grey, smooth as skin. Ushahin poled the skiff underneath its vast canopy. There was a rope knotted through an iron ring in its prow. He laid down his pole and knelt on the forward bench to loop the rope around the trunk of the palodus, securing the skiff. Mud-crabs scuttled among the thrusting roots of the palodus, and waterbugs skittered here and there on the surface of the water. The setting sun gilded the swamp, lending a fiery glory to the murky waters. Some yards away, the charred skeleton of a mangrove shed quiet flakes of ash, long past the smouldering stage. How many hours had he lost, falling through the dragon's mind?

It didn't matter.

Overhead, the first pale stars of twilight began to emerge and the ravens of Darkhaven fluffed their feathers, settling on their perches and calling to one another with sleepy squawks. All was quiet in the Delta, and at its heart, a pair of yellow-green eyes hung like lanterns in the dimness, hinting at the enormous bulk beyond. Ushahin gave one last tug on the bilge-sodden rope, and smiled. "Mother of Dragons." He bowed to her, then sat, feeling the skiff rock a little beneath his shifting weight. "I am listening."

"In the beginning," said Calanthrag the Eldest, "there was Urulat . . . "

"PULL!" SPEROS SHOUTED.

The Gulnagel groaned, hauling on the ropes. They were heroic figures in the red light of the setting sun, broad backs and shoulders straining, the muscles in their bulging haunches a-quiver. The chunk of rock they labored to haul moved a few paces on its improvised skid, built of a dented Fjel buckler and rope salvaged from the Well. It hadn't been on a pulley, either; just a straight length of it, impossible to draw. He'd had to send one of the Fjel back down the Well to sever it and retrieve as much as was possible.

"Pull!" Speros chanted. "Pull, pull, *pull!*"

With grunts and groans, they did. It moved, inch by inch, grinding across the hard-packed sand. He joined his efforts to theirs at the end, rolling it manually to the lip of the Well. It wasn't easy. The standing monoliths of Stone Grove had shattered when toppled, but even the pieces into which they had broken were massive. Atop the mound of the Well, Speros stood shoulder to shoulder with the Gulnagel, heaving.

"All right, lads," he panted, loosening the rope with dirty fingers. "Now *push.*"

It fell with a satisfying crash, landing only a few yards below. Their long labors showed results at last; the shaft of the Well was well and truly clogged. Speros flopped onto the cooling sand, giving his aching muscles a chance to recover.

"More, boss?" One of the Gulnagel hovered over him.

"A few more, aye." With difficulty, Speros rose, gathering the rope. It was vine-wrought, but sturdy beyond belief. Those poor old Yarru had woven it well. "*One* more," he amended, weaving toward a distant boulder. "Bring the skid."

Stout hearts that they were, they did. He helped them lever the next rock onto the concave buckler and wrapped the rope around it, securing the boulder in place, lashing it to the handles. "Once more, lads," he said encouragingly, helping the Gulnagel into harness. "Remember, push with the legs!"

One grinned at him, lowering his shoulders and preparing to haul. Freg was his name; Speros knew him by the chipped eye-tusks that gleamed ruddily in the sunset. There were marks on his shoulders where the rope's chafing had worn the rough hide as smooth as polished leather. "You drive a team hard, boss."

"Aye, Freg." Speros laid a hand on the Fjel's arm, humbled by his strength and endurance. Never once, since the Marasoumië had spat them out, had he heard one complain. "And you're the team for it. Pull, lads, *pull!*"

Groaning and straining, they obeyed him once more. Taloned feet splayed, seeking purchase on the churned sand. Yellowed nails dug furrows on top of furrows, strong legs driving as the Fjel bent to the harness, and the buckler moved, iron grating and squealing as it was dragged across the desert.

How many times had they done this? Speros had lost count. It had seemed impossible on the first day. Boulders were like pebbles, dropped into the Well of the World. On the first day they had merely fallen an impossible distance, shattering, dispersing fragments into the cavern of the dead Marasoumië. He had been uncertain that the Well could be blocked. It had taken all his cunning to achieve it; rigging the skid, utilizing the full strength of the Fjel, moving the largest pieces first.

Even then, he had been unsure.

And yet . . . and yet. In time, it had happened.

The last boulder crashed like thunder as they rolled it over the lip. Speros straightened, putting his hands at the small of his back. His lower back ached, and his nails were torn and bloodied. "Good job, lads," he gasped. "Fill in the rest with loose rock and sand, make it look natural. That ought to do it."

The Gulnagel surrounded the shallow mouth of the Well, backing up to it and squatting low. Sand and shale flew as they dug dog-wise, shoveling a flurry of debris betwixt their rear legs, braced and solid. The remaining feet of the Well's open throat dwindled to inches.

"Good job, lads," Speros repeated, eyeing the rising level and trying to remain steady on his feet. "Remember to make it look natural."

One of them grunted; Freg, perhaps. It was hard to tell from the rear. Speros clapped a hand on the nearest Fjel appendage and let his staggering steps take him down the mound. The earth was churned and torn. He had to tread with exhausted care to avoid turning an ankle. All around the desert floor, the jagged stumps of the monoliths remained, raw and accusatory.

General Tanaros was seated on one, sharpening his sword and gazing westward.

Speros wove toward him. "Lord General!" He drew himself up in a weary salute. "The Well is filled."

"Thank you, Speros." The General spoke in a deep voice, absentminded. "Look at that, will you?" He pointed with the tip of his sword; to the west, where a red star hung low on the horizon. "Dergail's Soumanië still rises. What do you think it means?"

"War." Speros' quivering legs folded, and he sat abruptly. "Isn't that what they say? It is in the Midlands, anyway." He rubbed his eyes with the heels of his hands, trying to scrub away the exhaustion. "The red star, reminder of Dergail's defeat. It's the Sunderer's challenge, a declaration of war."

"So they do," the General mused. "And yet, Lord Satoris did not raise the star. He thought it a warning. A sister's kindness."

"Does it matter?" Speros fumbled for the waterskin lashed to his belt and managed to loosen the stopper. It sloshed, half-empty, as he raised it to his lips and took a sparing mouthful.

"Betimes, I wonder." General Tanaros drew his whetstone down the length of his sword. "I fear we have not chosen our battlefield wisely, Speros."

Speros glanced up at him. "Beshtanag, sir? Or Darkhaven?"

"No." The General shook his head. "Neither. I mean the hearts and minds of Men, Speros." He examined one edge of his ebony blade, testing it with his thumb. "Do you suppose it would have made a difference?"

"Sir?"

"The Bearer." Sheathing his sword, General Tanaros turned his attention to the Midlander. "He made the only choice he was offered. Would it have made a difference, do you think, if we had offered another one?"

"I don't know, Lord General."

"I wonder." Tanaros frowned. "But what would we have offered him, after all? Wealth? Power? Immortality? Those are merely bribes. In the end, it all comes down to the same choice."

Speros shrugged. "A reason to say no, I suppose."

"Yes." General Tanaros glanced across the Stone Glade. The smaller mound that had been erected outside the circle of broken monoliths was barely visible in the deepening twilight. It had taken the Gulnagel less than an hour to dig a grave large enough to contain the corpses of the slaughtered Yarru elders. "I suppose so."

"Sir." Speros cleared his throat. "Will there be a lot of . . . that sort of thing?"

Tanaros smiled bleakly. "You told me you'd shed innocent blood before, Midlander."

"Aye." He held the General's gaze, though it wasn't easy. "But not gladly." A creeping sense of alarm stirred in his heart. Was the General thinking of dismissing him? Speros ran his tongue over his teeth, feeling the gap where one had been lost in the dungeons of Darkhaven. He had gambled everything on this. He thought about the Midlands and the disdain his name evoked, the disappointment in his mother's eyes. He thought about how General Tanaros had deigned to meet him as an equal on the sparring-field. He thought of the camaraderie of the Fjel, and their unfailing admiration and loyalty, and knew he didn't want to lose it. Not for this, not for anything. What did the death of a few old Charred Folk matter? They'd brought it on themselves, after all. The Lord General had asked them to give him a reason to spare them. A reason to say no. It wasn't that much to ask. His hands clenched involuntarily into fists, and he pressed one to his heart in salute. "I failed you, I know. It won't happen again."

It was the General who looked away first. "I almost would that I'd failed myself in this," he murmured, half to himself. "All right." He sighed, placing his hands flat on his thighs. "You say the Well is filled?"

"Aye, sir!" Speros sprang to his feet, light-headed with relief. "It would take a team of Fjel a lifetime to unblock it!"

"Good." General Tanaros stood and gazed at the twilit sky. It seemed larger, here in the desert, and the red star of Dergail's Soumanië pulsed brighter. "We'll take a few hours' rest, and leave ere dawn." Turning, he poked Speros' half-empty waterskin. "The water-hole here is deep; Ngurra told me it never runs dry. So don't stint yourself, Midlander, because I don't know how lucky we'll be crossing the desert."

"Aye, sir." Speros raised the skin and took an obliging swallow.

"I mean it." The General's eyes were shadowed and his face was hard. What had transpired here in the Unknown Desert had taken its toll on him. For a moment it seemed he might speak of it; then he shuddered, gathering himself. He fixed Speros with a clear gaze. "Drink while you can, and see to it that every waterskin we can salvage is filled to bursting. I mean to get us home alive."

"Aye, sir!" Speros smiled, relishing the word. "Home."

TWENTY-NINE

"DON'T LOOK."

Blaise Caveros' voice was low as he attempted to interpose his mount between her and the sight of the fallen dragon. It was a futile courtesy. Calandor's bulk loomed beyond the gap in Beshtanag's wall like a second mountain. There was no way Lilias could avoid seeing him as the train of Haomane's Allies made their way down the slope, passing through the broken wall.

It was true, what the old legends claimed. In death, the dragon had turned to stone. The glittering scales had faded to dull grey, veined with a reddish ore. Already, the clean, sinuous lines of his form had grown weathered and vague. Lilias' hands trembled on the reins as she tried to trace his shape with her gaze.

There, she thought; the smaller ridge is his tail, and those are his haunches. How did he land? Oh Shapers, that crumpled part underneath is a wing! It must have broken in the fall.

Without thinking, Lilias drew rein and dismounted, tugging blindly at robes that caught and tore on the buckle of her mount's girth. "Sorceress!" Blaise's call seemed distant and unimportant. She stumbled across the battlefield into the shadow of Calandor's body, hands outstretched. There. That was his shoulder, that was one of his forelegs against which she had so often leaned, feeling the warmth of his mighty heart radiating against her skin.

"Calandor," she whispered, laying her hands on the harsh grey stone. It was sun-warmed. If she closed her eyes, she could almost pretend. The long ridge of his neck slanted along the ground, ending in the dim outline of his noble head, chin resting on the earth. Only knobs of dead stone remained where his green-gilt eyes had shone. Oblivious to the waiting train, Lilias embraced as much of the fallen dragon as her arms could encompass, and wept.

Hoofbeats rattled on the stony ground behind her, and leather tack creaked. "Sorceress," Blaise said. "It's time to go."

Lilias rested her brow against the sun-warmed rock. If she tried, she could almost imagine the pulse beating in her own veins was the steady throb of the dragon's heart. "Can you not allow me even a moment of grief?"

"No. Not here. Not now."

She turned slowly to face him, squinting through tear-swollen eyes. He sat impassively in the saddle, leading her mount by the reins. Beyond him, Haomane's Allies waited in shining, impatient panoply. At the head of the column, Aracus Altorus was frowning, the Soumanië bright on his brow. A coterie of Ellylon and a handful of Borderguard surrounded him. The woman Archer was watching her with distrust, an arrow loosely nocked in Oronin's Bow. A long line of soldiery—Pelmarans, Midlanders, Vedasians—stretched behind them, mounted and on foot, all regarding her with triumphant contempt.

It was too much to bear.

Averting her head, Lilias left the dragon's side and fumbled for the stirrup. Someone laughed aloud as she struggled to mount without the aid of a block. Blaise reached over and hauled her unceremoniously into the saddle. He kept control of her reins, leading her back toward the train. Aracus gave the signal and progress resumed.

Behind them, a cheer arose as a Pelmaran foot-soldier passing in the ranks jabbed at the ridge of Calandor's tail with the butt-end of his spear. It set a trend. Sick at heart, Lilias twisted in the saddle to watch as each passing man ventured a thrust or a kick, bits of stone crumbling under their blows. One of them spat.

"Darden." Blaise beckoned to one of the dun-cloaked Borderguardsmen. "Tell them to stop."

The man nodded, turning his horse's head and riding back down the line. The order was received with grumbling, but it was obeyed. After the battle, few of Haomane's Allies would venture to disobey one of the Borderguard.

"Thank you." Lilias spoke the words without looking at him.

Blaise shrugged, shifting his grip on the twin sets of reins. "He was one of the Eldest. If nothing else, that is worthy of a measure of respect."

The train continued, passing over the well-trodden ground of its own encampment. The vast city of tents had been struck and folded, but the ravages of their occupation remained. Trees had been clear-cut for siege-engines and battering rams, leaving raw stumps and scattered debris. Ashes and bones littered the sites of a hundred campfires. Gazing at it, Lilias shook her head. "He was only trying to protect his home," she said. "To protect *me*."

Blaise gave her a hard look. "Tell that to the mothers and widows of the men he roasted alive in their armor."

In the forefront of the vanguard, their column narrowed as Aracus Altorus entered the verge of the forest. The pine shadows muted his red-gold hair and gave a watery green tint to the silver armor of the Rivenlost who surrounded him.

"You could have withdrawn," Lilias said quietly. "It would have been enough."

"And you could have surrendered!" A muscle worked in Blaise's jaw. "What do you want from me, Sorceress? Pity? You chose to take part in the Sunderer's scheme. You could have surrendered when it failed, and pleaded for honest clemency."

She laughed mirthlessly. "Would my fate be different, Borderguardsman?"

"Yours?" He raised his brows. "No."

"So." She rubbed her cheeks, stiff with the salt of drying tears. "It doesn't matter, does it? Nothing matters, in the end. Let us leave it at that, Borderguardsman. If you would speak, speak of something else."

He shrugged as they entered the shadow of the pines. "Aracus entrusted me with the task of warding you. I have no need to speak."

The horses' hooves thudded softly on the broad, beaten path, gaining speed as Aracus Altorus stepped up the pace to a slow trot. Soon, the vanguard would pull ahead of the foot-soldiers, leaving them behind. An occupying force of Regent Martinek's men remained to oversee Beshtanag's affairs. The remaining Pelmarans would assemble a council of Regents to determine what aid they could send westward; in the south, the Vedasian knights would seek to rally their own overlords. Duke Bornin of Seahold would gather the forces of the Midlands. As for the rest of them, they were bound for the Rivenlost haven of Meronil and the counsel of Ingolin the Wise; to seek news of Malthus, to attempt to unlock the power of the Soumanië, to plan an assault upon Darkhaven.

And their prisoner, Lilias of Beshtanag, who held the answers to two of these matters, would be carried along with them like a twig in a flood.

Turning in the saddle, Lilias glanced behind her one last time. Already the fortress was invisible from this angle. She caught a glimpse of the dull grey hummock of Calandor's remains before low pine branches swept across her field of vision, closing like a curtain upon Beshtanag.

"Good-bye," she whispered. "Good-bye, my love."

In her quarters, Cerelinde balked.

"Thank you, Lord Vorax," she said stiffly. "I pray you tell his Lordship I decline his invitation."

The madling Meara hissed with alarm in the corner. Vorax the Glutton grimaced, planting his heavy hands on the gilded belt that encircled his girth; which had, in fairness, grown considerably less than it had been when he greeted her at the gates of Darkhaven. "Do you think I fancy being his errand-boy, Lady? I have more important duties. Nonetheless, his Lordship's invitations are not *optional.*"

"Very well." She laid aside the lace-work with which she had been occupying her hours. "As his Lordship *commands.*"

Vorax held open the door to her chambers with a sardonic bow, smiling in such a way as showed his sturdy teeth above his beard. Small scabs stippled his brow and cheeks. Cerelinde repressed a shudder at having to pass close enough to feel the heat of his body. "You are too kind, Lady."

"Not at all." She returned his false smile, watching the Staccian's eyes narrow. It was a relief, in some ways, to deal with him instead of Tanaros. Vorax the Glutton did not confuse her senses or her thoughts, and however he had spent the long years of his immortality, it had inured him to the allure of the Ellylon. He would as lief see her dead as alive, and made little effort to disguise the fact.

"To the garden, then." His thick fingers took impersonal possession of her arm, and he steered her down the halls. The pace he set was fast enough to make her stride hurried. Here and there, where tapestries hung, there was a scurrying sound in the walls, and Cerelinde had been in Darkhaven long enough to guess it was Meara, or the other madlings, at work. There seemed no end to their knowledge of the passages that riddled Darkhaven.

She noted, as they passed, that the Mørkhar Fjel of the Haven-guard saluted Vorax with less alacrity than they had Tanaros. It filled her with a sense of uneasy pride.

"Here." Vorax led her into the narrow corridor, with the door of polished wood and silver hinges at the end of it. Cerelinde shrank back against the wall as he fumbled at his belt for a ring of keys. He shot her a wry glance. "Don't worry, I'm only fulfilling his Lordship's wishes. I've no interest in aught else."

Cerelinde straightened. "I'm not afraid."

"Oh, aye." He smiled dourly, fitting a small key to the lock. "I can see that."

It stung her pride, enough to make her reach out and lay gentle fingers on the scabbed skin of his brow. If she had possessed the ancient magics Haomane's Children were said to have before the world was Sundered, she might have healed him. She watched his eyes widen at the delicate touch of Ellylon flesh against his rude skin. "Are you injured, Lord Vorax?"

"No," he said shortly, pulling away from her and opening the door. "Go on," he added, giving her an ignominious shove. "His Lordship is waiting."

Lifting her skirts, Cerelinde stepped across the threshold and raised her face to the night sky, breathing deep. Arahila's moon rode high overhead, a silvery half-orb; and yet, it was not the same garden she had visited with Tanaros. There was a sulfuric tang to the moist air that caressed her skin, with an underlying odor of rot. Dead patches pocked the grass, pallid by moonlight.

It hurt to see it, which surprised her.

"My Lord?" Cerelinde called.

"I am here," the deep voice answered. "Come."

There, where a dark form blotted out the stars. Stumbling over the dying grass, she made her way toward him. A faint sound shivered the night; bells, crying out. On slender stalks the bell-shaped blossoms shivered, heedless of the acid rain that had pierced their petals, leaving yellowish holes with seared edges. The sound they emitted was a plangent and sorrowful alarum, sounding without cease.

"Oh!" Cerelinde stooped, reaching for them. "Poor blossoms."

"Clamitus atroxis." Lord Satoris gazed at the stars revolving in their slow dance. "Sorrow-bells, sounding for every act of senseless cruelty in Urulat. Were they as loud, when you heard them before?"

"No." She bent her head over the flower bed.

"Nor I." The Shaper sighed. "Though I fear it is I who has set them ringing, I do not relish the sound, Cerelinde."

Cerelinde stroked the seared petals of the sorrow-bells, feeling them shudder under her fingertips. *Aracus.* "What have you done, my Lord?" she murmured, the blood running cold in her veins at the Shaper's words.

"There was time when I did," he mused. "It was sweet to my ears, a gratifying reminder that you Lesser Shapers are more than capable of wounding one another to the quick without my aid. And yet, I find it not so sweet when I am the cause. Vengeance sours quickly upon the palate when it fails to find its rightful target. It was never my wish to be what fate has made me, Lady."

Cerelinde straightened and took a step forward. *"What have you done?"*

"Have no fear." A hint of contempt edged his voice. "The Son of Altorus is safe enough. It was no one you knew, Lady. Victims of Haomane's Wrath, once. Now victims of mine. This time, they brought it upon themselves."

"The Charred Folk." The knowledge brought relief, and a different sorrow. "Ah, my Lord. Why?"

"Will you tell me you do not know?" the Shaper asked.

"My Lord." Cerelinde spread her hands. "I do not."

"Senseless." Reaching down, Lord Satoris wrenched a handful of sorrow-bells from the earth. Throttling them in his grip, he regarded the thin, trailing roots twitching below. The fragile petals drooped against his dark flesh, still emitting a faint peal. "How so?" he asked the shuddering blossoms. "I Shaped you and gave you existence. Why do you sound for *their* deaths? Senseless? How so, when they seek to use the Water of Life to extinguish the marrow-fire? How so, when they seek to destroy me?"

Hope leapt in Cerelinde's breast, warring with unease. "Haomane's Prophecy," she breathed.

"Haomane's Prophecy." He echoed the words with derision, tossing the wilting plants at her feet. "My Elder Brother's Prophecy is the framework of his will, nothing more, and you are the tools with which he builds it. Do not be so quick to hope, Lady. I have a will of my own, and tools at my disposal."

Root tendrils writhed over the toes of her slippers and the dying bells' ringing faded to a whimper, while those left in the bed keened anew in mourning. The Sunderer was in a strange mood, untrustworthy and fey. The copper-sweet tang of his blood mingled with the lingering odor of sulfur. If he were willing to turn upon Darkhaven itself, what hope was there for her? Cerelinde repressed a shudder, mortally tired of living on the knife-edge of fear.

"Why not end it?" she asked, feeling weary and defeated. "If it's the Prophecy you fear, why not simply take my life? Your Vorax would be glad enough to do it."

"No," he said simply. "I will not."

"*Why?* Is it because there is another?" Her pulse beat faster, remembering what he had told her before, the words she had been certain were lies. It would be easier to accept death if they were not. "Is it true? That Elterrion's line continues elsewhere?"

"No, Lady." The Shaper gave a bitter laugh. "Oh yes, that part was true. There are others. There will be others. Other heroes, other heroines. Other prophecies to fulfill, other adversaries to despise. There will be stories told and forgotten, and reinvented anew until one day, perhaps, the oldest are remembered, and the beginning may end, and the ending begin. Ah, Uru-Alat!" He sighed. "Until the sorrow-bells fall silent forever, there will be others."

"I do not understand," she said, confused.

"What if I asked you to stay?" His mood shifted, and the red light of malice glinted in his eyes. "You might temper this madness that comes too soon upon me, this anger. There would be no need for war were you to choose it willingly. You have seen, Daughter of Erilonde; there is beauty in this place. There would be more, did you choose to dwell here." He extended a hand to her. "What would you say if I asked it?"

What if they were not lies?

Moonlight cast the shadow of his mighty hand stark on the dead and dying grass. Cerelinde thought of the years of uneasy truce her acquiescence might bring, and measured it against the hope, the eternal hope, of the Rivenlost. Of Urulat, of all the world; but most of all, of her people. It was the ancient dream, the hope bred into their ageless flesh ever since the world was Sundered, of the Souma restored, the land made whole. It was nearer now than ever it had been, and she was willing to die to make it so. She could not allow herself to believe otherwise.

"I would say no," she said softly.

"So." He let his reaching hand fall back to his side. "It is no less than I expected, Lady. No less, and no more."

"Why did you refuse?" The words sprang impulsively from her lips, and Cerelinde wished them unsaid the moment she uttered them. But having been uttered, they could not be taken back. She forged onward. "This . . . rift, the Shapers' War. Haomane First-Born asked you three times to withdraw your Gift from Arahila's Children. Why did you refuse?"

"Why?" Thunder rumbled in the distance and clouds began to gather above the Vale of Gorgantum, obscuring the stars. Lifting his head, the Shaper watched as scudding wisps occluded the sundered disk of the silvery moon. In the dim light that remained his throat was an obsidian column, his breast a shield of night and the slow tide of seeping blood that glimmered on his thigh and trickled down one leg was oily and black. Something in his stance, in his *presence,* reminded her that he was one of the Seven Shapers; reminded her of the unbearable torment glimpsed when he had donned the Helm of Shadows. "Ask my Elder Brother, Lady. It is him you worship."

"He is not here to ask," Cerelinde said humbly, clasping her hands together.

"No." Slowly, Lord Satoris lowered his head to regard her, and his eyes glowed as red as blood, or dying embers. "He is not, is he?"

The clamitus atroxis shivered in resonant grief as the Shaper turned away, head held low, the dark bulwark of his shoulders rising like the swell of a wave. Cerelinde struggled against a sense of loss. A loss, but of what? Of a moment lost, an opportunity passing. Something slipped away, slipped between her slender fingers and through the gaps in her keen Ellylon mind as He who had Sundered the world trudged across the garden, leaving droplets of dark blood on the dying grass in his wake.

"My Lord!" she cried aloud in despair. "*Why?*"

A gentle rain began to fall as Satoris walked away from her, his words floating back to reach her. "Whatever stories they tell of me, Cerelinde, they will not say I slew you out of hand. That, at least, I may ensure."

Left standing alone in the garden, she flinched as the first drops struck her, but it was an ordinary rain. Water, no more and no less, leaving damp spots on her silk robes. It fell like a soft balm on the moon-garden, washing away the stench of sulfur, the dark traces of the Shaper's blood. In a nearby bed, pale flowers opened like eyes to welcome the clean rain, and the poignant odor of vulnus-blossom wafted in the air.

Their scent evokes memory. Painful memory.

Tanaros' words.

It was an aroma like nothing else, delicate and haunting. Cerelinde stumbled, backing away from the source, not wishing to see what it had evoked before: Lindanen Dale on her wedding day, Aracus struggling under the deadly onslaught of the Were, her kinsmen and his falling, slaughtered, and Tanaros looming before her on his black horse, reaching for her, blood staining the length of his black blade.

"No," she whispered.

It didn't come. Instead, she saw again the dark silhouette of the Shaper; Satoris Banewreaker, Satoris the Sunderer, with the shadow of his extended hand on the dying grass between them.

"I do not understand!" Turning her face to the night sky, Cerelinde let the rain wash away the gathering tears. "Lord-of-Thought," she pleaded, "I pray you lend me wisdom."

"Lady." A bulky figure trudged across the garden toward her, its path marked by the yellow glow of a bobbing lantern. "The Mørkhar said his Lordship had left you. Come on, I've not got all night." Holding the lantern aloft, Vorax sniffed. "Vulnus-blossom," he said in disgust. "You're better off avoiding the foul stuff. After a thousand years, I can tell you, some things are best forgotten."

"Lord Vorax." Cerelinde laid one hand on his arm. "What do you see?"

He turned his broad face toward her, illuminated by the lantern's glow. It was a Man's face, an ordinary Staccian face, plain and unhandsome. For all that, it was not a mortal face; the eyes that regarded her had watched a thousand years pass, and gazed without blinking at all the long anguish contained within the Helm of Shadows.

"You," he said bluntly. "I see you."

USHAHIN TURNED HIS FORKED STICK, rotating the slow-lizard's gutted carcass.

It was an unlikely breakfast, all the more so for being prepared by virtue of a dragon's courtesy. The lizard was roasting nicely in the outer verges of the searing flame she provided, held under careful control. Its charred hide was beginning to crackle and split, tasty white flesh bulging in the seams. Ushahin brought it in for inspection and scorched his fingers wedging loose a chunk of flaky meat. It had a sweet and mild flavor, with a smoky undertone. "Very pleasant," he said, extending the stick. "And done, I think. Will you not share it, Mother?"

The twin-sourced jet of flame winked into nonexistence as Calanthrag the Elder closed the iron-scaled valves of her nostrils, blinking with slow amusement. "My thanksss, little ssson. As I sssaid, I have eaten."

"Anyone I know?" He picked out another chunk of roasted lizard.

"Perhapssss." The dragon shifted one submerged claw.

Ushahin paused in the act of raising the piece to his mouth. "Vorax's Staccians."

"Perhapssss."

He chewed and swallowed the bite, conscious of the fact that he owed its delectation to her hospitality. "And yet you spared me."

"Are you sssorry?"

"No." He thought about it and shook his head. "Of a surety, I regret their deaths. Yet if you had not devoured them, I do not think I would be sitting here. And you would not have told me such mysteries as stagger the mind."

The nictitating lids blinked. "Even ssso."

The morning sun slanted through the mangrove and palodus trees, its warmth dispersing the vapors that rose from the swamp's waters in the cool hours of night. Insects chirred and whined. Overhead, birds flitted, dining on the prodigious swarms. Here and there the raucous *kaugh* of a raven punctuated their calls. Filled with a deep sense of contentment, Ushahin Dreamspinner sat in his skiff and ate roasted slow-lizard, until his belly was as full as his thoughts.

When he was finished, he laid his roasting stick carefully in the skiff beside his pole and the makeshift spear with which he had slain the lizard. The restless ravens settled in the trees, watching and waiting. The dragon was watching too, endless patience in her inhuman eyes. Ushahin touched his chest, feeling the scar's ridges through the fabric of his shirt, remembering the pain and the ecstasy of his branding. The scar throbbed beneath his touch, exerting a westward tug on his flesh. He thought of Lord Satoris, left with only one of his Three at his side, and the urge grew stronger.

Raising his head, he watched the ravens fluff and sidle, catching the tenor of their feathered thoughts. A winding wall encircling a vale, dark towers rearing under an overcast sky, yellow beech leaves and messy nests.

Home, home, home!

Calanthrag's voice hissed softly. "Do you ssstruggle againsst your dessstiny, Sson of No One?"

"No." He shook his head. "What you have told me, I will hold close to my heart, Mother, and ponder for many years. But it is Lord Satoris who gave meaning to my existence. I am his servant. I cannot be otherwise."

"He is the Sssower. Ssso it mussst be. Ssso it is."

There was a tinge of sulfur and sorrow in the dragon's exhalation. Turning away, Ushahin knelt in the skiff and worked at the knot in the rope he had tied around the palodus tree. His crooked fingers were unwontedly nimble. Oh, there was power in this place! It sang in his veins, heating his blood and rendering irrelevant the myriad aches that were his body's legacy. There was a part of him that was reluctant to leave. He sighed, bowing his head and winding the rope, laying it coiled in the prow. Straightening, he grasped the pole and stood, meeting the dragon's gaze. "Do you know how my story will end, Mother?"

"No." Calanthrag did not blink. "Only the Great Ssstory, little ssson."

Whether or not it was true, Ushahin could not say, for he had learned truth and lies were but two sides to the same fabric for dragonkind, inextricably interwoven. He thought of the things the dragon had shown him in the long night he had passed in the Delta; of the Chain of Being looped and looped and looped again, gathering him in its coils. A mighty consciousness, fragmenting, sighed and consigned itself to its fate. A world was born and died, and dying was born anew. Across the vastness of the stars, in the hidden bones of the earth. Nothing was born but that died; nothing died but was born. Fragmented. Striving, all in ignorance, at cross-purposes and folly. Waiting, all unknowing, for magic to pass from the world, for the deep fires to be extinguished, until there was only the hunger, the memory and *wanting*.

Such were the things the Eldest knew; the Eldest remembered.

Only then; only then would the cycle have come full circle, and true sentience reemerge, ready to be reborn.

Ushahin's hands tightened on the pole. "Will it truly come to pass, Mother?"

The dragon's jaws parted in a laugh, a true laugh, punctuated with jets of smoke. "Yesss," Calanthrag the Elder said. "Oh, yesss. Sssome day. Without usss, it shall not passs. Yet may it come later than sssooner for ssuch as I and you."

"So." Ushahin nodded. "I will play such a role as I may."

Plumes of smoke rolled and roiled, dark and oily, coiling around the branches of the palodus tree and obscuring its spatulate leaves. Ushahin coughed and the ravens of Darkhaven rose in a ruckus into the cleaner air above, chattering with annoyance.

When the smoke cleared, the dragon regarded him. "Go, little Ellyl-Man," she said. "It is time. Go, and remember." She moved one foreleg, then another; legs like columns, churning the mire.

The vast hummock shuddered, moving. Murky water surged as Calanthrag's plated breast emerged from the swamp, mossy and dripping. Along the dragon's sides, vaned pinions stirred, revealing their sharp angles, hinting at their folded spans. The thick, snaking column of her neck arched, spines jutting erect as her head reared into the sky to brush the uppermost branches of the tall palodus tree. Gilt-green eyes glowed from on high and the massive jaws parted, revealing rows of jagged teeth, darkened with the Delta's corrosion. A forked tongue, red as heart's blood, flickered between them. "Remember the plasse of the Sssower's birth," Calanthrag hissed. Behind those terrible jaws, the opening of the dragon's iron-grey gullet glowed like the glory-hole of a kiln. "Remember *I* am here!"

The skiff rocked under the dragon's shadow. Ushahin Dreamspinner rode it out, legs braced, holding tight to his pole and craning his neck, caught between awe and terror. "I will not forget, Mother!" he shouted. "I will not!"

"Go!" the Eldest roared in a gout of fire.

Ushahin crouched, jamming the pole into the submerged roots of the palodus and shoving hard, launching his skiff into the waterways. A blue-white ball of flame passed low over his head, singeing his pale hair. Above, the ravens gathered in a flock launched themselves like an arrow in a southern trajectory, heading for the outskirts of the Delta.

"GO!"

He went, hard and fast, arms a blur planting and moving the pole. Dip and push; dip and push. The pain that wracked his ill-set bones was never more forgotten. Dip and push; dip and push. The skiff hummed over the waters, Darkhaven's ravens fanned out before it in a flying wedge. They found a path; he followed. How far was far enough? Mangrove and palodus ignited in their wake, bursting into flame in this unlikely, water-sodden place. In moments they had left the heart of the Delta behind them. Ushahin poled the skiff without thinking, winding his way through the narrow waterways, his gaze fixed on the flying wedge before him; small figures, darkly iridescent in the sunlight, beating frantically, tilting the knife-edges of their wings to catch and ride the wind.

He followed.

Stand upon stand of mangrove passed uncounted, measuring the distance they traveled. Two, four, eight . . . how far was far enough? Whatever the distance, they traversed it. Gouts of fire gave way to tendrils of smoke, until its reaching fingers crumbled, fading into nothingness in the bright air.

The glade, with its tall palodus tree and its strange hummock, was behind them.

Stillness settled over the Delta.

Ushahin leaned upon his pole, panting. After a moment, he laughed softly.

Amid the quiet hum of insects, the ravens settled around him, closer than they had dared in the dragon's presence. One spread its wings and dropped, landing neatly on the top of his pole, fine talons clutching the raw wood. He cocked his head, eyeing the half-breed; an effect rendered comical by an irregular tuft of feathers.

"Greetings, Fetch." Ushahin smiled. "I thought it was you I saw among the flock. Have you learned something of the uncertain nature of dragons? So have I, little brother; so have I." He dragged his sleeve across his forehead, smearing the residue of unwonted sweat. "I thank you for guiding me to that place, and I thank you for guiding me out of it. I am glad to leave it alive."

The raven squawked and wiped its beak on the pole, quick and nervous.

"Tanaros?" Ushahin's brows rose. "He travels the Unknown Desert, or so his Lordship says. Would you seek him, Fetch? There is no water there."

The raven bobbed its head, sidling from foot to foot.

"Very well." He shrugged, too weary to argue the matter. "Go, if you will. I have companions enough to guide me home, and much to contemplate along the way."

Fetch squawked once more and launched himself in a flurry of feathers, dark wings beating. Ushahin Dreamspinner watched him go, bemused. "Why?" he asked aloud. "Is it *love?* What a strange conceit, little brother!" There was no answer, only the stares of the other ravens, hunched and waiting, the sheen of their feathers purple in the swamp-filtered sunlight. Ushahin sighed, planting his pole. "Home," he said to them, giving a strong shove. "Home, it is. Onward, brethren!"

The remaining ravens took wing, arrowing for the fringes of the Delta. Somewhere ahead, where the mangrove thinned and the swamp turned to marshy plains, there was a mount awaiting; a steed of Darkhaven, with arched neck and preternatural intelligence in its eyes. Ushahin poled his skiff and followed, navigating the waterways.

Only once did he pause and gaze behind him.

The Great Story that encompassed the world was vaster than he had reckoned; than any had reckoned. Even Lord Satoris, who had listened to the counsel of dragons, could not hold the whole of it in his sight, enwrapped as he was in his Elder Brother's enmity. It was older than time, and it would outlive the Shapers' War, and perhaps Ushahin's role in it had only begun.

"I will not forget, Mother," he whispered.

In the glade at the heart of the Delta, Calanthrag the Eldest chuckled, settling her bulk into the swamp. Twin plumes of smoke trailed above as her sinuous neck stretched, her head lowered. Sulfurous bubbles arose as her nostrils sank below the water's surface, breaking foamy and pungent. Nictitating lids closed, filmy and half-clear, showing the unearthly gleam of gilt-green orbs below until the outer lids shut like doors. The last ripple spent itself atop the waters.

Beneath the tall palodus tree, the hummock in the heart of the Delta grew still, and the bronzed waters reflected sunlight like a mirror.

Calanthrag the Eldest slept, and laughed in her dreams.

THIRTY

❖

FOR THE FIRST TIME, SKRAGDAL of the Tungskulder Fjel was ill at ease underground.

It was a short journey through the Vesdarlig Passage, one he had made before. All of them had. It was the oldest route through the tunnels to southwestern Staccia. It was a good tunnel, broad and straight. The walls were wide, the ceiling was high. The floor had been worn smooth by the passing tread of countless generations of Fjel. The Kaldjager patrolled it ruthlessly, ensuring that its egresses remained hidden, that its safety remained inviolate, that its ventilation shafts remained clear. It should have been a haven of comfort. It would have been, before.

It was Blågen, one of the Kaldjager who noticed it, loping back from a scouting excursion. His broad nostrils flared and his yellow eyes gave Skragdal an assessing glance. "You have the reek."

Skragdal grunted. "I was in the Marasoumië."

Blågen shrugged. "Ah."

The Men had it too, but Men often reeked of fear, except for General Tanaros. It didn't seem to bother the Nåltannen or the Gulnagel, and the Kaldjager hadn't been there for the terrible moment when the world had gone away in a rush of red light and stone had closed in upon them all. And now all that was gone, too, and the old wizard trapped inside it. The Men were talking about it, had been talking about it since they entered the tunnels, talking without cease, talking over one another, releasing nervous energy.

" . . . tell you, I'd rather be above ground, where you can see what's coming at you. Who knows what's down here *now?*"

"Yah! What, are you afraid the wizard's gonna get you?"

" . . . keep *telling* you, he's not dead, not with a Soumanië on him. He'll be back."

" . . . love of his Lordship's weeping wound, they're not even the same *tunnels,* the Ways aren't the same as our tunnels!"

"Sometimes they are, sometimes they aren't."

" . . . Kaldjager would catch him a mile away!"

" . . . even *hear* what happened? The old bugger's got a *Soumanië,* he can come out of nowhere and turn our arses to stone!"

" . . . Godslayer!"

" . . . back in the marrow-fire, where it belongs."

"And a right lot of good it'll do *us* there."

"Shut it, Einar." Osric, delivering an order. "That's treason you're talking."

"Lieutenant, I'm just *saying*—"

"Shut it!"

Skragdal wished Men wouldn't talk so much. Their restless minds grasped at thoughts like squirrels at nuts, gnawing and stuffing, dashing here and there, burying some and discarding others. And then words. Words! An endless stream, spewing from their lips, wasted with careless ease. It stemmed from Haomane's Gift, he supposed, and he ought to envy it. That's what Men and Ellylon said.

Only Lord Satoris had ever said otherwise.

They made camp in a vast cavern that night, a day's ride away from the Vesdarlig Door. Countless thousands had camped there before; Skragdal had done it himself, as an eager young pup on the way to honor the Fjel oath. The sleeping-places were worn smooth, broad grooves in the cavern floor, with suitable rough spots left untrammeled. He took comfort in seeing his fellows situated, freed from their cumbersome armor, rumbling and grumbling, working backs and shoulders against the stone. There was comfort in the evidence of countless members of the tribes who had done the same, leaving faint traces of their scent. It felt good to scratch itching hides against the rock.

Osric's Men took the southern quadrant, as was tradition.

They scratched the rock, too; only differently. Marks, etched with shards onto the cavern walls. Men lit fires, huddling under the ventilation shafts, sharing their fears and dreams, griping about the journey's hardship. Ruddy flames danced on the walls, showing the marks clearly. Scritching lines, narrow and perplexing. Sometimes they formed characters; sometimes, only shapes. Always, the lines shifted and changed, taunting him with elusive meaning.

Skragdal studied them, blinking.

"You can't read, can you?"

He glanced down at the Staccian commander. "I am Fjel," he said simply. "We do not share Haomane's Gift."

Osric's brow wrinkled. "You've tried, then?"

"No, lieutenant." He did not tell the story. None of the Fjel did; not to Men, not to anyone. Only to their pups. A long time ago they had wanted to learn. Neheris' Children had wanted it badly enough to plead with the wounded Shaper who had fled to their lands. And during the long years of his recuperation from Haomane's Wrath, Lord Satoris had tried to teach his people. In the end, it came to naught. The meaning of scratched lines—on stone, on parchment—was too evasive. How could a handful of symbols, which bore no intrinsic meaning, represent all the myriad things in the world? What relationship did they bear to the thing itself? It was a pointless endeavor.

Osric glanced at the scratchings. "Well, you're not missing much. Lads' folly for the most part, writing their names to let the ones who come after know they were here. That, and empty boasts. You'll have the Kaldjager stand watch again tonight?"

"Aye, lieutenant."

"Good man. Get some sleep."

He tried. Others slept, rumbling and snoring, comforted by stone's solid presence. It did not bother them that they had seen stone turn to an engulfing enemy in the red flash of a Soumanië's power. It should not bother him. Fjel had the gift of living in the present. Only important things were carried in the heart; only sacred memories, passed from generation to generation. All that was not worth carrying—fear, envy, hatred—was left to be washed away and forgotten in the flowing rivers of time.

Do not mourn for the Gift Haomane withheld from you. Did Neheris-of-the-Leaping-Waters not Shape her Children well? This I tell you, for I know: One day Men will covet your gifts. Treasure them, and rejoice.

Lord Satoris' words.

Those were the words that had restored Fjel pride and faith, the ones they passed on to their offspring. Those were the words that had inspired their ancient oath. Skragdal had heard them as a pup. He had carried them in his heart with pride, but he had never understood them as he did now, lying sleepless beneath the earth. Could such gifts be lost? Could the nature of the Fjel change, tainted by long exposure to the ways of Men? Was it the burden of command that weighed upon him, shaping his thoughts into fearful forms? Would he, if he could, scratch his name upon the wall?

No, he thought. No.

Reaching into a pouch that hung from his belt, Skragdal withdrew a half-carved lump of green chalcedony and examined it in the dim light of the cavern. There were flaws in the stone, but the fluid form of the *rhios* was beginning to emerge, a sprite as blithe as water flowing through a river bend. This is a thing that is not the thing itself, he thought. Yet it has a shape. I can hold it in my hands, and I can coax a truer shape from it. It is a stone, a real thing. It is a green stone that looks like water. These things I understand. He cupped the *rhios* in his hands and whispered a prayer to Neheris-of-the-Leaping-Waters. "Mother of us all, wash away my fear!"

There was an ease in saying the words. Words held power when they were spent with care. He felt a measure of fear ebb. The surrounding stone became a kinder companion. The memory of the Marasoumië faded, taking with it the image of the wizard with his terrible, glaring eyes, his lips working in the thicket of his white beard as he spoke the words to command the Ways, the red gem of the Soumanië ablaze on his chest. He would not forget, but neither would he carry it with him.

Skragdal sighed.

It was a gift.

Lord Satoris was right, had always been right. How wise were the Elders who had seen it! Did the Fjel not slumber in peace while Men whimpered in their dreams?

It was so, it had always been so.

"ARE WE GOING TO DIE here, Lord General?" Speros' voice cracked on the question, and his eyes rolled in his head, showing dry white crescents below the brown iris. The noonday sun stood motionless overhead. His footsteps had begun to stagger, leaving a meandering trail in the sand. Their water supply had been gone since last night, and hours of trekking had taken their toll.

"No." Tanaros gritted his teeth, grabbing the Midlander's arm and hauling it across his shoulders. Lowering his head, he trudged onward, taking up the weight that sagged against him. "Come on, lad. Just a little way further."

Speros' breath was hot and ragged against his ear. "You said that before."

"And I will again," he retorted, still trudging.

"General!" one of the Gulnagel shouted. "Water-hole!"

The staggering cavalcade made its way across the wasteland of the Unknown Desert. They fell to their knees and dug by hand in the scrubby underbrush, marking the signs the Yarru had taught them. There, where thorn-brush grew and the termites built their mounds. There was life, ounce by precious ounce. Moisture darkened the sand and collected, gleaming, where they dug. An inch of water, perhaps more. Sand flew as the Fjel widened the hole, then scooped assiduously at the gathering moisture with Tanaros' helmet, husbanding every drop. They had carried the general's armor on their backs, reckoning it too precious to leave.

A lucky thing, since it made a good bucket.

"Sir?" A Gulnagel held out his helmet. It looked small in his massive hands. An inch of water shone at the bottom. "Drink."

Tanaros licked his dry lips, squinting at the sky. It was blue and unforgiving, the white sun blazing in it like Haomane's Wrath. "Let him have it," he said, nodding at Speros, whom he had laid gently in what scant shade the thorn-brush afforded. "What is left, take for yourselves."

"All right, boss." The Fjel squatted on the parched earth, cradling Speros' head in his lap and tilting the helmet. "Drink," he said, coaxing.

The Midlander drank, his throat working, then sighed.

What was left, the Gulnagel shared. It amounted to no more than a sip apiece. One of them approached the largest termite mound and thrust a thorny branch into the opening at the top, stirring and teasing. The others gathered around the dry tower as indignant insects emerged in a marching line, pinching with deft talons and popping them into their mouths, crunching antennae and legs and swollen thoraxes with relish.

"Eat, General." Freg, grinning through his chipped eyetusks, approached him. His horny hands were cupped and filled with squirming bounty. "They're *good*."

Tanaros shook his head. "You have them, Freg. You've earned them."

"You're sure?" The Gulnagel seemed anxious.

"Aye." He nodded.

Better that the Fjel should eat, and imbibe whatever moisture the termites held. It was not that Tanaros disdained the meal. They needed it; as much as Speros, though they reckoned it less. He knew. He knew Fjel. They were Neheris' Children, born to a land of mountains and leaping rivers, not made for desert travel. The hides of the Gulnagel had grown desiccated and stark on this journey; leeched of color, dry and cracking.

Still, they would go and go and go, obedient to his orders, legs churning, never a complaint among them.

They ate until there were no more termites.

"We're ready, General." Freg stooped over the Midlander's supine form. "You want I should carry him? I've strength enough for it."

"Aye." Tanaros drew a deep breath, feeling the arid air burn in his lungs. If his eyes had not been so dry, he might have wept. The lad had followed him out of a sense of belonging. He should never have been allowed to pledge his loyalty; he did not deserve to be left. "Aye, Freg. Carry him while you can."

The Gulnagel did, hoisting Speros onto his own back. The Midlander's limbs dangled, jostled by each wayward step. Onward they staggered, over the parched earth. Tanaros led the way. He knew it; knew it as the migrating swallow knows its way. His branded heart served as compass. *There.* There it was before him. Darkhaven. Home, where Lord Satoris sat on his Throne and Godslayer hung blazing in the marrow-fire. It exerted its own pull, guiding his faltering steps across the shortest route possible, no matter how inhospitable the land.

Alas, in the Unknown Desert, the shortest route was not always the best. The Yarru had known as much. The Unknown was crossed one water-hole at a time, one place of sustenance after another. They knew the way of it. If he had let them live, they might have guided him.

Better not to think about it.

Thus did they sojourn, onward and onward. The sun moved in immeasurably small increments across the sky. If there were shade, they would have traveled by night; but they had found no shade, not enough to shelter them. The Gulnagel panted like dogs, with open mouths and labored breathing. Even so, none would lay down his burden.

Tanaros forced his legs to move. One step, then another and another. After all, what did it cost him? He would not die in this place. It was like the Marasoumië. It might kill him, in time; it would take a long time. He could lie on the desert floor, dying of thirst, for ages. He had time. Let him set an example, instead. The black blade of his sword banged against his hip as he trudged onward through the empty desert, leading his staggering band.

The burning sun sank its leading edge below the horizon. Night would follow, with no water in sight. No chance of finding it by starlight; the signs were too subtle. He wondered, grimly, how many would live to see the dawn.

"Lord General!" One of the Gulnagel flung out a rough-hewn hand, pointing.

Wings, the shadow of wings, beating. They were cast large upon the parched earth and there was something familiar in the sound. Tanaros lifted a head grown heavy with exhaustion, raising an arm.

"Fetch!" he cried.

A familiar weight, settling. Talons pricked his arm, and a tufted head bobbed, cocking a beady eye at him. *"Kaugh!"*

"Fetch," Tanaros murmured. A feeling in his heart swelled, painful and overlarge. It was foolish. It didn't matter. He stroked the raven's feathers with one forefinger, overwhelmed with gratitude. "How did you find me?"

Something nudged at his thoughts, a scrabbling sensation.

Surprised, he opened his mind.

A patchwork of images flooded his vision; sky, more sky, other ravens. A fecund swamp, leaves and bark and beetles. Ushahin Dreamspinner standing in the prow of a small boat, squinting through mismatched eyes. A dragon's head reared against the sky, ancient and dripping. Darkness; darkness and light. The world seen from on high in all its vastness. Laughter. A dragon's jaws, parting to breathe living fire.

"You saw this?" Tanaros asked.

"Kaugh!"

A green blur of passing swamp, bronze waters gleaming. Wings beating in a flying wedge; a pause, a caesura. Ushahin wiping sweat from his brow. A lofting, the downbeat of wings. Aloneness. Tilting earth, marsh and fertile plains, a shadow cast small below. It wavered, growing larger, then smaller. A blur of night and stars, pauses and launches. Blue, blue sky, and the desert floor.

The shadow held its size, held and held and held.

Greenness.

A drought-eater; no, three! Thick stalks, succulent leaves. Green-rinded fruits hung low, ripe with water. The shadow veered, growing large, then veered away again.

Desert, parched desert, beneath the lowering sun.

Tanaros and his company seen from above.

"Oh, Fetch!" His dry eyes stung. "Have you seen this? Can you show me?"

"Kaugh!" Bobbing and chuckling, the raven launched itself from Tanaros' arm, setting a northward trajectory.

"Follow him!" Marshaling his strength, Tanaros forced himself in the direction of the raven's flight, departing from his heart's compass. With mighty groans and dragging steps, the Gulnagel followed. Speros, unconscious, jounced on Freg's back, ungainly as a sack of millet and thrice as heavy.

It was not a long journey, as Men reckon such things. How long does it take for the sun to set once the outermost rim of its disk has touched the horizon? A thousand beats of a straining heart; three thousand, perhaps, here where the desert lay flat and measureless. With the distance half-closed, Tanaros saw the silhouettes of the drought-eaters, stark and black against the burning sky. Hope surged in his heart. He set a steady pace, exhorting the Gulnagel with praise and curses. If they had stuck to their course, they would have passed them by to the south, unseen.

But there was water ahead, *water!* The plants held it in abundance.

For a hundred steps, two hundred, the drought-eaters appeared to recede, taunting, ever out of reach. And then they were there, and Fetch settled atop a thick trunk, making a contented sound. The raven ruffled his feathers. A dwindling sliver of flame lit the western horizon and the scent of moisture seeped into the arid air. With rekindled strength, Tanaros strode ahead, drawing his sword to sever a green-ripe fruit from its fibrous mooring and holding it aloft.

"Here!" he cried in triumph. "Water!"

One by one the Gulnagel staggered into his presence, each burdened with a piece of his armor. Each laid his burden on the sand with reverence; all save the last.

With heavy steps, Freg of the Gulnagel Fjel entered the stand of drought-eaters, a loose-limbed Speros draped over his back like a pelt. Freg's taloned hands held the Midlander's arms in place where they were clasped about his neck. His dragging tread gouged crumbling furrows in the dry earth. One step, then another and another, following Tanaros' example. The drought-eaters cast long shadows across his path. Freg's face split in a proud, weary smile.

"General," he croaked, pitching forward.

"Freg!"

In the dying wash of light, Tanaros crouched beside the Gulnagel and rolled him onto his back. He spread his hands on the broad expanse of the Fjel's torso, feeling for the beat of his sturdy heart. There was nothing. Only dry hide, harsh and rough to the touch. The heart that beat beneath it had failed. Freg's chipped grin and empty eyes stared at the desert sky. Tanaros bowed his head. The other Gulnagel murmured in tones of quiet respect, and Fetch ducked his head to preen, picking at his breast-feathers.

Thrown free by Freg's fall, Speros stirred his limbs and made a faint noise.

"Water," Tanaros murmured, extending one hand without looking. A severed drought-fruit was placed in it. He tipped it and drank; one swallow, two, three. Enough. He placed it to the Midlander's parched lips. "Drink." Water spilled into Speros' mouth, dribbled out of the corners to puddle on the dry earth. Tanaros lifted his head and gazed at the watching Gulnagel. "What are you waiting for?" he asked them, blinking against the inexplicable burn of tears. "It's water. Drink! As you love his Lordship, drink."

Stripping the plants, they hoisted drought-fruit and drank.

It was a mighty stand, and an old one. The plants seldom grew in pairs, let alone three at once. The Yarru must have told stories about such a thing. There was enough water here to quench their thirst, enough water here to carry. Tanaros fed it in slow sips to Speros until the Midlander's eyes opened and consciousness returned, and he shivered and winced at the cramps that gripped his gut. Under starlight he scanned the remaining Fjel with a fevered gaze, and asked about Freg. His voice sounded like something brought up from the bottom of a well.

Tanaros told him.

The Midlander bent over with a dry, retching sob.

Tanaros left him alone, then, and walked under the stars. This time he did not brood on the red one that rose in the west, but on the thousands upon thousands that outnumbered it. There were so many visible, here in the Unknown Desert! Arahila's Gift against the darkness, flung like diamonds across the black canopy of night. Nowhere else was it so evident. There was a terrible beauty in it.

It made him think of Ngurra's calm voice.

It made him think of Cerelinde, and her terrible, luminous beauty.

It made him think of his wife.

Alone, he pressed the heels of his hands against his closed lids. Her eyes had shone like that at the babe's birth. Like stars; like diamonds. Her eyes had shone like that when he killed her, too, glistening with terror as his hands closed about her throat. And yet . . . and yet. When he sought her face in his memory, it was that of the Lady of the Ellylon he saw instead. And there was no terror in her eyes, only a bright and deadly compassion.

"My Lord!" he cried aloud. "Guide me!"

Something rustled, and a familiar weight settled on his shoulder, talons pricking through his undertunic. A horny beak swiped at his cheek; once, twice. *"Kaugh?"*

"Fetch." It was not the answer he sought, but it was an answer. Tanaros' thoughts calmed as he stroked the raven's feathers; calmed, and spiraled outward. "How did you know to find me, my friend? How did you penetrate the barrier of my thoughts? Was it the Dreamspinner who taught you thusly?"

"Kaugh," the raven said apologetically, shuffling from foot to foot.

An image seeped into Tanaros' mind; a grey, shadowy figure, lunging, jaws open, to avenge an ancient debt. Always, there were her slain cubs, weltering in their blood. A sword upraised between them, and Aracus Altorus' face, weeping with futile rage as her weight bore him down, half-glimpsed as Tanaros wheeled his mount to flee and the Lady Cerelinde's hair spilled like cornsilk over his thighs. The Grey Dam of the Were had died that day, spending her life for a greater gain.

"Ah."

Ushahin's words rang in his memory. *Do you know, cousin, my dam afforded you a gift? You will know it, one day.*

"Yes, cousin," Tanaros whispered. "I know it." And he stroked the raven's feathers until Fetch sidled alongside his neck, sheltering beneath his dark hair, and remembered the broken-winged fledgling he had raised; the mess in his quarters, all the small, bright objects gone missing. And yet, never had he known the raven's thoughts. A small gift, but it had saved lives. On his shoulder, Fetch gave a sleepy chortle. Tanaros clenched his fist and pressed it to his heart in the old manner, saluting the Grey Dam Sorash. "Thank you," he said aloud. "Thank you, old mother."

Vengeance. Loyalty. Sacrifice.

Such were the lodestones by which his existence was charted, and if it was not the answer he sought, it was answer enough. Thrusting away the thoughts that plagued him, Tanaros turned back toward the drought-eaters, walking slowly, the raven huddled on his shoulder.

There were not enough stones to build a cairn, so the Fjel were digging. Shadows gathered in the mouth of the grave. Dim figures looming in the starlight, the Gulnagel glanced up as he entered the encampment, continuing without cease to shift mounds of dry sand and pebbles. Tanaros nodded acknowledgment. No need for speech; he knew their ways.

The unsteady figure of Speros of Haimhault labored alongside them. "Lord General," he rasped, straightening at Tanaros' approach.

"Speros." He looked at the fever-bright eyes in the gaunt face, the trembling hands with dirt caked under broken nails. "Enough. You need to rest."

The Midlander wavered stubbornly on his feet. "So do they. And he died carrying *me*."

"Aye." Tanaros sighed. The raven roused and shook its feathers, launching itself from its perch to land on the nearest drought-eater. "Aye, he did." Casting about, he spotted his helmet amid the rest of his armor. It would hold sand as well as water, and serve death as well as life. One of the Gulnagel grunted, moving to make room for him. "Come on, then, lads," Tanaros said, scooping at the grave, filling his helmet and tossing a load of sand over his shoulder. "Let's lay poor Freg to rest."

Side by side, Man and Fjeltroll, they labored beneath Arahila's stars.

IT WAS ON THE VERGES of Pelmar, a half day's ride outside Kranac, that the Were was sighted. Until then, the journey had been uneventful.

The forest was scarce less dense near one of the capital cities, but the mounted vanguard had been moving with speed since leaving Martinek's foot-soldiers behind, weaving in single-file columns among the trees. If she had not despised them, Lilias would have been impressed at the woodcraft of the Borderguardsmen. Plains-bred they might be, but they were at ease in the forest. The Ellylon, of course, were at home anywhere; Haomane's Children, Shaped to rule over all Lesser Shapers. Although they acknowledged him as kin-in-waiting and King of the West, even Aracus Altorus treated them with a certain respect. Always, there was an *otherness* to their presence. Grime that worked its way into the clothing and skin of Men seemed not to touch them. The shine on their armor never dimmed and an ever-willing breeze kept their pennants aloft, revealing the delicate devices wrought thereon. Under the command of Lorenlasse of Valmaré, the company of Rivenlost rode without tiring, sat light in the saddle, clad in shining armor, guiding their mounts with gentle touches and gazing about them with fiercely luminous eyes, as if assessing the world of Urulat and finding it lacking.

In some ways, she despised them most of all.

And it was an Ellyl, of course, who spotted the scout.

"*Anlaith cysgoddyn!*" It was like an Ellylon curse, only sung, in his musical voice. He stood in the stirrups, one finely shaped hand outflung, pointing. "*Were!*"

She saw; they all did. A grey, slinking figure, ears flattened to its head, ducking behind a thick pine trunk. Once sighted, it moved in a blur, dropping low to the earth, fleeing in swift, leaping bounds. Patches of sunlight dappled the fur on its gaunt flanks as it lunged for deeper shadow.

Aracus Altorus gave a single, terse order. "Shoot it!"

"Wait!" Lilias cried out in instinctive protest, too late.

A half dozen bowstrings twanged in chorus. Most were Ellylon; one was not. Oronin's Bow sounded a deep, anguished note, belling like a beast at bay. This time, it shot true against its maker's Children. The same fierce light that suffused the eyes of the Rivenlost lit the Archer's face as she turned sideways in the saddle, following her arrow's flight with her gaze. Its path ended in a howl of pain, cut short in a whimper. The underbrush rustled where its victim writhed.

"Blaise," Aracus said implacably. "See what we have caught."

"Stay here," Blaise muttered to Lilias, relinquishing the reins of her mount and dismounting in haste.

Since there was nowhere to go, she did. With a sick feeling in the pit of her stomach, she watched as he beckoned to other Borderguardsmen, as their dun cloaks faded into the underbrush. And, sitting in the saddle, she watched as they tracked down their prey and brought him back.

He was slung between them like a hunter's quarry, a Borderguardsman attached to each outspread limb. It was a pathetic sight, a Were stripped of all his shifting glamour. The haft of a yellow-fletched arrow protruded from the right side of his narrow, hairy breast. His chest heaved with each shallow breath, the wound burbling. Where they passed, crimson droplets of blood clung to the pine-needles.

"*Phraotes!*" Lilias whispered.

The one-time Were ambassador was panting. He hung in his captors' grip, jaws agape. His amber eyes, meeting hers, rolled.

There were foam and blood on his muzzle. "Sorceress," he gasped. "It seems, perhaps, I should not have fled."

Aracus Altorus raised his eyebrows. "You know this creature?"

"Yes." A tide of anger rose in her. "*Yes!*" she spat. "I know him, and I know he has done you no harm! He is the Grey Dam's ambassador to Beshtanag, O King of the West, and he brought to me the news that his folk would do nothing to oppose your passage. *Nothing.*" Lilias drew a breath. "What harm has he done you now, that you would slay him out of hand? Nothing!"

"Lilias," Blaise said. One of four, he maintained a cruel grip on Phraotes' right foreleg, keeping the Were's hairy limbs stretched taut. "Enough."

"What?" she asked sharply. "No, I will speak! For a thousand years the Were dwelled in Beshtanag in peace. What do I care for your old quarrels?" She stared at the faces of her captors, one by one. "What did he care? Is there to be no end to it?" Against her will, her voice broke. "Will Haomane order you to slay everything that lives and does not obey his command?"

For a moment, they stared back at her. The Ellylon were expressionless. Blaise's face was grim. Fianna, the Archer of Arduan, turned away with a choked sound. Aracus Altorus sighed, rumpling his red-gold hair. "Sorceress—" he began.

"We were attacked," a soft voice interjected; an Ellyl voice. It was Peldras, of Malthus' Company, who alone among his kind traveled in worn attire. He gazed at her with deep sorrow. "I am sorry, Lady of Beshtanag, but it is so. Blaise and Fianna will attest to it. On the outskirts of Pelmar, in deepest night, the Were fell upon us. Thus was Malthus lost, and the Bearer, fleeing into the Ways of the Marasoumië. Thus did one of our number fall, giving his life so that we might flee."

"Hobard of Malumdoorn," Blaise murmured. "Let his name not be forgotten."

"Even so." Peldras bowed his head.

"Phraotes?" Lilias asked in a small voice. "Is it true?"

"What is truth?" The Were bared his bloodstained teeth. "A long time ago, we made a choice. Perhaps it was a bad one. This time, we were forced into a bad bargain. Yet, what else was offered us? Perhaps *you* made a bad bargain. I am only an ambassador. I would be one to this Son of Altorus did he will it."

Aracus frowned. "Do you gainsay the testimony of my comrades? Your people attacked Malthus' Company under cover of night, unprovoked. A valiant companion was slain, the wisest of our counselors was lost, the greatest of our hopes has vanished. You have shown no honor here, no remorse. Why should I hear your suit?"

"Why not?" The Were's head lolled, eyes rolling to fix his gaze on him. "It was a favor extracted by threat, nothing more. We failed; it is finished. We did not make war upon you in Beshtanag, Arahila's Child. The Grey Dam fears the wrath of Satoris Third-Born, but Haomane's is more dire. We seek only to be exempted from the Shapers' War. Yea, I feared to approach in good faith, and I have paid a price for it. Will you not listen before it is paid in full?"

Angry voices rose in reply; in the saddle, Aracus Altorus held up one hand. "Set him down." He waited while Blaise and the others obeyed. Phraotes curled into a tight ball and lay panting on the pine mast. His ears were flat against his skull and the shaft of the arrow jerked with each breath, slow blood trickling down his grey fur, but his visible eye was watchful. The Were did not die easily. Aracus gazed down at him, his expression somber. "There remain many scores between us, not the least of which is Lindanen Dale. And yet you say you are an ambassador. What terms do you offer, Oronin's Child?"

With a sound that was half laugh, Phraotes coughed blood. His muzzle scraped the loam. "The Grey Dam is dead; the Grey Dam lives. Though she carries her memories, the Grey Dam Vashuka is not the Grey Dam Sorash." One amber eye squinted through his pain. "What terms would you accept, King of the West?"

"Son of Altorus!" There was a stir in the ranks, and the gilded bee of Valmaré fluttered on its pennant as Lorenlasse rode forward, glittering in his armor, to place a peremptory hand on Aracus' arm. "Dergail the Wise Counselor *died* through the treachery of Oronin's Children," he hissed, "and Cerion the Navigator was lost! The Lady Cerelinde would be your bride if they were not faithless. You may forget, but *we* remember. Will you treat with them and be a fool?"

Plain steel sang as Blaise Caveros unsheathed his sword. "Unhand him."

Finely chiseled Ellyl nostrils flared. "What manner of villain do you take me for, traitor-kin?" Lorenlasse asked in contempt. "Our way is not *yours*. We do not slay out of misguided *passion*."

"Enough!" Aracus raised his voice. "Blaise, put up your sword. My lord Lorenlasse, abide." He sighed again and rubbed his temples, aching beneath the Soumanië's weight. "Would that Malthus was here," he muttered. "Sorceress!"

Lilias glanced up, startled. "My lord Altorus?"

"Advise me." He brought his mount alongside hers and looked hard at her. "You know them; you have made pacts with them, and lived. I do not forget anything, but I have erred once in mistaking my true enemy, and innocent folk have died. I do not wish to err twice. Are the Were my enemy?"

"No." She shook her head. "They wish only to be let alone."

"Whence Lindanen Dale?"

He was close, too close. Their horses' flanks were brushing. His presence crowded her, yet there was no room to shrink away on the narrow path. Lilias swallowed. "It was your kinsmen slew her cubs. Do you not remember?"

"I was not born." His face was implacable.

"Faranol," Phraotes rasped. "Prince Faranol."

"Yes." Lilias drew a shallow breath, wishing Aracus would give her space to draw a deeper one. He was close enough that she could smell him, the tang of metal and the sharp odor of human sweat. This urgency, the exigencies of mortal flesh, pressed too close, reminded her too keenly of the limits that circumscribed her own existence, of her own aching, aging body. "Faranol of Altoria slew the offspring of the Grey Dam Sorash. A hunting party in Pelmar. Surely you must know."

"Yes." Because he did not need to, he did not say that Faranol was a hero to the House of Altorus. "I know the story."

"Hence, Lindanen Dale," she said simply.

"So." Aracus' fingertips pressed his temples. "It is a cycle of vengeance, and I am caught up in it by accident of birth." With a final sigh he dropped his hands and cast his gaze upon the Were. "You are dying, Oronin's Child. What power have you to make treaties? Why should I believe you?"

Lying curled upon the ground, Phraotes bared his bloody teeth. "We have walked between life and death since the Glad Hunter Shaped us, blowing his horn all the while. Death walked in his train as it does in yours. We are a pack, son of Altorus, and our Shaper's Gift lies in those dark corridors. Though Oronin's Horn now blows for me, the Grey Dam hears me; I speak with her voice. Ushahin-who-walks-between-dusk-and-dawn is banned from our company. The fetters of old oaths are broken, we are despised in Urulat, and Oronin has raised his hand against us this day. New oaths may be made and honored. What will you, King of the West?"

"Sorceress?"

His eyes were wide, demanding. Demanding, and trusting. For

the first time, Lilias understood why they had followed him; Man and Ellyl alike. The knowledge made her inexplicably weary. "For so long as the Grey Dam Vashuka endures," she said, speaking true words to him, "the Were will abide by what bargain you strike. I have no other counsel."

"It is enough." He nodded. "Thank you."

Something in her heart stirred at his thanks. The mere fact of it made bile rise in her throat. Lilias looked away, not watching as Aracus left her side. He dismounted, walking away a small distance. Others followed, raising voices in argument: gilded Ellylon voices, the deeper tones of the Borderguard, the pleading voice of the woman Archer. Lilias glanced across the backs of milling, riderless horses. Aracus listened to the arguments without speaking, his broad shoulders set, his head bowed under the useless weight of the Soumanië. She wondered if they would regret having sworn their fealty to him this day. There was a twisted satisfaction in the thought.

"He'll do it, you know."

Glancing down, she saw Blaise standing beside her mount, gathering its reins in his capable hands. "Do what?"

"Forge a truce." He handed the reins up to her, his fingers brushing hers. Blaise's eyes were dark and intent. Her chestnut mare snuffled his hair, and he stroked its neck absently, still watching her. "He's big enough for it, Lilias, despite their fears. I ought to know."

Lilias shook her head, unsettled in the pit of her stomach. What did it matter that Aracus Altorus had forgiven Blaise Caveros his immortal ancestor's betrayal? Calandor, her beloved Calandor, was no less dead for it. On the ground, Phraotes coiled tight around a knot of pain and waited. Only the wrinkled, foam-flecked lips of his muzzle gave evidence to his slow death throes. He met her gaze with a glint of irony in his amber eye. He was the only creature here she understood. "It's easy to be magnanimous in victory, Borderguardsman," she said.

"No." Sighing, Blaise straightened. "No, it's not. That's the thing."

In time, the arguments fell silent and Aracus returned, retracing his path with heavy steps. The Rivenlost were amassed behind him, a quiet, glittering threat. A concord had been reached. Aracus Altorus stood above the dying Were, gazing downward, his face in shadow. His voice, when he spoke, sounded weary. "Will you hear my terms, Oronin's Child? They are twofold."

Phraotes' sharp muzzle dipped and lifted. "Speak."

"One." Aracus raised a finger. "You will foreswear violence against all the Shapers' Children, in thought and deed, in property and in person. Only such simple prey as you find in the forest shall be yours. You shall not conspire upon the soil of Urulat in any manner. You will disdain Satoris the Sunderer and all his workings."

The Were ambassador exhaled, crimson blood bubbling through his nostrils. It might have been a bitter laugh; the arrow in his breast jerked at the movement. "The Grey Dam Vashuka accedes. So it shall be. Do you swear us peace, we will retreat unto the deepest forests to trouble the Lesser Shapers no more, and be forgotten."

"Two." Aracus raised a second finger. "You will abjure the Sunderer's Gift."

Behind him, Lorenlasse of the Valmaré smiled.

So, Lilias thought; it comes to this. That offering, which Haomane disdained for his Children, he cannot bear another's to possess. The Shapers' War continues unending, and we are but pawns within it. Silent atop her mount, she thought of the things Calandor had shown her in his cavern atop Beshtanag Mountain, the things that filled her heart with fear. *One day,* he had said, *when his own are gone, Haomane will adopt Arahila's Children as his own. Until then, he will eliminate all others.*

She wondered if Oronin Last-Born would protest, or if he were willing to sacrifice his Children on the altar of Haomane's pride for the sin of having aided Satoris Banewreaker. In the silence that followed Aracus' pronouncement, it seemed that it must be so. Like Neheris-of-the-Leaping-Waters, the Glad Hunter would abide.

"No cubs?" Phraotes rasped. "No offspring?"

Aracus Altorus shook his head. "None."

It took longer to obtain an answer. The Were's eyes rolled back into his head, his body writhing upon the loam. Whatever path his thoughts traveled, it was a difficult one. Phraotes gnashed his teeth, blood and foam sputtering. His body went rigid, then thrashed, the protruding arrow jerking this way and that, his clawed hands digging hard and scoring deep gouges in the pine mast.

"Lord Aracus," Peldras the Ellyl whispered. "Such a request, whether you will it or no, embroils the Were in the Shapers' War . . ."

Aracus raised one hand, intent. "Such are my terms."

Say no, Lilias thought, concentrating her fierce will. *Say no, say no, say NO!*

"Yea!" Phraotes, panting, opened slitted eyes. "The Grey Dam Vashuka accedes. Do you leave us in peace, Oronin's Children will abjure the Gift of Satoris Third-Born, and procreate no more in her lifetime. Like Yrinna's Children, we shall not increase; nor shall we remain. We shall dwindle, and pass into legend. Like—" his amber gaze fell upon Lorenlasse, "—like Haomane's Children, in all their pride." Head lolling, he gave his bloody grin. "Is it a bargain, King of the West? Will you swear to leave us in peace, and guarantee the word of all who are sworn to your allegiance?"

"I will," Aracus said simply. "I do."

There was a moment of silence, broken only by the sound of horses shifting, stamping restless hooves, cropping at foliage. It didn't seem right, Lilias thought. There should have been a vast noise; a shuddering crash such as there had been when Calandor fell, an endless keening wail of Oronin's Horn. Not this simple quietude. She wanted to weep, but there were no tears left in her, only a dry wasteland of grief.

"So be it." Phraotes closed his eyes. "Oronin has wrought this and the Were consent. With my death, it is sealed. Draw out the arrow, King of the West."

Aracus knelt on one knee beside the crumpled figure, placing his left hand on the Were's narrow chest. With his right, he grasped the arrow's shaft. Murmuring a prayer to Haomane, he pulled, tearing out the arrow in one hard yank. Blood flowed, dark and red, from the hole left by the sharp barbs. Phraotes hissed, tried to cough, and failed. His lids flickered once and, with a long shudder, he died.

"All right." Aracus Altorus climbed to his feet, looking weary. He rubbed at his brow with one hand, leaving a smear of blood alongside the Soumanië. "Give him . . . give him a proper burial," he said, nodding at the still figure. "If the Were keep their word, we'll owe him that much, at least."

There was grumbling among the Borderguard; the Ellylon made no complaint, assuming that the order was not intended for them. But it was Lilias who found her voice and said, "No."

Aracus stared at her. "Why?"

"The Were do not bury their dead," she said harshly. "Leave him for the scavengers of the forest if you would do him honor. It is their way."

He stared at her some more. "All right." Turning away, he accepted his reins from a waiting Borderguardsman and swung into the saddle. "Blaise, send a rider to Kranac to notify Martinek of this bargain. Tell him I mean to keep my word, and do any of the Regents of Pelmar break it, I will consider it an act of enmity. By the same token, do the Were break it, they will be hunted like dogs, until the last is slain. Let it be known."

"Aye, sir." Blaise moved to obey. In a few short minutes a rider was dispatched and the remainder of the company was remounted, preparing to depart. There was barely time for Lilias to take one last glance at Phraotes. It was hard to remember the Were ambassador as he had been; a keen-eyed grey shadow, gliding like smoke into the halls of Beshtanag. Dead, he was diminished, shrunken and hairy. His eyes were half slitted, gazing blankly at the trees. His muzzle was frozen in the rictus of death, wrinkled as if at a bad scent or a bad joke. Phraotes did not look like what he had been, one of the direst hunters ever to touch the soil of Urulat.

We shall dwindle, and pass into legend.

Lilias shuddered. "I'm sorry," she whispered, horribly aware that if she had not given counsel to Aracus, the bargain might never have been struck. "I didn't know what he would ask. Phraotes, I'm sorry!"

There was no answer, only the Were's dead, sharp-toothed grin.

If it were a bad joke, she hoped it was on Haomane's Allies.

THIRTY-ONE

A HALF DOZEN RAVENS PERCHED in the green shadows of the outermost edges of the Delta, drowsy in the midday sun. Beneath them, Ushahin Dreamspinner crouched, watching horses grazing on sedge grass.

He had been raised by the Grey Dam Sorash and, outcast or not, a part him would always be kindred to the Were. He knew the paths the Were trod; the dark paths of the forest, the dark paths of the pack mind. Although his path had diverged, he heard the echoes of their thoughts. When Oronin's Bow was raised against one of his Brethren, he felt it, and shuddered at the killing impact. When a dire bargain was struck, he bowed his head and grieved.

"You are too hasty, Mother," was all he whispered.

It was her right, the Grey Dam Vashuka. And he understood, oh yes, the thought behind it. Oronin's Children had never sought anything but solitude; the right to hunt, the right to be left alone. Still, he thought, she had surrendered too much, too soon. Perhaps it was a trick; yes, perhaps. The bargain held only as long as the Grey Dam lived. And she might live many hundreds of years upon the hoarded years her brethren sacrificed to her. His dam, the Grey Dam Sorash, had done so.

Or she might not. It was yet to see.

Ushahin watched the horses.

They did not care for him, horses. Although he was of the blood of two races, Lesser Shapers whose mastery of the lower orders of being went unquestioned, it was his years among the Were that had shaped him the most. Horses sensed it as if it were an odor on his skin. Ushahin, the predator. They carried him reluctantly at best, and when all was said and done, he preferred to travel on his own two feet. It had been a fine arrangement, until his Lordship had closed the Ways. Now, Ushahin had need of speed. Darkhaven was waiting; and the horses of Darkhaven lay to hand.

They were splendid creatures, there was no denying it. Their inadequate disguises had long since worn off; ill-cropped manes and tails regrown in flowing splendor. They were poorly groomed, aye, but they had shed winter's shaggy coat, and their summer hides gleamed with good health.

He had his eye on the best of the lot, an ill-tempered bay with a coat the color of drying blood, a black mane and tail. It had been Hunric's mount, if his memory served. A long-legged stallion with a fine, wedge-shaped head and snapping teeth to boot. The others bore scars of his temper.

The horses of Darkhaven had sharper teeth than those bred elsewhere.

Ushahin waited until dusk, when his own abilities edged toward their height. It was then that he emerged from the verges of the Delta, a length of rope in his crooked hands. It had served to secure his skiff; it would serve for this.

"Come," he crooned. "Come to me, pretty one."

It didn't, of course. His target stood poised on wary legs, showing the whites of its eyes, aware of his intent. He had to use the glamour, a Were trick, catching its mind in the net of his thoughts. Once it was done, the horse stood still and trembled, its hide shuddering as if flystung. Ushahin limped from his place of concealment, placing the rope around its neck, winding a twist about its soft muzzle and knotting it to create a makeshift hackamore.

"So," he whispered. "Not so bad, is it?"

The blood-bay stallion shuddered. So close, their hair was intertwined; Ushahin, leaning, his fine, pale hair mingling with the horse's black mane. He could smell the sweat, the lather forming on the horse's blood-dark hide. Its defiance would only be held in check so long, unless he wanted to fight it all the way to Darkhaven. He did not. Now, or never. Ignoring the pain in his crooked limbs, he slid one arm over its neck and hauled hard, pulling himself astride, and clamped hard with both thighs.

"Home!" he shouted, casting aside the net of thought that bound it.

The bay exploded beneath him: bucking, sunfishing, limbs akimbo. Ushahin laughed out loud and clung to its back. It hurt, hurt beyond telling, jarring his ill-mended bones. Yet he was one of the Three, and he had breakfasted with a dragon. No mere horse would be his undoing, not even one of the horses of Darkhaven.

It was a long battle nonetheless. Almost, the bay stallion succeeded in unseating him. It plunged toward the Verdine River and planted its forelegs in a halt so abrupt Ushahin was thrown hard against its neck. The other horses watched with prick-eared interest as the bay twisted its head around to snap at him. It charged, splashing, into the fringes of the Delta and sought to jar him loose against the trunk of a palodus tree, bruising and scraping his flesh.

None of it worked.

By the time the bay's efforts slowed, stars were emerging in the deep-blue twilight. The capitulation came all at once; a slump of the withers, the proud head lowering. It blew a heavy breath through flared nostrils and waited.

"Home," Ushahin said softly, winding his thoughts through the stallion's. Leaning forward, he whispered in one backward-twitching ear. "Home, where the Tordenstem guard the Defile as it winds through the gorge. Home, where the towers of Darkhaven beckon. Home, tall brother, where your attendants await you in the stable, with buckets of warm mash and *svartblod,* and silken cloths for your hide."

The blood-bay stallion raised its head. Arahila's gibbous moon was reflected in one liquid-dark eye. It gave a low whicker; the other two horses answered. From verges of the Delta, a half dozen ravens launched themselves, flying low on silent wings over the moon-silvered sedge grass.

Ushahin laughed, and gave the bay its head. "Go!" he shouted.

With great strides, it did. Bred under the shrouded skies of the Vale of Gorgantum, it ran with ease in the pale-lit darkness, and thundering on either side were two riderless horses. One was a ghostly grey, the color of forge-smoke; the other was pitch-black. And before them all, the shadowy figures of the ravens of Darkhaven forged the way.

Homeward.

DANI HAD SLIPPED.

It was as simple as that. He did not know that the terrain he and his uncle traversed was called the Northern Harrow, but he did not need to be told that it was a harsh and forbidding land. He knew that bare feet toughened by the sun-scorched floors of the desert were a poor match for the cruel granite and icy clime of the northern mountains. And he had discovered, too late, that ill-sewn rabbitskin made for clumsy footwear. When the cliff's edge had crumbled under his footing, he slid over the edge with one terrified shout.

Unmindful of the pain of broken and bending nails, he clung to the ledge he had caught on his downward plunge, fingertips biting deep. Below him, there was nothing. It was an overhang that had broken his fall; beneath it, the cliff fell away, cutting deeply back into the mountain's peak. His kicking feet, shod in tattered rabbit-skin, encountered no resistance. There was only a vast, endless drop, and the churning white waters of the Spume River below.

"Uncle!" Craning his neck, Dani fought terror. "Help me!"

Uncle Thulu—*lean* Uncle Thulu—peered over the edge of the cliff, and his eyes were stretched wide with fear in his weather-burnt face. "Can you pull yourself up, lad?"

He tried, but something was wrong with the muscles of his arms, his shoulders. There was no strength there. It might, Dani thought, have had to do with the popping sound they'd made when he caught himself. "No."

"Wait." Uncle Thulu's face was grim. "I'm coming."

Since there was nothing else for it, Dani waited, dangling from his fingertips and biting his lip at the pain of it. Overhead, Uncle Thulu scrabbled, finding the braided rope of rabbit-hide he'd made, looking for an anchor rock to secure it.

"Hang on, lad!" Thulu called over his shoulder, letting himself down inch by careful inch, a length of rope wrapped around his waist, his bare feet braced against the mountainside. "I'm coming."

The rope was too short.

Dani's arms trembled.

At home, the rope would be made of thukka-vine. There was an abundance of it. It was one of the earliest skills the Yarru-yami learned; how to braid rope out of thukka. Here, there was only hide, only the scant leavings of one's scant kills, poorly tanned in oak-water. And if Uncle Thulu had not tried to make him shoes, Dani thought, the rope would be longer.

"Here!" Plucking his digging-stick from his waistband, Thulu extended it, blunt end first. "Grab hold, lad. I'll pull you up."

Dani exhaled, hard, clinging to the ledge with the fingers of both star-marked hands. Against his breastbone, the clay flask containing the Water of Life shivered. A fragile vessel, it would shatter on the rocks below, as surely as his body would. What then, if the Water of Life was set loose in Neheris' rivers, where her Children dwelled? It was the Fjeltroll who would profit by it. "Take the flask, Uncle!" he called. "It's more important than I am. Use your stick, pluck it from about my neck!"

"No." Thulu's face was stubborn. "You are the Bearer, and I will not leave you."

Gritting his teeth, Dani glanced down; down and down and down. Far below, a ribbon of white water roared over jagged rocks. It seemed it sang his name, and a wave of dizziness overcame him, draining his remaining strength. "I can't do it," he whispered, closing his eyes. "Uncle, take the flask. As I am the Bearer, I order it."

Without looking, he heard the agonized curse as his uncle reversed the stick. He felt the pointed end of his uncle's digging-stick probe beneath the cord about his neck, catch and *lift*. For an instant, there was a sense of lightness and freedom, so overwhelming that he nearly laughed aloud.

And then; a gasp, a sharp *crack* as the tip of the digging-stick broke under the impossible weight of the Water of Life. The flask thudded gently against his chest, returning home to the Bearer's being, nestling against his flesh.

"Dani." Thulu's voice brought him back, at once calm and urgent. "It has to be you. Grab hold of the stick."

Fear returned as he opened his eyes. Once again, it was the blunt end of the stick extended. The braided leather rope, stretched taut, creaked and groaned. "The rope's not strong enough to hold us both, Uncle."

"It is." Uncle Thulu's face was contorted with effort, his own arms beginning to tremble under the strain. "Damn you, lad, I wove it myself. It has to be! Grab hold, I tell you; grab hold!"

"Uru-Alat," Dani whispered, "preserve us!"

The end of the peeled baari-wood stick was within inches of his right hand. It took all his courage to loose his grip upon the steady ledge, transferring it to the slippery wood. What merit was there in the mark of the Bearer? Dani's palm was slick with terror, slipping on the wood. The vertiginous drop called his name. He struggled to resist its call as Uncle Thulu's digging-stick slid through his grasp, scraping heedlessly past the Bearer's starry markings.

Slid; and halted.

Against all odds, Dani found a grip; there, near the end, where the slick wood was gnarled. It wasn't much, but it was enough. Clinging to the rope with one arm, Uncle Thulu hauled hard with the other, grunting and panting with the effort. The leather rope thinned and stretched, thwarting their efforts . . . but it held and did not break. The muscles of his arm quivered as, inch by torturous inch, Thulu of the Yarru-yami pulled his nephew from the abyss. When his head reached a level with the overhang, Dani clawed at the rock with his free hand, ignoring the pain in his shoulders and levering himself upward until he got a foot beneath him, toes digging hard against the granite, and drew himself up onto the ledge to stand on wavering legs.

"Oh, lad." Uncle Thulu embraced him with one arm, weeping. "Oh, lad!"

"Truly, Uncle," Dani said, his voice muffled against Thulu's shoulder, "if I am the Bearer, I could ask no better guide."

It took a long time to get from ledge to cliff-top. When it was done, both were trembling with a mix of exertion and the aftermath of fear. Uncle Thulu unwound the rope from his waist and unknotted it from the anchor, a proud jut of granite. He kissed the rope in gratitude, and for good measure, the stone itself. "Uru-Alat be praised," he said fervently, shoving his digging-stick into his waistband.

"Truly," Dani murmured, collapsing onto the chilled stones. His arms ached and his shoulders felt half-pulled from their sockets. "How much farther, Uncle?"

Uncle Thulu paced the edge of the cliff, eyeing the river below. "We'll find another route." His voice was decisive. "A *better* route, Dani. The Spume is a key, I'm sure of it. There are . . . traces, a foulness in the current." He stroked his digging-stick, humming absently for a moment, then stopped. "There is a branch underground that leads to the Defile. That much I sense for, even here, the waters are tainted." Pausing in thought, he tapped his lips. "It must happen some leagues to the west. Perhaps, if we abandon the heights and cut westward . . . yes. Such is the pattern of Uru-Alat's veins." Thulu glanced at his nephew, who sat huddled in his cloak, cradling his aching limbs. "Have you the strength, lad?" he asked gently.

"Aye." Dani shuddered, and laughed. "At least," he said, "we've not encountered the Fjeltroll."

"WE HAVE RECEIVED NO REPORTS of such travelers."

Their host spoke smoothly; but then, Coenred, Earl of Gerflod, was a smooth man. His auburn hair was smooth, flowing over his shoulders. His beard was groomed and silken, and his ruddy lips were smooth within their tidy bracket of facial hair.

Osric nodded. "Like as not, they've not been spotted yet."

"Like as not," Earl Coenred agreed, hoisting a tankard of ale. His fingers, with their smooth nails, curved about the bejeweled tankard. He nodded to one of the serving-maids. "Gerde, fill our guests' cups. Drink up, lads, the mutton's yet to come!"

Bobbing a nervous curtsey, she obeyed, circulating around the long trestle table. It took a long time to serve the Staccian lord's contingent and Osric and his men. There were a great number of the former, clad in handsome attire. Another servant brought her a fresh jug of ale. As she reached the far end of the table, where the Fjeltroll were seated, her steps began to drag, and her hand trembled visibly as she poured.

Osric and Coenred spoke in murmurs, ignoring both her anxiety and its source. While the earl had extended hospitality to the Fjel in a gesture of allegiance, it did not include taking them into the counsel of Men.

With an attempt at a benign smile, Skragdal extended his tankard. For Lord Satoris' sake, Skragdal was doing his best to honor the earl's hospitality, hunkering on the tiny chair provided him. It was built to Men's scale and he perched awkwardly on it, broad thighs splayed, his rough-hided knees bumping the edge of the table. It was not his fault it was too small, nor that his taloned grip dented the soft metal of his tankard, rendering it lopsided. He tried to convey these things with his smile; easy and apologetic, wrinkling his upper lip and baring his eyetusks in a gesture of goodwill.

The serving-maid squeaked in terror, and the lip of her jug rattled against his tankard. Ale splashed over the rim. Setting the half-empty jug upon the table with a bang, she fled. Earl Coenred glanced up with brief interest, beckoned to another serving-maid to bring another jug, then resumed his conversation, intent on Osric, spinning a web of smooth words.

Skragdal frowned.

"I . . . do not like how this smells."

A deep voice; a Fjel voice, speaking their tongue. He glanced up sharply to see the young Tungskulder Thorun, sitting with shoulders hunched, a posture of uncertainty. "Speak," he said.

Thorun's hunched shoulders shrugged as he peered out from under his heavy brow; his eyes were red-rimmed and miserable. "I do not trust my senses."

"Ah." Skragdal remembered; there was a story, one that mattered. "Bogvar."

Thorun nodded. They remembered it together—Thorun who had lived it, Skragdal who had heard it, left behind to command as field marshal in Hyrgolf's absence. Cuilos Tuillenrad, the City of Long Grass, where the Lady of the Ellylon had awoken the wraiths of the dead. There, confused by the magic she had awakened, Thorun had mistaken his comrade Bogvar for an Ellyl wraith. Death, a foul death, had been the result. Thorun had offered his axe-hand in penance. The Lord General had refused it.

Skragdal flared his nostrils, inhaling deeply. "There is no enchantment here," he said calmly. "Only fear, only greed. Such are the scents of Men. Speak, Tungskulder."

"Lies." Thorun shuddered in his hide. "This earl reeks of lies."

The Nåltannen were squabbling over the fresh ale-jug, laughing as their steely talons clashed in the effort, drinking deep and making toasts. The Gulnagel were little better, hunkering over the table with slitted eyes and rumbling bellies, awaiting platters of mutton. And the Kaldjager . . . the Cold Hunters would not commit themselves to any hall built by Men. They remained outdoors and kept a safe distance, scouting the perimeter of Gerflod. Neither the earl nor his Men knew of their existence.

For once, Skragdal was glad for their distrust.

He flared his nostrils again, inhaling softly, letting the delicate odors of Men's emotions play over his palate. There was Osric, dogged and determined, grateful for Earl Coenred's kindness. There were Osric's Men, dreaming of gain and glory, hoping the serving-maids would return. There were Coenred's Men, nervous and wary in their thoughts. And there . . .

Skragdal smelled the lie.

It was smoothly spoken. There had been no word—no word—since their company had emerged from the Vesdarlig Passage. No one knew what had transpired in Beshtanag, how badly their plans had gone awry. How not? It was his Lordship's business. His Enemies were slow. And yet . . . and yet. Here, mere leagues south of Neherinach, where Osric's Men and Skragdal's Fjel would part ways, word had emerged.

Earl Coenred had heard news, dire enough to undermine his loyalties. All was known. Nothing was said. The lie was there in every smooth denial, every polite inquiry. The Earldom of Gerflod had turned.

Skragdal exhaled with regret. He wondered how it had happened. A traitor among the Staccians? It could be so. Fjel had never trusted them. Men did not remember the way the Fjel did, trusting carelessly to their ink-scratched markings to preserve memory. And what manner of loyalty was it that could be purchased for mere gold? He did not doubt Lord Vorax, no—he was one of the Three, and beyond doubt. Yet his countrymen . . . perhaps.

He dismissed the thought. What mattered was at hand.

"You smell it," Thorun said.

"Aye." Skragdal realized he was staring at the earl; Coenred had noticed it, a nervous sheen of sweat appearing on his brow. His smooth mask was slipping, and the sour tang of ill-hidden fear tainted the air. Skragdal looked away. Relieved, the earl called in a loud voice for more ale, more ale. Once again, fresh jugs were set to circulating, born by a procession of nervous servants. At least they made no pretence of hiding their fear.

"Should we kill them?" Thorun asked simply.

It was a hard decision. Hyrgolf, he thought, would approve it; he would not hesitate to trust a Tungskulder's nose. Would General Tanaros? No, Skragdal thought. He would not hesitate to believe, but nor would he sanction violence against an ally who had not betrayed his hand. So, neither will Osric turn on a fellow Staccian on my word alone. I cannot count on his support.

That left only the Fjel.

As platters of mutton were brought to the table, heaped high and steaming, Skragdal cast his gaze over his comrades. They tore into the meal with tooth and talon, terrifying the earl's staff. The Nåltannen had drunk deep, and continued to heft their tankards, alternating between mutton and ale. The Gulnagel ate with a will, smearing grease on their chops as they lifted slabs of meat with both hands, gnawing and gnawing, eyes half-lidded with pleasure.

Such was the Fjel way; to gorge until replete, to rest upon satiation. Those were the dictates of life for Neheris' Children, raised in a harsh clime where summer's bounty inevitably gave way to barren winter. Survival dictated it.

What was disturbing, Skragdal thought, was that Earl Coenred knew it. This abundance had been deliberately provided. He watched his comrades gorge and pondered the expression of satisfaction that spread, slow and sleek, over the earl's features. What were the odds? There were sixteen Fjel in the Great Hall of Gerflod Keep, and all of them unarmed. Their arms and armor were stacked in a stable lent them for shelter; a cunning stroke, that. How many Men? Coenred must have two hundred within the walls.

It could be done, of course. Skragdal hunched his shoulders and flexed his talons, feeling his own strength. He had labored in the mines and in the smelting yards. He knew the weaknesses of metal, where armor was willing to bend and break. With his talons, he could peel it from them, piece by piece. Men were soft, as General Tanaros had taught them. Men died easily, once their soft flesh was exposed.

"Boss?" Thorun's red-rimmed eyes were hopeful.

Reluctantly, Skragdal shook his head. "No. Lying comes easily to Men. We have no proof that they mean us harm because of it," he said softly. "General Tanaros would want *proof* in this matter. But I will speak to Osric of it."

It proved harder than he had anticipated. Once the meal was consumed, Earl Coenred rose, tankard in hand. He made an elegant speech in Staccian about Gerflod's loyalty to Darkhaven, the long arrangement by which Staccia prospered and dwelled in peace alongside the Fjel border. He praised Osric's diligence and vowed Gerflod's aid in the quest. He made much of thanking the Fjel for their unflagging bravery and support. " . . . and it is my hope that you have enjoyed my hospitality tonight, as poor token of those thanks," he added.

The Nåltannen roared in approval, banging their tankards.

I should not have let them drink so much, Skragdal thought.

Earl Coenred raised his free hand for silence. "I apologize that Gerflod has no quarters to adequately house you, but Lieutenant Osric assures me that the stable we have provided will suffice," he said. A contingent of Men entered the hall, wearing light armor underneath the livery of Gerflod. "My men will escort you there forthwith," the earl continued, "and with them, a full keg of ale!"

Ah, but it is hard, thought Skragdal. How am I to command their appetites, when it is how Neheris Shaped us? I am not General Tanaros, to preach the joys of discipline. He is one of the Three. On his tongue, it sings with glory; on mine, it would be a lie. Must I betray what I am to command my brethren?

All around him the Fjel roared with goodwill, surging to their feet to follow Coenred's Men. Already, they were halfway out the door, following the promise of more drink and sweet slumber. And why not? They had earned it. And yet, there was Thorun with his hopeful gaze. There was the earl smiling, with his smooth beard and his combed hair, the lie stinking in his teeth.

Skragdal sighed and rose from his chair. Leaning over the table on his knuckles, he took a deep breath and raised his voice. "*Os-*

ric!" He was no Tordenstem, to make his enemies quake to the marrow of their bones with the Thunder-Voice, but the shout of a Tungskulder Fjel could rattle any rafters built by Men. In the fearful silence that followed, Skragdal added, "We must speak."

It was an awkward moment. The smooth mask of the earl's expression slipped, revealing fear and annoyance. He made a covert gesture to his Men, who stepped up their pace in escorting the Fjel from the Great Hall. Skragdal nodded at Thorun, not needing to speak his thoughts. Thorun nodded in return, following the exodus quietly. Skragdal waited. Osric, flushed with embarrassment, made his way around the table. Although his head only came to Skragdal's breastbone, his fingers dug hard into the flesh of his arm, drawing him into the far corner of the hall's entryway. "They're our *hosts,* Tungskulder!" he hissed under his breath. "Have a care for Staccian courtesy, will you?"

"Osric." Ignoring the Staccian's importunate grip, Skragdal dropped his voice to its lowest register, a rumble like large rocks grinding. "This earl is lying."

Osric blew out his breath impatiently, smelling of ale. "About what?"

"He knows." How to communicate it? There were no words in Men's tongues to explain what he knew, or why; no words to describe the scent of a lie, of ill-will behind a smooth smile, of danger lying in wait. "More than he is saying. Osric, we should leave this place. Now. Tonight."

"Enough." The Staccian lieutenant's voice was sharp. He released his grip on Skragdal's arm, taking a step backward and craning his neck to glare at the Fjel. "We part ways at Neherinach, Tungskulder. Until then, by Lord Vorax's orders, you are under my command. Your Fjel have embarrassed Darkhaven enough for one night. Go with them, and keep them under control. Do not embarrass his Lordship further by insulting our host."

Skragdal flared his nostrils, smelling the lie. "Osric . . . "

"Go!"

He waited.

"Go!"

With a curt bow, Skragdal went. Behind him, he heard one of the earl's Men make a cutting comment, and the wave of laughter that answered; then Osric's voice, at once dismissive and apologetic. *What can you expect? They are little better than brutes, after all. But his Lordship insisted on it. We need the tribes, you know.*

It galled him, prickling his hide all along the ridge of his spine.

Skragdal made his way down the halls of Gerflod Keep, past the earl's startled guards, to emerge outdoors. It was quiet in the narrow courtyard. He took deep breaths of night air, filling his lungs and seeking calm. He had thought better of Osric. That was his mistake. Staccia was not Darkhaven. Here, the balance had shifted. Arahila's Children were reminded of their superiority, compelled to exercise it.

"Hey." One of the earl's Men peered tentatively at him beneath the steel brim of his helmet. With the point of his spear, he gestured toward a stable across the courtyard, where lamplight poured through the crack of the parted door. Faint sounds of Fjel merriment issued from within, muffled by sturdy wood. "Your lodgings are that way, lad."

Skragdal rumbled with annoyance.

"As . . . as you will." The Gerflodian guard's words ended on a rising note of fear.

Shaking his head, Skragdal trudged across the courtyard. A patch of gilded lamplight spilled over the paving-stones. He flung open the stable door and was hailed by shouts. Thorun, who had donned his armor, met his gaze with a shrug; he had done his best. The Gulnagel, having gorged deepest on the meat, were half asleep, bellies distended. Everywhere else, it seemed, Nåltannen lounged on bales of clean straw, their kits strewn about the stable, tankards clutched in their talons. They raised their tankards in salute, shouting for him to join them.

"Shut up!" With an effortless swipe, Skragdal slammed the door closed behind him. In the echoing reverberation, the Fjel fell silent. "Where is the ale-keg?"

One pointed.

"Good." He trudged across the floor, pausing to catch up his axe. Bits of straw stuck between his toes as he approached, hefting the axe over his shoulder. It only took one mighty swing to breach the keg, splintering its wooden slats. Brown ale foamed over the straw, rendering the whole a sodden mess.

"Awww, boss!" someone said sadly.

"Shut up." Skragdal pointed with the head of the axe. "Listen."

They obeyed. For a moment only the hiss of foaming ale broke the silence; then, another sound. A slow scraping as of wood against wood, a gentle thunk.

"That," Skragdal said, "was the sound of the earl's Men barring the stable door." Tramping across the straw, he kicked a dozing Gulnagel in the ribs in passing, then began to rummage in earnest through his pile of arms and armor. "Get up, Rhilmar," he said over his shoulder, donning his breastplate and buckling it. "All of you. Up and armed."

They gaped at him.

"Now!" he roared.

There was a scramble, then; deep Fjel voices surging in dawning anger, metal clattering as armor was slung in place, arms were hefted. It was just as well. To Men's ears, the sounds of Fjel preparing for battle would be indistinguishable from the sounds of Fjel at their leisure. Skragdal smiled grimly.

"What now?" a Nåltannen growled.

"We wait." Watching the barred door fixedly, Skragdal settled the haft of his battle-axe on one armor-plated shoulder. "There's no harm in it. We've waited this long, lads, and the Kaldjager will be keeping watch from the borders. We'll wait until the earl's Men show their hand. And then . . . " He bared his eyetusks in another smile, " . . . we'll see what there is for a Fjeltroll to *learn* here."

They cheered him for it, and Skragdal's heart swelled at the sound. His words had struck them where they lived, speaking to the old unfairness, the old hurt. Although his name might be forgotten in the annals of Men and Ellylon—no one would write down this night's doings, and if they did, they would not record the name of Skragdal of the Tungskulder Fjel—if it was worth the telling, Neheris' Children would remember the story.

It was a long wait, and a dull one. Outside, the stars moved in their slow dance and, in the west, the red star ascended over the horizon. Inside, the lamps burned low, and there were only the slow breathing of the Fjel, and the sound of straw rustling underfoot as this one or that adjusted his stance. Funny, Skragdal thought, that Men were so anxious to bar the door, yet so fearful to attack. If they had waited longer for the former, it might not have tipped their hand.

But it had, and the Fjel were patient. Even drunk, even sated, the Fjel knew how to be patient. Now they had shaken off their torpor. They were awake, waiting and watching. If it took all night, they would wait all night. One did not survive, hunting in a cold clime, without patience.

In armed silence, they waited.

And in the small hours, there were new sounds.

There were footsteps, and whispering and hissing. Men's voices, tight with fear and urgency. Liquid sounds, splashing. Skragdal's nostrils widened, inhaling the sharp odor of seep oil. It was the same oil used in the lamps, only more, much more.

"Boss . . . " someone murmured.

He hoisted the axe in his right hand and settled his shield on his left arm, General Tanaros' words ringing in his memory. *Keep your shields up!* "Soon," he promised. "Keep your shields high, lads."

They were alert, all of them. The Earl was a fool if he reckoned them slaves to their appetites; Skragdal's words had done the trick. Words; Men's tools. He had used them well. In guttering lamplight, Fjel eyes gleamed under heavy brows. It made him proud to see the determination in Thorun's visage; a fellow Tungskulder, here at his side. Broad shoulders for heavy burdens; so Neheris had said when she Shaped them.

Krick . . . krick . . . krick . . .

"A flint-striker," one of the Gulnagel said unnecessarily.

Outside, flames whooshed into the air, licking at the dry, oil-soaked tinder. Inside, there were only slivers of brightness, showing between the planks. Smoke, grey and choking, crept under the door. Someone coughed.

"Now!" Skragdal shouted, hurling his weight at the door.

He remembered, and kept his shield high. It hit the stable door with splintering force, the full might of his charge behind it. The door burst outward in an explosion of sparks, singeing his hide. They were minor wounds; he had endured worse when the acid rain fell over Darkhaven, an understandable expression of Lord Satoris' ire. He kept his head low, letting his charge carry him into the courtyard.

"Who is first?" Skragdal bellowed, axe in hand. *"Who is first to die?"*

There was no shortage of volunteers. It had been a dozen Men, no more, who had undertaken the mission. They died easily at the bite of his axe, dropping empty jugs of lamp-oil, cowering in their armor. Skragdal laughed aloud, feeling blood splash his arms, slick and warm on his hide. It felt good, at last, to do what he did best. He strode sure-footed across the cobblestones, laying about him like a Midlander harvesting hay. The earl's Men poured through the doors of Gerflod Manor, emerging in scores, even as Fjel after Fjel leapt from the burning stable, joining him in the massacre until the narrow courtyard was churning and it was hard to find fighting-space. Over and over he swung his axe, rejoicing in the results. By the leaping flames of the stable he saw the terror in his attackers' faces. It didn't last long. Their swords and spears clattered ineffectually against his shield, against the heavy plates of his armor, glancing blows scratching his tough hide where it was unprotected. Neheris had Shaped her Children well. Meanwhile, the keen blade of his axe, swung by his strong arm, sheared through the thin metal of their armor, until the head was buried deep in soft flesh. Again and again, Skragdal struck, wrenching his axe loose to strike again. As their warm blood spilled, ebbing from their bodies, terror gave way to the calm stare of death.

Men died so easily.

"Sir! That was the last of them!" Someone was grappling with him; one of his own. A shield locked with his; over its rim, he met Thorun's gaze. "You spoke of *learning*," the Tungskulder reminded him.

"Aye." Panting, Skragdal disengaged. "Aye, I did. My thanks." He gave his head a shake, clearing the haze of battle-frenzy, and lowered his axe. The stable was engulfed in flame, blazing toward the heavens, throwing heat like a forge and illuminating a courtyard awash in blood. Everywhere the bodies of the earl's Men lay strewn and discarded, pale flesh gouged with gaping wounds. Here and there, one groaned. The Nåltannen hunted through the dead, dispatching the dying. There were too many to count, but he reckoned a good number of the earl's Men had died in the courtyard. More than the earl had intended to risk. Turning his head, he saw the doors of Gerflod Keep standing open and unbarred. "So," he said. "Let us *learn*."

Once the words were uttered, there was no stopping the Fjel. The Gulnagel, blood-spattered, howled, racing for the doors in great, bounding leaps. Even as they entered the Keep, Nåltannen caught up the cry and streamed after them, weapons clutched in gleaming steel talons, half-forgotten shields held low and dangling.

Skragdal sighed. "Summon the Kaldjager," he said to Thorun. "We'll need to leave this place. *Swiftly.*" Thorun nodded, thrusting his axe through his belt-loop, moving with steady deliberation through the flame-streaked darkness. A good lad, Skragdal thought, watching him go. A good one.

Gerflod Keep lay waiting, its open doors like the mouth of a grave.

Shouldering his axe, Skragdal trudged across the courtyard. He paused in the open door and cocked an eye toward the stable. Its roof sagged as a beam collapsed somewhere inside the burning structure, sending up a huge shower of sparks. Safe enough, he reckoned. Gerflod Keep was stone; stone wouldn't burn.

He entered the Keep, his taloned feet leaving bloody prints on

its marble floors, mingling with the tracks of the Fjel who had gone
before. He followed their trail, opening his nostrils wide.

The stink of fear and lies had given way to the reek of terror
and the stench of death. All along the way, Men lay dying; Gerflod's Men, Earl Coenred's men. Here and there, where they were
unarmored and wore only livery, the Nåltannen had given in to old
instincts, slitting their bellies with the swipe of a steel-taloned paw.
Those Men groaned, dying hard. The Nåltannen had been in a
hurry.

Skragdal snorted at the odor of perforated bowels, bulging and
blueish through the rents in soft mortal flesh, oozing fecal matter.
Those Men, clutching at their spilling entrails, still had terror in
their eyes. Murmuring a prayer to Neheris, he raised his axe to dispatch them, one by one. Some of them, he thought, were grateful
for it.

In the Great Hall, he found Osric and his Men. None of them
were alive. Osric was leaning backward in his chair, grinning. A
half-empty tankard sat in front of him and the hilt of a belt-knife
protruded from his throat. It was a small knife, made for a Man's
hand, with the earl's insignia on the hilt. A trail of blood lay puddled in his lap.

"Ah, Osric," Skragdal said, with genuine sorrow. "I tried to tell
you."

The Staccian lieutenant continued to grin at the ceiling, wordless
and blind. Near the head of the table there was a low groan and a
scraping sound, a hissed curse. Skragdal trudged over to investigate.

On the floor, Earl Coenred writhed in his shadow, one hand
clamped to his throat. Blood seeped through his fingers, where the
rending marks of Nåltannen talons were visible. He did not, Skragdal thought, look so smooth with red blood bubbling on his ruddy
lips. Stooping, he leaned in close enough to grasp a handful of the
earl's auburn hair and ask the question.

"Why?"

The earl's eyes rolled up in his head, showing the whites. "The
Galäinridder!" he gasped, catching his breath in a burbling laugh.
"The Bright Rider, the Shining Paladin!" Droplets of blood spewed
from his lips in a fine spray. "We did not welcome him, but he
came. Out of nowhere, out of the mountains, he came, terrible to
behold, and he told us, told us everything. Haomane's Wrath is
coming, and those who oppose him will pay. Even here, even in
Staccia. There is nowhere to hide." The earl's face contorted as he

summoned the will to spit out his last words. "You are *dead*, Fjel-troll! Dead, and you don't even know it!"

"Not as dead as you," Skragdal said, releasing his grip and straightening. Raising his axe, he brought it down hard, separating the earl's head from his body.

The edge of his axe clove through flesh and bone and clanged on marble, gouging a trough in the floor and making his arms reverberate. Skragdal grunted. The earl's head rolled free, fetching up against a table leg. There, it continued to stare at him under drooping lids.

Dead, and you don't even know it.

"Fjel!" Skragdal roared, straightening, adopting General Tanaros' words without even thinking. "Fall out! *Now!*"

THIRTY-TWO

❖

IT WAS DUE TO THE raven that no one else had yet died in the Unknown Desert.

Tanaros didn't count the days; none of them did. What would be the point? None of them knew how long it would take to cross the desert on their meandering, uncharted course. When they could find shade, they rested by day and traveled by night. When there was no shade, which was most of the time, they marched beneath the white-hot sun. He put his trust in Fetch, in the gift of the Grey Dam Sorash, and led them staggering onward. Better, he reckoned, to walk toward death than let it find them waiting.

It didn't.

Again and again, Fetch guided them to safety; to shade, to water. Hidden water-holes, drought-eaters, rocky ledges that cast deep shade, anthills, basking lizards, nests of mice: all these things the raven found. Tanaros followed his shadow across the parched earth, the raven's squawk echoing in his ears, until they reached the place where the raven alighted. Again and again, Fetch preened with satisfaction upon their arrival, as they found themselves in a place where sustenance was to be had.

"How do you know?" Tanaros mused on one occasion, studying the raven where it perched on his forearm. "No raven ever traveled this desert, nor any Were. How do you *know?*"

The bright eyes gleamed. *"Kaugh!"*

It was a jumbled impression of thoughts that the raven projected; water, beetles and a tall palodus tree, a dragon's head, rearing above the treetop. Over and over, the dragon's head, ancient and iron-grey, dripping with swamp-water and vegetation, its jaws parted to speak or breathe flame.

"I don't understand," Tanaros told him.

Hopping onto a thorn-branch, Fetch settled and rattled his feathers.

"And *why?*" he asked the raven.

One bright eye cracked open a slit, showing him his quarters in Darkhaven, customary order giving way to mess and disarray. An injured nestling. A pair of hands, strong and capable, made to grip a sword-hilt, shaping themselves to cup feather and hollow bone with an unaccustomed tenderness.

"For that?" He swallowed. "It was a whim. A small kindness."

"Kaugh." The raven closed both eyes and slept.

In the end, he supposed, it didn't matter. What mattered was that they survived, step by step, day by day. But it opened a chink in his heart, that might have sealed itself like stone against the thought of love. When the somber faces of Ngurra and the Yarru-yami haunted his dreams, it gave him a tiny brand to hold the darkness at bay.

A small kindness, a confluence of compassion, had saved his life. Was that strength, or a weakness?

Tanaros could not say. If there had been compassion in his heart the day he learned Calista and Roscus had betrayed him, perhaps he would have found the strength to walk away. What brought them together? Passion? Compassion? They had lacked the strength to resist desire. And yet that thought, too, was anathema. In their hearts, they had already made a cuckold of him. Had they been stronger, he would have spent his life living an unwitting lie, and the world would be a different place.

He did not know if it would be a better one.

Nothing was simple.

"Lord General?" Another day without shade, another day's trek. If there were a chink in the wall of his heart, it was Speros who thrust a wedge into it. Recovered from the ravages of dehydration, the Midlander had shown surprising and stubborn resilience, regaining sufficient strength to place one foot in front of the other, day after day, refusing the aid of the Gulnagel. Now he turned a sunburnt face in Tanaros' direction, his voice wistful. "What's the Lady of the Ellylon like?"

"Like a woman," he said shortly. "An Ellyl woman."

"Oh." Speros returned his gaze to the desert floor, watching his feet trudge across the sand. It crunched rhythmically under their boots, under the taloned feet of the Gulnagel, who traded glances over their heads. "I've never seen an Ellyl," he said eventually. "I just wondered . . . "

"Yes." Tanaros took a deep breath, the desert's heat searing his lungs. "They're very beautiful. *She* is very beautiful. Do you want to know how much?" He remembered Cerelinde in her chamber, the night he had bade her farewell, and how she had shone like a candle-flame, pale hair shining like a river against her jeweled robes as she turned away from him. *Go then, and kill, Tanaros Blacksword! It is what you do.* "So much that it hurts," he said harshly. "So much it makes you pity Arahila for the poor job she made of Shaping us. We're rough-hewn clay, Speros, a poor second next to her Elder Brother's creation. So much it makes you despise Arahila for trying and falling so short, yet giving us the wit to know it. Is that what you wanted to hear?"

Speros glanced wryly at him. "Not exactly, my lord."

"Well." Despite himself, Tanaros smiled. The unfamiliar movement made the skin of his dry lips split. "You've seen Ushahin Dreamspinner."

"No." Speros shook his head. "I've only heard tales."

"Ah." Tanaros licked his split lip, tasting blood. "Well, he is a paltry, cracked mirror through which to behold the beauty of the Ellylon, but I imagine you'll see him in time. And if the Dreamspinner isn't Ellyl enough for you, unless I am much mistaken, you'll encounter Ellylon aplenty on the battlefield, and be sorry you did, for they're doughty fighters beneath their pretty hides."

"Aye, Lord General." For a few moments, the Midlander was silent. "I would like to see the Lady, though," he mused. "Just to see her."

Tanaros made no reply.

Speros glanced at him again. "Will Lord Satoris kill her, do you think?"

"No." The word leapt too quickly from his cracked lips. Tanaros halted, rubbing his hands over his face. It felt gritty with sand and grime. His head ached from the effort of walking, from Speros' questions, from too little food, and too much light. Once, in Beshtanag, he had welcomed the sight of it. Now he yearned for the dim, soothing light of Darkhaven, for the familiarity of its gleaming black walls and corridors. After the endless sunlight of the Unknown Desert, he wouldn't be sorry if he never left the cloud-shrouded Vale of Gorgantum for another mortal lifespan. "Speros, save your breath. We've a long way to go yet today."

"Aye, Lord General."

This time the Midlander was properly subdued, and his silence lasted what Tanaros gauged to be the better part of a league. He set as brisk a pace as he dared, rendering further speech impossible. He wished he could outpace his own thoughts. There were too many words etched into his memory, chasing themselves around and around in his mind. Cerelinde's voice, his Lordship's, Ngurra's . . . and now Speros', his voice with its broad Midlands accent, asking a question in innocent curiosity.

Will Lord Satoris kill her, do you think?

The thought of it made his palms itch and bile rise in his throat. He remembered altogether too well how his wife's face had looked in death; blind eyes staring, all her lively beauty turned to cold clay. Even in his fury it had sickened him. The thought of seeing Cerelinde thusly was unbearable.

He was glad when the landscape made one of its dull, inhospitable shifts from rippled sand to barren red earth, dotted here and there with thorn-brush. Loose rocks and scattered boulders made the footing tricky, and it was a relief to have to concentrate on the task of walking. Fetch's shadow wavered on the uneven ground, then vanished as the raven veered westward, becoming a tiny black dot in the unbroken blue sky, then disappearing altogether. Tanaros led his company in the direction the raven had taken, keeping its flight-path fixed in his mind and placing his feet with care. There was little else to relieve the tedium. Once, a hopping-mouse broke cover under a thorn-brush, bounding into the open in unexpected panic.

With a grunt, one of the three remaining Gulnagel dropped his burden and gave chase, returning triumphant with a furry morsel clutched in his talons. Despite the fact that he was panting with the effort, he offered it to his general.

"No, Krolgun," Tanaros said, remembering Freg, and how he had offered him a handful of termites. "It's yours." He looked away as the Fjel devoured it whole, hoping the scant nourishment was worth the effort.

Another hour, and another. Tanaros slowed their pace, scanning the skies with growing concern. He forgot to watch his steps, fixing his gaze on the sky. Had he kept their path true to the trajectory of Fetch's flight? He thought so, but it was hard to tell in the featureless desert. They had been too long on the march, and their waterskins were dwindling toward empty. Nearby he could hear Krolgun still panting, his steps beginning to drag. The others were little better and, crane his neck though he would, there was no sign of the raven.

Only the empty blue skies, filled with the glare of Haomane's Wrath.

"Lord General?" Speros' voice, cracked and faint.

"Not now, Speros," he said impatiently.

"Lord General!" The Midlander's hand clutched his arm, dragging his attention from the empty skies. Speros' mouth was working, though no further words emerged. With his other hand, he pointed westward, where a line of twisted forms broke the horizon. "Look!" he managed at length.

Frowning, Tanaros followed his pointing finger. "Are those . . . trees?"

"Aye!" Releasing his arm, Speros broke into a mad, capering dance. "Jack pines, Lord General!" he shouted. "Good old Midlands jack pines! General!" There were tears glistening in his eyes, running down his sunburnt face. *"We've reached the edge!"*

It was the Gulnagel who broke ranks with an exuberant roar, abandoning his command to race toward the distant treeline. What sparse reserves of energy the Lowland Fjel had hoarded, they expended all at once. Their packs bounced and clanked as they ran, powerful haunches propelling their massive bodies in swift bounds. With a wordless shout, Speros discarded his near-empty waterskins and followed them at a dead run, whooping in his cracked voice.

Four figures, three large and one small, raced across the barren landscape.

Tanaros Blacksword, Commander General of Darkhaven, shook his head and hoped his army of four would not expire before reaching the desert's edge. He gathered up Speros' waterskins and settled them over his shoulder, then touched the hilt of the black sword that hung from his belt. It was still there, the echo of his Lordship's blood whispering to his fingertips. Back on course, the compass of his branded heart contracted.

Westward.

He set out at a steady jog, watching the treeline draw nearer, watching the racing figures ahead of him stagger, faltering and slowing. It was farther than they thought, at least another league. Such was always the case. Though his feet were blistered and his boots were cracking at the heels, he wound his way across the stony soil and kept a steady pace, drawing abreast of them in time. He dispensed waterskins and an acerbic word of reprimand, accepted with chagrin. They kept walking.

Their steps grew heavier as they walked, all energy spent. Heavy, but alive.

Tanaros' steps grew lighter, the nearer they drew.

Jack pines, stunted and twisted, marked the western boundary of the Unknown Desert. Beyond, sparse grass grew, an indication that the content of the soil was changing, scorched desert slowly giving way to the fertile territories of the Midlands.

In the shadow of the jack pines, Fetch perched on a needled branch, bobbing his head in triumphant welcome. His black eyes were bright, as bright as the reflection of sunlight on the trickling creek that fed the pines.

A small kindness.

CROUCHED UPON THE BACK OF the blood-bay stallion, Ushahin Dreamspinner floated above the horse's churning stride, borne aloft like a crippled vessel on the waves of a wind-tossed sea. And yet, there was power in him, far beyond the strength of his twisted limbs. Riding, he cast the net of his mind adrift over the whole of Urulat, and rode the pathways between waking and dreaming.

It was a thing he alone knew to do.

The Were had taught it to him; so many believed. It was true, and not true. The Grey Dam Sorash had taught him the ways of the Were, in whose blood ran the call of Oronin's Horn. Because there was Death in their Shaping, there were doors open to them that were closed to the other races of Lesser Shapers.

Ushahin had heard Oronin's Horn. It had blown for him when he was a child and his broken body had lain bleeding in the forests of Pelmar. Somewhere, there was a death waiting for him. But the Grey Dam had claimed him, grieving for her lost cubs, and whispered, *not yet*.

So she had claimed him, and taught him. Yet he was not Were, and their magic twisted in his usage. The Were, like the Fjeltroll, could smell Men's fear; unlike the Fjel, they could hear a Man's heart beat at a hundred paces and taste the pulse of his fear. Ushahin, in whose veins ran the blood of Haomane's Children, could sense Men's *thoughts*. And it was their thoughts—their dreams, their unspoken terrors and wordless joys—that formed the pathways along which he traveled. It was a network as vast and intricate as the Marasoumië, yet infinitely more subtle. He had walked it many a time. This was the first time he had ridden it.

Ushahin-who-walks-between-dusk-and-dawn.

Thus had the Grey Dam Sorash named him in the tongue of the Were, who had no other words for what he was. It was his name, the one he had borne for many times the length of a mortal life-span. Although the Were reviled him and the Grey Dam Vashuka had repudiated his claim upon their kinship, it was the name he would keep.

It had been given him in love.

Once, he had had another name; a Pelmaran name, given him by one long dead. His father's mother, he thought; there was some vague memory there. A widow of middle years, with hair gone early to grey, a lined face and a sharp tongue. *After all, we've got to call him something.* His father, a tall shadow, turning away with averted face. The Pelmaran lordling, his life ruined for a moment's passion, did not care what his son was called. He retreated into memory, reliving the moment. It was something few Men could claim, to have expended a lifetime of desire on Ellylon flesh.

That, Ushahin remembered.

Not what they had called him.

When he tried, he saw light; bright light, the light of Haomane's sun. It had stood high above the marketplace in Pelmar City the day the other children had run him down and held him at bay. He'd stood his ground for a long time, but in the end there had been too many of them. The children of Pelmar City did not like his bright eyes, that saw too keenly their squalid thoughts; they did not like his pale hair, the way his limbs moved or his sharp cheek-bones; slanted, strange and unfamiliar. It made them afraid, and they knew, in the way children know things, that his father's guilt would keep his lips sealed, and his mother's people had gone far, far away.

Better none of it had ever happened.

So, with cobblestones wrenched from the market square, they had set out to make it so. The first few were thrown, and he had dodged them. If they had not cornered him, he would have dodged them all; but they had. They had run him to ground.

He remembered the first blow, an errant stone. It had grazed his cheek, raising a lump and a blueish graze, breaking his fair skin. Had it cracked the bone? Perhaps. It didn't matter. Worse had come later. They had closed in, stones in fists. There had been many blows, then. Ushahin did not remember the ones that had broken his hands, raised in futile defense. He had curled into a ball; they had pounced upon him, swarming, hauling his limbs straight. A trader's shadow had darkened the alley, and withdrawn. There would be no intervention in the quarrels of children. Someone—he did not remember who had done it, had never even seen their face—had stomped gleefully on his outstretched arms and legs, until the bones had broken with sounds like dry sticks snapping in half.

The last blow, he remembered.

There had been a boy, some twelve years of age. Kneeling on the cobblestones, a mortal boy on scabbed knees. A rock in his fist, crashing down upon Ushahin's temple. At that blow, bone had shattered, a dent caving the orbit of his eye. The boy had spat upon his broken face and whispered a name. What it was, he didn't remember. Only the long crawl afterward, moving his broken limbs like a swimmer on dry land, and the trail of blood it left behind him in the marketplace; the gentle succor of the forest's pine mast floor, and then the Grey Dam, giving him a new name.

Ushahin-who-walks-between-dusk-and-dawn.

The blood-bay's muscles surged beneath him, compressing and lengthening, stride after stride. It should have grown weary, but there was no weariness in dreams. Somewhere, distantly, Ushahin felt its astonishment. His power had grown during his sojourn in the Delta. He wondered why Satoris had never returned to the source of his birth, if his Lordship had ceded it to Calanthrag the Eldest as the price for the dragons' aid during the Shapers' War. Whatever regenerative mystery remained, it had infused him with strength. Even now he felt it course through his veins. The bay's nostrils flared, revealing the scarlet lining; still, it ran, its strides consuming the leagues. Beneath the dim starlight the marshes of outer Vedasia fell behind them, and they continued onward.

They ran as swift as rumor, following the curve of Harrington Inlet. The road was pale dust under their hooves, and before them flew ravens in a wedge. To their left and to their right ran a riderless horse; one ghost-grey, and one night-black. In their wake, they left nightmares, and along the coast the Free Fishermen of Harrington Inlet tossed in their beds, waking upon sweat-dampened pallets to their wives' worried faces and the cries of fretful children.

It made Ushahin smile.

But there was bigger game afoot. Casting his nets, he caught Men's dreams in a seine, sifting through them. Behind him, yes. Behind him was that which was known, Aracus Altorus and his com-

pany, riding hot toward the west. Ellylon blood and Ellylon pride
ran high and hot, as did that of the Men of Curonan. Still, they
would not dare to cross the Delta. Their thoughts veered away
from it, filled with fear. They would lose time crossing open water
rather than chance the Delta. Thinking of Calanthrag the Eldest,
who dwelled in its heart, Ushahin smiled again. He spared a moment's hate for Aracus Altorus, who had won a bitter victory from
the Were. He spared a moment's pity for the Sorceress of Beshtanag, doomed to rot in mortal flesh. He spared a moment's curiosity for Blaise Caveros, who so resembled his ancestor, Tanaros.

Then, he gazed ahead.

To Meronil, he did not dare look. Ingolin the Wise kept its
boundaries with care, maintaining all that remained of the old Ellyl
magics, and even Ushahin Dreamspinner dared not walk the
dreams of the Ellylon who dwelt within. But before Meronil was
Seahold, a keep of Men, and north of Seahold lay the fertile territories of the Midlands.

There, rumor stalked.

It came from the north; from the mountains of Staccia, winding
its way in a whisper of thought, passed from lip to ear. Curious,
Ushahin followed it to its source, tracing its path through the
mountains, back to the ancient battlefield of Neherinach, where a
node-point of the Marasoumië lay dead and buried. Dead, yes, but
no longer buried. The node-point lay raw and exposed, granite
cooling in the northern sun. Something had disturbed it, blasting it
from the very earth.

The *Galäinridder.*

Such was the word in the Staccian tongue; such was the image
that disturbed their dreams, filtering its way from the mountains to
the plains, distant as a dream. A rider, a warrior; the Shining Paladin, who rode upon a horse as white as the foam on the crest of a
wave. Although his hands were empty, brightness blazed from his
robes and the clear gem upon his breast, which shone like a star.
His beard crackled with lightning, and power hung in every syllable of the terrible words he spoke, catching their consciences and
playing on their fears of Haomane's Wrath.

Ushahin frowned.

What he had found, he did not like; what he had failed to find,
he liked less. Where, in all of this, was the Bearer? A little Charred
lad, accompanied only by his mortal kin. He should have been
easy to find, his terrors setting the world of dreams ablaze. Only
Malthus' power had protected him, enfolding him in a veil. If the

Counselor were truly trapped in the dying Marasoumië, his power should be failing, exposing the Bearer. Yet . . . it was not.

"Malthus," Ushahin whispered. *"Galäinridder."*

East of Seahold, his thoughts turned. Was it Haomane's Counselor they feared? He would give them something better to fear, the grief of their mortal guilt, come back to turn their dreams into nightmares. Ushahin's lips twisted into the bitter semblance of a smile. Were Arahila's Children so sure of *right* and *wrong?* So. Let their nights be filled with mismatched eyes and shattered bone, the terrible sight of a rock held in a child's fist, descending in a crushing blow.

Let them awake in the cold sweat of terror, and wonder *why*.

The flying wedge of ravens altered its course, forging a new path through the twilight, in the borderlands between waking and sleeping. One heel nudged his mount's flank, the rope rein of the hackamore lying against a foam-flecked neck. Obedient, the bloodbay swerved; obedient, the riderless horses followed, shadowing his course.

Together, they plunged into the Midlands.

"THEY ARE COMING, VORAX."

"Very good, my Lord." If he had thought it hot in the Throne Hall, it was nothing to the Chamber of the Font. Sweat trickled down his brow, stinging the half-healed blisters he had sustained in the burning rain. Vorax swiped at it with a gauntleted hand, which only made it worse.

"Do you hear me?" Lord Satoris, pacing the perimeter of the Font, gave him a deep look. "Ushahin Dreamspinner comes. Tanaros Blacksword comes. It is only a matter of time. My Three shall be together once more, and then my Elder Brother's Allies shall tremble."

"Aye, my Lord." He tugged his jeweled gorget, wishing he were not wearing ceremonial armor. It would have been better to meet in the Throne Hall. At least his Lordship had not donned the Helm of Shadows. It sat in its niche on the wall, the empty eyeholes measuring his fear. He was glad nothing worse filled it, and glad he had not had to wear it himself since the day Satoris had destroyed the Marasoumië. Still, it stank of his Lordship's unhealing wound in the Chamber, a copper-sweet tang, thick and cloying, and Vorax wished he were elsewhere. "As you say. I welcome their return. Is there something you wish me to do in preparation?"

"No." Lord Satoris halted, staring into the coruscating heart of the Font. His massive hands, hanging empty at his sides, twitched as if to pluck Godslayer from its blue-white fire. "What news," he asked, "from Staccia?"

Vorax shook his head, droplets of sweat flying. "No news."

"So," the Shaper said. His head bowed and his fingertips twitched. But for that, he stood motionless, contemplating the Shard. Dark ichor gleaming on one thigh, seeping downward in a slow rill to pool on the flagstones. "No news."

"No news," Vorax echoed, feeling a strange twinge in his branded heart. "I'm sorry, my Lord, but I'm sure naught is amiss. It will take some time, finding a pair of errant mortals in all of the northlands. We expected no less." He paused. "Shall I send another company? Do you wish me to lead one myself? I am willing, of course."

"I . . . no." Lord Satoris shook his head, frowning. "I cannot spare you, Vorax. Not now. When Tanaros returns . . . perhaps. And yet, I am disturbed. There is . . . something. A bright mist clouds my vision. I do not know what it means."

Vorax scratched at his beard. "Have you . . . ?" He nodded at Godslayer.

"Yes." The Shaper's frown deepened, and he continued to gaze fixedly at the dagger, hanging pulsing and rubescent in the midst of the blazing Font. "To no avail. If something has passed elsewhere in Urulat, it is a thing not even the Souma may show me. And I am troubled by this. Godslayer has never failed me, when I dared invoke its powers in full. Not upon Urulat's soil."

"Break it," Vorax shrugged. "Maybe it's time. It would solve a lot of problems."

The words were out of his mouth before he knew he meant to speak them. In the brief, shocked silence that ensued, he knew it for a mistake. Certain things that might be thought should never be spoken aloud, not even by one of the Three.

"*What?*" Lord Satoris' head rose, and he seemed to gather height and mass in the sweltering Chamber. He took a step forward, hands clenching. The flagstones shuddered under his feet. Overhead, massive beams creaked. Shadows roiled around Satoris' shoulders and red fury lit his eyes. "*WHAT?*"

"My Lord!" He backed across the Chamber and raised his gauntleted hands; half pleading, half placating. "Forgive me! I am thinking of us, of all of us . . . of you, my Lord! If Godslayer were shattered, if it were rendered into harmless pieces . . . why, it would no longer be a threat, and . . . and the Prophecy itself couldn't be fulfilled!"

"Do you think so?" The Shaper advanced, step by thunderous step.

"I, no . . . aye, my Lord!" Vorax felt the edge of a stair against his heel, and retreated up one spiraling step, then another, and another. He was sweating under his armor, sweat running in rivulets. "It could be like the Soumanië!" he breathed, clutching at the idea. "A piece for each of us, for each of the Three, and we could wield them in your defense, aye; and the largest one for you, of course! We would have more than they, yet no piece keen nor large enough, no dagger left to, to . . . " His words trailed off as Lord Satoris reached the base of the stair, leaning forward and planting his enormous hands on either side of it. His dark face was on a level with Vorax's, eyes blazing like embers. The reek of his blood hung heavy in the close air.

"To slay a Shaper," Lord Satoris said. "Is that it? Only pieces, broken pieces of the Souma. Is that what you propose, my Staccian?"

"Aye!" Vorax almost laughed with relief, wiping his brow. "Aye, my Lord."

"*Fool!*"

For a long moment, his Lordship's eyes glared into his, measuring the breadth and depth of his loyalty. A miasma of heat emanated from his body, as if Haomane's Wrath still scorched him. It seemed like an eternity before the Shaper turned away, pacing back toward the Font. When he did, Vorax sagged on the spiral stairway, damp and exhausted.

"It is Godslayer that keeps my Elder Brother at bay," Satoris said without looking at him. "Have you never grasped that, Staccian? *Because* it is capable of slaying a Shaper. That which renders me vulnerable is the shield that protects all of Darkhaven. Without it, Haomane would have no *need* to work through Prophecy, using mortal hands as his weapons." His voice held a grim tone. "Do you think the gap that Sunders our world is so vast? It is nothing. The Lord-of-Thought could abandon Torath and cross it in an instant, bringing all of my siblings with him onto Urulat's soil. But he will not," he added, reaching one open hand into the Font to let the blue-white flames of the marrow-fire caress it, "nor will they, while I hold *this*."

His hand closed on Godslayer's hilt. Vorax's heart convulsed within its brand, sending a shock of ecstatic pain through his flesh.

Halfway up the winding stair, he went heavily to one knee, feeling the bruising impact through his armor. "Aye, my Lord," he said dully. "I am a fool."

"Yes," Satoris murmured, contemplating the dagger. "But a loyal one, or so I judge." He released the hilt, leaving the Shard in the Font. "Ah, Haomane!" he mused. "Would I slay you if I had the chance? Or would I sue for peace, if I held the dagger at your throat? It has been so long, so long. I do not even know myself." Remembering Vorax, he glanced over his shoulder. "Begone," he said. "I will speak to you anon, my Staccian. When my Three are united."

"Aye, my Lord." He clambered to his feet with difficulty, and bowed. "I will await your pleasure." There was no response. Vorax grunted with relief and turned around, making his way up the spiral stair. He kept one gauntleted hand on the glimmering onyx wall, steadying himself until he reached the three-fold door at the top of the stair.

Which way? The Staccian hesitated. The door to the right was *his* door, leading through the back passages of Darkhaven to his own quarters. He thought of them with longing; of their rich appointments, booty gained by right of spoil over the centuries. All his things were there, all his luxuries.

No. It was too soon. He stank of fear and dripped with sweat under his armor, and he did not want to bring it into his quarters. That had been a bad misstep in the Chamber. He needed to walk the back ways, to clear his mind and temper his heat.

There was the middle door; Tanaros' door.

No. He did not wish to meet Tanaros Blacksword's Fjel guards upon emergence, and watch their nostrils widen at his stink. Not now.

Vorax laid his gauntleted hand upon the left door, Ushahin's door. Recognizing his touch as one of the Three, the veins of marrow-fire within it brightened. It swung open, then closed behind him as he stepped through it, sealing without a trace.

The air was markedly cooler, and he breathed it in with gratitude, letting his eyes adjust to new darkness. Only a faint trace of the marrow-fire lit his way, veins buried deep in the walls. Sounds filled the dark corridors; Ushahin's madlings, scratching, babbling, scrambling. Vorax smiled, setting out in the direction of the sounds.

The Dreamspinner's folk understood fear. They would forgive.

How many years had it been since he had ventured into Ushahin's passageways? He could not remember. Ten? More like fifty, or a hundred even. There had been no cause, during the long years of peace; or neutrality, which passed for peace. While Haomane's Allies sulked and left Lord Satoris unmolested, the Three tended to their separate ways, keeping Darkhaven's affairs in order. Vorax limped on his bruised knee and counted his strides, one hand hovering over his hilt. At a hundred paces, the corridor forked. He paused, listening, then took the right fork.

It forked, again and again.

Vorax followed the voices.

It was the Fjel who had built Darkhaven, in accordance with his Lordship's design; but these passages were not built to a Fjel's scale. They were behind the walls, the province of rats and scuttling madlings. Rats, Vorax had expected. He was amazed at the progress Ushahin's madlings had made; widening breaches in the masonry to open connections between passages where none were meant to exist, forging exits and entrances where none were intended. There was no danger to his Lordship, of course; no madling would touch dare the three-fold door and risk his wrath. Still, it made him uneasy to think how extensively they had penetrated the fortress. He wondered if Ushahin knew.

At one point he encountered a deep chasm in a passageway, and had to sidle across the verge of it on his heels, both hands outflung to grasp the dimly veined walls, toes hanging out over empty nothingness. His knees creaked with the effort of balancing. Pausing to steady his nerves, Vorax looked down, gazing past his boot-tips. Dry heat blasted upward in a column.

The chasm went down and down, deeper than a mineshaft. Somewhere, far below, was a flickering light cast by blue-white flames and a roar like that of a distant forest fire, or dragons. Vorax shuddered, and edged clear of the chasm, back onto solid ground. That was no work of madlings. He wondered what fault in Darkhaven's foundation had permitted the chasm to open. It was as close as any man should get to the Source; and a far sight closer than any Staccian ought. He'd had enough infernal heat to last him an immortal lifetime. It was *cool* in Staccia.

Betimes, he missed it.

Perhaps, when this latest threat had passed, it would be time to consider passing on his mantle. To retire to a pleasant estate, where the sun shone in a blue sky over a white, wintery landscape, and the wolf tracked the hare through new-fallen snow. He could continue his duties in Staccia, binding the earls and barons in fealty, negotiating lines of supply and men for Darkhaven, negotiating the companionship of their pretty younger daughters for himself, spinning out his days in soft, blissful comfort, freed from the constraints of his vow-branded flesh to age his way into easeful death, pillowing his head in the laps of Staccian maidens. It was not a bad idea, after all, to have a presence in Staccia. It had been too long since he had made himself *known* there.

The path took an upward turn. Trudging doggedly up the steep incline, he tried to imagine if his Lordship would ever agree to such a thing. He rather thought not. After all, Staccia's very peace and prosperity were dependent upon the bargain Vorax had struck with his Lordship so many years ago. He had not imagined, then, that there could ever come a day when immortality would become burdensome.

Ah, well. It was a pleasant thought.

Ahead, voices echoed; a madlings' clamor, but with something else running through it, a single voice like a silver thread. The incline had ended at last, the path level beneath his feet. Frowning, Vorax quickened his stride. There was light ahead; not marrow-fire, but candlelight, warm and golden. Through a narrowing passage, he glimpsed it. He picked his way with care, easing shoulder-first into the gap. His armor scraped along the rocks, getting scratched and dented in the process.

Unexpectedly, the passage widened.

Vorax stumbled into open space, catching himself. It was a rough-hewn chamber, a natural space vastened by the efforts of a hundred generations chipping at the stone walls. Everywhere, buttends of tallow candles burned, wedged into every available niche and crevice. Scraps and oddments of carpet covered the floor, and the walls were covered with scratched messages; some legible, most a garble of words. There must have been a dozen madlings gathered, light glimmering from their eyes. All of them whispered, hissing and muttering to one another.

One was kneeling before the figure who stood in the center of the chamber, grimy fingers plucking at the hem of her blue robe as he raised a face filled with hope. "Me?" he said. "Me? Lady see me?"

The Lady Cerelinde bent her head, cupping the madling's face with both hands. Her hair spilled forward, shimmering in the candlelight, veiling her features. "Ludo," she said softly, her silvery voice ringing. "You were a wheelwright's son. I see you, Ludo. I see what might have been. I see you with a plump wife, smiling, and laughing children chasing one another in your father's yard."

"Lady!" He gasped the word, face shining and distorted with tears, and rocked back and forth, wringing the hem of her robe. "Lady, Lady, yes!"

Cerelinde released him with a gentle smile, lifted her head—and froze.

The madlings wailed in chorus.

"Lady." Vorax took a further step into the chamber, his sword rasping free of its scabbard. He met her oddly fearless gaze, and the blood seemed to sing in his veins, a high-pitched tone ringing in his head. He raised the blade, angling it for a solid blow, watching her expose the vulnerable column of her throat as her gaze followed the sword. His voice, when he spoke, sounded strange to his ears. "What is it you do in this place?"

"I might ask you the same," she said calmly. "Do you desire a glimpse of *what might have been*, Lord Vorax? It is a small magic, one of the few which the Rivenlost are afforded, but I am willing to share it. All you must do is consent in your heart to know."

He gritted his teeth. "That, I do not."

"So." She watched the candlelight reflecting on the edge of his sword. "I do not blame you, given what you have chosen. They do. It gives them comfort to know, poor broken creatures that they are. Is there harm in it, my Lord? Have I trespassed? I was brought to this place."

"Who—?"

"Get out!" From the shadows a figure flung itself at him, wild-eyed, arms windmilling. Astonished, Vorax put up his sword, taking a step backward. He had a brief impression of sallow features beneath a mat of tangled hair. "Get out!" the madling shrilled, flailing at him. *"You* brought her here, but this is *our* place! *Ours!* Get out!"

Catching her thin wrists in one gauntleted hand, he held her at bay. It took a moment to put a name to her, but he had seen her before; one of Tanaros' favorites, or one who favored him. There was no telling, with madlings. "Meara," he said. "What do you do here? *Why?"*

She sagged in his grasp, then twisted to scowl at him through her dark, matted hair. "We batter our hearts, my lord, against the specter of what might have been. Don't you see?" There were tears in her eyes, at odds with her expression. "I warned him, my lord," she said. "I did. I tried to tell him. But he didn't want to know, so he left, and Ushahin left, and we were left alone. Isn't it clear?"

"No." Vorax released his grasp, letting her crumple on the

chamber floor. "No," he said again, "it's not." He eyed them; Meara, her face averted, the lad Ludo, weeping. Others wept, too. Only the Lady Cerelinde stood, dry-eyed. "Listen," he said to the madlings. "This place, all places, belong to Lord Satoris. What might have been . . . is not. Do you understand?"

Wails of assent arose in answer. One of the madlings was banging his head against an outcropping of rock, bloodying his forehead. "His blood!" he moaned. "His Lordship's blood!"

"Aye." Vorax gave them a hard look. "That which he shed to defend us all, and sheds every minute of every day in suffering. Do you disdain it?" They wailed denial. "Good," he said. "Because Ushahin Dreamspinner, who is your master, returns anon. And, too, there will come Tanaros Blacksword, who makes his way home even now. Do you wish them to find you weeping over *what might have been?*"

Perhaps it was the right thing to say; who could tell, with madlings? They dispersed, wailing, into the passageways of Darkhaven. Only Meara and the Ellyl woman were left, the one still huddled, the other still standing.

Vorax exhaled hard, dragging his arm across his brow, and sheathed his sword. "Meara," he said conversationally, "I suggest you return the Lady to her chambers, and do not allow her to venture out again unless his Lordship summons her. If I find you here again, I will not hesitate to strike. And if you think my mercy is cruel, remember what Ushahin Dreamspinner might do to her. He has no love for her kind."

"Aye, my lord." Meara stood sullenly, plucking at Cerelinde's sleeve.

The Lady of the Ellylon stood unmoving. "General Tanaros is coming?"

"Aye."

There was a change; a subtle one. She did not move, and even her lids did not flicker. Yet beneath her fair skin, a faint blush arose, tinting her cheeks. Something knotted in Vorax's belly, and he stepped into her space, crowding her with his bulk.

"Lady," he said softly. *"Leave him be."*

Her chin rose a fraction. "You were the one to offer me Lord Satoris' hospitality, my lord Glutton. Will you break it and be foresworn?"

"I would have slain you the instant Beshtanag fell." He watched fear seep into her luminous gaze, and favored her with a grim smile. "Make no mistake, Lady. Neither hatred nor madness drives me, and I know where the margin of profit lies. If his Lordship heeded me, you would be dead." He drew his sword a few inches clear of the scabbard, adding, "I may do it yet."

"You wouldn't dare!" Her eyes blazed with terrible beauty. "Aracus—"

"Aracus!" Vorax laughed, shoving the hilt back in place. "Oh, Lady, whatever happens, we've ages of time here behind the walls of Darkhaven before the Son of Altorus becomes a problem. No, if you want to invoke a protector, I suggest you stick with his Lordship. And mind, if I find you plying Tanaros with Ellylon glamours and magics, I *will* see you dead."

The Lady Cerelinde made no answer.

"Good." Vorax nodded. "Get her out of here, Meara, and do not bring her again. Mind, I will be speaking to the Dreamspinner."

He watched them go, the madling leading, tugging at the Ellyl's sleeve. The sight did nothing to dispel the knotted, sinking feeling in his belly. It was providence that had made him choose the left-hand door, alerting him to untold danger. On the morrow he would assemble a patrol of his own men to scour the passages behind the walls, sealing off the madlings' secret corridors, or as many as they could find. Something was wrong within the edifice of Darkhaven, crumbling even as the chasm had opened in the floor under his feet. He remembered the moon-garden by half-light, a shining figure beneath the stars, the heady scent of vulnus-blossom mingling with sulfur in the damp air, evoking painful memory.

Lord Vorax, what do you see?

Vorax shook his head and blew out the candle-butts. By the glimmer of the marrow-fire he pressed onward, leaving the chamber behind and picking his path through the tangled maze of narrow passages until he reached an egress. It was a sanctioned door, opening to his touch behind a niche in one of Darkhaven's major hallways. One of the Havenguard snapped to attention as he emerged; a Mørkhar Fjel, axe springing into one hand, shield raising, dark bristles prickling erect. "Lord Vorax, sir!"

"At ease," he sighed.

The Mørkhar stared straight ahead. Ignoring him, Vorax made his way down the towering halls, limping steadily back to his own quarters. It was a blessed relief to reach the tall ironwood doors, carved with the twin likenesses of a roaring Staccian bear, and a pair of his own Staccian guardsmen lounging against them. The fear-sweat had dried to a rime beneath his armor, and he was only tired, now. Beyond those doors lay comfort and easement. His belly rumbled at the thought of it.

"Let me in, Eadric."

"Aye, sir!" The senior guardsman grinned, fumbling at his belt for a key. "Good ease to you, sir!"

The tall ironwood doors swung open, and Vorax entered his quarters. Within, it was another world, rich and luxuriant, far removed from everything in Darkhaven; the stark grandeur of its halls, the fearful heat of the Chamber of the Font, the scrabbling mysteries behind its walls. Lamplight warmed rich tapestries, gleamed upon gilded statuary, sparkled on jewel-encrusted surfaces. He had had ten mortal lifetimes to amass the treasures contained within his quarters. Somewhere, music was playing. It paused as he entered, then resumed, the harpist bowing her head over the ivory-inlaid curve of her instrument, fingers caressing the strings. Three Staccian handmaids rose to their feet, surrounding him with solicitous care, their deft fingers unbuckling his ceremonial armor.

"My lord, you are weary!"

"My lord, you must rest!"

"My lord, you must eat!"

It was not, after all, so much to ask. For a thousand years he had guaranteed the safety of their nation. In the bathing-room, Vorax let them strip him and stood while they brought warm water and sponged the stink of sweat and fear from his skin. Water ran in rivulets, coursing through the ruddy hair on his chest, over the bulge of his stomach, down the thick columns of his legs. Their hands were gentle. They understood his needs and were paid well for their terms of service, their families recompensed in titles, lands and money. Did a man deserve any less, after a thousand years?

They robed him and led him, gently, to his great ironwood chair. It, too, was carved in the likeness of a bear. That had been his family's insignia, once. Now it was his, and his alone. He sank into it, into the familiar curves, the ironwood having conformed over long centuries of wear to his own shape. One of his handmaids fetched a pitcher of Vedasian wine, pouring him a brimming goblet. He quaffed half at a gulp, while another handmaid hurried to the door, her soft voice ordering a message relayed to the kitchen. A meal in nine courses, including soup to whet his appetite, a brace of pigeon, a whole rack of lamb, grilled turbot, a cheese course and sweets to follow. His belly growled plaintively at the prospect. This day called for sustenance on a grand scale. He drank off the rest of the goblet's contents, held it out to be refilled, and drank again. Warmth spread throughout him from within. The wine began to ease his stiff joints, rendering the throbbing bruise on his knee a distant ache. His free arm lay in magisterial repose over the top of the chair's, fingers curling into the bear's paws. His feet were propped on soft cushions. He groaned as another of his handmaids knelt, kneading his stockinged soles with her thumbs.

"Is it good, my lord?" Her blue-grey eyes gazed up at him. There was a spattering of freckles over the bridge of her nose. They would have been innocent, those eyes, save for a reflection of gold coin held cunning in their depths. The youngest daughter of a Staccian lordling, she knew where her family's margin of profit lay. "Your supper will arrive anon."

"Aye," he said gently, thinking of the Lady Cerelinde's blush, of her terrible beauty, and the scent of vulnus-blossom. Some things were better measured in coin. "'Tis good, sweetling."

A scratch at the door announced the arrival of his supper. Vorax inhaled deeply as the dishes were uncovered and the savory aroma of food filled his quarters. His Staccian handmaids helped him to the table, filled to groaning with his repast. They brought the wine-pitcher, placing his goblet in easy reach. Eyeing the repast, he selected a bowl of consommé and raised it to his lips with both hands.

It would take a mountain of food to ease the memory of his misstep in the Chamber, of Lord Satoris' anger, of the silence out of Staccia, of the madlings' gathering, of the Lady of the Ellylon's presence among them, and above all, of that gaping chasm in the secret heart of Darkhaven.

Drinking deep from the bowl, Vorax began.

"GO, LADY, GO!" MEARA ACTUALLY shoved her from behind, then snatched her hands back as if the touch burned. Caught unawares, Cerelinde stumbled over the threshold of the hidden door, pushing the heavy tapestry aside to enter her quarters.

It was blessedly quiet within.

She sat on the edge of her bed, willing her heartbeat to slow, remembering candlelight reflecting from the edge of Vorax's sword and meditating upon the nearness of death. This must be, she thought, the way warriors felt in the aftermath of battle; a strange mix of latent terror and exhilaration. Meara paced the boundaries of the room, peering anxiously into every corner. Where she trod upon the soft carpets, the scent of bruised heart-grass followed in a ghostly reminder of the Ellylon weavers who had woven them long ago.

"It is safe," she pronounced at length. "No one is here."

"That is well." Her calm restored, Cerelinde inclined her head. "Forgive me, Meara. Perhaps the venture was ill-advised. I would not wish any of you to be placed in danger."

The madling shot her a glance. "He's right, you know. Lord Vorax is. You should leave the Lord General alone. There's nothing but death in it, death and blood and more madness. You should leave *us* alone. Why don't you? Why did he have to bring you here?"

"Meara." She spread her hands, helpless. "To that, I cannot speak. You know I am a hostage here. It is a small gift, a small kindness. You asked me to share it. Since it is all I have to offer, I did."

"I know." Meara hunkered at the foot of the bed. "Aye, I know, I did. We are the broken ones, we who want to know. They should not have left us, and they should not have brought you. They should have known better, and you should never have shown me kindness, no." She gnawed on her thumbnail, then asked abruptly, "Lady, what would you have seen for Lord Vorax? Would you have shown him what the shape of Urulat would be if he had chosen elsewhere?"

"No." Cerelinde shook her head. "A glimpse of the life he might have had, nothing more; a life that would have ended long, long ago. More than that, I cannot say. We are only afforded a faint glimpse, Meara, beyond the greatest of branchings in a single life. It is a small gift, truly."

"*Why?*"

She gazed at the madling with sorrow and compassion. "We are Rivenlost, Meara. We were left behind upon the shores of Urulat, while the Bright Ones, those among his Children whom Haomane held dearest, dwell beside him upon the crown of Torath. In curiosity, in innocent desire, those of us who are the Rivenlost wandered too far from Haomane's side, and we were stranded when the world was Sundered. This small gift was won in bitter hours, when the eldest among us wondered and sought to pierce the veil. What if we had been more diligent? What if we had stood at the Lord-of-Thought's side during the Sundering? It has been passed down, this gift. We, too, batter our hearts against *what might have been*."

"What do you see?" Meara whispered.

"Brightness." Cerelinde smiled, glancing westward. "Brightness, and joy."

"So." Squatting, Meara wrapped both arms about her knees and tucked her chin into her chest, hiding her face. "You cannot see the *small* might-haves."

"No." She thought, with regret, of a myriad small might-have-beens. What if she had consented to wed Aracus in the sturdy mortal confines of Seahold? What if Aracus had consented to their wedding vows being held in the warded halls of Meronil, under the aegis of Ingolin the Wise? What if . . . *what if* . . . she had never agreed to wed him at all? "I would that I could, Meara. But, no. The tapestry is too vast, and there are too many threads woven into it. Pluck at a small one, and others unravel. Only Haomane the Lord-of-Thought is vouchsafed that knowledge."

Meara tilted her head. Her eyes, peering through a thicket of hair, held a cunning gleam. "What about his Lordship?"

"Lord . . . Satoris?" Without thinking, Cerelinde stiffened. In memory's eye, she saw the Shaper's form blotting out the stars, the shadow of his extended hand lying stark and black on the desiccated grass of the moon-garden, patiently proffered for her inevitable refusal.

"Aye." Meara nodded sharply.

Cerelinde shook her head. "He is a Shaper. He is beyond my ken."

"There was a . . . what do you call it? A great branching." Studying the floor, Meara plucked at the carpet, then sniffed at the sweet odor of heart-grass on her fingertips. "When he refused, three times, to withdraw his Gift from Arahila's Children." Her sharp chin pointed upward, eyes glancing. "What might have been, had he not? You could see *that* for him."

A chill ran the length of Cerelinde's spine. "I do not think," she said gently, "his Lordship would consent to seek this knowledge."

"You could ask." Meara straightened abruptly, tossing back her hair. "It would be interesting to know, since *some* of Arahila's Children disdain it. His Lordship's Gift, that is. Which is odd, since it is all they have that *you* do not; and all I do, too. I do, you know." Placing her hands on her hips, she fixed the Lady of the Ellylon with a disconcerting stare. "I will go now. Thank you, for what you did. It meant very much to some people. I am sorry to have placed you in danger, but I do not think Lord Vorax will kill you. Not yet, anyway."

"Good," Cerelinde said simply, staring back.

When the madling had gone, Cerelinde buried her face in her hands and took a deep, shuddering breath. When all was said and done, there was too much here beyond her comprehension. She had been grateful for Meara's request. She had hoped, in sharing this small gift, to bring a measure of compassion to the stark halls of Darkhaven, to the meager lives of those who dwelled within its walls. It had seemed a kindness, a simple kindness, to offer comfort in lieu of the healing she could not effect.

Now, she was not so sure.

Seeking comfort of her own, she thought of Aracus, and tried to imagine his understanding. There was nothing there, only the memory of his gaze, wide-set and demanding, stirring her blood in unaccustomed ways, filling her with hope and pride and the dream of the Prophecy fulfilled.

In this place, it seemed very far away.

She thought of Tanaros instead, and remembered the old madling woman Sharit they had met in the halls of Darkhaven, and how gently he had taken her hand; how proudly she had stood, gripping it tight. Whatever had passed here this day, Tanaros would understand it.

He was not what she would have expected him to be, at once both less and more. Less terrifying; a Man, not a monster. And yet he was more than a Man. Immortal, as Aracus was not. Like the El-lylon, he understood the scope of ages.

Cerelinde wondered what he had been like, so long ago, as a mortal Man. Not so different, perhaps, from Aracus. After all, Tanaros was related by ties of distant kinship and fosterage to the House of Altorus. He must have been as close to his liege-lord as Blaise Caveros was to Aracus. Had he been as fiercely loyal? Yes, she thought, he must have been. The betrayal would not have wounded him so deeply if he were not.

He must have loved his wife, too. What manner of passion had led her to commit such a grievous betrayal? She thought about Aracus, and the quick, hot drive that blazed within him. And she thought about Tanaros, steady and calm, despite the ancient, aching grief that lay behind his dark gaze. Though he was her enemy, he treated her with unfailing courtesy. She did not know the answer.

He was coming.

They were all coming. Vorax the Glutton's words had confirmed it. Somewhere, in the world beyond Darkhaven's walls, the tides of fate had shifted. Beshtanag had fallen. Tanaros Kingslayer and Ushahin the Misbegotten were on their way, soon to reunite the Three. And on their heels would be Aracus Altorus, the Border-guard and her kinsmen in his train, intent on storming Darkhaven.

She was the Lady of the Ellylon and his betrothed, the key to fulfilling Haomane's Prophecy. They would not relent until she was freed or the plains of Curonan were churned to red mud with the last of their dying blood.

And Lord Satoris in his immortal pride and folly would revel in it.

Death was the only certainty. Whatever else transpired, the ravens of Darkhaven would feast on the flesh of foes and allies alike. The thought of it made her shudder to the bone. The hand of Haomane's Prophecy hovered over her, a bright and terrible shadow, filled with the twinned promise of hope and bloodshed. Although she wished it otherwise, she could see, now, how they were intertwined.

All things were as they must be. Light and dark, bound together in an inextricable battle. The paths that led them here were begin-ning to narrow. Soon, it would not matter *what might have been.* Only what *was.*

She was afraid, and weary of being alone with her fear.

Hurry, Cerelinde prayed. *Oh, hurry!*

And she was no longer sure, in that moment, to whom or for what she prayed.

Of all the things that had befallen her in Darkhaven, this was surely the most fearful.

GODSLAYER

ONE

ALL THINGS CONVERGE.

In the last Great Age of the Sundered World of Urulat, which was once called Uru-Alat after the World God that gave birth to it, they began to converge upon Darkhaven.

It began with a red star rising in the west; Dergail's Soumanië, a polished stone that had once been a chip of the Souma itself—that mighty gem that rested on the sundered isle of Torath, the Eye in the Brow of Uru-Alat, source of the Shapers' power.

Satoris the Shaper took it for a warning, a message from a sister who had loved him, once upon a time; Arahila the Fair, whose children were the race of Men. His enemies took it as a declaration of war.

Whatever the truth, war ensued.

Haomane, First-Born among Shapers, long ago uttered a Prophecy.

"When the unknown is made known, when the lost weapon is found, when the marrow-fire is quenched and Godslayer is freed, when a daughter of Elterrion weds a son of Altorus, when the Spear of Light is brought forth and the Helm of Shadows is broken, the Fjeltroll shall fall, the Were shall be defeated ere they rise, and the Sunderer shall be no more, the Souma shall be restored and the Sundered World made whole and Haomane's Children shall endure."

It began with the rising of Dergail's Soumanië. Cerelinde, the Lady of the Ellylon, a daughter of Elterrion's line, plighted her troth to Aracus Altorus. It was the first step toward fulfilling Haomane's Prophecy; Arahila's Children and Haomane's conjoined, their lines inextricably mingled. But in Lindanen Dale, their nuptials were disrupted.

Bloodshed ensued.

It was a trap; a trap that went awry. It seemed at first that all the pieces fell into place. Driven by vengeance, the Grey Dam of the Were spent her life in an attack, and the half-breed Ushahin Dreamspinner unleashed madness and illusion. Under its cover, Tanaros Blacksword abducted the Lady Cerelinde and took her to Darkhaven.

Haomane's Allies were misled. Pursuing a rumor of dragons, under the command of Aracus Altorus, they raised an army and launched an assault on Beshtanag and Lilias, Sorceress of the East. And there the trap went awry. The Ways were closed, and the Army of Darkhaven was turned back, their company's leadership scattered. In Beshtanag, Haomane's Allies took to the field.

There, they prevailed.

They were not supposed to do so.

They were coming; all of them.

They came on foot and on horseback and by sailing ship, for the Ways of the Marasoumië had been destroyed. Lord Satoris had done this in his wrath. The Dragon of Beshtanag was no more, slain by the Arrow of Fire; the lost weapon, found. Bereft of her Soumanië, the Sorceress of the East was nothing more than an ordinary woman; Lilias, mortal and powerless. The Were had struck a bitter bargain with Aracus Altorus, ceding to his terms; defeated ere they rose. Aracus was coming, his heart filled with righteous fury, knowing he had been duped.

Malthus the Wise Counselor, trapped in the Ways, had vanished beyond the sight of even Godslayer itself . . . but rumor whispered of a new figure. The Galäinridder, the Bright Rider, whose words bred fear in the hearts of Men, inspiring them to betray their ancient oaths to Lord Satoris.

But Haomane's Allies had not won yet.

On the westernmost verge of the Unknown Desert, Tanaros Blacksword, Commander General of the Army of Darkhaven, made camp alongside a creek. There he slaked the thirst of his long-parched flesh and made ready to rally his surviving troops and set his face toward home. Immortal though he was, he could have died in the desert. Thanks to a raven's gratitude, he lived.

When he dreamed, he dreamed of the Lady Cerelinde.

On the back of a blood-bay horse, Ushahin Dreamspinner rode the pathways between waking and dreaming, plunging into the

Midlands and leaving a trail of nightmares in his wake. A wedge of ravens forged his path, and on either side, a riderless horse flanked him; one a spectral grey, the other as black as coal.

If he had dreamed, which he did not, he would dream of the counsel of dragons.

Vorax the Glutton, muttering over his stores, awaited them in Darkhaven.

The immortal Three were soon to be reunited.

Haomane's Prophecy was yet to be fulfilled.

In the mighty fortress of Darkhaven, where the Lady Cerelinde endured imprisonment and fought against a rising tide of doubt, the marrow-fire yet burned. Within it hung the dagger, Godslayer; ruby-red, a Shard of the Souma. Once, it had wounded Satoris; the wound that would not heal. Godslayer alone could end a Shaper's life; the life of Lord Satoris, the life of any of the Shapers. And while the marrow-fire burned, no mortal hand could touch it. None but a Shaper would dare.

Only the Water of Life, drawn from the Well of the World, could extinguish the marrow-fire. The Water had been drawn, but its Bearer was lost.

Thrust out of the Ways by Malthus the Counselor in a desperate gambit, abandoned and lost, Dani of the Yarru wandered the cold lands of the Northern Harrow, deep in Fjeltroll territory, with only his uncle to guide him. Together, they sought to follow the rivers, the lifeblood of Urulat, to Darkhaven.

And they, too, were being hunted. . . .

Led by Skragdal of the Tungskulder, the Fjel were on the hunt. Their loyalty to Lord Satoris was beyond question. Haomane's Prophecy promised them nothing but death. No matter where it led them, they would not abandon their quest. They would succeed or die trying.

All things converge.

NEHERINACH WAS A GREEN BOWL cradled in the mountain's hands. Here and there, small boulders breached its surface; elsewhere, a half dozen small hillocks arose, covered in flowering ivy. A small river, spring-fed, wound through the center of it, meandering westward to sink belowground. Low mountains, sloping upward with a deceptively gentle grade, surrounded it. Patches of gorse offered grazing to fallow deer, shelter to hare that crouched in the shadow of small crags.

It was a peaceful place, and a terrible one.

On the verges, the Kaldjager scouts waited, glancing sidelong out of yellow eyes to watch the others' straggling progress. Skragdal, leading them, knew what the Kaldjager felt. This was where it had begun.

They assembled in silence on the field of Neherinach. The green grass was soft beneath their feet. Water sparkled under the bright sun. Birds stirred in the trees, insects took flight from grass stems.

"Come," Skragdal said quietly.

They crossed the field together, and the grass flattened beneath their approach, springing back once they had passed. It smelled clean and sweet. Skragdal felt his talons breach the surface of the soil beneath, rich and crumbling. It filled him with an ancient fury. There was old blood in that soil. Thousand upon thousand of Fjel had died in this place, fighting without weapons against a vast army of Men and Ellylon, attacked without quarter for the crime of giving shelter to the wounded Shaper who had taught them the measure of their own worth. The ivy-covered hillocks that dotted the field marked the cairns of Fjel dead; one for each of the six tribes.

In the end, they had won; by treachery and stealth, according to the songs of Haomane's Allies. It was true, they had laid traps, but what was treachery to a people invaded without provocation? It had been a bitter victory.

Near the riverbank, where the ground was soft enough to hold an impression, they found a trace of old hoofprints. Skragdal frowned. Only Men and Ellylon rode horses, and he did not like the idea of either despoiling Neherinach.

"A rider," Thorun said.

"Aye."

"The earl's Galäinridder?"

"Perhaps."

Led by the Kaldjager, they followed the tracks to their origin. At the northern tip of Neherinach, a node-point of the Marasoumië had lain buried in a hollow place. Now, a great crater had been gouged from the earth. Splintered rock thrust outward in every direction. Whatever had emerged had done so with great force. The innermost surfaces of the granite were smooth and gleaming, as if the rock itself had become molten. It had not happened all that long ago. There were fresh scratches on the rock, and the remnants of hoofprints were still visible on the churned ground.

"That's not good," Thorun said.

"No." Staring into the hole, Skragdal thought of Osric's Men gossiping in the tunnels, and of Osric in Gerflod Hall, grinning his dead grin at the ceiling. The ragged hole gaped like a wound in the green field of Neherinach, exposing the ashen remains of the node far below. Earl Coenred's final words echoed in his memory, making his hide crawl with unease. *Dead, and you don't even know it!* "It's not."

He thought about changing their course, setting the Kaldjager to track the Galäinridder; but General Tanaros had told them, again and again, the importance of obeying orders. It was important to obey orders, even those Lord Vorax had given. Anyway, it was already too late. Gerflod Keep lay a day behind them, and the Rider had some days' start. Not even the Gulnagel could catch him now.

But they could warn Darkhaven.

"Rhilmar," he said decisively. "Morstag. Go back. If General Tanaros has returned, tell him what we have seen here. Tell him what happened in Gerflod. If he is not there, tell Lord Vorax. And if he will not listen, tell Marshal Hyrgolf. No; tell him anyway. He needs to know. This is a matter that concerns the Fjel."

"Aye, boss." Rhilmar, the smaller of the two, shivered in the bright sun. In this place of green grass, sparkling rivers, and old bones, fear had caught up to him; the reek of it oozed from him, tainting the air. "Just . . . just the two of us?"

One of the Kaldjager snorted with contempt. Skragdal ignored it. "Haomane's Allies didn't fear to send only two, and smallfolk at that," he said to Rhilmar. "Go fast, and avoid Men's keeps." He turned to the Kaldjager. "Blågen, where is the nearest Fjel den?"

The Kaldjager pointed to the east. "Half a league." His yellow eyes gleamed. "Are we hunting?"

"Aye." Skragdal nodded. "We follow orders. We will spread word among the tribes until there is nowhere safe and no place for them to hide. Whoever—whatever—this Galäinridder is, he did well to flee Fjel territories and put himself beyond our reach." Standing beside the desecrated earth, he bared his eyetusks in a grim smile. "Pity the smallfolk he left behind."

THEY SPENT AN ENTIRE DAY camped beneath the jack pines, reveling in the presence of water and shade. Red squirrels chattered in the trees, providing easy prey for the Gulnagel. Speros, ranging along the course of the creek, discovered a patch of wild onion. Tanaros' much-dented helmet, having served as bucket and shovel, served now as a makeshift cooking pot for a hearty stew.

By Tanaros' reckoning, they had emerged to the southeast of Darkhaven. Between them lay the fertile territories of the Midlands, then the sweeping plains of Curonan. It was possible that they could locate an entrance to the tunnels on the outskirts of the Midlands, but there was still a great deal of open ground to cover. It would be an easy journey by the standards of the desert; but there was the problem of the Fjel. Two Men traveling in enemy territory were easily disguised.

Not so, three large Gulnagel.

"We'll have to travel by night," Tanaros said ruefully. "At least we're well used to it." He eyed Speros. "Do you still remember how to steal horses?"

The Midlander looked uncertain. "Is that a jest, sir?"

Tanaros shook his head. "No."

They passed a farmstead on the first night and stole close enough to make out the shape of a stable, but at a hundred paces the sound of barking dogs filled the air. When a lamp was kindled in the cottage and silhouetted figures moved before the windows, Tanaros ordered a hasty, ignominious retreat, racing across fields, while the Gulnagel accompanied them at a slow jog.

Not until they had put a good distance between themselves and the farmstead did he order a halt. Back on the dusty road, Speros doubled over, bracing his hands on his thighs and catching his breath. "Why . . . not just . . . kill them? Surely . . . farmers wouldn't be much trouble."

Tanaros cocked a brow at him. "And have their deaths discovered? We've leagues to go before we're in the clear, and all of the Midlands standing on alert. You were the one served in the volunteer militia, Speros of Haimhault. Do you want one such on our trail?"

"Right." Speros straightened. "Shank's mare it is, General."

They walked in silence for several hours. After the desert, Tanaros reflected, it was almost pleasant. Their waterskins were full, and the fields provided ample hunting for the Gulnagel. The air was balmy and moist, and the stars overhead provided enough light to make out the rutted road. On such a night, one could imagine walking forever. He thought about the farmstead they had passed and smiled to himself. While his motive for having done so was reasoned, there was a luxuriant pleasure in having spared its inhabitants' lives. Such choices seldom came his way. He wondered what story they would tell in the morning. They'd pass a sleepless night if they knew the truth. Likely the scent of the Gulnagel had set the dogs to barking; better to send Speros alone, next time. He wondered if Fetch, who had flown ahead, might be able to scout a likely candidate for horse-thievery.

"It's funny, isn't it?" Speros remarked. "I never could have imagined this."

"What's that?"

"*This.*" The Midlander waved one hand, indicating the empty road, the quiet fields. "Us, here. Tramping across the country like common beggars. I'd have thought . . . I don't know, Lord General." He shrugged. "I'd have thought there'd be more *magic.*"

"No." Tanaros shook his head. "There's precious little magic in war, Speros."

"But you're . . . one of the Three, sir!" Speros protested. "Tanaros Blacksword, Tanaros . . ." His voice trailed off.

"Kingslayer," Tanaros said equably. "Aye. An ordinary man, rendered extraordinary only by the grace of Lord Satoris." He touched the hilt of his sword. "This blade cannot be broken by mortal means, Speros, but I wield no power but that which lies in reach of it. Are you disappointed?"

"No." Speros studied his boots as he walked, scuffing the ruts in the road with cracked heels. "No," he repeated more strongly, lifting his head. "I'm not." He grinned, the glint of starlight revealing the gap amid his teeth. "It gives me hope. After all, Lord General, *I* could be you!"

As Tanaros opened his mouth to reply, one of the Gulnagel raised a hand and grunted. The others froze, listening. Motioning for silence, Tanaros strained his ears. Not the farmsteaders, he hoped. Surely, they had seen nothing. There had been only the warning of the dogs to disturb their sleep. Like as not, they had cast a weary gaze over the empty fields, scolded the dogs, and gone back to sleep. What, then? The Fjel had keener ears than Men, but all three wore perplexed expressions. Speros, by contrast, bore a look of glazed horror.

Tanaros concentrated.

At first he heard nothing; then, distantly, a drumming like thunder. Hoofbeats? It sounded like, and unlike. There were too many, too fast—and another sound, too, a rushing, pulsating wind, like the sound of a thousand wings beating at once. It sounded, he realized, like the Ravensmirror.

"Fetch?" Tanaros called.

"Kaugh!"

The fabric of the night itself seemed to split beneath the on-slaught as they emerged from the dreaming pathways into the wak-ing world; ravens, aye, a whole flock, sweeping down the road in a single, vast wing. There, at the head, was Fetch, eyes like obsidian pebbles. And behind them, forelegs churning, nostrils flaring . . .

Horses.

They emerged from darkness as if through a doorway, and starlight gleamed on their sleek hides. All around them, the ravens settled in the fields; save for Fetch, who took up his perch on Tanaros' shoulder. Their iron-shod hooves rang on the road, solid and real, large bodies milling. There were three of them; one grey as a ghost, one black as pitch, and in the middle, a bay the color of recently spilled blood.

And on its back, a pale, crooked figure with moonspun hair and a face of ruined beauty smiled crookedly and lifted a hand in greeting.

"Well met, cousin," said Ushahin Dreamspinner. "A little bird told me you were in need of a ride."

"Dreamspinner!" Tanaros laughed aloud. "Well met, indeed." He clapped one hand on Speros' shoulder. "I retract my words, lad. Forgive me for speaking in haste. It seems the night holds more magic than I had suspected."

Speros, the color draining from his desert-scorched skin, stared without words.

"I have ridden the wings of a nightmare, cousin, and I fear it has brushed your protégé's thoughts." Ushahin's voice was amused. "What plagues you, Midlander? Did you catch a glimpse of your own mortal frailties and failings, the envy to which your kind is prey? A rock, perchance, clutched in a boyish fist? But for an ac-cident of geography, you might have been one of *them*." His mis-matched eyes glinted, shadows pooling in the hollow of his dented temple. "Are you afraid to meet my gaze, Midlander?"

"Cousin—" Tanaros began.

"No." With an effort of will, Speros raised his chin and met the half-breed's glittering gaze. Clenching one hand and pressing it to his heart, he extended it open in the ancient salute. His starlit face was earnest and stubborn. "No, Lord Dreamspinner. I am not afraid."

Ushahin smiled his crooked smile. "It is a lie, but it is one I will honor for the sake of what you have endured." He nodded to his left. "Take the grey. Do you follow in my footprints, within the

swath the ravens forge, she will bear you in my wake, Tanaros." He
pointed to the black horse. "You rode such a one, once. Here is another. Can your Gulnagel keep pace?"

"Aye," Tanaros murmured, his assent echoed by the grinning
Fjel. He approached the black horse, running one hand along the
arch of its neck. Its black mane spilled like water over his hand,
and it turned its head, baring sharp teeth, a preternaturally intelligent eye glimmering. Clutching a hank of mane low on the withers,
he swung himself astride. Equine muscle surged beneath his thighs;
Fetch squawked with displeasure and took wing. Using the pressure of his knees, Tanaros turned the black. He thought of his own
stallion, his faithful black, lost in the Ways of the Marasoumië, and
wondered what had become of it. "These are Darkhaven's horses,
cousin, born and bred. Where did you come by them?"

"On the southern edge of the Delta."

Tanaros paused. "My Staccians. The trackers?"

"I fear it is so." There was an unnerving sympathy in Ushahin's
expression. "They met a . . . a worthy end, cousin. I will tell you of
it, later, but we must be off before Haomane's dawn fingers the
sky, else I cannot keep this pathway open. Night is short, and there
are . . . other considerations afoot. Will you ride?"

"Aye." Tanaros squeezed the black's barrel, feeling its readiness
to run, to feel the twilit road unfurling like a ribbon once more beneath its hooves. He glanced at Speros and saw the Midlander, too,
was astride, eyes wide with excitement. He glanced at the Gulnagel
and saw them readying themselves to run, muscles bunching in
their powerful haunches. "Let us make haste."

"Boss?" One held up Tanaros' helmet. "You want this?"

"No." Thinking of water holes, of shallow graves and squirrel
stew, Tanaros shook his head. "Leave it. It has served its purpose,
and more. Let the Midlanders find it and wonder. I do not need it."

"Okay." The Fjel laid it gently alongside the road.

Tanaros took a deep breath, touching the sword that hung at
his side. His branded heart throbbed, answering to the touch, to
the echo of Godslayer's fire and his Lordship's blood. He thought,
with deep longing, of Darkhaven's encompassing walls. He tried
not to think about the fact that *she* was there. A small voice whispered a name in his thoughts, insinuating a tendril into his heart, as
delicate and fragile as the shudder of a mortexigus flower. With an
effort, he squelched it. "We are ready, cousin."

"Good," Ushahin said simply. He lifted one hand, and a cloud
of ravens rose swirling from the fields, gathering and grouping. The

blood-bay stallion shifted beneath his weight, hide shivering, gathering. The road, which was at once like and *unlike* the road upon which they stood, beckoned in a silvery path. "Then let us ride."

Home!

The blood-bay leapt and the ravens swept forward. Behind them ran the grey and the black. The world lurched and the stars blurred; all save one, the blood-red star that sat on the western horizon. Now three rode astride, and two were of the Three. The beating of the ravens' wings melted into the drumming sound of hoofbeats and the swift, steady pad of the Gulnagel's taloned feet.

And somewhere to the north, a lone Rider veered into the Unknown Desert.

In the farmsteads and villages, Midlanders tossed in their sleep, plagued by nightmares. The color of their dreams changed. Where they had seen a horse as white as foam, they saw three; smoke and pitch and blood.

Where they had seen a venerable figure—a Man, or something like one—with a gem as clear as water on his breast, they saw a shadowy face, averted, and a rough stone clenched in a child's fist, the crunch of bone and a splash of blood.

Over and over, it rose and fell.

Onward, they rode.

LILIAS WAS SEASICK.

She leaned over the railing of the dwarf ship *Yrinna's Bounty* and spewed her guts into the surging waves. When the contents of her belly had been purged to emptiness, her guts continued to churn. There was no surcease upon these lurching decks, this infernal swell. The waves rose and fell, rose and fell, a constant reminder that the world she knew had vanished. Lilias retched and brought up bile until her very flesh burned with dry, bitter heat. It was no wonder she failed to hear the approach of the Ellyl behind her.

"Pray, steady yourself, Sorceress." A cool hand soothed her brow, and there was comfort and sweet ease in the touch. "'Tis but Meronin's waves that do disturb those accustomed to the solid ground of Uru-Alat."

"Get away!" Lilias, straightening, shoved him. "Leave me alone."

"Forgive me." The Ellyl took a graceful step backward, raising his slender hands; Peldras, one of Malthus' Companions. The one with the damnable shadow of sorrow and *compassion* in his gaze. "I meant only to bring comfort."

Lilias laughed, a sound as harsh as the calling of gulls. Her mouth was parched and foul. She pushed strands of dark hair, sticky with bile, out of her face. "Oh, comfort, is it? Can you undo what is done, Ellyl? Can you restore Calandor to life?"

"You know that such a thing cannot be." The Ellyl did not flinch, and the sorrow in his gaze only deepened. "Lady Sorceress, I regret the deaths at Beshtanag. Even, yes, perhaps even that of the Eldest. It grieves me to have come too late. Believe me, if I could have prevented them, I assure you, I would have. I did seek to do so."

"So." Lilias shrugged and glanced across the deck toward where Aracus Altorus bent his head, listening to the Dwarf captain, who was the picture of ease upon the pitching decks, with his short stature and his root-gnarled legs astraddle. She was unsure how or why Yrinna's Children had stood ready at Port Eurus to ferry Haomane's Allies over the waters. "You failed."

"Yes." Peldras bowed his head, fair, gleaming hair falling to curtain his somber brow. "Lady Sorceress," he said softly, "I do not think your heart is as black as it has been painted. I would speak to you of one I met, Carfax of Staccia, an agent of the Sunderer's will who by Arahila's mercy became a Companion in truth at the end—"

"No." Gritting her teeth and swallowing hard, Lilias pushed past him. "I don't want to hear it, Ellyl. I don't want your cursed pity. *Do you understand?"*

He took another step backward; avoiding her foul breath, no doubt. Once, even one of the Rivenlost would have stood awed in her presence. Now, there was nothing to her but bile and decay. This foulness, this mortality, it rotted her from the inside out. The stench of it bothered her own nostrils. "Forgive me, Sorceress," he breathed, still reaching out toward her with one pale, perfect hand. "I did not mean to offend, but only to offer comfort, for even the least of us are deserving. Arahila's mercy—"

"—is not something I seek," Lilias finished brusquely. "And what did Arahila the Fair know of *dragons?"*

It was something, to see one of the Ellylon at a loss for words. She took the image with her as she stumbled toward the cabin in which she had been allotted space. Haomane's Children, scions of the Lord-of-Thought. Oh, it gave them such pleasure to imagine themselves wiser than all other races, than all of the Lesser Shapers.

The air was hot and close inside the narrow cabin, but at least it blocked out the sunlight that refracted blindingly from the waves, making spots dance in her vision. Here it was mercifully dark. Lilias curled into a Dwarf-size bunk, wrapping herself around her sick, aching belly into a tight bundle of misery.

For a few blessed moments, she was left in solitude.

The door cracked open, slanting sunlight seeping red through her closed lids.

"Sorceress." It was a woman's voice, speaking the common tongue with an awkward Arduan inflection. The cool rim of an earthenware cup touched her lips, moistening them with water. "Blaise says you must drink."

"Get away." Without opening her eyes, Lilias slapped at the ministering hand; and found her own hand stopped, wrist caught in a strong, sinewy grip. She opened her eyes to meet the Archer's distasteful gaze. "Let *go!*"

"I would like to," the woman Fianna said with slow deliberation, "but I have sworn a vow of loyalty, and it is the will of the King of the West that you are to be kept alive. It is also the will of our Dwarfish hosts that no *Man* shall accompany one of our gender in closed quarters. So . . . drink."

She tilted the cup.

Water, cool and flat, trickled into Lilias' mouth. She wanted to refuse it, wanted to flail at the life-sustaining invasion. The Archer's hard gaze and the calloused grip on her wrist warned her against it. And so, with resentful gulps, she drank. The cool water eased the parched tissues of her mouth and throat, rumbling in her belly. Still, it stayed where it was put.

"Good." Fianna sat back on her heels. "Good."

"You should wish me dead," Lilias rasped. "Aracus is a fool."

"You know his reasons. As for me, I do." The Archer's voice was flat, and there was no burdensome compassion in her mien, only hatred and steady distrust. "Would you say elsewise of me?"

"No." Lilias drew herself up until her back touched the wall of the cabin. "Oh, no. I would not."

"Then we understand one another." She refilled the cup. "Drink."

Lilias took it, careful to avoid contact with the Archer's fingers. Those were the hands that had nocked the Arrow of Fire, those the fingers that had drawn back the string of Oronin's Bow. She did not want to feel their touch against her skin ever again. "Indeed, we do." She sipped at the water, studying Fianna's face. "Tell me, does Blaise Caveros know you are enamored of him?"

A slow flush of color rose to the Archer's cheeks; half-anger, half-humiliation. "You're not fit to speak his name!" she spat, rising swift to her feet.

Lilias shrugged and took another sip. "Shall I tell him?"

For a moment, she thought the other woman would strike her. Fianna stood, stooped in the tiny cabin, her hands clenching and unclenching at her sides. At length, the habit of discipline won out, and she merely shook her head. "I pity you," she said in a low voice. "I shouldn't, but I do. You've forgotten what it means to be a mortal woman." She regarded Lilias. "If, indeed, you ever even knew. And it's a pity because it's all that's left to you, and all that ever will be."

"Not quite." Lilias gave a bitter smile. "I have my memories."

"I wish you the joy of them!"

The door slammed on the Archer's retort. Lilias sighed, feeling her tense body uncoil. If nothing else, at least the confrontation had distracted her from her misery. It felt as though she might survive the sea journey after all. Aracus' will, was it? Well, let him have his way, then. It was nothing less than the Son of Altorus demanded. "I wish you the joy of it," Lilias whispered.

Finishing the water, she curled onto her side and slept.

When she awoke, it was black as pitch inside the cabin, and stifling hot. Somewhere, the sound of breathing came from another bunk, slow and measured. Was it the Archer? Like as not, since the Dwarfs maintained a prohibition on men and women sharing quarters.

The thought of it made her stomach lurch. Moving silently, Lilias clambered from the bunk and made her way to the door. It was unlatched and opened to her touch. She exited onto the deck, closing the door quietly behind her.

Outside, the sea breeze blew cool and fresh against her face, tasting of salt. She took a deep breath, filling her lungs. For a mercy, her stomach settled in the open air. It was almost pleasant, here beneath the vault of night. The stars seemed to shine more brightly than ever they did in the mountains, and the waxing moon laid a bright path on the dark waves. Here and there, lanterns were hung from the ship's rigging, lending a firefly glow. Dwarfish figures worked quietly by their light, tending to this and that, ignoring her presence.

It was bliss to have no keeper for the first time since Beshtanag. Lilias made her way to the prow of the ship, finding its swaying no longer discomforted her as it had earlier. To her chagrin, she found she was not alone; a tall figure stood in the prow, gazing outward over the water. His head turned at her approach, moonlight glinting on the gold fillet that encircled his brow.

She halted. "My lord Altorus. I did not mean to intrude."

"Lilias." He beckoned to with one hand. "Come here. Have you ever seen Meronin's Children?"

She shook her head. It was the first time he had addressed her thusly, and it felt strange to hear her name in his mouth. "No, my lord. Until this morning, I had never even seen the sea."

"Truly?" Aracus looked startled. "I would have thought . . . ah, 'tis of no mind. Come then, and see. Come, I'll not bite." He pointed as she came hesitantly to stand beside him. "See, there."

In the waters beyond the ship's prow, she saw them; a whole gathering, graceful forms arching through the waves in joyous leaps. Their sleek hides were silvery beneath the stars and there was a lambent wisdom in their large, dark eyes, at odds with the merry smiles that curved their slim jaws.

"Oh!" Lilias exclaimed as one blew a shining plume of spray. "Oh!"

"Wondrous, aren't they?" He leaned pensively on the railing. "It seems, betimes, a passing pleasant way to live. The world's strife does but pass across the surface of their world, leaving no trail. Though they will never be numbered among the Lesser Shapers, perhaps Meronin was wise to Shape his children thusly. Surely, they are happier for it."

"'And Meronin the Deep kept his counsel,'" Lilias quoted.

Aracus glanced at her. "You know the lore."

"Does it surprise you so?" She gazed at the graceful figures of Meronin's Children, describing ebullient arcs amid the waves. "I have never seen the sea, but I have lived for a thousand years on my mountain, Aracus Altorus, and the counsel of dragons is as deep as Meronin's."

"Perhaps," he said. "But it is false."

Lilias eyed him. "Do you know, my lord, that dragons number Meronin's Children among the Lesser Shapers? They say their time is not come, nor will for many Ages. Still, they say, Meronin has planned well for it. Who benefited most when the world was Sundered?"

He frowned at her. "You know well it was the Sunderer himself."

"Was it?" She shrugged. "Haomane First-Born says so, but Lord Satoris has lived like a fugitive upon Urulat's soil with ten thousand enemies arrayed against him. Meanwhile, Meronin's waters have covered the Sundered World, and his Children multiply in peace." Lilias nodded at the leaping forms. "Meronin the Deep keeps his counsel and waits. It may be that one day he will challenge the Lord of Thought himself."

"You speak blasphemy!" Aracus said, appalled.

"No." She shook her head. "Truth, as I know it. Truth that is not found in scholars' books or Shapers' prophecy. Whatever I may be, I am Calandor's companion, not Haomane's subject. You spoke of lore. There is a great deal I know."

"And much you will not share." His voice turned blunt. "Why?"

Lilias shivered and wrapped her arms around herself. "You speak of the Soumanië? That is another matter, and my lord knows *why*."

His gaze probed hers. "You understand a woman's life is at stake?"

"Yes." She met his gaze without flinching. "Would you believe me if I told you Satoris will not kill her?"

He raised his brows. "Surely you cannot pretend to believe such a thing."

She sighed. "I can, actually. Once upon a time, Satoris Third-Born, too, was much given to listening to the counsel of dragons; aye, and speaking with them, too. For good or ill, I know something of his nature. Although it is twisted, there is nobility in it— and pride, too. A Shaper's pride. He will not slay her out of hand."

"No." Aracus debated, then shook his head. "No!" Beneath the dull, emberless stone of the Soumanië, his face was set. "Do you see *that*?" With one stabbing finger, he pointed unerring at the red star that rode high overhead in the night skies. "It is a declaration of war, Sorceress. I saw the innocent dead at Lindanen Dale. I witnessed my betrothed wrenched away in vile captivity, and followed into a trap that would have slain us all, save for Haomane's grace. If the Sunderer spoke to you of mercy, he has ensnared your thoughts in his lies."

"No," Lilias said gently. "*You* declared war upon Satoris, my lord Aracus, when you pledged yourself to wed the Lady of the El-lylon. The red star merely echoes that deed. I do not absolve him of his actions, any more than I ask absolution for mine. Only . . . what else did you expect him to do?"

"It is Haomane's Prophecy." His hands gripped the railing until his knuckles whitened, and he stared over the waters, watching Meronin's Children disport themselves with a mix of unconscious envy and fresh unease. "I did not *ask* for this destiny."

"I know." Lilias watched him. "But you accepted it nonetheless." Moonlight cast faint shadows in the lines worry and weariness had etched into his features. He was young, yes; but he was a Man, and mortal. How would it be to watch his beloved endure, unaging, while his flesh withered and rotted? She, who had replaced scores of pretty attendants in her own ageless time, had the strangest urge to smooth his furrowed brow.

"What choice had I?" He turned his wide gaze upon her, filled with that compelling combination of demand and *trust*. "Truly, what had I?"

All things must be as they are, little sssister. All thingsss.

"I don't know, my lord," Lilias whispered, tears blurring her vision. Lifting one hand, she touched his cheek, laying her palm against it and feeling the warmth of his skin, the slight rasp of red-gold stubble. On his brow, the Soumanië pulsed with a brief, yearning glow at her nearness. It made her heart ache. "Tell me, do you love her?"

"Yes." His fingers closed on her wrist. "I do."

There were a thousand things he could have said; how Cerelinde's beauty put the stars to shame, how her courage made him curse his inadequacy. How he understood the sacrifice she had made for the Rivenlost, and how terrible the cost would be. Aracus Altorus said none of them, and yet all were present in his simple, blunt words, in his wide-set, demanding gaze. He was a warrior; oh, yes.

One who loved the Lady of the Ellylon.

"Well, then." Lilias opened her hand, letting him steer it away, deflecting her touch harmlessly. "You had no choice, did you?"

He stared at her. "You trouble me, Sorceress."

"Good." She smiled through her tears. "You *should* be troubled, my lord Altorus." Wrenching her hand free, she took a stumbling step away from him. "Thank you for sharing your vision of Meronin's Children with me. Whether or not it was true, it was a pleasant dream."

The disinterested Dwarfs watched her progress, and Aracus' stare followed her back to her cabin, until she closed the door onto stifling darkness and the Archer snoring in the second bunk.

Lilias closed the door, and wept.

TWO

FOR DAYS, THEIR PATH HAD taken them westward on an arid course through the Northern Harrow, following an underground branch of the Spume River.

Thulu led the way, probing with his digging-stick and listening, listening to the lifeblood coursing through Uru-Alat's veins, deep below the surface. Dani did not question his uncle's guidance. All children of the Yarru-yami were taught to follow the deep veins of Uru-Alat, but the skill was honed by age and practice, and this was a task for which the Yarru elders had trained his uncle for many years.

Although it was a hardship, at least it was one to which the Yarru were suited. Dani and his uncle sipped sparingly from their waterskins, their bodies accustomed to eking the most from every precious drop. When ordinary folk would have faltered, the Yarru pressed onward with only a touch of discomfort.

They kept to low ground, to dry gorges and valleys. Away from the leaping rivers there was scant sign of any other living thing, save the tall spruce that dotted the mountainsides. It was a mercy, for it meant they saw no sign of Fjeltroll. Here and there, Uncle Thulu found a tiny spring, like an unexpected gift of Neheris, a sparkling trickle of water darkening a narrow cleft amid the rocks.

Where there were springs, there was small game; hare and ptarmigan. Using Yarru-style slings Thulu had made with strips of hide, both of them took turns shooting for the pot. It was harder to get a clean shot than it was in the open desert, but to his pleasure, Dani found his keen eye held him in good stead as a marksman.

After clambering amid the mountain peaks, it was almost easy going. Their feet, already hardened by the desert, grew accustomed to the harsh terrain. The nights were cool, but nowhere near as chill as they had been in the heights. After some debate, they gauged it safe to build a brisk fire, which dispelled the worst of the cold; for the rest, they shared their wool cloaks and huddled together, doubling their warmth.

On the morning of the seventh day, they heard a distant roar. Uncle Thulu, leaning on his freshly sharpened digging-stick, turned to Dani with a grin. "That's it, lad. That's our river!"

The trail wound through a torturous series of switchbacks, and it was an afternoon's hard tramping before they reached the source, standing upon a promontory of rock and beholding what lay below.

When they did, Dani gazed at it with awe.

The Spume River burst out of the side of a mountain, plunging in a mighty cascade to the churning riverbed below. At close range, the sound of it was deafening. It was like a living thing, foam-crested and green-thewed, boiling around the boulders that dared disrupt its course. On the edge of the near bank, the barren limbs of a half-fallen spruce tree struggled desperately against the current.

"We're going to follow *that*?" Dani asked, agape.

"Aye, lad!" Uncle Thulu widened his nostrils and inhaled deeply. He shouted his reply. "Can't you smell the taint of it? One way or another, it will lead us to Darkhaven!"

Opening his mouth to respond, Dani gazed past his uncle and paused. Forty yards downriver, hunkered on a ledge, a squat figure was watching them.

At a passing glance, it looked like a boulder, perched and stolid, the color of dull granite; then it flung out one massive arm to point at them, its barrel chest swelled and swelled, increasing vastly in girth, and its mouth gaped to reveal a cavernous gullet.

The roar of a Tordenstem Fjel split the gorge.

Dani's blood ran cold.

It was a wordless roar, and it echoed between the walls of the gorge, drowning out the sound of the river, impossible though it seemed. Dani clapped both hands over his aching ears, his insides reverberating like a struck gong. His teeth, the very marrow of his bones, vibrated at the cacophonous howl.

"Fjeltroll!" he shouted unnecessarily.

Again the roar sounded, making his innards quiver. And, oh,

worse, even worse! On the ridge above it, other heads popped up, silhouetted against the sky; inhuman heads, misshapen and hideous. There were at least a score of them. The sentry repeated its deafening howl and the Fjeltroll began to descend with horrible speed, jamming talons into narrow fissures and swarming down the cliffs.

"Dani!" He could see Uncle Thulu's mouth shaping his name as he pointed toward the banks of the churning river. "This way!" Without waiting, Thulu plunged downward, slithering through a gap in the rocks.

"Don't leave me!" Fighting panic, Dani scrambled after his uncle. It was hard to hold a thought while his insides churned, and he could scarce feel his fingertips. The paralyzing roar sounded again. Glancing behind him, Dani saw the Fjel drawing closer. They wore nothing over their coarse hide, and their leathery lips were drawn back to reveal long tusks. Small yellow eyes glinted with ruthless cunning under their bulging brows. "Uru-Alat," he whispered, freezing.

"Come *on*!" Uncle Thulu shouted. At the bottom of the gorge, he had made his way to the fallen spruce and was wrenching at its uppermost branches, breaking them loose. "Dani, come *on*!"

Half-sliding, half-falling, the Water of Life banging against his chest in its clay flask, Dani made the descent. The plunging Spume boiled like a cauldron, then snarled and raged in its narrow bed, spitting geysers in his path. He stumbled across rocks slick with spray to his uncle's side.

"Hold these." Sparing a quick glance up the gorge, Thulu thrust a load of spruce branches into his arms. "No, like so. Good lad."

"Are they . . . ?" Dani clenched his jaw to still his chattering teeth.

"Aye. Fast." As calm as though he were braiding thukka-vine in the desert, Thulu wove a length of rabbit-hide rope amid the branches, deftly knotting and tightening. "We have to try the river, Dani. It's our only chance." He met Dani's gaze. "Whatever happens, hold tight to the branches. They'll keep you afloat."

Dani nodded, understanding.

"Good lad." With a single, quick motion, Thulu stooped and grabbed his digging-stick, shouldering past Dani. "Now *go*!"

The Fjeltroll were on them.

The path was narrow, and even the sure-footed Fjel could only attack two at a time. Uncle Thulu fought like a tiger at bay, wielding his stick in a blur. The unarmed Fjel hissed in fury, swiping with their terrible talons, unable to get within reach. The largest among them barked a guttural order, and two pair split away, clambering up the gorge in order to flank the older Yarru on his left. Dani, clutching his makeshift float, stared in horror. The one who had given the order grinned, a malicious intelligence in his yellow eyes.

"What are you waiting for?" Thulu shouted over his shoulder. "Go, Dani! *Go!*"

"*No.*" Deep within him, an unexpected wave of fury surged. Dani dropped the spruce bundle and reached for his sling. "Not without you!"

Busy fighting for his life, Uncle Thulu grunted.

It was a clean rage, clearing Dani's head and making the blood sing in his ears. Somehow, although fear was still present, it seemed distant and unimportant. He reached into his pouch and withdrew a smooth stone, fitting it into the sling. He spun it, taking careful aim at the nearest Fjeltroll approaching on the left. Uru-Alat, but they were hideous! With a grimace, the Fjel pointed at the flask on his chest with one grimy talon, saying something in its harsh tongue. Dani let fly with the sling.

His aim was true. Clasping one hand over its right eye, the Fjeltroll roared and staggered. Grabbing a handful of stones, Dani flung a barrage in quick succession, driving the Fjel several paces backward. The others regrouped, watching. "Leave us *alone!*" he shouted at them.

It was a brief respite. Lowering their heads, the uninjured Fjel renewed their approach, grimacing as Dani's sling-flung rocks bounced from their tough hides, from the dense ridge of bone on their brows. In a few seconds, they would reach him.

On his right, he heard rather than saw it; Thulu's sharp exclamation of pain, then a grunt of effort and a heavy thud. A Fjel voice roared in agony. An arm clamped hard about Dani's waist, wrenching him off-balance. "*Now,* lad!"

And then he was falling.

The river smacked him like a mighty fist. It *was* like a living thing; a malevolent one that sought his life at every avenue, seeking to extinguish the spark of vital fire that made his heart beat and his lungs draw breath. Water filled his eyes and ears and nose and mouth, more water then he had known in a lifetime. Dani flailed and the river rolled him over like a piece of debris, driving him into its depths.

If not for his uncle, he would surely have drowned. It was

Thulu's strong arm around his waist that hauled him up until his head broke water and he gasped for air. With his other arm, Uncle Thulu held tight to the spruce-branch float, his fingers wedged under the hide ropes. "Hold on!" he shouted above the river's din. "Hold on to the branches!"

Dani did.

It was barely large enough to let them keep their heads above water. The river spun them and Dani saw the Fjel on the banks, arguing amongst themselves. One lay fallen and motionless, Uncle Thulu's digging-stick jutting from its torso. On the ledge above the gorge, the lone sentry howled in fury, receding quickly from view.

The biggest Fjel, the one who had given the orders, gave pursuit.

"Uru-Alat!" Clinging to the float, Dani watched the Fjel race along the narrow path, using all four limbs, scrambling and hurdling. His heart sank. Its mouth was open and panting hard, but it was outpacing the very current. "Can they swim?"

"I don't know." His uncle grimaced. Glancing at him, Dani saw trails of blood winding through the foam that churned around his submerged chest.

"You're injured!"

"A scratch." Thulu pointed with his chin toward a bend in the river. "Here he comes. Kick with your legs, Dani! I don't think he *can* swim. If we can swing wide left, maybe the current will carry us past him."

There where the bend created a shallow apron of shoreline and the current slowed a fraction, the Fjel was fording the river, wading with dogged persistence to intercept their course. Water parted to surge around the mighty thews of its thighs, around its waist. The force of it would have swept anything else off its feet.

Not the Fjel.

Step by step, it continued its steady advance.

Dani kicked frantically, felt the float's course shift. His uncle grunted, beating at the river with one arm. The trails of red in the foam surrounding him spread and widened. Almost . . .

Neck-deep in the river, the Fjel raised one dripping arm and reached out with a taloned hand to catch a branch of their float, halting its progress. It had to tilt its chin to keep its mouth clear of the river's surface. It was close enough that Dani was staring into its slitted yellow eyes, mere inches away.

It said something in the Fjel tongue.

"Go *away*!" Dani kicked at it.

The Fjel grinned and said something else, reaching with its

other hand for the clay flask that hung about his neck. Water surged all around them on every side. Its taloned hand closed around the flask . . .

. . . and dropped, sinking below the surface of the river as though it held a boulder in its grasp. The Fjel sank, its head vanishing beneath the river. Its grip was torn loose from the float, and the current restaked its claim. Dani choked, feeling the thong tighten around his neck and burn his skin; then that, too, eased as the Fjel let go.

The float rotated lazily as it cleared the bend, its passengers clinging for dear life. Behind them, a column of bubbles broke the surface. The big Fjel rose, dripping, and staring after them.

Too late.

They had rounded the bend.

Struggling to stay afloat, Dani watched it until it was out of sight and wondered what the Fjel had said. And then the river's course took a steep drop and it turned once more to a white-water torrent, and he obeyed his uncle's desperate, shouted orders and clung to the float and thought of water and how to stay alive in it and nothing else, until the raging current flung them hard against a boulder.

Something broke with an inaudible snap, and Dani felt an acute pain in his shoulder and a dull one in his head. As the world went slowly black in his vision, he worked one hand free to fumble at the clay vial around his throat. It was intact.

It was his last conscious thought.

THE ROAR OF THE TORDENSTEM Fjel echoed through Defile's Maw, scattering the ravens into a circling black cloud, setting the shrouded webs of Weavers' Gulch to trembling, welcoming them back to Darkhaven.

Speros glanced at the figures crouching on the heights, remembering all too well his ungentle reception at their hands. He ran his tongue over his teeth, probing the gap where a front one was missing.

"Last chance, Midlander." General Tanaros drew rein beside him, an unfathomable expression in his dark eyes. "I mean it. Turn around now, and ride away without looking back. You can keep the horse."

Speros shook his head. "No."

"You know what's coming?"

"Aye, Lord General." He kept his gaze steady. "War."

Tanaros sighed. "If you had an ounce of sense, you'd take my advice and go."

"Where, sir?" Speros shook his head again. "There's no place for me out there. Should I join Haomane's Allies and ride against you? I would sooner cut off my right arm." Alarm squeezed his chest. "Do you seek to be rid of me? Is it because of what happened with the Yarru? I promised, I'll not fail you again. And I *did* help, after all; you'd not have gotten the Well sealed without my aid."

"Aye." The General's strong hand rested on his shoulder. "You're a good lad, Speros. I do you no kindness in accepting your loyalty."

"Did I *ask* for kindness?" Anger mixed with the alarm. "Sir?"

"No." The General lifted his gaze, watching the ravens circle overhead. An errant lock of hair fell over his brow. Behind his austere features was a shadow of sorrow. "Perhaps it is a piece of wisdom that you do not."

Something in Speros' heart ached. The General feared for him. His family had reckoned him shiftless, an idler whose goals would never amount to aught. They had never showed as much concern for his well-being as the General did. They cared nothing for the ideas that fired his imagination. He had met their expectations accordingly and paid the price for it.

General Tanaros was different. He had believed in Speros, taken a chance on him. He knew, in a wordless way, that he would do anything to see General Tanaros smile, to see his expression lighten with approval.

Even if it led to defeat, it would be worthwhile.

"I'm staying." Setting his heels to his mount's flanks, he shook off Tanaros' hand and jogged ahead before the Lord General could say aught else to dissuade him. One of the trotting Gulnagel grinned at him, and Speros grinned back, his sense of alarm fading. These were his comrades, his companions. One had given his life for him. They had given him the honor and respect his own family had denied him. They had labored side by side together, laying the dead to rest. How could he think of leaving?

He would find a way to prove himself to General Tanaros.

Ahead of him, Ushahin Dreamspinner rode astride, swaying as his blood-bay mount picked its way along the path of the Defile. Hearing Speros approach, he glanced languidly over his shoulder. "Weavers' Gulch, Midlander." He waved a crabbed hand at the sticky strands crossing the vast loom of the Defile, the scuttling weavers that spun the warp and weft of it. "Does it evoke fond memories for you?"

"Not especially, Lord Dreamspinner." Speros eyed the hanging veils of webbing and swallowed hard. He touched his bare neck, remembering the sharp sting of a spider's bite and awakening trussed and bound. "Not especially."

Ushahin gave his lopsided smile. "The ones who come to *me* pass through untouched. Such is the protection I afford them in the purity of their madness. Still, I think you must be a little bit mad to attempt it at all."

Speros shivered and fell back, following in the half-breed's wake, though it was no longer necessary now that they traveled by ordinary day, and not on the path between dreaming and waking that had carried them through the Midlands and across the plains of Curonan. "Perhaps," he said.

"Oh, I think it is more than *perhaps.*" Amid the ghostly veils of webbing, Ushahin smiled once more. "Tanaros Blacksword might disagree, but he's a little bit mad, too, isn't he? We will see, in time."

They made steady progress through the Defile. The Gulnagel breathed deeply through widened nostrils, inhaling the odor of the ichor-tainted waters, the welcome scent of home. Beyond the Weavers' Gulch, the Defile Gate and its flanking towers loomed amid the vast, encircling wall. Alerted by the Tordenstem, teams of Fjel were already at work opening the gate. Overhead, the ravens circled in grim triumph. The walls were crowded with Fjel, armed to the teeth, waving axes and maces in the air, shields held high. They were shouting.

"Tan-a-ros! Tan-a-ros!"

"Go on, cousin." Ushahin nodded. *"You're* the one they've been awaiting."

Giving him a deep look, General Tanaros nudged his mount forward. He lifted one hand as he rode between the gates, acknowledging the cries. He looked weary, Speros thought. And why not? He had done a hero's work, carrying out his Lordship's bitter orders, keeping them alive in the desert. He had earned a rest.

"You love him, don't you?" Ushahin asked in a low voice.

"No," Speros said automatically, then thought of the General's shoulder beneath his arm, urging him to keep going, step by torturous step. The General's hands, cradling his head, placing the drought-fruit to his lips. The General, stooping under the starlight, scooping sand in a battered helmet, helping dig a grave for poor

Freg. "Aye!" he said then, defiant. "I have a care for him. Why shouldn't I, after all? My own Da never did half as much for me as the Lord General's done."

"Ah, well, then." The Dreamspinner's mismatched eyes glittered. "There's a little piece of madness for you."

Speros flung his head back. "What would *you* know of it, my lord?"

"Love?" the half-breed mused. He shook his head, fair hair shimmering. "Not much, Speros of Haimhault. What love I had, I have betrayed. The Grey Dam Vashuka will attest to that. But heed my advice, and make a good job of it." He nodded at Tanaros. "There's a hunger in him for the son he never had. And there's a hunger in him for the woman whose love he lost. One, it would seem, is greater than the other. But who knows? If it comes to a choice, you may find yourself an unexpected fulcrum."

With that, Ushahin took his leave, passing through the Defile Gate. Speros stared after him while the Gulnagel who had accompanied them passed him by on either side. With a start, he touched his heels to his mount's flanks. It stepped forward, the color of smoke, obedient to his will.

The Gate closed behind them.

He was home.

It FELT STRANGE TO BE alone in his quarters. They had been tended, and recently; that much was clear. His dining table gleamed with hand-rubbed beeswax, the floors had been swept clean and the carpets beaten. The lamps were lit and a fire was laid. Hot water steamed in the tub in his bathing-chamber, but not a madling was in sight.

Tanaros hadn't been truly alone since he had birthed himself from the Marasoumië and climbed up the well-shaft of the Water of Life. The silence, the absence of another's heartbeat, was deafening. He found himself wishing Fetch had stayed with him, but the raven had rejoined his own kin.

Piece by piece, he removed his dirty, dented armor. The straps were stiff with grime. He placed each piece carefully on the stand, then unbuckled his sword belt and propped the sword in the corner. There was no scratch at the door, no madling coming to beg to touch the black blade tempered in his Lordship's blood. Tanaros frowned and sat on the low stool to pry off his boots.

It wasn't easy to get them off and it wasn't pleasant once he did. For a time, he simply sat on the stool. All the weariness of the long, long journey he had endured settled into his bones. There was no part of him that did not ache; save for his branded heart, which no longer tugged like a yearning compass toward the fortress of Darkhaven. He was home, and he was grateful beyond telling that his Lordship had given them a night's respite before requiring their report.

"Truly, my Lord is merciful." He spoke the words aloud, half-listening for a murmured chorus of agreement.

No one answered.

With an effort, Tanaros levered himself upright and padded to the bathing-chamber, where he peeled off clothing so filthy it defied description. From one pocket, he withdrew the *rhios* Hyrgolf had given him, setting it gently upon a shelf. Everything else he left in a stinking pile on the tiled floor.

Beneath the clothing, his naked body was gaunt. The Chain of Being only stretched so far; privation had taken its toll. His ribs made ridges along the sides of his torso. Skin that had not seen daylight for weeks on end was shockingly pale, grey as a ghost. Tanaros sank into the tub, watching the water turn cloudy.

A long, long time ago, when he would return from a hard day's labor of training Roscus Altorus' troops, Calista had drawn his bath with her own hands. At least, she had always made a show of pouring the last bucket of steaming water, smiling at him under her lashes. *See what I do for you, my love?* And then she would draw a stool alongside the tub so she might sit beside him and scrub his back and add a few drops of scented oil to the water. It had smelled like . . . like vulnus-blossom, only sweet and harmless.

The memory made his eyes sting. Tanaros ducked his head underwater and came up dripping. He grabbed a scouring cloth and a ball of soap and set to work mercilessly on his grimy skin. The water in which he sat grew murkier. Grey skin turned grub-white, in marked contrast to his strong, sun-scorched hands. He had wrapped those hands around her throat.

Slayer. The Yarru Elder Ngurra's voice stirred in his memory, prompted by the odor of vulnus-blossom. Dark eyes in a creased face, filled with wisdom and sorrow, beneath the hanging shadow of a black sword. Old men, old women, hanging back and clinging to one another's hands. *You do not have to choose this.*

Tanaros scoured harder.

He wished he were Vorax. It would be simpler, thus. He would have come home to a bevy of Staccian maidens and reveled in it.

Simple pleasures. The Staccian asked nothing more and never had. Only to enjoy them in abundance, forever. It was a good way to live. Even Ushahin had his madlings . . . oh, yes, of course.

That was where *they* were. Rejoicing in the return of their own particular master, in the camaraderie of souls twisted out of true. Settling back into the warm water, Tanaros closed his eyes. Since he was alone, he might as well indulge in his memories.

The bath-oil had smelled like vulnus-blossom . . .

He tried to summon it; the rage, the old, old anger. Calista's gaze meeting his as she lay in her birthing-bed, eyes stretched wide with guilty fear as she held the babe with red-gold hair close to her breast. Roscus, looking surprised, the hand he had extended so often in false brotherhood clutching uncomprehending at the length of steel that had pierced his belly. Remembering the scent of vulnus-blossom, Tanaros tried to summon the bitter satisfaction that moment had engendered.

It wouldn't come.

Too far away, and he was tired, too tired for rage. There was too much to be done, here and now. Calista had been dead for a long, long time; aye, and Roscus, too. Somewhere, somehow, the fearsome womb of the Marasoumië, the blazing sands and merciless sun of the Unknown Desert, had rendered their ghosts into pallid shadows. It was the living who commanded his attention. One, more than others.

Since the comfort of anger was denied him, he sought to turn his mind to matters at hand, to the report he must make on the morrow to Lord Satoris and the preparations for battle to come; but the odor of vulnus-blossom wove a distracting thread through his thoughts. He shied away from the memory of Ngurra's uplifted face and the old Yarru's words. Why was there such pain in the memory, enough to displace the murder of his wife? His thoughts fled to the moon-garden and he saw *her* face, luminous and terrible with beauty. The Lady of the Ellylon.

What did you see? he had asked her.

You. I saw you . . .

"No." Shaking his head, scattering droplets of water, Tanaros arose. He stepped dripping from the tub and toweled himself dry, donning a dressing-robe. Despite the fire laid in his hearth, he shivered. She was here in Darkhaven, separated from him only by a few thick walls, burning like a pale flame. Alone and waiting. Had she heard word of his return? Did she care if he lived or died? Or did she think only of Aracus Altorus? Gritting his teeth, he willed himself not to think of it. "Ah, no."

There was a crisp knock at the door to his chambers.

He padded barefoot to answer it, feeling the luxury of Rukhari carpets beneath his feet. Meara was there when he opened the doors, eyes downcast. Another madling accompanied her, carrying a tray. Savory odors seeped from beneath the covering domes.

"Meara!" His mood lightened. "'Tis good to see you. Come in." He opened the doors wider, inhaling deeply. His stomach rumbled in sympathy, hunger awakening in his starved tissues. It had been a long time since he had allowed himself a proper meal. "What have you brought? It smells delicious."

"Squab, my lord." Her tone was short. "And other things." She watched the second madling lay the table with care. "Forgive us, Lord General, that we cannot stay. Others will return in time to tend to everything."

Tanaros frowned. "Does the Dreamspinner demand your presence, Meara? Or is it that I have offended you in some way?"

She lifted her gaze to his. "Does my lord even remember?"

He did, then; her weight, straddling him. The smell of her; of womanflesh, warm and earthy. Her teeth nipping at his lip, her tongue probing. His hand, striking her face, hard enough to draw blood. Tanaros flushed to the roots of his hair.

He had forgotten.

"Aye." Meara nodded. "That."

"Please." He made a deep courtier's bow, according her the full measure of dignity any woman deserved. "Allow me to apologize again, Meara. Forgive me, for I never meant to strike you."

"Oh, and it's *that* you think demands apology the most, my lord?" She put one hand on her hip. "Never mind. I forgave you *that* from the beginning."

"What, then?" Tanaros asked gravely. "Tell me, and I will make amends."

"No." Gnawing her lip, she shook her head. "I don't think so, my lord. Not if you have to ask. Some things cannot be mended. I know, I am one of them." Meara shivered and gripped her elbows, then gave a harsh laugh. "Ask the Lady, if you want to know. She's heard word of your return. She is waiting, although she does not say it."

"Is she?" He kept his voice polite.

"Oh, yes." She eyed him. "She does not fear you as she does the others. I think she has seen some kindness in you that she believes might be redeemed. Be wary, my lord. There is danger in it."

Tanaros shrugged. "She is a hostage, Meara. She can do no harm."

The bitten lips curved in a mirthless smile. "Go to her, then. One day, you will remember I warned you. I did from the first. It was a mistake to bring her here." She beckoned to her companion and turned to depart.

"Meara," Tanaros called after her.

"I have to go, my lord." She walked away without looking back. "Use the bellpull if you have need of aught else."

He stared after her a moment, then closed the doors. The aroma of his supper called him to the table. Despite the accumulated hunger of weeks of privation, he delayed for a moment, savoring her words.

Cerelinde was waiting for him.

USHAHIN DREAMSPINNER SAT CROSS-LEGGED ON a high chopping block.

All around him, his madlings pressed and swarmed, jostling for position, reaching out to touch his knee or his foot in reassurance. He sat and waited for all of them to assemble—not just the cooks and servants, but the launderers, the maids, the stable lads. All of the folk who tended to his Lordship's glorious fortress.

His people.

Darkhaven's kitchens were roasting hot and greasy, redolent of cooking odors. For the madlings, it was a safe haven, one of the few places in the fortress in which they enjoyed the comfort of domestic familiarity. Here, they established their own society, their own hierarchy. Cooks possessed by mad culinary genius worked cheek by jowl with half-witted assistants and found common ground. All took pride in their labor, knowing that Darkhaven could not function without them; and the kitchens represented the pinnacle of that pride.

Ushahin did not mind being there. The atmosphere soothed his aching joints, reminding him of the moist, fecund air at the heart of the Delta. The belching ovens might have been Calanthrag's nostrils. The thought gave him pleasure, though he hid it from his madlings.

Their mood, at once ebullient and penitent, disturbed him. It came as no surprise, in light of what Vorax had told him. Sifting through the endless tangle of their waking thoughts, Ushahin saw a single image repeated: Cerelinde, the Lady of the Ellylon.

He kept a stern visage until all were assembled. When Meara and the lad who accompanied her returned from their errand, he raised one hand for silence. With whispers and broken murmurs, a sea of madlings obeyed. Their twitching faces were raised to listen, gleaming gazes fixed upon him.

"My children," Ushahin addressed them. "I have labored long and hard, through countless dangers, to return to you. And now I find Lord Vorax is wroth. How do you account for yourselves in my absence?"

A hundred faces crumpled, a hundred mouths opened to shape a keening wail of guilt. It surged through the kitchens, echoing from the grease-blackened rafters and the bright copper pots and kettles, scoured to an obsessive shine. Some went to their knees, hands outstretched in a plea for forgiveness.

"So." Ushahin nodded. "You know of what I speak. Did you bring her *here*?"

A wail of protest rose in answer. Heads shook in vehement denial, matted hair flying. No, no. They had not brought her here.

"Where?" he asked.

The wailing trickled into shuffling silence. Ushahin waited.

"A place." One of them offered it in a mutter, eyes downcast. "A place behind the walls, lord, that we made bigger."

Another looked up, pleading. "You said those were *our* places, lord!"

"The spaces in between." Ushahin nodded again. "I did. Those are the places we occupy, my children; those of us whom the world has failed to claim. No one knows it better than I. And I entrusted those places to you, with Lord Satoris' blessing. Why, then, did you bring the Ellyl woman there?"

The hundredfold answer was there in the forefront of their thoughts, in their hungry, staring eyes. None of them gave voice to it. It didn't matter; he knew. Lives of happy normalcy, wives and husbands, sons and daughters. An honest livelihood filled with the myriad mundane joys of living. *What-might-have-been.*

Oh, yes, Ushahin Dreamspinner knew.

"'Tis a bittersweet joy," he said softly, "is it not? What might have been. I, too, have wondered, my children. What might *I* have been, had my Ellyl kin claimed me?" He lifted his gnarled hands, gazing at them, then at his madlings. "A bridge, perhaps, with limbs straight and true, built to span the divide between Haomane's Children and Arahila's. Instead"—he shook his head—"I am the abyss. And when they seek to gaze into the spaces in between and stake a claim there, they will find *me* gazing back at them. I am the dark mirror that reflects their most fearful desires. I am the dark underbelly of Haomane's Prophecy."

The madlings were silent, rapt.

"Never forget." Ushahin's voice hardened. "It was the *Ellylon* who rejected me, who wanted no part of a child of mixed blood, gotten in violence and tainted—*tainted*, they say—by Lord Satoris' Gift. I am the very future they court in fear and loathing. I am the shadow that precedes the children of the Prophecy they seek to fulfill. And who can say that they will not despise their own offspring? For they, too, will carry the taint of Lord Satoris' Gift with them."

Someone hissed.

Ushahin smiled. "Oh, yes," he said. "For they despise his Lordship above all else; always and forever. They may grieve at your pain, and they may offer pleasant visions, but they are Haomane's Children, and they will not lift one finger"—he raised one crooked finger—"to aid you unless Haomane profits by it."

The kitchen erupted in indignant rage. Ushahin rode their anger like a wave, letting them seethe and rant until they subsided, turning toward him with expectant eyes, waiting to hear what he would say next. His madlings knew him. They understood him. He had been broken and had risen triumphant nonetheless; he bore the badges of his breaking—his uneven face, his twisted limbs—in painful solidarity with their aborted lives and shattered minds. It was for this that they loved him.

A vast tenderness infused his heart, and he wondered if Shapers felt thusly toward their Children. It seemed it might be so.

"It is well that you remember this," he told them, "for war comes upon us. And we may put faces to those enemies we know, but 'tis harder to put faces to the enemies among us. Who among you would betray Lord Satoris?"

No one, no one, arose the cries; at once both true and not-true. Somewhere, the seeds of betrayal had already taken root. Listening to the madlings' protestations, Ushahin thought of Calanthrag the Eldest and the things of which she had spoken. A shadow of sorrow overlay the tenderness in his heart. The pattern was fixed and inevitable. He could only serve his Lordship as best he might and pray that these spreading roots would not bear fruit for many generations to come. The Eldest herself had borne the same hope. He remembered her words, uttered in her knowing, sibilant hiss: *Yet may it come later than sssooner for ssuch as I and you.*

"Well done, my children," Ushahin said to his madlings. "Keep faith, and hope. Remember that it is his Lordship's mercy that protects us here." He held up his hand to quiet them and made his voice stern once more. "Now, who will speak to me of the hole that pierces the bowels of Darkhaven? How is it that a gap has opened onto the marrow-fire itself?"

This time, the silence was different.

"We didn't do it, my lord!" It was one of the stable lads who spoke, near the exits. He ducked his head with a furtive blush. "It was just *there*."

Madlings glanced at one another, catching each other's eyes. The question was asked and answered. There were nods and murmurs all around. Each time, it was the same. They had had naught to do with it.

A cold finger of fear brushed the length of Ushahin's crooked spine. He thought of how Darkhaven had been built, of how Lord Satoris had used the power of Godslayer to raise the mountains that surrounded the Vale of Gorgantum and laid the foundation of Darkhaven itself. What did it mean if the foundation was crumbling? What did it mean if Lord Satoris himself had allowed it to happen—or worse, was unaware?

For all things mussst be as they musst.

"No." He caught himself shaking his head, saying the word aloud. With an effort, Ushahin willed himself to stillness, breathing slowly. The madlings watched him with trepidation. "No, never mind, it's all right." He forced a lopsided smile. "You did no wrong, then. It is nothing that cannot be mended. All is well."

A collective sigh of relief ran through his madlings. With a final nod, Ushahin gave them license, permitted them to shuffle forward, a sea of humanity surging against the small island promontory of his chopping-block dais. He gave them his broken hands to clutch and stroke, offering no false promises nor comfort, only the sheltering shield of his stubborn, enduring pain.

"Oh, lord!" It was a young woman who spoke, eyes bright with emotion. She kissed his fingertips and pressed his hand to her cheek. "I tried, my lord, I did. Forgive me my weakness!"

"Ah, Meara." Bending forward, Ushahin caressed her cheek. He touched the surface of her thoughts and saw the shadow of Tanaros' face therein. He grasped a little of what it betokened and pitied her for it. What was love but a little piece of madness? "All is well. I forgive you."

She caught her breath in a gasping laugh. "You shouldn't. I

brought her there. We are weak. *I* am weak." She cradled his hand, gazing up at him. "You should kill her, you know. It would be for the best."

"Yes." Ushahin grew still, hearing his own thoughts echoed. "I know." For a moment, they remained thusly. Then his heart gave a twinge beneath the branded skin that circumscribed it, and he shook his head ruefully and withdrew his hand. "I cannot, little sister. I am sworn to his Lordship, and he would see her live. I cannot gainsay his will. Would you have it otherwise?"

"No." Unshed tears pooled like diamonds in her eyes.

"Remember what you are," he said gently to her, "and do not dwell on what-might-have-been. Remember that *I* love you for that-which-is."

"I will!" Her head bobbed, overbrimming tears forging swathes down her sallow cheeks. Meara sniffled and scrubbed at her tears. "I will try, lord."

"Good." Ushahin gazed past her at the faces of the madlings still awaiting his regard. "Well done, my child." So many of them! How had their numbers come to swell so large? Their pain made his heart ache. He understood them, understood their weaknesses. What-might-have-been. A rock, clutched in a boy's hand, descending. What if it had never fallen? A trader's shadow, darkening the alley before withdrawing; his father, a tall shadow, turning away with averted face. What if someone—anyone—had intervened? It was a dream, a sweet dream, a bittersweet dream.

He understood.

And as for the other thing . . .

Ushahin shuddered, thinking of the foundations of Darkhaven giving way beneath him. The passages were too narrow to allow the Fjel masons access, and any patchwork Vorax's Staccians had done was merely a stopgap. If the foundation crumbled, it was symptomatic of things to come. Only his Lordship could root out this decay—if he retained the will and the power and the sanity to do so. Ushahin would speak to him. He prayed his Lordship would hear his words and act upon them, for if he did not . . .

"May it come later than sooner," he whispered, opening his arms to his throng. "Oh, please, may it!"

THREE

ON THEIR SECOND DAY ON land, Haomane's Allies compared notes as they rode along the coastal road that lay between Harrington Bay, where the dwarf-ship *Yrinna's Bounty* had deposited them, and Meronil, the Rivenlost stronghold whence they were bound.

All of them had been plagued by strange visions in the night.

The Borderguardsmen spoke of it in murmurs, clustering together in their dun cloaks, bending their heads toward one another. Even the Ellylon spoke of it, when the tattered remnants of Malthus' Company found themselves riding together on the broad road.

"'Twas as if I dreamed," Peldras mused, "or so it seems, from what Men have told me; for we do not lose ourselves in sleep as Arahila's Children do. And yet it seemed that I did wander therein, for I found myself watching a tale not of my own devising unfold. And a great wind blew toward me, hot and dry as the desert's breath, and I beheld him emerge from it—the same, and not the same, for the Wise Counselor was somehow *changed*."

"Yes!" Fianna breathed, her face aglow. "That's what *I* saw!"

"'Twere as well if he were," Lorenlasse of the Valmaré said shortly, coming abreast of her. "For all his vaunted wisdom, Haomane's Counselor has led us into naught but folly, and we are no closer to restoring the Lady Cerelinde."

Nudging his mount, he led the Rivenlost past them. Sunlight glittered on their armor and their shining standards. Peldras did not join his fellows, but gazed after them with a troubled mien. At the head of the long column of Allies, Aracus Altorus rode alone and spoke to no one. His dun cloak hung down his back in unassuming folds, but his bright hair and the gold circlet upon it marked him as their uncontested leader.

"What did *you* see?" Blaise Caveros asked Lilias abruptly.

Bowing her head, she studied her hands on the reins— chapped for lack of salve, her knuckles red and swollen. She preferred to listen, and not to remember. It had been an unpleasant dream. "What do my dreams matter?" she murmured. "What did *you* see, Borderguardsman?"

"I saw Malthus," he said readily. "I saw what others saw. And you?"

Lifting her head, she met his dark, inquisitive gaze. What *had* she seen, dreaming beside the fire in their campsite? It had been a restless sleep, broken by the mutters and groans of Men rolled in their bedrolls, of Ellylon in their no-longer dreamless state.

A Man, or something like one; venerable with age. And yet . . . there had been something terrible in his eyes. Lightning had gathered in folds of his white robes beneath his outspread arms, in the creases of his beard. There was a gem on his breast as clear as water, and he had ridden into her dreams on the wings of a desert sirocco, on a horse as pale as death.

And he had raised one gnarled forefinger like a spear, his eyes as terrible as death, and pointed it at *her*.

"Nothing," Lilias said to Blaise. "I saw nothing."

On that night, the second night, the dream reoccurred; and again on the third. It kindled hope among the Men and unease among the Ellylon, and discussion and dissent among members of both races.

"This is some trick of the Misbegotten," Lorenlasse announced with distaste.

"I do not think he would dare," Peldras said softly. There were violet smudges of weariness in the hollows of his eyes. "For all his ill-gained magics, Ushahin the Misbegotten has never dared trespass in the minds of Haomane's Children."

On orders from Blaise Caveros, the Borderguard sent scouts to question commonfolk in the surrounding territories. They returned with a confusion of replies; yes, they had seen the Bright Rider, yes, and the other Rider, too, the horses the colors of blood, night, and smoke. A wedge of ravens flying, a desert wind. A stone in a child's fist, crushing bone; a clear gem, and lightning.

They were afraid.

Lorenlasse of Valmaré listened and shook his fair head. "It is the Misbegotten," he said with certainty. Others disagreed.

Only Aracus Altorus said nothing. Weariness was in the droop of his shoulders; but he set his chin against the weight of the Soumanië as he rode and glanced northward from time to time with a kind of desperate hope.

And Lilias, whom the visions filled with terror, watched him with a kind of desperate fear.

"You know more than you say, Sorceress," Blaise said to her on the fourth day.

"Usually." Lilias smiled with bitter irony. "Is that not why I am here?"

He studied her. "Is it Malthus?"

She shrugged. "Who am I to say? You knew him; I did not."

Blaise rode for a while without speaking. "Is it Ushahin Dream-stalker?" he asked at length, adding, "You knew him; I did not."

"I met him," Lilias corrected him. "I did not *know* him."

"And?" He raised his eyebrows.

"What would you have me do?" she asked in exasperation. "You are a courteous enough keeper, Blaise Caveros, but I am a prisoner here. Would you have me *aid* you, my lord? After you destroyed my life and rendered me"—Lilias held up her wind-chafed, reddened hands—"*this*?"

"What?" Leaning over in the saddle, Blaise caught her wrist in a strong grip. Their mounts halted, flanks brushing. "Mortal? A woman?" His voice softened. "It is the lot to which you were born, Lilias of Beshtanag. No more, no less. Is it so cruel?"

Ahead of them, the Rivenlost rode in glittering panoply, ageless features keen beneath their fluttering pennants. "Yes," Lilias whispered. "It is."

Blaise loosed his grip and retrieved his dropped rein, resuming their pace. "I do not understand you," he said flatly.

"Nor do I expect you to," she retorted, rubbing her wrist.

He stared across at her. "Did we not show you mercy?"

Unwilling laughter arose from a hollow place within her. "Oh, yes!" Lilias gasped. "As it suited you to do so. Believe me, you'll regret *that*, my lord!" She laughed again, a raw edge to the sound. "And the great jest of it is, I find that being forced to continue living, I have no desire to cease. I am afraid of dying, Blaise."

He looked away. "You, who have sent so many to their death?"

"Not so many." She considered his profile, stern and spare. "Beshtanag was left in peace, mostly. The Regents were afraid of Calandor. Do you think me a monster?"

"I don't know." Blaise shook his head. "As you say, I have met you, Sorceress. I do not *know* you. And of a surety, we are agreed: I do not understand you." He rode for a time without speaking, then asked, "What was he like?"

"Calandor?" Her voice was wistful.

"No." He glanced at her. "Ushahin."

"Ah." Lilias gave her bitter smile, watching her mount's ears bob and twitch. "So you would pick over my thoughts like a pile of bones, gleaning for scraps of knowledge."

He ignored her comment. "Is it true it is madness to meet his gaze?"

"No." Lilias thought about her meeting on the balcony, the Soumanië heavy on her brow, and her desire to Shape the Dreamer into wholeness, taking away his bone-deep pain. And she remembered how he had looked at her, and her darkest fears had been reflected in his mismatched eyes. Everything he had seen had come to pass. Another hysterical laugh threatened her. "Yes, perhaps. Perhaps it is, after all."

Blaise watched her. "Have you met others of the Three?"

"The Warrior." Seeing him look blank, she clarified, "Tanaros Kingslayer. Your kinsman, Borderguardsman."

"And?" His jaw was set hard.

"What do you wish me to say, my lord?" Lilias studied him. "He is a Man. Immortal, but a Man. No more, and no less. I think he gives his loyalty without reserve and takes betrayal hard." Out of the corner of her eye, she saw Fianna the Archer watching them with distaste and smiled. "And he does not understand women. You are much like him, Blaise Caveros."

Blaise drew in a sharp breath to reply, wrenching unthinking at the reins. His mount arched its neck and sidled crabwise.

But before he could get the words out, the fabric of the world ripped.

A hot wind blew across the coastal road, setting the dust to swirling. Haomane's Allies halted, their mounts freezing beneath them, prick-eared. Borderguardsmen shielded their eyes with their hands; Ellylon squinted. At the head of the column, Aracus Altorus lifted his chin.

A clap of lightning blinded the midday sun.

Out of the brightness, a figure emerged; the Galäinridder, the Bright Rider, astride a horse that shone like sea-foam in starlight. The horse's broad chest emerged like the crest of a wave, churning onto the world's shoals. The Rider's robes were white and his white beard flowed onto his chest. Nestled amid it was a gem as clear as water, as bright as a diamond, so bright it hurt to behold it.

"Borderguard!" Aracus' voice rang as his sword cleared its sheath. "Surround him!"

They moved swiftly to obey, dun cloaks fluttering in the breeze as they encircled the shining Rider, who calmly drew rein and waited. Blaise nodded at Fianna as he moved to join them, entrusting Lilias to her care. At a gesture from Lorenlasse, the Rivenlost archers strung their bows, moving to reinforce the Borderguard.

"How is this, Aracus?" The Rider smiled into his beard. "Am I so changed that you do not know me?"

"I pray that I do." Aracus nudged his mount's flanks, bringing him within striking range. His voice was steady, the point of his blade leveled at the Rider. "And I fear that I do not. Are you Malthus, or some trick of the Sunderer?"

The Rider opened his arms. "I am as you see me."

Sunlight dazzled on the clear gem. Lilias flinched. On her right, Fianna unslung Oronin's Bow and nocked an arrow, pointing it at Lilias' heart.

No one else moved.

Aracus Altorus broke into an unexpected grin. "That's a wizard's answer if ever I've heard one." He sheathed his sword, leaning forward to extend his hand. "Welcome back, my lord Counselor! We feared you dead."

"Ah, lad." Malthus' eyes crinkled as he clasped Aracus' hand. "I'm harder to kill than that."

The Borderguard gave a cheer, unbidden. There was no cheering among the Rivenlost, but they lowered their bows, returning arrows to their quivers. Turning her head, Lilias saw that Fianna kept an arrow loosely nocked, aimed in her direction. There was lingering distrust in her gaze.

"How?" Aracus asked simply.

"It took many long days," Malthus said, "for I spent my strength in maintaining the spell of concealment that hides the Bearer from the Sunderer's eyes. What strength remained to me, I lost in my battle with his Kingslayer. When the Sunderer destroyed the Marasoumië, I was trapped within it, scarce knowing who I was, let alone where. And yet, in the end, I won free." He touched the white gem on his breast, his face somber. "I fear the cost was high, my friends. As I am changed, so is the Soumanië. It is a bright light in a dark place, one that may illuminate Men's souls, but no longer does it possess the power to Shape."

A murmur of concern ran through the ranks of Haomane's Allies.

"Is that all?" Aracus Altorus laughed, and removed the gold fillet from his head. A gladness was in his manner for the first time since Cerelinde had been taken from him. "Here," he said, offering it. "The spoils of Beshtanag. It's useless to me. I'd thought to ask you teach me how to wield it, but it's better off in your hands, Malthus. I'm a warrior, not a wizard."

Toward the rear of the company, Lilias made a choked sound.

"Ah, lad." Malthus gazed at the fillet in Aracus' palm, the gold bright in the sunlight, the Soumanië dull and lifeless. "Truly," he murmured, "you have the heart of a king. Would that the gem could be given as easily. No." He shook his head. "It is not truly yours to give, Aracus. The Soumanië must be inherited from the dead or surrendered freely by a living owner. Until that happens, I can wield it no more than you."

Aracus frowned. "Then—"

"No one can wield it." Malthus lifted his head, and his gaze was filled with a terrible pity. With one gnarled forefinger, he pointed at Lilias, who sat motionless, conscious of the Archer's arrow pointed at her heart. "Not so long as the Sorceress of Beshtanag lives."

DANI OPENED HIS EYES TO see a dark blot swimming in a pool of light hovering above him. His head ached and the bright, blurred light made him feel nauseated. He blinked and squinted until his vision began to clear, and the dark blot resolved itself into the worried face of his uncle, silhouetted against the blue Staccian sky.

"Dani!" Thulu's face creased into a grin. "Are you alive, lad?"

There seemed to be a stone upon his chest. He tried an experimental cough. It hurt in a number of places. "I don't know," he whispered. "Are you?"

"Barely." Thulu sat back, nodding at him. "You can let go of it now, lad. It's safe enough."

"What?" He realized his right hand was clutching the flask containing the Water of Life so hard it ached, pressing it hard against his flesh. His fingers had cramped frozen, and it took an effort to open them. The pressure on his chest eased when he released the flask. He tried to sit and floundered, finding his left arm bound and useless.

"Careful." Uncle Thulu moved to assist him. "There you go."

"What's that for?" Sitting upright, Dani looked at his left arm in bewilderment. It was secured in a damp makeshift sling torn from one of their cloaks, knotted around his neck. He tried moving it. A jolt of pain shot through his shoulder. "Ow!"

"Careful," Thulu repeated. "What do you remember, lad?"

"The river." He could hear it roaring nearby. The sound of it cleared some of the mist from his thoughts. "The Fjeltroll. We were attacked." He blinked at his uncle, remembering red blood swirling in the river foam. "You were wounded."

"Aye." Uncle Thulu showed him the gashes, three lines gouged across his chest. He had packed them with clay from the riverbank to stop the bleeding. It had worked, but his skin had a greyish cast. "I had a time getting you out of the river."

"We hit a rock." Dani felt at his head, finding a painful lump. It throbbed beneath his fingertips. He winced.

"*You* hit a rock," his uncle corrected him. "*I* fished you out." He padded out of sight and returned to hand Dani a much-battered bowl. "Here. Drink."

Dani sipped broth, made from strips of dried hare boiled in river water, and felt a measure of warmth in his belly, a measure of strength return to his limbs. He glanced around the makeshift campsite. It was sparse, little more than a sheltered fire and a few garments drying on the rocks. Their pine-branch float was nowhere in sight. He shifted his shoulders and felt the pain lance through him. It was bad, but bearable. "How badly am I hurt?"

"I don't know." Thulu's gaze was unflinching. "I think you broke a bone, here." One calloused finger brushed Dani's collarbone on the left side. "I bound it as best I could. How's your head?"

"It hurts." Dani squinted. "We're not safe here, are we?"

"No." A deep compassion was in his uncle's gaze, as deep as the Well of the World. "They're after us, lad. They'll follow the river. It won't be long. If you mean to continue, we'll have to flee." He opened his empty hands. "Across dry land, those places the Fjel do not believe sustain life."

"You lost your digging-stick!" Dani remembered seeing it, the length of peeled baari-wood jutting from the rib cage of a Fjel corpse. It had saved his life. "Can you still find water's path beneath the earth?"

"I believe it." His uncle stared at his empty palms, then clenched them into fists. "We are Yarru-yami, are we not?" He bared his teeth in a grin made fearful by the loss of fatty flesh, his face gaunt and hollow. "As Uru-Alat wills, I am your guide, Dani. Though we cross dry land, and our enemies pursue us, we will survive. We will flee, cunning as desert rats, until we come to the source of illness. If it is your will to follow the veins of Uru-Alat, I will lead you."

"It is, Uncle." In a gesture of trust, Dani set down his bowl and laid his right hand open like an upturned cup over his uncle's clenched fists. The radiating lines that intersected his pale palm formed a half a star. "Lead, and I will follow."

Thulu nodded, swallowing hard. The apple of his throat moved beneath his skin, and tears shone in his dark eyes. "Finish your broth," he said gently, "then gather yourself. We dare not wait. The Fjeltroll will not be far behind."

"Aye, Uncle." Dani nodded and picked up the bowl, finishing the last of his broth. With his free hand, he levered himself to his feet. For an instant, the world swam around him—then it steadied, anchored around the pain in his left shoulder, and the weight that hung suspended from his throat. He drew a deep breath. "I am ready."

"All right, then." Rising from a squat, his uncle scattered the fire with one well-placed kick of a calloused heel. Seizing their lone cooking-pot, he trampled on the coals, grinding them beneath his feet, then kicked pebbles and debris over the site until nothing of it remained. The River Spume surged past, heedless. Thulu exhaled, hard, and doubled over, catching at his chest. Bits of clay mingled with blood flaked loose. "All right," he said, straightening. "Let's go, lad."

They went.

SKRAGDAL ROARED.

The Fjel under his command kept silent and out of his way, keeping to the walls of the Nåltannen moot-hall. A Tungskulder in a rage was a thing to be avoided. Skragdal stormed in a circle, stomping and roaring, waving his arms in an excess of rage. The Nåltannen Elders glanced uneasily at the trembling stalactites on the ceiling of their den's central chamber. The Gulnagel runner who had brought news of the sighting crouched and covered his head, waiting for Skragdal's fury to pass.

Eventually, it did.

The blood in his frustrated veins cooled from anger's boiling-point. Skragdal willed himself to stillness and drew a deep breath.

Rationality seeped back into his thoughts, the cool battle logic that General Tanaros had tried so hard to instill in him, that Field Marshal Hyrgolf had entrusted him to maintain.

"Tell me again," he rumbled.

Obliging, the Gulnagel stood and repeated his story. The smallfolk had been sighted in the southwestern verge of the Northern Harrow, where the Spume River reemerged from its journey underground. A Tordenstem sentry had given the alarm, and a pack under the command of Yagmar of the Tungskulder had cornered them beside the river. The smallfolk had held them off long enough to make an escape down the river.

"That," Skragdal said ominously, "is the part I do not understand."

The Gulnagel raised his hands in a shrug. "Who expects a cornered rabbit to fight? It was a narrow path and Yagmar's folk were taken by surprise. Besides"—he eyed Skragdal's plated armor, the axe and mace that hung at his belt, "they were not armed by Darkhaven."

"Still," Skragdal said. "They are Fjel."

"Yes." The Gulnagel shrugged. "It happened swiftly. Yagmar followed. He caught them where the river bends. He told them if they gave him the flask you seek, he would let them go. They paid him no heed."

Skragdal closed his eyes. "They are Men," he said softly. "Smallfolk from the desert. They do not speak Fjel."

"Oh!" The Gulnagel considered. "Some Men do."

"Staccians, yes." Skragdal opened his eyes. "These are not. And Yagmar should not have tried to bargain. His Lordship's orders are to kill them."

"Yagmar stood this deep," the Gulnagel said, placing the edge of one hand against his throat. "The river runs fast." There was a murmur of comprehension among the gathered Fjel. They appreciated the power of the northern rivers, which Neheris-of-the-Leaping-Waters had Shaped herself. Some could be forded; not all, not even by a Tungskulder. And none of them could swim. The density of their body-mass would not permit it.

Skragdal sighed. "So Yagmar tried to take the flask."

"Yes." The Gulnagel nodded. "And although it was no bigger than his thumb, it make him sink like a stone."

"Where are they now?" Skragdal stared at the messenger.

"Fled." The Gulnagel grimaced. "Away from the river, back into the dry mountains. It is what I am sent to tell you. Yagmar found their trail, but it leads away from water. After a day and a half, he had to turn back." He pointed at the waterskin slung from Skragdal's belt. "Neheris' bounty provides. We do not carry tools for hunting far from her rivers, where only small prey dwells."

"We are hunting small prey," Skragdal growled.

The Gulnagel gave another shrug. "What would you have us do?"

Skragdal considered the smaller Fjel, then glanced around at his companions. They returned his gaze impassively. None of them would dare advise him; not even Thorun, on whom he relied as a fellow Tungskulder. Dim light filtering through the air-shafts of the moot-hall glinted on their armor and weapons. This was the third den they had visited since leaving Neherinach. It felt strange to be among free-living members of his own people. They seemed vulnerable to him. It was not only the lack of arms, but the simplicity, the innocence. They remembered Neherinach—but that had been before Haomane had sent his Wise Counselors, armed with the Soumanië. Skragdal remembered what had happened in the Marasoumië, and the blasted node-point they had found, the carnage in Earl Coenred's hall. Those of Neheris' Children who did not serve Darkhaven had no idea of the forces arrayed against them.

He wished, very much, to be one of them.

The thought made him turn to the Nåltannen Elders. They were gathered in a group, watching and waiting to hear what he would decide. Skragdal bowed his head and addressed Mulprek, who was senior in this den. She was a female, her withered dugs giving testament to the myriad pups she had born. Her mate, he knew, was some years her junior. "Old mother," he said humbly. "Give me your counsel."

"Does the great warrior seek advice?" Mulprek wrinkled her lip and bared dull, yellowing eyetusks. She shuffled forward to peer up at him, laying a hand on his forearm. Her worn talons gleamed like steel against his hide, and she smelled of musk. Despite her age, her eyes were keen and bright. "This is a hunt, not a battle. Your prey has left a trail. You know where they are bound." She nodded at the Kaldjager Fjel in his company. "Use the Cold Hunters. Flush the prey, and herd them. Lay a trap. So we have always done. So I say."

It was good advice.

Skragdal nodded. "Let all the tribes remain vigilant," he said. "All hands may be needed for this." He turned to Blågen, whom he knew best among the Kaldjager. "Can your lads do this thing?"

"Aye. If you don't mind losing your scouts." The Kaldjager's eyes gleamed yellow. He slapped his waterskin. It made a heavy, sloshing sound. "We've no fear of dry land. If the Gulnagel will lead us to the trail, we'll hunt. We'll kill them if we can and herd them if we can't. Where do you want the smallfolk?"

The image of a green field dotted with vine-laced barrows rose in his mind. It lay on their route, and it would be a fitting place to make an end to it. Why these desert smallfolk had chosen to oppose his Lordship, he could not fathom. Already, they had paid a terrible price for their folly.

But it didn't matter, only that the thing was done.

"Neherinach," Skragdal said grimly. "Bring them to Neherinach."

A RIVER OF WINGS FILLED the Tower of Ravens, black and beating.

Flying in a circle.

Tanaros stood outside himself, watching through Fetch's eyes. He was part and parcel of the endless river, riding the silent current. Curving along the basalt walls. Wings, overlapping like scales, glossy feathers reflecting the blue-white flicker of the marrow-fire. He saw his brethren, bright eyes and sharp beaks. It was important that the wings overlap, beating in intricate layers.

His Lordship had summoned the Ravensmirror.

There he stood, at its center. A core of looming darkness, darkness visible. The Ravensmirror revolved around him. He had spoken the words in the ancient Shapers' tongue. His blood was a tang in the air.

Through doubled eyes, Tanaros beheld him; and the Three. He saw Vorax, who stood sturdy as a bulwark in the raven's gaze. To his eyes, the Staccian looked tired and worn. The news out of Gerflod had taken its toll. He saw Ushahin, who shone like a beacon in Fetch's eyes. Tanaros saw a feverish glitter in the half-breed's mien. There was power there, gathering and unspent. Where, he wondered, did it come from?

He saw himself.

A circling vision, glimpsed in the round. A pale face upraised, tracking the ravens' progress. A furrowed brow, a lock of hair falling, so. A pair of hands, strong and capable, gentle enough to cup a scrap of life wrought of hollow bones and feathers, a quick-beating heart. The fingers of one hand curled tenderly about the hilt of his black sword, holding it like a nestling.

Tanaros blinked, clearing his doubled vision. He tightened his grip on his sword-hilt, knuckles whitening.

Lord Satoris uttered the word. *"Show!"*

Around and around the ravens surged, and images formed in the reflection of their glossy wings.

None of them were good.

The last time Lord Satoris had summoned the Ravensmirror, it had shown armies of Haomane's Allies gathering. Now, they were on the move. In every quarter of Urulat, they had departed. In Pelmar, the Five Regents had assembled a massive delegation; they issued forth like a stream of ants, bent on honoring the pacts made at the overthrow of Beshtanag. In Vedasia, long trains of knights wound along the orchard-lined roads, flanked by their squires and attendants. A corps of archers marched forth from the tiny nation of Arduan. Along Harrington Inlet, the Free Fishers drew lots to determine who would stay, and who would fight. On the ruffled waters of the bay, ships hurried toward Port Calibus, where Duke Bornin of Seahold awaited with the foot soldiers under his command, returning from the Siege of Beshtanag.

Vorax cleared his throat. "They're coming here this time, aren't they?"

"Soon." Lord Satoris stared at the Ravensmirror. "Not yet." He turned his unblinking gaze on Vorax. "Shall we see what transpires in the north, my Staccian?"

The Ravensmirror tilted, images fragmenting, reforming in the shape of mountains and pines, leaping rivers. Where they bordered Fjel territory, the stone fortresses of Staccia were sealed tight in adamant defense. To the southwest, along a narrow swath . . .

Vorax grunted at the sight of Staccian lordlings arming themselves for battle, preparing to venture southward. "Too long," he said. "It has been too long since I went among them and reminded them of our bargain, and the peace and prosperity it has garnered Staccia."

"Do not despair." Tanaros watched the unfolding vision as it veered farther north. All across the peaks and valleys Neheris had Shaped, Fjel hunted; a collection of tough hide and bared eyeteeth, seeking their quarry. There were too many, and the territory too vast, for the ravens of Darkhaven to encompass, but it showed enough for hope. "The Fjel are loyal. If this Bearer is to be found, they will find him."

"But *Staccia*—"

"No." Ushahin shook his head. "Do not blame yourself, cousin. The Galäinridder made that path, bursting from the field of Neherinach, if my vision and the Fjel's tale holds true. I felt him as I rode, sifting through the dreams of Men."

Lord Satoris clenched his fists. "Malthus!"

The Three exchanged a glance.

"Where *is* he?" Tanaros asked aloud. "I thought him trapped and done." He bent his gaze on the shifting Ravensmirror. "Where's Aracus Altorus? Where are the Borderguard? Where are the *Rivenlost*?"

The fragmented visions shattered like a dark mirror, reforming to show something new. Wings beat and whispered, flitting among a copse of trees along the road, keeping a careful distance and staying hidden. The Arrow of Fire was spent, but the Archer's gaze endured. It was best to be wary. A group; a small group, measured against the numbers they had been shown, but a doughty one. There was the Borderguard of Curonan, in their dun-grey cloaks. There were the Rivenlost, tall and fair, radiant in silver armor. They were leaving Seahold behind them, with all its pennants flying. Toward Meronil they rode, the stronghold of Ingolin the Wise, steeped in Ellylon magic.

Tanaros drew in his breath in a hiss.

At the head of the company rode two Men; one mortal, with a Soumanië dull and ashen on his brow. He knew him, knew that demanding, wide-set gaze. And the other—the other it hurt to behold, robes rustling like a storm, a diamond-bright gem nestled in his white beard. Tanaros knew him, too. He remembered the shock that had resonated through his arms when the black blade of his sword had bitten deep into the old one's staff and stuck there. So close, it had been.

And then the Marasoumië had exploded.

"Malthus," he whispered, watching. "Would that I had killed you." The Counselor rode a mount as white as foam, and something in the arch of its neck, the placement of its hooves and the silvery fall of its mane, made his heart ache. Tanaros remembered it differently, cast in hues of night, as willful as this mount was tranquil. "That's my *horse*! What have you done to it?"

"What, indeed?" Lord Satoris' smile was like the edge of a knife. "Ah, Malthus! It is a violent resurrection you performed to escape entombment in the Ways. I did not believe it could be done. But it came at a price, did it not? Not dead, but almost as good."

Ushahin squinted crookedly at the vision in the Ravensmirror. "He's spent its power, hasn't he? The Soumanië. He's spent it all."

"Not all." The Shaper studied his adversary. "But that which remains is a brightness cast by the Souma, even as matter casts shadow. My Elder Brother's weapon Malthus no longer has the power to Shape matter, only the spirit."

"Dangerous enough," Tanaros murmured, thinking of the Staccian exodus they had witnessed, the tale Skragdal's Gulnagel had brought of Earl Coenred's betrayal. "Where the spirit wills, the flesh follows."

"Yes." Lord Satoris nodded. "But no longer is Malthus the Wise Counselor capable of bringing down the very gates of Darkhaven."

Vorax stirred. "He had such power?"

"Oh, yes, my Staccian." In the center of the tower room, the Shaper turned to him. "Malthus had such power, though not enough to defeat me in the bargain." His words hung in the darkling air. "For that, he would need an army."

"My Lord, he has an army," Vorax said bluntly. "And another Soumanië."

"Yes." Lord Satoris gave his knife-edged smile. "Useless to him, now. None can use it, unless its living holder surrenders it, or dies. It will be a fascinating thing to see, how my Brother's weapon deals with this dilemma." He turned back to consider the swirling visions, forgetful of the presence of his Three. "What will you do, Malthus?" he asked the Counselor's image. "Will you let the Sorceress live, seek to sway her heart, and endure the consequence if you fail? Or will you see her judged and condemned to death for her crimes?" The Shaper laughed aloud, a sound that made the foundations of Darkhaven vibrate. "Oh, it would be an amusing thing if it were the latter!"

A shudder ran over Tanaros' skin. He glanced sidelong at the Ravensmirror, where Aracus Altorus still rode alongside Malthus. There, farther back in the train, he saw her: Lilias of Beshtanag, the Sorceress of the East. She was much changed from the woman he had met in Beshtanag; pale and haggard, with fear-haunted eyes. Tanaros was aware of his heart beating within his branded chest, a solid and endless pulse.

He wondered what it would be like to have that stripped away after so long, to know, suddenly, that his heartbeats were numbered, that each one brought him a step closer to death.

In the Ravensmirror, the company of Malthus drew farther away, their image dwindling. They were passing the copse, into a stretch of open road. Among the ravens, a shared memory flitted from mind to mind: Arrow, arrow, arrow! Bodies tumbling from the sky. The ravens of Darkhaven dared not follow.

"Enough."

Lord Satoris made an abrupt gesture, and the Ravensmirror splintered into myriad bits of feathered darkness, scattering about the tower. Black eyes gleamed from every nook and cranny, watching as the Shaper paced in thought.

"It is bad, my Three," he said in time. "And yet, it is better than I feared. We have strong walls, and the Fjel to withstand their numbers. Malthus' power is not as it was. What we have seen is not enough to destroy us." He halted, a column of darkness, and tilted his head to gaze out the window toward the red star of Dergail's Soumanië. "It is what we have not seen that troubles me."

"The Bearer," Ushahin said.

"Yes." The single word fell like a stone.

"My Lord." Tanaros felt a pang of love constrict his heart. "The Fjel are hunting. He will be found, I swear it to you."

The Shaper bent his head toward him. "You understand why this thing must be done, my General?"

"I do, my Lord." Tanaros did not say it aloud; none of them did. The Prophecy hovered over them like a shroud.

"Perhaps the lad's dead." Vorax offered the words hopefully. "The travails of the Marasoumië, a hard journey in a harsh land— they're desert-folk, they wouldn't know how to survive in the mountains." He warmed to the idea. "After all, think on it. Why else would the damnable wizard head south, if his precious Bearer was lost in the northlands?"

"Because Malthus cannot find his Bearer, my Staccian." Grim amusement was in Lord Satoris' voice. "The lad is hidden by the Counselor's own well-wrought spell—from my eyes, and the eyes of Ushahin Dreamspinner. Now that the Soumanië is altered, Malthus cannot breach his own spell. And so he trusts the Bearer to the workings of my Elder Brother's Prophecy and goes to Meronil to plot war, and because there is a thing there he must retrieve."

No one asked. After a moment, Ushahin sighed. "The Spear of Light."

"Yes." Lord Satoris returned to the window, gazing westward. "I believe it to be true." His shoulders, blotting out the stars, moved in a slight shrug. "It matters not. Malthus has ever had it in his keeping."

Tanaros' mouth was dry. "What is your will, my Lord?"

The Shaper replied without turning around. "Send the runners back to Fjel territory, accompanied by as many Kaldjager as you can spare. The hunt must continue. Once they have gone, set a team to blocking the tunnels. Too many in Staccia know the way, and traitors among them. Tell the Fjel to return overland when they have succeeded." He did turn then, and his eyes glared red against the darkness. "Tell them to bring me the Bearer's head. I want to see it. And I want to see Malthus' face when it is laid at his feet."

Tanaros bowed his head. "My Lord."

"Good." The Shaper moved one hand in dismissal. "The rest you know, my Three. They are coming. Prepare for war."

They left him there, a dark figure silhouetted against darkness. Wet darkness seeped from his unhealing wound, trickling steadily to form a gleaming pool around his feet. Twin streaks of shadow streamed past his massive shoulders into the night as Ushahin bid the ravens to leave the Tower. Watching them go, Tanaros had an urge to call Fetch back, though he didn't.

"Well." Descending the winding stair, Vorax exhaled heavily and wiped his brow. "That's that, then."

"War." Ushahin tasted the word. "Here."

"Aye." Vorax grunted. His footsteps were heavy on the stairs. "I still think there's a fine chance that little Charred lad may be dead, and this a lot of fuss over nothing. It would be like that damnable wizard to play us for fools." He nudged Tanaros. "What do you say, cousin? Are the Charred Folk that hard to kill?"

Tanaros thought of the boy he had seen in the Ways, with a clay vial at his throat and a question in his eyes. He thought of the Yarru elders; of Ngurra, calm and sorrowful beneath the shadow of his black sword.

I can only give you the choice, Slayer.

"Yes," he said. "They are."

After that, the Three continued in silence. What his companions thought, Tanaros could not guess with any certitude. They had never spoken of what would befall them if Haomane's Allies were to prevail.

It had never seemed possible until now.

FOUR

◆

THE VALLEY IN WHICH THE Rivenlost haven of Meronil lay was a green
cleft shrouded in mist. By all appearances, it filled the valley to the
brim, moving in gentle eddies, sun-shot and lovely, a veil of rainbow droplets.

Lilias caught her breath at the sight of it.

Blaise Caveros glanced at her. "I felt the same when I first saw it."

She made no reply, watching as Aracus Altorus and Malthus the
Counselor rode to the valley's edge, peering into the mists. There,
they conferred. Aracus inclined his head, the Soumanië dull on his
brow. Mist dampened his red-gold hair, making it curl into ringlets
at the nape of his neck.

He needs a haircut, Lilias thought.

Aracus didn't look at her. She wished that he would, but he
hadn't. Not since the day the Counselor had appeared before them,
pointing his gnarled finger at her, and spoken those fateful words.

Not so long as the Sorceress of Beshtanag lives.

It was Aracus Altorus who had placed his hand on the Counselor's forearm, lowering his pointing finger. It was Aracus who
had raised his voice in a fierce shout, bidding Fianna the Archer to
lower her bow. And it was Aracus who had brought his mount
alongside hers, fixing her with his wide-set gaze. All the words that
had passed between them were in that gaze. He was not a bad
man, nor a cruel one. He had extended trust to her, and mercy, too.

"Will you not release your claim upon it, Lilias?" he had asked
her simply.

In the back of her mind there arose the image of Calandor as
she had seen him last; a vast mound of grey stone, the crumpled

shape of one broken wing pinned beneath him, the sinuous neck stretched out in death. To join him in death was one thing; to relinquish the Soumanië willingly? It would be a betrayal of that memory. While she lived, she could not do it. Tears had filled her eyes as she shook her head. "I cannot," she whispered. "You should have let me die when you had the chance."

Aracus had turned away from her then, giving a curt order to Blaise to ensure her safety. There had been dissent—not from Blaise, but among the others, and the Archer foremost among them. Arguing voices had arisen, calling for her death. In the end, Aracus Altorus, the would-be King of the West, had shouted them down.

"I will not become like our Enemy!"

Throughout it all, Malthus the Counselor had said nothing; only listened and watched. A horrible compassion was in his gaze, and Lilias flinched when it touched her. It had done so all too much since he had rejoined them. She wished he would turn his gaze elsewhere.

Now, on the edge of the valley, Malthus turned in the saddle, beckoning to the commander of the Rivenlost, Lorenlasse of the Valmaré. The clear gem at Malthus' breast flashed as he did so, making the mist that filled the valley sparkle.

Lorenlasse rode forward, placing the mouthpiece of a silver horn to his lips.

A single call issued forth, silvery and unsubstantial.

For a moment, nothing happened; then an echoing call arose from the valley's depths, and the mists parted like a veil, revealing that the paved road continued onward in descent. Below them lay the cleft green valley, divided by a gleaming river that widened as it flowed toward the sea harbor, spanned by an intricate series of bridges that joined fanciful towers spiring on either side. It was white, white as a gull's wing. White walls curved to surround both hemispheres, and the city itself was wrought of white marble, structures more delicate than Men's arts could compass.

Through it all ran the Aven River, toward the silvery sea. Sunlight gilded its surface, broken into arrowing ripples by the low, elegant boats being poled here and there. And on an island in the center of the river stood the Hall of Ingolin the Wise, his pennant flying from the highest tower, depicting the argent scroll of knowledge on a field of sage green. A trio of white-headed sea eagles circled the spire in a lazy gyre, borne aloft on broad wings.

"Meronil." There was deep satisfaction in Blaise's voice. "Have you ever seen anything so lovely?"

Lilias remembered Calandor alive and the majesty of his presence. How he had looked perched on the cliff's edge; sunlight glittering on his bronze scales, the glint of his green-gilt eyes, filled with knowledge. Love. A trickle of smoke, twin plumes arising in the clear air. The moment when he launched his mighty form into flight, the gold vanes of his outspread pinions defying the void below. So impossible; so beautiful.

"Perhaps," she murmured.

In the valley below, a company of Ellylon warriors emerged from the eastern gate, riding forth to meet them. They wore Ingolin's livery over their armor, sage-green tunics with his argent scroll on the breast. Their horses were caparisoned in sage and silver, and their hooves beat a rhythmic tattoo on the paving stones as they drew near.

The leader inclined his head. "Lord Aracus, Lorenlasse of Valmaré," he said, then inclined his head toward Malthus. "Wise Counselor. Be welcome to Meronil. My Lord Ingolin awaits you."

With a gesture, he turned his mount and his men fell into two lines, flanking their guests to form an escort. With Aracus, Lorenlasse, and Malthus at the head, the company began the descent.

Lilias found herself in the middle of the column; behind the Rivenlost, but at the forefront of the Borderguard of Curonan. She twisted in the saddle to look behind her, and Blaise, ever mindful, leaned over to claim her mount's reins. Riding at her immediate rear, Fianna the Archer gazed at her with smoldering distrust. Lilias ignored her, watching what transpired. As the last Borderguardsman cleared the lip of the valley, the pearly mist arose. Dense as a shroud, it closed behind the last man. Once again, the green valley was curtained; and yet, overhead the sky was clear and blue, the sun shining upon Meronil.

There was magic at work here she did not understand; Ellylon magic. What was true Shaping, and what was illusion? She could not tell, only that she was captive within its borders. Lilias shuddered. Without thinking, she lifted one hand to feel her brow, keenly aware of the Soumanië's absence.

"Are you well, Sorceress?" Blaise asked without looking at her.

"Well enough." Lilias dropped her hand. "Lead on."

They completed their descent. There was fanfare at the gate. Lorenlasse blew his silvery horn; other horns sounded in answer. The leader of their escort spoke courteously to the Gate's Keeper; the Gate's Keeper replied. Rivenlost guards stood with unreadable faces, crossing their spears. Aracus sat his mount with his jaw set and a hard expression in his eyes. The Gate's Keeper inclined his head. Malthus the Counselor smiled into his beard, fingering the bright gem at his breast. Fianna the Archer scowled, trying hard not to look overwhelmed by Ellylon splendor. Blaise conferred with his second-in-command, delegating. The bulk of the Borderguard withdrew to make camp in the green fields outside Meronil's eastern gate.

All of it gave Lilias a headache.

The Gate's Keeper spoke a word, and there was a faint scintillation in the air. The gate opened. They rode through, and the gate closed behind them.

They had entered Meronil.

The Rivenlost had turned out to see them. They were Ellylon; they did not gape. But they stood along their route—on balconies, in doorways, upright in shallow boats—and watched. Male and female, clad in elegant garb, they watched. Some raised their hands in silent salute; others made no gesture. Their age was unknowable. They were tall and fair, with grave eyes and a terrible light in their faces, a terrible grief in their hearts. Their silence carried a weight.

There should have been music playing.

Meronil was a city made for music, a symphony in architecture, its soaring towers and arching bridges echoing one another, carrying on a dialogue across the murmuring undertone of the Aven River.

Instead, there was only mourning silence.

In the city, Lorenlasse of the Valmaré dismissed his company. They parted ways, returning to their homes; to regroup, to await new orders. Lorenlasse bowed low to Aracus Altorus before he took his leave, promising to see him anon. Was there mockery in his bow? Lilias could not say.

Then, they were few. Haomane's Allies; Malthus' Company. There was Aracus and Malthus, and Blaise and Fianna, keeping watch over Lilias. Among the Ellylon, only Peldras accompanied them. Ingolin's escort led them across a wide bridge toward the island, while the River Aven flowed tranquilly below and the denizens of Meronil watched. No longer hidden amid a large party, Lilias shrank under their regard, feeling herself small and filthy beneath it, aware of the stain of her own mortality.

She imagined their disdain.

So this *is the Sorceress of the East?*

She reclaimed her reins from Blaise and concentrated on holding them, fixing her gaze upon her own reddened, chapped knuckles. It was better to meet no one's eyes. The Bridge's Keeper granted them passage. The company alighted on the island. When the doors to the Hall of Ingolin were thrown wide open, Lilias kept her gaze lowered. She dismounted at Blaise's quiet order and bore out the exchange of courtesies, the embraces given and returned, with little heed. None of it mattered. She wished she were anywhere in the world but this too-fair city.

"*Sorceress.*"

A voice, a single voice, speaking the common tongue, infused with deep music and bottomless wisdom, a host of magic at its command. It jerked her head upright. Lilias met the eyes of Ingolin the Wise, Lord of the Rivenlost.

He was old; so old, though it was not in his features, no. Or if it was, it was not in such a way that mortal Men understood. It was true, his hair was silver-white, falling like a shining river past his shoulders. Still, his shoulders were broad, and his features unlined. Time's footprints did not touch the Ellylon as they did the rest of the Lesser Shapers. But his eyes . . . ah!

Fathomless and grey, eyes that had seen the world Sundered.

They met hers, measured and *knew* her. They saw the hopeless tangle of grief and envy knotted in her heart. Ingolin was not called the Wise for nothing. He bent his head a fraction in acknowledgment of the status she had once held. "Lilias of Beshtanag. We welcome you to Meronil as our guest."

Others watched her; Aracus, with the dead Soumanië on his brow, filled with longing. Fianna, seething with resentment. Malthus and the Ellyl Peldras, both with that awful compassion. And Blaise; what of Blaise? He sat his mount quietly, scarred hands holding the reins, avoiding her eyes.

Lilias drew a deep breath. "You put a pleasant face upon my captivity, Lord Ingolin."

"Yes." Ingolin offered the word simply. "You know who you are, Sorceress; what you have been, what you have done. You know who we are and what we seek." He indicated the open door. "You will be granted hospitality within these walls; and sanctuary, too. Of that, I assure you. No more, and no less."

Lilias' head ached. There was too much light in this place, too much whiteness. She rubbed at her temples with fumbling fingers. "I don't want it."

There was no pity in his face, in the eyes that had beheld the Sundering of the world. "Nonetheless, you shall have it."

❖

"IT'S *HIM!*" MEARA HISSED.

Cerelinde's heart clenched in a spasm of fear. She willed herself to a semblance of calm before glancing up from the embroidery in her lap. "Has Lord Satoris summoned me, Meara?"

"Not his *Lordship!*" The madling grimaced and jerked her head at the doorway. "General Tanaros. He's *here.*"

This time, it was a surge of gladness that quickened her heart. It was more disturbing than the fear. Cerelinde laid aside her embroidery and folded her hands. "Thank you, Meara. Please make him welcome."

She did, muttering to herself, and made a hasty exit without apology.

And then he was there.

He was taller than she remembered; or perhaps it was the gauntness his travail had left that made him seem so. The room seemed smaller with him in it. Muted lamplight reflected dimly on the glossy surface of his ceremonial black armor. He bowed, exacting and courtly. "Lady Cerelinde."

"General Tanaros." She inclined her head, indicating the empty chair opposite her. "Will you sit?"

"Thank you." Encased in unyielding metal, Tanaros sat upright, resting his hands on his knees. He regarded her in silence for a moment, as though he'd forgotten what he'd come to say. "I trust you are well?"

"As well as I may be." Cerelinde smiled faintly. "Meara has obtained materials that I might indulge in needlework to alleviate the tedium. His Lordship has not permitted Lord Vorax to kill me."

"Vorax?" The straps of Tanaros' armor creaked as he shifted. "He wouldn't."

"He would like to."

"He won't."

Another silence stretched between them. Cerelinde studied him. He looked tired, his face bearing the marks of sun and wind. The hollows of his eyes looked bruised, and beneath the errant lock of dark hair that fell across his brow, there were furrows that had not been there before. It stirred pity in her heart, an emotion she sought to repress. He was Tanaros Kingslayer, one of the Three, Lord General of the Army of Darkhaven.

Still, he was here, sitting in her well-appointed prison cell, and he was the only sane person she had seen in this place who did not appear to wish her dead.

"In Haomane's name," she said quietly, "or any you might honor, will you please tell me what is happening?"

"War." Tanaros held her gaze without blinking. "Not yet, but soon. Even now, they are gathering in Meronil to plot strategy. They are coming for you, Lady."

Cerelinde nodded once. "Do they have a chance?"

He shrugged, making his armor creak. "Do I think they can take Darkhaven? No, Lady, I do not. But nothing in war is certain save bloodshed."

"It could be averted."

"By letting you go?" Tanaros gave a short laugh. "To wed Aracus Altorus?"

She made no reply.

"Ah, Lady." His voice roughened. "Even if your answer were no . . . how long? One mortal generation? Ten? How long do you suppose it will be until another scion of Altorus is born who sets your heart to racing—"

"Enough!"

"—and makes the blood rise to your cheeks?"

"Enough, my lord," Cerelinde repeated, flushing. "There is no need to be vulgar."

Tanaros raised his brows. "Vulgar?"

She opened her mouth, then closed it.

Tanaros sighed and rumpled his hair with one hand. "In the end, it matters naught. I do not think Haomane's Allies would ever be willing to forgo the Prophecy. And I am quite certain, in this instance, that his Lordship is not interested in negotiating."

"He could relent," Cerelinde said in a low, impassioned voice. "I have said it before, and it is still true. He could relent and surrender to Haomane's will. There is that. There is *always* that."

"No." Tanaros shook his head. "No, Lady, I don't think there is. I don't think there ever was."

"Why?" she asked steadily.

He shrugged again. "Ask *him*, if you truly want to know. Perhaps the answer lies in what-might-have-been."

"You heard of that?" Cerelinde flushed a second time. "I meant to speak to you of the incident. It is a small gift, a small magic. Vorax was wroth, but I did not mean to disturb, only to bring comfort. It eases them, to glimpse the paths they might have walked." She considered Tanaros and added softly, "I could show you, if you wished."

"No!" The word exploded from his lips. He took a slow breath, bracing his hands on his knees. "No," he repeated more gently. "Do you think I don't know, Lady? An ordinary cuckold's life, with all the small shames and painful sympathies attendant upon it. Believe me, I know what I abandoned."

"Perhaps. Perhaps not." Cerelinde looked at his braced hands, then raised her gaze to his face. "Is that why you killed her?"

"No." Tanaros lifted his hands, examining them in the dim lamplight. "I was angry." He met her gaze. "I held her hand through the birth. I wept tears at her pain. It was only afterward, when I saw the babe. I saw his red hair, and I remembered. How she and Roscus had smiled at one another. How they had fallen silent when I entered a room. A thousand such incidents, meaningful only now. I asked her, and she denied it. Lied. She lied to me. It was not until my hands were at her throat that she confessed. By then, my anger had gone too far." He paused. "You don't understand, do you?"

"No." She shook her head. "Neither portion, I fear."

"It is said the Ellylon cannot lie," he mused. "Is it so?"

"We are Haomane's Children," Cerelinde said, perplexed. "The Lord-of-Thought Shaped us. To think is to speak; to speak is to be. How can we speak a thing that is not true? We might as well unmake ourselves. It is not a thing I can fathom."

"Ah, well." Tanaros gave her a twisted smile. "We are Arahila's Children, and the truth of the heart does not always accord with that of the head. Be mindful of it, Lady, since you propose to wed one of us. If I am wrong, and we lose this coming war, it may matter."

"Aracus would not lie," she said certainly.

"Perhaps," he said, echoing her words. "Perhaps not."

Silence fell over the room like a shroud.

"Tanaros Kingslayer," Cerelinde said aloud. "Do you lay that death, too, at anger's doorstep? For it seems to me you must have loved him, once, for him to have wounded you so deeply."

For a long time, he was silent. "Yes," he said at length. "Anger, and love. It is the one that begat the other's strength, Cerelinde. He was my liege-lord; and for many years, like unto a brother to me." His mouth quirked into another bitter smile. "Do the Ellylon understand *betrayal?*"

"Yes." She did not tell him what was in her mind; that the Ellylon had known betrayal at the hands of Men. So it had been, since before the world was Sundered. From the dawning of the Second Age of Urulat, Arahila's Children had coveted the Gifts of Haomane's. And they had made war upon the Ellylon, believing in their folly that a Shaper's Gift could be wrested away by force. "We do."

"So be it." After considering her words, Tanaros give himself a shake, like a man emerging from a dream. He cleared his throat. "Forgive me, Lady. I did not come here to speak of such things."

"What, then?" Cerelinde asked simply.

His dark gaze was steady and direct. "To assure you that I continue to vouch for the safety of your well-being. No more, and no less."

She inclined her head. "Thank you."

"Well." Tanaros flexed his hands upon his knees. He made to rise, then hesitated. "Lady . . . if it might please you, there is something I might show you outside the walls of Darkhaven proper. On the morrow, perhaps?"

Outside.

For the third time in the space of an hour, Cerelinde's heart leapt. "Oh, yes," she heard herself whisper. "Please."

Tanaros rose, executing another crisp bow. "On the morrow, then."

Like a good hostess, she saw him to the door. He paused only briefly, searching her face. Something haunted was in his gaze, something that had not been there before. Then he took his leave, averting his eyes. The Fjeltroll on duty saluted him in passing, closing the door upon his departure.

It locked with an audible sound, sealing Cerelinde into her quarters.

Left alone, she placed her hand upon the ironwood door, contemplating her outspread fingers.

"ALL TOGETHER, NOW," SPEROS SAID encouragingly. "That's right, you've got it, lean on the lever. One, two, three . . . *yes!*" He let out a triumphant whoop as the great boulder settled into place with a resounding crash. "Oh, well *done*, lads!"

On the crude ramp, one of the Tordenstem let loose a reverberating howl, lofting the heavy, pointed log that had served as a lever. Delighted in their achievement, the others echoed his cry until loose pebbles rattled and the very air seemed to tremble.

Despite his aching eardrums, Speros grinned. "Hold on!" he shouted, prowling around the wooden rick on which the boulder rested. "Let's be sure it will hold."

It would. The thick branches groaned and the ropes lashing them together creaked, but in time they settled under the boulder's weight, ceasing their complaint. They would hold. High atop the crags above the Defile, Speros lay on his belly, squirming forward on his elbows, inching onto the overhanging promontory until he could peer over the edge.

Far, far below him lay the winding path that led along the desiccated riverbed. The mountains that Lord Satoris had erected around the Vale of Gorgantum were impassable, except perhaps to a determined Fjeltroll. With the tunnels blocked, the path was the only way into the Vale. If Haomane's Allies sought to penetrate Darkhaven's defenses, they would have to traverse it.

It would be difficult. Speros meant to make it impossible.

"Right." He squirmed backward and got to his feet. "We'll need to pile it high, with as much as it can hold. If we can get enough weight to take off the edge of this crag . . ." He made a chopping gesture with one hand. "It will block the path. But first we need to get our fulcrum in place." He glanced around, seeking a smallish boulder. "How about that one?"

"Aye, boss!" A Tordenstem Fjel padded cheerfully down the log ramp. It dipped under his heavy tread. He splayed his legs and squatted, lowering his barrel chest near to the ground, and wrapped powerful arms around the rock. It came loose in a shower of pebbles. "Where do you want it?"

"Here." Speros pointed to the spot.

The Fjel grunted and waddled forward. There was a second crash as he set down his burden at the base of the wooden rick. "There you are, then."

"That's done it. Shall we see if it will work?" Speros reclaimed the lever and tested it, lodging the pointed tip of the log beneath the mammoth boulder they had first moved. He positioned the midsection over the rock intended to serve as the fulcrum and leaned all his weight on the butt.

"Careful, boss," one of the Tordenstem rumbled.

"Don't worry." Speros bounced on the lever. Nothing so much as shifted. "Can *you* move it, Gorek?"

The Fjel showed the tips of his eyetusks in a modest smile. "Like as not." He approached the lever, taloned hands grasping the rough bark, and pushed.

It shifted, and the entire structure groaned.

"All right!" Speros said hastily. "One, then; or two of you at the most. We'll work it out later. Come on, lads, let's load the rick."

Hoofbeats sounded along the path that led from Darkhaven proper as the Fjel formed a chain, piling the wooden rick high with loose rocks and stones. Speros went out to meet the approaching rider. And there was Tanaros, clad in black armor, all save his helmet, astride the black destrier he had claimed in the Midlands, surveying his—*his*—accomplishments.

"Lord General!" Speros felt his face split in another grin. "Do you see what we've done here?"

"Indeed." Tanaros drew rein and took it in; the rick, the boulders, the lever, the Tordenstem padding their way up the crude ramp to deposit heavy stones. Dismounting, he strode to the edge of the promontory and gazed at the path below, gauging the trajectory. The wind stirred his dark hair. "Would it block the path entirely?"

"Long enough to give them trouble. There's another site that may work as well." Watching the General stand on the verge of the abyss gave Speros an uneasy feeling in the pit of his stomach. "Careful, my lord. There's not much holding that ledge up."

Tanaros raised his brows. "That's the point, isn't it?"

"Aye." Speros swallowed nervously.

"Don't worry. I've lived too long to die falling off a cliff." Tanaros came back to place a hand on Speros' shoulder. "Well done, Midlander. This was a fine thought you had."

"Thank you, sir!" His anxiety vanished in a surge of pride. "It came to me after we rode through the Defile. Why not use the strength of the Tordenstem to greater effect? It was filling in the Well of the World that gave me the idea. You recall how—"

"Yes." A shadow of sorrow crossed the General's face.

"—we used skids and levers . . ." Speros stopped. "Forgive me."

"No matter." Tanaros shook his head.

"I know, I failed you in the desert." Speros took a deep breath. "Believe me, Lord General, I have sworn an oath. I have said it before and will say it again. A thousand times, if need be. It will never happen—"

"Speros!" The General's grip on his shoulder tightened until it hurt. "Enough," he said quietly. "You will speak no more of it. I bear you no blame for what happened with the Yarru. What happened there . . ." He sighed and released Speros' shoulder, gazing out across the gorge of the Defile. "It will be good to fight an enemy who comes seeking a battle."

"Aye, sir." Speros followed the General's gaze uncertainly.

"Not *yet*, lad!" His mood shifting, Tanaros smiled at him. "They'll come soon enough. And I thank you for making us that much the readier for it."

"Aye, sir!" Speros smiled back at the General.

"You're a good lad, Speros of Haimhault." With another clap on the shoulder, Tanaros left him, striding across the stony ground to greet the Tordenstem. He knew them all by name. In another moment, he was gone, swinging astride the black horse and heading back toward the fortress, his figure dwindling beneath the dull grey sky.

Watching him go, Speros retained a lingering vision of the General standing on the edge of the cliff, the wind tugging at his dark hair, a specter of sorrow haunting his eyes. He wished there was something he could do or say to dispel that shadow.

He wished it *was* his own failure that had put it there.

It wasn't, of course. In his heart of hearts, he knew it. That was his own specter, the ghost of his father's voice, his family's disapproval. It had nothing to do with General Tanaros. That was something else altogether. He had heard what the old Yarru had said about the General's choice, and he had heard the General's reply, his final, agonized shout: *Give me a reason not to make it!*

But he hadn't. The old man had just stood there. *Choose*, he'd said; as if his people hadn't sent one of their own off upon a quest to fulfill Haomane's Prophecy, to destroy Lord Satoris and everything General Tanaros held dear. And what had followed afterward, the black blade flashing, the dull thud of Fjeltroll maces and blood sinking into the sand . . .

"What else was he supposed to do?" Speros asked aloud.

"Boss?" One of the Tungskulder glanced quizzically at him.

"Nothing." He squared his shoulders. There was one thing, at least, he could do. "Come on, lads, let's move. We've got another one of these to build before Haomane's Allies come a-calling."

FJELTROLL WERE HUNTING THEM AND Uncle Thulu was sick.

He had denied it for days; and long, thirsty, grueling days they were. After the first Fjeltroll to follow them had turned back, Dani had dared to hope. They worked their way slowly westward, avoiding all save the smallest water sources, concealing their trail as they went. It was slow and laborious, and he was increasingly worried about his uncle's condition, but at least they were spared the threat of Fjel.

Then they had seen another.

Dani had spotted it in the distance. It wasn't like the others that had attacked them. This one traveled alone, moving swiftly and silently. It worked its way back and forth across the terrain in purposeful arcs, pausing at times to lift a narrow, predatory head and scent the air. If it hadn't been for the glint of sunlight on its armor, he might have missed it.

Armor.

The Fjel hunting them was armed; worse, it carried a waterskin. Dani choked out a warning. Uncle Thulu clamped a hand over his mouth, casting around wildly for a place to hide.

Uru-Alat be thanked, he had found one—a cave, scarce more than a shallow depression, its opening partially hidden by pine branches. Uncle Thulu shoved Dani into it, scrambling after him and dragging the branches back in place. He stripped off a handful of needles as he did, grinding them hard between his palms.

"Here," he whispered, pressing half of the damp wad into Dani's good hand. "Rub it on your skin. It will help mask our scent."

Dani obeyed awkwardly, hampered by the cloth that bound his left arm. "I don't think he saw us," he whispered back. "Can they track by scent like the Were?"

"I'm not sure." Thulu peered through the branches. "But I suspect it's live prey rather than a cold trail he's sniffing after. If it wasn't, he'd be on us already." He settled back, adding grimly, "We'll find out soon enough, lad."

Pressed close to his uncle, Dani could feel the dry, feverish heat of his skin and hear the faint rattle in his chest as he breathed. Offering a silent prayer to Uru-Alat, he touched the clay vial at his neck like a talisman.

They waited.

The Yarru-yami were good at waiting. It took patience to survive in the desert. Many a time, Dani had squatted in front of a crevice in the rocks, a rock in his sling, waiting for hours for a lizard to emerge. He had never thought until now how much worse it must be for the lizard, hidden in darkness, unable to see or smell beyond the walls of its shelter, making the tentative decision to emerge without knowing whether a predator awaited it.

Dani strained his ears for the sound of heavy Fjel feet crunching on the rocks, the scrape of talons. Surely something that large could not move in total silence? Perhaps; perhaps not. There was no sound but the rattle of his uncle's breath. It seemed to be growing louder. His own mouth grew dry and parched. Dani sucked on a pebble to relieve the dryness and waited.

Beyond the spray of pine needles that curtained their hiding place, shadows moved across the ground. They stretched long and black, slanting toward twilight, before Uncle Thulu gauged it safe to investigate.

"I'll do it." Dani moved before his uncle could argue, parting the branches and wriggling out of the shallow cave and into open air.

With his heart in his throat, half-anticipating a blow, he scrambled to his feet and glanced around wildly.

There was nothing there, for as far as the eye could see. Only the slanting shadows; rocks and pine trees, and a mountain thrush warbling somewhere in the branches. Overhead, the sky was turning a dusky hue.

Dani laughed with relief. "He's gone, Uncle!"

The pine branches curtaining the cave rustled, then went still. Dani waited for a moment with a dawning sense of alarm. When Thulu failed to emerge, he wrenched the branches aside with his right hand, admitting light into the cavern.

"Uncle!"

The older Yarru squinted at him. "Sorry, boy. Thought the rest . . . do me good, at least." He made an effort to rise and grimaced. "Seems not."

A cold hand of fear closed around Dani's heart. In the lowering light of sunset, Uncle Thulu looked *bad*. His eyes were fever-bright and his face was drawn and haggard. His lips were dry and cracked, and his ashen skin seemed to hang loose on his bones.

Dani took a deep breath, touching the clay vial in an instinctive gesture. He willed his fear to subside. Without meaning to, he found himself thinking of Carfax the Staccian, who had found the courage to save him at the end, when the Were had attacked them. It seemed like a very long time ago.

Still, he found courage in the memory.

"Let me see." He knelt beside his uncle, untying the laces on the front of his woolen shirt. Folding back a corner to lay bare his uncle's chest, he hissed involuntarily through his teeth. The three gashes left by a Fjel's talons were angry and red, suppurating. Proud flesh swelled in ridges on either side, and a yellowish substance oozed from them.

"It's nothing." Uncle Thulu fumbled at his shirt. "I can go on, lad."

"No." Dani sat back on his heels. "No," he said again more strongly. "You can't." He nodded, mostly to himself. "But we're going to stay here until you can."

FIVE

◆◆◆

IT FELT GOOD TO HUNT with the Kaldjager.

Skragdal had shed his armor for the hunt; set aside his shield, unbuckled the leather straps to remove the unwieldy carapace of steel, laid down his battle-axe and his mace. Without them, he felt light as a pup, almost giddy with lightness.

Beyond the western outskirts of Drybone Reach, where the smallfolk had fled, ash trees grew and the White River tumbled from the heights in measured stages. Water gathered in foaming pools, a shining ribbon spilling over a worn granite lip only to gather and spill onward, lower and lower. In this fashion did it make its way to the field of Neherinach, several leagues hence.

It was beside one such pool that Skragdal crouched amid the roots of a tall ash, his talons digging into the rich loam. He was glad he had chosen to dally here. A cool breeze played over his exposed hide. He widened his nostrils, inhaling deeply.

There.

The odor of blood, living blood. A beating heart and the rank odor of fear, the distinctive scent of lanolin. He felt a keen hunter's smile stretch his mouth. Late summer, when the young males among the mountain sheep vied for precedence and territory, staking their claim for the winter to come.

The Kaldjager were driving one his way.

Lifting his head, he saw it. A ram, descending in bounds. Its coat was shaggy and greyish-white. A pair of ridged horns rose from its brow in looping, massive curves, as thick as a Tungskulder's forearm.

It saw him and froze.

And there were the Kaldjager, emerging from their pursuit, one on either side. They moved quickly and efficiently, sealing off the young ram's avenue of retreat. One of them saw Skragdal as he rose from his crouch, stepping from beneath the shadow of the ash tree. Even at a distance, his yellow eyes glinted. He hunched his shoulders, opening one hand in an overt gesture. *Tungskulder, the prey is yours.*

Skragdal spread his arms gladly. They felt so *light* without armor.

Beside the pool, the ram halted, setting its forelegs and planting its cloven hooves. It was breathing hard. It lowered its head, the heavy, curling horns tilting as it glanced behind it to either side, catching sight of the grinning Kaldjager.

There was no way out.

Skragdal lowered his head and roared.

Everything else went away when the ram charged. It came hard and fast, its scent filling his nostrils. At the last moment, it rose upon its hind legs. For an instant, the ram's head was silhouetted against the sky. He took in its amber-brown eyes, filled with determined fury of the will-to-survive, its narrow, triangular nostrils and oddly Man-like mouth set in a slender muzzle, the heavy, ridged spirals of its horns. It was for these moments that Fjel lived in the wild.

The ram descended.

Skragdal met it head-on; head to head, brow to brow. It made a clap like thunder breaking. The shock of it reverberated through the thick ledge of bone protecting his brow, through his whole body. His shoulders sang with echoing might. Digging his taloned feet into the loam, he reached out with both arms, filling his hands with lanolin-greasy wool.

They grappled, swaying.

And then the ram's legs trembled. Its amber-brown eyes were dazed. With another surge of strength, Skragdal roared and wrenched sideways, breaking its neck. He swiped at the ram's throat as he flung it to the ground. Red furrows gaped in the wake of his talons. The ram lay without moving, blood seeping slowly over the rocks without a beating heart to pump it.

Truly, Neheris had Shaped her Children well.

Skragdal grinned as the wild Kaldjager approached. "My thanks, brethren. That is how the Tungskulder hunt," he said to them. "What do the Kaldjager say?"

They eyed his kill with respect. "We say it is well done, Skragdal of Darkhaven," one of them said. "Our clan will feast well tonight; aye, and your lads, too. As for the rest?" He nodded to the east. "One comes. One of yours."

Skragdal straightened, feeling the tug of absent armor on his shoulders where the straps had worn his hide smooth and shiny. It was Blågen, coming at a trot, his arms and armor jangling, a half-empty waterskin sloshing at his belt. He was unaccompanied.

"Boss," Blågen said briefly, saluting as General Tanaros had taught them.

Everything that had gone away came crashing back. He was not free from the constraints of command. Skragdal sighed and pulled at the pointed lobe of one ear, willing the act to stimulate words, thoughts. "Where are they?"

"We lost their trail in Drybone Reach."

Skragdal stared at him. "How?"

Blågen shrugged, glancing sidelong at the dead ram. "It is a large area. They are Arahila's Children, cunning enough to hide and let us pass. Ulrig and Ruric have gone back to begin at the beginning. We will find them." He glanced then at the other Kaldjager and showed the tips of his eyetusks. "We could use the aid of our brethren if they are willing to undertake a different kind of hunt."

The wild Kaldjager exchanged slow smiles.

Skragdal considered them. "How many of you?"

"Twelve," one replied. He nodded at Blågen's waterskin. "If we had those. Twelve and your three would be enough to sweep the Reach. Your smallfolk could not hide." He pointed at the dead ram. "You see how we herd our prey."

Others from Skragdal's company began to arrive, straggling; Gulnagel, Nåltannen, the strapping young Tungskulder Thorun. Not taking part in the hunt, they had retained their arms, and their gear rattled and sloshed about them. Skragdal suppressed another sigh. He had hoped it would have ended sooner, more simply, but was not to be. He squinted at the sun, which seemed so *bright* after the Vale of Gorgantum. Although he misliked entrusting the task to Fjel he had not seen trained himself, too much time had passed to equivocate.

Anyway, old Mulprek was right. There were no better hunters than the Kaldjager. Although they were not as swift as the Gulnagel nor as strong as the Tungskulder, they were swifter and stronger than any of the other tribes. Kaldjager were strange and solitary for Fjel, living in roaming clans instead of proper dens, but they were unflagging in the chase, and utterly ruthless. Not even General

Tanaros could improve upon their skills. If the Cold Hunters could not do it, it could not be done.

"All right, then." Stooping, Skragdal picked up the ram's corpse and slung it over his shoulder. Its head lolled, blood gathering to fall in slow drops from its gashed throat. It had seemed like a gift, this fine, clean kill, and now it was spoiled. Feeling obscurely cheated, he glared at the other Fjel. "Why is it so hard to kill these smallfolk?"

For a long moment, no one answered.

"Don't worry, boss." Blågen broke the silence with the fearless insouciance of the Cold Hunters. "We'll find them."

"You had better," Skragdal said grimly. "It is the only thing his Lordship has asked of us." He held Blågen's gaze until the Kald-jager blinked. "Back to the clan's gathering-place," he said. "We will share out our gear there."

"Then we hunt?"

"Yes." Skragdal grunted, shifting the ram's corpse on his shoulder. "And we go to Neherinach to lay a trap."

THEY WERE WAITING FOR HER in the great hall.

Sunlight blazed through the tall windows that surrounded it, glistening on the polished amber wood of the long table and the marble floor with its intricately laid pattern of white and a pale, veined blue. In the center of the table was a gilded coffer inlaid with gems. Between the windows, pennants hung from gilded poles. The clear windows were bordered with narrow panes of sea-blue glass, and the slanting sunlight threw bars of cerulean across the room.

It looked, Lilias thought, like a beautiful prison-chamber.

Ingolin the Wise presided at the head of the table, with Malthus the Counselor at his right hand and Aracus Altorus at his left. The others were Ellylon. Lorenlasse of Valmaré she knew; the others, she did not, although their faces were familiar. All of it was familiar. One of the Ellylon was a woman, with features so lovely at close range that Lilias could have wept.

Instead, under the combined weight of their regard, she froze in the doorway.

"Go on." Blaise prodded her from behind. He pointed to an empty chair on one side of the table, isolated from the rest. "Take your seat."

Lilias took a deep breath and entered the room, crossing through the bars of blue light. She drew out the chair and sat, glancing back at Blaise. He had positioned himself like a guard beside the tall doorway. High above him, on the pediment that capped the entrance, was the room's sole imperfection: a shattered marble relief that had once depicted the head of Meronin Fifth-Born, Lord of the Seas.

The memory evoked pain—the splintering pain she had endured when the sculpture had been demolished—but it evoked other memories, too. Lilias raised her chin a fraction, daring to face the assembly.

"Lilias of Beshtanag," Ingolin said. "You have been brought here before us that we might gain knowledge of one another."

"Am I on trial here, my lord?" she inquired.

"You are not." His voice was somber. "We seek the truth, yes. Not to punish, but only to know. Willing or no, you are a guest in Meronil and I have vouched for your well-being." He pointed at the ruined pediment. "You see here that which was once the work of Haergan the Craftsman. I think, perhaps, that it is not unfamiliar to you, Sorceress. Did you speak to us in this place using Haergan's creation, claiming that the Lady Cerelinde was in Beshtanag?"

"Yes." She threw out the truth. Let them make of it what they would. Around the table, glances were exchanged. Aracus Altorus gritted his teeth. She remembered how he had reacted when she had made Meronin's head speak words he despised, leaping onto the table, hurling an Ellylon standard like a javelin.

"How did you accomplish such a thing?" Ingolin frowned in thought. "It is Ellyl magic Haergan wrought, and not sympathetic to Men's workings. Even the Soumanië should not have been able to command matter at such a distance."

"No, my lord." Lilias shook her head. "I used Haergan's mirror."

"Ah." The Lord of the Rivenlost nodded. "It was in the dragon's hoard." Sorrow darkened his grey eyes. "We have always wondered at Haergan's end. It is a difficult gift to bear, the gift of genius. A dangerous gift."

"To be sure," Lilias said absently. Although she did not know the details of Haergan's end, Calandor's words echoed in her thoughts, accompanied by the memory of his slow, amused blink. *I might not have eaten him if he had been more ussseful.*

"*Why?*" It was the Ellyl woman who spoke, and the sound of her voice was like bells; bells, or silver horns, a sound to make mortal flesh shiver in delight, were it not infused with anger. She leaned forward, her lambent eyes aglow with passion. *"Why would you do such a thing?"*

Her words hung in the air. No one else spoke. Lilias glanced from face to face around the table. Plainly, it was a question all of them wanted answered; and as clearly, it was an answer none of them would understand.

"Why do you seek to fulfill Haomane's Prophecy?" she asked them. "Tell me that, and perhaps we may understand one another."

"Lilias." Malthus spoke her name gently. "These things are not the same, and well you know it. Urulat is Sundered from itself. We seek that which Haomane the Lord-of-Thought himself seeks—to heal the land, so restore it to the wholeness and glory to which it was Shaped, and which Satoris Banewreaker has perverted."

"Why?" Lilias repeated. They stared at her in disbelief, except for Malthus, who looked thoughtful. She folded her hands on the table and met their stares. "I ask in earnest, my lords, my lady. Was Urulat such a paradise before it was Sundered?"

"We had the light of the Souma!" Lorenlasse of Valmaré's voice was taut with fury, his bright eyes glittering. "We are Haomane's Children and we were torn from his side, from all that sustained us." He regarded her with profound contempt. "You cannot possibly know how that feels."

"Lorenlasse," Ingolin murmured.

Lilias laughed aloud. There was freedom in having nothing left to lose. She pointed at the lifeless Soumanië on Aracus' brow. "My lord Lorenlasse, until very recently, I held a piece of the Souma itself. I stretched the Chain of Being and held mortality at bay. I had power to Shape the very stuff of life, and I could have twisted your bones like jackstraws for addressing me in such a tone. Do not speak to me of what I can or cannot know."

"My lord Ingolin." The Ellyl woman turned to the Lord of the Rivenlost. The rigid lines of her body expressed her distaste. "It seems to me that there is naught to be gained in furthering this discussion."

"Hold, Lady Nerinil." Malthus lifted one hand, forestalling her. "There may yet be merit in it. Lilias." He fixed his gaze upon her. Seated among Ellylon, he looked old and weary. "Your questions are worthy ones," he said. "Let me answer one of them. Yes, Urulat *was* a paradise, once. In the First Age, before the world was Sundered, when the world was new-made and the Shapers dwelled among us." Malthus smiled, gladness transforming his face. "When Men had yet to discover envy and delighted in the skills of the Ellylon; when the Were hunted only with Oronin's blessing and the Fjeltroll heeded Neheris, and the Dwarfs tilled the land and coaxed forth Yrinna's bounty." On his breast, the clear Soumanië blazed into life. "That is the world the Lord-of-Thought shaped," he said quietly. "That is the world we seek to restore."

Lilias blinked, willing away an onslaught of tears. "It may be, Counselor. But that world was lost long before Urulat was Sundered."

"Through folly," Aracus said unexpectedly. "Men's folly; *our* folly. What Haomane wrought, we unmade through covetousness and greed."

"Men did not begin the Shapers' War," Lilias murmured.

"I am not so sure." Aracus shook his head. "It was Men who made war upon the Ellylon, believing they withheld the secret of immortality from us. If we had not done so, perhaps Haomane First-Born would not have been forced to ask the Sunderer to withdraw his Gift from us."

Ingolin laid a hand upon Aracus' arm. "Do not take so much upon yourself. The House of Altorus has never been an enemy to the Ellylon."

"Perhaps not," Aracus said. "But I would atone for the deeds of my race by working to see Haomane's Prophecy fulfilled. And then perhaps, in a world made whole, we might become what once we were."

A silence followed upon his words. Even Lorenlasse of the Valmaré was respectful in the face of Aracus' passion.

Malthus smiled at Lilias. White light flashed in the depths of his transfigured Soumanië, casting scintillating points of brightness around the room. "Is your question answered in full, Lilias of Beshtanag?"

"Yes, Counselor." Lilias rubbed at the familiar ache in her temples. "Your point is made. I understand the purpose of this meeting. You may now ask me once more to relinquish the Soumanië."

"I do not ask on my own behalf." Resonant power filled Malthus' voice, making her lift her head to meet his eyes. "I ask it on behalf of the Lady Cerelinde, who suffers even as we speak. I ask it on behalf of the Rivenlost, who endure the pain of separation, dwindling year by year. I ask it on behalf of those noble Men who would atone for the misdeeds of their race. I ask it on behalf of all Urulat, that this vision we share might come to pass. And I ask it, yes, on behalf of those poor souls who have fallen into folly, through the lies of Satoris Banewreaker, that they might know redemption. The Soumanië that Aracus Altorus bears was Shaped by

Haomane himself, carried into battle by Ardrath the Wise Counselor, who was like unto a brother to me. Lilias of Beshtanag, will you release your claim upon it?"

"No." The word dropped like a stone from her lips. Despite the welling tears and the ache in her head, Lilias laughed. "It is a pleasant fiction, Counselor. But there is a problem with your story. You are Haomane's Weapon, Shaped after the world was Sundered. How can you claim knowledge of the First Age of Urulat?"

At the head of the table, Ingolin stirred. With a frown creasing his brow, the Lord of the Rivenlost bent his gaze on Malthus. "How do you answer, old friend?"

Something deep shifted in Malthus' eyes, and it was as if a veil had been withdrawn, revealing ancient and terrible depths. "I am as the Lord-of-Thought Shaped me," he said softly. "And I possess such knowledge as he willed. More than that, Sorceress, I cannot say, nor may I."

Lilias nodded. "Can you tell me, then, why Haomane refused when Satoris offered his Gift to Haomane's Children?"

"Because such a thing was not meant to be." Malthus shook his head, and the semblance of age and weariness returned to his mien. "Thus was the will of Uru-Alat, which only the Haomane First-Born, the Lord-of-Thought, sprung from the very brow of the world, grasps in its fullness."

"Except for dragons, of course. But perhaps it wasn't Haomane's will that you possess *that* knowledge." Lilias pushed back her chair and stood, gazing at their silent, watching faces. Her vision was blurred with the weak, foolish tears she couldn't seem to suppress. "You should have tried to woo me," she said to Aracus. "It might even have worked." Thick with tears, her voice shook. "I am a proud woman, and a vain one, and if you had begged me for the Soumanië I might have relented. But although I am flawed, I have lived for a very long time, and I am *not* a fool." She dashed at her eyes with the back of one hand, a choking laugh catching in her throat. "I'm sorry, Counselor," she said to Malthus. "It must disappoint you to learn that your Soumanië has not illuminated my soul."

"Yes." There was no mockery in Malthus' tone, only abiding sorrow. He gazed at her with profound regret. "It does."

"Yes, well." Lilias took another shaking breath. "Perhaps I am protected by the claim I have not relinquished, or perhaps this place suffers from a surfeit of brightness already. Perhaps, after all, my soul is not so black as it has been painted." She stood very straight, addressing all of them. "I know who I am and what I have done. I have endured your compassion, your mercy, your righteous outrage. But you should not have brought me here to humiliate me with your *goodness*."

"Such was not our intention, Sorceress," Ingolin murmured. "If that is your feeling—"

"No." She shook her head. "You claimed to want knowledge, Ingolin the Wise, but all you truly wanted was my repentance. And the Soumanië." Lilias smiled through her tears and spread her arms. "And yet, I cannot gainsay what I know. All things must be as they are. For the price of my life, the Soumanië is yours. Will you take it and be forsworn?"

The Lord of the Rivenlost exchanged glances with Aracus and Malthus. "No, Sorceress," he said with terrible gentleness. "We will not."

"Well, then." Lilias swallowed, tasting the bitter salt of her tears. "Then I will keep my claim upon it until I die of uselessness and shame." She turned to Blaise. "Will you take me back to my quarters, please?"

Blaise looked to Aracus, who gave a curt nod. Without a word, Blaise opened the door. She followed him through it.

Behind her, the silvery voices arose.

THE LADY CERELINDE SMILED AT him. "General Tanaros."

"Lady." He bowed in greeting, thinking as he straightened that perhaps it had been a mistake to come here. The impact of her presence was always greater than he remembered. "Are you ready?"

"I am."

Out of the courtly habit he had kept for over a thousand years, Tanaros extended his arm to her as he escorted her from her chamber. Cerelinde took it as she had done the night he brought her to the moon-garden, her slender, white fingertips resting on his forearm. He had forgone his armor, wearing only the black sword belted at his waist, and he could feel her touch through the velvet sleeve of his austere black doublet. Clear and distinct, each fingertip, as though she were setting her own brand upon him through some forgotten Ellyl magic; as powerful as Godslayer, yet more subtle.

What would it be like, that delicate touch against bare skin?

The thought came before he could quell it, and in its wake

arose a wave of desire so strong it almost sickened him, coupled with a terrible yearning. It was a nameless emotion, its roots as old as mortality; covetous envy thwarted, manifesting in the desire to possess something so other, so *fine*.

"Are you all right?" There was concern in her voice.

"Yes." Standing in the hallway outside her door, Tanaros caught the eye of the leader of the Havenguard quartet he had assigned to accompany them. The sight of the Mørkhar Fjel looming in armor steadied him. He touched the *rhios* that hung in a pouch at his belt, feeling its smooth curves, and willing his racing pulse to ease. "Krognar," he said. "This is the Lady Cerelinde. Your lads are escorting us to the rookery."

"Lady," Krognar rumbled, inclining his massive head.

"Sir Krognar." She regarded him with polite, fascinated horror.

Tanaros could feel the tremor that ran through her. "This way, Lady," he said.

The quartet of Mørkhar Fjel fell in behind them as he led her through the winding corridors of Darkhaven. The marble halls echoed with the heavy pad and scritch of their horny, taloned feet, accompanied by the faint jangle of arms.

"You needed no guard the night you brought me to see Lord Satoris' garden," Cerelinde said presently. Although her voice was level, her fingers clenching his forearm were tight with fear.

"The moon-garden lies within the confines of Darkhaven," Tanaros said. "The rookery does not. I am responsible for your security, Cerelinde."

She glanced briefly at him. Despite her fear, a faint smile touched her lips. "Do you fear I will use Ellyl magic to effect an escape?"

"Yes," he said honestly. "I do. I fear enchantments of the sort you invoked in Cuilos Tuillenrad. And I fear . . ." Tanaros took a deep breath. "I fear I do not trust myself to resist your beseechment, should you seek to beguile me. It is best that the Havenguard are here."

Color rose to her cheeks, and her reply was unwontedly sharp. "I did not *beseech* you to do this, Tanaros!"

"True." He disengaged his arm. "Shall we go back?"

Cerelinde hesitated, searching his face. "Is it truly *outside*?"

"Yes." He answered without hesitating, without pausing to consider the pleasure it gave him to answer her with the truth. "It is outside. Well and truly, Cerelinde."

She turned away, averting her gaze. Strands of her hair, as pale as corn silk, clung to his velvet-clad shoulder. "Then I would fain see it, my lord Blacksword," she murmured. "I would walk under the light of Haomane's sun."

Tanaros bowed. "Then so you shall."

They exited Darkhaven through the northern portal, with its vast doors that depicted the Council of the Six Tribes, in which the Fjeltroll Elders had voted to pledge their support to Lord Satoris; he to whom they had given shelter, he who had sought to teach the Fjel such Gifts as Haomane had withheld. Tanaros wished that Cerelinde had noticed the depiction and inquired about it. There was much he would have liked to discuss with her, including the quixotic nature of Haomane's Gift, the gift of *thought*, which only Arahila's Children shared.

But beyond the doors, there was daylight.

"Ah, *Haomane*!" Cerelinde breathed the word like a prayer. Relinquishing his arm, she ran on ahead with swift, light steps; into the daylight, into the open air. Although the sky was leaden and grey, she opened her arms to it, turning her face upward like a sunflower. And there, of a surety, was the sun. A pale disk, glimpsed through the clouds that hovered over the Vale of Gorgantum. "Tanaros!" she cried. "The *sun*!"

"Aye, Lady." He was unable to repress a smile. "'Tis where you left it."

Her face was alight with pleasure. "Mock me if you must, Tanaros, but the light of the sun is the nearest thing to Haomane's presence, without which the Rivenlost fade and dwindle. Do not despise me for taking joy in it."

"Lady, I do not." It seemed to him, in that moment, he could never despise her. "Shall we proceed?"

He escorted her down the paths that led into beechwood. Although the wood lay within the vast, encircling wall that surrounded Darkhaven, the dense trees blotted out any glimpse of its borders. Were it not that the trees grew dark and twisted, their trunks wrenched around knotted boles, they might have been anywhere in Urulat.

Once they were beneath the wood's canopy, Tanaros gave way, allowing Cerelinde to precede him, wandering freely along the trail. The Mørkhar padded behind them, heavy treads crunching on the beech-mast. Autumn was approaching and the leaves were beginning to turn. Elsewhere, they would have taken on a golden hue. Here in Darkhaven, a splotch of deepest crimson blossomed in the center of the jagged spearhead of each leaf, shading to dark green on the outer edges.

Cerelinde touched them, her fingertips trailing over glossy leaves and rutted, gnarled bark. "There is such pain in the struggle," she wondered aloud. "Even their roots groan at their travail. And yet they adapt and endure. These are ancient trees." She glanced at him. "What has done this to them, Tanaros? Is it that Lord Satoris has stricken them in his wrath?"

"No, Lady." He shook his head. "It is his blood that alters the land in the Vale of Gorgantum, that which flows from his unhealing wound. For thousands upon thousands of years, it has seeped into the earth."

"A Shaper's blood," she murmured.

"Yes." He watched her, his heart aching. In the muted, blood-shot light beneath the beech canopy, the Lady of the Ellylon shone like a gem. How finely they were wrought, Haomane's Children! No wonder that Haomane loved them so dearly, having taken such care with their Shaping. "Come, it is this way."

She paused for a moment as they entered the rookery, where a hundred ragged nests adorned the crooked trees, absorbing the sight in silence. The wood was alive with ravens, bustling busily about their messy abodes, sidling along branches and peering at the visitors with bright, wary eyes. When she saw the small glade and the table awaiting them, Cerelinde turned to him. "You did this?"

"Aye." Tanaros smiled. "Will you join me in a glass of wine, Lady?"

Another faint blush warmed her cheeks. "I will."

The table was laid with dazzling white linens and set with a simple wine service; a clay jug and two elegantly turned goblets. It was Dwarfish work, marked by the simple grace that characterized their labors. How it had made its way to Darkhaven, Tanaros did not know. Beneath the glowering light of the Vale, table and service glowed alike, filled with their own intrinsic beauty. And beside the table, proud and upright in plain black livery, stood Speros, who had undertaken the arrangements on his General's behalf.

"Speros of Haimhault," Tanaros said. "This is the Lady Cerelinde."

"Lady." Speros breathed the word, bowing low. His eyes, when he arose, were filled with tears. In the desert, he had expressed a desire to behold her. It was a wish granted, this moment; a wish that made the heart ache for the beauty, the *fineness*, that Arahila's Children would never possess. "May I pour you a glass of wine?"

"As you please." Cerelinde smiled at him, taking her seat. The Mørkhar Fjel dispatched themselves to the four quarters of the glade, planting their taloned feet and taking up patient, watchful stances. "Thank you, Speros of Haimhault."

"You are welcome." His hand trembled as he poured, filling her cup with red Vedasian wine. The lip of the wine-jug rattled against her goblet. With a visible effort, he moved to fill his General's. "Most welcome, Lady."

Tanaros sat opposite Cerelinde and beheld that which made the Midlander tremble. He pitied the lad, for a wish granted was a dangerous thing; and yet. Ah, Shapers, the glory of her! It was a light, a light that shone from within—it was Haomane's love, shining like a kiss upon her brow. It was present in every part of her; bred into the very fineness of her bones, the soaring architecture of the flesh. All at once, it enhanced and shamed its surroundings.

And she was pleased.

In all his prolonged years, he had never seen such a thing. One of the Ellyl; pleased. Her heart gladdened by what Tanaros had done. It was reflected in the gentle curve of her lips. It was reflected in her eyes, in the limitless depths of her pupils, in the pleated luminosity of her irises, those subtle colors like a rainbow after rain. And although her mood had not yet passed, it would. The thought filled him with a prescient nostalgia. Already he longed to see it once more; yearned to be, in word and deed, a Man as would gladden the heart of the Lady of the Ellylon and coax forth this brightness within her. Who would not wish to be such a Man?

"Cerelinde." He hoisted his goblet to her.

"Tanaros." Her smile deepened. "Thank you."

"Kaugh!"

Tanaros startled at the sound, then laughed. He extended an arm. In a flurry of black wings, Fetch launched himself from a nearby branch, alighting on Tanaros' forearm. "This," he said fondly, "is who I wanted you to meet." He glanced at Speros, feeling an obscure guilt. "Or *what*, I should say."

The Lady of the Ellylon and the bedraggled raven regarded one another.

"His name is Fetch," Tanaros said. "He was a late-born fledgling. Six years ago, I found him in his Lordship's moon-garden, half-frozen, and took him into my quarters." He stroked the raven's iridescent black feathers. "He made a fearful mess of them," he added with a smile. "But he saved my life in the Unknown Desert; mine, and Speros', too. We are at quits now."

"Greetings, Fetch," Cerelinde said gravely. "Well met."

Deep in his throat, the raven gave an uneasy chuckle. He sidled away from her, his sharp claws pricking at Tanaros' velvet sleeve.

"My apologies." Tanaros cleared his throat in embarrassment as Fetch scrambled to his shoulder, clinging to the collar of his doublet and ducking beneath his hair to peer out at Cerelinde. "It seems he is shy of you, Lady."

"He has reason." Her voice was soft and musical. "My folk have slain his kind for serving as the Sunderer's eyes, and the eagles of Meronil drive them from our towers. But it is also true that the Rivenlost do not begrudge any of the small races their enmity." Cerelinde smiled at the raven. "They do not know what they do. One day, perhaps, there will be peace. We hope for it."

Shifting from foot to foot, Fetch bobbed his tufted head. His sharp beak nudged its way through the dark strands of Tanaros' hair, and his anxious thoughts nudged at Tanaros' mind. Opening himself to them, Tanaros *saw* through doubled eyes a familiar, unsettling sensation. What he saw made him blink.

Cerelinde ablaze.

She burned like a signal fire in the raven's gaze, an Ellyl-shaped woman's form, white-hot and searing. There was beauty, oh, yes! A terrible beauty, one that filled Fetch's rustling thoughts with fear. Her figure divided the blackness like a sword. And beyond and behind it, there was a vast emptiness. The space between the stars, endless black and achingly cold. In it, as if through a crack in the world, stars fell; fell and fell and fell, trailing gouts of white-blue fire, beautiful and unending.

Somewhere, there was the roar of a dragon's laughter.

Tanaros blinked again to clear his vision. There was a sudden pressure upon his shoulder as Fetch launched himself, soaring with outspread wings to a nearby branch. The raven chittered, his beak parted. All around the rookery, his calls were uneasily echoed until the glade was alive with uneasy sound.

"Perhaps I am unwelcome here," Cerelinde said softly.

"No." At a loss for words, Tanaros quaffed his wine and held out his goblet for Speros to refill. He shook his head, willing the action to dispel the lingering images. "No, Lady. You are a guest here. As you say, they are fearful. Something happened to Fetch in the desert." He furrowed his brow in thought, pondering the strange visions that flitted through the raven's thought, the recurrent image of a *dragon*. Not just any dragon, but one truly ancient of days. "Or before, perhaps. Something I do not understand."

"It seems to me," said the Lady of the Ellylon, "many things happened in the desert, Tanaros." She gazed at him with the same steady kindness she had shown the raven, the same unrelenting pity with which she had beheld the madlings of Darkhaven. "Do you wish to speak of them?"

Speros, holding the wine-jug at the ready, coughed and turned away.

"No." Resting his elbows on the dazzling white linen of the tablecloth, Tanaros fiddled with the stem of his goblet. He studied the backs of his hands; the scarred knuckles. It had been a long, long time since he had known a woman's compassion. It would have been a relief to speak of it; a relief so deep he felt the promise of it in his bones. And yet; she was the Lady of the Ellylon, Haomane's Child. How could he explain it to her? Lord Satoris' command, his own reluctance to obey it. Strength born of the Water of Life still coursing in his veins, the quietude of Stone Grove and Ngurra's old head lifting, following the rising arc of his black blade. His refusal to relent, to give a reason, any reason. Only a single word: *Choose*. The blade's fall, a welter of gore, and the anguished cry of the old Yarru's wife. The blunt crunch of the Fjel maces that followed. These things, she would not understand. There was no place for them here, in this moment of civilized discourse. "No," he said again more firmly. "Lady, I do not."

"As you please." Cerelinde bowed her head for a moment, her features curtained by her pale, shining hair. When she lifted her head, a nameless emotion darkened her clear eyes. "Tanaros," she said. "Why did you bring me here?"

All around the rookery, ravens settled, cocking their heads.

"It is a small kindness, Lady, nothing more." Tanaros glanced around, taking in the myriad bright eyes. There was Fetch, still as a stone, watching him. A strange grief thickened his words. "Do you think me incapable of such deeds?"

"No." Sorrow, and something else, shaded her tone. "I think you are like these trees, Tanaros. As deep-rooted life endures in them, so does goodness endure in you, warped and blighted by darkness. And such a thing grieves me, for it need not be. Ah, Tanaros!" The brightness returned to her eyes. "There is forgiveness and Arahila's mercy awaiting you, did only you reach out your hand. For you, and this young Man; yes, even for the ravens themselves. For all the innocent and misguided who dwell beneath the Sunderer's shadow. Is it asking so much?"

He drew breath to answer, and the rookery burst into a flurry of black wings as all the ravens of Darkhaven took flight at once, a circling stormcloud. Without thinking, Tanaros found himself on his feet, the black sword naked in his fist. The Mørkhar Fjel came at a thundering run, bristling with weapons. Speros, unarmed, swore and smashed the Dwarfish wine-jug on the edge of the table, shattering its graceful form to improvise a jagged weapon. Red wine bled in a widening stain on the white linen.

"Greetings, cousin." Ushahin stood at the edge of the glade; a hunched form, small and composed. Above him, the ravens circled in a tightening gyre, answering to him as if to one of the Were. His uneven gaze shifted to Cerelinde. "Lady."

"Dreamspinner." Her voice was cool. She had risen, standing straight as a spear.

"Stand down." Tanaros nodded to Speros and the Fjel and shoved his sword back into its sheath. His hand stung and his chest felt oddly tight, as though the brand over his heart were a steel band constricting it. "What do you want, Dreamspinner?"

"I come on his Lordship's orders. 'Tis time to send the ravens afield again." Ushahin gave his tight, crooked smile. In Cerelinde's presence, he looked more malformed than ever. Here was the beauty of the Ellylon rendered into its component parts and poorly rebuilt, cobbled together by unskilled hands. "But there is a matter of which I would speak to you, cousin. One that concerns the safety of Darkhaven." He paused, and in the silence, Fetch descended, settling on his shoulder. "A matter of corruption."

He said no more, waiting.

Tanaros inclined his head. A moment had passed; an axis had tipped. Something had changed, something was lost. Something bright had slipped away from him, and something else had settled into place. Its roots were deep and strong. There was a surety, a knowledge of self, and the course he had chosen. Beneath its brand, his aching heart beat, each beat reminding him that he owed his existence to Lord Satoris.

A vast and abiding love.

He touched the pouch at his belt, feeling the contours of Hyrgolf's *rhios* through it, letting himself be humbled by the awesome

loyalty of the Fjel. The Fjel, to whom it seemed Arahila's forgiveness did not extend. On the far side of the glade, Ushahin's eyes
glittered as if he knew Tanaros' thoughts.

Perhaps he did.

"Permit me to escort the Lady Cerelinde to her quarters,"
Tanaros said to the half-breed. "Then I am at your disposal." Turning to Cerelinde, he extended his arm. "Lady?"

Cerelinde took his arm. "Thank you," she whispered, "for this
glimpse of sun."

"For that, Lady, you are welcome." Tanaros heard the unsteadi-
ness in his voice and despised it. He crooked his arm, capturing
her fair, white fingers against his torso and made his voice harsh.
"Now, come with me."

She went, making no protest.

Behind them came the padding footfalls of the Havenguard,
crunching upon the beech-mast. And all the way, Tanaros felt the
combined gaze of Ushahin and the ravens of Darkhaven upon him.
On his arm, Cerelinde's touch burned; on the outer edges of his
sight, Fetch's vision burned, a raven's fitful thoughts, backed by a
dragon's roar, and the gleam in Ushahin's mismatched eyes.

Somewhere between the two, lay his path.

So be it, Tanaros thought, conscious of the steady throb of his
beating heart, and all that he owed, every breath drawn, to Lord
Satoris.

A matter of corruption?

No. Never.

SIX

FROM HIS PERCH HIGH ATOP a pine tree, Dani saw the Fjel.

It was the fourth time that day he had clambered up the tree, using it as a vantage point to survey the barren reach. Each time, he whispered a prayer to Uru-Alat, praying to find the landscape empty as it had been the day before, and the day before it.

On the third day, his luck ran out.

Although it was hard to tell from so far away, they appeared to be the same kind he had seen before—lean and predatory, with smooth, grey hides that were blended into the rocky terrain. If he hadn't been keen-sighted, he might have missed them. But, no, there it was again—a steely flash in the distance, the northern sunlight glinting on armor plate. Clinging to the pine's trunk with his good right arm, he stared intently at the direction of the Fjel. There were more of them this time, though only one wore armor. Save for the waterskins strapped over their torsos, the rest were unadorned.

They were traveling in a pack and they were traveling swiftly. For a moment, Dani watched, mesmerized by their steady, tireless lope. Even at a distance, an awful grace was in it.

Then fear returned in a rush, the sour taste of it in his mouth. Using both feet and the one hand, Dani descended the pine tree in awkward haste, heedless of the prickling needles and rough bark, and hurried into the hidden cave.

"Fjeltroll?" Uncle Thulu's voice was faint and thready.

"Aye." He met his uncle's feverish gaze. "A dozen at least."

"Did they see you?"

"No." Dani shook his head. "They're pretty far south of us and moving fast, all in a pack. It doesn't even look like they're hunting.

I think they'll miss us," he added hopefully. "Maybe they're not even looking."

"No." Uncle Thulu coughed weakly and wheezed, one hand scrabbling at his chest. In the dim light, his shirt was stained dark with seeping fluids. Despite Dani's best efforts to clean and tend them, his wounds continued to fester. Yesterday, they had begun to slough dead flesh and the small space stank of it. "Help me sit."

With alacrity, Dani eased him into a sitting position, propped against the cavern wall. "Better?"

"Aye," Uncle Thulu whispered, licking his dry, cracked lips.

"Here." Moving deftly and quietly, Dani made his way to the mouth of the cave. There, in a shallow depression to one side, was a cache of moss he had gathered. It had sustained them during the past three days. Grasping a smooth stone, he ground the spongy moss into a damp paste. Scooping up a handful, he returned to squat beside his uncle. With gentle care, he spread the paste on the elder Yarru's parched lips. "Try to eat."

Uncle Thulu's mouth worked with difficulty, his sluggish tongue taking in the moss paste. Blinking back tears, Dani spread another fingerful on his lips. There was moisture in it, not much, but enough to live on. It was the only thing he had been able to find within half a day's journey of their hiding place. And if he had not seen a single lost elk grazing on it, he might never have thought to try the moss. It was all that had kept his uncle alive.

And barely, at that.

"Enough." Uncle Thulu grasped Dani's wrist with urgent strength and drew in a deep, rattling breath. "Dani, listen to me."

"Yes, Uncle." His chest ached with fear and love.

"They're starting over. That's why they're moving in a hurry. They're going back to pick up our trail from the beginning. And if they've added to their numbers, they're not going to miss us this time." Thulu's eyes were overbright in his wasted face. "Dani, you have to go. *Now.*"

"I won't." He refused to hear what Thulu was saying. "Not without you."

His uncle said it anyway. "I'm dying, Dani."

"What if we went back?" The thought struck him like an offer of salvation. "We could wait for them to pass, then head south! They wouldn't hunt for us once we passed out of Fjel territory, and the Staccians . . . well, they're just Men, we can hide from Men, Uncle! And get you home, where—"

"Dani." Uncle Thulu's grip tightened on his wrist. "I'm not going anywhere," he said gently. "Do you understand? This is where the journey ends for me. I'm sorry, lad. You've got to go on without me."

"No!" Pulling away, Dani clutched the clay vial around his neck. "For what?" he asked angrily. "For *this*? It's not worth it! It's not *fair*, uncle!" He yanked at the vial with all his strength. For a moment, the braided cord on which it was strung burned the skin of his neck; then it parted with a faint snap. Dani held the vial in one hand. Hot tears burned his eyes, and his voice trembled. "I didn't *ask* to be the Bearer! What's Satoris ever done to the Yarru-yami, anyway, that we should seek to destroy him? It's not *his* fault Haomane's Wrath scorched the desert, he was just trying to *hide* from it! And if he hadn't . . . if he hadn't, we wouldn't have found the Water of Life! We wouldn't be the keepers of Birru-Uru-Alat. We wouldn't even be what we *are*!"

The ghost of a smile moved Thulu's cracked lips. "These are fitting questions for the Bearer to ask," he whispered. "But you will have to answer them alone."

Dani unclenched his hand, staring at the vial. It lay on the starry, radiating lines of his grimy palm; a simple object, fragile and crude. Clay, gathered from a scant deposit at one of the Stone Grove's water-holes, fired with baari-wood and dung in a pit dug into the desert's floor.

Inside it was the Water of Life, water he had drawn from the Well of the World and dipped from the bucket, holding it in his cupped palms as old Ngurra had told him to do, filling the vial with care. The lifeblood of Uru-Alat, the World God; the secret the Yarru-yami held in trust. A gift only the Bearer could draw; a burden only the Bearer could carry. A choice in the making.

In the apple orchards of Malumdoorn, while the sun slanted through the trees and the Dwarfs stood watching, a single drop had caused a dead stick to burst into green life; planting roots, sprouting leaves and blossoms.

A dawning certainty grew in him. For the first time, Dani saw clearly the divided path before him and understood that the choice between them was his, and his alone, to make. Not for the sake of Malthus, whose impassioned words had swayed him; not for the sake of Carfax, who had given his life to save him. Not even for his uncle, who would gainsay it. The choice was his, and his alone. This, and not the Water itself, was the Bearer's true burden.

Dani lifted his head. "No, Uncle. Not just yet."

"Ah, lad!" There was alarm in Thulu's weak voice. "The Water of Life is too precious to waste—"

"Am I the Bearer?" Dani interrupted him. "You keep telling me it is my right to choose, Uncle, and yet you give me no guidance, no hint as to which choice is *right*. Well, I am choosing." With one thumbnail, he pried at the tight cork, working it loose. The faint scent of water, life giving and mineral-rich, trickled into the small cavern. With his heart hammering in hope and fear, Dani bent over his uncle and smoothed his brow, putting the vial close to his lips. "I choose for you to live."

Uncle Thulu exhaled one last, long, rattling breath and closed his eyes in surrender. "May it be as Uru-Alat wills," he whispered.

At close range, the stench of his suppurating wounds vied for dominance with the odor of water. Dani ignored it, concentrating on tilting the flask. Under his breath, he chanted the Song of Being, the story of Uru-Alat and how the World God died to give birth to the world. It was an act of prayer; a Yarru prayer, the oldest prayer, a story learned and told in the deep places of the earth, where the veins of life pulsed and the Yarru had hidden from Haomane's Wrath. It was an old story; older than the Shapers. It was as old as dragons, who were born in the deep places from the bones of Uru-Alat and carried a spark of marrow-fire in their bellies.

A single drop gathered on the clay lip of the vessel. It gathered and swelled; rounding, bottom-heavy. It shone like a translucent pearl, glimmering in the shadowy cavern, reflecting all the light in the world.

Beneath it were his uncle's parted lips. Dark flesh, fissured and cracked, smeared with moss-paste. The tip of his tongue, a pink supplicant lying quiescent on the floor of his thirsting mouth.

Dani tilted the vial.

One drop; two, three!

They fell like stars through the dark air into the mortal void of Uncle Thulu's waiting mouth. And, oh, Uru-Alat! A sweet odor burst forth as they fell, redoubled in strength; a scent like a chime, like the sharp clap of a pair of hands.

It happened almost too quickly for sight to follow. Uncle Thulu's eyes sprang open, wide and amazed. His chest heaved as he drew in a great, whooping gasp of air. Dani cried aloud in astonishment, scrambling backward and nearly spilling the Water of Life. He shoved the cork into the clay flask, then shoved his knuckles into his mouth, fearful that his outcry would draw the Fjeltroll.

"Ah, Dani, lad!" Uncle Thulu sat upright. The brightness in his eyes owed nothing to fever—it was the brightness of sunlight on clear waters, a promise of life and health. "If this is folly, what a glorious folly it is!" He grinned, showing strong white teeth, and yanked his shirt aside to expose his chest. "Tell me what you see!"

Beneath the foul-crusted wool, Thulu's skin was smooth and dark, gleaming with health. In the dim light, Dani could barely make out three faint lines, pale threads like long-healed scars. He sighed with relief. "They're well and truly healed, aren't they?"

"More than healed!" His uncle's voice reverberated joyously from the cavern walls. "Ah, lad! I've never felt better in my life! Why, I could—"

"Shhh!" Dani laid one hand over Thulu's lips. "The Fjeltroll."

"Right." His uncle nodded. "Aye, of course."

"I'll go look." Without waiting for Thulu to argue, Dani turned to wriggle out of the cavern's narrow opening. With the vial in one hand and the dirty sling still tied around his left arm, it was awkward going. He inched beneath the concealing pine branches and into the open, crawling on his belly until he had a clear view.

There, to the southeast, a moving smudge on the landscape; a dull glint of steel. He didn't even need to climb the tree to spot them. The Fjel had already passed them. They were moving fast . . . and they would be returning fast, too.

"Have they gone?"

Dani winced at the sound of his uncle's voice. Glancing over his shoulder, he saw Thulu standing in front of the cave. "Aye, barely. Uncle, get down, *please!*"

"Sorry, lad." Thulu drew a shuddering breath and dropped to a squat. In the open light of day, he looked even more hale—unnervingly hale. The muscles in his sturdy thighs bunched and twitched with vigor. "It's just . . . I don't know if I can explain, but it's like a fire in my veins, Dani. I can't hold still." He rubbed his face with both hands. "Just as well, isn't it? We've no time to waste."

"You'll have to sit for a minute." Dani sat in a hunched pose and concentrated on splicing the broken thukka-vine thong on which the vial was strung, braiding the strong fibers. "We're not going anywhere until those Fjeltroll are long out of sight."

"And where shall we go when we do, Bearer?" Despite it all, Uncle Thulu put the question to him gently, remembering the words Dani had spoken in fear and anger. "It seems, against the odds, that I am still here to guide you. Where is it you would go?"

Dani bowed his head, his coarse black hair hiding his expression. "Darkhaven," he murmured. "We go to Darkhaven, Uncle."

"You're sure?"

"Aye." He stroked the pit-fired clay vessel with one fingertip. "I made a choice, Uncle. I'm responsible for it now. And if there are questions the Bearer should ask . . ." He shrugged. "Perhaps I should ask them in Darkhaven."

Uncle Thulu watched him. "It is Darkhaven's agents who seek your life."

"I know." Dani tested the spliced thong's strength and gauged that it would hold. Raising his good arm, he slipped the vial around his neck, feeling it nestle into place against his chest. "I have given them reason."

"You know, lad." Uncle Thulu nodded at Dani's left arm, bound in its sling. "I know what I said before. But we've a long way to go, and Fjeltroll to outrun. Whatever questions you might ask, it's not going to alter their orders; not here and now. A single drop from that flask—"

"No." Dani shook his head. Fear had passed from him; in its wake, he felt tired and resigned. "You were right, Uncle. It *is* too precious to waste. And how terrible might we become if the Bearer chose to use it thusly? No," he said again. "It was my choice to use it to save your life. It is enough." He glanced behind him, surveying the horizon. There was no glint of sunlight on steel; the moving smudge had gone. "Shall we go?"

"Aye, lad." Uncle Thulu sprang to his feet, then paused. He fumbled at his chest with blunt fingertips, finding no wound, but only the pale ridges of long-healed scars. An expression of perplexity crossed his broad face. "What was I saying? It was a folly of some sort, I fear. Something has changed here, Dani, has it not? I should be dead, and yet I live. And you, you . . ."

"I am the Bearer," Dani finished softly. For the first time, he had a glimmering of what the words meant, and it made him feel very, very alone. With an effort, he used his good arm as a lever, clambering upright. Once standing, he touched the clay vial at his throat, aware of his burden. "Will you be my guide, Uncle?"

"I will," said his uncle. And he bowed, low. "Aye, lad, I will."

THE WALL WAS LIKE A dragon's spine, coiled and sinuous. It stretched for league upon league around Darkhaven, clinging with determination to every sinking valley and rising ridge in the Vale that surrounded Lord Satoris' fortress.

It was taller than the height of three men, and broad enough for four horsemen to ride astride atop it; or four Fjel to run at a trot. Within its confines lay all that Darkhaven encompassed. There, to the north, were the mines where the Fjeltroll labored, digging iron from the earth. There, closer, were the furnaces where it was smelted, the forges where it was beaten into steel. The Gorgantus River made its sluggish way beneath a pall of grey-black smoke, tapped by the cunning of Speros of Haimhault, who had built a waterwheel and made it serve Darkhaven's purposes.

There was the training-field, the expanse of beaten ground where Tanaros drilled his army, day upon day. And there, southward, were the pastures where Staccian sheep grazed on dark, wiry grass, fattening to fill Fjel bellies, drinking tainted water from the Gorgantus River and thriving upon it. From their blood the foul-smelling *svartblod*, dearly loved by the Fjel, was fermented.

And there, far to the west—a gleam in the distance—was the shoreline of the Sundering Sea, where Dergail the Counselor had met his death at the hands of the Were. Beyond it, somewhere in the shining sea-swell of the distance, lay Torath, the Crown of Urulat, home of the Souma, where the Six Shapers dwelled and Haomane First-Born ruled over them.

It was all visible from the wall, interrupted at regular intervals by the watchtowers, manned by the faithful Havenguard, who kept a watch over the whole of Lord Satoris' empire.

On an empty stretch of wall between towers stood Tanaros Blacksword, who was gazing at none of it. A brisk breeze whipped at his dark hair, lashing it against his cheeks. He was one of the Three, and he was dangerous. Lest it be forgotten, one hand hovered over the hilt of his black sword.

"Tell me," he said to his companion, "of this *corruption*."

His look and his tone would have intimidated any sane comrade. Ushahin Dreamspinner sighed and hugged himself instead, warding off the autumn chill. His thin arms wrapped about his torso, his sharp elbows protruded. Cold seemed to bite deeper since his time in the Delta. It had not been his choice to meet on the wall. "Tell me," he said to Tanaros, "what you know of Darkhaven's construction."

"What is there to know?" Tanaros frowned. "Lord Satoris caused it to be created. After the Battle of Curonan, he retreated to the Vale of Gorgantum and raised up these mountains, using Godslayer's might. And he conceived of Darkhaven, and the Fjel delved deep into the earth and built high into the sky, building it in accordance with his plan. So it was done, and we Three were summoned to it."

"Yes." Ushahin extended one crooked hand and waggled it in a gesture of ambivalence. "And no. Darkhaven was not built by Fjel labor alone, and it is made of more than stone and mortar. It is an extension of its Shaper's will. It exists here because it exists in his Lordship's mind. Do you understand?"

"No," Tanaros said bluntly. "Do you say it is illusion?" He rapped his knuckles on the solid stone ramparts. "It seems solid enough to me, Dreamspinner."

Ushahin shook his head. "Not illusion, no."

"What, then?" Tanaros raised his brows. "Is it Fjel craftsmanship you question, cousin? I tell you, I am no mason, but I would not hesitate to pit their labors against the craftsmanship of Men; aye, or Ellylon, either."

"Then why is it that in two thousand years the Fjel have never built anything else?" Ushahin asked him.

Tanaros opened his mouth to reply, then closed it, considering. "Why would they?" he asked at length. "The Fjel are delvers by nature, not builders. They built Darkhaven for *him*, for his Lordship, according to his design. I say they made a fine job of it, cousin. What is it that you say?"

Ushahin shrugged. "You are too much of one thing, Tanaros, and not enough of another. It is not a matter of questioning the Fjel, but a matter of what causes Darkhaven to *be*. There are places that exist between things; between waking and sleep, between being and not-being. Darkhaven is such a place."

"Perhaps. And perhaps you spend too much time among your madlings, cousin." Tanaros eyed him. "What has this do with corruption?"

"Come," said Ushahin. "I will show you."

He walked with Tanaros along the wall, past the watchtowers where the Fjel saluted them, descending the curving stair at the inner gates of the keep. By the time they reached the entryway, Ushahin's bones ached fiercely with the cold. It was a relief to enter Darkhaven proper, to hear the bronze-bound doors close with a thud and the bar drop into place, the clank and rattle of the Havenguard resuming their posts. The black marble walls shut out every breath of wind, and the flickering blue-white veins of marrow-fire warmed the halls and lit them with an eldritch gleam that was gentle to his light-sensitive gaze.

"This way." Ushahin led Tanaros toward the section of the fortress in which his own austere quarters were housed. Madlings skittered from their approach. Although their fealty was unquestioned, he seldom brought anyone this way and it made them wary—even of the Lord General.

"If you wanted to meet in your quarters—" Tanaros began.

"Here." Ushahin halted in front of a niche. The arch that framed it rose almost to the vast ceiling above. On the back wall of the niche was a sculpture depicting the Wounding of Satoris, standing out in high relief, the outer limbs reaching across the arch into open air to engage one another.

Two figures were in opposition, tall enough to dwarf even a Fjel onlooker; Oronin Last-Born, the Glad Hunter, and Lord Satoris, Third-Born among Shapers. They grappled like giants, both figures shimmering with a fine network of marrow-fire. Satoris' hands were raised to parry a blow, one catching Oronin's left wrist; Oronin's right leg was extended, indicating how he had slipped as he lunged, planting the Shard of the Souma in Satoris' thigh with his right hand. Where Godslayer's haft stood out from his Lordship's marble flesh, a node of marrow-fire shone, brighter than the rest, and a bright vein trickled down his thigh.

"Forgive me, Dreamspinner," Tanaros said. "It is a mighty piece of work, but I don't understand—"

"Look closely." Ushahin waited patiently as Tanaros examined the niche. It was not easy to spot the opening, a low, narrow doorway hidden in the recesses and rendered almost invisible by the deep shadow cast by the bright figures.

"Ah." Tanaros saw it at last. "One of your madlings' passageways?"

"Yes."

"What would you have me say?" Tanaros shrugged. "I would that there were none, cousin, but they do no harm as long as they are confined within the inner walls. Indeed, forbid it be so, but were Darkhaven ever to face invasion, they might serve a purpose. Did not Lord Satoris himself cede you such rights?"

"Yes," said Ushahin. "To the spaces in between, where creatures such as I belong. But Tanaros, who built the passageways?" Watching the other's expression, he shook his head. "They were not here when I was first summoned, cousin. My madlings did not build them; others, yes, but not one such as this, built into the very structure of the wall. It would require inhuman strength."

"The Fjel . . ."

Ushahin pointed at the narrow gap, accessible only between the braced legs of the two Shapers' figures. "What Fjeltroll could fit in that space? I have asked and the Fjel have no knowledge of it, not in any generation. It was not there, and then it was. Darkhaven *changes*, Tanaros; its design shifts as his Lordship's thoughts change. This is what I seek to tell you."

"Ah, well." Tanaros gazed at the sculpted face of Lord Satoris. The Shaper's expression was one of agony, both at Godslayer's plunge and the greater loss. Oronin's blow had dealt him his unhealing wound, that which had stolen his Gift. "He is a Shaper, cousin. Is it such a surprise?"

"No, Blacksword. Not *this*. I've known about *this* for centuries." Ushahin shook his head in disgust. Ducking beneath Oronin's outstretched arm, he opened the hidden door onto the passageways between the walls. "Come with me."

Once behind the walls, he led with greater confidence, following a winding path with a shallow downward slope. The air grew closer and hotter the farther they went, then leveled once more. Tanaros followed without comment, his footsteps crunching on rubble. When they reached the rough-hewn chamber the madlings had claimed for their own, Tanaros paused. The madlings had not gathered here since the day Vorax had found them with the Lady of the Ellylon, and his Staccians had cleared much of the debris, but the evidence of their presence remained—scratched gibberish on the walls, overlooked candle-butts wedged into crevices.

Tanaros sighed. "Will you tell me this is his Lordship's doing? I have spoken with Vorax, cousin; and I have spoken with Cerelinde, too. I know what happened here."

"Oh, I know you've spoken with *Cerelinde*, cousin." A dark tone edged Ushahin's voice. "No, it's not this. Further."

They squeezed through a narrow portion of the passage. A few paces beyond it, the level path dropped into a sharp decline. Ushahin led them onward, down and down, until a blue-white glow was visible ahead, as bright and concentrated as the sculpted node of Godslayer's dagger.

"Do you see it?" he asked.

"Aye." Tanaros' jaw was set and hard. "It is no more than Vorax told me."

A roaring sound was in the air, and an acrid odor, like the breath of dragons. Ushahin grinned, his mismatched eyes glittering with reflected marrow-light. "Come see it, then."

They descended the remainder of the way with Ushahin leading, sure-footed on the pathways that were his own, his aching joints at ease in the hot, stifling air. There, all the way to the bottom of the decline.

A new chasm had erupted.

There was the old one, patched over by Vorax's Staccians. They had made a fair job of it for mortal Men. The old path was clearly visible, scuffed with gouges where a slab of stone had been dragged with great effort, capping the breach. It was braced by beams that had been soaked in water, already faintly charred by the heat of the marrow-fire, but holding. Rocks and rubble had filled the gaps.

And there, to the left of it—a gaping wound, emitting a violent, erratic light. Above it, a vaulted hollow soared. At the bottom, far, far below, the Source of the marrow-fire blazed and roared like a furnace. Heedless of danger, Tanaros stood at the edge and looked downward.

The sides of the sheer drop beneath his feet were jagged and raw. The marrow-fire was so bright it seared his eyes. He gazed upward, where his shadow was cast large and stark, flickering upon the hollow chamber of the ceiling. It, too, appeared new, as though hunks of rock had been sheared away.

Tanaros frowned. "There is some fault in the foundation that causes this. Small wonder, cousin, when it is built upon *this*." He turned to Ushahin. "Have you spoken of it to his Lordship?"

"Yes," Ushahin said simply.

"And?"

In the stifling heat, Ushahin wrapped his arms around himself as if to ward off a chill. His voice, when he answered, held an unwonted note of fear. "His Lordship says the foundation is sound."

Tanaros returned his gaze to the fiery, seething depths of the chasm. For a long moment, he was silent. When he spoke, it was without turning. "I will ask again, Dreamspinner. What does this have to do with *corruption?*"

"There is a canker of brightness at the core of this place," Ushahin said quietly. "Even as it festers in the thoughts of my madlings, even as it festers in your very heart, cousin, it festers in his Lordship's soul, gnawing at his pride, driving him to stubborn folly. There is no fault in the structure, Blacksword. Lord Satoris *is* the foundation of Darkhaven. How plainly would you have me speak?"

"You speak treason," Tanaros murmured.

"He caused rain to fall like acid."

The words, filled with unspoken meaning, lay between them. Tanaros turned around slowly. His dark eyes were bright with tears. "I know," he said. "I *know*. He had reason to be wroth,

Ushahin!" He spread his arms in a helpless gesture. "There is madness in fury, aye. No one knows it better than I. Everything I have, everything I am, his Lordship has made me. Would you have me abandon him *now*?"

"No!" Ushahin's head jerked, his uneven eyes ablaze. "Do not mistake my meaning, cousin."

"What, then?" Tanaros stared at him and shook his head. "No. Oh, no. This is not *Cerelinde's* fault. She is a pawn, nothing more. And I will not gainsay his Lordship's orders to indulge your hatred of the Ellylon, cousin."

"It would preclude the Prophecy—"

"*No!*" Tanaros' voice rang in the cavern, echoes blending into the roar of the marrow-fire. He pointed at Ushahin, jabbing his finger. "Do not think it, Dreamspinner. Mad or sane, *his* will prevails here. And, aye, his pride, too!" He drew a shaking breath. "Would you have him become *less* than Haomane? I will not ask his Lordship to bend his pride, not for your sake nor mine. It has kept him alive this long, though he suffers agonies untold with every breath he takes. Where would any of the Three be without it?"

"As for that, cousin," Ushahin said in a low voice, "you would have to ask the Lady Cerelinde. It lies in the realm of what-might-have-been." Bowing his head, he closed his eyes, touching his lids like a blind man. "So be it. Remember, one day, that I showed you this."

Turning, he began to make his way back toward the upper reaches.

"I'll bring Speros down to have a look at it," Tanaros called after him. "He's a knack for such things. It's a flaw in the *structure*, Dreamspinner! No more and no less. You're mad if you think otherwise!"

In the glimmering darkness, Ushahin gave his twisted smile and answered without pausing, the words trailing behind him. "Mad? Me, cousin? Oh, I think that should be the least of our fears."

LILIAS SAT BESIDE AN OPEN window.

The chambers to which she was confined in the Hall of Ingolin were lovely. The parlor, in which she sat, was bright and airy, encircled with tall windows that ended in pointed arches; twin panes that could be opened or closed, depending on whether one secured the bronze clasps that looked like vine-tendrils. The Rivenlost did love their light and open air.

A carpet of fine-combed wool lay on the floor, woven with an intricate pattern in which the argent scroll insignia of the House of Ingolin was repeated and intertwined. It gave off a faint, sweet odor when she walked upon it, like grass warmed by the sun.

In one corner of the parlor was a spinning-wheel. A bundle of the same soft, sweet-smelling wool lay in a basket beside it, untouched. Ellylon noblewomen took pride in their ability to spin wool as fine as silk.

There had been a spinning-wheel in Beshtanag. In a thousand years, she had scarce laid a hand to it.

On the southern wall was a shelf containing half a dozen books, bound in supple leather polished to a mellow gleam. They were Rivenlost volumes—an annotated history of the House of Ingolin, the Lost Voyage of Cerion the Navigator, the Lament of Neherinach—crisp parchment pages inscribed with Ellylon characters inked in a flowing hand. Although Calandor had taught Lilias to speak and read the Ellylon tongue, she hadn't been able to bring herself to read any of them.

It was clear that these rooms were designed to house a treasured guest, and not a prisoner. Still, a lock was on the outer door, and beyond her lovely windows awaited a drop of several hundred feet.

The rooms were at the top of one of the outer towers. From her seated vantage point, Lilias could watch the sea-eagles circling the central spire. Their wings were as grey as stormclouds, but their heads and underbellies were pristine white, white as winter's first snowfall on Beshtanag Mountain.

Every thirty seconds, they completed another circuit, riding the updrafts and soaring past on vast, outspread wings. They made broad circles, coming so close it almost seemed she could touch them as they passed. Close enough to see the downy white leggings above their yellow feet, talons curved and trailing as they flew. Close enough to make out the fierce golden rings encircling the round, black pupils of their eyes. She felt their gaze upon her; watching her as she watched them. Like as not it was true. The Eagles of Meronil served the Rivenlost.

"And why not?" Lilias said, addressing the circling sea-eagles. "That is what we do, we Lesser Shapers. We impose our wills upon the world, and *shape* it to our satisfaction. After all, are you so different from the ravens of Darkhaven?"

The sea-eagles tilted their wings, soaring past without comment.

"Perhaps not." Since the eagles did not deign to reply, Lilias answered her own question, reaching out one hand to touch the glass panes of the open window. It felt cool and smooth beneath her fingertips. Far below, the Aven River beckoned, a silvery ribbon dividing to encompass the island upon which the Hall of Ingolin was built, winding its way toward the sea. "In the end, it is a question of who chooses to use you, is it not?"

There was a scraping sound; in the antechamber, the outermost door to her quarters was unlatched, swinging open.

"Lady Lilias."

It was an Ellyl voice, fluted and musical. There was much to be discerned from the layering of tones within it. That was one of the hardest parts of her captivity; enduring the unspoken disdain and muted hatred of those Rivenlost whom Ingolin had assigned to attend her. "Lady," yes; after a thousand years of rule, they would accord her that much. Not "my lady," no. Nobleborn or no, she was none of *theirs*. Still, it was better than their compassion. Her words in the great hall had put an end to that particular torment. Lilias got to her feet, inclining her head as her attendant entered the parlor.

"Eamaire," she said. "What is it?"

Her attendant's nostrils flared. It was a very fine nose, chiseled and straight. Her skin was as pale as milk. She had wide-set, green eyes, beneath gracefully arching brows. The colors of her irises appeared to shift, like sunlight on moving grasses, on the rustling leaves of birch-trees. "There is a Man here to see you," she said.

Blaise Caveros stood a few paces behind her. "Lilias."

"Thank you, Eamaire," Lilias said. "You may leave us."

With a rigid nod, she left. Lilias watched her go, thinking with longing of her quarters in Beshtanag with their soft, muted lighting, a warm fire in the brazier, and her own attendants, her pretty ones. If she had it to do over, she would do it differently; choose only the willing ones, like Stepan and Sarika, and her dear Pietre. No more surly charms, no.

No more like Radovan.

It hurt to remember him, a flash of memory as sharp and bright as the gleam of a honed paring-knife. On its heels came the crash of the falling wall and Calandor's voice in her mind, his terrible brightness rousing atop Beshtanag Mountain.

It is time, Lilias.

With an effort, she pushed the memory away and concentrated on Blaise. "My lord Blaise." She raised her brows. "Have you come to make one last plea?"

"No, not that." He looked ill at ease amid the graceful Ellylon furnishings. "I don't know, perhaps. Would it do any good?"

"No," Lilias said quietly. "But you could sit and talk with me all the same."

"You're a stubborn woman." Blaise glanced away. "I don't know why I came, Lilias. I suppose . . . I feel a responsibility for you. After all, I kept you from taking your life." He smiled bitterly. "You did try to warn me that I would regret it."

"Do you?"

"Yes." He met her eyes, unflinching. "Perhaps not entirely for the reasons you believe."

Lilias tilted her head, considering him. "Will you not sit and tell me why?"

He sat in one of the parlor's four chairs, which were wrought of a pale, gleaming wood that seemed not to have been carved so much as woven, the slender branches wrought into an elegant form with arms like the curled ends of a scroll. The chair, made for an Ellyl's slighter weight, creaked beneath him. Blaise ignored it, waiting for her.

She took her seat by the window. "Well?"

"It was something you said." He cleared his throat. "That you had the right to seek death in defeat. That I wouldn't have denied you a clean death on the battlefield if you had been a man."

"Nor would you," Lilias murmured.

"No." Blaise picked restlessly at a loose thread on the knee of his breeches. "There was a man I wanted to kill," he said abruptly. "A Staccian, Carfax, one of the Sunderer's minions. His men attacked us outside Vedasia. Malthus . . . Malthus handled the others. Him, we took prisoner. I thought he was too dangerous to live, especially . . ."

"In company with the Bearer?" Lilias suggested. She laughed tiredly at his wary glance. "Ah, Blaise! Did you think I didn't know?"

"I wasn't sure."

"So you let him live."

He nodded. "On Malthus' orders. And in the end . . . do you know that, too?"

"Yes." Lilias swallowed against the sudden swelling in her throat. Brightness, falling. All the brightness in the world. "I know all that Calandor knew, Blaise. I know it all, even unto the cruel end." She rubbed the tears from her eyes, contempt shading her voice. "Will you tell me now what lesson lies within your tale? How even I am not so far gone that Arahila's mercy cannot redeem me?"

"No." He shook his head. "That wasn't my purpose."

"What, then?"

Blaise shrugged. "To say . . . what? Although I maintain poison is an unclean death, I do regret depriving you of the dignity of your choice. It was unfairly done; perhaps, even, at cross-purposes with Haomane's will. Who can say?" He smiled crookedly. "If Malthus had not maintained that Carfax of Staccia had the right to choose, we would not be having this conversation."

"No," Lilias said quietly. "We wouldn't."

Blaise sighed and rumpled his hair. "I raised the hackles of your pride, Lilias; aye, and your grief, too. I know it, and I know what it has cost us. I know the Counselor's words in the great hall stroked you against the grain. I knew it when he spoke them. I am here to tell you it was ill-considered."

Lilias glanced out the window. The Eagles of Meronil soared past on tilted wings, watching her with their gold-ringed gazes. "Do you suppose any of this will change my mind?" she asked.

"No. Not really, no." There were circles around his eyes, too; dark circles, born of weariness and long effort. "Lilias . . ." He hesitated. "Did you know that Darkhaven's army wasn't coming?"

There must, she thought, be a great sense of freedom in riding the winds' drafts; and yet, how free were they, confined to this endless gyre? Lilias thought about that day, during the siege, when she had dared the node-point of the Marasoumië beneath Beshtanag and found it blocked, hopelessly blocked.

"Yes," she said. "I knew."

"Why didn't you surrender, then?" Blaise furrowed his brow. "That's the part I don't understand. The battle was all but lost. You could have *told* us that the Lady Cerelinde was in Darkhaven. And if you had—"

"*I know!*" Lilias cut him off, and drew a shuddering breath. "I would still be a prisoner, but Calandor would live. *Might* live. How many other things *might* have happened, Borderguardsman? If you had arrived a day later, Calandor would have prevailed against Aracus' army. Or we might have escaped together, he and I. Did you never wonder at that?" They could have fled; they could have hidden. *For a time, Liliass. Only that.* The too-ready tears burned her eyes. "Aye, I regret it! Is that what you want to hear? A few months, a few years. Would that I had them, now. But you had reclaimed the Arrow of Fire. Could it have ended otherwise?"

"No." Blaise Caveros murmured the word, bowing his head. A lock of dark hair fell across his brow. "Not really."

"Ask yourself the same question," Lilias said harshly. "What is it worth, this victory? Aracus could buy peace for the price of his wedding vows."

"Aye." He ran both hands through his dark, springing hair to push it back, peering at her. "For a time, Lilias. And then what? It begins anew. A red star appears on the horizon, and the Sunderer raises his army and plots anew to destroy us. If not in our lifetimes, then our children's, or their descendants'. You heard Malthus' words in the council, Lilias. You may disdain his methods, but it is a true dream; Urulat made whole, and the power to forge peace— a lasting peace—in our hands. Aracus believes it, and I do, too."

"Malthus . . ." Lilias broke off her words, too weary to argue. "Ah, Blaise! Satoris didn't raise the red star."

He stared at her, uncomprehending. "What now, Sorceress? Do you claim it is not Dergail's Soumanië?"

"No." Outside her window, the sea-eagles circled while the Aven River unfurled beneath them, making its serene way to the sea. She sighed. "Dergail flung himself into the Sundering Sea, Blaise. It was never Satoris who reclaimed his Soumanië."

There was genuine perplexity in his frown. "Who, then?"

"This is the Shapers' War," Lilias said in a gentle tone. "It has never been anything else. And in the end, it has very little to do with *us*."

"No." Blaise shook his head. "I don't believe it." Something mute and intransigent surfaced in his expression. "Aracus was right about you. 'Tis dangerous to listen to your words." He heaved himself to his feet, the chair creaking ominously under his weight. "Never mind. You've made your choice, Sorceress, insofar as you were able. In the end, well . . ." He gestured around her quarters. "'Tis yours to endure."

Lilias gazed up at him. "Aracus said that?"

"Aye." He gave her a wry smile. "He did. I'm sorry, Lilias. Would that I could have found words that would make your heart relent. In truth, it's not why I came here today. Still, I do not think it is a choice you would have regretted."

"*Blaise.*" Lilias found herself on her feet. One step; two, three, closing the distance between them. She raised her hand, touching the collar of his shirt. Beneath it, his pulse beat in the hollow of his throat.

"Don't." He captured her hand in his, holding it gently. "I am loyal to the House of Altorus, Lilias. It is all I have to cling to, all that defines me. And you have seen that brightness in Aracus, that makes him worthy of it." Blaise favored her with one last smile, tinged with bitter sorrow. "I have seen it in your face and heard it in your words. You find him worthy of admiration; perhaps, even, of love. If I understand my enemy a little better, I have you to thank for it."

"Blaise," she whispered again; but it was a broken whisper. Lilias sank back into her chair. "If you would but *listen*—"

"What is there to say that has not been said?" He gave a helpless shrug. "I put no faith in the counsel of dragons. Without them, the world would never have been Sundered."

It was true; too true. And yet, there was so much to explain. Lilias struggled for the words to articulate the understanding Calandor had imparted to her. From the beginning, from the moment the red star had first risen, he had shared knowledge with her, terrible knowledge.

All things musst be as they musst.

The words did not come; would never come. Fearful mortality crowded her thoughts. A void yawned between them, and the effort of bridging it was beyond her. "Go," she said to him. "Just . . . go, and be gone from here."

Blaise Caveros bowed, precise and exacting. "You should know," he said, hesitating. "The Soumanië, *your* Soumanië—"

"Ardrath's Soumanië," Lilias said wearily. "I know its provenance, Borderguardsman. Have you listened to nothing I say?"

"Your pardon." He inclined his head in acknowledgment. "You should know, having once possessed, having *still* possession of it— it is being set into a sword. It was Aracus' choice," he added, "with Malthus' approval. 'Tis to be set in the hilt of his ancestral sword, as a pommel-stone. Malthus is teaching him the use of it, that he might draw upon its power should your heart relent. Does it not, Aracus will carry it into battle against the Sunderer nonetheless."

"How men do love their sharp, pointy toys. I wish him the joy of it." Lilias turned her head to gaze out the window. "You may go, Blaise."

After a moment's hesitation, he went. "Good-bye, Lilias."

Although he did not say it, she knew he would not return. He would go forth to live or die a hero, to find love or squander it among others who shared the same fierce, hard-edged certainty of his faith. And so it would continue, generation upon generation, living and dying, his children and his children's children bound to the yoke of the Shapers' endless battle, never reckoning the cost of a war not of their making. She would tell them, if only they had ears to hear. It was not worth the cost; nor ever would be. But they would never hear, and Lilias, who had lived a life of immortality surrounded by mortals, was doomed to spend her mortality among the ageless.

Outside her window, the sea-eagles soared, tracing an endless parabola around the tower. Beyond her door, the sound of his receding footsteps began to fade.

Already, she was lonely.

SEVEN

❖

PEERING INTO THE CHASM, SPEROS gave a low whistle. The brilliant flicker of the marrow-fire far below cast a masklike shadow on his face. "*That's* what this place is built on?"

"That's it," Tanaros said. "What do you think? Is there aught we can do?"

The Midlander glanced up at raw rock exposed on the ceiling, then back at the chasm, frowning. "It's beyond my skills, Lord General. I can make a better job of patching it than Lord Vorax's Staccians did, but it's only a matter of time."

"Where does the fault lie?"

Speros shrugged. "There's no fault, not exactly. Only the heat of the marrow-fire is so intense, it's causing the rock to crack. Do you feel it? There's no forge in the world throws off that kind of heat. I'd wager it's nearly hot enough to melt stone down there at the Source."

Tanaros' brand itched beneath his doublet. He suppressed an urge to scratch it. "Aye, and so it has been for a thousand years and more. Why does it crack *now*?"

"I reckon it took that long to reach the breaking point." Speros stamped on the stony floor. "This is hard rock, Lord General. Or it may be . . ." He hesitated. "Hyrgolf said there was a rain that fell while we were away, a rain like sulfur."

"Aye," Tanaros said quietly. "So I heard."

"Well." The Midlander gave another shrug. "Rain sinks into the earth. It may have weakened the stone itself." He glanced at Tanaros. "Begging your pardon, Lord General, but why is it that Lord Satoris chose to erect Darkhaven above the marrow-fire?"

"Gorgantum, the Throat, the Pulse of Uru-Alat." Tanaros favored him with a grim smile. "You have heard of the dagger Godslayer, have you not, Speros of Haimhault? The Shard of the Souma?"

"General Tanaros!" Speros sounded wounded. "What manner of ignorant fool do you take me for? I know the stories well."

"I know what they say in the Midlands," Tanaros said. "I am telling you that the legends are true, lad. It is Godslayer that wounded his Lordship. It is Godslayer, and Godslayer alone, that holds the power to destroy him. And it is *that*"—he pointed into the flickering depths—"which protects it."

"From whom?" Speros gazed into the bright void.

"Anyone," Tanaros said harshly. "*Everyone*. Godslayer hangs in the marrow-fire in the Chamber of the Font because his Lordship placed it there. And there, no mortal hand may touch it; no, nor immortal, either. Believe me, lad, for I know it well. Your flesh would be burned to the bone simply for making the attempt, and your bones would crumble ere they grasped its hilt. So would any flesh among the Lesser Shapers."

"Even yours?" Speros asked curiously. "Being one of the Three and all?"

"Even mine," Tanaros said. "Mine, aye; and Lord Vorax's, and Ushahin Dreamspinner's. Godslayer's brand does not protect us from the marrow-fire." His scar burned with new ferocity at the searing memory. "Even the Lady Cerelinde, lest you ask it. Not the Three, not the Rivenlost. Another Shaper, perhaps, or one of the Eldest, the dragons." He shook his head. "Elsewise, no one."

"Ah, well." The Midlander tore his gaze away from the marrow-fire. "I can't imagine anyone being fool enough to try. I wouldn't, not if I had a hundred buckets of that cursed water."

"The Water of Life." Tanaros remembered the taste of the Water in his mouth; water, the *essence* of water, infusing him with vigor. If the Well of the World were before him now, he would dip his finger into it and sooth the burning tissue of his brand. "Did you taste it?"

"Are you mad?" Speros' eyes widened. "The cursed stuff nearly killed me. I wouldn't put it in my mouth for love nor money!" He laughed. "I can't imagine what those poor little Yarru folk think to do with it. Haomane's Prophecy doesn't exactly say *how* they're to use it, does it?"

"No," Tanaros murmured. "It doesn't."

"Well, then." Speros shrugged. "If you ask me, Lord General, I think you worry too much. This is a problem, aye, but you see that?" He pointed to the ceiling. "By my gauge, there's a good twenty fathoms of solid rock there. At this rate, it ought to hold un- til Aracus Altorus is old and grey. And by *that* time, Haomane's Al- lies may as well call off the siege—and make no mistake, Lord General, Darkhaven can hold out that long, fortified as it is!—be- cause now that I've seen her with my own two eyes, I don't see the Lady Cerelinde taking some doddering old mortal relic into her bed, Prophecy or no. So then it's too bad for them, try again in an- other generation or three, and meanwhile Lord Satoris can pluck Godslayer out of the marrow-fire and put this right. Do you see?"

Tanaros laughed. "Clear as day. My thanks, lad."

"Aye, sir." Speros grinned at him. "So what would you have me do here?"

"Seal the breach," Tanaros said. "If it is all we can do, we will do it."

BY THE SECOND DAY, IT seemed to Dani that his entire life had con- sisted of running, stumbling and exhausted, across a barren grey landscape. It was hard to remember there had ever been anything else. The sun, rising in the east and moving westward, meant noth- ing. Time was measured by the rasp of air in his dry throat, by one foot placed in front of another.

He would never have made it without Uncle Thulu. What vigor the Water of Life had imparted, his uncle was determined not to waste. He was Yarru-yami, and he knew the virtue of making the most of water. His desert-born flesh, accustomed to privation, hoarded the Water of Life. When Dani flagged, Uncle Thulu cajoled and exhorted him. When his strength gave way altogether, Thulu gathered moss while Dani rested, grinding it to a paste and making him eat until he found the will to continue.

On they went, on and on and on.

The terrain was unforgiving. Each footfall was jarring, setting off a new ache in every bone of Dani's body, every weary joint. His half-healed collarbone throbbed unceasingly, every step sending a jolt of pain down his left arm. On those patches of ground where the moss cushioned his steps, it also concealed sharp rocks that bruised the tough soles of his feet.

When darkness fell, they slept for a few precious hours; then there was Uncle Thulu, shaking him awake.

"Come on, lad." Rueful compassion was in his voice, coupled

with a reserve of energy that made Dani want to curl up and weep for envy. "You can sleep when you're dead! And if we wait, the Fjeltroll will see to it for you."

So he rose and stumbled through the darkness, clutching a hank of his uncle's shirt and following blindly, trusting Thulu to guide him, praying that no Fjel would find them. Not until the sky began to pale in the east could Dani be sure they were traveling in the right direction.

On the third day, it rained.

The rain came from the west, sluicing out of the sky in driving grey veils. And while it let them fill their bellies and drink to their heart's content, it chilled them to the bone. It was a cold rain, an autumn rain. It rained seldom in the reach, but when it did, it rained hard. Water ran across the stony terrain, rendering moss slippery underfoot, finding no place to drain in a barren land. And there was nothing, not hare nor ptarmigan nor elk, to be found abroad in the downpour.

"Here, lad." Uncle Thulu passed him a handful of spongy moss. They had found shelter of a sort; a shallow overhang. They stood with their backs pressed to the rock behind them. Rain dripped steadily from the overhang, a scant inch past the end of their noses. "Go on, eat."

Dani thrust a wad of moss into his mouth and chewed. The more he chewed, the more it seemed to expand; perversely, the rainwater he had drunk made the moss seem all the drier, a thick, unwieldy wad. The effort of swallowing, of forcing the lump down his throat, made the clay vial swing on its spliced thong, banging at the hollow of his throat.

Uncle Thulu eyed it. "You know, Dani—"

"No." Out of sheer weariness, he closed his eyes. With his right hand, he felt for the vial. "It's not *for* that, Uncle. Anyway, there's too little left." Though his lids felt heavy as stones, Dani pried his eyes open. "Will you guide me?"

"Aye, lad," Thulu said gruffly. "Until the bitter end."

"Let's go, then." Still clutching the clay vial, Dani stumbled into the rain and Uncle Thulu followed, taking the lead.

After that, it was one step, one step, then another. Dani kept his head down and clung to his uncle's shirt. The rain, far from relenting, fell with violent intent. It plastered his black hair to his head and dripped into his eyes. Overhead, clouds continued to gather and roil, heaping one upon another, building to something fearful. The dull grey sky turned ominous and dark.

Since there was no shelter, they kept going.

They were toiling uphill; that much, Dani could tell. The calves of his legs informed him of it, shooting protesting pains with every step he took. Still, he labored. Above them, the roiling clouds began to rumble with thunder. Lightning flickered, illuminating their dark underbellies. What had been a steady downpour was giving way to a full-fledged storm.

Beneath his feet, the steep incline was beginning to level. Although he could see nothing in the darkness, Dani's aching calves told him that they had reached the hill's crest. He began to breathe a bit easier.

"Still with me, lad?" Uncle Thulu shouted the words.

"Aye!" Dani tossed the wet hair from his eyes. "Still with you, Uncle!"

Thunder pealed, and a forked bolt of lightning lit up the sky. For an instant, the terrain was revealed in all its harsh glory. And there, looming in the drumming rain, was one of the Fjeltroll.

Its lean jaw was parted in a predator's grin. In the glare of the forked lightning, its eyes shone yellow, bifurcated by a vertical pupil. Rain ran in sheets from its impervious grey hide. It said something in its own tongue, reaching for him with one taloned hand.

Dani leapt backward with a wordless shout, grasping the flask at his throat. Beneath his bare feet, he felt the hill's rocky crest crumble. And then it was gone, and there was nothing but a rough groove worn by flooding and him tumbling down it, the afterimage of the horrible Fjel grin seared into his mind.

"Dani!"

Borne by sluicing water, he slid down the hill, his uncle's shout echoing in his ears, vaguely aware that Thulu had plunged after him. It was worse than being caught in the rapids of the Spume. Beneath the torrent of rainwater, rocks caught and tore at his flesh, tearing away the makeshift sling that had held his left arm immobilized. He grunted at the pain, conscious only of his momentum, until he fetched up hard at the base of the hill. There he lay in the pouring rain.

"Dani." Uncle Thulu, illuminated by flickering lightning, limped toward him. Reaching down, he grabbed Dani under the arms and hoisted him to his feet. Beyond them, a dark figure was picking its way down the slope. "Come on, lad, run. Run!"

He ran.

It was no longer a matter of pain. Pain was a fact of existence, a familiar sound in the background. His limbs worked, therefore no new bones were broken. The clay vial was intact, bouncing and thumping as he ran. For the first half a league, sheer terror fueled his flight. Then his steps began to slow.

It was a matter of exhaustion.

As hard as his lungs labored, Dani couldn't get enough air into them. He gasped convulsively. Lurid flashes of lightning lit the sky, blinding him, until he could see nothing in the pouring rain but scintillating spots of brightness everywhere. Pain blossomed in his side, a keen shriek piercing the chorus of aches. Though he willed himself to ignore it, he couldn't stand upright. Hunched and dizzy, he staggered onward until Uncle's Thulu's hands grasping his shoulders brought him to a halt.

"Dani."

He peered under his dripping hair and fought to catch his breath. Blinking hard, he could make out his uncle's face. "Yes, Uncle?"

"Don't argue with me, lad."

Before Dani could ask why, the last remaining air was driven from his lungs as Uncle Thulu hoisted him like a sack of grain and flung him over his shoulder. Without hesitating, Thulu set off at a steady trot.

In the darkness behind them, loping through the falling rain, the Kaldjager Fjel grinned and gave its hunting cry. Across the reach, its brethren answered, passing on the cry, until all had received the word.

Their prey was found.

MERONIL WAS FILLED WITH SONG.

A vast contingent of Haomane's Allies would be departing on the morrow. For the past two days, delegates from other nations had met in the great hall of Ingolin the Wise. Seahold, the Midlands, Arduan, Vedasia, Pelmar, the Free Fishers—all of them had sent pledges. Their armies were on the march.

They would converge on the southern outskirts of the plains of Curonan, and there their forces would be forged into a single army under the command of Aracus Altorus, the would-be King of the West. From there, they would march to Darkhaven.

While they would march under many banners, two would fly above all others. One was the Crown and Souma of Elterrion the Bold, and it would be carried by the host of the Rivenlost. Ingolin the Wise would command them himself, forgoing his scholar's robes for Ellylon armor, and the argent scroll of his own house would fly lower than that of Elterrion's.

The other banner was that of the ancient Kings of Altoria, a gilt sword upon a field of sable, its tangs curved to the shape of eyes. It would be carried by the Borderguard of Curonan, for their leader, Aracus Altorus, had sworn that he would take up the banner of his forefathers the day he led the Borderguard against Satoris Banewreaker. So it would be carried, as Aracus would carry the sword of his ancestors; the sword of Altorus Farseer, with its gilded tangs shaped like eyes and a Soumanië set as its pommel-stone. And at his side would be Malthus the Counselor, whose Soumanië shone bright as a diamond, who carried the Spear of Light, the last of Haomane's Weapons.

Tomorrow, it began.

Tonight, Meronil was filled with song.

It began as darkness encroached from the east and Haomane's sun settled in the west in a dwindling blaze of golden splendor. As the last rays faded like embers, purple dusk settled over Meronil, turning its ivory towers and turrets, its arching bridges, to a pale lavender that darkened to a violet hue.

At her lonely window, Lilias sat and watched.

Throughout the city, lights were kindled. Tiny glass lights, smaller than a woman's fist, burning without smoke. The Rivenlost placed them in fretted lamps; hung from doorways, in windows, on bridges, carried by hand. A thousand points of light shone throughout the city, as though Arahila the Fair had cast a net of stars over Meronil. And as the lamps were kindled, Ellylon voices were raised in song.

She had been right, it was a city meant for music. The sound was inhumanly beautiful. A thousand voices, each one as clear and true as a bell. Lilias rested her chin on one hand and listened. She was not alone. Even the Eagles of Meronil ceased their vigilant circling and settled on the rooftops to listen, folding their wings.

A city of Men would have sung war songs. Not the Ellylon. These were laments, songs of loss and mourning, songs of remembrance of passing glory. From each quarter of Meronil, a different song arose; and yet, somehow, they formed a vast and complex harmony. One melody answered another in a deep, resonant antiphony; the simple refrain of a third wound between the two, stitching them together and making them part of the whole. A fourth melody soared above the rest, a heartbreaking descant.

"And Haomane asks us not to envy them," Lilias whispered.

One by one, the melodies died and faded into silence. In the lucid stillness that followed, she saw the first barge glide onto the Aven River and understood. The Pelmaran delegates had brought more than a pledge of aid in the coming war. Traveling in the wake of Aracus and his swift-moving vanguard, they had come more slowly, bearing wagons in their train. They had brought home the casualties of the last war, the Ellylon dead of Beshtanag.

There were only nine of them. The Host of the Rivenlost was a small company, but a doughty one. They had fought bravely. Only two had been slain by her Beshtanagi wardsmen. Their faces were uncovered, and even from her tower chamber, Lilias could see that they were as serene and beautiful in death as they had been in life. The bodies of the Ellylon did not wither and rot with mortality as did those of Men.

Three barges, three dead to a barge. A single lamp hung from the prow of each vessel, their light gleaming on the water. The barges glided on a river of stars, moved by no visible hand. The bodies of the nine lay motionless. Seven of them were draped in silken shrouds, their forms hidden, their faces covered.

Those would be the ones Calandor had slain with fire.

Alone at her window, Lilias shuddered. "Why couldn't you just leave us *alone*?" she whispered, knowing it was a futile question, at once false and true. They had come to Beshtanag because she had lured them there. The reason did not alter their deaths.

A fourth barge glided into view, larger than the others. It was poled by Ellyl hands and it carried a living cargo. In the prow stood Malthus the Counselor, distinguished by his white robes and his flowing beard, holding a staff in one hand. On his right stood Aracus Altorus, his bright hair dimmed by darkness, and on his left stood Ingolin the Wise. Others were behind them: Lorenlasse of Valmaré, kindred of the slain. There was a quiet liquid murmur as the Ellylon polemen halted the barge.

Malthus raised his staff and spoke a single word.

It was no staff he bore, but the Spear of Light itself. As he spoke, the clear Soumanië on his breast burst into effulgence, radiating white light. It kindled the Spear in his hand. Tendrils of white-gold brilliance wrapped its length, tracing images on the darkness. At the tip, its keen blade shone like a star. By its light, all of Meronil could see the retreating sterns of the three barges making their silent way down the Aven River, carrying their silent passengers. The barges would carry them all the way to the Sundering Sea, in the hope that the sea would carry them to Torath, the Crown, where they might be reunited in death with Haomane First-Born, the Lord-of-Thought.

A voice, a single voice, was lifted.

It was a woman's voice, Lilias thought; too high, too pure to be a man's. The sound of it was like crystal, translucent and fragile. No mortal voice had ever made such a sound nor ever would. It wavered as it rose, taut with grief, and Lilias, listening, was caught by the fear it would break. It must be a woman's voice, for what man had ever known such grief? It pierced the heart as surely as any spear. Who was it that sang? She could not see. The voice held the anguish of a mother's loss, or a wife's.

Surely it must break under the weight of its pain.

But it held and steadied, and the single note swelled.

It soared above its own anguish and found, impossibly, hope. The hope of the dwindling Rivenlost, who longed for Haomane's presence and the light of the Souma. The hope of Aracus Altorus, who dreamed of atoning for Men's deeds with a world made whole. Hope, raised aloft like the Spear of Light, sent forth like a beacon, that it might give heart to the Lady Cerelinde and bid her not to despair.

Other voices arose, one by one. A song, one song. Raising their clear voices, the Ellylon sang, shaping hope out of despair, shaping beauty out of sorrow. Three barges glided down the Aven River, growing small in the distance. In the prow of the fourth barge, Malthus the Counselor leaned on the Spear and bowed his head, keeping his counsel. Ingolin the Wise, who had watched the Sundering of the world, stood unwavering. Aracus Altorus laid one hand on the hilt of his ancestors' sword, the Soumanië dull in its pommel.

Around and above them, the song continued, scaling further and further, ascending impossible heights of beauty. Inside the city, delegates from the nations of Men listened to it and wept and laughed. They turned to one another and nodded with shining eyes, understanding one another without words. In the fields outside Meronil's gates, the Borderguard of Curonan heard it and wept without knowing why, tears glistening on cheeks weathered by wind and sun. The Rivenlost of Meronil, grieving, made ready for war.

In her lonely chamber, Lilias of Beshtanag wept, too.

Only she knew why.

EIGHT

"TELL ME AGAIN."

The Shaper's voice was deep and resonant, with no trace of anger or madness. It loosened something tight and knotted in Ushahin's chest, even as the warmth of the Chamber of the Font eased his aching joints. The blue-white blaze of the Font made his head ache, but the pulse of Godslayer within it soothed him. Between the heat and the sweet, coppery odor of blood, the Chamber was almost as pleasant as the Delta. Ushahin sat in a high-backed chair, both crooked hands laced around one updrawn knee, and related all he had seen and knew.

Armies were making their way across the face of Urulat.

His ravens had scattered to the four corners and seen it. It would be better to recall them and summon the Ravensmirror, but they were yet too far afield. Still, Ushahin perceived their flickering thoughts. He could not render their multitude of impressions into a whole, but what glimpses they saw, he described for his Lord. Pelmarans, marching like ants in a double row. Vedasian knights riding astride, encased like beetles in steel carapaces. Arduan archers in leather caps, accorded a wary distance. Midlanders laying down their plows, taking up rusted swords.

A company of Rivenlost, bright and shining, emerging from the vale of Meronil. Behind them were the Borderguard of Curonan, grim-faced and dire. Above them flew two pennants; the Crown and Souma, and the gilt-eyed Sword of Altorus Farseer. And among the forefront rode Malthus the Counselor, who carried no staff, but a spear whose blade was a nimbus of light.

Lord Satoris heaved a mighty sigh. "So he has brought it forth. Ah, Malthus! I knew you had it hidden. Would that I dared pluck Godslayer from the marrow-fire. I would not be loath to face you on the field of battle once more."

Sitting in his chair, Ushahin watched the Shaper pace, a vast moving shadow in the flickering chamber. There was a question none of them had dared to ask, fearful of the answer. It had been on the tip of his tongue many times. And when all was said and done, the fears of Ushahin Dreamspinner, who had made a friend of madness, were not like those of other men. This time, he asked it. "Will it come to that, my Lord?"

"It will not." The Shaper ceased to pace and went still. Shadows seethed in the corners of the chamber, thickening. Darkness settled like a mantle on Satoris, and his eyes shone from it like twin coals. "For if it came to that, Dreamspinner—if it became necessary that I must venture onto the field of battle myself—it would mean we had already lost. It is not the defense I intended, nor have spent these many years building. Do you understand?"

"Perhaps, my Lord," Ushahin offered. "You have spent much of yourself."

"Spent!" Lord Satoris gave a harsh laugh. "Spent, yes. I raised Darkhaven, I bound it beneath a shroud of clouds! I summoned my Three and bent the Chain of Being to encompass them! I bent my Brother's weapon to my own will and tuned the Helm of Shadows to the pitch of my despair. I brought down the Marasoumië! I am a Shaper, and such lies within my reach. It is not what I have spent willingly that I fear, Dreamspinner."

The blue-white glare of the Font gleamed on the trickle of ichor that bled down the black column of the Shaper's thigh. At his feet, a dark pool was beginning to accumulate, spreading like ink over the stone floor. How much of the Shaper's power had his unhealing wound leached from him over the ages?

"My Lord." Ushahin swallowed, the scent of blood thick in his throat. "I spoke to you of my time in the Delta. There is power there, in the place of your birth. Might you not find healing there?"

"Once, perhaps." Satoris' voice was unexpectedly gentle. "Ah, Dreamspinner! If I had fled there when Haomane's Wrath scorched me, instead of quenching my pain in the cool snows of the north . . . perhaps. But I did not. And now it is Calanthrag's place, and not mine. The dragons have paid a terrible price for taking part in this battle between my brethren and I. I do not think the Eldest would welcome my return."

"She—" Ushahin remembered the endless vastness behind the dragon's gaze and fell silent. There were no words for it.

"You have seen."

Not trusting his voice, he nodded.

"All things must be as they must," the Shaper mused. "It is the one truth my Brother refuses to grasp, the one thought the Lord-of-Thought will not think. Perhaps it is easier, thus. Perhaps I should have spent less time speaking with dragons when the world was young, and more time among my own kind."

"My Lord?" Ushahin found his voice. "All of Seven . . . each of your brethren, they Shaped Children after their own desires, yet you did not. Why is it so?"

Lord Satoris, Satoris Third-Born, who was once called the Sower, smiled and opened his arms. In his ravaged visage, beneath the red glare of his eyes and his wrath-scorched form, there lay the bright shadow of what he had been when the world was young. Of what he had been when he had walked upon it and ventured into the deep places his brethren feared, and he had spoken with dragons and given his Gift to many. "Did I not?" he asked softly. "Hear me, Dreamspinner, and remember. *All* of you are my Children; all that live and walk upon the face of Urulat, thinking thoughts and wondering at them. Do you deny it?"

There was madness in it; and there was not. The madness of Shapers could not be measured by the standards of Men—no, nor Were, nor Ellylon, nor any of the Lesser Shapers. The foundations of Darkhaven shifted; the foundations of Darkhaven held. Which was true?

All things must be as they must.

Ushahin shuddered and glanced sideways, his gaze falling upon Godslayer. There it hung in the glittering Font, beating like a heart. A Shard of the Souma, its rough handle a knob of rock. It would fit a child's hand, such a child as might raise it and bring it crashing down, heedless of what it crushed. Heedless of what it pierced. The pattern, the Great Story, was present in every pulse of light it emitted.

Let it come later than sooner.

Tears made his vision swim, spiked the lashes that framed his uneven eyes. "Ah, my Lord! No, never. I would not deny it."

"Ushahin." There was tenderness in the Shaper's voice, a tenderness too awful to bear. "These events were set in motion long ago. Perhaps there was a better course I might have chosen; a wiser course. Perhaps if I had tempered my defiance with deference, my Elder Brother's wrath would not have been so quick to rouse. But I cannot change the past; nor would it change the outcome if I could. My role was foreordained ere the death of Uru-Alat birthed the Seven Shapers, both its beginning and its ending—and though I grow weary, when that will come, not even Calanthrag the Eldest can say with surety. Thus, I play my role as best I might. I honor my debts. I must be what I am, as long as I may cling to it. And when I cannot, I will not. Do you understand?"

Ushahin nodded violently.

"That is well." Satoris, moving without sound, had drawn near. For a moment, his hand rested on Ushahin's brow. It was heavy, so heavy! And yet there was comfort in it. Comfort, and a kind of love. "You see too much, Dreamspinner."

"I know," he whispered.

"Tell me, then, what you see to the north." The hand was withdrawn, the Shaper resumed his pacing. Where he had stood, the stones drank in his ichor and the dark pool vanished. Another portion of him had become part of Darkhaven. "Have your ravens found the Bearer? Have my Fjel dispatched him yet?"

"No." Ushahin shook his head. "Many of your Fjel gather in Neherinach. That much, my ravens have seen. I suspect the hunt is afoot. More, I cannot say." He hesitated. "There is another thing, my Lord."

The red glare of the Shaper's eyes turned his way. "Say it!"

"Staccians." Ushahin cleared his throat. "Those we saw in the Ravensmirror, arming, those along the path the Galäinridder forged . . . I have touched their dreams, and they make their way to the plains of Curonan, for it is the place toward which all the armies are bound. And yet the Staccians, they were the first to set out. By now they may have reached the outskirts."

Lord Satoris laughed. It was an unpleasant sound. "Might they?"

"Aye." Ushahin glanced involuntarily at the Helm of Shadows, sitting in its niche. Darkness filled its eyeholes like the promise of anguish. "I could learn more if you would give me leave to walk the plains—"

"No." Lord Satoris raised one hand. "No," he repeated. "I do not need to know what lies in the hearts of these *Men,* who beheld the flight of Malthus the Counselor and his colorless Soumanië, that is so strange and altered. Still, I may use them as an example. Let Staccia see how I deal with oath-breakers, and Haomane's Allies how I deal with those who would destroy me." He smiled. It was not a pleasant sight. "Go, Dreamspinner, and send General Tanaros to me. Yes, and Lord Vorax, too."

"As you will," Ushahin murmured, rising.

"Dreamspinner?" The Shaper's voice had altered; the unlikely gentleness had returned.

"My Lord?"

"Remember," Lord Satoris said. "Whatever happens. All that you have learned. All that you have *seen*. It is all I ask."

Ushahin nodded. "I will."

SOMEWHERE IN THE MIDDLE OF the night, Uncle Thulu's strength began to wane.

Dani felt it happen.

He had done his part; he had not argued. Once he had regained his breath, they had come to an accommodation. If Uncle Thulu would lower him from his shoulder, Dani would suffer himself to be carried on his uncle's back.

He had wrapped his legs around his uncle's waist, clinging to his neck. Uncle Thulu resumed his steady trot. It made Dani feel like a child again; only this night was like something from a child's nightmare. What did the desert-born know of rain? After the storm passed, it continued to fall, endless and drumming, soaking them to the skin. It was cold. He had not known it was possible to be so cold, nor so tired. Dani rested his cheek against Uncle Thulu's shoulder. The vial containing the Water of Life was an uncomfortable lump pressing into his flesh. Still, through the rough wool of his shirt, he could feel the warmth rising from his uncle's skin, warming him. It was one of the gifts the Water of Life had imparted.

When it began to fade, he felt that, too. Felt the shivers that raced through his uncle as coldness set into his bones. Felt his steps begin to falter and stagger. Slight though he was, Dani was no longer a child. His weight had begun to tell.

"Uncle." He spoke into Thulu's ear. "You must put me down."

It took another handful of staggering steps before his uncle obeyed. Dani slid down his back, finding his feet. His limbs had become cramped and stiff, and his right arm did not quite work properly. Every inch of flesh ached, bruised and battered by his flood-borne tumble down the rocky slope. Still, he was alive, and he had recovered enough strength to continue unaided.

"Can you go on?" he asked.

Uncle Thulu was bent at the waist, hands braced on his knees, catching his breath. At Dani's question, he lifted his head. A dull grey light had begun to alleviate the blackness of the eastern skies behind them. It was enough to make out the rain dripping steadily from his face, into his open, exhausted eyes.

"Aye, lad," he said roughly. "Can you?"

Dani touched the clay vial at his throat. "Yes."

Once more, they set out at a slow trot.

Several hundred yards behind them, the watching Kaldjager chuckled deep in their throats and fanned out behind their prey.

In the dim grey light that preceded dawn, Tanaros rose and donned his armor, piece by piece. Last of all, he settled his swordbelt and the black sword in its scabbard around his waist. There were to be no survivors. His Lordship had ordered it so.

He had misgivings at the thought of leaving Darkhaven unattended; though it wouldn't be, not truly. There was Ushahin Dreamspinner and his field marshal Hyrgolf, with whom Tanaros had spoken at length. And, too, there was Speros. Though the Midlander was loath to be left behind, he was grateful to be entrusted with a special task: ensuring the safety, in Tanaros' absence, of the Lady Cerelinde.

The sojourn would be brief; a quick strike, and then back to Darkhaven. The return journey would afford him a chance to check the perimeter of the Vale, to make certain that any tunnels leading beneath it were well and truly blocked. It would ease his mind to see it firsthand.

In the end, it didn't matter. Lord Satoris had ordered it; Tanaros would go.

And it felt good, after so long, to be *doing* and not waiting. He had slept deeply that night, nurturing the coal of hatred that burned at the core of his heart. This was a simple task, an *easy* task. The Staccians who had chosen to follow Malthus had betrayed their ancient accord. They were warriors. They had reckoned the price of their betrayal, as surely as they had reckoned the price of their fealty. It should be easy to kill them.

A ruddy light was breaking in the eastern skies when they assembled.

Vorax was there, splendid in his gilded armor. He rode a mount big enough to bear him, his thick thighs wrapped around its barrel.

An uncanny awareness was in his mount's eyes, echoed in the others'. Fifty mounted Staccians followed his lead, all of them riding the horses of Darkhaven. He grinned at Tanaros, his teeth strong and white in the thicket of his ruddy beard. "Shall we go a-hunting, cousin?"

"Aye." Tanaros glanced at the throng of Gulnagel that surrounded him, the muscles of their haunches twitching with eagerness. "Let us do so." He gave the command. "Open the gate!"

They made good time on the narrow path of the Defile. Tanaros rode with the ease of long familiarity, glorying in the freedom. There was the Weavers' Gulch; he ducked his head, laying his cheek alongside the black's neck. The heavy feet of the Gulnagel pounded along the rocks, their talons scoring stone. Here and there, the little weavers scuttled along their vast loom, repairing the torn veils, disapproval in the angle of their poisoned fangs. Behind him, Vorax and his Staccians thundered.

Overhead, the Tordenstem sentries roared. Though vibration of their voices displaced showers of rocks, it was a sound of approval. If it had not been, they would be dead. Tanaros craned his neck as he rode, noting the position of the Midlander's carefully laid traps with approval.

After the narrow paths came the plains.

"Go," Tanaros whispered, flattening himself on his mount's back. Pricked ears twitched backward, laying close to its skull. It heard, and ran. Long grass parted like the sea. Tanaros looked left and right. To either side, he saw the Gulnagel, running. They surged forward in great bounds, tireless. Behind them, the Staccian contingent pounded. Vorax, at their head, was shouting a battle-paean.

There should have been scouts. Ever since Altoria had fallen—ever since Tanaros had led forth an army, the Helm of Shadows heavy on his shoulders—there had been scouts. The Borderguard of Curonan, keen-eyed and deadly in their dun cloaks.

There were none.

There had been none since they had ridden to attend their leader Aracus Altorus upon his wedding in Lindanen Dale. As the sun moved slowly across the unclouded sky, they rode, unchallenged. All of the armies of Haomane's Allies were spread across the face of Urulat, moving slowly toward this place. Now, it was empty. The ghosts of Cuilos Tuillenrad lay still, only whispering at their passage.

Those who betrayed Lord Satoris would pay.

At sunrise, the rain ceased.

Dawn broke with surprising glory over the reach, golden light shimmering on the wet rocks, turning puddles of standing water into myriad, earthbound suns. Where the moss grew, it brought forth an abundance of delicate white flowers.

It revealed another surprise, one that Dani hailed with a low cry of joy. They had come to the western verge of the empty reach. Ahead lay a craggy decline in which green trees grew in profusion, and mountains rising to the north. Somewhere, there was birdsong and the sound of rushing water.

Uncle Thulu summoned a weary smile. "That's our river, lad. Shall we find it?"

"Aye." Dani took a deep breath. "Give me a moment." He turned behind him to gaze at the sun with gratitude. Although his sodden clothes made him shiver, the sun's first warmth dispelled some of the chill. The sky overhead was pale gold, the underbellies of the dispersing clouds shot through with saffron.

And there . . .

Dani froze. "Fjeltroll," he whispered.

They were coming, a long, ranging line of them. Distance made the figures small, but they were drawing steadily nearer, moving at the effortless lope that had not diminished in the slightest. Sunlight glinted on their hides, still wet from the night's rainfall; on a few, it glinted on armor. One of them hoisted a waterskin, raising it as if in mocking salute, then tilted it to drink deep. Its pace never faltered.

Uncle Thulu swallowed audibly. "Run!"

They ran.

At a hundred paces, they reached the verge and began scrambling down the crags. Dani used hands and feet alike, ignoring the scraping pain in his palms and soles. Something gave way with a tearing sound near his right shoulder and a fresh jag of pain wrenched at him. He ignored that, too.

"This way!" Thulu plunged into the trees at the base of the decline. Checking the clay flask at his throat, Dani ran after him. Behind him, he could hear the sound of talons on rocks and the hunting cries of the Fjel.

Under the canopy of trees, it was cool and green. The loamy ground was soft, muting their footfalls. Gilded shafts of sunlight pierced the green. Drops of gathered rain slid from the leaves overhead, shining as they fell. Over the sound of water and birdsong and the harsh breath rattling in his lungs, Dani could hear the calls of the Fjel as they spread out through the woods. He found a burst of new energy in fresh terror.

They ran.

"Come on." Uncle Thulu panted grimly, veering northward toward the sound of rushing water. "Maybe the river . . ." He slowed, saving his breath as they rounded the trunk of a massive ash tree and came upon it; the White River, plunging down from the mountains in a series of cataracts. Water gathered in pools, spilling downward. "Maybe . . ."

Dani stifled a shout and pointed.

Beside one of the pools, one of the Fjel crouched on its powerful haunches, grey and motionless as a boulder. Its yellow eyes gleamed in its narrow visage. The intelligence in them was almost human. It shook its head slowly, baring its eyetusks in a predator's grin.

"Go!" Thulu shoved Dani back the way they had come. "Go, lad, go!"

They fled due west, straining their ears for the sounds of pursuit. If any was forthcoming, it was inaudible over the river-sound and their own labored breathing. Dani, running hard, felt the sharp stitch of pain return in his left side.

"South," Uncle Thulu gasped. "We'll cut south and pick up the river later!"

For a time it seemed it would work. They ran unimpeded. The ground rose sharply, but the path ahead was clear. Dani ran half-doubled with pain, clamping his left elbow hard against his ribs. It eased the stitch, but a bolt of pain shot through his right arm with every stride. He grabbed his right elbow with his left hand and staggered onward, hugging his rib cage. He had to lower his head to make the incline, bare toes digging into the loam, step by exhausted step.

Near the top, Uncle Thulu loosed a wordless cry and grabbed his arm. Dani lifted his head wearily.

One of the Fjeltroll awaited them, sitting in an easy crouch, loose-limbed and ready. It pointed west with one taloned hand and said something in its guttural tongue, smiling a terrible smile. Its tongue lolled in its mouth, grey-green and pointed.

"Back, back, back!" Thulu suited actions to words, scrambling backward down the incline, heedless of the dirt that smeared his skin.

Dani followed, breathing hard. "Can we get behind them?"

His uncle nodded grimly. "Let's try."

It was no good.

They doubled back, retracing their steps; there was another Fjeltroll, two Fjeltroll, stepping out from behind the massive tree-trunks. There was a cunning light in their yellow eyes; almost amused. One spoke to the other, and both laughed. Sunlight glinted on their eyetusks. They pointed westward.

Westward they ran; zigging and zagging to the north and south, fleeing like coursing hares. As they ran, cries resounded through the wood. And at the end of every avenue of flight that did not run true west along the rushing course of the White River, they found one of the Fjeltroll waiting. Looming among the leaves. Waiting, and pursuing at leisure.

All the same kind, with smooth grey hide, yellow eyes, and a predator's smile.

All pointing west with infinite patience.

"Uncle." In the middle of the woods, Dani staggered to a halt. The golden light of dawn had given way to the sinking amber hues of sunset. Under the leafy canopy, insects whined and flitting birds uttered high-pitched calls. Keeping his arms wrapped tight around his aching midsection, he lifted haunted eyes to meet his uncle's gaze. "I think we are being driven."

"Aye." Uncle Thulu nodded heavily. "I think you are right, lad."

"Well, then." The giddiness of despair seized Dani. Somewhere to his right, to the north, the White River was running, burbling over rock and stone. Around them, unseen, the Fjeltroll were closing, making ready to drive them farther westward. "There's no point in running, is there?"

"No." Thulu shook his head with sorrow. "No, lad. No point at all."

Dani touched the vial at his throat. "Then we won't."

Together, they began to walk.

NINE

THE STACCIAN TRAITORS HAD ESTABLISHED a tidy campsite on the southern outskirts of the plains of Curonan. One of the wide-ranging Gulnagel spotted it first in the late afternoon of their second day. Tanaros gave the order for the halt, lifting the visor of his helm and staring across the waving sea of grass. Shouts of alarm were borne on the wind, high and faint, as the Staccians caught sight of the attackers.

"Why do you delay?" Vorax drew alongside him. Through the slits in his visor, his face was flushed with betrayal and battle-rage. "Did you not hear what happened in Gerflod? I say we strike *now*, Blacksword, before they are ready!"

"No." Tanaros thought of the news out of Gerflod; of Osric and his men slain out of hand. He weighed it against the memory of Ngurra, the Yarru Elder, unarmed beneath the shadow of his sword. "They are warriors. We will give them a warrior's death."

Vorax made a sound of disgust. "They are dogs and deserve to die like dogs."

Tanaros looked hard at him. "Do you contest my command, cousin?"

"Not yet." Vorax wheeled his mount, taking his place at the head of his Staccians. "Your word you'll give me first strike!" he called.

"My word." Tanaros nodded.

Here and there, figures ran among the hide tents, racing to don armor. The Staccians had staked their horses some distance from their campsite, strung in a long line that each might have ample room to graze. Tanaros frowned and wondered what they had been thinking. Had they supposed they would be safe here on the plains? Had they expected Malthus to be here waiting, offering his protection? Did they believe Darkhaven would not take the risk of striking against them?

If so, they had made a grave error in judgment.

Perhaps, he thought, they had had no choice at all. Malthus the Counselor had ridden past them like the wind, cutting a swath through Staccia; the Galäinridder, risen from the ruined depths of the Marasoumië, the Bright Rider with a gem on his breast that shone like a star. It no longer held the power to Shape matter; only spirit. Which was more terrible? Had they chosen to betray Lord Satoris and their old bargain? Or had they merely been caught in the net of Malthus' power, compelled to follow Haomane's Weapon as the tides followed Arahila's moon?

"Boss?" One of the Gulnagel interrupted his thoughts. "They're in formation, Lord General, sir."

Tanaros blinked. "Krolgun," he said, remembering. Hyrgolf had assigned to this task all three of the Gulnagel who had accompanied him during their awful trek through the Unknown Desert. He laid a gauntleted hand on the Fjel's bulky shoulder. "We'll do this for Freg, eh?"

"Aye, boss!" Krolgun gave a hideous, delighted grin. "He'd like that, he would!"

"First strike to Lord Vorax and his lads," Tanaros reminded him.

"Aye, Lord General!"

"And keep your shields *up.*"

"Aye, Lord General, sir!" There was a rattle along the ranks of the Gulnagel as their shields were adjusted. Some hundred and fifty yards away, the enemy had mounted, forming a dense wedge, bristling with spears. There were nearly two hundred of them, outnumbering Vorax's company four to one. Even counting the forty Gulnagel, the treasonous Staccians held the advantage in numbers. Still, it was a mistake, Tanaros thought. Numbers did not tell the whole tale. He had gauged this task's needs with care. Better for them if they had formed a circle and made ready to fight back-to-back.

Then again, what did the Staccians know? They may have skirmished against unarmed Fjel in the wilds. They had never fought a unit of Fjel trained by *him*.

"Blacksword!" Vorax's voice was impatient. He had his men in a wedge formation, too. Behind their visors they were grim-faced, ready to avenge the affront to their own loyalty. They, too, had lost comrades since the red star had risen. "Will you take all day, cousin?"

Hatred. Hatred was clean. It swept aside doubt. Tanaros thought about Osric of Staccia, dying in the Earl of Gerflod's banquet hall, an unsuspecting guest. He thought about the Gulnagel Freg, carrying Speros' weight and staggering to his death in the desert. Malthus the Counselor had caused these things. If these Staccians wished to follow him, let them die for him. They were Arahila's Children, and Haomane First-Born had given them the Gift of thought. Whether they used it or not, they had *chosen*.

His sword rang clear of its sheath as he gave the signal. "Go!"

Vorax roared, clapping his heels to his mount's flanks. He was a formidable figure; sunlight glittered on his gilded armor. He, too, had long been kept idle. His men streamed after him, hair fluttering beneath steel helms. At a hundred yards, the Staccian leader gave the command. The plains of Curonan shuddered beneath pounding hooves as the two wedges surged toward one another.

"Traitors!" Lord Vorax's bellow rose above the fray as the two forces collided. *"Traitors!"*

Tanaros watched as Vorax's company plunged into the Staccian wedge, sowing chaos and turning the neatly ordered formation into a disordered melee. These were not men who had trained together on the drilling field, day after day. Riders milled across the plains, trying in vain to regroup and bring their short spears to bear on the enemy that had split their ranks. Vorax's men thundered through them and past, swinging wide, their wedge still intact. The horses of Darkhaven held their heads high and contemptuous as Vorax brought his company around for a second assault.

"Let's go, lads," Tanaros said to his Fjel. *"Go!"*

With great, bounding strides and shields held high, the Gulnagel raced into battle. The long grass parted in their wake; some of them swung their axes like scythes, shearing grass out of an excess of high spirits as they ran. Twenty to one side, twenty to the other. The Staccian traitors turned outward in alarm, too late; Vorax and his men were back in their midst. And now there was no time to regroup. There was no guarding their backs, where spears and swords were waiting to thrust, finding the gaps in their armor. No guarding their fronts, where the Gulnagel wielded axe and cudgel, using their shields to parry, ducking with ease on their powerful thighs, bounding to strike from unexpected angles. They fought with concerted, trained efficiency. Their axes slashed at Staccian spears until they drooped like broken stems of grass, heavy-headed. Their cudgels dented steel with mighty blows.

Horses fell, shrieking beneath the onslaught. There were broken limbs, spouting arteries. Astride his black mount, Tanaros pounded into the fray, laying about him with his black sword. This battlefield, any battlefield, was his home. For a thousand years, he had been honing his skills. There was no blow he could not parry, no contingency he failed to anticipate. The blood sang in his veins and a clean wind of hatred scourged his heart. Where he struck, men died. His sword had been tempered in the blood of Lord Satoris, and it sheared through steel and flesh alike.

He wondered if Cerelinde knew. He wondered if she worried. The thought quelled his battle-ardor, leaving a weary perplexity in its wake.

"You." Tanaros came upon the Staccian leader; unhorsed, dragging himself through the long grass, blood seeping under his armpit. He pointed with the tip of his sword. "Why?"

The man fumbled at his visor, baring a grimacing, bearded visage. "You are dead, Darkling!" he said, and spat bloody froth onto the plains. "So the Bright Paladin told us. Dead, and you don't even know it!"

A sound split the air. The butt-end of a short spear blossomed from the Staccian's chest. Its point, thrown with furious force, had pierced his breastplate. He stared unseeing at the sky.

Tanaros looked sidelong at Vorax.

"Not so dead as him," Vorax said impassively. "Are we done here, cousin?"

"Aye." Tanaros drew a deep breath and glanced around him. "Very nearly."

They left no survivors. It went quickly, toward the end. A few of the Staccians threw down their arms and pleaded, begging to surrender. Tanaros left those to Vorax, who shook his head, steady and implacable. His Staccians slew them where they knelt, swinging their swords with a will and taking their vengeance with dour satisfaction. Lord Satoris' orders would be obeyed. Elsewhere, the axes of the Gulnagel rose and fell, severing spinal columns as easily as blades of grass. They had no difficulty in dispatching the wounded.

Riderless horses milled, whinnying.

"Let them be." Tanaros raised one hand. "This day is no fault of theirs."

"And the Men?" Vorax asked grimly.

"We leave them for Haomane's Allies to find," Tanaros said. "And leave a warning. It shall be as his Lordship willed."

There had been no casualties in their company. A shrewd commander, Tanaros had planned wisely and well. There were wounded, and they were tended in the field. But the dead . . . it would fall to the wives and daughters of the Staccian traitors to number them. With the aid of the Fjel, they piled the dead, headless body upon headless body. It made a considerable heap, all told. Tanaros set Krolgun to ranging the plains until he found a chunk of granite that would serve as a marker. When it was set in place, Tanaros drew his dagger and used its point to scratch a message in the common tongue on the grey surface.

To Malthus the Counselor, who led these men into betrayal; mark well how they are served by your deeds. Do you assail Satoris the Sower, Third-Born among Shapers, expect no less.

In the day's dying light, the scratched lines shone pale against the dull grey rock. Behind the stone lay the heaped dead.

"Is it well done?" Tanaros asked Vorax.

"It is." The Staccian's voice rumbled deep in his chest. His gilded armor, kindled to mellow brightness by the setting sun, was splashed with blood. He spared Tanaros a heavy glance. "Do you think it will dissuade them?"

Tanaros shook his head. "No," he said gently. "I do not."

"So be it." Vorax gave a slight shrug, as if to adjust a weight upon his shoulders, then lifted his chin. His bearded profile was silhouetted against the dying sun. "Our task is finished!" he bellowed. "Let us leave this place!"

Tanaros, swinging into the saddle, did not gainsay him; he merely raised one hand to indicate his agreement, signifying to Men and Fjel alike to make ready to leave. There was time, still. The long, slanting rays of the setting sun would allow them leagues before they rested.

The plains of Curonan rang with thunder as they departed.

Behind them, the heaped dead kept their silence.

THE GREEN GRASS OF NEHERINACH, still damp with the night's rain, sparkled in the afternoon sun. The ivy that covered the burial mounds twined in rich profusion, nourished by the rainfall. Birds flitted among the trees, hunting insects that seemed to have multiplied overnight. Overhead, the sky had cleared to a deep autumnal blue.

It was a lovely day, despite the bones that lay buried here.

Skragdal had chosen to make his stand before the largest of the burial mounds. Since the Kaldjager were driving the smallfolk here, let them see. Let them hear of how Haomane's Allies had slain unarmed Fjel by the thousand. Let them grasp the greater meaning of their quest. Let them understand why they met their death in this green and pleasant place, where ancient blood soaked the earth.

He felt at peace for the first time since leaving Darkhaven. It would have been terrible to fail at this task. Field Marshal Hyrgolf had recommended him; Hyrgolf, who was trusted by General Tanaros himself, Lord General of the Army of Darkhaven, right hand of Lord Satoris. Since Osric's death, Skragdal had been carrying the entire trust of Darkhaven on his shoulders. Broad though they were, it was a mighty weight. It would be good to have done with it.

"Today is a good day," he said to Thorun.

The other Tungskulder nodded. "A good day."

One of the Kaldjager emerged from the tree line, loping alongside the sparkling river. Catching sight of them, he veered across the field. It was Glurolf, one of those sent from Darkhaven to join them.

"Boss." He saluted Skragdal. "They're on their way."

Skragdal nodded. "How long?"

"Not long." Glurolf grinned. "A bit. They're moving slow. We ran them hard."

They waited with the steady patience of Fjel. Skragdal was glad to have Thorun at his side. Tungskulder understood one another. On either side of them, the Nåltannen were arrayed in a long line. Their hands rested on their weapons, steely talons glinting in the bright sun. It did not seem possible that two bone-weary smallfolk could prove dangerous, but Skragdal was not minded to take any chances.

In a little while, other Kaldjager began emerging from the tree-covered slopes. They paused, waiting. Skragdal counted them and nodded in satisfaction. There were three yet afield. They must have the smallfolk well in hand. He widened his nostrils, trying to catch the scent of their prey. Men called them the Charred Ones. He wondered if they would smell of smoke.

They didn't.

There it was; a tendril of scent, one that did not belong in this place of Neheris' Shaping. It was the scent of Men—the yeasty odor of their flesh, their living blood, warm and salty. It was the reek of fear, a bitter tang, and of stale sweat. But there was something else, too, elusive and haunting. Skragdal parted his jaws, tasting the odor with his tongue. It was familiar, and not.

He turned to Thorun. "Do you know?"

"Water," the other Tungskulder said. "*Old* water."

Skragdal saw them, then.

It was as Lord Vorax had said; there were two of them. They emerged from the cover of the trees, walking slowly. When they saw Skragdal and his lads waiting, they stopped. They looked very small, and very, very tired.

"Neheris!" Thorun snorted. "Mother of us all! *This* is what we've been searching for?"

"Do not judge in haste." Skragdal fingered his carved *rhios* uneasily, thinking about the crater at the northern end of Neherinach where the Galäinridder had burst from the earth. He had been there in the Ways when the wizard expelled them from the Marasoumië, his gem blazing like a terrible red star. "Perhaps it is a trick."

"Perhaps," Thorun said.

There was no trick. Three more Kaldjager emerged from the trees to come behind the smallfolk. On either side, the others began to close in upon them. The Kaldjager were in high spirits, baring their teeth and showing their pointed tongues. It had been a good hunt. One of them pointed toward Skragdal and spoke. Weary and resigned, the smallfolk began trudging across the field.

Skragdal folded his arms and watched them come, slow and halting. It was true they were dark-skinned, though not so dark as a Mørkhar Fjel. The bigger one moved as though he were bowed beneath a great weight. Skragdal understood the feeling. There were tears on that one's haggard face, and he no longer reeked of fear, but of despair.

The smaller one held one arm clamped to his side. With his other hand, he clutched at a small clay flask strung about his neck on a braided vine. For all that, his head was erect, and his dark eyes were watchful and grave.

"Not much more than a pup," Thorun observed.

"No," Skragdal said. "Bold, though."

By the time the smallfolk reached the burial mound, they were wavering on their feet. The bigger one tried to shield the smaller. Aside from belt knives and a tattered sling at the little one's waist, they weren't even armed. They did not belong in the place. And yet, there was the flask, as Lord Vorax had said it would be. The smell of water, of *old* water, was stronger. If everything else was true, it was more dangerous than a sword; than a thousand swords. Skragdal shook his head, frowning down at them.

"Do you know where you are?" he asked in the common tongue. They gaped at him in astonishment. "This place." He indicated the field. "Do you know it?"

"You *talk!*" the smaller one said in wonderment.

One of the Nåltannen made a jest in his own tongue; the others laughed. "Enough." Skragdal raised his hand. "We do not make jests in this place. Smallfolk, this is Neherinach, where Haomane's Allies killed many thousand Fjel. We carried no arms. We sought only to protect Satoris, Third-Born among Shapers, who took shelter among us. Do you understand? You will die here to avenge those deaths."

The bigger one rested his hands on the shoulders of the smaller, whispering to him. The smaller shook him off. "Why?" he asked simply.

Anger stirred in Skragdal's belly, and his voice rose to a roar as he answered. "You would carry the Water of Life into Darkhaven and you ask *why?*"

The small one flinched, clutching his flask, but his gaze remained steady on Skragdal's face. "Why did you protect Satoris?"

Skragdal gave a harsh laugh, a sound like boulders rolling down a mountainside. "Does it matter to you, Arahila's Child? Ah, no." He shook his head. "Haomane gave *you* the Gift of thought, not us. You have come too far to ask that question. Better you should have asked it before you began. Perhaps you would not be dying here today. Perhaps your people would not have been slain for your actions."

"*What?*" Blood drained from the small one's face, turning his skin the color of cold ashes. He stared at Skragdal with stricken eyes. The bigger one made a choked sound and dropped to his knees. "Uru-Alat, no! *No!*"

"Aye, lad. Did you not expect his Lordship to strike against his enemies?" It was hard not to pity the boy; no more than a pup, truly. How could he have understood the choices he'd made? Skragdal signaled to the others. The Kaldjager moved in close behind the smallfolk. Thorun and the nearest Nåltannen slipped axes from their belts, nodding readiness. "It will be swift, I promise you." Skragdal held out his hand for the flask. Lord Vorax had told him to spill it on barren ground. "Give me the Water, and we'll be done with it."

The boy closed his eyes, whispering feverishly under his breath. It was no language Skragdal knew; not the common tongue, but something else, filled with rolling sounds. He was clutching the flask so hard that the lines on his knuckles whitened. Skragdal sighed, beckoning with his talons.

"Now, lad," he said.

With trembling hands, the boy removed the cord from about his neck. His eyes, when he opened them, glistened with tears. They were as dark and deep as Skragdal thought the Well of the World must be. The boy cupped the flask in both hands, then held it out, his skinny arm shaking. It was a simple object to have caused so much trouble; dun-colored clay, smoky from its firing. A cork carved from soft desert wood made a crude stopper, and the braided vine lashed around its neck looked worn and mended. It couldn't possibly hold much water; no more than a Fjel mouthful.

"Here," the boy whispered, letting go.

Skragdal closed his hand on the clay vial.

It was heavy; impossibly heavy. Skragdal grunted. A bone in his wrist broke with an audible snap as the weight bore him to the ground. The back of his hand hit the earth of Neherinach with shuddering force.

There, the flask held him pinned.

It was absurd, more than absurd. He was Skragdal, of the Tungskulder Fjel. He got his feet under him, crouching, digging his talons into the soil. Bracing his injured wrist with his other hand, he set his shoulders to the task, heaving at the same time he thrust hard with his powerful haunches, roaring.

He could not budge his hand. There was nothing, only a pain in his wrist and a deeper ache in the center of his palm. And water, the smell of water. *Old* water, dense and mineral rich, the essence of water. It rose like smoke from a dragon's nostrils, uncoiling in the bright air and filling him with alarm. All around, he could hear his lads milling and uncertain, unsure how to proceed without orders. And beneath it, another sound. It was the boy, chanting the same words. His voice, ragged and grief-stricken, gained a desperate strength as it rose.

With an effort, Skragdal pried his fingers open.

The flask, lying on his palm, had fallen on its side. Worse, the cork had come loose. Water, silver-bright and redolent, spilled over the rough hide of his palm, trickling between his fingers, heavy as molten iron, but cool. It sank into the rich, dark soil of Neherinach and vanished.

The vines on the burial mound began to stir.

"Thorun!" Skragdal scrabbled at the flask with his free hand, tugging and grunting. This was not a thing that could be happening. His talons broke and bled as he wedged them beneath the flask's smooth surface. "Blågen, lads . . . *help me!*"

They came, all of them; obedient to his order, crowding round, struggling to shift the flask from his palm, struggling to lift him. Fjel faces, familiar and worried. And around them the vines crawled like a nest of green serpents. Tendrils grew at an impossible rate; entwining an ankle here, snaring a wrist there. Fjel drew their axes, cursing and slashing. Skragdal, forced to crouch, felt vines encircle his broad torso and begin to squeeze, until the air was tight in his lungs. Snaking lines of green threatened to obscure his vision. No matter how swiftly his comrades hacked, the vines were faster.

He turned his head with difficulty. There was the smallfolk boy, the stricken look in his eyes giving way to fierce determination. His lips continued to move, shaping words, and he held both hands before him, cupped and open. Odd lines in his palms met to form a radiant star where they met.

It seemed the Bearer was not so harmless as he looked after all.

"Forget me." Unable to catch his voice, Skragdal hissed the words through his constricted throat. *"Kill the boy!"*

They tried.

They were Fjel; they obeyed his orders. But there were the vines. The entire burial mound seethed with them, creeping and entangling. And there was the older of the smallfolk, finding his courage. He had caught up a cudgel one of the Nåltannen had dropped, and he laid about him, shouting. If not for the vines, Skragdal's lads would have dropped him where he stood; but there were the vines, surging all about them in green waves.

It wasn't right, not right at all. This place marked the Fjel dead. It was a terrible and sacred place. But the Water of Life was older than the Battle of Neherinach. That which was drawn from the Well of the World held no loyalties.

Skragdal, pinned and entwined, watched it happen.

There was Thorun, who had never forgiven himself his error on the plains of Curonan where he had slain his companion Bogvar. Green vines stopped his mouth, engulfing him, until he was gone. No more guilt for him. There were the Nåltannen, casting aside their axes to slash with steel talons, filled with the fury of instinctive terror, the rising reek of their fear warring with the Water's scent. But for every severed vine that dropped, two more took its place, bearing the Nåltannen down, taking them into the earth and stilling their struggles. The largest burial mound on the field of Neherinach grew larger, and its vines fed upon the dead.

There were the Kaldjager, disbelieving. Nothing could stand against the Cold Hunters. Yellow-eyed and disdainful, they glanced sidelong at the creeping tide of vines and shook their hands and kicked their feet, contemptuous of the green shackles, certain they would wrest themselves free.

They were wrong.

It claimed them, as it had claimed the others.

Skragdal wished the vines had taken him first. It should have been so. Instead, they left him for the end. Neherinach grew quiet. He was crouching, enshrouded; a statue in green, one hand pinned to the earth. It ached under the terrible weight. He panted for air, his breath whistled in his constricted lungs. A wreath of vine encircled his head. The loose end of it continued to grow, wavering sinuously before his eyes. Pale tendrils deepened to green, putting out leaves. Flowers blossomed, delicate and blue. It would kill him soon.

A hand penetrated the foliage, thin and dark. Skragdal, rolling his eyes beneath the heavy ridge of his brow, met the smallfolk's gaze. He wished, now, he had answered the boy's question.

"I'm sorry," the boy whispered. "You shouldn't have killed my people."

His hand, quick and darting, seized the flask, plucking it from Skragdal's palm. He lifted it effortlessly and shook it. A little Water was left, very little. He found the cork and stoppered it.

Then he was gone and there was only the vine.

It struck hard and fast, penetrating Skragdal's panting jaws. He gnashed and spat at the foliage, clawing at it with his freed hand, but vines wound around his arm, rendering it immobile as the rest of his limbs. In his mouth, vine proliferated, still growing, clogging his jaws. A tendril snaked down his throat, then another. There was no more air to breathe, not even to choke. Everything was green, and the green was fading to blackness. The entangling vines drew him down toward the burial mound.

In his last moments, Skragdal thought about Lord Satoris, who had given the Fjel the gift of pride. *Did Neheris-of-the-Leaping-Waters not Shape her Children well? This I tell you, for I know: One day Men will covet your gifts.*

He wondered if the boy would have understood.

Dying, Skragdal lived in the moment of his death and wondered what the day would be like when Men came to covet the gifts of the Fjel. He wondered if there would be Fjel left in the world to see it.

With his dying pulse thudding in his ears, he hoped his Lordship would know how deeply it grieved Skragdal to fail him. He wondered what he had done wrong, where he had gone astray. He smelled the reek of fear seeping from his vine-cocooned hide and thought of the words of a Fjel prayer, counting them like coins in his mind. Words, precious and valued.

Mother of us all, wash away my fear.

Dying, he wondered if it was true that Neheris-of-the-Leaping-Waters would forgive the Fjel for taking Lord Satoris' part in the Shapers' War, if she would understand that Satoris alone upon the face of Urulat had loved her Children, whom she had Shaped with such care, tuning them to this place where she was born; to stone and river and tree, the fierce, combative joy of the hunt. The clean slash of talons, the quick kill and hot blood spilling. The warm comfort of a well-worn den with a tender, cunning mate and sprawling pups upon the floor, playing at carving *rhios*. All those things that he had been Shaped to be, all those things that were no longer his to know.

As the slow throb of his strong heart ceased, he hoped so.

Skragdal of the Tungskulder Fjel was no more.

TEN

TANAROS CHECKED THE VESDARLIG PASSAGE last. Of all the tunnels, it concerned him the most. There were others, farther south, that would be more accessible to Haomane's Allies, but they were well-kept secrets. The Vesdarlig Passage was an old route, and the Staccians had known of it for many years. Once, that would not have worried him.

No longer.

Patient Gulnagel held torches aloft for him. He had sent Vorax and his Staccians home, keeping only the Fjel to aid him. This deep below the earth, the torches cast wide pools of light, flickeringly only slightly as the draft from the ventilation shafts stirred the dense air. Tanaros examined the pile of rocks and boulders that sealed the tunnel.

It appeared sound. There were boulders there that only a Fjel could move unaided. If he was certain of nothing else, he was certain of their loyalty. With the butt-end of a borrowed spear, he poked at the mound, wedging it in various crevices and shoving hard. A few pebbles skittered to the cavern floor, but he met nothing behind the rock save more rock.

"How deep is it piled?" he asked Krolgun.

The torchlight wavered at the answering shrug. "Fifty paces?" The Gulnagel grinned. "Real paces, boss, not smallfolk strides like yours."

Tanaros smiled, gauging the distance in his head. It should be well over fifty yards; farther, if Krolgun meant a Gulnagel's bounding stride. If Haomane's Allies wanted to cart fifty yards' worth of stone out of the tunnels, they were welcome to try. Without Fjel aid, it would take weeks, perhaps months. He would enjoy sending out sorties to pick them off meanwhile.

"All right, lads. Let's go home."

Although he felt better for having inspected each of the blocked tunnels in person and Vesdarlig Passage most of all, it was a relief to emerge into open air. A cool wind blew across the plains, the tawny grass rippling in undulating waves. Haomane's Allies were coming. This vast, open expanse would be filled with them. He didn't like being unable to see across it, even with sentries posted. The Staccian traitors were no anomaly; they were the un-witting vanguard, the first skirmish in what promised to be a long war. He could not afford to be less than wary.

It was dangerous enough that his concentration had drifted in the skirmish.

Overhead, the sun was shining, moving to the west. The moun-tains ringing the Vale of Gorgantum cast a stark shadow on the plains. Tanaros skirted the shadow as they headed for Defile's Maw, ranging unnecessarily wide. It was the last time he would see sunlight for a long, long time. After the Unknown Desert, it had been hard to imagine he'd ever miss it . . . and yet.

He remembered his first sight of it atop Beshtanag Mountain, gilding the peaks of the trees. After so long, it had gladdened his heart. He thought of Cerelinde, turning her face skyward, opening her arms. Even a glimpse of Haomane's sun, dim and cloud-shrouded, had brought her joy.

"We are not so different, are we?" he said aloud.

"Boss?" Krolgun, loping alongside him, raised a quizzical face.

"Naught of import." Tanaros shook his head. "I'm just . . . think-ing. What difference is there, truly, between us and Haomane's Al-lies, Krolgun? We breathe, we eat, we sleep. Would you have known one of Lord Vorax's Staccians from the traitors if your eyes were sealed?"

"Sure, Lord General!" Krolgun flashed his eyetusks and tapped his snout with one wicked yellow talon. "So would you, if you were Fjel. Or Were. The Were can hunt blind, they say. I wouldn't mind seeing that."

Tanaros smiled ruefully. The Were would not be aiding them; not soon, maybe never. They had paid too dearly for it. "That's not what I meant, lad."

"Sorry, boss." The Gulnagel shrugged. "I'm not one for think-ing. Haomane's Gift, you know. Ask Marshal Hyrgolf, he's got the knack of it." He laughed. "Making decisions and the like, all you made him into."

"Made him?" Tanaros was startled.

"Aye, boss." Krolgun glanced cheerfully at him. "Did you not mean to?"

"No," Tanaros said slowly. "Or, yes, I suppose." He frowned at his hands, going about their own capable business, maintaining a steady grip on the reins. They were still sun-dark from his sojourn in the desert, scars pale on his knuckles. "It's just that I never thought of it thusly."

"Ah, well." Krolgun gave another shrug. "All the same in the end, isn't it?"

"Perhaps." Tanaros nodded. "Perhaps it is."

Krolgun grinned. "There you are, then!"

HAOMANE'S ALLIES WERE ENCAMPED IN the Midlands.

Their campfires spread wide and far, a hundred twinkling lights echoing the multitude of stars that spangled the canopy of night. It was not the whole of their company; not yet. Pelmaran troops and the knights of Vedasia were still en route. But Seahold's forces had gathered, and those from the small holdings of the Midlands were there, or flocking to gather. Many of them came with wagon trains of supplies, all that could be spared from the fall harvest.

The Free Fishers were there, laconic and weather-beaten. A company of Arduan archers had arrived fired with pride at the deed of their countrywoman, who had slain the Dragon of Beshtanag. If neither company was willing to fully accept Aracus Altorus' sovereignty over their respective republics, still they were eager to fight at his side, prizing freedom above all things. As King of the West, Aracus would respect their independence; the Sunderer, they were certain, would not. Had he not shown as much in laying his trap in Beshtanag?

But the heart of the army was those who had ridden forth from Meronil; the Host of the Rivenlost and the Borderguard of Curonan. And it was their commanders who assembled in a hushed meeting in the tent of Ingolin the Wise; their commanders, and those who remained from the Company that had ridden forth with Malthus.

It was a spacious tent, wrought of silk rendered proof against the elements by Ellylon arts. Three banners flew from its peak, and lowest of all was the argent scroll of the House of Ingolin. Above it fluttered the gilt-eyed sword of Altorus Farseer. And above that, the Crown and Souma of the House of Elterrion flew, in defiant tribute to the Lady Cerelinde, in the defiant belief that she yet lived.

Inside, it was quiet, dimly lit by Ellylon lamps.

Those who were present gathered around the table, eyeing the closed coffer. It was inlaid with gold, worked with the device of the Crown and Souma. The gnarled hands of Malthus the Counselor rested on its lid. So they had done at every gathering, since the first in Meronil. Soon, he would open it.

Within the coffer lay a tourmaline stone. Once, it had been tuned to the pitch of Malthus' Soumanië. Now, it was tuned to the Bearer and his burden. It had been one of Malthus' final acts when he had thrust the lad and his uncle into the Marasoumië, binding them under a spell of concealment.

Malthus the Counselor had wrought his spell with skill; with his Soumanië altered, not even he could break it. But the gem would tell them whether the Bearer yet lived.

"Haomane grant it be so," Malthus said, opening the coffer.

Pale blue light spilled forth into the tent. There on the velvet lining of the coffer, the tourmaline yet shone, shedding illumination from deep within its blue-green core. The cool light like water in the desert, and those gathered drank it in as though they thirsted. For a moment, no one spoke, the atmosphere still taut. Ingolin's gaze lifted to meet Malthus'. The Counselor shook his head, the lines on his face growing deeper.

Aracus Altorus broke the silence, abrupt and direct. "It's grown dimmer." He glanced around the tent, gauging the brightness. "Half again as much as yesterday eve."

"I fear it is so," Malthus replied somberly.

"Why?"

Malthus sighed. "Would that I knew, Aracus."

"I was supposed to protect him." Blaise's voice was harsh. "Even that old man among the Yarru said it. Guardian, he called me." He stared at the shard of tourmaline, clenching and unclenching his fists. "What does it mean?" He looked to Malthus for an answer. "Does it mean Dani is injured? Dying?"

Malthus and Ingolin exchanged a glance, and the Lord of the Rivenlost answered, "We do not know, Blaise Caveros. No Bearer has ever carried the Water of Life outside the Unknown Desert before." Ingolin's silvery hair rustled as he shook his head. "What link binds him to that which he Bears? That is a thing only the Yarru may know, and even they may not. We cannot say."

"That poor boy," Fianna the Archer murmured. "Ah, Haomane!"

"Do not be so quick to mourn him." Malthus' voice deepened, taking on resonance. He summoned a smile, though a shadow of sorrow hovered beneath it. In the depths of his Soumanië, a bright spark kindled. "He is stronger than you reckon, and more resourceful. Take hope, child."

Fianna bowed her head in acquiescence, even as Lorenlasse of Valmaré lifted his in defiance. "Child!" he said scornfully. "A mortal may be, but *I* am not, Counselor. If you had protected this Bearer better, we would not have to cling to this desperate hope. Better still if you had spent your vaunted wisdom in protecting the Lady Cerelinde, on whom Haomane's Prophecy depends."

"Lorenlasse." Peldras touched the Ellyl warrior's arm. "Listen—"

"Let me be, kinsman." Lorenlasse shook off his touch.

"Child." Malthus' voice, gaining in power, rolled around the confines of the tent. He closed the lid of the coffer with a thud, extinguishing the light of the tourmaline. "*Haomane's* Child. Do not mistake what we do here! Our hopes ride upon the Bearer as surely as they do upon the Lady; indeed, even more."

Lorenlasse of Valmaré stared at him with bright Ellyl eyes. "It is too small a hope, Counselor."

"No." Malthus spoke the word softly, and although he damped the power in his voice, it surged through his being, emanating from the Soumanië on his breast. He laughed; an unexpected sound, free and glad, his arms spreading wide. Despite fear, despite sorrow, he opened his arms in embrace. The light he had quenched upon closing the coffer resurged threefold, dazzling, from the clear Soumanië. "No, Haomane's Child. While hope lives, it is *never* too small."

They believed, then; they *hoped*. All around the tent, backs straightened and eyes kindled. Only Aracus Altorus sighed, bowing his red-gold head. A mortal Man, he felt the burden of those lives he must send into battle.

"Counselor," he said heavily. "It is in my heart that you are right. The Bearer's quest is his own, and there is no aid we may give him. All we can do is afford him the opportunity, by pursuing our own goals." His mouth twisted in a wry smile. "At least insofar as we may. The Sunderer has had many years in which to render Darkhaven unassailable."

A silence followed his words, but Malthus smiled and the clear light of his Soumanië was undimmed. "Trust me, Son of Altorus," he said. "I know Satoris Banewreaker. I have a plan."

❖

THEY FLED FOR SEVERAL LEAGUES before they rested, following the hidden route of the White River, which went to earth outside Neherinach. Once they did, Dani found himself shuddering all over. He felt unfamiliar in his own skin. Within his narrow breast, his heart pounded like a drum.

He could not forget it, the sight of the vines coming to life, engulfing the Fjeltroll. Rampant life, breeding death. Dragging them down, one by one, stopping their mouths, piercing their entrails. It must have been a horrible death. He did not like to imagine it.

But they had killed his people.

Did you not expect his Lordship to strike against his enemies?

He hadn't.

No one remembered the Yarru. Even Haomane First-Born had forgotten them, bent on pursuing his vengeance. It didn't matter. The Yarru had survived, and understood. It was the Shapers' War. They had fled beneath the earth and forgiven Haomane his Wrath; they had understood. That was the greater knowledge with which they had been charged, the understanding of how Uru-Alat, dying, had Shaped the world. And of the Well of the World, and what it meant.

Dani had not reckoned on Satoris' anger.

He willed his trembling to subside, his breathing to slow. At his side, Uncle Thulu did the same. They had not spoken to one another since Neherinach. Now his uncle glanced sidelong at him, a slow smile spreading over his face. He patted himself down, feeling for wounds and finding none.

"Well done, lad," he said. "*Well* done!"

"Was it?" Dani murmured.

Uncle Thulu frowned at him. "Would you have done elsewise?"

"No." Dani shivered, remembering the way the vine-wrapped Fjeltroll had rolled his eyes to meet his when he had plucked the vial from its palm. It had spoken the common tongue. He hadn't expected that. Malthus should have warned him. They were more than mere beasts.

Killers, nonetheless.

Perhaps your people would not have been slain for your actions.

He shivered harder, wrapping his arms around himself, wondering how they had died. Quickly, he hoped. The Fjeltroll had offered him as much.

There was no pursuit; not that day, nor the next. They turned southward, making their way through a dense forest of spruce. The trees were ancient, their trunks covered with green moss, so vast Dani and Thulu could not have encircled them with joined arms. Ferns grew thick on the forest floor, turning brown and brittle with the advent of autumn. It was hard to walk without them crackling underfoot. With each crunching footfall, Dani felt the skin between his shoulder blades prickle.

Still, they saw no Fjeltroll. On the third day, they learned why.

No boundary stone marked the border between Fjel territory and Staccia, a nation of Men. They had no way of knowing they had crossed it until they emerged from the forest to find a vast structure of grey stone; a stone Keep, built by Men's hands. Dani froze, staring at it uncomprehending. After endless days without a glimpse of human life, something so big seemed impossible.

"Back into the woods, lad," Uncle Thulu muttered. "Quick and quiet, before we're seen!"

Too late. Behind them, the ferns crackled.

"*Vas leggis?*" It was a woman's voice, sharp with anger. "*Vas jagen?*"

Dani turned slowly, showing his open hands. The woman was young, scarce older than he, clad in leather hunting gear, with blonde hair tied in a braid. As she glared at him, he saw fear and confusion in her face; but it was resolute, too. She reminded him a little bit of Fianna, for she held a hunting bow, an arrow nocked and aimed at his heart, and he did not doubt that she knew how to use it.

"I am sorry," he said in the common tongue. "We do not speak your language. We are lost. We will go." Moving cautiously, he tapped his chest then pointed into the forest. "We will go, leave."

"No." She shook her head, gesturing toward the Keep with the point of her arrow. Her brow furrowed as she searched for words. "Go *there*."

Dani glanced at his uncle.

"Go *there!*" The arrow gestured with a fierce jerk.

"I don't think she means to give us a choice, lad," Uncle Thulu said.

If his skin had prickled in the forest, it was nothing to what he felt here, crossing open territory with the point of a drawn arrow leveled at his back. The Keep loomed before them, grey and ominous. A reek of charred wood was in the air, as though a hundred campfires had been extinguished at once.

As they drew nearer, Dani saw the source. There was a

wooden building in the courtyard, or had been, once. Where the foundation had stood, there was nothing but a heap of ash and debris, strewn with scorched beams. He touched the vial at his throat for reassurance, glancing over his shoulder at the woman. "What happened here?"

She stared at him. "Fjeltroll."

At the tall doors of the Keep, she rapped for entry, speaking in Staccian to the woman who opened the spy-hole to peer out at her. The spy-hole was closed, and they waited. Dani eyed the doors. They were wrought of massive timbers, wood from the forest. Here and there, pale gouges showed where Fjel talons had scored them.

"I thought the Fjeltroll and the Staccians were allies," he whispered to his uncle.

"So did I," Uncle Thulu whispered back. "Keep quiet, lad; wait and see."

The doors were unbarred and flung open with a crash. Dani jumped and felt the point of an arrow prod his back. Their captor repeated her words, mangling the syllables with her thick accent. "You go there!"

They entered the Keep.

Inside, a dozen women awaited them, hands grasping unfamiliar weapons. Dani glanced about him. Women, all women. Where were the men? There were only women. From what little he knew of life outside the desert, the genders did not dwell apart any more than they did within it. On each of their faces, he saw the same emotions manifested: a resolute anger, belying the shock and horror that lay beneath it.

He knew that look. It plucked a chord within him, one that had sounded at the Fjeltroll's terrible words, one that was only beginning to settle into his flesh in the form of fearful knowledge.

Something bad, something very, very bad had happened here.

At their head was a woman of middle years, holding a heavy sword aloft in a two-handed grip. She had brown hair, parted in the center and drawn back on either side, and her face was a study in grim determination.

"Who are you?" She spoke the common tongue, spitting the words in distaste. "What seek you here?"

"Lady." Uncle Thulu spoke in a soothing voice. "Forgive us. We are travelers, far from home. What is this place?"

"Gerflod," she said grimly. "It is Gerflod, and I am Sorhild, who was wed to Coenred, Earl of Gerflod. Darklings, dark of skin; you do not come from Staccia, and I do not believe you come lost.

What do you want?" Holding the sword aloft, she gritted her teeth. "Did *Darkhaven* send you?"

"No, lady." Dani spoke before his uncle could reply. He met Sorhild's blue-grey gaze, holding it steadily. "It is Darkhaven we seek, but Darkhaven did not send us. We are Yarru, from the place you call the Unknown Desert."

"Dani!" Uncle Thulu's protest came too late. The damage, if it were damage, was done.

Sorhild's eyes widened and something in her expression shifted; hope, painful and tenuous, entered. The sword trembled in her hands. "The Unknown Desert?"

Dani nodded, not trusting his voice.

"'When the unknown is made known . . .'" Sorhild quoted the words of Haomane's Prophecy and gave a choked laugh, covering her face with both careworn hands. Her sword clattered against the marble flagstones as it fell. "Let them enter," she said, half-stifled. "It is the Galäinridder's will they serve."

At her insistence, Dani and Thulu spent the night in Gerflod Keep and learned what had transpired there. They heard the tale of the Galäinridder, who had come upon Gerflod in terror and splendor; of his white robes and his pale horse, of the blazing gem upon his breast, and the horrible warning he bore. War was coming, and Haomane would fall in his wrath upon all who opposed him; those who did were already marked for death. They heard how the Galäinridder, the Bright Paladin, had changed the hearts of the Staccians who beheld him, charging their spirits with defiance.

"Was it Malthus?" Dani whispered to his uncle. "Why didn't he come for us?"

"Who can say, lad?" Thulu shrugged. "The ways of wizards are deep and strange."

They learned of dissension in Staccia, and how the lords along the Galäinridder's route had gathered themselves for battle, making ready to ride to the plains of Curonan to await the coming war, filled with the fire of their changed hearts. And they learned how Earl Coenred had stayed, reckoning he guarded a more important thing.

Vesdarlig Passage.

It was a tunnel, a very old tunnel, leading to Darkhaven itself. Staccians and Fjel had used it from time out of mind. And from it, a company had come; Men and Fjel. Earl Coenred had seen them emerge and knew they were bound for his estate. He had sent away the women and children of Gerflod, bidding them take shelter at a neighboring manor house.

"There was a slaughter." Sorhild, wife of Coenred, told the story sitting at the head of the long table in the Great Hall, her eyes red-rimmed from long nights of weeping. "It is all we found upon our return. Bodies stacked like cordwood, and bloody Fjel footprints upon the floor, everywhere." She smiled grimly. "My husband and his men fought bravely. There were many human dead among those Darkhaven had sent. But they were no match for the Fjel."

"No," Dani murmured. "They would not be."

In the small hours of the night, her words haunted him. It was too easy, here, to envision it; it was written in the grieving visages of the women, in the bloodstained cracks of the floors. And if it was real here, it was real at home, too. He thought about Warabi, old Ngurra's wife, always scolding to hide her soft heart. It was impossible to think she was not there in the Stone Grove, awaiting their return. And Ngurra, ah! Ngurra, who had tried to teach him all his life what it meant to be the Bearer, patient and forbearing. Dani had never understood, not really.

Now, he wished he didn't.

"We cannot linger here," he whispered, hearing his uncle toss restlessly on the pallet next to him. "If there is pursuit, we would lead the Fjel to their doorstep."

"I know, lad." Uncle Thulu's voice was somber. "We'll leave at first light. What do you think about this *tunnel* she spoke of?"

"I don't know." Dani stared at the rafters overhead, faintly visible in the moonlight that filtered through the narrow window. It made him uneasy, all this wood and stone above him. The thought of being trapped beneath the earth for league upon league made his throat feel tight. "Are there more Fjel hunting us, do you think?"

"We cannot afford to assume otherwise," Thulu said. "But from which direction?"

"If they come from the north, the tunnel is the last place they would think to look for us. But if they come from Darkhaven . . ." Dani rolled onto his side, gazing in his uncle's direction.

Uncle Thulu's eyes glimmered. "We'd be trapped like rabbits in a burrow."

"Aye." Dani shuddered. "Uncle, I am afraid. You must choose. You are my guide, and I trust you. Whichever path you choose, I will follow."

In the darkness, Thulu nodded. "So be it. Leave me to think upon it, and I'll name my choice come dawn."

ELEVEN

◆◆

MEARA REACHED FOR THE SOUP ladle.

"Not that one." Thom, who cooked the soups, didn't look up from the turnip he was chopping. "The Lady's is in the small pot. Mind you don't confuse them."

Despite the sweltering heat of the kitchen, Meara shivered as though an icy finger had run the length of her spine. "What are you saying?" she whispered. "What are you doing, Thom?"

"What is best." He worked the knife at blurring speed, thin, pale slices of turnip falling away from the blade.

"On whose orders?"

The knife went still then, and he did look at her. "By our lord's will."

He meant Ushahin, who was *theirs*. Who summoned them and gave them succor, who made a place for those who had no place. He had listened to the words she had spoken. There was a bitter taste in Meara's mouth, and she was afraid to swallow. "He is one of the Three! He cannot gainsay his Lordship's will!"

"No." Thom regarded her, lank hair falling over his brow. "But we can do it for him." He nodded at the door. "Hurry. Lord General Tanaros returns soon."

She filled the tray in haste, ladling soup from the small pot into a clay crock. It was of Dwarfish make, simple and fine. The soup was a clear broth with sweet herbs. It steamed innocently until Meara placed the lid on the crock, sealing in its heat. She selected three pieces of white bread, wrapping them in a linen napkin, then hurried out of the kitchen.

In her haste, she almost ran into Lord Ushahin.

"Meara!" He steadied her. "Is your errand so urgent, child?"

"I don't know, my lord." She lifted her gaze to meet his eyes; the one with its pale, splintered iris, the other solid pupil. In its dilated blackness was that understanding beyond understanding of all the spaces between, all the lost souls who had been thrust into them and forgotten. It was beautiful to her, and comforting. "Is it?"

He saw the tray then and understood that, too. Ushahin Dreamspinner shook his head gently, releasing her. "Do not speak to me of what you carry, Meara. Whatever it is, I may not know it for certain."

"I'm . . . I'm not certain, my lord. But whatever it is, is it worth . . ." She swallowed, tasting the bitter taste. "Defying his Lordship?"

"Out of loyalty, yes." A somber expression settled over his uneven features. "Do not fear. Whatever you do, I will protect you. Betimes it falls to madness to preserve sanity, child. Too many things have transpired, and now, in Neherinach, something further. An entire company of Fjel is missing." He shook his head once more, frowning into the unseen distance. "I sent my ravens too far afield, seeking the Bearer, and there were none that saw. It was an error. Yet there are too few of them for all of Haomane's Allies afoot, and the Bearer's pace swifter than I reckoned. How was I to know?"

"My lord?" Meara was confused.

"Never mind." Lord Ushahin smiled at her. "Serve the Lady her supper, Meara."

The halls had never seemed so long. She would have taken the secret ways, but General Tanaros had barred from within the entrances that led into the Lady's chambers. He was wary of her safety. Meara's rapid footfalls echoed, setting off a series of endless reverberations. She caught glimpses of her reflection in the shining black marble with its glimmering striations of marrow-fire; a hunched figure, scuttling and fearful. She remembered the might-have-been that the Lady Cerelinde had shown her: a pretty woman in an apron kneading dough, her hands dusty with flour. A man had entered the kitchen, embracing her from behind, whispering something in her ear that made her laugh. He was tall and handsome, with dark hair.

It was a fierce hurt to cling to. The Lady Cerelinde should never have shown her something that *nice*. It hurt too much. Kindness was not always kind, even when people begged for it.

A pair of Havenguard were posted outside the Lady's door;

Mørkhar Fjel, black and bristling. They were loyal to General Tanaros. Meara held her breath as they examined her tray, lowering their massive heads, sniffing at it with flared nostrils. She kept her head low, tangled hair hiding her face. She knew they could smell her fear, but the Fjel would not think it strange, not in one of Darkhaven's madlings, who were prey to all manner of terror. She did not know if they could smell poison; or if, indeed, there *was* poison.

There must be poison.

If there was, it was nothing the Fjel could detect; nothing that was deadly to *them*. Little could harm the constitution of a Fjeltroll. They unbarred the door and granted her admittance into the Lady's chamber.

Maybe there was no poison.

And then she was inside, and there was the Lady Cerelinde, tall and shining. All the light in the room seemed to gather around her, clinging to her as though it loved her. It shimmered down the length of her golden hair, clung to her silken robes, rested on her solemn, beautiful face in loving benison. Unfair; oh, unfair! It filled her with a terrible yearning for all the lost beauty of the world, all that might have been, and was not. No wonder General Tanaros' face softened when he gazed upon her. Meara ducked her head and ground her teeth, remembering how he had spurned her advances.

She was a fool; no, *he* was a fool. She would have been content with a little, with so little. Was there madness in it, or a desperate sanity? She could no longer tell. Love, soup, poison, loyalty, folly. Which was which?

The Lady smiled at her as she placed the tray upon the table. "Thank you, Meara."

What did it cost her to be gracious? It was all the same in the end. She was one of the Ellylon. They had turned their back on Lord Ushahin when he was no more than an innocent babe, because he was not good enough, though their blood ran in his veins. Tainted by violence, tainted by the seed of Arahila's Children, who had accepted Lord Satoris' Gift. No one was good enough for them. For *her*.

Not Meara, who was only to be pitied.

Not General Tanaros, who protected her.

Not even his Lordship, no; Lord Satoris, who turned no one away. Whose Shaper's heart was vast enough to embrace *all* of them, even though he bled. Who saw in Ushahin Dreamspinner something rare and wonderful, who understood his pain and respected it. Who offered all of those whom the other Shapers had abandoned this sanctuary, who gave them a reason to live and to serve, who valued the least of their contributions.

Meara loved him; she did.

And still her tongue cleaved to the roof of her mouth as the Lady of the Ellylon lifted the lid from the crock, steam escaping. Was it right? What was right? Did it matter? The thought made her uneasy, setting a tide of gibberish rising in her mind, the words she had spoken echoing in the vault of her skull.

You should kill her, you know. It would be for the best.

The Lady Cerelinde lowered her silver spoon, filling it with broth, and lifted it to her lips, blowing gently across the steaming surface. Meara would have done the same. It wasn't fair. Were they so different, Arahila's Children and Haomane's? Thought chased itself around her mind, mingling with her words, her shattered visions and fragmented memories, until a dark pit opened before her. It was as it had been since she was a child of twelve. The world tilted and her thoughts spiraled helplessly, sliding into a chaos of repetition and babble, seeking to give voice to a pattern too vast to compass.

The spoon halted on its journey. "Meara?"

She clutched her head, seeking to silence the rising tide within it.

Be for the best for the best of the rest for the best for the blessed beast for the rest the beast blessed for the beaten breast of the blessed rest be eaten lest the breast be wrest for the quest of the blessed for the best beast that blessed the rest . . .

Words, slipping between her clutching fingers, slipping onto her seething tongue, sliding between her clenched teeth.

. . . eaten lest the blessed beast be beaten lest the beaten rest be left bereft lest the breast bereft be cleft lest the blessed be wrest . . .

Words and words and words crawling like insects in her mind, dropping from her lips, a rising tide of them; and somewhere, more words, *other* words, resonant and ringing, words as bright and straight and orderly as the blade of a sword.

The Lady Cerelinde was standing, was speaking; Ellylon words, words of power and ancient magics, words like a sword, bright and blazing. Each syllable rang like a bell, driving back the dark tide of madness, and Meara wept to see it go, for the awful remorse that came in its stead was worse.

In the silence that followed, the Lady turned back to the table. Droplets of broth had spattered the white linen. In a slow, reluctant gesture, she extended one hand above the steaming crock and

whispered a soft incantation. There was a ring on her finger, set
with a pale and glowing moonstone. Even as Meara watched, the
stone darkened, turning a remorseless shade of black.

If it could have spoken, it would have uttered a single word:
Poison.

"Oh, Meara!" The Lady's voice was redolent with sorrow.
"Why?"

"Lady, what is it?" Meara scuttled forward, despising herself for
her flinching movements, for the remorse she felt. She clapped the
lid on the crock, making the poison vanish. "Is it not to your liking,
the soup?" she asked, feigning anxiety. "Thom did but try a new
recipe. If you do not like it, I will bring another."

"Meara." A single word, breathed; her name. All the gathered
light in the room, all the gathered light of Darkhaven, shone in the
Lady's eyes. She sighed, a sigh of unspeakable weariness, bowing
her head. "What must I do?"

"I don't know," Meara whispered, sinking to her knees.
"Lady . . ."

"Perhaps I should drink it." Cerelinde regarded the blackened
gem upon her finger. "Do you say so, Meara? It is the simplest so-
lution, after all. If I were no more, all of *this* would cease to be."
Her gaze settled on Meara. "Would it be for the best, Meara of
Darkhaven?"

"I don't know!" The words burst from her in agony; she raised
her head to meet the terrible beauty of the Lady's gaze. "I don't
know."

"Perhaps I should, after all," the Lady said softly. She lifted the
lid from the crock and picked up the spoon.

"No!" Meara darted forward, snatching away the tray. The Lady
touched her cheek. The skin of her hand was soft, impossibly soft,
and her touch burned with cool fire. A bottomless pity was in her
luminous eyes.

"Ah, Meara!" she said. "See, there is goodness in you yet, despite the Sunderer's corruption. Would that I could heal you. I am
sorry I have only this poor Rivenlost magic to offer, that affords but
a moment's respite. But take heart, for all is not lost. While goodness exists, there is hope. What I cannot do, Malthus the Wise
Counselor may. He could heal you, all of you. He could make you
whole, as Urulat itself could be made whole."

There were words, more words, spinning into skeins of answers, filling Meara's head until the pattern of her thoughts was as
tangled as the webs in the Weavers' Gulch. She wanted to tell the

Lady that it was too late, that Malthus should have cared for them long ago instead of letting them be lost and forgotten. That they had chosen the only love anyone ever offered them, that Ushahin Dreamspinner understood them, for he was one of them; yes, and so was Lord Satoris, in all his wounded majesty. That all pride was folly; the pride of Ellylon, of Men, yes, even of Shapers. That they had chosen the folly they understood best. Mad pride; a madling's pride, broken, but not forgotten.

There were words, but none would come.

Instead, something else was coming; fury, rising like a black wind from the bowels of Darkhaven. Lord Satoris knew; Lord Satoris was angry. The touch of Ellylon magic had alerted him. Beneath the soles of her feet, Meara felt the floor vibrate. His fury rose, crawling over her skin, making her itch and tremble. The lid on the crock rattled as she held the tray in shaking hands.

"Dreamspinner!"

The roar shook the very foundations of Darkhaven. It blew through Meara's thoughts, shredding them into tatters, until she knew only terror. The promise of Lord Ushahin's protection held little comfort.

The Lady Cerelinde felt it. Meara could tell; her face was bloodless, as stark and white as the new-risen moon. And yet she trembled only slightly, and the pity in her gaze did not fade. "So it is Ushahin the Misbegotten who wishes me dead," she murmured. "He uses his servants cruelly, Meara."

There were footsteps in the hall, coming at a run. It would be Speros, the Midlander. General Tanaros trusted him. Meara glanced involuntarily at the closed door, thinking of the Havenguard beyond it. Her actions would be reckoned a betrayal.

In a swift, decisive movement, the Lady Cerelinde yanked aside the tapestry that concealed the hidden passage into her quarters, throwing back the bolts that barred the door and opening it. "Fly," she said. "Fly and be gone!"

Meara wanted to stay; wanted to explain. Did not want to be indebted to the Lady of the Ellylon, to whom she had served a bowl of poisoned broth. But the Lady's face was filled with compassionate valor, and terror was at the door.

"I told him you would break our hearts," Meara whispered, and fled.

❖

Vines crawled down the face of the rock, concealing the entrance to the Vesdarlig Passage. The sight of them made Dani feel queasy. He swallowed hard, tasting bile as the women of Gerflod parted the dense curtain of vine to expose the dark, forbidding opening. He would feel better if they weren't touching the vines.

Uncle Thulu whistled between his teeth. "We'd never have found *that* on our own, lad!" He scanned the ground with a tracker's eye. "Fjel have been here, but not since the rains. I'd not have seen any sign if I hadn't known to look."

"That's good." Dani's voice emerged faint and thready.

Uncle Thulu gave him a hard look. "Are you sure you've got the stomach for this, Dani?"

He touched the clay vial at his throat, but there was no comfort in it; not with the women's careworn hands clutching the vines, patiently waiting. There was only the memory of writhing barrows and green death. He drew strength instead from their faces, from their terrible grief and the fierce, desperate hope to which they clung. Taking a deep breath, he answered, "I'm sure."

His uncle's look softened. "Then we'd best not delay."

Dani nodded, settling his pack on his shoulders. It held a warm blanket and as much food as he could carry; dried and salt-cured provender, laid up for the winter. They were dressed in sturdy, clean attire; warm woolens from the clothing-chests of men whose blood had stained the flagstones of Gerflod Keep. A fresh sling had been tied around his arm, giving respite to his still-aching shoulder. Their waterskins were full. In his pack, Uncle Thulu carried a bundle of torches soaked with a rendered pitch that burned long and slow.

The women of Gerflod had been generous.

"Thank you, Lady." Dani bowed to the Lady Sorhild. "We are grateful for your kindness."

She shook her head. "It is very little. I pray it is enough, and not too late. Still, I am grateful to have had this chance. We have many years of which to repent." Tears were in her blue-grey eyes. With a choked laugh, she gave him the traveler's blessing. "May Haomane keep you, Dani of the Yarru!"

"Come, lad." Uncle Thulu touched his arm.

Together they went forward, passing beneath the vine curtain. Dani glanced at the face of one of the women holding the vines. It was the young woman who had captured them, the one who had reminded him of Fianna. There were tears in her eyes, too, and the same desperate hope. She was whispering something in Staccian, the words halting on her lips. A prayer, maybe.

It had been a long time since anyone had prayed to Haomane First-Born in Staccia.

He wanted to tarry, to ask her name, to ask what it was the Galäinridder had said to make her so certain of the rightness of their quest, despite the fearful consequences. But they did not speak the same tongue, and there was no time. Already Uncle Thulu was moving past him, taking one of the torches from his bundle. There was a sharp, scraping sound as he struck the flint, a scattering of sparks, and then the sound of pitch sizzling as the torch flared to life.

Yellow torchlight danced over the rocky surfaces. It was a broad tunnel and deep, sloping downward into endless darkness. Beyond the pool of light cast by the torch, there was only black silence.

If they were lucky, that would hold true.

"Shall we go?" Thulu asked quietly.

"Aye." Dani cast one longing glance behind him. The vines were still parted, and he could see the Lady Sorhild holding up one hand in farewell. The hope in her face, in all their faces, was a heavy burden to carry. He sighed, setting his face toward the darkness, hearing the soft rustling of the vine curtain falling back into place. "Lead me to Darkhaven, Uncle."

"HE DID *WHAT?*" LIGHT-HEADED WITH fury, Tanaros grasped the front of Vorax's doublet, hurling the old glutton against the wall and pinning him there. "Is he *mad?*"

"Peace, cousin!" the Staccian wheezed, trying to pry Tanaros' grip loose. His bearded face was turning red. "As to the latter, need you ask?"

A cry of agony thrummed through the stones of Darkhaven, wordless and shattering; once, twice and thrice. It sounded raw and ragged, a voice that had been screaming for a long time. Somewhere, Ushahin Dreamspinner was suffering the consequences of having attempted to circumvent Lord Satoris' will.

Tanaros swore and released Vorax, who slumped to the floor, rubbing his bruised throat. "What did you have to do with it?"

"Nothing!" The Staccian scowled up at him. "Did we not just ride together, you and I? Did we not do his Lordship's bidding? Vent your anger elsewhere, cousin!"

Tanaros drew his sword, touching the point of it to Vorax's

chest. The hilt throbbed in his grip, resonating to the anger of Lord Satoris, in whose blood its black blade had been tempered. The same beat throbbed in his chest, the scar over his heart pulsing with it. "Poison deadly enough to slay one of the Ellylon is not obtained with ease. Don't lie to me . . . cousin."

Vorax raised his hands. "Ask your Lady, since you value her so much."

Tanaros nodded once, grimly. "So I shall."

He sheathed the sword before he strode through the halls of Darkhaven. It didn't matter. His fury, Lord Satoris' fury, beat from him in waves, white-hot and searing. No one would stand in its way. Madlings and Havenguard alike fell back before it; the former scuttling to hide, the latter falling in at his back, exchanging glances.

The door to her quarters was ajar.

That alone was enough to fill him with rage. Tanaros flung the door wide open, striding through as it crashed. The sight of Cerelinde in all her beauty speaking to Speros rendered him momentarily speechless.

"General Tanaros."

"Lord General!"

They both rose to their feet to greet him. Cerelinde's face was grave and guarded; Speros' was open and grateful. Tanaros struggled for control. Somewhere, there was the scent of vulnus-blossom.

No.

It was imagination, or memory. Once, he had come upon them thusly; not these two, but others. Calista, his wife. Roscus Altorus, his lord. Not these two.

"What happened here?" Tanaros asked thickly. "Tell me!"

"It was one of the Dreamspinner's madlings, boss." Speros watched his face warily, standing clear of his sword; the blade Tanaros had no memory of having drawn since he had left Vorax. "Tried to poison her, near as I can figure. His Lordship's in a proper fury. The Lady says she doesn't know which one it was that brought the poison."

With an effort, Tanaros brought his breathing under control, pointing the tip of his blade at Cerelinde. "Who was it?"

Her chin rose. "I cannot say, General."

She was lying; or as near to a lie as the Ellylon came. She knew. She would not say. Tanaros stared at her, knowing it. Knowing her, knowing she would seek to protect those she perceived as lesser beings, loving her and hating her at once for it. His wife had offered him the same lie, seeking to protect her unborn child, but he had seen the truth in the child's mien and read it in her gaze. He could do no such thing with the Lady of the Ellylon.

"So be it." He pointed his sword at Speros. "Keep her safe, Midlander. It is his Lordship's will."

"Lord General." Speros gulped, offering him a deep bow. "I will."

"Good." Tanaros shoved his sword back into his scabbard, turning on his heel and heading in the direction of the cry. It had come from the Throne Hall. Whether or not his Lordship had summoned him, he could not have said; it was where his fury compelled him to go. His armor rattled with the swiftness of his strides, its black lacquered surface reflecting light cast by the veins of marrow-fire in a fierce blue-white glare. For once, the Havenguard had to hurry to keep pace with him.

Even as he approached the massive doors depicting the Shapers' War, the pair of Mørkhar Fjel on duty opened them. A slender figure stumbled between the doors, crossed the threshold, and fell heavily to its knees, head bowed, clutching its right arm. Lank silver-gilt hair spilled forward, hiding its features.

"Dreamspinner," Tanaros said drily.

Ushahin lifted his head with an effort. His face was haggard, white as bone. When he spoke, his voice was hoarse. "Cousin."

The hilt of the black sword pulsed under Tanaros' hand. He did not remember reaching for it a third time. Breathing slowly, he made himself release it. If Ushahin was alive, it meant his Lordship did not want him dead. He stared at the half-breed's pain-racked face, concentrating on breathing and willing himself to calm. "This was very foolish. Even for you."

One corner of Ushahin's mouth twisted. "So it would appear."

"What did he do to you?"

Moving slowly, Ushahin extended his right arm. Nerves in his face twitched with the residue of pain as he held his arm outstretched, pushing up the sleeve with his left hand. His right hand was clenched in a fist, nails biting into the palm. He opened his stiff fingers, a sheen of sweat appearing on his brow.

The arm was whole and perfect; more, it was beautiful. Strength and grace were balanced in the corded muscle, the sleek sinews. His skin was milk-white and flawless. A subtle pool of shadow underscored the bone hillock of his wrist, unexpectedly poignant. His hand was a study in elegance; a narrow palm and long, tapering fingers, only the bloody crescents where his nails had bitten marring its perfection.

"His Lordship is merciful," Ushahin said tautly. "He allows me to bear his punishment that my madlings might be spared it."

Tanaros stared, bewildered. "This is punishment?"

Ushahin laughed soundlessly. "He healed my sword-arm that I might fight at your side, cousin." A bead of sweat gathered, rolling down the side of his face. "You'll have to teach me how to hold a sword."

Tanaros shook his head. "I don't understand."

"Oh, he broke it, first." Ushahin licked lips parched from screaming. "Inch by inch, bone by bone. He ground them into fragments, and then he Shaped them anew, as slowly as he destroyed them. Does that help make it clear for you?"

"Yes." Tanaros swallowed against a wave of nausea. "It does."

"Good." Ushahin closed his eyes briefly. "You were right, it was foolish. Not the attempt, but its aftermath." He opened his eyes. "He drew on Godslayer's power to do this, Tanaros, and spent his own in the bargain. I shouldn't have taken the risk of provoking such a thing. He's precious little to spare."

"Dreamspinner." Somewhere, the anger had drained from Tanaros. He considered Ushahin and sighed, extending his hand. "Get up." Despite the tremors that yet racked Ushahin, Tanaros felt the strength of the half-breed's new grip through his gauntleted hand as he helped him to his feet. "After a thousand years, why does he want *you* to wield a sword?"

"Ah, that." Ushahin exhaled hard, clutching Tanaros' shoulder for balance. "It is so that I may be of some use in the battle to come, since I am to be denied the Helm of Shadows." Their gazes locked, and Ushahin smiled his crooked smile. "You've worn it before. I may bring a greater madness to bear, but you bring the purity of your hatred and a warrior's skill. Wield it well, cousin; and ward it well, too. There is a prophecy at work here."

. . . and the Helm of Shadows is broken . . .

Tanaros took a deep breath. "It is a heavy burden."

"Yes." Ushahin relinquished his grip, standing on wavering feet. He flexed his newly Shaped sword-arm, watching the muscles shift beneath the surface of his pale skin. "I gambled, cousin, and lost. We will have to make do." He nodded toward the Throne Hall. "As you love his Lordship, go now and deliver news he will be glad to hear."

It was thrice a hundred paces to walk the length of the Throne Hall. The torches burned with a fierce glare, sending gouts of marrow-fire toward the rafters, casting stark shadows. His Lordship sat unmoving in his carnelian throne. Godslayer shone in his hands, and upon his head was the Helm of Shadows.

The sight of it struck Tanaros like a blow. It was never easy to bear, and hardest of all when Lord Satoris wore it, for it was tuned to the pitch of his despair—of the knowledge he alone bore, of the role he was fated to play. Of the anguish of a brother's enmity, of the loss of a sister's love. Of immortal flesh seared and blackened, of Godslayer's prick and his unhealing wound. Of generation upon generation of mortal hatred, eroding the foundations of his sanity.

There was a new pain filling the dark eyeholes: the agony of betrayal, the whirlwind of fury and remorse bound inextricably together, tainted with self-loathing. Tanaros felt tears sting his eyes, and his heart swelled within the constraint of his brand.

"Tanaros Blacksword." Lord Satoris' voice was low and weary.

"My Lord!" He knelt, the words bursting fiercely from him. "My Lord, I swear, I will never betray you!"

Beneath the shadow of the Helm, the Shaper's features shifted into something that might have been a bitter smile. "You have seen the Dreamspinner."

"He should never have defied your will." Tanaros gazed up at the aching void. "He should never have added to your pain, my Lord."

The Shaper bowed his head, studying Godslayer as the shard pulsed between his hands, emitting a rubescent glow. "It was not without reason," he mused. "And yet . . . ah, Tanaros! Is there no way to survive without becoming what they name me? I have fought so hard for so long. Ushahin Dreamspinner sought to take the burden on himself, but there is no escaping the pattern of destiny. Oh, loving traitor, traitorous love!" He gave a harsh echoing laugh, making the torches flare. "It is always the wound that cuts the deepest."

Tanaros frowned. "My Lord?"

"Pay me no heed." Lord Satoris passed one hand before his helm-shadowed eyes. "I am in darkness, my faithful general. I am surrounded by it. It is all I see, and it grows ever deeper. Pay me no heed. It is your time that is coming, the time of the Three. It is for this that I summoned you, so many years ago. I wonder, betimes, which one . . ." Glancing at Godslayer, he paused and gathered himself. "Vorax reports that it was done and the Staccian traitors dispatched. Have you ensured that the tunnels have been sealed?"

"Aye, my Lord." Tanaros touched the hilt of his sword for comfort, feeling its familiar solidity. "I pray you, know no fear. Darkhaven is secure."

"That is good, then." The Shaper's head fell back onto his carnelian throne as though it cost him too much to keep it upright. His shadowed eyes glimmered in the uptilted sockets of the Helm. He held Godslayer loosely in his grip. "Tell me, my faithful general. Did I ask it, did I return Godslayer to the Font, would you swear your oath anew?"

Tanaros stared at the beating heart of the dagger; the rough knob of the hilt, the keen edges, ruby-bright and sharp as a razor. The scar on his chest ached at the memory. It had hurt when his Lordship had plucked the dagger from the marrow-fire and seared his flesh with the pact of binding—more than any mortal fire, more than any pain he had ever known. He raised his gaze. "I would, my Lord."

"Loyal Tanaros," Lord Satoris whispered. "It is to you I entrust my honor."

"My Lord." Tanaros bowed his head.

The Shaper gave another laugh, weary and edged with despair. "It is no boon I grant, but a burden. Go, now, and tend to your duties. I must . . . I must think." He glanced once more at Godslayer, a bitter resentment in his gaze. "Yes, that is it. I must think."

"Aye, my Lord." Rising to his feet, Tanaros bowed and made to take his leave.

"Tanaros." The whisper stopped him.

"My Lord?"

Beneath the Helm, the Shaper's shadowed features shifted. "Teach the Dreamspinner to hold a blade," he said softly. "He may have need of the knowledge before the end."

TWELVE

❖

Days passed in Meronil.

One, Lilias discovered, was much like the other. Sometimes the days were clear and the sun outside her tall windows sparkled on the Aven River far below. Betimes it rained; a gentle rain, silvery-grey, dappling the river's surface.

Little else changed.

There was no news; or if there was, no one did her the courtesy of telling her. Still, she did not think there was. It was too soon. Somewhere to the north, Haomane's Allies would be converging, gathering to march across the plains of Curonan and wage their great war. But in the west, the red star still rose in the evenings, a harbinger unfulfilled. It seemed so very long ago that she had watched it rise for the first time.

What does it mean, Calandor?

Trouble.

She had been afraid, then, and for a long time afterward. No longer. Everything she had feared, every private terror, had come to pass. Now there was only waiting, and the slow march of mortality.

She wondered what would happen in the north, but it was a distant, impersonal curiosity. Perhaps Satoris Banewreaker would prevail; perhaps he would restore her to Beshtanag. After all, she had kept their bargain. Perhaps he would even return into her keeping the Soumanië that she had wielded for so long, although she suspected not. No, he would not give such a gift lightly into mortal hands.

It didn't matter. None of it mattered without Calandor.

How was it that in Beshtanag, days had passed so swiftly? Days had blended into weeks, weeks into months, months into years. A decade might pass in what seemed, in hindsight, like the blink of an eye. Ah, but it was a dragon's eye, slow-lidded and amused, filled with amusement born of fathomless knowledge, gathered since before Shapers strode the earth.

Here, the days passed slowly.

Meronil was filled with women. There were a few men of the Rivenlost; an honor guard, rudimentary and sparse. Lilias watched them from her window as they passed, riding astride without need for saddle or reins. They looked stern and lovely in their bright armor. She wondered at their being left behind; wondered if they had volunteered, if they had been injured in previous battles. Perhaps they were reckoned too young to be on the front lines of a dire war; it was hard to gauge their age.

Mostly, though, there were women.

No children, or none that she saw. Few, precious few, children had been born to the Rivenlost in the last Age of Urulat. Few children had *ever* been born to the Ellylon; Haomane's Children, created by the Lord-of-Thought, who had rejected the Gift of his brother Satoris Third-Born.

And for that he was worshipped.

The thought made Lilias shake her head in bemusement. She did not understand—would *never* understand. How was it that Men and Ellylon alike refused to see that behind their endless quarrels lay the Shapers' War? It was pride, nothing but pride and folly; two things she had cause to know well.

The women of Meronil spoke seldom to her. There were handmaidens who tended to her needs; Eamaire and others, who brought food, clean water to bathe, linens for her bed. They no longer bothered with disdain, which in some ways was even harder to bear. Captive and abandoned, her power broken, Lilias was beneath their notice; a burden to be tended, nothing more.

When her heart was at its bleakest, Lilias imagined Meronil beset by the forces of Lord Satoris. She envisioned a horde of rampaging Fjel, besmirching its white towers and bridges with their broad, horny feet; bringing down its very stones with their powerful taloned hands, while Tanaros Kingslayer, the Soldier, sat astride his black destrier and watched and the Ellylon women fled, shrieking in disbelief that it come to this at the last.

Betimes, there was a fierce joy in the vision.

At other times, she remembered Aracus Altorus, with his wideset gaze; trusting, demanding. She remembered Blaise, dark-eyed Blaise, in all his fierce loyalty. They had treated her fairly, and in her heart of hearts she no longer wished to see them slain, lying in a welter of their own gore. It would not bring Calandor back, any more than Lord Satoris' victory. When all was said and done, they were her people; Arahila's Children. And yet both of them *believed*, believed so strongly. A hope, a vision, a world made whole; a faint spark nurtured and blown into a careful flame by Malthus the Wise Counselor, who was Haomane's Weapon.

Those were the times when Lilias leaned her forehead against the lintel of her window and wept, for she had too little belief and too much knowledge.

One day alone was different, breaking the endless pattern of tedium. Long after Lilias had assumed such a thing would never happen, an Ellyl noblewoman paid a visit to her quarters. It was the Lady Nerinil, who had sat in at Malthus' Council, who represented the scant survivors of the House of Numireth the Fleet, founder of Cuilos Tuillenrad, the City of Long Grass.

She came announced, filling the tower chamber with her unearthly beauty. Lilias had grown accustomed to the handmaidens; the Lady Nerinil was something else altogether. How was it, Lilias wondered, that even among the Rivenlost, one might outshine another? Perhaps it was a form of glamour, a remnant of the magics they had lost when the world was Sundered. She was glad she had asked the handmaidens to remove all mirrors from her room.

"Sorceress of the East!" Nerinil paced the chamber, unwontedly restless for one of her kind. Her tone was bell-like and abrupt. "There is a thing that troubles me."

Lilias laughed aloud. "Only one, Lady?"

The Lady Nerinil frowned. It was an expression of exceeding delicacy, the fine skin between her wing-shaped brows creasing ever so slightly. "In the Council of Malthus, I asked a question of you; one to which you made no reply."

"Yes." Lilias remembered; the sweet, ringing tones filled with anger and incomprehension. *Why would you do such a thing?* She looked curiously at her. "I answered with a question of my own. It was you who did not wish the conversation furthered, Lady. Why, now, do you care?"

Nerinil's luminous eyes met hers. "Because I am afraid."

Lilias nodded. "You have answered your question."

"Fear?" The Ellyl noblewoman gave a short, incredulous laugh. "Only fear? I am afraid, Sorceress, but I do not condemn thousands to death because of it."

"Yes," Lilias said wearily. "You do. You, and all of Haomane's Allies. What do you think will happen when they march upon Darkhaven?"

The Lady Nerinil shook her head, her dark hair stirring. Tiny diamonds were woven into it, and it gleamed like the Aven River reflecting stars at night. "Your question was asked and answered, Sorceress. You know our plight and our dream. We march upon Darkhaven despite our fear, and not because of it."

Lilias shrugged. "Doubtless that will prove great comfort to the wives and mothers of the slain. I'm sure they will be pleased to know a Midlander farmer's son died so that the Rivenlost may behold the face of Haomane once more."

A flash of anger crossed the Lady Nerinil's features. "You are swift to condemn Haomane's Allies for leading soldiers to take arms against the Sunderer, Sorceress. And yet you deceived us and sought to lead us into the Sunderer's trap to be slaughtered. Is this not hypocrisy? The Rivenlost had done nothing to threaten or harm you."

"No," Lilias agreed, gazing out the window. "But I would have been next."

There was silence, then. For a long time, the Lady Nerinil said nothing, for the Ellylon were incapable of lying. "Perhaps," she said at last, and her voice was low and melodious. "Like the Sunderer, you were a dragon-friend."

"I was that." Lilias swallowed, tasting the salt of her tears. *Oh, Calandor!*

"And your life was worth the lives of thousands?"

"It was to me." Lilias turned her gaze on the Ellyl noblewoman. "As you say, Lady, I had done nothing to threaten or harm you. I wished only to be left in peace. Did Beshtanag deserve to be destroyed because of it?"

"For that, no," the Lady Nerinil said quietly. "But the Soumanië was never meant to be yours to wield, and never in such a manner. You set yourself against Haomane's will when you did so. Surely you must have known such defiance could not go unanswered forever."

"Ah, Haomane." Lilias curled her lip. "We spoke of *fear*, Lady. What is it Haomane fears? Why is he so jealous of his power that he will not share even the smallest portion of it with a mortal woman?" She paused. "Or is it *knowledge* the Lord-of-Thought fears? Even Haomane's Allies seem passing fearful of the wisdom of dragons. Perhaps it is *that* he sought to extinguish."

"No." The Ellyl spoke tentatively, then frowned and repeated the word more strongly. "*No.*" Scintillant points of light danced around the room as she shook her head once more. "I will not fall prey to your sophistry and lies. You seek but to justify your actions, which served only your own ends."

"Can Haomane First-Born claim otherwise?" Lilias laughed shortly, feeling old and haggard, and wishing the Ellyl would depart. "At least, unlike the Lord-of-Thought, I know it. Have I ever denied as much?"

The Lady Nerinil looked at her with a fathomless expression in her dark, lambent eyes. "It seems to me that you spoke true words in the Council of Malthus, Sorceress. You are a proud woman, and a vain one."

"Yes," Lilias said. "I know."

"Arahila the Fair bids us to be compassionate," the Lady Nerinil mused. "May she in her infinite mercy forgive me, for I cannot find it in my heart to pity you, Lilias of Beshtanag."

The words carried a familiar sting. "I do not want your pity," Lilias murmured.

"I know." The Lady Nerinil of the House of Numireth the Fleet inclined her head with grace. "But it is all that you deserve."

THE TUNNEL WENT ON FOREVER.

After the unforgiving terrain of the northern Fjel territories, it should have been easy. Beyond the initial descent, the tunnel was level. Its floor was worn almost smooth by the passage of countless generations; broad Fjeltroll feet, the booted feet of Men, even horses' shod hooves, for it was vast enough for two Men to ride abreast. It was warmer beneath the earth than it was above it, out of the elements of wind and rain. They had food and water, and torches to light their way.

Set against that was a sense of stifling fear, and Dani would have traded all of the comforts the tunnel afforded to be rid of it. In the desert, one could see for leagues all around. Here, there was only the endless black throat of the tunnel. Stone below and stone above, ton upon ton of it. They used the torches sparingly, a tiny pool of firelight moving through the darkness.

Once, Dani had watched an enormous blacksnake swallow a hopping-mouse. Its hind legs were still twitching as it disappeared into the snake's gullet. Afterward, it made a visible lump as it moved through the long, sinuous body.

That was what it felt like.

The tunnel smelled of Fjeltroll; musky, faintly rank. Old or fresh? There was no way of knowing. They could see nothing beyond the edge of the torchlight. Every step forward was fraught with tension. If they could have done without the torches, they would have, but it was impossible. They would have been bumbling into the walls with every other step; or worse, wandered into one of the smaller side tunnels.

From time to time, they came upon ventilation shafts cut into the ceiling high above. When they did, they would pause, breathing deeply of the clean air and gazing upward at the slanting rays of daylight filtering into the tunnel. Uncle Thulu would snuff his torch, and for a precious span of yards they would continue by virtue of the faint illumination, no longer an excruciatingly visible target.

Then the air would grow stale and darkness thicker, until they could no longer see their hands before their faces, and they would pause again, straining their ears for any sound of approaching Fjeltroll. The sound of the flint striking, the violent spray of sparks as Uncle Thulu relit the torch, always seemed too loud, too bright.

There was no way of marking the passage of days. Although they tried counting the ventilation shafts, they had no idea how far apart they were. When they grew too weary to continue, they rested, taking turns sleeping in shifts, huddled in one of the side tunnels. Sometimes in their endless trudging, they felt a whisper of cool air on their faces though the darkness remained unalleviated. When that happened, Dani reckoned it was night aboveground.

In the tunnel, it made no difference.

They found resting-places where the forces of Darkhaven had made camp; broad caverns with traces of old campfires. There they found supply-caches, as Sorhild of Gerflod had told them. At the first such site they reached, Dani lingered beneath the ventilation shaft, studying marks scratched onto the cavern wall above the cold ashes of an abandoned campfire.

"Can you read what it says, Uncle?" he asked.

Uncle Thulu shook his head. "No, lad. I don't have the art of it."

Dani traced the markings with his fingertips, wondering. "Is it a spell, do you think? Or a warning?"

His uncle gave them a second glance. "It looks like clan markings as much as anything. Come on, let's be on our way."

Afterward, they did not linger in these places, for the scent of Fjeltroll was strongest where they had eaten and slept, but took aught that might be of use and hurried onward. Dani found himself thinking about the marks; wondering who had written them, wondering what they meant. It was true, they did look like clan markings. Among the Six Clans of the Yarru-yami, it was a courtesy to leave such signs in territories they hunted in common, letting others know where a new drought-eater had taken root, when a waterhole had silted closed, where a patch of *gamal* might be found. Or it could simply be a sign to let Lizard Rock Clan know that the Stone Grove had already passed through, hunting such prey as might be found.

It hurt to think of home.

He wondered what would be worth marking in the endless tunnel. Caches, perhaps; or perhaps it was notes about the other tunnels, the side tunnels Sorhild had warned them not to venture far into. Maybe it was nothing, only marks to show someone had passed this way. It was easy, in the tunnels, to believe the outside world could forget you ever existed.

He wondered if there was anyone *left* in the outside world to remember him. Surely the Fjeltroll could not have slain *all* of the Yarru-yami, not unless all of the Six Clans had remained at the Stone Grove. The desert was vast and Fjeltroll were not suited to traveling in an arid clime. Perhaps some of the Yarru lived.

Or perhaps they did not. Who, then, would remember Dani of the Yarru and his fat Uncle Thulu if they died beneath the earth? Blaise? Fianna? Hobard? Peldras, the Haomane-gaali? Carfax, who had saved him after all? He held out little hope that any of them had survived. There had been too few of them, and the Were too swift, too deadly. Even Malthus had deemed it imperative to flee.

There was Malthus, if it was true, if he was the Galäinridder after all. Dani thought he must be, even though the gem was the wrong color. But the Galäinridder had gone south without looking for them. He must think they were dead already, or lost forever in the Ways.

He was still thinking about it when they broke for a rest, laying their bedrolls a short, safe distance inside one of the side tunnels. It took a bit of searching to find a stone with a sharp point that fit nicely in the hand.

"What are you doing, lad?" Uncle Thulu, rummaging through their packs, eyed him curiously. "We're in enough danger without leaving a sign to point our trail."

"With the two of us marching down the tunnel plain as day, I don't think we need to worry about it, Uncle." Scratching on the tunnel wall, Dani drew the marking of the Stone Grove clan, five monoliths in a rough circle. He frowned, settling back to squat on his heels, then leaned forward to sketch a small vessel with a cork stopper in it, adding a digging-stick for good measure. "There."

Against his will, Uncle Thulu smiled. "There we are."

"Aye." Dani set down the stone and met his uncle's gaze. "It's just . . . if we fail, if we're caught and slain out of hand, maybe someday someone will find this; Malthus, or one of the Haomane-gaali; they have long memories. Or maybe a Staccian from Gerflod who remembers the Lady Sorhild's stories. And they will say, 'Look, the Bearer was here and his Guide was with him. Two Yarru-yami from the Stone Grove clan. They made it this far. They tried. Can we not do as much?'"

"Ah, lad!" Thulu's voice was rough. "I wish I had my digging-stick with me now. There may be no waterways to trace down here, but I hated to leave it in that Fjeltroll."

"You'll make another," Dani said. "I'll help you find it. After we go home. We'll rise before dawn and chew *gamal* together, then when the stars begin to pale, we'll go to the baari-grove and watch the dew form and pick just the right one." He smiled at his uncle. "One with a thirst for water, straight and strong, that peels clean as a whistle and fits firm in the hand, so you can lean on it once you've grown fat again."

Thulu laughed softly, deep in his chest. "Do you think so?"

"No." Dani's smile turned wistful. "But we can pretend."

"Then we shall." Thulu stroked the clan markings on the wall with his strong, blunt fingertips. "And, aye, lad, I promise you. Whatever happens, one day the world will say, 'Dani the Bearer was here, and his fat Uncle Thulu, too. They did their best. Let us do the same.'"

USHAHIN DREAMSPINNER SAT CROSS-LEGGED ON a high crag overlooking the plains of Curonan, squeezing a rock in his right hand. The heavy sheepskin cloak he wore cut the worst of the wind, but his bones still ached in the cold.

All except his right arm.

It felt strange; a foreign thing, this straight and shapely limb that moved with effortless grace. This finely made hand, the fingers capable of nimble manipulation and a powerful grip alike. Gone was the familiar stiffness of joint and bone-deep ache that plagued the rest of his body. In its place was an easy, lithesome strength and the memory of an agony that surpassed any pain the rest of his body had known, living like a phantom beneath the surface of his skin. The bones did not merely ache. They remembered.

Tanaros had told him to squeeze the rock. It would strengthen the new sinew and muscle, toughen the soft skin of his palm and fingers. It seemed unnecessary to Ushahin, but it gave a focal point to the pain; to the memory of pain. So he squeezed, and each time his hand constricted around the rock, it sent a pulse through fiber and bone that remembered its own slow pulverization. There was a macabre comfort in it; and irony, too. Another memory, an image that lay over him like a shadow, and it, too, carried a pain his bones remembered. Now, a thousand years later, here he was, a rock clenched in his fist. It was strange the way time brought all things full circle. Ushahin wished he could speak to Calanthrag about it. The Eldest would have understood.

But time itself was the problem, for there was none to spare. Not for him, not for any of them. His ravens were streaking across the face of Urulat. Ushahin sat, squeezing a rock in his right hand, and gazed through the fragmented mosaic of their myriad eyes. He could not say which filled him with the most fear: that which they saw, or that which they did not.

Hoofbeats sounded on the winding, treacherous path behind him, drawing him out of his distant reverie. "Lord Dreamspinner?"

"Speros of Haimhault." Ushahin acknowledged him without looking.

"General Tanaros has asked me to take you to the armory." Although he was doing his best to conceal it, the Midlander's voice held a complex mixture of emotions. Ushahin smiled to himself.

"Do you wonder that I still live?" he asked, dropping the rock and getting to his feet. "Is that it, Midlander? Would you see me dead for defying his Lordship's wishes?"

"No, my lord!" Speros' brown eyes widened. He sat astride the horse he had ridden during their flight to Darkhaven; the ghostly grey horse Ushahin had lent him. Behind him was the blood-bay stallion, its head raised and alert. "I would not presume to think such a thing."

"No?" Ushahin made his way to the stallion's side. Its once rough hide was glossy with tending, a deep sanguine hue. He felt it shudder beneath his touch, but it stood without flinching and let him mount, slewing around one wary eye. It was much easier to pull himself astride with one strong right arm. "How is it, then? Are you, like our dear general, ensorcelled by the Lady of the Ellylon's beauty?"

Speros kneed his horse around to face Ushahin, his jaw set, a flush creeping up his cheeks. "You do me an injustice," he said through gritted teeth, "and a greater one to the Lord General."

Ushahin gazed at him without answering, reaching out to sift through the Midlander's thoughts. Ignoring Speros' jolt of horror at the invasion, he tasted the deep and abiding awe with which the young man had first beheld the Lady of the Ellylon, weighing it judiciously against his fierce loyalty to Tanaros, born of their travail in the desert and his own inner demons. "So," he said softly. "It is loyalty that wins. Or need I search further? Shall I tell you your deepest fears, your darkest nightmares?"

"Don't." Speros choked out the word. The blood had drained from his face, and his wide-stretched brown eyes were stark against his pallor. "Please don't, my lord! It hurts."

Ushahin sighed and released him. "Then speak truth to me, Speros of Haimhault. What troubles you?"

Speros shuddered, tucking his chin into the collar of his cloak; heavy sheepskin like Ushahin's own. "You betrayed him," he said in a low voice. "Lord Satoris."

"No." Ushahin shook his head, gazing past the Midlander toward the plains. "I defied him, which is a different matter altogether." He looked back at Speros. So young, and so mortal! Why was it that he seemed so much more vulnerable than his own madlings? He had come here unwelcome, had braved far worse than his madlings, who were admitted unharmed. And yet. There was something touching about it; his fear, his loyalty. "Do you know what is coming, child?"

"War." Speros lifted his chin defiantly, the color returning to his face. "I'm not a *child*, Lord Dreamspinner."

"War," Ushahin echoed. "War, such as the world has not seen since the Fourth Age of the Sundered World." He pointed to the east. "Do you know what I have seen today, Midlander? Dwarfs, on the march. An entire company, following a column of Vedasian knights."

Speros laughed. "Dwarfs, my lord?"

"You laugh," Ushahin murmured. "Yrinna's Children have broken their Peace, and you laugh. You should not laugh, Midlander. They are strong and stubborn, as sturdy as the roots of an ancient tree. Once, long ago, before the world was Sundered, they made war upon the Ellylon."

"They are very . . . short," Speros said cautiously. "Or so it is said."

Ushahin gave him a grim smile. "We are all smallfolk to the Fjel, and yet they can be defeated. Do you know what I have not seen? An entire company of Fjel sent to hunt a pair of smallfolk. Not to-day, nor yesterday, nor for many days now. So, yes, Midlander, I defied his Lordship. I am uneasy at the signs converging upon us. I do not have a Shaper's pride; no, nor even a Man's, to scruple at a dishonorable course. If there was another chance to avert Hao-mane's Prophecy at a single stroke, I would take it."

For a long moment, Speros was silent. "I understand," he said at length.

"Good." Ushahin turned his mount. "Then take me to the ar-mory."

They rode in single file along the path, and the Tordenstem Fjel on sentry duty saluted them as they passed. Speros glanced at the fortifications he had built at the edge of the Defile; the wooden ricks laden with boulders, levers primed and ready. "Darkhaven *is* well-guarded, Lord Dreamspinner," he said. "I do not discount your fears, but we are prepared for any army, whether it be Men, Elly-lon, or Dwarfs."

"What of Shapers?" Ushahin inquired.

Speros shot him an alarmed look. *"Shapers?"*

"To be sure." Ushahin laughed mirthlessly. "Who do you think we are fighting, Speros of Haimhault? Aracus Altorus? Malthus the Counselor? The Lord of the Rivenlost?" He shook his head. "Our en-emy is Haomane First-Born."

"I thought the Six Shapers would not leave Torath!"

"Nor will they," Ushahin said. "Not while his Lordship holds Godslayer. But make no mistake, this war is of Haomane's making. It is the wise man who can name his enemy."

The Midlander was quiet and thoughtful as they made their way back to within Darkhaven's walls and rode toward the armory. Alongside the Gorgantus River, the waterwheel built at Speros' sug-gestion creaked in a steady circle, powering the bellows. Grey-black smoke was churning from the smelting furnaces, and nearby, the forges were going at full blast, sending up a fearful din and clatter. Teams of Fjel handled the work of heating and reheating cast-iron rods and plates, beating and folding them back onto themselves until the iron hardened. Elsewhere, red-hot metal was plunged into troughs of water, sending up clouds of acrid steam, and grinding wheels shrieked, scattering showers of sparks. The

Fjel worked heedless amid it all, their thick hides impervious. A Staccian smith clad in a heavy leather apron strolled through the chaos, supervising their efforts.

In the presence of so much martial clamor, Speros' spirits rose visibly. "Come, my lord," he shouted. "We'll find you a weapon that suits!"

Inside the armory, the thick stone walls diminished the racket outside. Weapons were stacked like firewood; piles of bucklers and full-body shields, racks of spears, bits and pieces of plate armor on every surface. Whistling through his gapped teeth, Speros strode toward a row of swords, hefting one and then another, pausing to eye Ushahin. At last he nodded, satisfied, and offered one, laying it over his forearm and extending the hilt. "Try this one, my lord."

It was strange to watch his hand, his finely made hand, close on the hilt. Ushahin raised the sword, wondering what he was supposed to discern from it, wondering what his Lordship expected him to do with it.

"Very nice!" Speros grinned at him. "Shall I teach you a few strokes, my lord?"

"I have seen it done," Ushahin said wryly.

"Ah, come now, Lord Dreamspinner." Speros plucked another blade from the row and tossed aside his sheepskin cloak, taking up an offensive stance. "If I were to come at you thusly," he said, aiming a slow strike at Ushahin's left side, "you would parry by—"

Ushahin brought his blade down hard and fast, knocking the Midlander's aside. "I have seen it done, Speros!" The impact made every misshapen bone in his body ache. He sighed. "This war will not be won with swords."

"Maybe not, my lord." The tip of Speros' sword had lodged in the wooden floor. Lowering his head until his brown hair spilled over his brow, he pried it loose and laid the blade back in its place. "But it won't be lost by them either."

"I pray you are right," Ushahin murmured. "You have done your duty to Tanaros, Midlander. I am armed. Go, now, and leave me."

After a moment's hesitation, Speros went.

Ushahin gazed at the blade in his right hand. The edges were keen, gleaming blue in the dim light of the armory. He wished, again, he knew what his Lordship expected of him. Since he did not, he found a scabbard for the blade and a swordbelt that fit about his waist and left the armory.

Outside, the blood-bay stallion was waiting, its reins looped over a hitching rail. Beneath the murky pall of smoke that hung over the place, its coat glowed with dark fire, as though it had emerged molten from the furnace and were slowly cooling. It stood unnaturally still, watching him with its wary, intelligent gaze.

"Have we come to a truce, you and I?" Ushahin asked aloud. "Then we are wiser, in our way, than our masters."

Perhaps it was so; or perhaps Ushahin, who had been abjured by the Grey Dam, no longer carried the taint of the Were on him like a scent. It grieved him to think it might be so. The horse merely gazed at him, thinking its own abstruse equine thoughts. He did not trouble its mind, but instead stroked its mane, wondering at the way his fingers slid through the coarse, black, hair. It had been a long time since he had taken pleasure in *touch*, in the sensation of texture against his skin.

"All things must be as they must," he said to the stallion, then mounted and went to tell Lord Satoris that the Dwarfs had broken Yrinna's Peace.

THIRTEEN

◆◆

"Lady." Tanaros bowed. "Are you well?"

She stood very straight, and her luminous grey eyes were watchful and wary. Her travail in Darkhaven had only honed her beauty, he thought; paring it to its essence, until the bright flame of her spirit was almost visible beneath translucent flesh.

"I am," she said. "Thank you, General Tanaros."

"Good." He cleared his throat, remembering how he had burst into the room and feeling ill at ease. "On behalf of his Lordship, I tender apologies. Please know that the attempt upon your life was made against his orders."

"Yes," Cerelinde said. "I know."

"You seem very certain."

Her face, already fair as ivory, turned a paler hue. "I heard the screams."

"It's not what you think." The words were impulsive. Tanaros sighed and ran a hand through his hair. "Ah, Cerelinde! His Lordship did what was necessary. If you saw Ushahin's . . . punishment . . . you would understand."

Her chin lifted a notch. "The Ellylon do not condone torture."

"He healed his arm," Tanaros said abruptly.

Cerelinde stared at him, uncomprehending. "Forgive me. I do not understand."

"Slowly," Tanaros said, "and painfully. Very painfully." He gave a short laugh. "It matters not. Ushahin understood what he did. He bore his Lordship's punishment that his madlings might not. He did not want them to suffer for serving his will." A stifled sound came from the corner; turning his head, Tanaros saw Meara huddled there. A cold, burning suspicion suffused his chest. "Do you have something to say, Meara?"

She shook her head in frantic denial, hiding her face against her knees.

"Let her be." Cerelinde stepped between them, her face alight with anger. "Do you think I would permit her in my presence did I not trust her, Tanaros?"

"I don't know," he said quietly. "*Do* you trust her?"

The Ellylon could not lie. She stood close to him, close enough to touch, her chin still lifted. He could feel the heat of her body; could almost smell her skin. Her eyes were level with his. He could see the pleated irises, the subtle colors that illuminated them; violet, blue, and green, and the indeterminate hue that lies in the innermost curve of a rainbow.

"Yes," Cerelinde said, her voice steady and certain. "I do."

There was a sob, then; a raw sound, wrenched from Meara's throat. She launched herself toward the door with unexpected speed, low to the ground and scuttling. Taken by surprise, Tanaros let her go. He caught only a glimpse of her face as she passed, an accusatory gaze between strands of lank, untended hair. Her hands scrabbled at the door, and the Mørkhar Fjel beyond it allowed her passage.

"What passes here, Lady?" Tanaros asked simply.

"You frighten her." Cerelinde raised her brows. "Is there more?"

"No." He thought about Meara; her weight, straddling him. The heat of her flesh, the touch of her mouth against his. Her teeth, nipping at his lower lip. The memory made him shift in discomfort. "Nothing that concerns you."

Cerelinde moved away from him, taking a seat and keeping her disconcerting gaze upon him. "You do not know me well enough to know what concerns me, Tanaros Blacksword."

"Lady, I know you better than you think," he murmured. "But I will not seek to force the truth you are unwilling to reveal. Since I am here in good faith, is there aught in which I may serve you?"

Yearning flared in her eyes and she took a deep breath, letting it out slowly. Her voice trembled as she answered, "You might tell me what passes in the world beyond these walls."

Tanaros nodded. "I would thirst for knowledge, too, did I stand in your shoes, Cerelinde. Never say I denied you unkindly. Yrinna's Children are on the march."

"What?" Yearning turned to hope; Cerelinde leaned forward,

fingers whitening on the arms of the chair. There were tears in her bright eyes. "Tanaros, I pray you, play no jests with me."

He smiled sadly at her. "Would that I did."

"Yrinna's Children have broken her Peace!" she marveled. "And . . ." Her voice faltered, then continued, adamant with resolve. "And Aracus?"

"He is coming." Tanaros sighed. "They are all coming, Cerelinde."

"You know it is not too late—"

"No." He cut her off with a word. It hurt to see such hope, such joy, in her face. When all was said and done, it was true; he was a fool. But he was a loyal fool, and his loyalty was to Lord Satoris; and to others, who trusted him. Tanaros fingered the *rhios* that hung in a pouch at his belt. "Save your words, Lady. If you have need of aught else, send for me, and I will come."

With that he left her, because it was easier than staying. The Mørkhar Fjel at her door gave him their usual salute. Tanaros stared hard at them. Too much suspicion and longing was tangled in his heart.

"See to it that no one passes unnoted," he said. "Even the Dreamspinner's madlings, do you understand? It was one such who served the Lady poison."

"Lord General." It was Krognar, one of his most trusted among the Havenguard, who answered in a deep rumble. "Forgive us. One looks much like another."

"Do they *smell* alike?" Tanaros asked sharply.

The Mørkhar exchanged glances. "No," Krognar said. "But you did not ask us to note their scent. They are Lord Ushahin's madlings. You never troubled at them before."

"I'm asking you now."

The Mørkhar bowed. "It will be done," said Krognar.

Leaving them, Tanaros paced the halls. His heart was uneasy, his feet restless. He half-thought to track down Meara and question her, but there was no telling where she might be in the maze of corridors behind the wall. And did it matter? She was Ushahin's creature. If it had been her, she had only been doing his bidding. He had paid the price for it; for all of them. His Lordship was content. Could Tanaros be less?

Since he had no answers, he went to see Hyrgolf instead.

There was always merit in inspecting the barracks. Tanaros exited Darkhaven proper, making his way to the Fjel delvings north of the fortress. He strode through tunneled corridors, pausing here and there to visit the vast, communal sleeping chambers. They were glad of his visit, proud of their preparations, showing him armor stacked in neat readiness, weapons honed to a killing edge. Word traveled ahead of him, and he had not gone a hundred paces before the Fjel began spilling into the corridors, baring eyetusks in broad grins and beckoning him onward.

"Hey, Lord General!"

"Hey, boss!"

"Come check *our* weapons!"

"When are we going to war?"

The sheer weight of their enthusiasm settled his nerves and made him smile. The Fjel, who had the most to lose in accordance with Haomane's Prophecy, were with him. No sign of faltering there; their loyalty was unswerving. "Soon enough, lads!" he shouted to them. "I'm off to see Marshal Hyrgolf."

They cheered the mention of his name. One of theirs, one of their own.

And then there was Hyrgolf, standing in the entryway of his private chamber, his broad shoulders touching on either side of it. His leathery lips were curved in a smile of acknowledgment, but the squinting eyes beneath the heavy ridge of his brow held a deeper concern.

"General Tanaros," he rumbled. "Come."

VORAX WALKED ALONG THE NORTHEASTERN wall of the auxiliary larder, touching items stacked alongside it; kegs of Vedasian wine, vast wheels of cheese wrapped in burlap piled into columns. Sacks of wheat, bushels of root vegetables; so much food it could not be stored within the confines of Darkhaven proper, but space must be found outside its walls. The towering cavern was filled to bursting with them.

All his, all his doing.

He was proud of it. There was no glamour in it; no, nor glory. There was something better: sustenance. Glutton, Haomane's Allies called him. Let them. He had earned his appetite, earned his right to indulge it. For a thousand years, Vorax had provided *sustenance.* Food did not fall on the plate and beg to be eaten, no matter who you were; peasant, Rivenlost lord, or one of the Three.

No, it had to be obtained; somehow, somewhere. In Staccia, they had always understood it. Precious little could be grown in the northern mountains. Neheris had not Shaped her lands with Men in mind. There was fish and game, and sheep and goats were tended. Never enough, not for as many Men dwelled in Staccia. For aught else, they had to trade; and they had little with which to trade. There was proud living in the mountains, but it was hard living, too. It had made them hungry, and it had made them shrewd.

And Vorax was the hungriest and shrewdest of them all. He had made the bargain to end all bargains—and he had kept it, too. Staccia had done naught but profit by it, and Darkhaven done naught but prosper. The betrayal of the Staccian lordlings incited by the Galäinridder was the only blot on his record, and that had been dealt with swiftly and irrevocably. He had earned the right to be proud.

"Do you see this, Dreamspinner?" He slapped a wheel of cheese with one meaty hand. It made a resounding echo in the vaulted cavern. "We could feed the Fjel for a month on cheese alone!"

"I don't imagine they'd thank you for it," Ushahin muttered, wrapped in his sheepskin cloak. Darkhaven's larders were built into the mountains of Gorgantum, deep enough that they remained cool even in the warmth of summer; not Fjel work, but older, part of the tunnel system that lore held was dragon-made.

"They would if their bellies pinched," Vorax said pragmatically. "And it may come to it, does this siege last. Meanwhile, who procured the flocks that keeps them in mutton?"

"Would you have me sing your glory?" The half-breed shivered. "I would as soon be done with it, Staccian."

"As you will," Vorax grumbled, and went back to counting kegs. "Third row, fifth barrel . . . here." He reached between the wooden kegs, grunting, and drew forth a parcel thrice-wrapped in waxed parchment, which he tossed onto the stony floor. "I had to bargain dearly for it, Dreamspinner. Are you sure we ought to destroy it?"

"I'm sure." Ushahin squatted next to the packet, bowing his head. The ends of his pale hair trailed on the ground; he glanced upward with his mismatched eyes. "We had our chance and took it. The time has passed. Do you want to risk Tanaros finding it? He is asking questions, cousin, and in time he may think of your outermost larder, or learn it from my madlings. Do you want his Lordship to know your involvement? Would you risk *that*?"

"No." Vorax shook his head and shuddered. "No, I would not."

"So." With his newly deft right hand, Ushahin unfolded the parcel. A scant pile of herbs lay in the center of the creased parchment. There had been more, once. He inhaled, his nostrils flaring. "All-Bane," he murmured. "Sprung from the death-mound of a Were corpse. I have not smelled it since I dwelled in the forests of Pelmar."

"Aye," Vorax said. "Or so the Rukhari swore. I demanded it in compensation for our aborted bargain. They were loath to part with it." He shrugged. "Do you think it would have killed her?"

"Yes," the half-breed said. "Oh, yes, cousin. All-Bane, Oronin's Foil. To taste of it is to hear the Glad Hunter's horn call your name. Death rides in his train, and not even the Ellylon are exempt from its touch." He regarded the herbs with his twisted smile. "Would that Oronin Last-Born had protected his Children as well in life as he does in death. The Lady would have died had she sampled the broth."

"Pity," Vorax said, reaching for a torch. "It was a noble effort."

"Yes." Ushahin straightened and rose. "It was."

Vorax touched the torch to the parcel. The waxed parchment ignited with a flare. Fire consumed it, and soon the dried herbs were ablaze. Tendrils of smoke arose, dense and grey, with a faint violet tint, more smoke than one would have thought possible from such a scant handful. It coiled along the floor, rising where it encountered living flesh.

"It smells . . . almost sweet," Vorax said in wonder. "No wonder the Fjel did not recognize it as a poison." A pleasant lassitude weighted his limbs and his eyelids felt heavy. He inhaled deeply. "What is the aroma? Like vulnus-blossom, only . . . only the memory it evokes is pleasant. It reminds me of . . . of what, Dreamspinner?" He smiled, closing his eyes and remembering. "Childhood in Staccia, and goldenrod blooming in the meadows."

"Out. *Out*, cousin!"

The words came to him filtered through a haze; a gilded haze of swimming light, violet-tinged, the air filled with pollen. Vorax opened his eyes and frowned, seeing Ushahin Dreamspinner's face before him, skin stretched taut over the misshapen cheekbones. "What troubles you, cousin?" he asked in a thick voice.

Pale lips, shaping a curse in the tongue of the Were; he watched with mild interest, watched the shapely right arm swing back, then forward, tendrils of smoke swirling in its wake. It all seemed so slow, until it was not. Vorax rocked on his heels at the impact of the half-breed's palm against his bearded cheek.

"Enough!" he roared, anger stirring in his belly. "Do not try my patience!"

Ushahin's eyes glittered through the smoke. One was black, drowning-black, swallowed by pupil; the other was silver-grey, fractured into splintered shards, like a mirror broken into a thousand pieces of bad luck, with a pinprick of black at the center. His hand, his right hand, fell upon the Staccian's shoulder with unexpected strength, spinning him. "Vorax of Staccia, *get out of this place!*"

There was a shove, a powerful shove between the shoulder blades, and Vorax went, staggering under the impetus, placing one foot after the other until he reached the outermost opening with its narrow ledge. There the air was cold and clean and he breathed deeply of it, gazing at Darkhaven's holdings until his head began to clear. There was edifice; there was the encircling wall, vanishing to encompass them. There was the Gorgantus River. There, in the distance, were the pastures and the mines; there, nearer, were the furnaces and forges, beneath their pall of smoke.

It made him glance involuntarily behind him; but the smoke of the All-Bane had not followed him. There was only Ushahin, huddled in his sheepskin cloak, looking raw with the cold.

"Are you well, cousin?" he asked in a low voice.

"Aye," Vorax said roughly. With his chin, he pointed at the Dreamspinner's hidden right arm. "Who would have thought there was such strength in that wing of yours. So is . . . *that* . . . what you might have been?"

"Perhaps." Ushahin gave a terse laugh. "I am the Misbegotten, after all."

"Ah, well. You would have made a doughty warrior, cousin." There was nothing else in those words he wanted to touch. Vorax breathed slow and steady, watching the sluggish flow of the Gorgantus River below them. The waterwheel Tanaros' Midlander protégé had built turned with excruciating slowness, murky water dripping from its paddles. Still, it did its job, powering the bellows. "Is it done?" he asked presently.

Ushahin shrugged his hunched shoulders. "Let us see."

They did, returning step by step, side by side. There was the larder, lined with kegs and loaves and wheels. There, on the floor, a tiny pile of ashes smoldered, no longer smoking. Side by side, they stared at it.

"Is it still dangerous?" Vorax asked.

"I do not believe so." Ushahin glanced into the darkness at the rear of the larder, where the chamber narrowed into a winding tunnel. "There is no one there to heed Oronin's Horn. The passages are too low, even for my madlings." He shrugged again. "Even if they were not, the tunnels leading from here link to the Vesdarlig Passage, and it is blocked, now. No one travels to or from your homeland, cousin."

"I pray you are right." Vorax stamped on the smoldering pile with a booted heel, grinding the remnants into harmless powder until nothing remained but a faint sooty smear. "There," he said with satisfaction. "All evidence of our conspiracy is gone."

Ushahin considered him. "Then we are finished?"

"Aye." Vorax met his gaze unflinching. "I lack the courage of your madness, Dreamspinner. Already, you have shielded me from his Lordship's wrath. I will not risk facing it a second time." He shook his head. "Haomane's Prophecy is no certain thing. His Lordship's fury is. Do you cross his will again, there will be no mercy. I would sooner die in his name than at his hands."

Ushahin nodded. "As you will, cousin."

"URU-ALAT!" DANI WHISPERED. "A ROCKFALL?"

There was a sick feeling in the pit of his stomach. Beside him, Uncle Thulu was silent, staring in disbelief. By the wavering torchlight, the pile of boulders before them reached all the way to the ceiling.

"No." Thulu spoke at last, his voice heavy. "No, this was done on purpose. There's no damage to the tunnel itself." He gave a hollow laugh. "Of course it was. Why wouldn't they block it? One less entrance to guard."

It was too much to encompass. How many days had they been traveling beneath the earth? Weeks, at least; it may have been longer. Each step filled with fear and trepidation, each curve in the tunnel harboring the potential of a Fjel attack. All for nothing. There had been no Fjel. There was no egress. The tunnel was blocked.

"Can we move them?" Dani asked. "Or climb over it?"

Uncle Thulu squared his shoulders, shaking off the yoke of despair. "I don't know, lad. Let's try."

They wedged the torches into the pile and began working, shifting the smaller rocks and digging out around the larger, concentrating their efforts on one several feet off the tunnel floor that appeared to be supporting the weight of others.

"Ready, lad?" Uncle Thulu asked, once he could wrap his arms around it.

Dani nodded grimly, taking hold of the boulder. "Ready."

On a count of three, they hauled together, tipping it. The massive stone's weight did the rest, rolling loose. As they leapt clear of its path, a small section of the pile shifted, other boulders settling in a cascade of smaller rocks.

Otherwise, it was unchanged.

"No good." Thulu shook his head. "This is Fjeltroll work. It may go on for yards; scores of them, is my guess. After all, they're trying to keep an army out, not just a couple of weary Yarru-yami."

Dani took a deep breath. "I'll see if we can climb over it."

He went slowly, testing each hand- and foothold with care. The boulders, disturbed by their efforts, shifted beneath his weight. For once, he was glad that he was unshod, feeling the subtle movement of the rocks beneath the soles of his bare feet. Although he no longer needed the sling, his left shoulder was imperfectly healed and ached with the strain. The muscles of his legs quivered; partly with effort, and partly with nerves. The clay vial strung around his neck had never seemed so vulnerable. One wrong step, and he would set off a rockslide. Whether or not Dani survived it, he doubted the fragile vessel would.

Endless as it seemed, he eventually reached the top.

"What do you see, lad?" Uncle Thulu called from the base of the pile, holding his torch as high as possible.

"Nothing." Dani braced his palms on the ceiling of the tunnel and sighed. The pile was solid. There was no gap at the top; or at least, only inches. "We could *try* making a passage from here." He reached forward with one hand to pry a few stones loose and tried to imagine it. Moving through the darkness, shifting rocks a scant few at a time, wriggling back and forth on their bellies, pinned against the ceiling. It was not a hopeful prospect.

"It might be quicker to walk back to Staccia," Thulu said dourly. "And safer, too. Come down, Dani. We'll find another way."

"Wait." There was something; a faint current of air, moving. Dani went still, holding his outspread hand over the rocks. He could feel it, a whisper against his skin. "There's an air shaft."

"Are you sure?"

"I'm sure." Taking a better stance, Dani slid the vial around and tucked it under his collar at the back of his neck. "Stand clear, Uncle!"

It felt good, after days and days of grinding sameness, to be *doing*. He burrowed steadily into the pile, working with both hands, grabbing rocks and tossing them to either side. Those at the uttermost top were smaller, easier to move. They bounced down the rockpile in a rattling, satisfying procession. The larger ones were trickier. The first one he managed to expose was at chest height, twice as large around as his head. Whispering a swift prayer to Uru-Alat, Dani worked it loose.

Unbalanced, the pile shifted. His footholds vanished, sending him sliding and scrabbling downward on his belly, nails clinging ineffectually to stone. Bruised and banged, he fetched up hard, jarring one hip against a solid, immobile boulder.

"Dani!"

"I'm all right!" He checked the clay vial and found it safe, then peered upward. The hole had widened considerably. He could feel the air on his face now. Dani inhaled deeply. "Uncle! I smell *grass*!"

The light cast by Thulu's torch flickered wildly. "Dani, lad, I'm coming up."

It was painstaking. Once Thulu completed the treacherous journey, laden with packs and torches and moving with infinitesimal care, they set to work in tandem. They worked as swiftly as they dared, widening the hole one rock at a time, working in the direction of the air current. Torchlight aided, but it posed a hazard, too. Every time the rock-pile settled and their balance slipped, there was the added risk of setting themselves ablaze.

"All this work, and I don't suppose we've any idea how big the shaft is," Uncle Thulu observed. "It will be a hard blow if we don't fit."

Covered in rock dust, Dani grinned at him. "Maybe it's a good thing you're not so fat anymore!"

After further hours of labor, there was no jest left in either of them. Feeling with careful fingertips, they found the bottom of the ventilation shaft, clearing around and beneath it. There was no sign of daylight, which hopefully meant nothing worse than that night had fallen while they worked. The shaft was wide enough, barely; a scant three feet across. Whether it narrowed and how high it went was another matter.

"You found it," Thulu said somberly. "You look."

"All right." Returning the flask to its customary place at his throat, Dani eased himself onto his back and ducked his head under the opening. At first, his eyes grown used to torchlight, he saw only blackness and his heart sank. But gradually, his vision cleared, and he laughed aloud. The shaft was deep, but it cut an unswerving path through the solid rock. And far, far above him . . .

"What do you see?"

"Stars!" A patch of starlight, faint and distant. He ducked back out, eyes shining. "We can do this, Uncle. It's a long climb, but we can do it."

Uncle Thulu gave him a worried smile. "We'll try."

Squatting atop the rock-pile, they sorted through their gear, paring down supplies to the barest of essentials. A parcel of food and a waterskin apiece lashed around their waists, belt daggers, and the warm Staccian cloaks the Lady of Gerflod had given them. Dani kept his slingshot, and Thulu his flint striker. Everything else, they would leave.

"I'm smaller and lighter," Dani said. "I'll go first."

Thulu nodded, fidgeting with his pack. "You know, lad, a drop of the Water—"

"No." Dani shook his head, touching the flask. "We can't, Uncle. I don't dare. I don't even know if there's enough left for . . . for what I'm supposed to do. Will you at least try? If I can do it, you can."

Uncle Thulu sighed. "Go on, then."

There was only one way to do it. Squirming under the opening, Dani stood up inside the ventilation shaft. If he craned his head, he could see the stars. It seemed a longer way up than it had at first glance. Setting his back firmly against one wall of the shaft, he braced his legs on the opposite wall and began to inch his way upward.

It was torturous going. He had underestimated; underestimated the distance, the difficulty, the sheer exhaustion of his muscles. Within minutes, his legs were cramping and his breath was coming hard. It made him thirsty, and he could not help but think about the Water of Life and the scent of it, the scent of all life and green growing things. Three drops, and Uncle Thulu had healed almost as completely as though he had never been injured, had gained the energy to run and run and run without tiring, carrying Dani on his back. It wouldn't take that much to make this climb infinitely easier.

One drop. How much harm would it do to take one drop of the Water? To restore vigor to his weary body, to uncramp his painful muscles, to quench his parched tissues, to erase the plaguing ache near his collarbone.

The temptation was almost overwhelming. Gritting his teeth, Dani remembered how much had spilled in Neherinach, where the Fjeltroll had caught them. Rivulets of water, gleaming silver in the sunlight, trickling over the Fjel's horny palm. If it hadn't . . . perhaps. But it had, and there was too little left to waste; not unless it was a matter of life or death. It wasn't, not yet.

He forced himself to keep inching upward, to remember instead the look of stark disbelief in the eyes of the last Fjel to die, the one who had spoken to him. The Water of Life was not to be taken lightly; never, ever. Old Ngurra had told him that many times. In the womb of the world, Life and Death were twins. To invoke one was to summon the other's shadow.

Inch by inch, Dani of the Yarru resisted temptation and climbed.

He had not known his eyes were clenched shut until he felt the tickle of grass upon his face and a cold wind stirring his hair and realized he had reached the top of the shaft. An involuntary cry escaped him as he opened his eyes.

"Dani!" Uncle Thulu's voice sounded ghostly far below. "Are you all right?"

"Aye!" He shouted down between his braced legs. "Uncle, it's beautiful!"

In a final surge of strength, he wriggled upward a few more inches and got his arms free of the shaft, levering his body out and onto solid earth. For a moment, Dani simply lay on his back, willing his muscles to uncramp. The sky overhead seemed enormous, a vast black vault spangled with a million stars, and Arahila's moon floating in it like a pale and lovely ship. In the distance there were mountains, tall and jagged, but all around there was nothing but grass; a sea of grass, sweet-smelling, silvery in the moonlight, swaying in waves.

"All right, lad!" Thulu's words echoed faintly from the shaft. "My turn."

Dani rolled onto his belly and peered down. "One inch at a time, Uncle." Reaching to one side, he tore out a handful of grass. "Just keep moving."

It was impossible, of course. He had known that before he'd made it halfway up the shaft. Uncle Thulu, he suspected, had known it all along. He was thin enough to fit in the shaft, but too big to make the climb. His longer limbs would be too cramped. His muscles, supporting his greater weight, would begin to quiver. He would be forced to give up and tell Dani to continue on his own.

Dani should have given him a drop of the Water of Life. Now, it was too late.

Sitting upright, Dani began plaiting grass.

It was not as sturdy as thukka-vine, but it was strong and pliant. Head bowed, he worked feverishly. Over and under, fingers flying. It was one of the earliest skills the Yarru learned. From time to time he paused, wrenching up more handfuls of the tough, sweet-smelling plains grass, weaving new stalks into his pattern. Arahila's moon continued to sail serenely across the sky, and a length of plaited rope emerged steadily beneath his hands.

"Dani." Uncle Thulu's voice, low and exhausted, emerged from the shaft. "Dani, lad."

"I know." He peered over the edge and saw his uncle's figure lodged in place. Thulu had not quite made it halfway. "Stay where you are." Kneeling, he paid out the rope, hand over hand. It dangled, a few inches too short. "Can you hold on a little while longer?"

"Dani, listen to me . . ." Angling his head, Thulu saw the rope and fell silent. Moonlight caught the glimmer of tears in his eyes. "Ah, lad!"

"Hold on," Dani repeated, coiling the rope. "A little while."

The words of the Song of Being whispered through his mind as he worked. Although his lips were silent, he spoke them with his fingertips, plaiting grass into rope; each strand, each loop, each growing inch a prayer to Uru-Alat. He did not measure a second time. The rope was a prayer. It would be as long as the prayer. That was the length that was needed.

When it was done, he knelt beside the shaft and lowered the rope. Wedged between the walls, Uncle Thulu braced himself in place with his legs and lashed the rope around his waist, tying it securely.

"Ready?" Dani called.

Thulu nodded. "Ready."

Dani got to his feet. He could feel the words of the Song of Being beneath his hands, chanting in his veins. As he hauled, slowly and steadily, hand over hand, he listened to them. There was wisdom in them, old Ngurra had said; the secrets of Life and Death, twined together in the death of Uru-Alat the World God and the birth of the world. Dani was not wise enough to understand them. But he was trying.

It was part of the Bearer's burden.

Arahila's moon was riding low when Thulu clambered clear of

the shaft. As Dani had done, he could do no more than roll onto the grass and stare at the stars. For his part, Dani dropped where he stood and sat heavily in the grass. He felt as though his limbs were made of stone. It was a long time before he could summon the strength to speak. "Where are we, Uncle?"

Thulu sat up with an effort, rubbing the aching, cramped muscles of his legs and glanced around him. "The plains of Curonan, lad."

"And Darkhaven?"

Thulu pointed westward across the plains, toward the distant mountains that rose, black and jagged, blotting out the stars. "There."

THE CANDLES BURNED LOW IN Hyrgolf's chamber, until the rocky niches held little more than blue flames dancing above puddles of tallow. For long hours, they had conferred on matters regarding the defense of Darkhaven; the posting of sentries, scouting parties of Gulnagel, inspections of the tunnels, manning of the fortifications, battle-tactics useful against Men and Ellylon and Dwarfs. The night was already old when Hyrgolf rummaged in a corner, bringing forth a half-empty skin of *svartblod*.

"General," he said, holding it forth in one enormous hand. "Drink."

Tanaros hesitated, then accepted it. Uncorking the skin, he took a deep swig. It burned all the way down to his belly, and the foul taste made his eyes water. "My thanks!" he gasped, handing it back.

The Tungskulder Fjel studied him. "I have never smelled fear on you before."

"Fear." Tanaros gave a harsh laugh, his throat seared by the *svartblod*'s heat. "Hyrgolf, my skin crawls with it. There is too much I mislike afoot in this place."

"The Dreamspinner's betrayal troubles you," Hyrgolf said.

"Yes." Tanaros met his eyes; the Fjel's familiar gaze, small as a boar's and steady as a rock. "More than I can say, for I fear there is reason in his madness. Would you do such a thing, Hyrgolf? Would you defy his Lordship's will and betray his wishes if it would avert Haomane's Prophecy at a single stroke?"

"No," Hyrgolf said simply. "I do not have the wisdom to meddle in the affairs of Shapers. The Fjel made their choice long ago, General. Haomane's Prophecy binds us to it." He smiled with hideous gentleness. "How did you tell me it went? *The Fjeltroll shall fall.*"

"Yet you do not fear," Tanaros murmured.

"Death in battle?" Hyrgolf shook his massive head. "No, not that. Lord Satoris . . ." He paused, raising the skin to drink. "He made us a promise, once. He said one day Men would covet our gifts." Lowering the skin, he handed it back to Tanaros. "He said Neheris-of-the-Leaping-Waters Shaped us well."

"She did." Tanaros took another scalding swig. "She did at that, Marshal." He wiped his lips and sighed. "Do you think we are so different in the end, Hyrgolf? You and I, Haomane's Allies?"

"No." The Fjel shrugged his heavy shoulders, gazing past Tanaros at the crudely carved *rhios* in a niche behind one of the dwindling candles. His boy's first effort. *Not bad for a mere pup, eh?* "Not in the end, General." He smiled ruefully, a shadow beneath the dense ridge of his brow. "Problem is, we seem to be somewhere in the middle, don't we?"

"Aye." Tanaros got unsteadily to his feet, returning the skin to Hyrgolf. He clapped one hand on the Fjel's shoulder, reassured by the solid warmth of it, the unwavering loyalty. "His Lordship has the right of it, Hyrgolf. Even now, I envy you."

"General." Hyrgolf heaved his massive body upright. His taloned hands were surprisingly delicate as they closed around Tanaros' arm. "Go, and sleep. You have need of it. His Lordship has need of you."

"He entrusted me with his honor," Tanaros whispered.

"Aye." Hyrgolf nodded. "He is wise that way. And you entrust us with yours."

Tanaros shivered. "At what price, Hyrgolf?"

The Fjel smiled one last time, sad and slow. "I do not think that is ever given to us to know, General. We rejoice in it, for it is all we have, all we have chosen." He gave Tanaros a gentle shove, and the advice given to the rawest of recruits. "Go now, and sleep. You will feel better once the battle is joined."

Tanaros went, stumbling slightly. Outside, the cold air struck like a blow, diminishing the intoxicating effects of the *svartblod* he had drunk. He gazed at the horizon, where Arahila's moon swam low, a tarnished silver coin, and remembered the night his Lordship had first called them to the tower to see the red star that had arisen. His soft words, the pain in his voice.

Oh, Arahila!

"Why didn't you stay at his side?" Tanaros, wavering on his feet, addressed the moon. "You, any of you! Neheris, whom the Fjel still worship! Were you frightened? Is that it? Was Haomane Lord-of-Thought that powerful? What did you know that his Lordship did not?"

There was no answer, only a pair of Mørkhar Fjel on patrol, confirming his identity and giving him a wide berth.

Tanaros laughed softly. The air was cold, but the *svartblod* in his veins insulated him from it. Although he was not drunk, his flesh felt warm. "Or what did *he* know that Haomane First-Born did not?" he asked the moon. "Tell me that, O my Shaper!"

Light, only light; the light of the Souma, a lesser light, but no less lovely for it. It shed its silent benison. Things grew by it; things that blossomed in his Lordship's gardens. Tanaros sighed and set his feet on a homeward course.

"He loves you still," he informed the moon, glancing over his shoulder. "But he has made his choices. As I have made mine, as the Fjel have made theirs. The difference is, we made them freely. And *he* allowed us to do it. The Lord-of-Thought would not have done as much."

The moon, the beautiful moon, made no reply.

FOURTEEN

❖

Dawn broke over the plains of Curonan, a glorious and terrifying sight. The sun's red orb crept slowly over the eastern horizon, staining the waving grass until it resembled a sea of blood. To the west, the mountains of Gorgantum threw up a defiant challenge, their implacable peaks shrouded in darkness.

At night, drenched in silvery moonlight, the plains had been a safe and magical place. It was different by daylight, with the eye of Haomane's Wrath opening in the east and the baleful shadow of Gorgantum to the west. Caught between the two on the vast, open space of the plains, Dani felt horribly conspicuous.

"Which way, lad?" Uncle Thulu asked quietly.

Grasping the clay flask that hung about his neck, Dani bowed his head. Sunlight, he knew. Haomane's Wrath could be terrible and impersonal, but he knew it. He was Yarru, and he understood. Darkness was another matter. Darkness, in which the Sunderer awaited; Satoris Banewreaker, who had slain his people, who wanted nothing more than for Dani to die so he could spill the Water of Life upon barren ground.

And more than anything else, Dani did not want to enter the shadow of those mountains. But he was the Bearer, and the burden of choice was upon him.

"Darkhaven," he said. "We go toward Darkhaven."

Uncle Thulu nodded. "So be it."

They set out at a steady walk, the sun at their backs, trampling their shadows into the sweet-smelling grass. They did not speak of how entrance might be gained into the Vale of Gorgantum. For the moment, the journey alone sufficed.

Hours later, the mountains scarcely seemed closer. Distances were as deceiving on the plains as they were in the desert. What it was that made Dani glance over his shoulder toward the eastern horizon, he could not have said. Regret, perhaps, or simple longing. It had crossed his mind that if the plains were not so immense, they might find Malthus in the east; Malthus, whose wisdom could guide him.

What he saw made him shudder.

"Uncle." His nails bit into Thulu's arm. "Look."

Ravens; a flock of ravens. A long way off, a smudge of darkness against the bright sky, but coming fast. Dani remembered how a trio of ravens had found them in the marshy land on the outskirts of Vedasia, circling high above them. How Malthus' voice had risen like thunder, giving warning. *The eyes of the Sunderer are upon us!* How Fianna had leapt from the saddle; the Archer of Arduan, the longbow singing in her hands. One, two, three, and her arrows had streaked skyward, striking down the Sunderer's spying eyes.

Not here.

"Run," said Thulu, and they ran without thought, sprinting over the plains, the long grass lashing their legs. There was no cover, not so much as a shrub. Nowhere to hide. Once the ravens spotted them, there would be Fjeltroll; hundreds of them. Thousands. And the Slayer, the man on the black horse, who had drawn his black blade to kill Malthus in the Marasoumië. Dani's heart pounded in his chest. In the forests of Pelmar, he had watched mice scurry beneath the shadow of a hunting owl's wings. Perhaps it was a swifter death than being swallowed by a snake, but the terror was worse.

If there was any chance he survived this ordeal, he decided, he would never hunt hopping-mice again.

The thought made him careless; his foot struck something hard and stony, hidden by the thick grass, and he fell headlong. Both hands rose instinctively to protect the clay vial as he struck the ground hard, the impact jarring the breath from him. He fumbled at the vial. It was unbroken, but the cork stopper had been knocked partially loose, and moisture gleamed on its exposed surface. With frantic fingers, Dani shoved it back in place. Only then did the constriction in his chest ease, and his breath returned in a sobbing gasp. He could smell the Water of Life in the air, its clean, mineral essence rising like a beacon.

"Are you all right?" Uncle Thulu's voice was taut.

"Aye." Dani glanced down at the object that had tripped him. It was the lip of a ventilation shaft. He felt for the grass rope he had woven, coiled in his pack. "Uncle. Surely we must have cleared the blockage."

Their eyes met, a spark of hope leaping between them; then Thulu shook his head. "Without the rockpile beneath us, the rope's too short," he said wearily. "The fall from the shaft would kill us. Even if it wasn't"—he gestured around—"there's naught to anchor the rope, lad."

Dani bowed his head, stroking the rope's plaited length. A trace of moisture glistened on his fingertips. His pulse quickened, and he began to chant the Song of Being under his breath.

"Lad," Thulu began, then fell silent as the rope began to grow beneath Dani's fingertips, stalks seeding and sprouting, stretching and growing in ever-lengthening plaits, young and strong and green. One end sprouted roots, pale tendrils questing in the open air.

Still chanting, Dani risked a glance toward the east. The ravens were coming; no longer a smudge, but a wedge-shaped cloud, soaring and wheeling, mighty enough to cast a shadow on the plains. It rode before them on the grass, darkness moving over the waves, veering in their direction. Something had caught their attention; perhaps movement, perhaps the scent of the Water of Life itself, faint and rising.

His voice faltered, then continued. There was no other avenue of escape. In one swift gesture, he stabbed the rope's end into the cold soil, feeling the tendrils take root, sending their shoots into the dark earth. The plaited stalks continued to lengthen and twine, whispering like a snake's coils between his palms. He tugged once, experimentally. The rope was firmly rooted.

"It will never hold us," Uncle Thulu said flatly.

"It will," Dani said. "It has to."

He did not offer this time, but simply went, clearing away the overgrown grass and clambering into the shaft. The rope felt sturdy in his hands, though he could hear the hoarse, dry rustle of its growth echoing in the shaft.

Hand over hand, Dani lowered himself into darkness.

It was a narrower shaft than the other. His elbows scraped the sides, and he prayed Uncle Thulu would fit. It was a relief when he cleared the shaft, dangling in the empty darkness. Ignoring his aching shoulder for the hundredth time, he went as quickly as he dared, fearful despite his assurance that the rope would end before his feet touched the floor of the tunnel.

It didn't.

"Uncle!" he called. "Hurry!"

What faint light the shaft admitted was blocked by Thulu's body. Muffled sounds of scraping and banging ensued, accompanied by a muttered stream of Yarru invective. Dani clutched the rope to hold it steady, his heart in his throat until he saw daylight once more and, at the apex of the tunnel, his uncle's battered figure clinging to the rope, lowering himself at a dangerous pace.

Then he was down, a broad grin visible on his dark face. "Think I left half my skin on that damned rock, lad!"

"Did they see us?" Dani asked anxiously.

Thulu shook his head. "I don't think so. Uru-Alat, boy! You were as quick as a rabbit. I followed as best I could." He touched Dani's shoulder. "Well done, Bearer."

"I'm glad you're safe." He hugged Uncle Thulu, wrapping both arms around his solid warmth, feeling his embrace returned. For a moment, the world was a familiar place, safe and loving.

"So am I, Dani." Thulu's breath stirred his hair. "So am I." Squeezing Dani's arms, he released him. "You know it only gets harder, don't you?" His expression had turned somber. "We left the torches in the other tunnel. In a dozen paces, we'll be traveling blind into Darkhaven. And I do not know the way, or what branchings lie along it."

"I know. And I am afraid. But you are my guide, and I trust you to guide me." Dani laughed softly, stroking the grass-plaited rope that hung beside him. "I have been traveling blind from the beginning, Uncle. It is only now I begin to see, at least a little bit."

The plaited rope shivered beneath his touch. It was dwindling, the sere grass stalks crackling as they returned to their natural length. There had not been enough of the Water of Life to sustain its impossible growth, not with winter's breath at their necks. Dani released it, and the Yarru watched in silence as it shrank, the loose end retreating into the dimly lit shaft high above their heads.

There it hung, brittle and useless. There would be no pursuit from that quarter—and no escape.

Thulu shuddered. "I told you it wouldn't hold us!"

"Aye." Dani grasped the flask at his throat, feeling at the cork to ensure it was firmly in place. "But it did." He squared his shoulders beneath the burden of the Bearer's responsibility and set his face toward the unknown. "Let's go."

Together, they set out into the impenetrable dark.

THEY WERE COMING.

In the swirling, gleaming darkness that encircled the Tower of Ravens, it was all the Ravensmirror showed.

It was nothing they had not seen before, in bits and pieces. And yet here it was in its entirety. The promise of the red star had come to fruition. Upon the outskirts of Curonan, Haomane's Allies had converged into an army the likes of which had not been seen since the Fourth Age of the Sundered World.

And perhaps not even then, Tanaros thought, watching the images emerge. *Dwarfs.* Yrinna's Children, who had maintained her Peace since before the world was Sundered. They had turned their back on Lord Satoris' Gift, refusing to increase their numbers, refusing to take part in the Shapers' War, tending instead to the earth's fecundity, to the bounty that Yrinna's Gift brought forth.

No more.

He gazed at them in the Ravensmirror; small figures, but doughty, gnarled and weathered as ancient roots, trudging through the tall grass alongside the gleaming knights of Vedasia. Their strong hands clutched axes and scythes; good for cutting stock, good for shearing flesh. What had inspired them to war?

"Malthus," Lord Satoris whispered, his fists clenching. "What have you done?"

Malthus the Wise Counselor was there, the clear gem ablaze on his breast, the Spear of Light upright in his hand; he was there, they all were. Aracus Altorus, riding beneath the ancient insignia of his House; Blaise Caveros beside him, steady and loyal. There was the Borderguard of Curonan, with their dun-grey cloaks. There were all the others; Pelmarans in forest-green, Duke Bornin of Seahold in blue and silver, a motley assortment of others. Midlanders, Free Fishers, Arduan Archers. Ah, so many! Ingolin the Wise, and his Rivenlost Host, shining in stern challenge. There was no attempt to hide. Not now, no longer. Even the archers paid the circling ravens no heed; conserving their arrows, concealing nothing.

They were coming, parting the tall grass as they rode.

"Come," Lord Satoris crooned. *"Come."*

The Ravensmirror turned and turned, and there was a reflection of ravens in it; a twice-mirrored image of dark wings rising in a beating cloud, carried on a glossy current of dark wings. Tanaros frowned and blinked, then understood. They had been feasting on the pile of Staccian dead he had left on the plains for Haomane's Allies to find. There were the headless bodies, heaped and abandoned. There were Haomane's Allies, reading the message he had scratched onto the marker stone. A ripple ran through their ranks. There was Malthus, bowing his head in sorrow, grasping his gem and murmuring a prayer, white light blazing red between his fingers. There was Aracus Altorus, turning to face them, drawing his sword and speaking fierce words; an oath of vengeance, perhaps.

Vorax licked dry lips and glanced sidelong at Tanaros. "How long?"

"A day's ride," Tanaros said. "At their pace, perhaps two." He watched fixedly, trying to decide which of them he despised the most. Aracus Altorus, with his arrogant stare and Calista's faithless blood running in his veins? Malthus the Counselor, Haomane's Weapon, the architect of this war? Or perhaps Ingolin the Wise, Lord of the Rivenlost. What an honor it was he had deigned to lead his people into battle, how conscious he was of it!

And then there was Blaise of the Borderguard; his own kinsman, many generations removed. How proud he was to be at the right hand of the Scion of House Altorus! How determined he was to make amends for his ancestor's treachery! Tanaros narrowed his eyes, studying the Borderguardsman's seat, the way his hand hovered near his hilt, gauging his skills.

"You're better than he is, aren't you?" Tanaros murmured. "I was always better than Roscus, too. But we must keep the positions to which we were born, mustn't we?" Hatred coiled like a serpent in his entrails. "All things in their place," he said bitterly. "Order must be preserved as the Lord-of-Thought decrees."

"Haomane." The Shaper's low voice made the stones vibrate. In the center of the Tower, he gave a mirthless laugh. "Enough! I have seen enough."

The Ravensmirror dispersed.

"You know your jobs." Lord Satoris turned away. "Prepare."

A weight settled on Tanaros' shoulder; he startled, seeing Fetch's eye so near his own, black and beady. There had been none of the disconcerting echo of doubled vision he had experienced before. "Fetch!" he said, his heart gladdening unexpectedly. "I did not know you were here."

The raven wiped its beak on his doublet. Its thoughts *nudged* at his own. Grass, an ocean of grass, the swift, tilting journey across the plains of Curonan to report . . . and, what? A stirring, a tendril of scent wafting on the high drafts. Water, all the fresh water the raven had ever seen; the sluggish Gorgantus, the leaping flume of the White, the broad, shining path of the Aven. A hidden Staccian lake, a blue eye reflecting sky; a water-hole in the Unknown Desert. Rain, falling in grey veils.

Water, mineral-rich, smelling of life.

Green things growing.

Tanaros swallowed. "What do you seek to tell me?"

The raven's thoughts flickered and the plains rushed up toward him, stalks of rustling grass growing huge. Rustling. Something was sliding through the grass; a viper, sliding over the edge of a stone lip. No. A length of braided rope, vanishing.

Then it was gone and there was only the wind and the plains, and then that too was gone, and there was only Fetch, his claws pricking Tanaros' shoulder. His Lordship had gone, and Vorax, too. Ushahin alone remained in the Tower of Ravens with them, his new sword awkward at his side, a glitter of fear in his mismatched eyes.

"You saw?" Tanaros asked hoarsely.

"Yes."

Tanaros pressed the heels of his hands to his eyes. "Do we tell his Lordship?"

"It is for you to decide, cousin." Ushahin's voice was quiet. "You know well the course I would advocate."

"No." Tanaros lowered his hands. On his shoulder, Fetch chuckled uneasily deep in his throat. "She has nothing to do with this, Dreamspinner."

Ushahin shrugged and said nothing.

"All right." Tanaros took a deep breath. "I will tell him."

He made his way through the fortress, following his Lordship's path. To his surprise, Fetch remained with him, riding his shoulder with familiar comfort. Where the Shaper had passed, his presence hung in the air, the copper-sweet tang of his blood mixed with the lowering sense of thunder. Approaching the threefold doors to the Chamber of the Font, Tanaros felt as though he were swimming in it, and his branded heart ached with love and sorrow. Through the door, he heard his Lordship's summons.

"Come, Blacksword."

The Font's brilliance hurt his eyes. Facing away from it and squinting, he told Lord Satoris what he had sensed in Fetch's thoughts. In the Tower, it had seemed a fearful concern with which to burden his Lordship, but as he spoke the words, they began to sound foolish.

"A scent," the Shaper said thoughtfully. "A rope."

"My Lord, I believe it was the odor of the Water of Life," Tanaros said, remembering the Well of the World. "And the rope . . . the rope was of Yarru making. I have seen its like before." He was grateful for the slight weight of the raven on his shoulder, steadying him. "My Lord, I fear the Bearer is making his way toward Darkhaven."

"Yes." In the darkness beyond the Font, the Shaper sighed and the shadows seemed to sigh with him. "He is coming, Tanaros Blacksword. They are all coming, all my Elder Brother's little puppets."

"My Lord?"

"They are always coming, and they have always been coming, since long before the world was Sundered, since before there was a world to dream of Sundering. I have always known. It is only the when of it that remains uncertain; even here, even now. But they are mistaken if they believe this is the end. This time, or any other time. There is no end, save in beginning. Even the Lord-of-Thought cannot change this pattern." The Shaper drew near, waves of power emanating from him. "Curious little raven," he said to Fetch. "Whose thoughts have *you* been thinking?"

Fetch chuckled.

"Ah." A long, silent moment passed between them. The dark ghost of a smile crossed Lord Satoris' ruined visage. "Thank you, loyal Tanaros, for bringing me this small guest." He inclined his head. "For this small kindness."

"My Lord?" Tanaros repeated, confused and fearful that his Lordship was succumbing to madness after all.

"It comes and goes, my general, the way of all things." The Shaper raised one hand in a gesture of dismissal. "As you, now, shall go."

"What of the Bearer, my Lord?"

"Malthus' spell hides him even from the eyes of the Souma." Lord Satoris shook his head. "There is nothing *I* can do. Would you have me tell you your business, Blacksword? Double your patrols in the tunnels between here and the blockage."

"My Lord." Bowing carefully, mindful of Fetch, Tanaros took his leave.

Aboveground once more, he made his way to the great entrance, where the Havenguard admitted him passage through the tall doors. It was another cold, clear night. Standing in the courtyard, he moved Fetch to his forearm and stood for a moment, thinking about the oncoming army, about a length of plaited rope, old Ngurra's face beneath the shadow of his sword, and the dark-skinned boy he had seen in the Ways, the questioning look on his face. He thought about Cerelinde in her chambers, praying for rescue, and his Lordship's strange mood, and about Fetch.

"Whose thoughts *have* you been thinking?" he asked the raven, stroking him with one finger. Fetch ducked his head, shifting from foot to foot. "What happened to you before you found me in the desert?"

For an instant, Tanaros saw himself once more through the raven's vision: a stark, noble figure with haunted eyes, mantled in passions that flickered like dark fire around the edges of his being, a doom he carried like embers in his cupped hands. Scarred hands and a scarred heart, capable of tenderness or violence, and behind him stars falling endlessly, lovely and dying.

Somewhere, a dragon roared.

"So be it," Tanaros whispered. "Go, little brother, and find shelter from the coming storm." Lifting his arm, he watched the raven take flight, black wings glossy in the starlight. "Good-bye, Fetch."

A small kindness.

His eyes stung; touching them, he found them wet with tears. Hyrgolf was right, he would feel better once the battle was joined. Gathering himself, Tanaros went to rouse Speros and give him new orders.

IN THE SMALL HOURS OF the night, Malthus the Wise Counselor sat silently on a narrow folding stool in a corner of Aracus Altorus' tent, watching the pupil he had taught for so many years pace its confines, restless and unable to sleep.

"Out with it," he said at last. "You cannot afford to ride into battle already weary, Aracus."

Aracus' gaze lit, as it had many times that night, on the coffer that held the tourmaline stone linked to the Bearer of the Water of Life. "It was dimmer," he said. "Not by much, but a little. Others did not notice, but I did. I saw it, Malthus."

"Yes." The Counselor folded his hands in his sleeves. "I know."

"Does it mean the Bearer is failing?" His tone was harsh. *"Dying?"*

"I cannot say, Aracus," Malthus replied quietly. "No more than I could before. I lack the knowledge, for this is a thing that has never been done. But if you would ask what thought is in my heart, it is that the Water of Life dwindles as the Bearer perseveres. Dani used it in Malumdoorn to answer the Dwarfs' challenge of the Greening. He knows its power."

"Dwindles," Aracus repeated, following a path worn by his restless feet. He shot a glance at the Counselor. "By how much, Malthus? How much is required to extinguish the marrow-fire? How much remains? Enough?"

Malthus shook his hoary head. "I know not, and cannot say."

"No?" Aracus eyed him. "How many times have you withheld the fullness of your knowledge from me, Malthus? Your plots have ever been deep-laid. I wonder, betimes, what you fail to tell me now."

"There is nothing." Malthus touched the gem on his breast. Its clear blaze underscored the deep lines graven on his features. "Forgive me, Son of Altorus. The Lord-of-Thought's will is set in motion, and I, like this Soumanië I bear, will soon be spent. There is some service I may yet do to lure the Sunderer's minions from his lair. But I have no more knowledge to conceal." He smiled sadly. "*The unknown is made known.* There is nothing more I may tell you."

"Would that there was!" The words burst from Aracus. He fetched up before Malthus and flung himself to his knees, his face pale and strained. "Wise Counselor, I am leading men, good men, unto their deaths; Men, aye, and Ellylon and Dwarfs. Whatever else happens, this much is certain. And they are trusting me to do it because I was born to it; because of a Prophecy spoken a thousand years before my birth." He gave a choked laugh, his wide-set eyes pleading. "Tell me it is necessary, Malthus! Tell me, whatever happens, that it is all worthwhile."

A man's face, holding the phantom of the boy he had been, reckoning the cost of youth's dreams. How many generations had it taken for one such as him to come? Malthus the Counselor reached out, cupping the cheek of the boy he remembered, speaking to the man he had become.

"All things," he said gently, "must be as they are."

Aracus bowed his head, red-gold hair falling to hide his expression. "Is that all the comfort you have to offer?"

"Yes," Malthus said, filled with a terrible pity. "It is."

"So be it." Aracus Altorus touched the hilt of his sword; the sword of his ancestors, a dull and lifeless Soumanië set in its pommel. "Strange," he murmured. "It seems to me I have heard those words before, only it was the Sorceress who spoke them. Perhaps I should have listened more closely."

"We all choose our paths," Malthus said. "Unless you wish to follow hers, soaked in innocent blood, it is the better part of wisdom to pay her words scant heed; for such truth as they held, the Sorceress twisted to justify her own deeds. Yet there was more folly in her than evil, and even one such as she may have a role to play in the end. Do not discount Lilias of Beshtanag."

"You counsel hope?" Aracus lifted his head.

"Yes," said Malthus. "Always." He smiled at Aracus. "Come. Since sleep evades you, let us review the ways in which the Soumanië's power may be invoked and used, for it is my *hope* that such knowledge may yet be needful."

With a sigh, Aracus Altorus began to repeat his mentor's teaching.

FIFTEEN

THE GULNAGEL WERE IN HIGH spirits, and Speros' lifted accordingly. He was grateful for the assignment, grateful for the show of trust on General Tanaros' part. And truth be told, he was grateful to be away from Darkhaven and the presence of the Lady Cerelinde. It made him feel at once awestruck and insignificant, vile and ashamed, and between the General's fierce glare and Ushahin Dreamspinner's insinuations, it was altogether too unnerving.

This, now; this was more the thing. The camaraderie of the Fjel and a purpose to achieve. A warrior's purpose, serving Darkhaven's needs. He'd had only a small glimpse of the tunnels underlying Urulat when they'd traveled through the Ways. The Vesdarlig Passage was bigger than he could have imagined; wide enough for two Fjel to run abreast, tall enough for Speros to ride his tall grey horse.

Ghost, he had named her, because of her coloring. She moved like one, smooth and gliding. After his first mount had been lost in the Ways, Speros had thought he might never be given another such to ride, but the General had let him keep Ghost for his own. She bore him willingly, though Speros was uncertain whether she liked him. She had a trick of gazing at him out of the corner of one limpid eye as if wondering how he would taste, and her teeth were unnaturally sharp.

That was all right. He didn't know whether he liked her. He was, however, quite certain that he loved her.

They moved swiftly, the Gulnagel at their steady lope, with one pair scouting ahead and Ghost keeping pace with the others at a swift canter. Streaking torchlight painted the walls with a shifting fresco of light and shadow, and it felt strange and exciting, a little like the unforgettable ride through the Midlands when Ushahin Dreamspinner had led them along the paths between waking and dreaming.

How odd it was to think that the plains of Curonan were above them. In another day, Haomane's Allies might be riding over their heads and never even know it.

If there had been more time, Speros mused, perhaps it would have been better to *use* the tunnels rather than block them. How long would it take to move the army in a narrow column? He calculated in his head, trying to estimate how large an opening it would require to allow them egress, how far away it would have to be to enable them to assemble unseen, yet close the distance and fall upon the enemy before they could rally.

A sound from the darkness ahead broke his reverie. For an instant, it sounded like a hound baying, and Speros was confused, remembering a dusty road and a small farmstead, trying to steal horses with the General.

But no, there were Ghost's tireless muscles surging beneath him, and there was one of the Fjel grinning upward, eyes reflecting torchlight, and the sound was deep, far too deep and resonant to issue from any hound's throat. It was the hunting-cry of the Gulnagel Fjel.

"Quarry, boss!"

Speros whooped aloud in triumph, setting his heels to Ghost's flanks. She surged forward, and the Gulnagel quickened their pace. They burst down the tunnel like a wave, prepared to sweep away everything before them.

"There, boss!" A taloned finger, pointing down a side tunnel. Speros wrenched Ghost's head, and she sank onto her haunches like a cat, skidding and turning, her iron-shod hooves sparking against the stones while the Gulnagel bounded ahead.

He followed them, their torches bobbing like fireflies, while the tunnel grew steadily narrower. Here and there it branched, then branched again, doubling back toward Darkhaven. The air grew hot and close. The feeling of triumph gave way to unease. As the walls closed in upon them and the ceiling lowered, he slowed Ghost to a trot, then a walk, slower and slower, until the walls of the tunnel were brushing his knees.

When he could ride no farther, Speros dismounted and felt

along the wall until he found a crevice into which he could jam
Ghost's reins. He continued on foot, stumbling over the tunnel's
floor. Unlike the main passage, worn smooth over centuries, it was
rocky and uneven. Sweat beaded on his brow, and he wondered
why he had bothered to wear full armor in pursuit of a pair of
Charred Folk.

Ahead, the torches swarmed and separated, growing more distant. The sound of baying had ceased. It was hard to breathe, and
harder to see. Speros fought back a spasm of panic. How many
branchings had he taken? He hadn't kept track. If the Gulnagel left
him, he wasn't sure he could find his way back.

"Hold up, lads!" he shouted.

To his relief, a pair of torches lingered unmoving. He made his
way down the tunnel, forced to walk bent and doubled under the
sloping ceiling. The Gulnagel were crouching, resting their weight
on the knuckles of one hand, torches held awkward in the other.
As Speros arrived, other Fjel were returning from farther tunnels,
some nearly crawling. The narrow space was crammed with flesh
and hide, rife with the acrid tang of smoke, the musty odor of Fjel,
and something faint and sweet beneath it.

"Any luck?" Speros asked grimly.

"Sorry, boss." It was Krolgun who answered, blinking. His eyes
looked bleary. "Our mistake. Thought we scented Man-prey close
at hand, but it's gone."

"You're sure?" Craning his bent neck, Speros tried to peer past
the hulking forms. There was nothing but tunnels and more tunnels, a maze of tunnels, each one narrowing like a funnel into the
darkness beneath the mountains.

"Sure enough." Krolgun shrugged. "Can't smell prey, and the
tunnels are too small to go farther." He chuckled low in his throat.
"Maybe it was you we caught a whiff of."

"What *is* that smell?" Speros sniffed the air, trying to identify the
underlying odor. It reminded him of his boyhood, long ago; before
he had ever filched a coin or borrowed an untended horse, before
his father had disavowed his name. A heady odor, like ripe, sun-
warm strawberries in the fields of Haimhault.

Krolgun gave another shrug. "Sheep?"

"No, not sheep." Speros frowned, then shook himself. The
torches were guttering for lack of air and his thoughts were doing
the same. "Never mind. Let's get out of here before we suffocate,
lads. We'll double back, retrace our steps. Maybe it was a trick."

If it was a trick, it was well-played. The Fjel searched every turn and blind alley and found nothing. Speros made his way back through the smoke-wreathed air to where Ghost stood awaiting him with unnatural patience, baring her teeth at his return. He took care to avoid them as he mounted. There was no room to turn her and he had to back her down the tunnel, watching uneasily as the dark maze before him receded.

Surely, no living thing could survive in such a place.

The remainder of their search was uneventful. They traveled at a more moderate pace until they reached the massive rock-pile that blocked the Vesdarlig Passage. The Gulnagel glanced at one another and shrugged.

Speros sighed. "Back toward Darkhaven, lads. Slow and careful, eyes and ears! Aye, and noses, too."

There was nothing to be found. Hours later they emerged to murky daylight in the Vale of Gorgantum. Speros relayed orders regarding doubled patrolling of the tunnels, then rode toward the fortress to stable Ghost before reporting to General Tanaros. Despite the futility of his mission, open air and Ghost's smooth, gliding pace cheered him. He wished the news were better, but perhaps it had been a fool's errand after all, chasing after something a raven had not quite seen. A plaited rope? It may have been, or it may have been the wind in the tall grass. Like as not, it had been. At least he could set the General's mind at ease. Soon, battle would be upon them and there would be no more need for mucking about after bits and pieces of Haomane's cursed Prophecy.

Riding toward Darkhaven, Speros of Haimhault smiled and dismissed from his memory the scent of strawberries ripening on the sun-warmed earth.

"GO!" THULU HISSED BETWEEN HIS teeth. "Go, lad, *go!*"

On his hands and knees, Dani scrambled as fast as he could, heedless of the rocks bruising and tearing his skin, horribly aware of the pounding feet and baying voices of the Fjeltroll that pursued them.

Attempting to navigate the Vesdarlig Passage in darkness had been a fearful task, but they had worked out a system. He had taken one wall, and Uncle Thulu the other. As long as each of them kept one hand on their respective walls, they could warn the other of gaps and confer, pooling their knowledge to avoid straying into the side tunnels.

Ominous though the darkness had been, it had saved their lives; or at least prolonged them. With their dark-accustomed eyes, they had seen the torches of the oncoming Fjel in enough time to hide deep in the very side tunnels they had been avoiding.

But the Fjel had caught their scent, and there was nothing for it but to flee and flee and flee, racing ahead of the pursuing torches, the howling Fjel, twisting and turning, deeper into the narrowing maze, running bent, then doubled, then forced to crawl in single file as the tunnels closed in upon them, too small to allow the Fjel to enter.

It was the chance fate afforded them, and they took it.

For what seemed like hours, Dani crawled blindly, scurrying. Terror fueled his flight. He chose at random unseen branches, head lowered and shoulders hunched, protecting the clay vial hanging from his throat, never certain when he would collide headfirst with a wall. Sometimes it happened. His head throbbed, his knees ached, and his hands were slick with blood.

And then there was silence, broken only by the sound of their ragged breathing. There was no sign of pursuit. They had entered a blackness so absolute, it seemed all the light in the world—every candle, every spark, every distant, glimmering star—had been extinguished. Dani slowed, then halted. Like a hunted animal, he crouched in his burrow.

"Do you hear anything?" he whispered.

"No," his uncle whispered back. "I think we've lost them."

"I think we've lost *us*." The words were not as frightening as they should have been. Wriggling, Dani maneuvered his body into a sitting position. If he drew his knees up tight to his chest and scrunched low, he could rest his back against the tunnel wall. Just a rest to catch his breath, he thought. It was a relief to have his weight off his bruised knees. The enfolding blackness was reassuring, warm and familiar. And why not? Dying was like being born, after all; so the Song of Being told. Inside the womb there was perfect blackness, although Dani did not remember it.

He remembered his mother, who had died before he was two years old. He remembered warm flesh, soft and dusky, smelling sweetly of milk. In the darkness, Dani smiled. Mother's milk, the odor of *love*. She had loved him very much. He remembered his father telling him so, and afterward, after his father was gone, Warabi and old Ngurra, who had raised him, the scent of mother's milk and warmed flesh, the sharp tang of a wad of well-chewed *gamal*.

Truly, the blackness was not so terrible.

"Do you smell that, lad?" Uncle Thulu said dreamily. "It's like the scent of baari-wood, newly peeled, slick with morning dew. Nothing like it, is there?" He laughed softly. "I must have been about your age when I cut my first digging-stick. 'Learn to follow the veins of the earth,' old Ngurra told me. 'The Bearer will have need of your skills.'" Another soft laugh. "Even the wise are wrong sometimes."

A faint sense of alarm stirred in Dani. "Baari-wood?"

"Peeled clean as a whistle, sweet as dawn." Uncle Thulu squirmed into place and slumped back against the wall beside him, their shoulders brushing companionably in the darkness. "You'll see, we'll go to the grove together, and you'll see." He inhaled deeply, then yawned. "You can almost see it now, if you try."

It was wrong, all wrong. There was no scent of baari-wood in the tunnels, only mother's milk and desert-warm flesh, and that was wrong, too, because his mother was long dead and his father, too, and there was nothing here save stone and darkness.

"Uncle." Dani shook Thulu's unresponsive shoulder. "Something's not right. We've got to keep moving. Please, Uncle!"

"To where, lad?" Thulu asked, peaceable and sleepy. "Back where the Fjel are waiting? That path is gone. Onward to starve in darkness? There's no way out of here. Better to rest, and dream."

"No." Gritting his teeth, Dani wiped the blood from his sticky hands and fumbled for the clay flask, trying to work the cork loose. It was tight; he had made sure of it after his fall had jarred it loose on the plains. His palms burned, his fingers felt thick and clumsy, and it was hard to get a grip on the cork. For a moment he thought, why not rest? Uncle is right, we are lost forever, it's better to rest and dream.

Then the cork gave way and the scent of the Water of Life arose, and it was clear and clean and potent, heavy with minerals, almost a weight on the tongue, shredding the veils that clouded his mind. With his head heavy and low, Dani took a deep breath, tasting life, verdant and alive, and understood anew how precious and precarious it was, and how tenuous their grasp upon it here in the bowels of the earth.

"Here." He thrust blindly into the blackness, shoving the flask in the vicinity of his uncle's nose. "Breathe, Uncle. Breathe deep."

Thulu did, and shuddered as though awaking from a dream. "Dani?" he murmured. "Dani, lad?"

"I'm here, Uncle." Retracting the flask, Dani felt for the lip and replaced the cork, banging it in tight with the heel of his wounded palm, repressing a wince. All around them was blackness, and there was no longer any comfort in it. "It's time."

"Time?"

"Time to follow the veins of the earth," Dani said gently. He felt for Thulu's arm and squeezed it. "We're under the mountains, Uncle; at least, I think we are. You're right, there's no going back, but there's still forward. Somewhere, these tunnels must emerge, and somewhere there is a river, the Gorgantus River."

"Yes." In the blackness, Thulu's voice was muffled, hands pressed to his face. "Perhaps. Ah, Dani! It's hard, so hard, buried alive beneath the earth. I wish I had my digging-stick to sense the way. Maybe then . . ."

"You don't need it." Beneath his fingertips, Dani felt the sinews of his uncle's arm shifting, the blood pulsing steadily under his skin. "Please, Uncle! You can do it, I know. It is what you trained all your life to do. Guide us."

For a time, an endless time, there was only silence. And then, faint and ragged, a tuneless song. It rose from his belly, rumbling deep in his lungs. In the black bowels of the earth, Thulu of the Yarru-yami sang of water, closing his blind eyes and tracing the veins of the earth, singing the song of its course through the stony flesh of the World God, Uru-Alat. And his voice, at first uncertain and desperate, slowly grew in strength, syllables rolling from his lips like cataracts leaping from a mountain ledge.

"Forward," he said at last. "You'll have to lead, lad; there's not enough room for me to pass you. Forward, and when the path forks, bear to the right."

Eyes open onto utter blackness, Dani got back onto his hands and knees and began to crawl.

"HIS LORDSHIP WISHES TO SEE you."

In the doorway of her chambers, Cerelinde took a step backward, but having delivered his message, the Havenguard remained waiting in silence, huge and impassive, three of his fellows behind him. Cerelinde glanced behind her at the tapestry with its hidden door.

"It is his Lordship's custom to send a madling at such times," she said, temporizing. The prospect of being accompanied solely by the Fjel filled her with deep unease. Damaged and unpredictable though the madlings were, they were not without reverence for the Lady of the Ellylon.

The Havenguard's features creased, his leathery upper lip drew back to reveal the tips of his eyetusks. "No more since one tried to kill you, Lady."

On another race, the expression might have passed for a smile. Cerelinde studied him, wondering if it was possible that the Fjel-troll was amused. "What does his Lordship desire?"

The Havenguard shrugged, indicating the irrelevance of the question. He was Mørkhar Fjel, with a dark, bristling hide beneath the gleaming black armor. Whatever his Lordship ordered, he would do. "You."

Cerelinde fought back a surge of fear and inclined her head. "As he commands."

They led her through the halls of Darkhaven, along corridors of gleaming black marble, laced with the blue-white veins of the marrow-fire. Their heavy weapons, polished to a bright shine, rattled against their armor. She found herself wishing Tanaros was there, for the Fjel respected and obeyed him. They had no reverence for the Lady of the Ellylon, no awe. Other races among the Lesser Shapers held the Ellylon in high regard. Not so the Fjel, for whom they held little interest.

It was not that she felt it her due, but it was familiar; understood. There was a measure of comfort was in it.

What a terrible thing it was, Cerelinde thought, to be deprived of Haomane's Gift, the gift of thought. She pitied the Fjel insofar as she was able. It was difficult to pity the pitiless, and the fierce Fjel seemed to her lacking in all sympathy, even for their own plight. It was Satoris' doing, she supposed, but it made the Fjel no easier to comprehend. Envy, she understood. All of the Lesser Shapers envied Haomane's Children, for the Chain of Being bound them but loosely and the light of the Souma was their birthright.

Disinterest was another matter, and incomprehensible.

She walked amid the Havenguard, feeling uncommonly small and insignificant. The least among them topped her by head and shoulders, and the Ellylon were a tall folk. Why had Neheris-of-the-Leaping-Waters seen fit to make her children so huge?

Such thoughts, while not comforting, were a welcome distraction, for altogether too soon they emerged through the middle of the threefold doors and descended the spiral stair into the Chamber of the Font. There it was, close and hot, reeking of ichor; the glittering Font, the beating ruby heart of Godslayer, the shadows crowding the corners. There *he* was, a shadow among shadows, speaking to the Fjel in their own guttural tongue, in a voice so low and resonant it lent a harsh beauty to the words. There were the Fjel, saluting and withdrawing. And then there was only Cerelinde and the Shaper.

"Cerelinde." He said her name; only that. The shadows sighed.

"My Lord." She lifted her chin and sought not to tremble.

Satoris, Third-Born among Shapers, laughed, and the shadows laughed with him. It was a low laugh, insinuating. "Are you so afraid, Lady of the Ellylon? Have I been such a poor host?" He gestured toward a chair, shadows wreathing his arm. "Sit. I mean you no harm. I would but converse with you upon the eve of battle. Who understands it as do we two?"

Cerelinde sat stiffly. "Do you jest?"

"Jest?" His eyes gleamed out of the shadows, twin coals. "Ah, no, Daughter of Erilonde! I made you an offer, once. Do you recall it?"

She remembered the garden by moonlight, the Sunderer's hand extended, its shadow stark upon the dying grass. *What if I asked you to stay?* Her own refusal, and the shivering sound of the sorrow-bells. "I do, my Lord."

"We reap the fruits of our pride, Cerelinde." He sighed. "And it is a bloody harvest. I ask again; who understands as do we two?"

"It is not pride, my Lord." Cerelinde shook her head. "It is *hope.*"

"Hope?" he echoed.

"Hope." She repeated the word more firmly. "For a world made whole, healed. For the Souma, made whole and glorious, and order restored. For the Lesser Shapers to become our better selves." The words, the vision, gave her strength. She remembered a question Meara had posed her, and wondered if she dared to ask it after all. "What is it you are afraid to confront, my Lord?" Cerelinde asked, feeling the stir of ancient Ellylon magics creeping over her skin, the scant remnant of gifts the Rivenlost had ceded to the Sundering. "I, too, posed you a question. I do not believe you answered it."

"Did I not?" the Shaper murmured.

What might-have-been . . .

Unexpectedly, Cerelinde found tears in her eyes. She swallowed. "Your crossroads, my Lord. There have been many, but only one is foremost. Three times, Haomane Lord-of-Thought asked you to withdraw your Gift from Arahila's Children. I asked why you refused him, and you did not answer. Do"—she hesitated—"do you wish to know what might have been if you had acceded?"

Satoris lowered his head, and the shadows roiled. His shoulders hunched, emerging like dark hills from the shadowy sea. His hands knotted into fists, sinew crackling. There was another sound, deep and hollow and bitter, so filled with anger that it took Cerelinde a moment to recognize it as laughter.

"Ah, Cerelinde!" He raised his head. The embers of his eyes had gone out; they were only holes, empty sockets like the Helm of Shadows, filled with unspeakable sorrow. "Do *you?*"

"Yes." She made herself hold his terrible gaze. "Yes, my Lord. I do wish to know. I am Haomane's Child, and we do not thrive in darkness and ignorance."

"Nothing," the Shaper said softly. "*Nothing*, is the answer. I need no trifling Ellyl gift to tell me what I have known for far, far too long."

"My Lord?" Cerelinde was perplexed.

"Not immediately." He continued as though she had not spoken, turning his back upon her and pacing the confines of the chamber. "Oh, the world would have gone on for a time, Daughter of Erilonde; Urulat, rigid and fixed. An echelon of order in which Haomane's Children reigned unchallenged, complacent in their own perfection. A sterile world, as sterile as I have become, ruled by the Lord-of-Thought, in which nothing ever changed and no thing, no matter what its passions, no being, no *creature*, sought to exceed its place. And so it would be, on and on and on, generation upon generation, age upon age, until the stars fell from the sky, and the earth grew cold, and died." His voice raised a notch, making the walls tremble. *"Is that what you wish?"*

"No," she whispered. "Yet—"

"Look!" Rage thundered in the air around him. He drew near, looming over her, smelling of blood and lightning. "Do you not believe me? Use your paltry Rivenlost magics, and *see*."

Shrinking back in her chair, Cerelinde stared into his eyes and saw a barren landscape of cold stone, a dull grey vista stretching on endlessly. There were no trees, no grass, not even a trickle of water. Nothing moved. Nothing breathed. Nothing lived. Overhead there was only a void; perfect blackness, the space between the stars, aching with the pressure of emptiness. Cold, so cold! Her teeth chattered, her flesh like ice, her bones aching to the marrow.

"Please," she got out through a clenched jaw. "Please!"

"Life *quickens*, little Ellyl." Granting her mercy, he turned away. "Quickens unto death, quickens into *generation*. Living and dying, giving birth unto ourselves. Everything. Even Shapers," he added in a low voice. "Even worlds."

Cerelinde rubbed her arms, trying to restore warmth to her flesh. "Is this the famous wisdom of dragons, my Lord? They twist truth into lies and they are not to be trusted."

"They are older than the Lord-of-Thought, you know." His head averted, the Sunderer laughed softly. "Ah, Haomane! We are but parts, scattered and broken; heart and head, limbs and organs. None of us perceives the whole, not even you, my Elder Brother. They do. What they think, what they feel . . . I cannot say. But they *know*. And I, I spoke to them, and I am cursed with knowledge for it. Skeins of lies, woven with threads of truth; that is the world we have Shaped. You need me. *Urulat* needs me; Urulat, Uru-Alat that was, that will be again. I did not choose this role. I do what I must. All things, in the end, must be as they are. Is it not so?"

Uncertain whether he spoke to her or to the specter of Haomane First-Born, Cerelinde gazed at the Shaper's back; the taut sinews, the wrath-blackened flesh. "Forgive me, but I do not understand."

"No," he said. "No, I suppose not. And yet it is in the *striving* that understanding begins, and that is the seed of generation that begets worlds." Again, Satoris gave his soft, dark laugh. "You should strive, little Ellyl; as all of us should. He made you too well, my Elder Brother did. Mortality serves a purpose. Oronin's Horn blows seldom for Haomane's Children. No urgency quickens your flesh, no shadow of exigency spurs your thoughts. What would you have to *strive* for, were it not for me?"

"You pretend you do us a service," Cerelinde murmured.

"No." The Shaper's shoulders hunched, rising like stormclouds. "I do the *world* a service. By my very existence, by this role not of my choosing."

"The world," Cerelinde echoed, feeling weariness settle upon her. She was tired; tired of fear, tired of lies. Lies, piled upon lies; half-truths and evasions. Some things were known. Some things were true. "My Lord, if you cared so much for the world, why did you Sunder it?"

"I DID NOT SUNDER THE WORLD!"

Satoris Banewreaker's fist crashed against the wall of the chamber; shadows roiled and sinews cracked, and Darkhaven shuddered from its foundation to its towers. The Font leapt, spewing blue-white fire, shedding sparks on the stone floor. Within its flames, Godslayer pulsed. He stood, breathing hard, his back to her. Ichor ran in rills down his inner thigh, black and oily.

"I did not Sunder the world," he repeated.

And Haomane smote the earth with his sword, and the earth was divided and the heat of Uru-Alat severed from the body. And in accordance with Meronin's will, the Sundering Sea rushed in to fill the divide, and so it was done.

"You shattered the Souma," Cerelinde said in a small voice.

"Not alone." Satoris Third-Born, who was once called the Sower, sighed. Lifting his head, he gazed toward the west, as though he could see through the stone walls of Darkhaven to the isle called Torath, the Crown, where the Six Shapers dwelled in the broken glory of the Souma. "Never alone." He shivered, lowering his head. "Go, little Ellyl, Daughter of Erilonde. I was wrong to summon you here. There is no hope, no hope at all."

"There is always hope," Cerelinde said.

"Will you ever harp upon it?" Satoris pitted his furrowed brow with his fingertips. "For your kind, perhaps. My Gift, the Gift my Elder Brother refused . . . it lies awaiting you in the loins of the Scion of Altorus. There are ways and ways and ways. Perhaps, then; perhaps not. It is your sole chance. Why else do you suppose Haomane's Prophecy is as it is?" He smiled grimly. "For me, there is nothing. And yet you are all my Children in the end. Make no mistake, I have sown the seeds of my own regeneration. In one place or another, they will take root."

"My Lord?"

"Go." He waved one hand. "Go, and begone from my sight, for you pain me."

Summoned by arcane means, the Havenguard appeared at the top of the spiral stair. There they waited, impassive in the flame-shot darkness.

The Sunderer pointed. *"GO!"*

Cerelinde climbed the stair slowly, her limbs stiff with the residue of fear and bone-deep cold. Below, Satoris Banewreaker resumed his pacing, disturbing the shadows. He glanced often toward the west and muttered to himself in a strange tongue, filled with potent, rolling syllables; the Shapers' tongue, that had not been heard on Urulat since the world was Sundered. One word alone Cerelinde understood, uttered in a tone of anguish and betrayal.

"Arahila!"

And then the Fjel led her away and the threefold door closed behind her, and Cerelinde of the House of Elterrion was escorted back to her chambers to await the outcome of the war that would decide her fate.

In the empty garden, beneath Arahila's moon, sorrow-bells chimed unheard.

SIXTEEN

❖

HAOMANE'S ALLIES HAD GONE ON the march under cover of darkness. Dawn broke over the plains to find them encamped a short distance from the foot of the Gorgantus Mountains. The mountains trembled at the roars of the Tordenstem sentries, summoning the Three and their chosen companions.

"By the Six!"

Tanaros heard Speros' shaking oath behind him. Another time, perhaps, he might have reprimanded the Midlander for it. In Darkhaven, one did not swear by the Six Shapers. Today it seemed meet.

The army covered the plains of Curonan, armor gleaming in the bloody light of dawn. Nothing glimpsed in the Ravensmirror had prepared him for the sight. Even from the overlook high atop the crags, it was immense.

Side by side by side, the Three gazed at the army.

So many companies! There they were, gathered at last in one place, arrayed for battle. The Rivenlost formed the vanguard. It surprised Tanaros, a little; but then, it was the Lady of the Ellylon over whom this war was waged. Perhaps it was a matter of honor.

"Well," Vorax said. "There they are."

"Indeed," Ushahin said drily.

Vorax leaned over in the saddle and spat. "And there they can sodding well stay, as far as I'm concerned. Maybe they'll go home when they begin to starve." At his rear, a pair of Staccians chuckled.

Tanaros said nothing, squinting, trying to pick out individuals. The companies were still milling and unsettled. Yes, there; glint of red-gold, a rider moving among the disparate companies, gesturing, giving orders, attempting to stitch them into a cohesive whole. Some of them had fought together at Beshtanag, but many of them had not. Coordination would be difficult in the field.

"You look like you're sizing them up for battle, cousin." Ushahin's remark sounded casual. "Do you lack faith in our fortifications?"

"No." Tanaros wondered why Haomane's Allies had bothered to waste a precious hour or two of sleep to arrive at dawn. He exchanged a glance with Hyrgolf, who shrugged. There was no element of surprise to be gained. Did they imagine the sight would shock Darkhaven into surrendering? He frowned, studying the army. There, there was another figure he knew, riding to the forefront as the ranks parted to allow him passage. White-robed and white-maned, the tip of his spear shining like the last star of the morning, a spark of brightness nestled in his snowy beard. He rode astride a horse as white as foam, with an arched neck and hooves that fell with deft precision.

"Is that . . . him?" Speros asked in a low voice.

"Malthus the Counselor." Tanaros confirmed it absently, still frowning. "What did you *do* to my horse, damn you?"

As if in answer, the figure of Malthus spread his arms wide. The clear Soumanië on his breast burst into a blaze of light, bathing him in white radiance. On either side of him, Rivenlost heralds in bright armor raised horns to their lips and blew long blasts, high and clarion, shivering and silvery in the dawn.

On the plains of Curonan, Malthus the Wise Counselor lifted his voice, and whether it was through some vestigial magic of the Soumanië or the wizard's own arts, given to him by Haomane himself, his voice carried above the plains, as powerful and resonant as any Tordenstem Fjel; as his Lordship himself.

"Satoris Third-Born, whom Men and Ellylon have named Sunderer and Banewreaker, we have come in answer to your challenge! In the name of Haomane First-Born, Lord-of-Thought, I command you to face us, or be forever branded a coward!"

His words broke like a thunderclap over the mountains, accompanied by a blinding wash of brilliant white light. Tanaros rocked back in the saddle as though he had been struck. It felt like it. Fury flooded his veins, drowning rational thought; for an instant, he nearly spurred his mount over the edge of the crag into thin air. He found he was laughing, his teeth bared in a grimace of defiance, one hand on the hilt of his black sword. The Fjel were roaring, Vorax was roaring, the Staccians and Speros were shouting promises of bloody death. Tanaros shook his head, trying to clear it. There was only one way down to the plains; back, back to Darkhaven and down through Defile's Maw. Yes, that was the way.

"Tanaros! *Tanaros!*"

A hand was on his arm; Ellyl-fair, tangling his reins and detaining him as he sought to turn his mount. Impatient, he tried to shake it off, but there was unexpected strength in the grip.

"You were right." Ushahin's voice was taut. "There is as much danger in the power to Shape spirit as matter."

The words penetrated slowly. Tanaros took a shaking breath, aware of his heart threatening to burst from his branded chest, of hungering for the scent of blood. Ahead of him, Fjel and Men alike were scrambling along the path toward Darkhaven. "Malthus' Soumanië," he said thickly, understanding. "Why should *you* be immune?"

"To this?" Ushahin Dreamspinner gave his bitter smile. A vein throbbed in his dented temple and his dilated eye was black as a void, seeping meaningless tears at the painful onslaught of light. "It is only another form of madness." He nodded down the path. "You had better halt your troops."

Cursing, Tanaros lashed his mount's haunches with his reins. He rode them down, plunging amid them, shouting. "Turn back, turn back! Hyrgolf! Vorax! Speros! Turn back!"

Hyrgolf heeded him first, coming to himself with a mighty shudder. He waded through the milling troops to plant himself in their path, setting his shoulders and roaring orders until the headlong rush stalled into aimless chaos.

"What was that?" Speros sounded confused, half-awake.

"That," Tanaros said grimly, "was Malthus."

The Midlander blinked befuddled brown eyes at him. "What happens now?"

They were all gazing toward him for an answer. Tanaros shook his head, wordless. Behind and beyond them, above the looming edifice of Darkhaven's fortress, stormclouds were gathering; black and roiling. One atop another they piled, bruise-colored and furious, until the air was heavy with tension. Wind blew in every direction, cold and cutting as a knife.

A peal of thunder answered Malthus' challenge. It began deep and low, so low it was little more than a tremor felt in the pit of the belly, then built in burgeoning fury, built and built in rolling peals, culminating in a booming crack, the likes of which had not been heard since the foundation of the world was Sundered. Even the horses of Darkhaven staggered, and Men and Fjel lifted their hands to cover their ears.

A fork of lightning split the dirty clouds, blue-white as the marrow-fire, and its afterimage was as red as the beating heart of Godslayer.

Then there was silence, until it was broken again by the silvery horns of the Rivenlost, casting their tremulous, valiant challenge aloft on a surge of light, sowing fresh unrest in their enemies' souls.

"What *now*?" Speros of Haimhault's voice broke. "Ah, Shapers! What now?"

"War." Ushahin Dreamspinner rode up the path with shoulders hunched against the biting winds. Under the lowering skies and their murky light, the mount that consented to bear him was the color of old blood, spilled and drying. Tanaros watched him come; half-breed, half-healed, his gilt hair lank with disdain. Ushahin met his eyes, but it was Speros he answered. "It is what it has always been, Midlander. War."

"We will give them *war*!" Vorax growled, and the Staccians echoed assent. "Supplies be damned! We will fall upon them and make them wish they had never been born."

Tanaros raised his hand, halting them. "It is for his Lordship to decide."

"It is in my heart that he has already decided," Ushahin murmured to him. "The Soumanië is persuasive, and his Lordship was not unwilling to be persuaded in the matter. I hope you took their measure well, cousin."

Tanaros glanced back toward the plains, longing to answer the horns' call. "Well enough, cousin, if it comes to it." He steeled himself. "We'd best make haste. The fortress is likely to be in an uproar. Can I trust you all to hold firm?"

There were grim nods all around. Bloodlust itched in all of them, but the initial madness of Malthus' spell had been broken. What remained could be resisted.

It was well, for his prediction proved an understatement. They arrived at Darkhaven to find it boiling with battle-frenzy. Fjel poured from the barracks, abandoned their posts along the wall, streaming toward the Defile Gate. Only their sheer mass prevented them from passing through it and entering Defile's Maw. So many Fjel were pressed up against the Gate it was impossible to open it. Enraged and slavering, partially armed or not at all, they flung themselves against the stone walls.

"Shapers!" Speros looked ill.

"Marshal Hyrgolf." Tanaros kneed his mount forward, taking a position atop the high path where all could see him. He gazed down at the seething mass of bodies. "Get me one of the Tordenstem." There was a slight commotion behind him, and then one of the Tordenstem, the Thunder Voice Fjel, was at his side, squat and grey as a boulder, offering a steady salute. Tanaros nodded at him. "Tell them their General commands their attention."

The Tordenstem took a great breath, his barrel-shaped torso swelling visibly, and loosed his voice in a mighty roar. *All heed the Lord General Tanaros! Tan-a-ros! Tan-a-ros! All heed the Lord General!*

Stillness settled, slow and gradual. The long training of the Fjel had instilled the habit of obedience in them. They ceased flinging themselves at the impervious stone and gazed upward at Tanaros, a semblance of sanity returning to their features.

"Brethren!" Tanaros raised his voice; an ordinary Man's voice, possessed of no special might, but pitched to carry over battlefields. "Who is it that has ordered this assault?" There was no answer. The Fjel shuffled and looked at their horny feet. "No?" Tanaros asked. "Then I will tell you: Malthus. It is Malthus the Counselor who orders it, and Malthus alone you obey if you heed this madness!"

They looked shame-faced and Tanaros felt guilty at it. He, too, had been caught up in the frenzy. If not for the Dreamspinner's intervention, he would be down there among them. But it would avail nothing to confess it. Now was the time to provoke their pride, not assuage it.

"Listen to me," he said to the Fjel. "This"—he gestured—"this mayhem, this undisciplined ferocity, *this* is how Haomane's Allies see you. This is what they wish the Fjel to be; mindless, unthinking. Ravening beasts. Do you wish to prove them aright? Is that how Neheris Shaped her Children?"

A roar of denial rose in answer. Tanaros smiled and drew his black sword. Its hilt pulsed in his grip, attuned to the hatred that throbbed in his veins. It glowed with its own dark light under the shrouded skies.

"By this sword!" he called. "By the black sword, quenched in his Lordship's blood, I swear to you! We will obey his Lordship's orders and see his will is done. And if his will be *war*, Haomane's Allies will know what it means to face the wrath, and the might, and the *discipline* of Darkhaven!"

Their cheers drowned out the distant call of Ellylon horns.

Tanaros sheathed the black sword and turned to Hyrgolf. "Summon your lieutenants and restore some semblance of order. Tell the lads to remain on alert."

"Aye, General." Hyrgolf paused. "You think his Lordship means to do it?"

"I don't know." Tanaros leaned over in the saddle, clasping the Tungskulder's shoulder. "We shall see, Field Marshal."

LILIAS STARTLED AWAKE FROM A dream of Beshtanag.

She had been dreaming of the siege, the endless siege, watching her people grow starved and resentful, waiting for an army that would never come, hearing once more the silvery horns of the Rivenlost blow and the herald repeating his endless challenge. *Sorceress! Surrender the Lady Cerelinde, and your people will be spared!*

Waking, she found herself in her pleasant prison-chamber, sunlight streaming through the high windows. Beshtanag was far, far away. And still she heard horns, a faint and distant call echoing through Meronil's white bridges and towers.

For a terrified moment, she thought it was Oronin's Horn summoning her to death. In Pelmar it was said those of noble birth could hear it; of a surety, the Were could. But, no, those were Ellylon horns.

"Eamaire." Swallowing her pride, Lilias pleaded with the attendant when she arrived. "What passes in the world? Is Meronil besieged?"

"While Haomane's Children draw breath on Urulat's soil, Meronil stands, Lady." A cool disdain was in the Ellyl's leaf-green eyes, as though she had borne witness to Lilias' darkest fantasies of destruction. "The Lord of the Rivenlost travels with the Host. You do but hear their horns sounding in the distance."

Lilias took a sharp breath. "Darkhaven?"

The Ellyl hesitated, then shook her head. "It may be. We cannot know."

She departed, leaving Lilias alone with the memory of her dream and the awful knowledge that it was true, all true, that Beshtanag was lost, everything was lost, and she was to blame. The horns sounded again, reminding her.

Perhaps Oronin's Horn would not have been so terrible after all.

Lilias sat at her window seat and watched the broad silver ribbon of the Aven River unfurl far, far below, thinking about her dream. Perhaps, she thought, she would sleep and dream it again. As awful as it was, it was no worse than the reality to which she had awakened, the reality she was forced to endure. At least in the dream, Beshtanag had not yet fallen, Calandor still lived, and Lilias was immortal.

There were worse things than death and dreams.

THE THRONE HALL WAS ABLAZE with marrow-fire. It surged upward from the torches to sear the mighty rafters and laced the walls in stark blue-white veins; earth's lightning, answering to Lord Satoris' rage. The Shaper was pacing the dais in front of his carnelian throne, a vast and ominous figure, unknown words spilling from his lips.

The Three glanced at one another and approached.

"My Lord." Tanaros went to one knee, bowing his head. From the corner of his eye, he saw Vorax do the same. Ushahin, unaccountably, remained standing. "We come to learn your will."

"My *will*." Lord Satoris ground out the words. He ceased his pacing and his eyes flashed red as coal-embers. "Did you not hear the challenge Malthus raises? My *will*, my Three, is to take up Godslayer and split open the very earth beneath his feet until he is swallowed whole by Urulat itself, and my Elder Brother's allies with him!"

His words echoed throughout the Throne Hall, echoed and continued to echo. Tanaros kept his head bowed, feeling the Shaper's wrath beating in waves against his skin. The air was filled with the acrid odor of blood and thunder, so dense he could taste it in his mouth.

"Can you, my Lord?" It was Ushahin, still standing and gazing up at Satoris, who asked the question. There was a strange tenderness in his voice. "Can we yet delay this hour?"

The Shaper sighed. His shoulders slumped and his head lowered. A beast brought to bay; and yet no beast had ever stood so motionless, so still. The last echo of his words faded, until there was only the sound of the Three breathing, the crackle and hiss of the torches, and the slow, steady drip of ichor pooling on the dais.

"I cannot." Satoris whispered the words, turning out his empty hands. "Oh, my Three! I am not what I was. It is a terrible burden to bear. I have borne it too long and spent too much." A shudder ran through him. "Was I unwise? I cannot say."

"Not unwise." Ushahin wiped at his dilated eye, watering in the marrow-fire's painful glare. "Never that, my Lord."

"No?" Satoris laughed, harsh and hollow. "And yet, and yet. Ah, Dreamspinner! What did you *see* in the Delta? Too much, I think; too much. I destroyed the Marasoumië and I reckoned it worth the cost, for it would destroy Haomane's Weapon within it. And yet he lives, he places himself within my grasp, no longer able to Shape matter, and I . . ." He glanced at his empty hand. "I cannot seize him. I bleed, I diminish. Clouds I may summon; smoke and fire, signifying nothing. Godslayer beckons, but I cannot rise to its challenge. I cannot Shape the earth. I spent myself too soon."

"My Lord!" Unable to bear it any longer, Tanaros rose to his feet. "We are here to serve you," he said passionately. "Tell us your will, and we will accomplish it."

"My will." Lord Satoris glanced around him, surveying his creation. "These mountains, this fortress . . . oh, my Three! Years, it bought me, bought us; ages. How much of myself did I spend to erect them? What folly beckons me to betray them? Ah, Malthus! You are a formidable foe. And I . . . I am *tired*. Uru-Alat alone knows, I am tired." He heaved another sigh. "I would see it ended."

Tanaros bowed to the Shaper. "My Lord, you have not erected Darkhaven in vain. It can withstand this siege. But if it is your wish to give battle, my Fjel are eager and ready."

"Can we win?" Vorax asked bluntly. He glanced sidelong at Tanaros and clambered to his feet. "Folly, aye, there's no question it's folly. Less of one if we stand a chance of winning."

"Our chances are good." Tanaros pictured the army of Haomane's Allies in his mind. "They are many, but poorly coordinated. It is the effects of Malthus' Soumanië I fear the most."

"Malthus will not be so quick to assail your soul once you take to the field wearing the Helm of Shadows, cousin," Ushahin murmured. "He will be hard-pressed to quell the terrors in his own people."

"You are eager to do battle for one who can scarce wield a blade, Dreamspinner." Vorax shook his head. "No, there is too much risk, and too little merit. I like my flesh too well to offer it to the swords of Haomane's Allies when I have strong walls to protect it. That way lies madness."

"Madness," Ushahin said drily. "Not an hour ago, you were charging toward the Defile, willing to mount a single-handed assault. Whose madness was that?"

Vorax flushed brick-red. "Malthus', and you well know it!"

Ushahin shrugged. "It will come again, and again and again. The Counselor is powerful, and Haomane's will lends him strength.

He will use the Soumanië to weaken our resolve." He smiled crookedly. "We have weapons to counter such an attack, but none to defend against it."

"It is his Lordship's choice," Tanaros said.

They looked to the dais and waited.

Lord Satoris sank into his throne. "Choice," he said bitterly. "What *choice* have I ever had? The pattern binds me fast, and I alone suffer the knowledge of it." He clutched his thigh, fingers digging deep into the wounded flesh. When he raised his hand, it dripped with black ichor, glistening wetly in the light of the marrow-fire. "Drop by drop, year by year, age upon age," he mused. "What will be left of me if I refuse this choice? For it will come again, and again and again, and there will be less of me to meet it. Did you know, Oronin Last-Born, when you planted God-slayer's blade in my flesh? Will you sound your Horn for me?" He laughed softly. "And what will happen when you do? Who will sound the Horn for *you*? For make no mistake, the day will come. Fear it, as you fear to cross the Sundering Sea. I will be waiting for it. I will be waiting for you *all*. I have placed my stamp upon the world, as I was meant to do."

"My Lord." Tanaros sought to return the Shaper's wandering thoughts to the present. "Your will?"

"You are insistent, my General." The Shaper lifted his hand, his ichor-wet hand, dragging his splayed fingertips down his face. Broad trails gleamed, black on black. "Malthus," he said in a calm voice, "wants a battle; so my Elder Brother bids him. It is my *will* that he shall have it, and I wish them all the joy of their desire." Lord Satoris met Tanaros' eyes. "Send an envoy. Let them retreat to a fair distance, and we will meet them in battle. And then . . ." He smiled. "Destroy them."

Tanaros bowed. "My Lord, it will be done."

NOT A MOUSE, BUT A worm.

A worm, a lowly worm, crawling blindly through the earth; that was what Dani felt himself to be. Only Thulu's intermittent directions whispered from behind reminded him otherwise. It was easier, in a way. It kept the terror at bay, the suffocating fear that stopped his throat when the walls closed in tight and he had to wriggle on his belly to keep going, never certain whether the tunnel would widen beyond, grow ever narrower, or end altogether.

At times it happened and they had to backtrack, slow and

painful, to the last fork they had taken. And then Thulu had to pause, singing the veins of the earth in a ragged voice, reorienting himself toward distant *water*.

I am a worm, Dani thought, a worm.

There was air, though not much. It was close and stifling. They breathed in shallow breaths, trying to dole it out in precious lung-fuls. Dani wondered how worms breathed as they inched through the black earth. Through their skin, perhaps.

Neither could have said how long their journey through the labyrinth of narrow tunnels lasted. At least a day; perhaps more. When seconds seemed to last minutes and minutes hours, it was impossible to say. It felt like an eternity. They crawled until they had the strength to crawl no farther, then they rested, sharing the last of their dwindling supplies; dry mouthfuls of food moistened by sparing sips of water.

They wasted no precious air in conversation. What was there to say? Either they would succeed or they would die, here beneath countless tons of rock, crawling in the pitch-black until the last of their supplies were gone and their strength failed and there was nothing left to do but lie down and die.

When the sound of human voices filtered into the tunnels, faint and distant, Dani thought at first that he had slipped into a waking dream; or worse, fallen into madness. Such a thing had been known to happen. Men had gone mad in the desert from an excess of sun, wandering dazed and speaking of things that did not exist. If light could cause such madness, surely darkness could do no less.

It was hard to make out words, but from the broad tone it seemed the voices were speaking the common tongue, which was irksome. Not since Gerflod had he used the hard-learned language, and after days upon days with only Uncle Thulu's company, Dani found it hard to comprehend. If he were going mad, he thought, he would prefer to do it in Yarru. Even a worm deserved that much.

He crawled toward the voices, a vague notion in mind of complaining to them.

"Dani!" Behind him, Uncle Thulu called his name. "Slow down, lad."

Dani paused, touching the clay vial dangling from his throat. It was solid and reassuring beneath his abraded fingers. What was he doing? "Uncle." He tried his voice, finding it hoarse and strange. He had not spoken in *any* tongue since they had first begun crawling, however long ago it was. "Listen."

They listened, breathing quietly. "Voices," Uncle Thulu said. "I hear voices."

In the blackness, Dani wept with gladness. "You hear them, too!"

"Aye, lad." His uncle's hand touched his ankle. "Go toward them, but slowly, mind. Whoever it is, they're not likely to be a friend."

Dani crept forward forgetting his aching knees and torn hands, the lingering pain in his shoulder. The tunnel continued to twist and turn, forking unexpectedly. He followed the sound of the voices, backtracking when they grew fainter. The path sloped upward, emerging gradually from the bowels of the earth. Turn by turn, the sound grew steadily louder.

Voices, a symphony of voices. As the tunnel widened, he could hear them; some high, almost flittering, some low, a bass rumble. Most were speaking in the common tongue, but here and there were Staccian tones he had heard among the women at Gerflod Keep, and there, too, was the Fjeltroll tongue, which sounded like rocks being pulverized.

The words in the common tongue had to do with food.

It was enough to make Dani wonder anew at his sanity; but then something else changed. The impenetrable blackness lessened. From somewhere, from wherever the voices spoke, *light* was seeping into the tunnels. He saw the dim outline of his own hands before him as he crawled, and kept going. He would have crawled into a den of Fjeltroll if it meant seeing the sun once more.

The light grew stronger; torchlight, not sunlight. It was enough to make him squint through eyes grown accustomed to utter blackness. When he could make out distant shadows moving across the rocky floor, Dani regained sense enough to freeze.

The tunnel, still low, had widened enough for Uncle Thulu to squirm alongside him. They lay on their bellies, watching the shadows move.

"Do you reckon we dare look?" Thulu whispered presently.

"I'll go," Dani whispered back.

He wriggled forward, inch by frightening inch. The tunnel sloped upward. The voices had grown clear as day, accompanied by scuffling and thudding, a steady series of grunts. Narrowing his eyes to slits, Dani peered over the crest of the incline.

The tunnel emerged onto a vast cavern, its walls stacked with foodstuffs. A throng of figures filled the space, Men and Fjeltroll alike, engaged in a concerted effort to shift the supplies. A steady stream were coming empty-handed and going laden, and an imposing figure, burly and bearded, directed their efforts. "An army travels on its belly!" he roared, slapping his own vast belly, clad in gilded plate-armor, for emphasis. "Come on, lads, *move*! I've more important matters on my plate!"

Dani winced and wriggled backward into the safety of the deep shadows, careful not to let the clay vial bang against the stony floor. In a soft whisper, he told Uncle Thulu what he had seen.

"Darkhaven's larder." Thulu gave a soundless chuckle. "Ah, lad! Time was I could have put a dent in it."

"What should we do?" The thought of retreating into the tunnels made Dani shudder all over his skin. "Try to find another route to the river?"

"We wait." Thulu nodded toward the cavern. "The river lies a distance beyond. No point tempting fate; I don't know if there *is* another route. Whatever they're doing, it can't take forever. Wait for silence and darkness, and then we'll see."

Once, Dani would have thought it a bleak prospect; lying on cold, hard stone for untold hours, hungry and thirsty. With fresh air to breathe, the tunnels behind him, and Darkhaven before him, it seemed like bliss. "And after that?" he asked.

Uncle Thulu glanced at him. "I don't know." He shook his head. In the dim light, his eyes were wide and dark in his worn face. "After that it's up to you, lad."

SEVENTEEN

THE THREE QUARRELED ABOUT IT, but in the end, Vorax won. He would serve as his Lordship's envoy. It had to be one of the Three; on that, they agreed. No one else could be trusted with a task of paramount importance. They did not agree it should be Vorax.

It was the logical choice, though Tanaros Blacksword and the Dreamspinner refused to see it, arguing that he was needed in Darkhaven, that they could ill afford the delay. Vorax listened until he could abide no more of their foolishness, then brought his gauntleted fists crashing down upon the table in the center of the Warchamber.

"We are speaking of driving a *bargain*!" he roared. "Have either of you an ounce of skill at it?"

They didn't, of course, and his outburst made them jump, which made him chuckle inwardly. It wasn't every day any of the Three was startled. There was menace in the old bear yet. In the end, they relented.

He spent the morning supervising the creation of a supply-train, shifting most of the contents of the larder, arranging for it to be carted down the Defile. Meat was a problem, but it could be hastily smoked; enough to provide for the Fjel, at least. There was food aplenty. Vorax had prepared for a siege of weeks; months. As long as it took. A battle on open ground, that was another matter.

It was folly, but it was his Lordship's folly. And in truth, although his head was loath, the blood in his veins still beat hard at the thought of it, remembering the maddening call of the Ellylon horns.

Still, it would take a cool head to negotiate the matter. That ruled out Blacksword, who was like to lose his the moment he clapped eyes on Aracus Altorus, and the Dreamspinner . . . well. The half-breed could be cool enough when he chose, and betimes he spoke sense in his foolhardy madness, but he was as unpredictable as spring weather in Staccia.

No, it had to be Vorax.

When the matter of supplies had been dealt with to his satisfaction, he retired to his chambers and ate a hearty dinner, enough to give him ballast for the task to come. He kissed his handmaids good-bye and fancied he saw a shadow of concern in the eyes of the youngest. An old bear was entitled to his fancy. It heartened him when he went to speak to the Ellyl bitch.

Cool heads; now, there was one. She didn't bat a lash at his query, just stared at him with those unsettling eyes and said, "Why should I assist you, Lord Vorax? It is not in my interest to give you tools with which to bargain."

He shrugged. "Lady, your only chance lies in this battle. If I'm not satisfied with the negotiations, it will not happen. Do you want to take that chance?"

She turned her head. What thoughts were passing beneath that smooth white brow, he could not have said. "Is Lord Ingolin in the field?"

"Your Rivenlost Lord?" Vorax scratched his beard. He hadn't picked him out from atop the crag, but the Ravensmirror had shown him leading the Host of the Ellylon. "Aye, Lady. He's there."

"Then tell them I said Meronil must have rung with the sound of horns this morning." She spoke without deigning to look at him. "By that token, they will know I live."

"Ladyship." He bowed with an ironic flourish. "My thanks."

He took his leave of her, accompanied by a pair of Havenguard. Tanaros had insisted upon it. The General might be hotheaded, but he was cautious of the Ellyl bitch's safety. Wisely enough, since Vorax would as lief see her dead.

His escort was waiting at the Defile Gate; ten of his Staccians, a company of thirty Fjel including a pair of Kaldjager scouts, and the young Midlander Speros. Vorax had his doubts about the lad—he was untried, desert travail or no—but he knew when to hold the line and when to quibble. It was what made him a shrewd bargainer; that, and the fact that he didn't *look* shrewd.

It felt strange to pass through the Gate, to abandon the safety of the thick walls and unscalable heights and enter the narrow Defile. There was little danger here—the Defile was well guarded from above—but it brought home the reality of the folly of his Lordship's decision; aye, and the excitement, too. His skin crawled at the same time he found himself humming battle-paeans.

"If it be folly, let it be a glorious one," he said aloud.

"Sir?" The Midlander glanced at him.

"Battle, lad. This battle."

They passed through the Weavers' Gulch without incident, the Kaldjager striding ahead to part the sticky veils. Vorax regarded the scuttling spiders with distaste. The Dreamspinner was fond of them, finding some arcane beauty in the patterns they wove. Small wonder he was mad, though it was a madness he shared with Lord Satoris. One of several, perhaps.

For the remainder of the descent, they spoke little, paying close heed to the dangerous trail. The Kaldjager had vanished, but Vorax could hear their sharp, guttural cries and the answer of the Tordenstem sentries above, low and booming. He wished they had more Kaldjager. The Cold Hunters were tireless in the chase, and if there was any weakness in their enemy's rearguard that could be exploited, they would find a way to circle around and sniff it out.

Too many lost in the northern territories, chasing down a rumor, a whisper of prophecy. Vorax would have given up his youngest handmaid to know what had truly happened there. Some trick of Malthus', like as not. There was simply no way a pair of desert-bred Charred Folk could have evaded the Kaldjager and defeated an entire company of Fjel.

The Kaldjager were waiting at the last bend, before the Defile opened its Maw, crouched like a pair of yellow-eyed boulders. They nodded at him, indicating the way was clear.

"All right, lads." Vorax settled his bulk more comfortably in the saddle and pointed with his bearded chin. "Let's drive a bargain."

They filed ahead of him, rounding the bend. Eigil, his Staccian lieutenant—the last one so appointed—carried their banner, the black banner of Darkhaven with the red dagger of Godslayer in the center. He was young for the task, but what else was Vorax to do? He had lost his best man, Carfax, in the decoy flight to Beshtanag; Osric had fallen to Staccian treachery. His blood still boiled when he thought about it. Speros of Haimhault carried the parley-banner; a pale blue oriflamme, unadorned. He took his job seriously, knuckles white on the banner's haft.

A silvery blast of horns sounded the instant they were seen. Vorax scowled into his beard. Trust the damned Ellylon to make a production of war. He waited for Eigil's answering shout.

"Lord Vorax of Darkhaven will entertain a delegation!"

He rode around the bend, traversing the final descent, lifting one hand in acknowledgment. It was a shock to see Haomane's Allies at close range. There were so *many*, covering the plains, arrayed no more than fifty yards from the Maw itself. His company was clustered at its base, the Fjel with their shields held high, prepared to defend his retreat if necessary.

Haomane's Allies stirred, conversing among themselves. He watched figures gesticulating, wondering if they argued as did the Three.

They knew the protocol. Three figures relinquished their arms with ceremony and rode forward, accompanied by an escort of forty Men and Ellylon. Half wore the dun-grey cloaks of the Borderguard; half the bright armor of the Rivenlost. There were no archers among them. If it came to a fight, it would be fair.

Vorax waited.

Malthus, Ingolin, Aracus; Haomane's Counselor, the Lord of the Rivenlost, and the Scion of Altorus. Vorax took their measure as they approached, riding from sunlight into the mountain's shadow. Their escort fanned out in a loose circle. His remained where they stood; shields high, bristling with weapons. The pale blue oriflamme in Speros' hands trembled, then steadied.

"Vorax of Staccia!" Aracus Altorus' voice was hard and taut. One hand rested on the hilt of his ancestral sword, drawing attention to the dull red gem set in its pommel. "We have come to demand that the Lady Cerelinde be restored to us."

Vorax laughed. "Why, so you have, little Man. Will you go if she is?"

It made the would-be King of the West uncertain; he frowned hard, staring. Malthus the Counselor exchanged a glance with Ingolin the Wise and shook his white-maned head.

"Vorax." His voice was gentle; almost kind. The clear Soumanië on his breast sparkled. "Do not insult us with false promises. Your Dark Lord knows what we are about. Why does he send you? What is his will?"

Vorax smiled. It was always good to establish the principal agent in any bargain. "One that should please you, wizard. For a small price, it is his Lordship's *will* to give you what you desire."

"Cerelinde!" Aracus Altorus breathed.

"War," the Rivenlost Lord said gravely.

"War," Vorax said, agreeing with the latter. Broadening his smile, he opened his arms. "What else have you courted so assiduously? You have swayed him, wizard; you have swayed us all! His Lordship is willing to meet the forces of Haomane's Allies upon the plain. And yet, we must have certain assurances."

Aracus Altorus raised his brows. "Why should we bargain with you?"

"Ah, little Man!" Vorax bent a benign glance upon him. "Do you see these heights?" He pointed toward the Gorgantus Mountains. "They cannot be scaled. There is but one passage, and believe me, if you believe nothing else I say, when I tell you it is well guarded. You have no leverage here."

"What is the Sunderer's price?" Malthus asked.

"Fall back." Vorax shrugged. "As I said, it is a small one. You seek battle; his Lordship is willing to give it. Fall back . . . half a league, no more. Allow our forces to assemble and meet yours in fair combat upon the plains. No attack shall begin until the signal is given."

The Counselor nodded. "And if we do not agree?"

"Look around you." Vorax indicated the plains with a sweep of his hand. "Can you fill your bellies with grass, like horses? I think not, Haomane's Counselor. Darkhaven can outwait you. Darkhaven *will* outwait you."

Malthus smiled, wrinkles creasing his face. The Soumanië nestled in his beard brightened, starry. "Will you?" he asked. "Oh, I think not, Vorax of Staccia. The Sunderer's will is fixed."

Vorax squinted sidelong at the Soumanië, feeling the urge to battle quicken his blood. "You're handy with that, Counselor," he observed. "Makes me pity my countrymen, those you led into betrayal. I trust you found them waiting, as promised. Doubtless Haomane is pleased." Bloodlust thickened his tongue, and he nodded at the gem. "Have a care. I come to bargain in good faith."

"And yet you perceive your weakness," Malthus said gently.

"Mine, aye." With an effort, Vorax tore his gaze from the Soumanië. "Funny thing, Counselor. Seems your pretty brooch doesn't work on the Dreamspinner." He forced his lips into a smile. "Something in his nature renders him proof against its folly, and he's right eager to see the Lady Cerelinde dead, is Ushahin Dreamspinner. He doesn't mind defying Lord Satoris to do it. He's quite mad, you know."

Aracus Altorus swore; Malthus passed his hand over the Soumanië, quenching its light.

Ingolin of the Rivenlost, who had sat motionless in the saddle, stirred. "You touch upon my fears, Vorax of Staccia. You are quick to use the Lady Cerelinde's life as a bargaining chip, yet it is in my heart that the Sunderer has little reason to have spared it to date."

"Oh, aye, she lives." Breathing easier, Vorax laughed. "For now, Ellyl lordling. His Lordship," he added contemptuously, "has staked his *honor* upon it."

Ingolin's melodious voice deepened. "I put no trust in the honor of Satoris Banewreaker. Let her be brought forth, if you would have me believe. Let us see with our own eyes that the Lady Cerelinde lives!"

"See, I thought you might ask that." Vorax scratched at his beard. "Problem is, Ingolin my friend, she's our safeguard. I don't put a great deal of trust in *your* word." He gave the Lord of the Rivenlost a friendly smile. "Why, you might break it, if you reckoned it were for the greater good!"

"I would not," the Ellyl Lord said stiffly. "The Ellylon do not lie."

"Maybe, maybe not." Vorax shrugged. "Someone else might break it for you, eh? The Lady stays in Darkhaven. But I asked her for a token, whereby you might know she lives. She asked me if you were in the field. When I said you were, she said, 'Tell them Meronil must have rung with the sound of horns this morning.' Does that suffice?"

Ingolin bowed his head, silver hair hiding his features. "Cerelinde," he whispered.

"Cerelinde," Vorax agreed. "Whose life hangs by this bargain, and your ability to honor it to the word. Shall we strike it?"

"How do we know you will keep your word?" Aracus Altorus' eyes blazed. "Perhaps this bargain is but a mockery. What safeguard do *you* offer, Glutton?"

Vorax glanced around, his gaze falling on the Midlander. "Speros of Haimhault." He beckoned. "Are you willing to serve?"

"My lord!" The Midlander looked ill. "Aye, my lord."

"Here you are, then." Vorax clapped a hand on his shoulder. "He's the architect of Darkhaven's defense. Try the Defile, and see what he's got in store for you! Word is he engineered the means to let General Tanaros fill in that pesky Well in the Unknown Desert, though you might know more of it than I. Any mind, he's been Tanaros Blacksword's right-hand Man for some time. Will he suffice?"

They looked shocked; all save Malthus. Did nothing on the face of Urulat shock the damned Counselor? He inclined his head, white beard brushing his chest.

"He will suffice," Malthus said somberly.

"Good." Vorax glanced at the sky, gauging the angle of the sun. "You'll withdraw your troops by dawn on the morrow, on pain of the Lady's death?"

"We will."

"Then we will meet you ere noon. You'll know our signal when we give it." He grinned. "Gentlemen, I will see you anon!"

His Staccians closed in tight, following as he turned his mount and headed into Defile's Maw, the Fjel guarding their retreat, step by backward step, shields held high. Below them, Speros of Haimhault sat on his ghost-grey mount and watched them go with desperate eyes.

It was, Vorax thought, a well-struck bargain.

SILVER HOARFROST SPARKLED ON THE sere grass in the moon-garden, shrouded its plants and trees in cerements of ice. No drops fell from the pale pink blossoms of the mourning-tree, and the corpse-flowers' pallid glow was extinguished. The mortexigus did not shudder in the little death, shedding its pollen, and the shivering bells of the clamitus atroxis waited in silence. Even the poignant scent of vulnus-blossom had been stilled by the cold.

Tanaros wrapped his cloak tighter and wondered if Cerelinde would come. He could have gone to her, or he could have ordered her to come. In the end, he had chosen to ask. Why, he could not have said.

Overhead, the stars turned slowly. He gazed at them, wondering if Arahila looked down upon Darkhaven and wept for her brother Satoris' folly, for the bloodshed that was certain to follow. He wondered if poor Speros, unwitting victim of Vorax's bargain, was watching the same stars. He was angry at Vorax for his choice, though there was no merit in arguing it once it was done. Other matters were more pressing; indeed, even now, he wasted precious time lingering in the garden. Still, his spirit was uneasy and an ache was in his heart he could not name.

After a time, he became certain she would not come; and then the wooden door with the tarnished hinges opened and she was there, flanked by the hulking figures of the Havenguard. They remained behind, waiting.

Her gown was pale, its color indeterminate in the starlight. A dark cloak enfolded her like green leaves enfolding a blossom's pale petals. Its sweeping hem left a trail in the frosted grass as she approached him.

"Tanaros," she said gravely.

"Cerelinde." He drank in the sight of her. "I didn't know if you would come."

"You have kept your word of honor, and I am grateful for the protection you have given me." She studied his face. "It is to be war, then?"

"Yes. On the morrow. I wanted to say farewell."

She laid one hand on his arm. "I wish you would not do this thing."

He glanced at her hand, her slender, white fingers. "Cerelinde, I must."

"No." She shook her head. "You have a choice, Tanaros. Even you, even now. Perhaps it is too late to stem the tide of battle, but it need not be, not for you. There is goodness in you; I have seen it. It is yours to reclaim."

"And do what?" Tanaros asked gently. "Shall I dance at your wedding, Cerelinde?"

The matter lay between them, vast and unspoken. She looked away. In that moment, he knew she understood him; and knew, too, that unlike his wife, the Lady of the Ellylon would never betray the Man to whom she was betrothed. The ache in his heart intensified. He laid his hand over hers, feeling for a few seconds her smooth, soft skin, then removed her hand from his arm.

"I'm sorry," he said. "I cannot."

"There are other things!" She looked back at him and starlight glimmered on her tears. "The world is vast, Tanaros. You could . . . you could help Staccia rebuild its ties to the rest of Urulat, or the Beshtanagi in Pelmar, or hunt Were or dragons or Fjeltroll—"

"Cerelinde!" He halted her. "Would you have me betray what honor I possess?"

"*Why?*" She whispered the word, searching his face. "Ah, Tanaros! What has Satoris Banewreaker ever done that he should command your loyalty?"

"He found me." He smiled at the simplicity of the words. "What has he not done to be worthy of my loyalty, Cerelinde? When love and fidelity alike betrayed me, when the world cast me out, Lord Satoris found me and summoned me to him. He understood my anger. He bent the very Chain of Being to encompass me, he filled my life with meaning and purpose."

"*His* purpose." Her voice was low. "Not yours."

"Survival." He spread his hands in a helpless gesture. "He seeks to survive. What else do any of us seek? Because he is a Shaper, the stakes are higher. I tell you this, Cerelinde. His Lordship is *here*. Wounded and bleeding, but *here*. And he has given shelter to all of us, all whom the world has bent and broken, all who yearn for a Shaper's love, all whom the world has despised. He demands our loyalty, yes, but he allows us the freedom to question the order of the world, to be who and what we are. Can you say the same of Haomane Lord-of-Thought?"

"You do not understand." Cerelinde's voice trembled. "He is . . . everywhere."

"For you, perhaps." Tanaros touched her cool cheek. "Not for me."

For a time, they stood thusly; then Cerelinde, Lady of the Ellylon, shuddered like the petals of the mortexigus flower and withdrew from his touch. Wrapped in her dark cloak, she gazed at him with her glorious eyes.

"Tanaros," she said. "I will not pray for your death on the morrow."

"Lady." He bowed low and said no more.

The Havenguard reclaimed her, and she went.

SPEROS OF HAIMHAULT FOUND SLEEP difficult.

It had all happened so *fast*. One moment, he had been concentrating on acquitting himself bravely, holding the parley-flag and assessing the forces of Haomane's Allies to report to the General; the next, he was agreeing to be a hostage.

At least they had been civil.

They were that; he had to admit. Back in the old days, when he was but a piddling horse-thief, he had never been treated with such care. The architect of Darkhaven's defense! It was a prodigious title, even if Lord Vorax had invented it.

To be honest, their triumvirate of leaders seemed to sense it; *they* were dismissive. Once they returned to the campsite, white-bearded Malthus made it clear he had greater concerns on his mind, which was just as well. Speros had no desire to find the wizard's attention focused on him. Aracus Altorus merely looked him up and down as if gauging his worth and finding it wanting. As far as Ingolin, Lord of the Rivenlost, was concerned, Speros might as well not exist.

But others were at the campsite; hangers-on, no doubt. Blaise Caveros, the Borderguard commander with an unsettling look of the General about him, took Speros to be a legitimate threat. He as-

signed a pair of guards fitting to his purported station to him; some
minor Ellyl lordling and an Arduan archer. They took turns keeping
watch over him. A woman, no less! She had a strange bow made of
black horn, which she cosseted like a babe. At nightfall she
brought him a bowl of stew from the common kettle. After he had
eaten, Speros grinned at her, forgetful of the gaps where he was
missing teeth.

"Very nice," he said, nodding at her weapon. "Where did you
get it?"

She stared blankly at him. "This is Oronin's Bow."

"Oh, aye?" He whistled. "So where did you get it?"

The archer shook her head in disgust. "You tend to him," she
said to the Ellyl, rising to survey the campsite.

"Did I say somewhat to offend her?" Speros asked the Ellyl,
who smiled quietly.

"Fianna the Archer slew the Dragon of Beshtanag with that
bow," he said. "Surely the knowledge must have reached Darkhaven's gates."

"It did." Speros shrugged. "I was in the desert at the time."

"Indeed." The Ellyl, whose name was Peldras, laced his hands
around one knee. "Your Lord Vorax spoke of your efforts concern-
ing a certain Well when he offered you into the keeping of the
Wise Counselor."

"You know it?" Speros repressed a memory of the General's
black sword cleaving the old Yarru man's chest, the dull thud of the
Gulnagels' maces.

"I do." Peldras regarded him. "You seem young and well-
favored to have risen high in the Sunderer's service, Speros of
Haimhault."

He shrugged again. "I've made myself useful."

"So it seems." Peldras raised his fair, graceful brows. "Although
I fear you may have outlived your usefulness, or Vorax of Staccia
would not have been so quick to surrender you. Did I stand in
your shoes, young Midlander, I would find it a matter of some concern. The Sunderer's minions are not known for their loyalty."

Speros thought of Freg, carrying him in the desert; of the General himself, holding water to his parched lips. He laughed out
loud. "Believe as you wish, Ellyl! I am not afraid."

"You were not at Beshtanag," Peldras murmured. "I witnessed
the price the Sorceress of the East paid for her faith in Satoris
Banewreaker, and the greater toll it took upon her people. Are you
willing to pay as much?"

"That was different." Speros shook his head. "I was in the Ways when your wizard Malthus closed them upon us. We would have aided her if we could."

"The Sunderer could have reopened the Ways of the Mara-soumië if he chose." The Ellyl glanced westward toward the shadowy peaks of the Gorgantus Mountains. "With the might of Godslayer in his hands, not even Malthus the Counselor could have prevented it. He chose instead to destroy them."

"Aye, in the hope of destroying Malthus with them!" Speros said, exasperated. "You forced this war; you and all of Haomane's Allies! Will you deny his Lordship the right to choose his strategies?"

"No." Peldras looked back at him. Under the stars, illuminated by the nearby campfire, his features held an ancient, inhuman beauty. "Ah, Speros of Haimhault! On another night, there is much I would say to you. But I fear sorrow lies heavy on my heart this night, and I cannot find it in me to speak of such matters when on the morrow, many who are dear to me will be lost."

"Did I ask you to?" Speros muttered.

"You did not." Rising, the Ellyl touched his shoulder. "Forgive me, young hostage. I pray that the dawn may bring a brighter day. Yet the world changes, and we change with it. It is in my heart that it is Men such as you, in the end, who will Shape the world to come. I can but pray you do it wisely."

Speros eyed him uncertainly, trying to fathom what trickery lay in the words. "Me?"

"Men of your ilk." Peldras gave his quiet smile. "Builders and doers, eager for glory, willing to meddle without reckoning the cost." Tilting his head, he looked at the stars. "For my part, I wish only to set foot upon Torath the Crown, to enter the presence of Haomane First-Born, Lord-of-Thought, and gaze once more upon the Souma."

Since there seemed to be no possible reply, Speros made none. The Ellyl left him then, and the Arduan woman Fianna returned. She pointed out a bedroll to him and then sat without speaking, tending to her bowstring. The scent of pine rosin wafted in the air, competing with the myriad odors of the campsite.

Speros wrapped himself in the bedroll and lay sleepless. The frostbitten ground was hard and uncomfortable, cold seeping into his bones. Oronin's Bow gleamed like polished onyx in the firelight. He wondered what sound it made when it was loosed, if echoes of the Glad Hunter's horn were in it.

At least the Ellylon horns were silenced by night, although one could not say it was *quiet*. The vast camp was filled with murmurous sound; soldiers checking their gear, sentries changing guard, campfires crackling, restless horses snuffling and stamping in the picket lines. He could make out Ghost's pale form against the darkness, staked far from the other cavalry mounts. Haomane's Allies gave her a wide berth, having learned to be wary of her canny strength and sharp bite.

There was a tent nearby where the commanders took counsel; too far for Speros to hear anything of use, but near enough that he saw them coming and going. Once, he saw it illuminated briefly from within; not by ordinary lamplight or even the diamond-flash of Malthus' Soumanië, but something else, a cool, blue-green glow. Afterward, Blaise Caveros emerged and spoke to Fianna in a low tone.

"Haomane be praised!" she whispered. "The Bearer lives."

At that, Speros sat upright. Both of them fell silent, glancing warily at him. It made him laugh. "He knows, you know," he said conversationally. "Lord Satoris. The Charred Folk, the Water of Life. There is no part of your plan that is unknown to him."

"Be as that may, Midlander," Blaise said shortly. "He cannot prevent Haomane's Prophecy from fulfillment."

"He can try, can't he?" Speros studied the Borderguardsman. "You know who you've a look of? General Tanaros."

"So I have heard." The words emerged from between clenched teeth.

"He says you're better with a sword than Aracus Altorus," Speros remarked. "Is it true?"

"It is," Blaise said in a careful tone, "unimportant."

"You never know." Speros smiled at him. "It might be. Have you seen the Lady Cerelinde? She is . . . how did the General say it? We spoke of her in the desert, before I'd seen her with my own eyes. 'She's beautiful, Speros,' he said to me. 'So beautiful it makes you pity Arahila for the poor job she made of Shaping us, yet giving us the wit to know it.' Is it not so? I think it would be hard to find any woman worthy after her."

Blaise drew in his breath sharply and turned away. "Be watchful," he said over his shoulder to Fianna. "Say nothing in his hearing that may betray us."

She nodded, chagrined, watching as the Borderguardsman strode away. Speros lay back on his bedroll, folding his arms behind his head. "Do you suppose he harbors feelings for his lord's betrothed?" he wondered aloud. "What a fine turn of events that would be!"

"Will you be *silent*!" the Arduan woman said fiercely. Her nervous fingers plucked at the string of Oronin's Bow. A deep note sounded across the plains of Curonan, low and thrumming, filled with anguish. Speros felt his heart vibrate within the confines of his chest. For a moment, the campsite went still, listening until the last echo died.

"As you wish," Speros murmured. Closing his eyes, he courted elusive sleep to no avail. Strangely, it was the Ellyl's words that haunted him. *Men of your ilk, builders and doers.* Was it wrong that he had taken fate in his own hands and approached Darkhaven? He had made himself useful. Surely the General would not forget him, would not abandon him here. Speros had only failed him once, and the General had forgiven him for it. His mind still shied from the memory; the black sword falling, the maces thudding. The old Yarru folks' pitiful cries, their voices like his grandmam's. His gorge rising in his throat, limbs turning weak.

But the General had not wanted to do it, any more than Speros had. The Ellyl was wrong about that. He did not understand; *would* not understand. Though Speros did not want to remember it, he did. The General's terrible sword uplifted, the cry wrenched from his lips. *Give me a reason!*

Opening his eyes, Speros blinked at the stars and wondered why so many questions were asked and went unanswered, and what the world would be like if they were not.

TOTAL DARKNESS HAD FALLEN BEFORE Dani and Thulu dared venture from the tunnels. They crept blindly, bodies grown stiff with long immobility, parched with thirst and weak with hunger, fearful of entering a trap.

But no; by the faint starlight illuminating the opening, the larder appeared empty of any living presence. The supplies stacked within it had been diminished, but not stripped. They fell upon what remained, tearing with cracked and broken nails at the burlap wrapping on a wheel of cheese, gnawing raw tubers for the moisture within them. They stuffed their packs with what scraps and remnants remained. The kegs of wine alone they left untouched, fearing that breaching one would leave evidence of their presence behind.

Only after they had assuaged their hunger and the worst of their thirst did they dare peer forth from the opening of the cavern onto the Vale of Gorgantum.

"Uru-Alat!" Dani felt sick. "*That's* Darkhaven?"

The scale of it was unimaginable. For as far as the eye could see, the Vale was encircled by a massive wall, broken by watch-towers. It vanished somewhere behind them, blocked by the swell of the slope, reemerging to encompass a small wood of stunted trees. A broad, well-trodden path led from the larder-cavern to the rear gates of the fortress itself. It was huge; impossibly huge, a hulking edifice blotting out a vast segment of the night sky. Here and there, starlight glinted on polished armor; Fjeltroll, patrolling the gates.

"Aye," Uncle Thulu said. "I don't suppose they're likely to let us in for the asking. Any thoughts, lad?"

Dani stared across the Vale. He could make out the Gorgantus River by the gleam of its tainted water. Other lower structures squatted alongside it, lit within by a sullen glow. He could smell smoke, thick and acrid in the air. "What are those?"

"Forges, I think. For making weapons and armor."

"Do you reckon they're guarded by night?"

"Hard to say." Thulu shook his head. "They're not in use or we'd hear the clamor. But the fires are still stoked, so they're likely not unattended. It's a long scramble, and there are guards on the wall, too."

"Aye, but they're looking outward, not inward. If we don't make any sound, move slowly, and keep to the shadow, they'll not spot us. It's the armor that gives them away. At least it would get us closer." Dani studied the fortress. Darkhaven loomed, solid and mocking, seemingly impenetrable. He wished he knew more about such matters. "There has to be another entrance *somewhere*, doesn't there?"

"I don't know." Uncle Thulu laid one hand on Dani's shoulder. "But truth be told, I've no better ideas. This time, lad, the choice is yours."

Dani nodded, touching the clay vial at his throat for reassurance. "We can't stay here forever. Let's try. We'll make for the river and follow it."

It was a nerve-racking journey. They emerged from the mouth of the cavern, abandoning the broad path to clamber down the mountain's slope where the shadows lay thickest. Both of them moved slowly, with infinite care. One slip of the foot, one dislodged pebble, and the Fjel would come to investigate.

If it had done nothing else, at least their long travail had prepared them for this moment. The inner slopes of the Gorgantus Mountains were gentler than the unscalable crags that faced outward, no more difficult to traverse than the mountains of the northern territories. They had learned, laboring atop the rock-pile, how to place their feet with the utmost care, how little pressure it took to shift a loose stone. Their night vision was honed by their time in the tunnels.

Once they reached level ground, it was another matter. Atop the incline to their right, they could see the curving shoulder of the encircling wall. The distant spark of torches burned in the watchtowers. Dani pointed silently toward the wood. Inching along the base of the slope, they made toward it. From time to time, the low tones of Fjeltroll drifted down from above.

The wood was foreboding, but the gnarled trees would provide cover and allow them to leave the wall. Dani breathed an inaudible sigh of relief when they reached the outskirts. Tangled branches, barren of leaves, beckoned in welcome. He entered their shadow and stepped onto the hoarfrosted beech-mast, grimacing as it crackled faintly beneath his feet.

Uncle Thulu grabbed his arm, pointing.

Dani froze and squinted at the trees.

There, a short distance into the wood, a ragged nest. There were others beyond it, many others. He thought of the dark cloud that had winged toward them on the plains, so vast it cast a shadow, and his heart rose into his throat.

Uncle Thulu pointed toward the left.

There was nowhere else to go. Step by step, they edged sidelong around the wood. The trick was to do it slowly, lowering their weight gradually with each step until the warmth of their bare soles melted the hoarfrost and prevented it from crackling. It seemed to take forever, and with each step Dani feared the woods would stir to life. He imagined a beady eye in every shadow, a glossy black wing in every glimmer of starlight on a frosted branch. He kept an anxious eye on the sky, fearing to see the pale light of dawn encroaching.

It seemed like hours before they had covered enough ground to put the wood between them and the wall. They backed away from it, away from the danger of sleeping ravens and waking Fjeltroll, and made for the river.

Here was open territory, unguarded. They crossed it as swiftly as they dared. The Gorgantus River cut a broad, unnatural swath through the Vale. Once, it had flowed southward down the Defile, where only a trickle remained. Lord Satoris had diverted it to serve his purposes, but it flowed low and sluggish, resentful despite untold ages at being deprived of its natural course.

And for other reasons.

They crouched on the bank, staring at the water. It looked black in the starlight, moving in slow eddies, thick as oil. An odor arose from it; salt-sweet and coppery.

"Do you reckon we can drink it?" Dani whispered.

Uncle Thulu licked his parched lips. "*I* wouldn't." He glanced at Dani. "You mean for us to get in that filth, lad?"

"Aye." He touched the flask, steeling his resolve. "The banks will hide us."

"So be it." Thulu slid down the bank.

Dani followed, landing waist deep in the tainted water. Cold mud squelched between his toes. Here, at least, they would be invisible to any watching sentries; merely a small disturbance on the river's oily surface. Lowering their heads, shivering against the water's chill, they began to make their way downstream. For all their efforts at caution, they slipped and slid, until they were wet, mud-smeared, and bedraggled, all the supplies they carried spoiled by the tainted water.

The sky *was* beginning to pale by the time they reached the buildings where the forges were housed; not dawn, not yet, but the stars were growing faint and the unalleviated blackness between them was giving way to a deep charcoal. And other obstacles, too, forced them to halt. Ahead of them on the river, a strange structure moved; a mighty wheel, turning steadily, water streaming from its broad paddles. Beyond it lay the low array of buildings; furnaces and forges, and a ramshackle structure that seemed to have been erected in haste. Despite the fact, it was the site of the greatest activity. Smoke poured from it, dim figures moving in its midst, going to and fro.

For the first time since the tunnels, Dani knew despair.

"What do you suppose that is?" Thulu whispered, leaning on the muddy bank. He sniffed the air. "Smells like . . . like a *meal*!"

"I don't know," Dani murmured. With an effort, he stilled his chattering teeth and studied the buildings. The nearest one seemed the most abandoned. He nodded at it. "We'll make for there. It may be we can find a place to hide."

"Aye, lad." Thulu extricated himself from the sucking mud. "Come on."

It was hard to move, cold as he was. Dani took his uncle's strong hand, bracing his feet against the bank and hauling himself out of the river. They shook themselves, wringing the foul water from their clothes. There was nothing to be done about the mud.

The entire place was wreathed in smoke. It did, Dani realized, smell like a meal; like roasting flesh, at once greasy and savory. His belly rumbled. Attempting to lead the way, he found himself stumbling.

"Hey!" A figure emerged from the smoke, soot-blackened and filthy, with unkempt hair and wild, red-rimmed eyes. It clutched a haunch of meat. "Lord Vorax says it's done enough for Fjel," it said in the common tongue, freeing one smeared hand to point. "Hurry, we've got to get it all moved!"

Tensed for flight, Dani stared in bewilderment as the figure—man or woman, he could not tell beneath the grime—beckoned impatiently. The slow realization dawned on him that in the dark, covered in filth as they were, no one could tell a Yarru from an El-lyl. He exchanged a glance with his uncle.

"You heard him, lad." Thulu wiped his forearm over his face, leaving a muddy smear that further obscured his features. "Lord Vo-rax said to hurry!"

Dani nodded his understanding. Keeping their heads low, they plunged into the billowing smoke to follow the beckoning madling.

Darkhaven had invited them inside after all.

EIGHTEEN

THE ARMY OF DARKHAVEN ASSEMBLED at dawn.

Tanaros scanned the scene before him with a seasoned eye. What he saw pleased him. Tens of thousands of Fjel were arrayed in orderly ranks, awaiting his command. They were eager, but contained. Vorax's Staccians, five hundred strong, were mounted and ready.

There was chaos in the rearguard where the supply-wagons were still being loaded, but he trusted Vorax would see all was in order. Beside him sat Ushahin Dreamspinner astride his blood-bay stallion, the leather case containing the Helm of Shadows wrapped in his arms.

Together, they waited.

The orange rim of the sun rose above the easternmost peaks of the Gorgantus Mountains to meet the enshrouding cloud cover above the Vale of Gorgantum, and the sound of Ellylon horns rent the air, uttering their silvery summons. The ranks stirred. Tanaros raised one gauntleted hand.

They waited.

A distant Tordenstem roared, then another.

Haomane's Allies were withdrawing.

Tanaros clenched his hand into a fist, and Hyrgolf bawled an order to the Fjel maintaining the Defile Gate. The bar was lifted. Two teams of Fjel put their backs into the task, and the massive doors, depicting the Battle of Neherinach, creaked slowly open.

"To war!" Tanaros shouted.

The long column began its descent into the Defile.

❖

Speros of Haimhault, the architect of Darkhaven's defense, was acutely aware that he was little more than baggage.

For all their unwieldy composition, the myriad companies of Haomane's Allies executed their withdrawal with a disturbing precision. Dawn broke, the horns sounded, and they were on the move.

Much of it, loath though he was to admit it, was due to Aracus Altorus. Somehow, he managed to be *everywhere* on the field; conferring with the Lord of the Rivenlost, with the Pelmaran Regents, with Duke Bornin of Seahold, with whoever commanded the knights of Vedasia and the company of Dwarfs. He was tireless. Everywhere Speros looked, there he was; a red-gold needle, stitching the army together with the thread of his will.

It was an orderly withdrawal. Companies of infantry—Midlanders, Dwarfs, Free Fishermen, Arduan archers, Pelmarans— marched stolidly, trampling the plains grass. The mounted companies—the Borderguard of Curonan, the Vedasian knights, the Host of the Rivenlost—rode at a sedate jog.

Speros rode with them, watched by his minders, the Ellyl Peldras and the Arduan woman Fianna. He was glad to be astride Ghost, whose snapping teeth kept the others at bay. He thought more than once of turning her head and fleeing, giving her free rein across the plains. No mount here could catch her, unless it was Malthus'. But if he did, it would give Haomane's Allies cause to break their bargain.

So he went with them, casting glances over his shoulder as he rode.

His heart rose when he first caught sight of Darkhaven's army, worming its way down the Defile. It was *vast.* Rank upon rank of Fjel, marching in twos. High above them, Tordenstem sentries perched on the peaks, roaring out the signal for all clear.

The vanguard reached the plains and spread out, aligning themselves to reform in precise configurations and making ready to accommodate others, who kept coming and coming. Aye, and there were the Staccians; a crack troop of five hundred, all mounted on the horses of Darkhaven, taking the left flank. There was Lord Vorax coming from the supply-train at the rear to take his place at their head, gilded armor flaming in the morning light.

And there—there was General Tanaros, astride his black mount, still and dark and ominous. *He* did not need to ride herd on a divided force. He sat tall in the saddle, bare-headed, giving orders and watching them obeyed with alacrity.

Speros grinned.

"Something pleases you, Midlander?" Blaise Caveros swerved near him.

"How not?" Speros spread his arms. "It is a fine day for a battle!"

Blaise eyed him grimly. "Haomane willing, you shall have one."

At a distance of some half a league, Haomane's Allies turned and made their stand. Speros, mere baggage, was relegated to the rearguard. Ghost was taken from him and picketed once more by wary handlers. It frustrated him, for he could see little but an sea of armor-clad backsides as the troops moved into formation.

His minders were going into battle, leaving Speros under the undignified watch of the attendants and squires who composed the rearguard. It seemed they would not fight together; Blaise was to lead the Borderguard, while Peldras would join the Host of the Rivenlost, and Fianna the Arduan force. He watched as they made a solemn farewell, standing in a circle with their right hands joined in the center. There was a story there; he wondered what it was.

The Bearer lives. . . .

Speros thought about the chase through the tunnels leading from the Vesdarlig Passage, the scent the Fjel had lost, the scent of sun-warmed strawberries he had all but forgotten. He glanced uneasily toward Darkhaven and wondered what manner of guard the General had left in place. Surely, one that would suffice; the General was no fool. Still, Speros wished he could speak to him.

There was no time. Across the plains a mighty din arose; a howl uttered by tens of thousands of Fjel throats, the clangor of tens of thousands of Fjel beating their weapons upon their shields. The horns of the Ellylon blew in answer, high and clear.

The battle was beginning.

"IT IS TIME."

Tanaros nodded to Ushahin Dreamspinner, who opened the leather case he held. The Commander General of the Army of Darkhaven lifted forth the Helm of Shadows and donned it.

Darkness descended like a veil over his vision. The sun yet shone, but it was as though it had been wrapped in sackcloth. Everything around him stood out vividly on a shadowy background. A throbbing pain seared his groin; a ghostly pain, the Helm's memory of Lord Satoris' burden. Inside his armor, Tanaros could feel ichor trickling down his thigh. Such was the price of the Helm of Shadows.

The ranks of Fjel parted to allow him passage. They were silent now, watching him from the corners of their eyes. Hyrgolf, solid, blessed Hyrgolf, met his gaze, unafraid. He saluted. Tanaros returned the salute, touching the little pouch that hung at his belt, containing the *rhios* Hyrgolf had given him.

A small kindness.

Vorax's Staccians averted their eyes. It was harder for Men. But they were astride the horses of Darkhaven, who watched him with fearless, gleaming eyes. There was Vorax at their head, saluting. The bulk of his work was done; the bargain struck, the supply-train in place. This was Tanaros Blacksword's hour.

He jogged his mount to the forefront of the army. There could be no leading from the rear, not wearing the Helm of Shadows. The black moved smoothly beneath him, untroubled by the added burden of armor it bore; armor that echoed his own, lacquered black and polished until it shone like a midnight sun. Madlings had tended to it with love. Corselet and gorget, cuisses and greaves and gauntlets for the Man. Glossy plate at the horse's chest, flanks, and neck, covering its crupper, a demi-chaffron for the head.

Black horse, black rider.

Black sword.

It glowed darkly in his vision as he drew it; a wound in the morning sky. A shard of shadow, the edge glittering like obsidian. It had been quenched in the blood of Lord Satoris himself and was strong enough to shatter mortal steel.

Tanaros drew a deep breath; past the ache in his branded heart, past the phantom pain of his Lordship's wound. He had given speeches on the training-field, rousing his troops. Now that the hour had come, there was no need. They knew what they were about. When the air in his lungs burned, he loosed it in a shout.

"Forward, Darkhaven!"

With a second roar, his army began to advance. Across the plains, the Ellylon horns answered and Haomane's Allies moved forward to meet them.

Tanaros kept the pace slow, gauging his enemy's forces. Aracus Altorus had rearranged them, placing the Arduan archers in the vanguard ahead of the Rivenlost. The move was to be expected. Darkhaven had no archers; it was not a skill to which the Fjel were suited, and Staccians disdained the bow for aught but hunting. He signaled to Hyrgolf, who barked out an order. His bannermen echoed it with sweeping pennants. A company of fleet Gulnagel shifted into place on either side of him, the muscles in their thighs bunched and ready. They bore kite-shaped shields that covered their whole bodies, and they had trained for this possibility.

What else?

Aracus had put the Vedasian knights on his right, in direct opposition to Vorax's Staccians. They formed a solid block, clad from head to toe in shining steel, their mounts heavily armored. Well-protected, but slow to maneuver. Tanaros nodded to Vorax, who nodded back, grinning into his beard. Let the Vedasians see what the horses of Darkhaven were capable of doing. No need to worry about them.

The Host of the Rivenlost was clustered behind the archers, in their midst a starry glitter that made his head ache. Malthus? Tanaros squinted. Yes, there he was among them; clad in white robes, disdainful of armor. He carried the Spear of Light upright, and the clear Soumanië shone painfully on his breast, piercing the darkness. Behind him was the Borderguard of Curonan, with Aracus Altorus and Blaise Caveros, and massed behind them, countless others; Seaholders, Midlanders, Pelmarans.

Behind the Helm of Shadows, Tanaros smiled.

Let him come, let them all come. He was ready for them. He had a legion of Fjel at his back. Ushahin Dreamspinner was among them; protected, he hoped, by Hyrgolf's Tungskulder Fjel. He was not worried. The Dreamspinner would find a way to ward himself.

The gap between them was closing. On the far side of the plains, an order was shouted. The Arduan archers went to one knee.

"Shields up!" Tanaros cried, raising his own buckler.

The air sang with the sound of a hundred bowstrings being loosed at once, and amid them was surely the sound of Oronin's Bow, a deep, belling note of sorrow. A cloud of arrows filled the sky, raining down upon their raised shields. The clatter was horrible, but the armor of Darkhaven was well-wrought and the arrows did little harm.

"Left flank, hold! Right flank, defensive formation!" Tanaros shouted. "Center, advance at my pace! All shields up!"

He could hear Hyrgolf roaring orders, knew his lieutenants and bannermen were echoing them. Tanaros nudged the black into a walk. On either side of him, the Gulnagel tramped forward behind their shields.

Slowly and steadily, the center began to advance.

This was the true test of his army's mettle; indeed, of his own. At close range, the arrows of the Arduan archers could pierce armor, foul their shields. If they kept their heads, they would hold until the last possible moment. Tanaros watched the Arduan line through the eye-slits of the Helm of Shadows. They could see it now, he could see their fingers trembling on their bowstrings. Still, any closer and he would be forced to halt.

The archers' nerve broke. A second volley of arrows sang out, ragged and discordant. Tanaros heard a few howls of pain, felt an arrow glance off his buckler. "Gulnagel, *go!*" he shouted. "Strike and wheel!"

On either side the Gulnagel surged forward, bounding on powerful haunches. They came together in a wedge; a difficult target, tight-knit and armored, driving toward the line of kneeling archers, closing the distance too swiftly for them to loose a third volley. There was shouting among Haomane's Allies as they scrambled to part ranks and allow the Arduans to fall back.

Too late. They had not anticipated so swift an attack. The wedge of Gulnagel split, wheeling along both sides of the Arduan line. They struck hard and fast, lashing out with mace and axe at the unprotected archers. Flesh and bone crunched, bows splintered. As quickly as they struck, they turned, racing back toward the formation.

A lone archer stood, loosing arrow after arrow at the retreating Fjel. The sound of Oronin's Bow rang out like a baying hound; one of the Gulnagel fell, pierced from behind. Tanaros gritted his teeth. "Left flank, on your call! Right flank, ward! Center, advance and strike!"

The horns of the Ellylon answered with silvery defiance.

Haomane's Allies had begun to regroup by the time Darkhaven's forces fell upon them; the advance of the Tungskulder and the Nåltannen was plodding, not swift. But it was steady and inevitable, and it was led by Tanaros Blacksword, who wore the Helm of Shadows.

This was not the battle he would have chosen; but it was his, here and now. Tanaros felt lighthearted and invulnerable. *I will not pray for your death on the morrow.* At twenty paces, he could see the faces of the enemy; Ellylon faces, proud and stern, limned with a doomed brightness in the Helm's vision.

Her kin; his enemy. Not the one he wanted most to kill, no. The time of the Rivenlost was ending; so the Helm whispered to him. But beyond them were the Borderguard of Curonan in their dun-colored cloaks. *He* was in their midst; Roscus' descendant, proud Aracus.

Malthus, with the Spear of Light.

At twenty paces, Tanaros gave a wordless shout and charged.

The Rivenlost gave way as he plunged into their ranks. They beheld the Helm of Shadows, and there was horror in their expressions. He broke through their line, dimly aware of them reforming behind him to meet the onslaught of the Fjel, that his charge had carried him into the thick of Haomane's Allies.

White light blazed, obliterating his Helm-shadowed vision. Tanaros turned his mount in a tight circle, striking outward with his black sword, driving down unseen weapons. He clung grimly to the pain of his phantom wound, to the pain that filled the Helm; the hatred and anguish, futile defiance, the bitter pain of betrayal. The scorching torment of Haomane's Wrath, the impotent fury, the malice fed by generation upon generation of hatred. He fed it with his own age-old rage until he heard the cries of mortal fear around him and felt Malthus' will crumble.

Darkness slowly swallowed the light until he could see.

The battle had swirled past him, cutting him off from his forces. A ring of Pelmaran infantrymen surrounded him, holding him warily at bay. Malthus the Counselor had ceded the battle in favor of the war; there, a bright spark of white-gold light drove into the ranks of Fjel.

Somewhere, Hyrgolf was roaring orders. The right flank of Fjel was swinging around to engage Haomane's Allies. Ignoring the Pelmarans, Tanaros stood in his stirrups to gaze across the field.

"Ah, no!" he whispered.

VORAX OF STACCIA PATTED HIS armor-clad belly. When all was said and done, there was nothing like the excitement of a battle to work up a man's appetite. He was glad he could rest content in the knowledge that the army was well-supplied. If nightfall came with neither side victorious, they'd all be glad of it.

At the moment, it bid fair to do just that. He watched Tanaros' charge carry him into the midst of enemy ranks and shook his head. Better if his Lordship had given the Helm of Shadows to the Dreamspinner.

The battlefield was getting muddled. In the center, Rivenlost and Borderguard were fighting side by side, pressing Marshal Hyrgolf's line in a concerted effort. The right flank was a mess, with two companies of Nåltannen Fjel wreaking havoc among hapless Midlanders.

And in front of him, the damned Vedasian knights were holding their ground. They were arrayed in a square, smirking behind their damned bucket-size helmets as though their armor made them invincible. On your call, Tanaros had ordered. Vorax sighed. If he waited any longer, he'd be faint with hunger.

"All right, lads!" he called in Staccian. "On my order. Nothing fancy; fan out, circle 'em, strike fast and regroup. Speed's our ally. Once they break formation, we'll pick off the bucket-heads one at a time." Raising his sword, he pointed at the Vedasians. "Let's go!"

Vorax set his heels to his horse's flanks. A Staccian battle-paean came to his lips as he led the charge. Five hundred voices picked it up, hurling words in challenge. Vorax felt a grin split his face. If Haomane's Allies thought their wizard had pulled Staccia's teeth, they were about to find they were sore mistaken.

Behind him, his lads were fanning out; each one astride a horse swifter, more foul-tempered, more glorious than the next. Vorax picked himself a likely target, a tall Vedasian knight with the device of an apple-tree on his surcoat.

Even as he was thinking it was considerate of the Vedasians to provide such an immobile target, the front line of their square folded inward to reveal a second company concealed within their ranks.

The Dwarfs, Yrinna's Children.

They ran forward to meet Vorax's Staccians, long spears clutched in their sturdy hands. Not spears, no; scythes, pruning hooks.

Some of the Staccians swerved unthinking. Others attempted to plow onward. Neither tactic worked. Everywhere, it seemed, there were Dwarfs; small and stalwart, too low to be easy targets, dodging the churning legs of the horses of Darkhaven and swinging their homespun weapons to terrible effect.

Horses foundered and went down, squealing in awful agony. Men who could stand struggled to gain their feet and combat the unforeseen menace. Others moved weakly, unable to rise. The Vedasian knights began to move toward the field, ponderous and inexorable.

In the midst of the impossible carnage, Vorax roared with fury, leaning sideways in the saddle, trying to strike low, low enough to reach his nearest assailant. He could see the Dwarf's face, grim and resolute, silent tears gleaming on the furrowed cheeks. Yrinna's

Child, aware of the awful price of breaking her Peace in such a manner.

Too far, out of reach.

And then he was falling; overbalanced, he thought. Too fat, too damned fat. But, no, it was his mount collapsing beneath him. Hamstrung, one knee half-severed.

They went down hard, the impact driving the breath from Vorax's body. He was trapped beneath the horse's flailing weight, unable to feel his legs. On the field, the Dwarfs were laying down their arms, bowing their heads. Here and there, overwhelmed Staccians fought in knots. A handful of Vedasian knights were dismounting to dispatch the wounded.

Vorax felt his helmet removed. He squinted upward at the faceless figure above him. It was brightness, all brightness; sunlight shining mirror-bright on steel armor. The figure moved its arms. He felt the point of a sword at his throat and tried to speak, but there was no air in his lungs.

No more bargains.

No more meals.

The sword's point thrust home.

No more.

ON THE PLAINS OF CURONAN, Ushahin-who-walks-between-dusk-and-dawn was present and not present.

His Lordship's will had placed him here for the sin of his defiance; his Lordship's will had placed a blade in Ushahin's right arm. And so he rode onto the battlefield for the first time in his long immortal life and beheld the pathways between living and dying, casting his thoughts adrift and traveling them.

Present and not present.

A squadron of Tungskulder Fjel formed a cordon around him. Twice, Rivenlost warriors broke through their line. Ushahin smiled and swung a sword that was present and not present, cutting the threads that bound their lives to the ageless bodies. What a fine magic it was! He watched them ride dazed away to meet their deaths at Fjel hands. One day, Oronin's Horn would sound for him, as it had sounded long ago when he lay bleeding in the forests of Pelmar. Today he whispered what the Grey Dam had whispered to him, *Not yet.*

There were things to be learned, it seemed, upon the battlefield.

And then death came for Vorax of Staccia, Vorax the Glutton, and the shock of it drove Ushahin into the confines of his own crippled body. One of the Three was no more.

The horns of the Rivenlost sounded a triumphant note.

Over the Vale of Gorgantum, an anguished peal of thunder broke.

TANAROS FLUNG BACK HIS HEAD and shouted, "Vorax!"

There were no words to describe his fury. It was his, all his, and it made what had gone before seem as nothing. There was no need to hold it, to feed it. It was a perfect thing, as perfect in its way as beauty and love. It filled him until he felt weightless in the saddle. The Helm of Shadows, his armor, the black sword; weightless. Even his mount seemed to float over the field of battle as he broke past the Pelmarans and plunged into the ranks of Haomane's Allies.

His arm swung tirelessly, a weightless limb wielding a blade as light as a feather. Left and right, Tanaros laid about him.

Wounded and terrified, they fell back, clearing a circle around him. What sort of enemy was it that would not engage? He wanted Aracus Altorus, wanted Malthus the Counselor. But, no, Haomane's Allies retreated, melting away from his onslaught.

"General! *General!*"

Hyrgolf's voice penetrated his rage. Tanaros leaned on the pommel of his saddle, breathing hard, gazing at his field marshal's familiar face, the small eyes beneath the heavy brow, steady and unafraid. He had regained his army.

Across the plains, combatants struggled, continuing to fight and die, but here in the center of the field a pocket of silence surrounded him. The battle had come to a standstill. Hyrgolf pointed past him without a word, and Tanaros turned his mount slowly.

They were there, arrayed against him, a combined force of Rivenlost and Borderguard at their backs. Ingolin, shining in the bright armor of the Rivenlost. Aracus Altorus, bearing his ancestor's sword with the lifeless Soumanië in the pommel. Malthus the Counselor, grave of face. Among them, only Malthus was able to look upon the Helm of Shadows without flinching away. The Spear of Light was in his grasp, lowered and level, its point aimed at Tanaros' heart.

"Brave Malthus," Tanaros said. "Do you seek to run me through from behind?"

The Counselor's voice was somber. "We are not without honor, Tanaros Kingslayer. Even here, even now."

Tanaros laughed. "So you say, wizard. And yet much praise

was given to Elendor, son of Elterrion, who crept behind Lord Satoris to strike a blow against him on these very plains, ages past. Do you deny it?"

Malthus sat unmoving in the saddle. "Does Satoris Banewreaker thus accuse? Then let him take the field and acquit himself. I see no Shaper present."

"Nor do I," Tanaros said softly. "Nor do I. And yet I know where my master is, and why. Can you say the same, Wise Counselor?"

"You seek to delay, Kingslayer!" Aracus Altorus' voice rang out, taut with frustration. "You know why we are here. Fight or surrender."

Tanaros gazed at him through the eyes of the Helm of Shadows, seeing a figure haloed in flickering fire; a fierce spirit, bold and exultant. Still, his face was averted. "I am here, Son of Altorus." He opened his arms. "Will you stand against me? Will you, Ingolin of Meronil? No?" His gaze shifted to Malthus. "What of you, Counselor? Will you not match Haomane's Spear against my sword?"

"I will do it."

The voice came from behind them. Blaise Caveros rode forward, unbuckling his helm. He removed it to reveal his face, pale and resolute. With difficulty, he fixed his gaze upon the eyeholes of the Helm of Shadows and held it there. Beads of sweat shone on his brow. "On one condition. I have removed my helm, kinsman," he said thickly. "Will you not do the same?"

Malthus the Counselor lifted his head as though listening for a strain of distant music. The tip of the Spear of Light rose, wreathed in white-gold fire, and the Soumanië on his breast sparkled.

Aracus Altorus drew a sharp breath. "Blaise, stand down! If this battle belongs to anyone, it is me."

"No." Blaise looked steadily at Tanaros. "What comes afterward is your battle, Aracus. I cannot wed the Lady Cerelinde. I cannot forge a kingdom out of chaos. But I can fight this . . . creature."

Tanaros smiled bitterly. "Do you name me thus, kinsman?"

"I do." Blaise matched his smile. "I have spent my life in the shadow of your infamy, Kingslayer. If you give me this chance . . . an *honorable* chance . . . to purge the world of its blight, I will take it."

Tanaros pointed toward Malthus with his blade. "Do you speak of honor, kinsman? Let the Counselor relinquish yon Spear."

"Tanaros," a voice murmured. He turned his head to see Ushahin Dreamspinner, his mismatched eyes feverish and bright. "There is madness in this offer."

"Madness, aye," Tanaros said quietly. "Madness to risk the Helm; madness, too, for Malthus to surrender a weapon of Haomane's Shaping while Ushahin-who-walks-between-dusk-and-dawn is afoot."

The half-breed shivered. "I do not know. Vorax's death—"

"—cries for vengeance. Let us provide it for him." Tanaros reached up to unbuckle the Helm of Shadows. Even through his gauntlets, its touch made his hands ache. Behind him, the Tungskulder Fjel murmured deep in their throats. "What say you, Counselor?"

Malthus' hand tightened on the Spear of Light. With a sudden move, he drove it downward into the earth. "Remove the Helm and lay it upon the ground, Kingslayer," he said in his calm, deep voice. "And I will release the haft and honor this bargain, if it be your will to make it."

A bargain was a fitting way to honor the death of Vorax of Staccia. Tanaros glanced around. Word had spread, and stillness in its wake. Across the plains, weary combatants paused, waiting. Some of Haomane's Allies were using the respite to haul the wounded from the field; behind their lines, figures hurried to meet them. The sturdy Dwarfs aided, carrying wounded Men twice their size. The dead lay motionless, bleeding into the long grass. There were many of them on the left flank, clad in Staccian armor.

There were no wounded Fjel to be tended. Wounded Fjel fought until there was no more life in them. There were only the living and the dead.

"Marshal Hyrgolf." Tanaros beckoned. "Order the Nåltannen to regroup, and move the second squadron of Gulnagel in position to harry the Vedasians. Tell them to hold on your orders. Give none until provoked."

"Aye, Lord General, sir!" Hyrgolf saluted.

Tanaros smiled at him. "Once I remove this Helm, I want your Tungskulder lads to guard it as though their lives depended on it. Does any one of Haomane's Allies stir in its direction, strike them down without hesitation or mercy. Is that understood?"

Hyrgolf revealed his eyetusks in a broad grin. "Aye, Lord General, sir!"

"Good." Tanaros offered a mocking bow to Blaise Caveros. "Shall we meet as Men, face-to-face and on our feet? Men did so once upon the training-fields of Altoria, before I razed it to the ground."

Color rose to the Borderguardsman's cheeks; with an oath, he dismounted and flung his head back. "Come, then, and meet me!"

Tanaros sheathed his sword and dismounted. Six Tungskulder stepped forward promptly to surround him. With careful hands, he lifted the Helm of Shadows from his head. He blinked against the sudden brightness, the disappearance of the phantom pain in his groin, the ache in his palms. Astride his foam-white horse, the Wise Counselor watched him, still gripping the planted shaft of the Spear of Light.

"What did you do to my horse, Malthus?" Tanaros called to him.

"All things are capable of change," Malthus answered. "Even you, Kingslayer."

"As are you, Counselor; for we are Lesser Shapers, are we not? Change is a choice we may make." Stooping, Tanaros laid the Helm on the trampled grass. "And yet I do not think you gave such a choice to my horse."

There was a moment of fear as he straightened; if Haomane's Allies were to betray their bargain, it would be now. But, no; Malthus had kept his word and released the Spear of Light. There it stood, gleaming, untouched by any hand, upright and quivering in a semicircle of Haomane's Allies. The eyeholes of the Helm of Shadows gazed upward from the ground, dark with pain and horror. Beyond the Tungskulder, Ushahin nodded briefly at him, his twisted face filled with sick resolve.

"So." Tanaros stepped away. A cold breeze stirred his damp hair, making him feel light-headed and free. His world was narrowing to this moment, this hard-trodden circle of ground. This opponent, this younger self, glimpsed through the mirror of ages. He gave the old, old salute, the one he had given so often to Roscus; a fist to the heart, an open hand extended. *Brother, let us spar. I trust my life unto your hands.* "Shall we begin?"

Blaise Caveros drew his sword without returning the salute. "Do you suggest this is a mere exercise?" he asked grimly.

"No." Tanaros regarded his gauntleted hand, closing it slowly into a fist. He glanced up to meet the eyes of Aracus Altorus; fierce and demanding, unhappy at being relegated to an onlooker's role. Not Roscus, but someone else altogether. "No," he said, "I suppose not."

"Then ward yourself well," Blaise said, and attacked.

NINETEEN

DARKHAVEN'S KITCHENS WERE FILLED WITH a fearsome clatter.

That was where Dani and Thulu found themselves herded once the long work of loading half-smoked sides of mutton onto the endless supply-wagons was done. It had been a long nightmare, filled with blood and smoke, the both of them staggering with laden arms along the stony trails. It seemed impossible that no one should notice them, but amid the horde of toiling madlings, they might as well have been invisible. Back and forth, back and forth, until the work was done and the army departed for the plains below.

And when it was, they were herded into the kitchens under the careless eye of a pair of Fjeltroll guards, who had larger matters on their minds. Darkhaven was buzzing like a hornets' nest; no one paid heed to a pair of filth-blackened Yarru huddled in a corner. The kitchens swarmed with such figures, swarthy with smoke and pitch and dried blood from the long night's labors.

Madlings.

Dani heard the word without understanding. In the kitchens, he understood. The inhabitants—the *human* inhabitants—of Darkhaven were mad. They had no way to cope with what transpired. It was clear to him, and to Thulu, that the bulk of Darkhaven's forces had abandoned the premises. Still, the madlings must cook; must prepare, must tend and be useful.

Pots boiled on stoves. Dishes roasted in ovens. It did not matter that there was no one to eat them. There was a kind of fearful safety amidst the mayhem, but it was not one that could last.

"Where to, lad?" Uncle Thulu whispered.

Dani, who had sunk his head onto pillowed arms, raised it with
an effort. "I don't know," he said dully. "I would ask . . . I would
ask . . ." He shook his head. "I'm tired."

Thulu regarded him. "Would you ask, lad, or *do*?"

"I don't know." Dani raked his hands through his lank black
hair. "Before . . . ah, Uncle! I wanted to *ask*. What has the Sunderer
done to the Yarru that I should seek to destroy him? And yet . . ."
He was still, remembering. *Perhaps your people would not have
been slain for your actions.* "I fear perhaps we have passed such a
point, and Malthus the Counselor had the right of it all along."

"Hey!" A figure shouted at them, glowering, brandishing a ladle
in one hand. "What idleness is this? Does it serve his Lordship?" A
platter was thrust forward, a silver salver with a dish-dome upon it.
"Here," the figure said roughly. "Take it to her Ladyship. She's been
near forgotten in the uproar. Few enough folk want to take the risk
of waiting on her now, but you'll do in a pinch."

Dani rose to his feet and took it unthinking, hunching his shoulders and ducking his head; Uncle Thulu was a step behind him.

"Well?" The cook's figure loomed. "What are you waiting for?
Go!"

They went.

Darkhaven's halls made its kitchens seem a haven of comfort.
They were massive and windowless, wrought entirely of gleaming
black stone. No gentle lamplight alleviated the darkness; only veins
of blue-white fire glittering in the walls. Cradling the tray against
his hip, Dani laid one hand upon one wall and found it warm.

"Marrow-fire," he murmured. "It must be."

"Aye, but where's the Source?"

"I don't know." Dani shook his head. "*Below*, Malthus said.
Somewhere in the depths of the earth, below Darkhaven's foundation."

"I've seen no stair." Thulu sighed. "We'll have to search, Dani.
Best we find a place to hide that tray and ourselves before our luck
runs out."

"The tray." Dani glanced at it. "For her Ladyship, he said. Do
you suppose . . ."

"The Lady Cerelinde?" Uncle Thulu whistled softly.

"She would know what to do," Dani said, for it seemed to him
it must be true. The Haomane-gaali Peldras had been wise; not as
wise as Malthus, but wise and gentle, filled with the knowledge of
his long years. Surely the Lady of the Ellylon must be no less! The
thought of laying the burden of decision on the shoulders of some-

one wiser than he filled him with relief. "All we have to do is find her."

The task proved easier than they reckoned. After a few more turns, they rounded a corner to see a quartet of Fjeltroll posted outside a door halfway down the hall. They were hulking Fjel with black, bristling hides and gleaming black armor. A madling was speaking to them; a woman.

Dani stopped with a mind to retreat. It was terrifying enough to have passed to and fro under the noses of the Fjeltroll amid a reeking crowd. This was too dangerous.

And too late.

The woman caught sight of them and raised her voice. "Time and more you came! Would you have her Ladyship starve?" She beckoned, impatient, as they stood frozen and staring. "Well, come on!"

Dani and his uncle exchanged a glance, then proceeded slowly.

For a moment, a brief moment, he thought they would get away with it. The madling woman snatched the tray from his hands, giving it to the Fjeltroll to inspect. One lifted the domed cover, and another leaned down to smell the dish. Dani began to back away unobtrusively, Thulu behind him.

"Wait." One of the Fjel guards spoke. They froze where they stood. It sniffed the air, broad nostrils widening. "These two are new," it said in its low, guttural voice. "What did the General say to do?"

Dani wished they had run, then; had run, had hidden, had never tried to find the Lady Cerelinde. The madling came toward them. Her eyes glittered with an unholy glee as she drew near, near enough that he could smell her, rank and unwashed.

"Who are you?" she asked. "Has General Tanaros been looking for *you*?"

Neither of the Yarru answered.

Slow and deliberate, the madling held up one hand and licked her forefinger, then swiped it down the side of Dani's face. He held himself still and rigid, staring at her. A layer of soot and river mud came away, revealing the nut-brown skin beneath it.

"If I were you," the madling said almost kindly, "I would run."

They took her advice, pelting down the hall. Behind them came the clamor of a laden tray falling, and the deep roar of Fjel pursuit.

❖

Meara watched the Charred Folk run. The sight made her laugh as few things did in these dire times. Lord Ushahin Dreamspinner would be proud if he were here; even *Tanaros* himself would be proud. She took a moment to imagine it—his hands on her shoulders, his dark eyes filled with fondness, a rare smile on his lips as he said, "Meara, today your deeds fill me with pride."

Of course, the Fjel had to catch them first. The thought caused her laughter to falter and vanish, replaced by a frown. She shouldn't have told them to run. She hadn't thought they really would. The Mørkhar Fjel of the Havenguard were tireless, but not swift, not like the Gulnagel.

But then, if the Charred Folk hid, the madlings could find them. Meara brightened at the thought. There was nowhere in Darkhaven anyone could hide that the madlings could not find them. Her smile was quite restored by the time the Lady opened the door.

Suddenly, Meara did not feel proud anymore.

The Lady Cerelinde looked at the silver dishes, the remains of her meal spattered over the gleaming marble floor of the hall. "Meara, what has happened here?" she asked in her gentle voice.

"Danger, Lady." She ducked her head and mumbled. "Strange Men. The Fjel will find them."

"What Men?" The Lady's voice rose when Meara remained silent. It was not harsh, no, it could never be harsh, but it held an edge as keen and bright as a sword. "Meara, what Men?"

"Charred Folk," Meara whispered, lifting her head.

The Lady Cerelinde took a sharp breath, and something in her face changed. A connection was made, a piece of the puzzle falling into place at last. It was nothing Meara understood, and yet she bore witness to it. "The Unknown Desert!" The Lady's slender fingers closed on Meara's arm, unexpectedly strong. "Come inside."

Meara followed, helpless and obedient. Behind closed doors, the Lady laid her hands on Meara's shoulders. It was just as she had imagined, only it was wrong, all wrong. No General Tanaros, no warm glow of pride. Only the Lady Cerelinde, her face filled with bright urgency. The world seemed to tilt and sway as she spoke. "Tell me about these Men. Did they come bearing anything that you might have noted? Waterskins? Vessels?"

Meara gaped at her. "No, Lady! They were . . . Men, dirty Men!"

The Lady's face changed again as hope went out of it, and it was as though someone had blown out all the lamps in the room. "Thank you, Meara," she said, releasing her.

"I'll go see about your dinner, Lady," Meara said humbly. Everything was normal and the world was no longer tilting; and yet it seemed as though something precious had been lost. A memory came unbidden and she offered it up. "The younger one did have a flask, Lady. A little one made of clay, tied on a thong around his neck."

There was a long pause, a not-daring-to-hope pause. "You're certain of this, Meara?"

She nodded, miserable. She should not have spoken.

The world spun crazily as hope returned in a blaze; brightness, brightness in the room, brightness in the Lady Cerelinde's face. The Lady was speaking, more words that rang like swords, bright and terrible, and Meara longed for the black pit to open, for the tide of gibberish to rise in her head, silencing words she did not want to hear. Anything, anything to drown out the awful charge. But no black pit opened, no tide arose. The voices were silent, driven into abeyance by the Lady's fierce glory.

". . . must find them, Meara, seek them out and find them, hide them from the Sunderer's minions! Give them what aid you may, for unless I am sore mistaken, the fate of the world rests upon their shoulders." She stooped to gaze into Meara's face. "Do you understand?"

Meara freed her tongue from the roof of her mouth to answer. "No," she whispered.

"I speak of healing the world," the Lady Cerelinde said gravely. She touched Meara, cupping her head in her fair, white hands. "All the world, Meara; Urulat and all that lies within it. Even you. All that might have been may yet be."

Fire, cool fire. Why did Haomane have to Shape such majesty into his Children? Why must it be given to us to know, to compare? No wonder Tanaros ached for her; and he did, he did. Meara knew he did. *I told him you would break our hearts.* She felt tears well in her eyes, her nose running. Ugly, unglamorous; a filthy madling, no more. She longed to wipe it, longed to break away from the horrible burden of trust in the Lady's glorious eyes.

"I can't!" she gasped. "I can't!"

"You can." Still stooping, the Lady Cerelinde touched her lips to Meara's damp brow. An oath, a promise, a lance of cool fire piercing her fevered brain. "Haomane's Prophecy is at work here. And there is goodness in you, Meara of Darkhaven. In that, I believe."

She staggered when the Lady loosed her; staggered and caught herself, staring dumbfounded as the Lady went to the tapestry that concealed the hidden passage, drawing back its bolts. So she had done once before, saving Meara from certain discovery. A debt had been incurred, returning threefold. She had not wanted it, had not wanted any of it. And yet, still it was.

Cerelinde, Lady of the Ellylon, stood upright and tall, shining like a candle in the confines of Darkhaven. She breathed a single word; but all the pride, all the hope, all the terrible, yearning beauty of the Rivenlost lay behind it.

"Please."

Stumbling and numb, wiping her nose, Meara went.

TWENTY

❖

BEHIND THE LINES OF HAOMANE'S Allies, no one was paying attention to the abandoned piece of baggage that was Speros of Haimhault.

On the battlefield, a strange hiatus had occurred; the armies had fallen back, regrouping, their attention centered on a knot of disturbance at its core. What it was, Speros could not have said. He knew only that he was forgotten. There were wounded incoming; scores of them, hundreds. Men, Men like him, and women, too, injured and groaning, carried on makeshift stretchers wrought out of spears, carried over the shoulders of hale comrades. Arduan's archers, limbs pulped by Fjel maces; Midlanders with crushed skulls, splintered ribs protruding from their pale flesh.

Such was war.

The sight made him sick and uneasy; and yet, and yet. War was war. Where did the true battlefield lie?

The smell of strawberries ripening in the sun . . .

He had promised the Lord General that he would not fail him again, and he believed he had kept his word. He had built the waterwheel, improved the furnaces, created the carefully balanced defenses above the Defile. General Tanaros had not asked him to do any of those things, but he had done them anyway and done them well. Still, he had failed anyway. Some enchantment had been at work that day in the tunnels. The Fjel had been right the first time around; the Bearer had been there.

He might still be there; or worse, seeking entry into Darkhaven.

Speros paced restlessly behind the lines, glancing over at Ghost. No one was paying her any heed, either. She met his gaze, her wicked eyes calm and bright. The picket stakes that held her were pounded loosely into the plains. A thought took shape in his mind. He drifted closer to her, waiting for one of his minders to shout at him, to order him back.

No one did.

There was no further need for him to serve as a hostage. Haomane's Allies had kept their word and withdrawn; the battle was engaged, his usefulness was ended. There would be no repercussions for Darkhaven if he failed in the attempt. The Ellyl Peldras was wrong; the General *would* come for him. Still, how much more impressed would he be if Speros proved himself in no need of rescue? And moreover, with a valuable warning to give.

I will not fail you again.

Speros took a deep breath. It would need to be done swiftly, but that was all right. He had stolen horses before. This wouldn't be much different, except that Ghost was *his* horse. He wished he had a dagger to cut the picket lines, but Haomane's Allies had taken his weapons. That was all right, too. Ghost was not an ordinary horse. She wouldn't panic.

It was a piece of luck that they had not bothered to remove her bridle; too fearful of her snapping teeth. Speros sidled close, watching her eye roll around at him. "Be sweet, my beauty," he murmured, low and crooning. "For once in your life, as you love his Lordship, be gentle."

Her ears pricked forward. With two quick yanks, Speros dragged the picket stakes from the earth. Ghost had already begun to move when he grasped her mane and hauled himself astride.

They were ten strides away from the encampment before an alarm was shouted. Speros laughed and flattened himself against Ghost's grey hide, feeling her muscles surge beneath him as she accelerated. Her neck stretched out long and low, coarse mane whipping his face. They were all shouting now, Haomane's Allies, shouting and pointing. Too late. Ghost's hooves pounded the tall grass, haunches churning, forelegs reaching, heedless of the dangling picket lines bouncing in her wake.

The plains rolled by beneath him. Speros' eyes watered. He blinked away the wind-stung tears and saw the rearguard of Haomane's Allies turning their attention toward him. A lone Ellyl horn wailed a plangent alarm. He sent Ghost veering wide around them, around their attendants still carting the wounded from the field. No hero's charge, this; no fool, he. He only wanted to warn General

Tanaros. If he could get behind Darkhaven's lines, he could send word. *Something is wrong, very wrong. Let me investigate. I will not fail you again.*

Or better yet, he would return directly to Darkhaven. There was no need to ask the General's permission. It would be better if he went himself in all swiftness. After all, if the Bearer had managed to penetrate Darkhaven's walls, there was only one place he would go—to the very Source of the marrow-fire itself. General Tanaros admired his initiative, he had told him so. He would still send word, so the General would know.

What a wondrous thing it would be if Speros of Haimhault were to avert Haomane's Prophecy!

The thought made Speros smile. He was still smiling when one of Haomane's Allies, kneeling beside a wounded Arduan archer, rose to her feet and unslung her bow, nocking an arrow. Speros' smile broadened to a grin. He reckoned he was too far away and moving too fast to be within range.

Of a surety, he was too far away to see that the archer was Fianna and the bow in her hands was wrought of black horn, gleaming like onyx. It was no mortal weapon, and its range could not be gauged by mortal standards.

Oronin's Bow rang out across the plains; once, twice, three times.

Speros did not feel the arrows' impact, did not feel the reins slip from his nerveless fingers. The earth struck him hard, but he didn't feel that, either. He blinked at the sky overhead, filled with circling ravens. He wondered if Fetch, who had saved them in the desert, was among them. He tried to rise and found his body failed to obey him. At last, he understood, and a great sorrow filled him.

"Tell him I tried," he whispered to the distant ravens, then closed his eyes. He did not reopen them, nor ever would.

Whickering in dismay, a grey horse raced riderless across the plains.

THE FIGHT FILLED TANAROS WITH a stark, pitiless joy.

There was a purity in it, one that no one who was not born and raised to the battlefield could understand. Two men pitted against one another; weapon to weapon, skill against skill. The world, with all its burdens and paradoxes, was narrowed to this circle of trampled grass, this single opponent.

He would win, of course. The outcome was not in question, had never been in question. Haomane's Allies were fools. They were so blinded by the terror the Helm of Shadows invoked that they had overlooked the other weapon he bore: the black sword, tempered in the marrow-fire and quenched in his Lordship's blood. It could shear through metal as easily as flesh, and it would do so when Tanaros chose.

Blaise Caveros was good, though. Better than his liege-lord, yes; better than Roscus had been, too. It was in his blood. He circled carefully, trying to get the sun in Tanaros' eyes; it worked, too, until a flock of ravens careened overhead, blotting out the sun like a vast black cloud. He kept his shield high, prepared to ward off blows at his unprotected head. He stalked Tanaros with patience, striking with deft precision. Tanaros was hard-pressed to strike and parry without using the edge of his blade and make a believable job of it.

The fight could not end too soon. If Ushahin had any chance of claiming the Spear of Light, it would have to last awhile. From the corner of his eye, Tanaros could see that the Dreamspinner was not where he had been; where he was, he could not say. Only that it was necessary to delay.

It helped that his skills were rusty. Tanaros had a thousand years of practice behind him, but it had been centuries since he had engaged in single combat in the old Altorian fashion. Only a single sparring match with Speros, shortly after the Midlander's arrival. He hoped the lad was well. It was a foul trick Vorax had played him, though Tanaros could not find it in his heart to fault the Staccian. Not now, while his grief was raw. After all, there had been merit in the bargain, and Haomane's Allies would not harm the lad. Their sense of honor would not permit it. Other things, oh, yes! They saw the world as they wished to believe it and thereby justified all manner of ill deeds. But they would not kill a hostage out of hand.

There was a dour irony in it, Tanaros thought, studying his opponent. There was nothing but hatred and determination in Blaise Caveros' face; and yet they looked alike, alike enough to be near kin. His son, if his son had been his, might have resembled this Man who sought his life. Quiet and determined, dark and capable.

But, no, his *son*, his wife's child, had been born with red-gold hair and the stamp of the House of Altorus on his face. Speros of Haimhault, with his irrepressible gap-toothed grin and his stubborn desire to make Tanaros proud, was more a son than that babe had ever been to him.

Blaise feinted right, and Tanaros, distracted, was almost fooled. He stepped backward quickly, catching a glancing blow to the ribs. Even through his armor and the layers of padding beneath it, the impact made him grimace. Behind him, the Fjel rumbled.

"You grow slow, Kingslayer," Blaise said. "Does the Sunderer's power begin to fail you?"

Tanaros retreated another pace, regaining his breath and his concentration. Beneath the armor, his branded heart continued to beat, steady and remorseless, bound to Godslayer's pulse. "Were you speaking to me?" he asked. "Forgive me, I was thinking of other matters."

The Borderguardsman's dark, familiar eyes narrowed; still, he was too patient to be baited. He pressed his attack cautiously. Tanaros retreated before it, parrying with sword and buckler, trying to catch a glimpse of the Spear of Light. Was there a rippling disturbance in the air around it? Yes, he thought, perhaps.

Somewhere, toward the rear of Haomane's Allies, there was shouting. Their ranks shifted; a single Ellyl horn sounded. The sound made him frown and parry too hastily. Blaise Caveros swore as his blade was notched, an awful suspicion beginning to dawn on his face.

Overhead, the ravens of Darkhaven wheeled and veered.

Three times over, Oronin's Bow sang its single note of death and anguish.

For a fractured instant, Tanaros' sight left him, taking wing. In an urgent burst, Fetch's vision overwhelmed his thoughts. Tanaros saw the plains from on high; saw the tall grass rippling in endless waves, the small figures below. Saw the lone horse, grey as smoke, her brown-haired rider toppling, pierced by three feathered shafts. Saw his lips move, his eyes close, a final stillness settle.

First Vorax, now Speros.

"Damn you!" Blinded by grief and visions, Tanaros lowered his guard. The injustice of the Midlander's death filled him with fury, *"He wasn't even armed!"*

Haomane's Allies—Haomane's Three—were looking to the south, seeking to determine what had transpired. Unwatched, unguarded, Blaise Caveros moved like a flash, dropping his sword and snatching the Spear of Light from the earth with one gauntleted hand. With a faint cry, Ushahin Dreamspinner emerged from nothingness; on his knees, his face twisted with pain, his crippled left hand clutched to his chest. He had been reaching for the Spear with it.

Too late, too slow.

Tanaros flung up his buckler, heard Hyrgolf roar, saw the Fjel surge forward. On the frozen ground, the Helm of Shadows stared with empty eyeholes. Blaise Caveros never hesitated. Hoisting the Spear like a javelin, he hurled it not at Tanaros, but at the empty Helm, hard and sure.

Light pierced Darkness.

The world exploded. Tanaros found himself on his hands and knees, deafened. He shook his head, willing his vision to clear.

It did, showing him the Helm of Shadows, cracked clean asunder, its dark enchantment broken. As for the Spear of Light, it was gone, vanished and consumed in the conflagration.

Tanaros climbed to his feet, still clutching his sword-hilt. "For that, you die," he whispered thickly, "kinsman." He nodded at the ground. "Pick up your sword."

Blaise obeyed.

There was a peaceful clarity in the Borderguardsman's dark eyes as he took up a defensive pose. He held it as Tanaros struck; a long, level blow, swinging from the hips and shoulders, the black sword shearing through metal and flesh. Cleaving his blade, slicing through his armor. Blaise sank to his knees, holding his shattered weapon. His face was tranquil, almost glad. Blood, bright blood, poured over his corselet.

He was smiling as he folded and quietly died.

Word was spreading; through the ranks of Haomane's Allies, through the Army of Darkhaven. Holding his dripping sword before him, Tanaros backed away. He stood guard over Ushahin Dreamspinner, who rose to retrieve the two halves of the broken Helm. Aracus Altorus stared at him as though made of stone, tears running down his expressionless face. Malthus the Counselor had bowed his head.

Word spread.

In its wake came wild cheers and cries of grief.

"Go," Tanaros said harshly, shoving Ushahin. "Take what remains of the Helm back to Darkhaven, Dreamspinner! You will do more good there than here." He found his mount without looking, mounted without thinking. He reached out his hand, and someone placed a helm in it. A mortal helm, made of mere steel. He clapped it on his head, his vision narrowed but unchanged.

Four Borderguardsmen had dismounted. One removed his dun-colored cloak, draping it over the body of Blaise Caveros. Together, they lifted him with care and began walking from the field. Tanaros let them go unmolested.

Aracus Altorus pointed at Tanaros with his sword. "You seal your own fate, Kingslayer. Haomane help me, I will kill you myself, enchanted blade or no."

Tanaros gave his bitter smile. "You may try, Scion of Altorus. I will be coming for you next."

Malthus the Counselor lifted his head, and the sorrow in his eyes was deep, deep as the Well of the World. But from a scabbard at his side, he drew forth a bright sword of Ellylon craftsmanship. The clear Soumanië on his breast blazed and all the horns of the Rivenlost rang forth in answer at once. Against the silvery blare of triumph a lone horn sounded a grieving descant, the tones intermingling with a terrible beauty.

From Darkhaven, silence.

When the Helm of Shadows is broken . . .

Tanaros exchanged a glance with Hyrgolf, saw the same knowledge reflected in his field marshal's gaze. He thought of the crudely carved *rhios* in Hyrgolf's den. *Not bad for a mere pup, eh, General?*

Hyrgolf smiled ruefully, extending one hand. "For his Lordship's honor, Lord General?"

Tanaros clasped his hand. "For his Lordship's honor."

On his order, the army of Darkhaven charged.

MERONIL WAS FILLED WITH THE sound of distant horns.

Lilias of Beshtanag stood before the tall windows in her tower chamber, opening them wide onto the open air to catch the strains of sound. Throughout the day, it seemed they blew without cease.

The clarion call of challenge she heard many times over; and the undaunted call of defiance. Once, there was a peal of victory, brief and vaunting; but defiance and a rallying alarum followed, and she knew the battle was not ended.

This was different.

Triumph; a great triumph, resonant with joy, and a single note of sorrow threaded through it. Haomane's Allies had won a great victory, and suffered a dire loss.

Lilias rested her brow on the window-jamb, wondering who had died.

She had been a sorceress, once; the Sorceress of the East. It was the Soumanië that had lent her power, but the art of using it she had mastered on her own merit, guided by Calandor's long, patient teaching.

It could not be Aracus Altorus who had fallen. Surely, she would sense it through the faint echo of the bond that remained, binding her to the Soumanië he bore. What victory had Haomane's Allies won, and at what cost?

A longing to *know* suffused her. Lilias clenched her fists, lifting her head to stare out the window. Below her the Aven River flowed, serene and unheeding. Around the tower, the sea-eagles circled on tilted wings, mocking her with their freedom. She hated them, hated her prison, hated the rotting mortal confines of the body in which she was trapped, bound tight in the Chain of Being.

Closing her eyes, Lilias whispered words of power, words in the First Tongue, the Shapers' Tongue, the language of dragons.

For a heartbeat, for an exhilarating span of heartbeats, her spirit slipped the coil of flesh to which it was bound. She was aware, briefly, of the Soumanië—Ardrath's Soumanië, *her* Soumanië—set in the pommel of Aracus Altorus' sword, the hilt clenched tight in his fist. She saw, briefly, through his eyes.

Blaise, dead.

The Helm of Shadows, broken.

And war; carnage and chaos and war, Men and Fjel and Ellylon swirling and fighting, and in the midst of it Tanaros Blacksword, Tanaros Kingslayer, the Soldier, looming larger than life, coming for Aracus astride a black horse, carrying a black blade dripping with Blaise's blood, a blade capable of shearing metal as easily as flesh.

No longer did it last, then Lilias was back, huddled on the floor, exhausted and sickened, trapped in her own flesh and weary to the bone. She saw again Blaise Caveros' body, limp and bloodied; felt Aracus' terror and determination, the desperate love that drove him. She remembered how Blaise had told her to look away when they passed what remained of Calandor, how he had forbidden the Pelmarans to desecrate the dragon's corpse. How Aracus had shown her Meronin's Children aboard the Dwarf-ship and treated her as an equal.

It was hard, in the end, to hate them.

"Calandor," she whispered. "Will you not guide me once more?"

There was no answer; there would never be an answer ever again. Only the echo, soft and faint, of her memory. *All things musst be as they are, little sssister.*

All thingsss.

Lilias rose, stiff and aching. The horns, the horns of the Riven-lost were still blowing, still rising and falling, singing of victory and loss, of the glory of Haomane's Prophecy and the terrible price it exhorted. And yet it seemed to her that beneath it all another note sounded, dark and deep and wild, filled with a terrible promise. It reminded her of her childhood, long, long ago, in the deep fastness of Pelmar, where Oronin the Glad Hunter had once roamed the forests, Shaping his Children to be swift and deadly, with keen jaws and amber eyes.

It sang her name.

Over and over, it sang her name.

"So be it," Lilias whispered. A weary gladness filled her. The stories that were told in Pelmar were true after all. That was his Gift; Oronin Last-Born, the Glad Hunter. She was mortal, and she was his to summon.

She could resist his call, for a time. Hours, perhaps days. She was the Sorceress of the East and her will was strong. It might be enough to tip the outcome on the battlefield . . . and yet, in her heart, she no longer believed it. The Helm of Shadows was broken. The things that Calandor had shown her were coming to pass, and while the world that followed might not be the one that Haomane's Allies envisioned, surely it would be one in which there was no place for Lilias of Beshtanag.

It would be a relief, a blessed relief, to slip the coil of mortality forever. She had tried. She had cast her die and lost, but it did not matter. Not in the end. Whether Haomane's Prophecy was fulfilled or thwarted, there was no winning for mortals in the Shapers' War.

And on the other side of death, Calandor awaited her.

There were things even the Shapers did not know.

Lilias embraced that thought as she climbed onto the window seat. She swayed there, leaning forward and spreading her arms. It was a clear day in Meronil, the white city sparkling beneath the sun. The wind fluttered her sleeves, her skirts. A sea-eagle veered away with a harsh cry, making her laugh. Far, far below, the silvery ribbon of the Aven River beckoned, flowing steadily toward the sea.

It was a relief, a blessed relief, to lay down the burden of choice.

"Calandor!" Lilias cried. "I am coming!"

She stepped onto nothingness and plummeted.

TWENTY-ONE

❖

DANI RACED DOWN THE HALLS of Darkhaven, his bare feet pounding the marble floors. Behind him, he could hear Uncle Thulu, breathing hard as they ran, accompanied by the blurred rush of their dim reflections in the glossy black walls, fractured by blue-white fire.

The sound of the pursuing Fjeltroll was like a rockslide at their backs; roaring, thudding, jangling with weaponry. But they were slow, thanks be to Uru-Alat, they were *slow!* Massive and ponderous, not like the Fjel who had hunted them in the north, driving them like sheep to the slaughter.

Still, they kept coming, tireless.

And they summoned others.

At every third corner Dani rounded, it seemed another squadron was advancing, grim and determined, forcing him to backtrack and pick another route. There were Fjel at entrances, guarding doors, joining the slow hunt. Soon, there would be no avenues left down which to flee . . . and he still had no idea how to find the marrow-fire.

Sheer desperation led him to the alcove. They had passed it once already; a tall, arched niche inset with a sculpture in high relief. He glimpsed it briefly, caught a vague impression of two vast figures struggling. When more Fjel were around the next corner, Dani doubled back, nearly colliding with Thulu, only to hear the clamor of pursuit coming from the other end of the hall.

"Here!" he gasped. "Hide!"

Suiting actions to words, he flung himself toward the alcove in a slide, skidding feet-first on the slippery floor, passing beneath the locked arms of the grappling figures, between their planted legs into the shadowy recess behind them.

There he found a small, hidden doorway, one that opened to his tug.

Scrambling onto his bruised knees, Dani grabbed Thulu's arm and hauled him into the alcove, into the narrow, hidden passage he had found. There was no time to close the door. He clamped one hand hard over his uncle's mouth, stifling his panting breath.

Together they huddled motionless, peering out of the shadows and watching the horny, taloned feet and the thick, armor-clad legs of the Fjel churn past. The parties met, with a sharp, frustrated exchange. Orders were barked and the Fjel separated, trotting back toward opposite ends of the hall, intent on further search.

When all was silent, Dani closed the door carefully and pointed farther down the passage. Thulu nodded. Clambering to their feet, they began to explore behind the walls of Darkhaven.

The air was hot and close, growing hotter the farther they progressed. The narrow, winding path, rubble-strewn, slanted downward in a shallow slope. Where it branched, Dani took the lowermost path. From time to time, he heard skittering, scrabbling sounds in the other passages, but they saw nothing. Periodic nodes of marrow-fire, emerging in thick, pulsing knots from the walls, illuminated only darkness.

Below, Malthus had said.

Surely, this was below.

Dani touched the clay vial at his throat, glancing uneasily at the walls. So much marrow-fire! If what permeated the fortress and its foundation was any indication, he could not imagine what lay at its Source. And he could not imagine how the scant mouthful of the Water of Life that remained in the vessel could have even the slightest impact upon it, beyond raising a brief puff of steam.

Your courage will be tested, young Bearer, beyond anything you can imagine.

Malthus had said that, too. At the time, Dani had accorded it little weight. It was the sort of tiresome warning Elders used to scare foolish boys into being cautious when there was an opportunity to do something worth doing, an opportunity for glory.

Later, in the barren reaches, when he had come to understand something of the true nature of the Bearer's burden, he had thought he understood it better. In the northern forests, in the terrible tunnels, he had been sure of it.

In the bowels of Darkhaven, he realized he had not even begun to grasp it.

Malthus had spoken truly. It was beyond anything he could imagine. In the stifling heat, Dani shivered to the bone. He had not expected to survive this journey, not for a long time. Still, the nearer he came to its end, the harder it was to continue.

The path grew level, the passage wider. Rounding a bend, Dani froze.

Ahead of him was a cavern; a rough-hewn chamber, enlarged by the crude efforts of many generations of human hands. Everywhere, lit candles flickered; butt-ends wedged into crevices. Writing was scratched and scrawled upon the walls, and scraps of carpet were strewn about.

In the center of the room, the madling woman who had bid them to run sat waiting for them on an overturned crate. Her hands were folded in her lap, her skirts tucked around her ankles. Beneath her lank hair, her brow shone with sweat and her gaze was fever-bright.

"You have found our place," she said to them. "I thought you would. After all, you must be a little bit mad to have come here."

Dani took a step backward, bumping into Uncle Thulu.

The madling woman shook her head. "No, not now. It's not time to run, now. Behind the walls, they are all around you. They are coming. Do you not hear?" Her mouth twisted in a rictus of a smile. *"They. We.* Will you come hither or be taken?"

"What do you want?" Dani asked cautiously.

She laughed, a harsh and terrible sound, and he realized tears were in her eyes. "Me? *Me?* Does it matter?"

"I don't know." Dani gazed at her. "Does it?"

"Yes." She whispered the word as though it hurt. "I think maybe it does. I think maybe it matters a great deal."

In the passages all around them, the sounds Dani had heard before were growing louder, drawing nearer. Scrabbling sounds, skittering sounds. Madlings, madlings behind the walls, coming for them. It didn't matter. There had never been a way back, not after coming this far. There was only forward. The madling woman beckoned. Dani took a deep breath. Reaching behind him, he found the solid warmth of his uncle's hand and clasped it hard.

Together, they entered the chamber.

❖

MEARA WATCHED THE CHARRED FOLK enter.

What do you want?

Oh, she could have laughed, laughed and laughed, while the tears streamed down her face. Such a grimy little youth! What did she want? She wanted to raise an alarm, to summon the other madlings to hurry, hurry, take them now. She wanted to whisper in the Charred lad's ear, tell him Darkhaven's secrets.

He was gazing at her with wide, dark eyes; liquid-dark, desert eyes. They should have been filled with innocence, but they weren't. There was too much sorrow, too much knowledge. If he had been a boy once, he was no longer.

The madlings could take them, take them both.

General Tanaros would be proud, so proud . . . but he had never trusted her, never *seen* her. She had offered herself to him; her heart, her body, the passion that was his Lordship's Gift to Arahila's Children. But Tanaros was a Man and a fool, wanting what he could never have. What would he do once the burst of pride faded? Turn away, forgetting Meara, longing after *her*.

The Lady Cerelinde's kiss burned on her brow.

Please, she had said.

The other Charred One watched her warily, holding the lad's hand. He looked as battered and exhausted as the lad. Clearly, they had been through much together. It was a pity. She did not want to betray them. She did not want to save them, either.

Give them what aid you may . . .

Not both of them, no. It was too much. Her head ached at the thought, splitting. She shook it hard and rose, approaching them. They stood fast, though the older tried to shield the younger. Meara ignored him, concentrating on the lad.

"You're a mess, you know," she said, trying on a tone of tenderness, a tone she might have used on a lover or a child, if things had been otherwise. Lifting a corner of her skirt, she scrubbed at the lad's face. They were almost exactly the same height. He stood very still, his narrow chest rising and falling. Dropping her skirts, she touched the clay vial that hung about his throat. It was an unprepossessing thing, crudely made, tied with a greasy thong. "Is this what his Lordship desires?"

"Yes," he said softly. "I reckon it is."

"Dani," the other said warningly.

"Dani." Meara touched his face. His skin was soft and warm, and though he was afraid, it was not her that he feared. "Is that your name?"

"Yes. What's yours?"

"Meara. Do you like it?"

He smiled. "I do."

"Why are you here, Dani?" she asked curiously.

He let go the other's hand, raising both of his and cupping them, palms together. The skin was pale, paler than the rest of him. It was marred by dirt and calluses, a myriad of scrapes and half-scabbed wounds. Still, she could discern radiating lines creasing his palms. They met, converging on the joined edges, forming a starburst.

"I am the Bearer," he said simply. "It is mine to do."

Meara nodded. She did not understand, not really; and yet, she did. Madlings heard things. The Charred lad was a piece of a puzzle, a terrible puzzle that should never be assembled. For the second time in her life, she wished the tide of madness would arise, the black pit would open.

Again, it did not happen. The Lady's kiss burned on her brow, a silvery mark, keeping the tide at bay. She had branded Meara as surely as his Lordship had branded his Three, but there was no gift in it. There was only this moment, this crux, and Meara balanced upon it as if on the edge of a blade. The splitting pain in her head intensified, until it felt as though it would cleave her very skull in twain. She wished it would.

The others were drawing nearer. Shuddering, Meara spoke.

"You are going to have to choose." The words came quickly, spilling from her lips. It was the only way to make the pain stop. "I cannot do this, not all of it. *Please*, the Lady said. And I owe her, I owe her, but I owe his Lordship, too. His Lordship and Lord Ushahin, who has always understood what we are." They did not understand, but it didn't matter. Like her, they understood enough. Meara pointed toward the far end of the chamber. "What you seek lies beyond. And in a moment, I am going to scream and betray you. One of you." She felt her face twist into a smile. "One may flee. One must stay. Do you understand?"

The Charred Folk exchanged a glance, silent.

Meara's voice rose. *"Do you understand?* Now, now, or I betray you both! You will die, the Lady will die, all of you, all of Haomane's Allies, dead, you should be dead." She swiped angrily at her weeping eyes. "Do you understand? I am breaking, broken, I cannot do this!"

The older one laid his hands upon the shoulders of the younger, speaking urgently in their tongue. His face was somber, filled with pride. So much love there! It twisted in Meara's guts like a serpent. She hated them both; hated them, hated Tanaros, hated the Lady, hated the very world that had brought her to such an im- passe. Ah, what-might-have-been! She might have been elsewhere, might have been a pretty woman in an apron, kneading dough, while a handsome man embraced her, laughing. It would have been a good life, her life, but it was not to be. It never had.

"Go," she said, grinding out the word. "Go!"

The Charred lad sent her a single glance, and fled.

Meara drew in her breath, filling her lungs. The other, the older Charred One, stood braced with his legs astraddle, waiting for what would come. There was a calm acceptance in his dark eyes.

Loosing her breath, Meara screamed.

BLINDED BY TEARS, DANI RAN.

It felt like leaving a piece of himself behind. It *was* leaving a part of himself behind. He felt the rocks of the passage tear at his skin, scraping away patches. It seemed only fair, having left the better part of himself to the madlings' mercy. He heard Meara's scream arise, awful and piercing, filled with all the pain of her di- vided soul. He heard the shrieks descend, the sound of shouting and struggling.

Uncle Thulu!

A thousand memories crowded his thoughts; Uncle Thulu, guiding and protecting him; Uncle Thulu, teaching him to hunt; Uncle Thulu, still fat, laughing as he tried to mount a horse for the first time, floundering so badly even Malthus laughed, too; Uncle Thulu, fighting Fjeltroll by the river; Uncle Thulu, carrying him on his back in the dry reaches.

What would the madlings do to him?

Better not to know, better not to think. The path sloped sharply downward. Dani navigated it blindly, feeling the way with both hands. It was hot, so hot. He dragged his forearm across his brow, clearing his vision.

There was a fissure in the earth.

It was impossibly, unfathomably deep. It had broadened and grown despite efforts to seal it. The remnants of charred beams and broken slabs of rock clung to its sides. Blue-white light blazed up- ward, casting stark shadows on the ceiling. Dani fell to his hands and knees, crawling forward to peer over the edge.

The marrow-fire roared. He had found the Source.

He felt faint and rolled onto his back, clutching the clay vial. His lips moved as he murmured the Song of Being.

There was no turning back. There had never been a way back, only forward. The drop was jagged and raw, but it would afford hand- and footholds, provided the heat did not kill him. It shouldn't. He was the Bearer, desert-born, Dani of the Yarru, whose people had endured Haomane's Wrath and learned the secrets of Uru-Alat.

Uncle Thulu had sacrificed himself for this.

Still praying, eyes clenched tight, Dani began to descend.

TWENTY-TWO

THE BATTLE WAS JOINED ONCE more.

For all his fury, Tanaros kept his wits about him. The Helm of Shadows was broken. His army was one of the last things standing between Haomane's Allies and fulfillment of the Prophecy, and he would take no careless risks. With deliberate forbearance, he let the Fjel charge precede him and sow chaos in the ranks of Haomane's Allies. The Tungskulder waded among them, roaring, laying about with axe and mace.

Men and Ellylon alike fell beneath their onslaught; unhorsed, wounded, trampled. Tanaros smiled grimly. On the left flank, his Gulnagel essayed sorties against the Vedasian knights, striking and wheeling as he had taught them. On the right flank, the Nåltannen were wreaking havoc amid the motley infantry.

But Aracus Altorus was no fool. Wheeling his mount, he shouted orders. His troops rallied, changing tactics. On the front line, fleet riders of the Rivenlost and the Borderguard dodged and swerved, striking at the slow Tungskulder with quick, slashing blows until Hyrgolf was forced to order his Fjel to regroup in a tighter defensive formation. The Dwarfs had retired from the field, but a handful of archers remained in the fray, and these Aracus moved to his right, slightly behind the front lines, setting them to picking off stray Gulnagel. Malthus the Counselor was everywhere, his white Soumanië a beacon of hope.

Still, Tanaros thought, the edge was his.

Darkhaven's army was too strong, too well trained. The Borderguard and the Host of the Rivenlost might stand against them, but the others—the Seaholders, the Midlanders, the Free Fishermen—were slowly being slaughtered. Even the Pelmarans, flush from victory in Beshtanag, and the Vedasian knights in their heavy armor, had not reckoned with the awesome might of the Fjel.

They fought so beautifully! The sight of them filled Tanaros with fierce pride. They kept their shields high, they held their formations, pressing forward, slow and inexorable. What a thing it would be, what a glorious thing, if Haomane's Prophecy were yet to be averted—by this, by strength of arms, by dint of long training. Lord Satoris had not *sought* this war. Haomane's Allies had pressed it upon him the moment Cerelinde agreed to wed Aracus Altorus. But he had prepared for it for many long years.

As had Tanaros. And though there was little room in his heart for hope, he meant to try nonetheless. He owed Lord Satoris no less.

If Aracus Altorus died, there could be no victory for Haomane's Allies. Not now, nor ever. There would be no Son of Altorus left living to wed a Daughter of Elterrion. No more royal Altorian bloodline tainted with the betrayal of Tanaros Caveros' faithless wife.

The sun was high overhead, moving toward the west. How long had the battle lasted? Hours, already. And yet, Tanaros felt no weariness. His mind was clear and keen, as though all his anger, all his grief, had been distilled into a single point of brightness. All he needed was an opening, a single opening.

Tanaros watched his enemies tire as the euphoria of their brief victory faded. The Rivenlost showed no sign of slowing, but the battle was taking its toll on the Men. Their faces were white with exhaustion, their horses lathered. The battlefield stank of blood and ordure.

When the Borderguard began to falter, Tanaros signaled to Hyrgolf.

His field marshal roared orders in the Fjel tongue, and his lieutenants and bannermen conveyed them. On the right flank, a banner rose and dipped in acknowledgment. Two squadrons of Nåltannen abandoned their careful discipline and plunged into the ranks of Haomane's Allies, cutting a swath through the infantry to mount a rear attack on the combined forces of the Borderguard and the Rivenlost.

Tanaros saw Aracus Altorus turn to meet this new threat and signaled again. With a mighty roar, the Tungskulder forged forward, and Tanaros with them.

In this new surge of chaos, it was all hand-to-hand fighting. The battle lines had crumbled. The black sword sang as Tanaros cut his way through the Rivenlost vanguard. An Ellyl warrior was in his path, his shining armor smeared with mud and gore. Tanaros swung his blade, felt it bite deep, and continued without pausing, letting the black horse carry him past, deeper into the fray.

Pennants were all around him; not signal-banners, but the standards of the Rivenlost, carried high above the mayhem, still proud, still glittering. Tanaros ignored them, keeping his gaze fixed on one that lay beyond: no Ellyl badge, but a gilt sword on a field of sable, the arms of the ancient Kings of Altoria.

"Aracus!" he shouted. "Aracus!"

The pennant turned in his direction.

More Ellylon, seeking to assail him on either side. Tanaros slashed impatiently at the one on his right, took a sharp blow to the shoulder from the other, denting his spauldron; and then one of the Tungskulder was there, dragging the Ellyl from the saddle by sheer force. The Tungskulder grinned at his General, then grunted as the unhorsed Ellyl lunged upward, his blade piercing a gap in his armor.

No time for sorrow. Tanaros plunged onward; toward the Altorian banner, toward the dun-grey cloaks of the Borderguard of Curonan.

"Aracus Altorus!"

And he was there, waiting, his standard-bearer beside him. His Men had turned back the Nåltannen attack. It had been a costly diversion, but worthwhile. Tanaros reined his mount, saluting with his sword. "Aracus."

"Kingslayer." The word was filled with unutterable contempt. Behind the eyeslits of his helm, Aracus Altorus stared at him. The sword in his hand echoed the one on his standard; his ancestor's sword. Once upon a time, Tanaros had known it well. The only difference was the lifeless Soumanië in its pommel. "You come at last."

"As I promised, Son of Altorus," Tanaros said softly.

Aracus nodded, taking a fresh grip on his sword-hilt. Beneath the contempt, he looked tired and resolute. It seemed like a very long time since they had first laid eyes on one another in the shattered nuptial ceremony in Lindanen Dale. "Shall we put an end to it?"

Tanaros inclined his head. "Nothing would please me more, Son of Altorus."

There should have been more to say, but there wasn't.

Settling their shields, they rode at one another.

They struck at the same instant, both catching the blows on

their bucklers. Tanaros felt the impact jar his arm to the shoulder. He felt, too, Aracus' buckler riven beneath the force of his blow, metal plate giving way, wood splitting. Tanaros laughed aloud as the would-be King of the West was forced to discard his useless shield.

"Shall it be now?" Tanaros asked, and without waiting for a reply, struck another blow.

Aracus Altorus parried with his ancestral sword, the sword Altorus Farseer had caused to be forged, the sword Roscus Altorus had borne before him long ago. A symbol, nothing more. It shattered in his grip, leaving him clutching the useless hilt with its curved tangs and dull Soumanië, a few jagged inches of steel protruding from it.

He lifted his bewildered gaze. He had believed, somehow, it would not happen.

Tanaros had thought to taunt him, this Man who sought to wed the Lady of the Ellylon, who sought to destroy Lord Satoris. He had thought to find satisfaction in this moment; and yet, having reached it, he found none. Aracus' gaze reminded him too much of Roscus' at the end; dimly surprised, uncomprehending.

He hadn't found it in killing Roscus, either.

"I'm sorry," he said, raising the black sword for the final blow. There was no choice here, only duty. "But you brought this upon yourself."

At that moment, the Soumanië in the pommel of Aracus Altorus' shattered sword blazed wildly into life.

HALFWAY UP THE DEFILE PATH, Ushahin felt it happen.

The world gave a sickening lurch and his mount staggered beneath him. An unaltered Soumanië, with the power to Shape matter, had passed to a new owner. Ushahin's vision veered crazily, and he saw the Defile loom beneath him, pebbles skittering beneath his blood-bay stallion's scrabbling hooves, bouncing down the crags toward the riverbed below.

He righted himself with an effort that made every ill-set bone in his body ache, twisting in the saddle to glance behind him.

It was bad.

The tide of battle was shifting, surging against them. The horns, the damned Ellylon horns, were raised in their clarion call, echoing and insistent. Everywhere, figures were reeling; the very *earth* was in motion, the plains lifting in a vast, slow surge, rippling like a wave.

Ushahin tasted bile.

"Oh, my Lord!" he whispered. "You should have let me kill her!"

It was not too late, not yet. Lashing the blood-bay stallion with his reins, Ushahin raced toward Darkhaven.

TANAROS' FINAL BLOW NEVER LANDED.

For the space of a few heartbeats, they simply stared at one another, wide-eyed and astonished, the Soumanië blazing between them. Then Aracus Altorus whispered a word and the world erupted in rubescent light.

The earth surged and Tanaros found himself flung backward, losing ground, half-blinded and lurching in the saddle as his mount squealed in rage and fought to remain on its hooves. In some part of him, Tanaros understood what must have happened. Somehow, somewhere, the Sorceress Lilias had died; the Soumanië's power was passing to its wielder: Aracus Altorus, who had been mentored by Malthus the Counselor, whose reserves of inner strength the Soumanië required had never been tapped.

In that instant, everything changed.

Haomane's Allies knew it. The horns of the Rivenlost rang out joyously, maddeningly. New vigor, new *hope* infused them, gave them strength. They had a new ally. The very plains themselves rose up in rebellion against the Army of Darkhaven; churning, fissuring.

And in the center of the battlefield, Aracus Altorus sat astride his mount, untouchable, both hands clasped around the hilt of his shattered sword. He had removed his helm to afford a clearer field of vision, and in the wash of ruby light pouring from the Soumanië, his face was at once agonized and transcendent. Malthus had reached his side in a flurry of white robes, was lending him strength and counsel.

And Ingolin, Lord of the Rivenlost, was rallying his troops.

All the hatred Tanaros had been unable to summon on the verge of dealing Aracus his death blow returned tenfold. With no thought in his mind but finishing the job, he spurred his mount back toward Aracus.

It was to no avail. His Lordship's brand afforded protection against the Soumanië itself, but the earth rose against him in waves, softened beneath him. At twenty paces away, his mount floundered, sunk to its hocks.

Malthus the Counselor gazed at him, grave and implacable.

Tanaros could draw no closer.

With a curse, he wrenched his mount's head around; and cursed again to see what transpired on the battlefield. The surging earth favored Haomane's Allies, bore them up. The infantry massed against his Nåltannen, whose numbers had been decimated by the charge Tanaros had ordered. Somewhere, Oronin's Bow was singing; mired Gulnagel twisted futilely, raising their shields as the archers circled. Riding the crest of its waves, the Rivenlost fell upon the Tungskulder. Still floundering, Tanaros was forced to watch as the Host of the Ellylon rode down his beloved Fjel.

"Hyrgolf!"

The word escaped him in a raw gasp. Hyrgolf knew what had happened, what *was* happening. He had chosen to meet the charge and buy time for his lads. He stood bravely, knee-deep in a sudden mire, baring his eyetusks in a fierce grin. It took four Ellylon to bring him down, and one was Lord Ingolin himself, who struck the final blow. With a peaceful sigh, Hyrgolf died, measuring his length on the trampled grass of the plains, the last ounces of his life bubbling from his slashed throat.

Tanaros swore, laying about him on either side with his black sword at the warriors who came for him. He gouged his mount's flanks with his heels, driving it mercilessly onto solid land. He rode unthinking, swerving to follow the shifting crests, killing as he went.

"Retreat!" he bellowed, seizing the nearest Fjel, shoving him toward home. "Retreat to Darkhaven!"

Overhead, the ravens screamed and wheeled.

Someone took up the call, then another and another. *"Retreat! Retreat! Retreat!"*

It was not in the nature of the Fjel to retreat. Some obeyed, the ragged ends of Tanaros' discipline holding true. Elsewhere, it frayed at last and Fjel stood, fighting until the end, dying with bitter, bloody grins. And then there were many, too many, trapped by the treacherous earth, who had no choice but to fight and die.

Tanaros wept, unaware of the tears trickling beneath the faceplate of his helm, mingling with his sweat. On the far outskirts of the battlefield, he took a stand, watching the staggering columns of Fjel file past. The earth was stable here; even with Malthus' aid, Aracus' strength extended only so far.

It had been far enough.

The horns of the Rivenlost sounded and a company detached to ride in pursuit of the fleeing remnants of Darkhaven's army.

They came swiftly, carrying their standards high, armor glittering beneath the mire, dotted here and there with the dun-grey cloaks of the Borderguard. And at the forefront of them all was the argent scroll of the House of Ingolin the Wise, Lord of the Rivenlost.

"Go!" Tanaros shouted at the retreating Fjel. "Go, go, *go!*"

They went at a stumbling jog, slow and wounded, passing the supply-trains that Vorax of Staccia had so diligently mustered. Useless, now. Tanaros pushed the memory aside and glanced at the sky. "One last kindness," he whispered, trying to catch Fetch's winged thoughts. "One last time, my friend."

Turning his mount, he charged the oncoming company. The black horse of Darkhaven was not the mount he had trained for many years, but it had born him willingly into battle and it ran now with all the fearlessness of its proud, vicious heart.

A dark cloud swept down from the sky.

Wings, all around him, black and glossy. It was like being in the center of the Ravensmirror, save that the path before him was clear. In front of him, Tanaros saw alarm dawning on the faces of his enemies. And then the ravens were among them, clamoring, obscuring their vision, wings battering, claws scrabbling.

In the chaos, Tanaros struck once, hard and true. Blue sparks flew and metal screeched as his black sword pierced bright Ellylon armor, sinking deep, deep into the flesh below.

"For Hyrgolf," he whispered, wrenching his blade free.

He did not linger to watch the Lord of the Rivenlost die, though the image stayed with him as he wheeled and raced toward the Defile; Ingolin's eyes, fathomless and grey, widening in pain and sorrow, the light of Haomane's regard fading in them. Behind him, the horns went silent and a great cry arose from the Host, echoed mockingly by the rising ravens.

From Darkhaven, nothing.

Fear, true fear, gripped Tanaros, then. Beneath his armor, the brand on his chest felt icy. Worse blows even than this could be dealt against Darkhaven. He remembered his Lordship's voice, low and strange. *He is coming, Tanaros Blacksword. They are all coming, all my Elder Brother's little puppets. . . .*

At the base of Defile's Maw, he caught up with the Fjel and shouted, "Follow as swiftly as you can! I go to his Lordship's aid!"

They nodded wearily.

Tanaros glanced behind him. A handful of Ellylon warriors remained with their fallen Lord. The rest were coming, swift and deadly, with hearts full of vengeance. The Defile could be sealed against them; but it would take time for the slower Fjel to get clear, more time than their pursuers allowed. He looked back at his lads, stolid and loyal, even in defeat. "Defile's Maw must be held. Who among you will do it?"

Twelve Tungskulder stepped forward without hesitation, saluting him. "For as long as it takes, Lord General, sir!" one said.

"Good lads." Tanaros' eyes burned. "I'm proud of you."

Spurring his black horse, he plunged into the Defile.

THE HAVENGUARD WERE SLOW TO open the Defile Gate.

Ushahin shouted with rare impatience; to no avail, for it took two teams of Fjel to shift the gates and one team was absent. Something had passed within the fortress, something that had the Havenguard in an uproar.

A bitter jest, to be powerless before mere stone, while on the plains below, a Man, a stupid mortal brute of an Altorus, wielded the power to Shape matter itself. Ushahin shivered in the saddle, wrapping his arms around the case that held the sundered Helm of Shadows and waiting.

He saw the ravens return, pouring like smoke above the Defile. He knew, then, that the army would follow and prayed that Tanaros would stay with them, would be a good commander and remain with his troops.

But, no; Tanaros Blacksword was one of the Three. Like Ushahin, he knew too well where danger lay at the end. As the Defile Gate began to creak open at last, hoofbeats sounded. And then the General was there, blood-spattered, the black blade naked in his fist.

"Dreamspinner," he said. "There is a thing that must be done."

Ushahin raised his head, daring to hope. "The Lady—"

"Damn the Lady!" Tanaros' voice cracked. "She's a pawn, nothing more!" Removing his borrowed helm, he passed a vambraced forearm over his face. For an instant, Ushahin imagined that he wiped away tears. "You were right," he said in a low tone. "The foundation . . . the foundation is crumbling, and Ushahin, I think he's coming. The Bearer. It's all happened, piece by piece. And I need to stop him."

"All we *need* to do—" Ushahin began.

"They're *coming*, Dreamspinner!" Tanaros took a deep breath. "We have to seal the Defile. Rally the Tordenstem, get them to those ricks Speros built. They won't think to do it on their own, they'll need orders. My lads' lives depend on it, those that are left."

"Tanaros," Ushahin said, shifting the case in his arms. "With the Soumanië, Aracus Altorus can—"

"Time," Tanaros said abruptly. "Aracus is a mortal Man, he can only do so much. It will purchase time, Ushahin! And lives, too; my *lads'* lives. I beg you, don't let all their sacrifices be in vain." A muscle in his jaw twitched. "And I pray you, do not make me do more than beg."

The Defile Gate stood open. They stared at one another.

"All right, cousin," Ushahin said gently. "You know well that I lack the strength to oppose you. For the moment, I will do your bidding. And afterward, in this *time* we have earned, you will heed my words."

"My thanks, Dreamspinner." Tanaros extended his free hand.

Ushahin clasped it with his right hand, his strong, healed hand. "Go, then, and protect the marrow-fire! I will see your Fjel home safely, all those who remain."

Together, they passed through the Defile Gate.

Ushahin watched Tanaros lash his mount, sprinting for the fortress. He shook his head as he turned the blood-bay stallion's course toward the high path along the Defile, thinking of the Grey Dam Sorash, who had raised him as her own, who had given her life to this venture.

It was folly, all folly. Yet he knew well, too well, the cost Tanaros bore this day.

Forgive me, Mother, he thought.

The Tordenstem were glad to see him; pathetic, bounding like dogs, squat, boulder-shaped dogs. Everything had gone wrong, confusing them. Ushahin sighed, riding to the verge of the crags where the easternmost rick was stationed and peering over the edge.

Tanaros' Fjel were coming, a straggling line of them. It shocked him to see how few they were, how slowly they moved. At the Defile's Maw, a scant dozen had made a stand, barring the path to Haomane's Allies, there where it was narrow enough to be defended. They were wielding maces and axes to deadly effect, roaring in defiance.

"Tan-a-ros! Tan-a-ros!"

It wouldn't last. A spark was moving on the plains; a red spark, a Soumanië, twinned with a diamond-brightness. Aracus Altorus was coming, and Malthus the Counselor with him. They were all coming, all of Haomane's Allies.

Ushahin sighed again. "How did it come to this?"

Levers in hands, the Tordenstem exchanged confused glances. "Boss?"

"Pay me no heed." Ushahin shook his head, impatient. "On my word, make ready to loose the first rockslide."

"Aye, boss!" They positioned their levers.

Ushahin watched, raising one hand. The Fjel were hurrying, hurrying as best they could. Aracus Altorus had arrived at the base of the Defile. He forged a swath through Haomane's Allies, his Soumanië flashing. Malthus the Counselor was at his side. The path began to crumble beneath the Tungskulder defenders' feet.

"Tell the others to hurry," Ushahin murmured to the Tordenstem.

One filled his lungs, his torso swelling. *"Snab!"* he howled. *"Snab!"*

The Fjel column hurried, even as the defenders began to fall and die, and Haomane's Allies to push past them. Not daring to wait, Ushahin let his hand drop. "Now!" he cried.

The Tordenstem heaved on their levers. Rocks tumbled, boulders fell, all in a great rumbling rush, bouncing down the crags, blocking the Defile.

For a time.

Below, the red spark of the Soumanië gleamed, and pebbles began to shift, slow and inexorable.

For a third time, Ushahin sighed. "Let us go to the next station. Perhaps this time we can manage to crush a few of Haomane's Allies."

There was scant consolation in the thought, but at least it would take him a step closer to Darkhaven. Glancing uneasily toward the fortress, Ushahin prayed that it would not be too late, that it was not already too late. He remembered the Delta and the words of Calanthrag the Eldest.

Yet may it come later than sssooner for ssuch as I and you. . . .

In his heart, he feared it had not.

TWENTY-THREE

◆◆◆

TANAROS STRODE THROUGH DARKHAVEN LIKE a black wind.

The shock of his arrival rippled through the fortress with a palpable effect. The Havenguard hurried from far-flung quarters of Darkhaven to meet him, falling over one another in their haste. His abrupt, awful news shocked them into momentary silence, and he had to shout at them twice before they were able to tell him what had transpired in his absence.

Two Men, Charred Folk, madlings caught one . . .

He wasted precious minutes hurrying into the dungeon, clattering down the slippery stair, hoping against hope to see the Man the madlings had caught. It gave him an unpleasant echo of the memory of Speros, hanging in chains, grinning crookedly with his split lips. Not Speros, no; not the Bearer, either. It was the other Yarru, his protector. Manacled to the wall, scratched and beaten and bloodied, he hung limp, lacking the strength to even stir. The Fjel had not been gentle. Only the slight rise and fall of his scarred torso suggested he lived.

"Where's the boy?" Tanaros asked, prodding him. *"Where's the boy?"*

Unable to lift his head, the prisoner made a choked sound. "Slayer," he said in a slow, thick voice. "Where do you think?"

Tanaros cursed and ran from the dungeon, taking the stairs two at a time.

He made his way behind the walls, through the winding passages, through the rising heat, to the chasm. To the place he had known he must go. The madlings had scattered, abandoning the places behind the walls, hiding from his fury, from the terrible news. There was only the heat, the light-shot darkness, and the chasm like a gaping wound.

There, he gazed over the edge.

Far below, a small, dark figure was descending laboriously.

Straightening, Tanaros shed his gauntlets. With deft fingers, he unbuckled the remainder of his armor, removing it piece by piece. When he had stripped to his undertunic, he replaced his swordbelt, then lowered himself into the chasm and began to climb.

It was hot. It was scorchingly, horribly hot. The air seared his lungs, the blue-white glare blinding him. Narrowing his eyes to slits, Tanaros willed himself to ignore the heat. It could be done. He had done it in the Unknown Desert. He was one of the Three, and it could be done.

Fear lent his limbs speed. Hands and feet moved swift and sure, finding holds. He took risks, careless risks, tearing and bruising his flesh. The worst thing would be to fail for being too *slow*, to be halfway down and find the marrow-fire suddenly extinguished.

It did not happen.

Reaching the bottom, Tanaros saw why.

The Source, the *true* Source, lay some paces beyond the chasm itself. It was not so large, no larger than the circumference of the Well of the World. Indeed, it was similar in shape and size; a rounded hole in the foundation of the earth itself.

But from it, the marrow-fire roared upward in a solid blue-white column. High above, at its core, a spit of flame vanished through an egress in the ceiling. The Font, Tanaros thought, realizing he was beneath his Lordship's very chambers. Elsewhere, the marrow-fire fanned outward in a blue-white inferno, flames illuminating the chasm, licking the walls, sinking into them and vanishing in a tracery of glowing veins.

And at the edge of the Source stood the Bearer.

It was the boy, the Charred lad he had seen in the Marasoumië. He had one hand on the clay vial strung about his throat and a look of sheer terror on his face. Even as Tanaros approached, he flung out his other hand.

"Stay back!" he warned.

"Dani," Tanaros said softly. He remembered; he had always been good with names, and Malthus the Counselor had spoken the boy's. So had Ngurra, whom he had slain. "What is it you think to do here, lad?"

Despite the heat, the boy was shivering. His eyes were enormous in his worn face. "Haomane's will."

"Why?" Tanaros took a step closer. The heat of the column was like a forge-blast against his skin. "Because Malthus bid you to do so?"

"In the beginning." The boy's voice trembled, barely audible above the roaring of the marrow-fire. "But it's not that simple, is it?"

"No." Something in the lad's words made Tanaros' heart ache, longing for what-might-have-been. In a strange way, it was comforting to hear them spoken by an enemy. It was true, after all was said and done, they were not so different. "No, lad, it's not." He drew a deep breath, taking another step. "Dani, *listen*. You need not do this. What has Haomane done that the Yarru should love him for it and do his bidding?"

The boy edged closer to the Source. "What has Satoris the Sunderer done that I should heed his will instead?"

"He left you in peace!" Tanaros said sharply. "Was it not enough? Until—" His voice trailed off as he watched the boy's expression change, terror ebbing to be replaced by profound sorrow. Somehow, the boy knew. The knowledge lay there between them. In the roaring marrow-fire, it seemed Tanaros heard anew the pleas and cries of the dying Yarru, the sound of Fjel maces crunching. And he knew, then, that whatever conversation he might have hoped to hold with the lad, it was too late.

"Did you kill them yourself?" Dani asked quietly.

"Yes," Tanaros said. "I did."

The dark eyes watched him. "Why? Because Satoris bid you to do so?"

"No." Gritting his teeth, Tanaros drew his sword and drew within reach of the boy. "I begged him. Old Ngurra, the old man. *Give me a reason!* Do you understand, lad? A reason to spare his life, his people; a reason, any reason! Do you know what he said?"

Dani smiled through the tears that spilled from his eyes, glittering on his brown skin. "Aye," he whispered. "Choose."

"Even so." Tanaros nodded. "And I am sorry for it, as I am sorry for this, but his Lordship did not ask for this battle and I have a duty to do. Now remove the flask, and lay it gently upon the stone, Dani. *Gently.*"

The boy watched the rising arc of the black sword and his dark eyes were like the eyes of Ngurra, filled with knowledge and regret. "I will ask you what you asked my grandfather," he said. "Give me a reason."

"Damn you, I don't *want* to do this!" Tanaros shouted at him. "Is your *life* not reason enough? Relinquish the flask!"

"No," Dani said simply.

With a bitter curse, Tanaros struck at him. The black blade cut a swathe of darkness through the blinding light. Loosing his grip on the flask, Dani flung himself backward, teetering on the very edge of the Source, almost out of reach. The tip of Tanaros' sword shattered the clay vessel tied around the lad's throat, scoring the flesh beneath it.

Fragments of pit-fired clay flew asunder.

Water, clear and heavy, spilled from the shattered flask; spilled, glistening, in a miniature torrent, only to be caught in the Bearer's cupped palms.

The Water of Life.

Its scent filled the air, clear and clean, heavy and mineral-rich, filled with the promise of green, growing things.

There was nothing else for it; no other option, no other choice. Only the slight figure of the Bearer silhouetted against the blazing column of blue-white fire with the Water of Life in his hands, his pale, scarred palms cupped together, holding the Water, the radiating lines joining to form a drowned star.

"I'm sorry," Tanaros whispered, and struck again.

And Dani the Bearer took another step backward, into the Source itself.

HE FELT THEM DIE, ALL of them.

So many! It should not have mattered, not after so long; and yet, he had imbued so much of himself in this place. This place, these folk, this conflict. An infinite number of subtle threads bound him to them all; threads of fate, threads of power, threads of his very dwindling essence.

Godslayer hung in the Font of the marrow-fire, pulsing.

It tempted him. It tempted him well nigh unto madness, which was a cruel jest, for he had been losing that battle for many a century.

One of the first blows had been the hardest. Vorax of Staccia, his Glutton. One of his Three, lost. Oh, he had roared at that blow. The power that had stretched the Chain of Being to encompass the Staccian was broken, lost, bleeding into nothingness. Ah, he would miss Vorax! He was all the best and worst of Arahila's Children combined; tirelessly venal, curiously loyal. Once, long ago, Vorax of Staccia had amused him greatly.

He would miss him.

He would miss them all.

Their lives, the brief lives—Men and Fjel—blinked out like candles. So they did, so they had always done. Never so many at once. Many of them cried his name as they died. It made him smile, alone in his darkness, and it made him gnash his teeth with fury, too.

Godslayer.

He remembered the feel of it in his palm when he'd taken to the battlefield ages ago. Striding, cloaked in shadow, blotting out the sky. Pitting its might against Haomane's Weapons, his vile Counselors with their bloodred pebbles of Souma. There had been no Three, then; only the Fjel, the blessed Fjel.

And they had triumphed. Yet it had been a near thing, so near. Already, then, he had endured many long ages sundered from the Souma, wounded and bleeding. An Ellyl sword, stabbing him from behind. He had dropped the Shard. If the courage of Men had not faltered, if a Son of Altorus had not sounded the retreat too soon . . .

His hand was reaching for Godslayer. He made himself withdraw it.

It was the one thing he dared not do, the one thing he *must* not do. He was weaker now, far weaker, than he had been. If he risked it, it would be lost. The Counselor would reclaim it in his brother's name, and Haomane would Shape the world in his image. That was the single thread of sanity to which he clung. He made himself remember what had gone before. The Souma, shattering. Oronin's face as he lunged, the Shard glittering in his fist.

A gift for his Gift.

He had called the dragons, and they had come. Ah, the glory of them! All the brightness in the world, filling the sky with gouts of flame and winged glory. No wonder Haomane had Sundered the earth to put an end to it. But what a price, what a terrible price they had all paid for the respite.

There would be no dragons, not this time.

He waited to see who would come instead.

Outside, the story retold itself, writing a new ending. The Helm of Shadows, that once he had claimed and bent to his own ends, was broken. The Counselor's Soumanië was clear, clear as water. The Son of Altorus did not flee, but wielded a bloodred pebble of his own. A weary lad carried a grimy clay vessel into the depths of Darkhaven itself. His faithful ones, his remaining minions, raced desperately to prevent them.

They were coming, they were all coming.

And there was naught to do but wait; wait, and endure. Per-

haps, in the end, it was as well. He was weary. He was weary of
the endless pain, weary of meditating upon the bitterness of betrayal, weary of the burden of knowledge, of watching the world
change while everything he had known dwindled and passed from
it, while he diminished drop by trickling drop, stinking of ichor and
hurting, always hurting; hurting in his immortal flesh, aching for his
lost Gift, diminishing into madness and hatred, a figure of impotent, raging despite.

Still, the story was yet to be written.

It was always yet to be written.

The thought pleased him. There were things Haomane First-
Born, the Lord-of-Thought, had never understood. He had not listened to the counsel of dragons. The death and rebirth of worlds
was a long and mighty business.

"You are all my Children."

He whispered the words, tasting them, and found them true. So
many lies, so few of them his! One day, perhaps, the world would
understand. He was a Shaper. He had been given a role to play,
and he had played it.

They were close now.

There was a sound; one of the threefold doors, opening. He
lifted his heavy head to see which of them had arrived first.

It was a surprise after all; and yet there were no surprises, not
here at the end. The Font burned quietly, spewing blue-white
sparks over the impervious stone floor. Within it, Godslayer, the
Shard of the Souma, throbbed steadily.

At the top of the winding stair, his visitor regarded him warily.

"My child," said Satoris Third-Born, who was once called the
Sower. "I have been expecting you."

USHAHIN RODE BACK AND FORTH along the edge of the cliffs high
above the Defile, gazing at the path far below.

The surviving Fjel had made a safe return to Darkhaven. If
nothing else, his actions had accomplished that much. But Haomane's Allies had managed to clear the first rockslide; and worse,
they had spotted the trap that would trigger the second one.

Now they waited, just out of range.

It was a maddening impasse. He wished Tanaros would return,
wished Vorax was alive, or Tanaros' young Midlander protégé; anyone who would take command of the disheartened Tordenstem.

There was no one. It shouldn't have mattered; Darkhaven was

a fortress, built to be defended. Time should be their ally, and a day ago, it might have been so. But now the army of Darkhaven was in tatters, the Helm of Shadows was broken, Haomane's Prophecy loomed over the Vale of Gorgantum, and Ushahin's very skin crawled with the urgent need to be *elsewhere*.

In the Weavers' Gulch, the little grey spiders scuttled across the vast loom of their webs, repairing the damage the Fjel had done in passing, restoring the pattern. Always, no matter how many times it was shredded, they restored the pattern.

Watching the little weavers, Ushahin came to a decision.

"You." He beckoned to one of the Tordenstem. "How are you called?"

The Fjel saluted him. "Boreg, sir!"

"Boreg." Ushahin pointed into the Defile. "You see Haomane's Allies, there. Watch them. At some point, they will begin to advance. When half their numbers have reached this bend in the path, I want you and your lads to trigger the rockslide."

"Aye, sir." The Tordenstem looked ill at ease with the command. "Will you not stay?"

"I cannot." Ushahin laid a hand on the Fjel's shoulder, feeling the rock-solid warmth of it. "General Tanaros trusts you, Boreg. Do your best."

"Aye, boss!"

Ushahin spared one last glance at Haomane's Allies. They were watching; a figure in the distant vanguard raised one hand, and the Soumanië flashed like a red star in the gloomy depths. Ushahin smiled contemptuously, certain that Aracus Altorus dared not waste a precious ounce of strength on assailing him, not with another rockslide and the Defile Gate awaiting. He did not know by what magic the power of the Souma was invoked, but he knew it took a considerable toll.

His Lordship was proof of that, and he was a Shaper.

"Enjoy this taste of victory, Son of Altorus," he murmured. "I go now to do what should have been done long ago."

Ushahin turned his mount's head toward Darkhaven. The blood-bay stallion caught his mood, its hooves pounding an urgent cadence as they made for the fortress. The case containing the sundered Helm jounced, lashed haphazardly to the saddle behind him. His right hand, healed and hale, itched for the hilt of his sword. He remembered how it had felt to move *between* life and death on the battlefield, to sever the threads that had bound the ageless Ellylon to their immortal souls.

He wondered how it would feel to cleave the life from the Lady Cerelinde's flesh.

The inner courtyard was jammed with milling Fjel, wounded and dazed, bereft of orders. Ushahin dismounted and pushed his way through the throng of Fjel, carrying the Helm's case, ignoring their pleas for guidance. There was nothing he could do for them. He was no military strategist.

Inside Darkhaven proper, it was quieter. The Havenguard, oddly subdued, had restored some semblance of order. None of his madlings were about, which gave him a moment's pause. He thought briefly of summoning them, then shook his head. There was no time.

It had to be done. It should have been done long ago.

There was madness in it; oh, yes. His right arm ached with the memory of his Lordship's wrath, the merciful cruelty that had Shaped it anew, pulverizing fragments of bone, tearing sinews asunder, a scant inch at a time. Ushahin had no illusions about the cost he would bear for this action.

And he had no doubt about its necessity.

He strode the halls, reaching the door to the Lady of the Ellylon's quarters. A pair of Havenguard sought to turn him away. With the case containing the broken Helm under his arm, he quelled them with a single, furious glance.

Chastened, they unbarred the door.

Ushahin stepped inside, smiling his bitter, crooked smile. "Lady," he began, and then halted.

Over a hidden passageway, a tapestry hung askew.

The chamber was empty.

"EXPECTING ME?" CERELINDE WHISPERED THE words. "How so, my Lord? For I did not expect to find myself here."

Some yards beyond the base of the stair, Satoris Banewreaker gazed upward at her with terrifying gentleness. "Will you seek after my knowledge now, little Ellyl? I fear it is too late." He beckoned. "Come."

She had never thought to get this far. As she'd paced restless in her chamber, the certainty that she must *try* had grown upon her. The weight of the burden Haomane's Allies had placed upon the Bearer, the burden she had laid on Meara's shoulders, were too great. It was unfair to ask what one was unwilling to give.

Meara might fail her.

The young Bearer's task might consume him.

And it had come to her that perhaps, after all, it was Haomane's plan that had placed her here, where she alone among his Allies held the key to fulfilling his Prophecy. Cerelinde knew the way to the threefold door.

She had not expected it to open to her touch. Surely, it must be a trap.

"Come." The Sunderer gestured at Godslayer. "Is this not what you seek?"

From her vantage point atop the stair, Cerelinde glanced at the dagger, pulsing in the Font. "You mock me, my Lord," she said quietly. "Though my life is forfeit for this error, do not ask me to walk willingly onto the point of your blade."

"There is no mockery." The Shaper smiled with sorrow, the red glow in his eyes burning low. "Can you not feel it, daughter of Erilonde? Even now, the Bearer is beneath us. Even now, he dares to risk all. Do you dare to risk less?"

"I am afraid," Cerelinde whispered.

"Indeed. Yet I have given my word that I will not harm you." The Shaper laughed softly, and there was no madness in it. "You mistrust my word, Lady of the Ellylon; yet if I am true to it, will you dare to become the thing you despise? Will you take that burden on yourself for the sake of your foolish, unswerving obedience to my Elder Brother's will?"

She shuddered. "I know not what you mean, my Lord Satoris."

"Come, then, and learn it." Once more, he beckoned to her, and an edge of malice crept into his tone. "Or will you flee and leave the Bearer to fail?"

"No." Cerelinde thought of the unknown Charred lad and all he had risked, all he must have endured. Gathering every measure of courage she possessed, she pushed her fear aside and gazed at the Shaper with clear eyes. In the coruscating light of the Font, he stood without moving, awaiting her. "No, Lord Satoris," she said. "I will not."

And though her legs trembled, she forced herself to move, step by step, descending the stair into the Chamber of the Font and the Sunderer's presence.

USHAHIN GATHERED HIS MADLINGS.

They came, straggling, in answer to his summons; his thoughts, cast like a net over Darkhaven, gathering all of those who were *his*.

They crowded, as many as could fit, into the Lady's chambers, others spilling into the hallways.

"What has happened here?" he asked.

They explained in a mixture of glee and terror; the hunt, the Charred Man, the Lord General's furious arrival, and how they had scattered before it.

"And the Lady?" he asked them. "How is it that she knew to flee?"

They exchanged glances, fell to their knees, and cried out to him, professing denial; all save one, who remained standing. And Ushahin's gaze fell upon her, and he knew what it was that she had done.

"Meara," he said gently. "How is it that I failed you?"

She shook her head, tears spilling down her cheeks. "Not you," she whispered. "Never you, my lord."

The others wailed.

Ushahin raised one hand. "No. I have failed you, all of you. I have been remiss in accepting my burden. But with your aid, it will end here."

The wailing continued; growing louder, interspersed with cries of fear and deeper, guttural shouts, the sound of pounding feet and jangling armor. Even as Ushahin opened his mouth to call for silence, one of the Havenguard burst into the room, forging a path through the kneeling madlings like a ship plowing through shallow waves. He was panting, the breath rasping harshly in the thick column of his throat. "Lord Dreamspinner!" He saluted. "Haomane's Allies approach the Defile Gate!"

"What?" Ushahin stared at the Fjel. "The rockslide—"

"Too late." The Havenguard shuddered. "The wizard, the white gem; I know not what he did, only that the lads were slow and the rocks fell too late." He paused, his small eyes beneath the heavy brow ridge bright with anxiety. "Will you come?"

They were gazing at him; all of them, his madlings, the Fjel, guilt-ridden Meara. Ushahin tasted despair.

"Listen," he said to them. "There is no time." He pointed toward the tapestried door. "The Lady of the Ellylon has passed behind the wall, and even now her kindred attempt a rescue." He paused, drawing his sword. "I go now in pursuit, for her death is our last hope, our only hope. My madlings, I charge you, all of you, with infiltrating every passage, every hidden egress in the fortress of Darkhaven. Do you come upon the Lady, halt her; kill her if you may. Any consequence that comes, I will accept. Do you understand?"

The madlings shouted their assent, leaping to their feet.

"Good." Ushahin pointed at the Havenguard with the tip of his blade. "Hold the Gate," he said grimly. "There is no other order I can give. Tell the lads they must resist if Malthus seeks to wield his Soumanië against them and sway their spirits. Bid them to cling to the thought of his Lordship's long suffering, bid them think of their fallen comrades. It may lend them strength. If it does not . . ." He glanced at Meara. "Bid them make ready to slay any comrade who seeks to betray us."

"Aye, boss!" Relieved to have orders, the Havenguard whirled to depart. The madlings went with him, surging out the door in a roiling, shouting mass. Ushahin watched them go.

Meara remained. "Will you not punish me?" she asked plaintively.

"What punishment will suit?" Ushahin asked. "Your penitence comes too late to aid his Lordship. I will deal with you anon, Meara of Darkhaven. Now go, and serve while you may."

Bowing her head, she went.

With a sword-blade naked in his strong right hand and the case containing the broken Helm tucked beneath his aching left arm, Ushahin thrust aside the tapestry and plunged into the passageways.

FOR A MOMENT, THE SOURCE continued to surge upward in a blazing column.

The Bearer, Dani the Bearer with his cupped hands, stood within it; stood, and lived. Through the sheets of blue-white flame, his gaze met Tanaros'. His lips, cracked and parched, whispered a word.

"Uru-Alat!"

And then his hands parted and the Water of Life fell, splashing, slow and glistening. The scent of water filled the cavern, sweet and clean and unbearable, as though all the water in the world was gathered in the Bearer's hands.

A handful; not even that, a scant mouthful.

It was enough.

The Source of the marrow-fire, the vast, roaring column of blue-white fire, winked out of existence. Tanaros, gaping, sword in hand, caught a final glimpse of the Bearer's figure crumpling to the ground.

And then he was trapped in darkness beneath the bowels of Darkhaven.

The Source was gone.

The marrow-fire had been extinguished.

For the space of a dozen heartbeats, Tanaros saw only blackness. He sheathed his sword, hands moving blindly. Slowly, his eyes adjusted to this new darkness, and when they did, he saw that traceries remained. The blue-white veins within the stony walls lingered, their light ebbing. *When the marrow-fire is quenched and Godslayer is freed* . . .

A new spasm of fear seized him. "Godslayer," Tanaros said aloud.

"URU-ALAT."

The word seemed to come from everywhere and nowhere, the World God's name whispered in every corner of the Chamber, all at once a prayer, a plea, a promise. It carried the scent of water, overwhelming for a moment the sweet charnel reek of ichor.

In the center of the room, Satoris Third-Born lifted his mighty head.

"Now," he said. "It is now."

In the blink of an eye, the glittering Font vanished, plunging the Chamber into gloom. For the span of a breath, Godslayer seemed to hang in the darkling air above the hole where the Font had blazed, then it dropped, clattering off the stones that ringed the empty pit. There it lay, unharmed, its lucid crimson radiance beating vividly against the darkness.

An involuntary cry escaped Cerelinde's lips. As swiftly as thought, she moved, darting toward the extinguished Font. All around her, shadows seethed. It seemed a penumbra of darkness gathered as the Shaper, too, moved forward. But if her mother was born to the House of Elterrion, her father was a scion of Numireth the Fleet, capable of outracing the darkness. Stooping, Cerelinde seized the rounded haft of the dagger.

Godslayer.

It throbbed against her palm, singing a wordless song of power that made the blood surge in her veins; a Shaper's power, power she did not know how to use. It didn't matter. It was a Shard of the Souma, and it had another purpose. Cerelinde straightened and whirled, prepared to fend off the Sunderer.

He had not moved.

"You see," he murmured. "I kept my word." He took a step toward her, turning his hands outward. "Finish your task."

Although she could not have said for whom she wept, there

were tears in her eyes, blurring her vision. Cerelinde tightened her
grip on Godslayer's haft. "Why?" she asked, her voice ragged with
grief. *"Why?"*

The Shaper smiled. "All things must be as they must, little sister."

He took another step forward and another, looming before her.
The clean aroma of water had vanished, and the sweet, coppery
scent of ichor filled her nostrils. A Shaper's blood, spilled many
Ages ago. An unhealing wound. Cerelinde raised the dagger between them. The Shard's deadly edges glimmered with its own
rubescent light. "Stay back!"

Satoris Third-Born shook his head. "One way or the other, you
will give me what is mine." He extended his hand as he had done
once before, in the moon-garden. "How do you choose, daughter
of Erilonde?"

Now, as then, there was no menace in the gesture; save that it
asked Cerelinde to betray all that she knew, all that she held dear.
The traceries of marrow-fire that illumed the walls of the Chamber
dimmed but slowly, revealing the Shaper's grave features. His
empty hand was outstretched and the vast expanse of his breast
was before her, immaculate and vulnerable, marrow-lit obsidian
flesh. Godslayer throbbed in her hand, a reminder of the dream of
the Rivenlost. The Souma made whole and Urulat healed, a world
no longer Sundered.

Will you dare to become the thing you despise?

"Arahila forgive me!" Cerelinde gasped.

Raising the dagger high, she plunged it into the Shaper's breast.

It sank with sickening ease, driving hilt-deep. Her clenched
knuckles brushed his immortal flesh, immortal no more. He cried
out; only once, a cry of such anguish, terror, and relief that Cerelinde knew it would echo in her ears for the remainder of her days.
For a moment they swayed, locked together; her hand on Godslayer's hilt, the Shaper's hands rising to cover hers.

Cerelinde saw things.

She saw the dawning of the world and the emergence of the
Seven Shapers within it and understood that it was at once an ending and a beginning; the death of Uru-Alat and the birth of a vast
divergence. She saw mountains arise and rivers burst forth. She
watched the world grow green and fruitful. She beheld the Shapers
at their labor, crafting their Children in love and pride. She saw
Satoris Third-Born walking alone and without fear in the deep
places of the earth, conversing with dragons.

And then she saw no more.

Godslayer's hilt slipped from her grasp. In the Chamber of the Font, the Sunderer had fallen to his knees, was slumping sideways. The shadow of a smile still hovered on his lips. In his breast, the dagger pulsed like a dying star.

"So," he whispered. "It begins anew."

TANAROS WASTED NO TIME EXAMINING the inert form of the Bearer. The lad's role was finished; it no longer mattered whether he lived or died. Moving swiftly in the dim light, Tanaros made his way to the outer wall of the chasm and began to climb.

If fear had impelled his descent, no word was large enough for the emotion that hastened his ascent. He was dizzy and unfeeling, his body numb with shock. His limbs moved by rote, obedient to his will, hauling him up the harsh crags until he reached the surface.

The passages behind the walls were growing dimmer, the veins of marrow-fire fading to a twilight hue. Tanaros paused to catch his breath and regain his sense of direction.

Then, he heard the cry.

It was a sound; a single sound, wordless. And yet it held in it such agony, and such release, as shook the very foundations of Darkhaven. On and on it went, and there was no place in the world to hide from it. The earth shuddered, the floor of the passage grinding and heaving. Tanaros crouched beneath the onslaught of the sound, covering his ears, weeping without knowing why. Stray rocks and pebbles, loosened by the reverberations, showered down upon him.

Although it seemed as though the cry would never end, at last it did.

Tanaros found himself on his feet with no recollection of having risen. Drawing his black sword, he began running.

WITHIN TEN PACES, IT HAPPENED.

There was no warning, no sound; only a sudden dim coolness as the veins of marrow-fire that lit the passages dwindled in brightness and the temperature in the stifling passages plummeted. Elsewhere in the passageways, he could hear his distant madlings uttering sounds of dismay and fear. Somewhere, the horns of the Rivenlost were calling out in wild triumph. Above Darkhaven, the ravens wheeled in sudden terror.

Ushahin shivered and pressed onward.

He was halfway to the Chamber of the Font when he heard the cry. It struck him like a blow, piercing him to the core. It was like no sound ever heard before on the face of Urulat, and he knew, with a horrible certainty, what it must portend. Ushahin stood, head bowed as rubble pelted him from above, his branded heart an agony within his hunched torso, arms wrapped around the useless case, and waited it out as another might outwait a storm.

Too late, always too late. The enemy was at the gate. The little weavers had completed their pattern. Haomane's Prophecy hovered on the verge of fulfillment.

Everything he feared had come full circle.

Almost . . .

In the silence that followed, Ushahin Dreamspinner stirred his ill-set, aching limbs. Step by painful step, gaining speed as he went, he began to follow the faint echoes of his Lordship's cry to their source.

TWENTY-FOUR

❖

ENTERING THE CHAMBER OF THE Font at a dead run, Tanaros halted, brought up short by the sight before him. "No," he said, uttering the word without thinking, willing it to be true, willing his denial to change what had happened and render it undone. "Ah, my Lord, *no!*"

It didn't change. Nothing changed.

Where the Font had burned for century upon century, there was nothing save a ring of scorched stone blocks surrounding an aperture in the floor of the Chamber. It seemed a small opening to have admitted such a gout of marrow-fire. Without the Font, the Chamber was dim-lit, the fading veins of marrow-fire that laced its walls filling it with a vague, subterranean twilight.

Lord Satoris lay supine upon the floor of the Chamber; shadows clustered the length of his awesome form. It seemed impossible, and yet it was so. Even fallen, he filled the space until it seemed little else could exist within it. The scent of blood that was not blood, of sweet, coppery ichor, was thick in the air.

The rough-hewn haft of Godslayer pulsed faintly, a ruby star, where it protruded from the bulwark of the Shaper's chest.

It moved, ever so slightly.

She stood in the far corner of the Chamber, beyond the ashen pit of the Font, shrinking away from it; from the Shaper, from her deed. Her eyes were stretched wide with horror, her hands upraised, sliding over her mouth as though to stifle a cry.

"Cerelinde," Tanaros said. The black sword was loose in his grip. *"Why?"*

Unable to answer, she shook her head.

Ignoring her, Tanaros went to his Lord. In the dying light of the marrow-fire, he knelt beside him. The flagstones were hard beneath his knees, tilted askew by the tremors that had shaken Darkhaven. Ichor puddled, soaking his breeches.

"My Lord," he said tenderly. "What must I do?"

At first there was no response, and he feared it was too late, that his Lordship was gone. And then the Shaper's head moved, as though his gaze sought the western horizon beyond the stone walls of his Chamber. "Arahila," he whispered, almost inaudible. "O my sister. What happens to *us* when we die?"

"My Lord, no!" Tanaros reached, touching the Shaper's vast breast, pressing the immortal flesh pierced by the glittering dagger, feeling ichor seep beneath his fingers. "Please, my Lord, what must I do to save you?"

Slowly, Satoris lifted one dragging hand, covering Tanaros', forcing his grip onto the dagger's burning hilt. "Draw it," he said with difficulty. "Let it be done."

Tanaros wept. "My Lord, no!"

In the corner, the Lady Cerelinde made an inarticulate sound.

"So it is not you, my General." With an effort, the Shaper turned his head. His eyes were dark and clear; clear as a child's, but far, far older. The red light of rage had faded in them, as though it had been extinguished with the marrow-fire. So they must have looked long ago, before the world was Sundered, when Satoris Third-Born walked in the deep places of the earth and spoke with dragons. His mouth moved in the faintest hint of a smile. "Not you, at the end."

With a crash, one of the threefold doors at the top of the spiral stair opened; the left-hand door, Ushahin's door. Even as he entered, wild-eyed, Tanaros was on his feet, the black sword in his hand.

"Dreamspinner," he said.

"Tanaros." At the top of the stair, Ushahin swayed and caught himself. "They are at the Gate." He gazed blankly around the Chamber. "My Lord," he said, his voice sounding strange and hollow. "Ah, my poor Lord!"

"He yet lives," Tanaros said roughly. "He bid me draw the dagger and end it."

Ushahin laughed, a terrible, mirthless sound. It held all the bitterness of his mad, useless knowledge, of the ending he had failed to prevent. "Are you not sworn to obey him in all things, cousin? Are you not Tanaros Blacksword, his loyal General?"

"Aye," Tanaros said. "But I think this task is yours, Dreamspinner."

They exchanged a long glance. For a moment, they might have been alone in the Chamber. The Shaper's words lay unspoken between them. They were of the Three, and some things did not need to be spoken aloud. "And her?" Ushahin asked at length, jerking his head toward Cerelinde. "Whose task is *she*?"

Tanaros raised his black sword. "Mine."

"So be it." Ushahin bowed his head briefly, then sheathed his blade and descended the stair. He crossed the crooked flagstones, dropping to his knees beside the Shaper's form, laying the leather case containing the broken Helm gently beside him.

"I am here, my Lord," he murmured. "I am here."

Sword in hand, Tanaros watched.

In the dusky light, the Shaper's body seemed wrought of darkness made manifest. Ushahin felt small and fragile beside him, his ill-formed figure a sorry mockery of the Shaper's fallen splendor; all save his right arm, so beautifully and cruelly remade.

It fell to him, this hardest of tasks. Somehow it seemed he had always known it would. When all was said and done, in some ways his lot had always been the hardest. He had seen the pattern closing upon them. He had spoken with Calanthrag the Eldest. It was fitting. Kneeling on the flagstones, Ushahin leaned close, the ends of his moon-pale hair trailing in pools of black ichor.

"What is your will, my Lord?" he asked.

The Shaper's lips parted. A terrible clarity was in his eyes, dark and sane, filled with knowledge and compassion. "Take it," he breathed in reply, his words almost inaudible. "And make an end. The beginning falls to you, Dreamspinner. I give you my blessing."

Ushahin's shoulders shook. "Are you certain?"

The Shaper's eyes closed. "Seek the Delta. You know the way."

With a curse, Ushahin raised his right hand. It had been Shaped for this task. It was strong and steady. He placed it on the Shard's crude knob of a hilt. Red light pulsed, shining between his fingers, illuminating his flesh.

It held the power to Shape the world anew, and he did not want it.

Even so, it was his.

"Farewell, my Lord," Ushahin whispered, and withdrew Godslayer.

Darkness seethed through the Chamber. The Shaper's form dwindled, vanishing as its essence coalesced slowly into shadow, into smoke, into a drift of obsidian ash. There was no outcry, no trembling of the earth, only a stirring in the air like a long-held sigh released and a profound sense of passage, as though between the space of one heartbeat and the next, the very foundation of existence had shifted.

Quietly, uneventfully, the world was forever changed.

Ushahin climbed to his feet, holding Godslayer. "Your turn, cousin," he said, hoarse and weary.

CERELINDE WEPT AT THE SHAPER'S passing.

It did not matter, in the end, who drew forth the dagger. She had killed him. He had stood before her, unarmed, and reached out his hand. She had planted Godslayer in his breast. And Satoris Third-Born had known she would do it. He had allowed it.

She did not understand.

She would never understand.

She watched as Ushahin rose to his feet, uttering his weary words. She saw Tanaros swallow and touch the raised circle of his brand beneath his stained, padded undertunic. Hoisting his black sword, he walked slowly toward her. Standing beneath the shadow of his blade, she made no effort to flee, her tears forging a broad, shining swath down her fair cheeks.

Their eyes met, and his were as haunted as hers. He, too, had sunk a blade into unresisting flesh. He had shed the blood of those he loved, those who had betrayed him. He understood the cost of what she had done.

"I'm sorry," he said to her. "I'm sorry, Cerelinde."

"I know." She gazed at him beneath the black blade's shadow. "Ah, Tanaros! I did only what I believed was needful."

"I know," Tanaros said somberly. "As must I."

"It won't matter in the end." She gave a despairing laugh. "There's another, you know. His Lordship told me as much. Elterrion had a second daughter, gotten of an illicit union. So he said to me. 'Somewhere among the Rivenlost, your line continues.'"

Tanaros paused. "And you believed?"

"No," Cerelinde whispered. "Such things happen seldom, so seldom, among the Ellylon. And yet it was his Gift, when he had one, to know such things." She shuddered, a shudder as delicate and profound as that of a mortexigus flower shedding its pollen. "I no longer know what to believe. He said that my mother prayed to him ere she died at my birth. Do you believe it was true, Tanaros?"

"Aye," he said softly. "I do, Cerelinde."

Ushahin's voice came, harsh and impatient. "Have *done* with it, cousin!"

Tanaros shifted his grip on the black sword's hilt. "The madling was right," he murmured. "She told me you would break all of our hearts, Lady." He spoke her name one last time, the word catching in his throat. "Cerelinde."

She nodded once, then closed her eyes. Whatever else was true, here at the end, she knew that the world was not as it had seemed. Cerelinde lifted her chin, exposing her throat. "Make it swift," she said, her voice breaking. "Please."

Tanaros' upraised arms trembled. His palms were slick with sweat, stinging from the myriad cuts and scrapes he had incurred in his climbing. He was tired, very tired, and it hurt to look at her.

Elsewhere in Darkhaven, there were sounds; shouting. His Lordship was dead and the enemy was at the gates.

A blue vein pulsed beneath the fair skin of Cerelinde's out-stretched throat.

He remembered the feel of his wife's throat beneath his hands, and the bewildered expression on Roscus' face when he ran him through. He remembered the light fading in the face of Ingolin the Wise, Lord of the Rivenlost. He remembered the Bearer trembling on the verge of the Source, his dark eyes so like those of Ngurra, the Yarru elder.

I can only give you the choice, Slayer.

None of them had done such a deed as hers. Because of her, Lord Satoris, Satoris Third-Born, who was once called the Sower, was no more. For that, surely, her death was not undeserved.

"Tanaros!" Ushahin's voice rose sharply. *"Now."*

He remembered how he had knelt in the Throne Hall, his branded heart spilling over with a fury of devotion, of loyalty, and the words he had spoken. *My Lord, I swear, I will never betray you!*

Wherein did his duty lie?

Loyal Tanaros. It is to you I entrust my honor.

So his Lordship had said. And Ngurra, old Ngurra . . .

Choose.

Breathing hard, Tanaros lowered his sword. He avoided looking at Cerelinde. He did not want to see her eyes opening, the sweep of her lashes rising as disbelief dawned on her beautiful face.

She whispered his name. "Tanaros!"

"Don't." His voice sounded as harsh as a raven's call. "Lady, if you bear any kindness in your heart, do not thank me for this. Only go, and begone from this place."

"But will you not—" she began, halting and bewildered.

"No." Ushahin interrupted. "Ah, no!" He took a step forward, Godslayer still clenched in his fist, pulsing like a maddened heart. "This cannot be, Blacksword. If you will not kill her, I will."

"No," Tanaros said gently, raising his sword a fraction. "You will not."

Ushahin inhaled sharply, his knuckles whitening as his grip tightened. "Will you stand against Godslayer itself?"

"Aye, I will." Tanaros regarded him. "If you know how to invoke its might."

For a long moment, neither moved. At last, Ushahin laughed, short and defeated. Lowering the dagger, he took a step backward. "Alas, not yet. But make no mistake, cousin. I know where the knowledge is to be found. And I *will* use it."

Tanaros nodded. "As his Lordship intended. But you will not use it today, Dreamspinner." He turned to Cerelinde. "Take the right-hand door. It leads in a direct path to the quarters of Vorax of Staccia, who died this day, as did so many others. No one will look for you there." He paused, rubbing at his eyes with the heel of his left hand. "If you are fortunate," he said roughly, "you may live."

Her eyes were luminous and grey, glistening with tears. "Will you not come with me, Tanaros?"

"No." If his heart had not been breaking at his Lordship's death, at the death of all who had fallen this day, it might have broken at her beauty. "Lady, I cannot."

"You *can*!" she breathed. "You can still—"

"Cerelinde." Reaching out with his free hand, Tanaros touched her cheek. Her skin was cool and smooth beneath his fingertips, damp with tears. A Man could spend an eternity loving her, and it would not be long enough. But she had slain his Lordship. Arahila the Fair might forgive her for it, but Tanaros could not. "No."

She gazed at him. "What will you do?"

"What do you think?" He smiled wearily. "I will die, Cerelinde. I will die with whatever honor is left to me." He moved away, pointing toward the right-hand door with the tip of his sword. "Now go."

"Tanaros." She took a step toward him. "Please . . ."

"*Go!*" he shouted. "Before I change my mind!"

The Lady of the Ellylon bowed her head. "So be it."

❖

Ushahin watched her leave.

As much as he despised her, the Chamber was darker for her absence. It had been a place of power, once. For a thousand years, it had been no less. Now it was only a room, an empty room with a scorched hole in the floor and an echo of loss haunting its corners, a faint reek of coppery-sweet blood in the air.

"What now, cousin?" he asked Tanaros.

Tanaros gazed at his hands, still gripping his sword; strong and capable, stained with ichor. "It was his Lordship's will," he murmured. "He entrusted me with his honor."

"So you say." Ushahin thrust Godslayer into his belt and stooped to retrieve the case that held the sundered Helm of Shadows. "Of a surety, he entrusted me with the future, and I would fain see his will done."

"Aye." Tanaros gathered himself. "Haomane's Allies are at the Gate?"

Ushahin nodded. "They are. I bid the Havenguard to hold it."

"Good." The General touched a pouch that hung from his swordbelt. His haunted gaze focused on Ushahin. "Dreamspinner. You can pass between places, hidden from the eyes of mortal Men. I know, I have ridden with you. Can you use such arts to yet escape from Haomane's Allies?"

"Perhaps." Ushahin hesitated. "It will not be easy. Not with the Host of the Rivenlost at our Gate, the Soumanië at work, and Malthus the Counselor among them."

Tanaros smiled grimly. "I mean to provide them with a distraction."

"It will have to be swift. If the Lady escapes to tell her tale, they will spare no effort to capture Godslayer." Unaccountably, Ushahin's throat ached. His words came unbidden, painful and accusatory. "Why did you do it, Tanaros? *Why?*"

The delicate traceries of marrow-fire lingering in the stone walls were growing dim. The hollows of Tanaros' eyes were filled with shadows. "What would you have me answer? That I betrayed his Lordship in the end?"

"Perhaps." Ushahin swallowed against the tightness in his throat. "For it seems to me you did love her, cousin."

"Does it?" In the gloaming light, Tanaros laughed softly. "In some other life, it seems to me I might have. In this one, it was not to be. And yet, I could not kill her." He shook his head. "Was it strength or weakness that stayed my hand? I do not know, any more than I know why his Lordship allowed her to take his life. In the end, I fear it will fall to you to answer."

A silence followed his words. Ushahin felt them sink into his awareness and realized for the first time the enormity of the burden that had settled on his crooked shoulders. He thought of the weavers in the gulch, spinning their endless patterns; of Calanthrag in her swamp with the vastness of time behind her slitted eyes. He laid his hand upon Godslayer's rough hilt, feeling the pulse of its power; the power of the Souma itself, capable of Shaping the world. The immensity of it humbled him, and his bitterness gave way to grief and a strange tenderness. "Ah, cousin! I will try to be worthy of it."

"So you shall." Tanaros regarded him affection and regret. "His Lordship bid me teach you to hold a blade. Even then, he must have suspected. I do not envy you the task, Dreamspinner. And yet, it is fitting. In some ways, you were always the strongest of the Three. You are the thing Haomane's Allies feared the most, the shadow of things to come." Switching his sword to his left hand, he extended his right. "We waste time we cannot afford. Will you not bid me farewell?"

Here at the end, they understood one another at last.

"I will miss you," Ushahin said quietly, clasping Tanaros' hand. "For all the days of my life, howsoever long it may be."

Tanaros nodded. "May it be long, cousin."

There was nothing more to be said. Ushahin turned away, his head averted. At the top of the winding stair, he paused and raised his hand in farewell; his right hand, strong and shapely.

And then he passed through the left-hand door.

TANAROS STOOD ALONE IN THE darkening Chamber, breathing slow and deep. He returned the black sword to his right hand, his fingers curving around its familiar hilt. It throbbed in his grip. His blood, his Lordship's blood. The madlings had always revered it. Tempered in the marrow-fire, quenched in ichor. It was not finished, not yet.

Death is a coin to be spent wisely.

Vorax had been fond of saying that. How like the Staccian to measure death in terms of wealth! And yet there was truth in the words.

Tanaros meant to spend his wisely.

It would buy time for Ushahin to make his escape; precious

time in which the attention of Haomane's Allies was focused on battle. And it would buy vengeance for those who had fallen. He had spared Cerelinde's life. He did not intend to do the same for those who took arms against him.

There were no innocents on the battlefield. They would pay for the deaths of those he had loved. Tanaros would exact full measure for his coin.

He touched the pouch that hung from his swordbelt, feeling the reassuring shape of Hyrgolf's *rhios* within it.

The middle door was waiting.

It gave easily to his push. He strode through it and into the darkness beyond. These were *his* passageways, straight and true, leading to the forefront of Darkhaven. Tanaros did not need to see to know the way. "Vorax. Speros. Hyrgolf," he murmured as he went, speaking their names like a litany.

TWENTY-FIVE

❖

THE PASSAGEWAY WAS LONG AND winding, and the marrow-fire that lit it grew dim, so dim that she had to feel her way by touch. But Tanaros had not lied; the passage was empty. Neither madlings nor Fjel traversed it. At the end, there was a single door.

Cerelinde fumbled for the handle and found it. She began to whisper a prayer to Haomane and found that the words would not come. The image of Satoris Banewreaker hung before her, stopping her tongue.

Still, the handle turned.

Golden lamplight spilled into the passage. The door opened onto palatial quarters filled with glittering treasure. Clearly, these were Vorax's quarters, unlike any other portion of Darkhaven. Within, three mortal women leapt to their feet, staring. They were fair-haired northerners, young and comely after the fashion of Arahila's Children.

"Vas leggis?" one asked, bewildered. And then, slowly, in the common tongue: "Who are you? What happens? Where is Lord Vorax?"

Tanaros had not lied.

It made her want to weep, but the Ellylon could not weep for their own sorrows. "Lord Vorax is no more," Cerelinde said gently, entering the room. "And the reign of the Sunderer has ended in Urulat. I am Cerelinde of the House of Elterrion."

"Ellyl!" The youngest turned pale. She spoke to the others in Staccian, then turned to Cerelinde. "He is dead? It is ended?"

"Yes," she said. "I am sorry."

And strangely, the words were true. Even more strangely, the three women were weeping. She did not know for whom they wept, Satoris Banewreaker or Vorax the Glutton. She had not imagined anyone could weep for either.

The oldest of the three dried her eyes on the hem of her mantle. "What is to become of us?"

There was a throne in the center of the room, a massive ironwood seat carved in the shape of a roaring bear. Cerelinde sank wearily into it. "Haomane's Allies will find us," she said. "Be not afraid. They will show mercy. Whatever you have done here, Arahila the Fair will forgive it."

Her words seemed to hearten them. It should have gladdened her, for it meant that there was hope, that not all who dwelled within the Sunderer's shadow were beyond redemption. And yet it did not.

What will you do?

What do you think? I will die, Cerelinde.

A great victory would be won here today. She would take no joy in it.

HAVENGUARD WERE AWAITING WHEN TANAROS emerged from the passageway, crowding Darkhaven's entry. The inner doors were shuddering, battered by a mighty ram. The enemy was past the Gate, had entered the courtyard. They were mounting an offense, coming to rescue the Lady of the Ellylon, coming to fulfill Haomane's Prophecy.

They would succeed.

And they would fail.

Tanaros grinned at his Fjel, watching them respond to it like a deep draft of *svartblod*, relishing their answering grins, broad and leathery, showing their eyetusks.

"Well, lads?" he asked them. "Shall we give our visitors the welcome they deserve? I'll give the greeting myself!"

They roared in acclaim.

"Be certain of it, lads, for it means your deaths!" He touched his branded chest, clad only in his padded undertunic. His armor was lost, vanished in the darkness of the crumbling passageways where the chasm gaped. "In his Lordship's name, I go forth to claim mine. I ask no one to accompany me who does not seek the same!"

The Havenguard Fjel laughed. One of them shouldered past the others, hoisting a battle-axe in one hand and a shield in the other. "I stand at your side, General," he rumbled. "I keep my shield high."

"And I!"

"And I!"

"So be it." The words brought to mind an echo of Cerelinde's farewell. Standing before the great doors, Tanaros paused. He felt keenly the lack of his armor. He wondered about Cerelinde, bound for Vorax's chambers, and how she would live with her deeds afterward. He wondered about the Bearer, if he lived or died. He wondered about the Bearer's comrade, who hung in chains in Darkhaven's dungeons, unable to lift his head. Somewhere, Ushahin was making his way through the hidden passages, Godslayer in his possession.

An Age had ended; a new Age had begun. The Shapers' War would continue.

The thought made Tanaros smile.

In the end, it didn't matter.

Haomane's Allies would Shape this tale as they saw fit. What mattered, what mattered the most, was that the tale did not end here.

"Open the doors," Tanaros ordered.

The Fjel obeyed, as they had always obeyed, as they had obeyed since his Lordship had fled to take shelter among them, sharing with them his vision of how one day, Men and Ellylon alike would envy their gifts, fulfilling the promise of Neheris-of-the-Leaping-Waters, who had Shaped them.

Tanaros strode through the open doors, flanked by a stream of Fjel. The Men wielding the battering-ram dropped back, gaping at his sudden appearance, at the doors behind his back, unbarred and thrown wide open.

Brightness in the air made him squint. The sun, the symbol of Haomane's Wrath, had pierced the veil of clouds that hung over the Vale of Gorgantum. It was low and sinking in the west, but it had prevailed.

Tanaros opened his arms.

They were there; they were all there amid the ragged, dying remnants of his Fjel. All his enemies, gathered. Aracus Altorus, grey-faced and exhausted, barely able to hold his shattered hilt aloft, his Soumanië flickering and dim. Malthus the Counselor astride his pale mount, his white robes swirling. The Rivenlost, at once bereft and defiant. The Archer of Arduan, a bow wrought of black horn in her hands.

Behind them, a legion of Haomane's Allies.

They were silent, watching him.

Gazing at them, Tanaros smiled.

When the last of his strength failed, when arrows pierced his breast, when their sheer numbers bore down his sword-arm and the black sword fell at last from his nerveless fingers, one of them would kill him. It didn't matter which one. All that mattered, here at the end, was that he would die with his Lordship's name on his lips, his honor intact in his heart. He would fulfill his duty.

"I am Darkhaven," he said. "Come and take me."

USHAHIN'S MADLINGS CLUNG TO HIM.

They surrounded him in a ragged tumult, weeping and apologizing for their failure to find the Lady of the Ellylon, begging him not to leave them. Some of them crawled, gasping at the sight of Godslayer; others sought to touch the case that held the severed Helm of Shadows, keening at Lord Satoris' death.

"Hush," Ushahin said, gentling them as he went. "Hush."

They wept all the harder, grasping his hands and kissing them, the healed and the broken alike.

"All things must be as they must," he said to them. "And I must leave you. Do not fear. Haomane's Allies will treat you gently."

He hoped it was true. They had not bothered to do so when they were ordinary people living ordinary lives. But perhaps the burden of *right* they had taken so violently on themselves would impel them to kindness.

It crossed his thoughts to send them to Vorax's quarters. There was time, yet, for the Ellyl bitch to pay for her sins. It would be a fitting ending for her. But the memory of the shadowed pain haunting Tanaros' eyes forestalled him.

Was it strength or weakness that stayed my hand?

Ushahin did not know. The question begged an answer, and he had an immortality in which to find it . . . if he lived through the next hour. If he did not, nothing would matter. And vengeance was unimportant in comparison with fulfilling his Lordship's will and taking his place in the pattern that bound him.

"Do you know which mount is mine?" he asked instead. "Bring it round to the postern gate near the kitchens."

The silent madling boy, the one who loved horses, pelted away at a dead run. Ushahin let the others escort him. His people, his wailing, keening throng. It would hurt to leave them. They passed through the kitchens, the fires burned down to unbanked embers, untended for the first time in memory, crowding through the door after him, surrounding him at the postern gate.

There was the stablehand, holding the bridle of his blood-bay stallion.

It was time.

Ushahin lashed the Helm's case to his saddle. He touched God-slayer's hilt, making certain it was secure in his belt. He mounted his horse.

"Remember," he said to them. "Remember Satoris, Third-Born among Shapers. Remember he was kind to you when the world was not."

The wailing throng swirled and parted, then Meara was there, clutching his stirrup, her tearstained face lifted upward.

"Forgive me," she gasped. "Oh please, oh please, my Lord, forgive me!"

He gazed down at her, thinking what a piece of irony it was that his Lordship's downfall should have hinged in part on such a small matter. It was true, Ushahin had failed his madlings. He alone had understood their longings, their vulnerability. He had let himself grow overly concerned with great dangers, forgetful of the small ones. Did he not owe Meara compassion? It was a fit counterpoint to the act of vengeance he had forgone.

An act of honor; a small kindness. Things his enemies would never acknowledge.

Leaning down in the saddle, Ushahin laid his misshapen left hand upon her head. "Meara of Darkhaven. In Satoris' name, I do forgive you."

Her eyes grew wide. Ushahin smiled his crooked smile.

"Farewell," he said to them. "When you remember his Lordship, think of me."

Straightening, he invoked the dark magic taught to him long ago by the Grey Dam of the Were, letting his waking awareness drift. The world shifted in his vision, leached of color. The madlings' voices faded, and Meara's last of all.

He beheld the paths between and set out upon them.

THE COURTYARD WAS A PLACE of slaughter.

It was too small to contain Haomane's Allies in their entirety. The bulk of their warriors were trapped behind the walls flanking the broken Defile Gate. The rest had fallen back before their onslaught, unprepared for fierce resistance.

Tanaros plunged into the thick of battle, laying about him on all sides.

There was no strategy in it, no plan. Men and Ellylon swarmed him and he swung his black sword, killing them. The Havenguard Fjel struggled to protect him, their shields high. Still the enemy came with sword and spear, piercing his guard, his unarmored flesh. For every one he killed, another took his place. He bled from a half a dozen wounds; from a dozen, from a score.

Still he fought, light-headed and tireless.

The flagstones grew slippery with blood. Horses slipped; mounted warriors dismounted, only to stumble over the bodies of fallen comrades. There was no magic here, only battle at its ugliest. Oronin's Bow was silent, for there was no way for the Archer to take aim in the milling fray.

Aracus Altorus had expended his strength.

But he was a born leader. He gathered his Men instead; the Borderguard of Curonan. Set them to fighting their way around the outskirts of battle, making for the open inner doors. Set them on a course to rescue Cerelinde, to penetrate the secrets of Darkhaven.

"Havenguard!" Tanaros shouted. "Ward the doors!"

They tried. They fought valiantly. He watched them go down, struggling under numbers even a Fjeltroll could not withstand. He watched a handful of Borderguardsmen slip past them, vanishing into the depths of the fortress. He would have led them, once.

It was a long time ago.

In the courtyard, his ranks were thinning. Here and there, bow-strings sang. More of Haomane's Allies streamed past the Defile Gate. Tanaros took a deep breath and squared his shoulders, meeting them.

Someone's blade grazed his brow. A young Midlander, his expression terrified. Tanaros shook his head, blinking the blood from his eyes, and killed him. He stood for a moment, wavering on his feet, thinking of Speros.

Another bow sang out; Oronin's Bow. Its fading echoes called his name. Tanaros felt a sharp punch to his midriff. When he lowered his hand, he found the arrow's shaft, piercing the padded, blood-soaked tunic over his ribs.

He looked for the Archer.

She was staring at him, her face fixed with hatred and grief. Another arrow was nocked in her bow, Oronin's Bow. Her arms trembled. Malthus the Counselor had dismounted to stand beside her, an Ellyl sword in his hand, the clear Soumanië on his breast, his aged face grave.

Tanaros blinked again.

Something was wrong with his vision, for the world seemed dim and strange. They stood out brightly, those two; and behind them, another figure. One who rode astride, giving the battle a wide berth and making for a gap in the forces entering freely through the Defile Gate. A Shard of terrible brightness burned at his hip, red as blood and urgent as the rising sun. He glanced in Tanaros' direction, a glance filled with vivid emotion that had no name.

Overhead, ravens circled and cried aloud.

"Ushahin," Tanaros whispered. "Go!"

The Counselor's head tilted, as though to catch a distant strain of sound. He began to turn, his gaze already searching. Tanaros struggled to fill his lungs, hearing his breath catch and whistle, feeling the arrow's shaft jerk.

"Malthus!" he shouted. "I am *here*!"

The Counselor's gaze returned, fixing him. His Ellyl blade swept up into a warding position. To Tanaros' vision, it seemed limned with pale fire. He laughed aloud, raising his own sword. It burned with dark fire; a wound in the sky, quenched in black ichor. Step by halting step, Tanaros advanced on them.

Oronin's Bow sang out, over and over.

Arrows thudded into his flesh, slowing him. There was pain, distant and unrelated. The air had grown as thick as honey. Tanaros waded through it, shafts protruding from his left thigh, his right shoulder, clustering at his torso. Ellylon and Men assailed him; he swatted their blades away, his black sword shearing steel. One step, then another and another, until he reached the Counselor.

Tanaros raised the black sword for a final blow.

"Malthus," he said. "I am here."

Or did he only think the words? The echoes of Oronin's Bow made it hard to hear. Tanaros fought for breath, his lungs constricted. He felt his grip loosen on the hilt of his sword; his hands, his capable hands, failing him at last. The black sword fell from his hands. The Counselor's face slid sideways in his vision. Malthus' lips were moving, shaping inaudible words. The light of the clear Soumanië he bore struck Tanaros with the force of Haomane's Wrath.

It hurt to look at it, so Tanaros turned his head, looking toward the Defile Gate. The world was growing dark. He understood that he was on his knees, swaying. The flagstones were hard, and sticky with blood; most likely his own. Here at the end, the pain was intense. All his myriad wounds hurt, and his branded heart ached with loss and longing. He fumbled at his breast, finding the shaft of another arrow.

He understood that he was dying.

There was shouting, somewhere, joyous and triumphant. There were Fjel in isolated knots, battling and dying. And there, beyond the Defile Gate, was a bright specter, moving unseen among the wraithlike figures of the living, bearing a spark of scarlet fire. Only Tanaros, caught between life and death, could see it.

He watched it dwindle and vanish, passing out of sight.

It seemed Ushahin Dreamspinner took the light with him, for darkness fell like a veil over his eyes. Tanaros thought of the events that had brought him to die in this place and found he could no longer conjure the old rage. The memory of his wife, of his liege-lord, had grown dim. Had they mattered so much to him once? It seemed very distant. He thought of Cerelinde standing beneath the shadow of his blade, awaiting death; and he remembered, too, how she had smiled at him in the glade of the rookery, making his heart glad.

He wished he could see her face once more and knew it was too late.

The sounds of the courtyard faded. The light of Malthus' Soumanië diminished, until it was no more troublesome than a distant star. The bonds that had circumscribed his heart for so long loosened, falling away. He had kept his vow. His Lordship's honor was untarnished. Godslayer, freed, would remain in Ushahin's hands. Tanaros had spent the coin of his death wisely.

His heart, which had beat faithfully for so many centuries, thudded; once, twice. No more. It subsided into stillness, a long-delayed rest.

There was only the long peace of death, beckoning to him like a lover.

Tanaros met it smiling.

ARACUS' VOICE CUT THROUGH THE clamor of ragged cheers and shouts that greeted her appearance, filled with relief and joy.

"Cerelinde!"

She stood on the steps of Darkhaven, gazing at the carnage in silent horror. Everywhere, there was death and dying; Men, Ellylon, Fjel. Aracus picked his way across the courtyard, making his way to her side.

She watched him come. He looked older than she remembered, his face drawn with weariness. His red-gold hair was dark with sweat, his armor splashed with gore. In one hand, he held the hilt of a shattered sword, set with a dimly flickering gem. A pebble of the Souma, smooth as a drop of blood. Her palm itched, remembering the feel of Godslayer pulsing against her skin.

"Cerelinde." Aracus stood before her on the steps, searching her eyes. The Borderguardsmen who had found her in Vorax's quarters began to speak. He silenced them with a gesture, all his urgent attention focused on her. "Are you . . . harmed?"

"No." She fought the urge to laugh in despair. "I killed him."

For a moment, he merely gazed at her, uncomprehending. "The . . . Sunderer?"

"Yes," she whispered. "The Shaper."

His Men did speak, then, relating what she had told them. Behind them, others emerged from the depths of Darkhaven, escorting Vorax's handmaids and an unarmed horde of weeping, babbling madlings. Aracus listened gravely to his Borderguard. "Get torches. Find the lad and his uncle," he said to them. "And Godslayer; Godslayer, above all. It lies in the possession of the Misbegotten, and he cannot have gotten far. Search every nook and cranny. He *will* be found." He turned back to Cerelinde. "Ah, love!" he said, his voice breaking. "Your courage shames us all."

Cerelinde shook her head and looked away, remembering the way Godslayer had sunk into Satoris' unresisting flesh. "I did only what I believed was needful."

Aracus took her hand in his gauntleted fingers. "We have paid a terrible price, all of us," he said gently. "But we have won a great victory, my Lady."

"Yes," she said. "I know."

She yearned to find comfort in his touch, in that quickening mortal ardor that burned so briefly and so bright. There was none. It had been the Gift of Satoris Third-Born, and she had slain him.

He had spoken the truth. And she had become the thing that she despised.

"Come," Aracus said. "Let us seek Malthus' counsel."

He led her across the courtyard, filled with milling warriors and dying Fjeltroll. They died hard, it seemed. A few of them looked up from where they lay, weltering in their own gore, and met her eyes without fear. They had seemed so terrifying, once. It was no longer true.

Malthus was kneeling, his robes trailing in puddles of blood.

He straightened at her approach. "Lady Cerelinde," he said in his deep voice. "I mourn the losses of the Rivenlost this day."

"I thank you, Wise Counselor." The words caught in her throat, choking her. She had seen that which his kneeling body had hidden. "Ah, Haomane!"

"Fear not, Lady." It was a strange woman who spoke. In one hand, she held a mighty bow wrought of horn. Though her face was strained with grief, her voice was implacable. "Tanaros Kingslayer is no more."

Cerelinde nodded, not trusting her voice.

Though half a dozen arrows bristled from his body, Tanaros looked peaceful in death. His unseeing eyes were open, fixed on nothing. A slight smile curved his lips. His limbs were loose, the taut sinews unstrung at last, the strong hands slack and empty. A smear of blood was across his brow, half-hidden by an errant lock of hair.

The scent of vulnus-blossom haunted her.

We hold within ourselves the Gifts of all the Seven Shapers and the ability to Shape a world of our choosing. . . .

Cerelinde shuddered.

She could not allow herself to weep for his death; not here. Perhaps not ever. Lifting her head, she gazed at Aracus. He was a choice she had made. He returned her gaze, his storm-blue eyes somber. There would be no gloating over this victory. His men had told her of the losses they had endured on the battlefield, of Blaise Caveros and Lord Ingolin the Wise, and many countless others.

She saw the future they would shape together stretching out before her. Although the shadow of loss and sorrow would lay over it, there would be times of joy, too. For the brief time that was alotted them together, they would find healing in one another, and in the challenge of bringing their races together in harmony.

There would be fear, for it was in her heart that neither Ushahin nor Godslayer would be found on the premises of Darkhaven. Haomane's Prophecy had been fulfilled to the letter, and yet it was not. Without Godslayer, the Souma could not be made whole, and the world's Sundering undone. The Six Shapers would remain on Torath, apart, and Ushahin would be an enemy to Haomane's Allies; less terrible than Satoris Banewreaker, for even with a Shard of the Souma, he would not wield a Shaper's power, capable of commanding the loyalty of an entire race. More terrible, for he did not have a Shaper's pride and the twisted sense of honor that went with it.

There would be hope, for courage and will had triumphed over great odds on this day, and what was done once might be done again.

There would be love. Of that, she did not doubt. She was the Lady of the Ellylon, and she did not love lightly; nor did Aracus. They would be steadfast and true. They would rule over Urulat with wisdom and compassion.

And yet there would be doubt, born out of her long captivity in Darkhaven.

Shouting came from the far side of the courtyard. More Border-guardsmen were emerging from Darkhaven, carrying two limp fig-ures. The Bearer and his uncle had been found and rescued. One stirred. Not the boy, who lay motionless.

"Aracus." Malthus touched his arm. "Forgive me, for I know your weariness is great. Yet it may be that the Soumanië can aid him."

"Aye." With an effort, Aracus gathered himself. "Guide me, Counselor."

In the midst of slaughter and carnage, Cerelinde watched them tend to the stricken Yarru, their heads bowed in concentration. The young Bearer was gaunt and frail, as though his travail had pared him down to the essence.

She tried to pray and could not, finding herself wondering, in-stead, if this victory was worth its cost. She longed to weep, but her eyes remained dry. She watched as the Bearer drew in a breath of air, sudden and gasping, his narrow chest heaving. She longed to feel joy, but felt only pity at the harshness with which Haomane used his chosen tools. She listened to the shouts of Men, carrying out the remainder of their futile search, and to the horns of the Rivenlost, declaring victory in bittersweet tones.

And she knew, with the absolute certainty with which she had once believed in Haomane's unfailing wisdom and goodness, that no matter what else the future held, in a still, silent place in her heart that she would never share—not with Aracus, nor Malthus the Counselor, nor her own kinfolk—she would spend the remain-der of her days seeing the outstretched hand of Satoris Third-Born before her, feeling the dagger sink into his breast, and hearing his anguished death-cry echoing in her ears.

Wondering why he had let her take his life; and why Tanaros had spared hers. Wondering if there was another scion of Elter-rion's line upon the face of Urulat. Wondering if her mother had prayed to Satoris on her deathbed.

Wondering why the Six Shapers did not dare leave Torath, and whether a world in which Satoris prevailed would truly have been worse than one over which Haomane ruled, an absent father to his Children.

Wondering where lies ended and truth began.

Wondering if she had chosen wisely at the crossroads she had faced.

Wondering, and never daring to know.

What might have been?

EPILOGUE

A SHADOW PASSED THROUGH THE Defile, disturbing the shroud of webbing that hung from the Weavers' Gulch in tattered veils. The little grey weavers chittered in dismay, scuttling furiously, setting about their endless work of rebuilding and repair.

No one else noticed.

Ushahin-who-walks-between-dusk-and-dawn rode the pathways between one thing and another; between waking and dreaming, between life and death, between the races of Lesser Shapers, between a dying Age and one being born.

He rode a blood-bay stallion, its coat the hue of drying gore, its mane and tail as black as the spaces between the stars. Lashed to his saddle was a leather case that contained a broken Helm, its empty eye-sockets gazing onto darkness.

And at his belt he bore a dagger wrought from a single Shard of the Souma, the Eye in the Brow of Uru-Alat. It was red, pulsing with its own inner light, and it would have betrayed his presence had he not wrapped it in shadow, in a cloak of the vague ambiguities that lay between victory and defeat, between pride and humility, between right and wrong.

Between all things.

He kept his thoughts shrouded as he rode, and no one challenged him as he passed beyond the Vale of Gorgantum.

Beyond him, the plains of Curonan stretched toward the east. He set out upon them, picking his way among the dead.

Overhead, there was a sound.

Glancing up, Ushahin-who-walks-between saw the raven circling and understood that it saw him in turn. He paused, waiting. It descended to land on his left shoulder, talons pricking. He sensed its sadness and looked into its thoughts as the Grey Dam of the Were had taught him long ago.

He saw death and knew he was the last of the Three.

The raven made a keening sound in its throat. He stroked its head, its errant tuft of feathers, with one crooked finger.

Soothed, the raven settled.

Ushahin-who-walks-between resumed his journey. He was pleased to have the raven's company. Later, he would give thought to vengeance, to the new pattern taking shape in the world, to the role that had befallen him, to the promise he had made to Lord Satoris, to the memory of the nameless child he had once been, before a rock in a stranger's fist had shattered his world.

Today, there was comfort in the simple communion of shared sorrow.

There would be time for the rest.

With his back to Darkhaven, Ushahin rode toward the Delta, where Calanthrag the Eldest awaited him.

In the Sundered World of Urulat, the sun set on an Age.

Tomorrow, a new one would dawn.

JACQUELINE CAREY is the author of the bestselling Kushiel trilogy (*Kushiel's Dart, Kushiel's Chosen,* and *Kushiel's Avatar*). A former researcher in art history, she resides in Michigan.